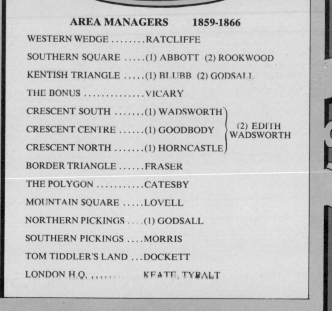

AREA MANAGERS   1859-1866

WESTERN WEDGE . . . . RATCLIFFE

SOUTHERN SQUARE . . . . .(1) ABBOTT (2) ROOKWOOD

KENTISH TRIANGLE . . . . .(1) BLUBB (2) GODSALL

THE BONUS . . . . VICARY

CRESCENT SOUTH . . . .(1) WADSWORTH ⎞
                                          ⎟ (2) EDITH
CRESCENT CENTRE . . . . . .(1) GOODBODY ⎬ WADSWORTH
                                          ⎟
CRESCENT NORTH . . . .(1) HORNCASTLE ⎠

BORDER TRIANGLE . . . . . . FRASER

THE POLYGON . . . . CATESBY

MOUNTAIN SQUARE . . . . . LOVELL

NORTHERN PICKINGS . . . .(1) GODSALL

SOUTHERN PICKINGS . . . . MORRIS

TOM TIDDLER'S LAND . . . DOCKETT

LONDON H.Q. . . . .   KEATE, TYBALT

Cal Sacks

A Horseman Riding By
The Green Gauntlet
The Avenue
Mr. Sermon

R. F. DELDERFIELD

God Is an Englishman

SIMON AND SCHUSTER

NEW YORK

THIRD PRINTING

SBN 671-20502-1
Library of Congress Catalog Card Number: 74-101871
Manufactured in the United States of America
Printed by The Murray Printing Company, Forge Village, Mass.
Bound by The Book Press, Brattleboro, Vt.

For My Wife, May
without whose affection,
oceans of coffee
and classical records
this would never have been finished.

Contents

Page

God Is an Englishman

Man with a Casket:
1857 - 1858

1

THEY stormed out of the dustcloud in a solid, scurrying mass, horse and foot in about equal proportions, but in no sort of formation; a mob of armed fugitives, with nothing in mind but to escape the hangman, or the bayonets of the Highlanders who had rushed the town at first light and had now fought their way as far as the Ranee's palace.

Swann, sitting his horse a few lengths in front of the extended squadron, recognised the badges and uniforms of the foremost, men of the 12th Native Infantry and the 14th Irregular Cavalry, the murderers of women who had entertained him here when he had ridden over from Allahabad less than a year ago. But before he could use his spurs the leading mounted man was bearing down on him and Swann noticed that he was encumbered by a curved-topped casket, balanced on the bow of his saddle.

The casket registered as an incongruity. It seemed ridiculous that a man flying for his life should encumber himself with luggage but this man had, so much so that his tulwar swung loose from his wrist on its sword-knot, and before he could find its hilt, Swann had sent him tumbling from the saddle with a single, backhanded slash. The box went flying, and even in that terrible uproar Swann heard the splintering crack of shattered wood as it bounced across the ground. Then he was engulfed, horse and foot streaming past him on either side, and his bay pivoted and was carried forward, gyrating and bucketing as her rider threw his weight this way and that parrying the random thrusts of sepoy bayonets and the sweep of the horsemen's swords.

The tumult was like the onrush of a bursting dam, its fury stunning the senses, so that he was unaware of the agency that brought him down in the midst of the press or how, pitching on hands and knees with his face in the dirt, he avoided being ridden over by the cavalry or bayoneted by the infantry. His sabre and *czapka* had gone and he was unable to rise on account of a crushing weight on his right leg, thrusting him forward and downward, so that his mouth and nostrils were plugged with red, pungent dust. Then, like the long sigh of the wind crossing Shirley Hills when he and Roberts had ridden up there to course a hare on an autumn afternoon, the

9

rout passed over him and went rippling away to the west. He had a single conscious thought. If this was death it was preferable to the tumult and discordancy of life.

* * *

When he opened his eyes the sun was at full strength and playing on his exposed neck like the steady lick of a torch. He found he could move his left arm, and pulled at the rucked up folds of his tunic in an attempt to ward off the glare and it was whilst he was thus engaged that he noticed his nose was almost touching the splintered fragments of the casket the horseman had carried into battle on his saddle bow.

He isolated this one piece of debris from the litter surrounding him, noting the intricate filigree pattern of the gilded hoops half-enclosing the lid, and because his mind was searching for a focus he set himself to contemplate it, wondering what it was doing there among so much military clutter. It symbolised a different sphere, a place of patient craftsmanship and gracious living, shunning its bearded carrier now sprawled on his face a yard or so further on, and the carcase of his horse that held Swann pinned by the leg in what seemed to be a cleft separating two ridges of naked rock.

Beyond it the dead and dying sloped away in a series of colourful furrows, white and scarlet, blue and pale yellow, with the red dust-cloud as their pall. The sour reek of blood and human sweat reached him so that nausea rose in his throat, but the spasm passed. He had seen many such fields, beginning with the Alma and ending, he supposed, here outside the walls of Jhansi in what would pass as a skirmish. Then the beat of an iron hammer began to fall on his temples like the long roll of Mahratta drums. He wondered how many wounds he had and where they were located. He felt no pain or distress other than the throb of his temples, and not a great deal of discomfort apart from the soft, immovable weight of the casket-carrier's horse on his thigh. He could thus resign himself to awaiting the arrival of the ambulance unit or the burial party and the prospect brought peace rather than panic; peace and a kind of wonder that the ultimate found him so still and soundless.

He must have dozed for a time for when he stirred again his leg was numb and the scent of sandalwood came to him from the splintered box, a sharp, tantalising whiff probing through the miasma of death, dust and wounds, and it was then, shifting his head slightly in a second attempt to ward off the glare, that he noticed something bright and lustrous coiled in the corner of the broken casket.

He did not know what it was but it suggested, at first glance, a handful of cobras' eyes, sullen and full of menace and yet, as he braced himself to outface them, possessed of a terrible beauty. For a long time he lay there contemplating them and thinking of nothing else, watching them catch and toss back the refracted light of the sun, seeming almost to challenge him to reach out and touch them and presently he did, lifting his hand very deliberately, as though to caress a nervous cat.

They did not shrink or bite, as he half-expected but slid softly and almost gratefully into his grasp. Then he saw that they were not cobras' eyes but jewels strung on a common thread and arranged in order of importance, the largest of them placed farthest from the clasp, the others tapering away until they met in a rectangle of thin, gold filigree. Holding them, and watching the sun play upon the hundreds of facets, he felt comforted and as though fearing the source of repose would be taken from him he drew his arm slowly across his chest and down the length of his thigh, groping below his empty scabbard until his thumb made contact with the catch of his sabretache. There was no need to fumble with the flap for it had burst open and he dropped the necklace inside, thrusting it down into the stiff, leather folds. The effort, small as it was, exhausted him. His hand fell away and in another moment he was still.

2

When he opened his eyes again he was trussed in a bed and facing a narrow, latticed window. It must have been towards evening for the shadows on the floor were long and steeply slanted. The room had whitewashed walls and very little furniture. Apart from the bed there was nothing but a stool and a bench, the latter encumbered with what looked like his valise and some of his blood-spattered accoutrements. He felt stiff and sore and at least two areas of his body were swathed in tight bandages but he was not aware of a particular pain. The Mahratta drumbeat still throbbed in his head but it was no more than an echo, the drums having moved a long way off. He was mildly astonished to find himself alive but was too drowsy to follow the thread of events beyond the point where he

11

had seen the casket-carrier ride out of a red fog, and the memory of this caused him to turn his head towards the bench, his eyes searching his kit for the sabretache. He could not see it but its absence caused him no particular concern. Within seconds he was asleep again.

The intermittent roll of drums, punctuated by the isolated boom of cannon, awoke him a second time and someone was holding a horn cup of lemonade to his lips. The drink had the qualities of nectar and he drained the beaker dry without looking beyond the brown, freckled hand that held it. Then he heard and recognised the short barking laugh of Roberts and raised himself, the movement sending rivulets of pain into the bruised areas around his back and shoulders and relaying them to his bandaged leg. He said, surprised by the thin timbre of his voice, "How bad is it, Bobs? Where am I hit?"

Roberts withdrew the beaker and stared down at him, thumbs hooked in his belt, small head cocked to one side.

"You weren't hit. Marryatt took a good look at you when he was here yesterday and I doubt if he'll bother to come back. Heavy bruising, a cut or two, and a touch of the sun. By God, Swann, the devil must have a lease on you! One of the lucky thirty-four again, eh? Even that damned fool Cardigan couldn't kill you."

He sat down on the stool, crossing his legs neatly and methodically, the way he did everything, the way Swann remembered from their Addiscombe days. A small, well-knit man, with skin the colour of newly-tanned leather and sharp intelligent eyes that smiled when Swann threatened to quarrel with his diagnosis.

"Canvass your system as carefully as you please, Adam, you'll find nothing to keep you here more than a day or two. 'Circus' Howard was killed, and about a dozen others. Your party had thirty-two casualties but most of them will live. 'Circus' was shot through the head when the first wave went in. That leaves just the two of us. It was hot for an hour or so before we blew in the gate but once the Highlanders got a footing in the town it was over in minutes."

"The squadron didn't stand a chance," Swann said, sullenly. "You told me I was to contain the stragglers. You didn't say there would be an army of them."

"I transmit orders, I don't write them. Two regiments have gone in pursuit, the 17th and your lot. They won't take prisoners. An hour or so after you were detached we found the mass grave of the garrison. It was Cawnpore over again, but no children, thank God."

12

Adam made no comment. He and Roberts had helped to empty the well at Cawnpore in July. In common with every other European in Havelock's relieving force they had since done what they could to seal the horror of the task in a remote attic of consciousness. Swann was surprised that Bobs should refer to it now.

Roberts said, "This is the end, Adam. The rest is no more than a mop-up. It's the end of something else, too. I missed watching the executions to come here and tell you."

"Well?"

"The Company rule is over. From here on India is the Crown's concern. It wasn't a rumour, after all. The news came from Delhi yesterday and Rose announced it as a near-certainty in the Mess. He wouldn't have done that if there was any doubt."

He waited and when Swann said nothing he looked vaguely irritated. "I don't have to tell you what difference this will make to all of us. Promotion will be speeded up, irrespective of our casualties. You're a fool if you don't take advantage of it." He paused, hopefully, looking directly at the bed.

Swann said, "I don't give a damn for our prospects here. If I needed confirmation I got it in that order you brought me just before that mob came storming down on us. Eighty men, posted in the open, to ambush two thousand! I'm lucky, you tell me. Well, maybe I am, but not in the sense that you meant it. First Cardigan's charge in the Crimea and now this. Nine solid months of senseless slaughter, encompassing the murder of God knows how many women and children. If I'm lucky it's because my contract has expired, and for no other reason that I can think of."

"It will be different now, Adam. Everything will change."

"Soldiering won't. Or your prospects either in the long run. You'll die, like all the rest of the '51 draft, shot down or speared in some Godforsaken village or river bottom with an unpronounceable name, and in what kind of cause, for God's sake?"

"In my own, Adam."

It was no more than a restatement of the old argument between them, an argument that would continue, if the paths ran parallel, for the rest of their lives. In as sense it crystallised their characters. Roberts, the dedicated careerist; Swann, the man who had taken a wrong turning but had never abandoned hope of finding his way out again. In the very early days of their association, when both were cadets, each had had a band of disciples. Roberts, starting out with many, had lost his one by one, a few from conviction but the majority

13

by death and gangrened wounds. Swann's converts had also gone and Roberts, the implacable, was not slow to remind him of the fate of two of them.

"There was Standford-Green and Badgery," he said, "they threw up their commissions in order to go home and make fortunes and what happened to them? Standford-Green put his hoarded savings in railway stock and lost it overnight, but he was luckier than Badgery. Badgery caught a chill in a London fog and was buried within four months of the farewell party we gave him in the Mess. If the fog hadn't killed him he would have starved, for at least Standford-Green could write a legible hand. They tell me he's working as a clerk in the Law Courts."

The man in bed was at a disadvantage but he had no intention of conceding Roberts his point. He never had and he never would. Respecting Roberts as a man he had never succeeded in exonerating him from bigotry. He said, deliberately, "I had no business in that last brush, Bobs. My contract expired more than a month ago. I could have asked for my passage before we moved up here, and because you and I are unlikely to dispute the claims of Queen and common-sense again I'll remind you why I'm lying here trussed up like a chicken. It's on your account, yours and 'Circus' Howard's. You were the very last of them and a man can't travel as far as we have without incurring obligations of a sort. But those obligations are personal and private, to me at any rate. They don't extend to Crown, Company or the City merchants, who pay us small change to enable them to milk a sub-continent and install fat wives in four-storey houses, with cook, parlourmaid, governess and basement."

"I know that," Roberts said, unexpectedly. "With you there has never been any other motive but comradeship, has there?"

"None. Just a dwindling batch of three-card-trick victims, relying on one another to stay sane and alive!"

Over in the square the drums rolled and the cannon boomed again. Roberts said, with his back to the bed, "You feel pity for those butchers out there?"

"They're not involved in what I'm trying to say, what I've always argued."

"But they are. We can hang a few hundred, and blow a few more from cannon, but there has to be a new beginning, here and elsewhere. How could that be achieved without a trained army standing behind the law?"

14

"You still believe in law? After all you've seen since the Mutiny began?"

"Yes, I believe in it. English law. And in my experience it makes a bad joke of everybody else's."

It struck Swann then that he might be seeing Roberts for the first time, that what he had always assumed to be an impersonal passion for rule-of-thumb, for precedent, for good order and discipline, was really something far more personal and fervent, a private creed, imbedded in a man who saw himself more as a missionary than a soldier. If it was so then it added a new dimension to their differences, setting them as far apart as the savage and the city sophisticate. Curiosity pricked him as he said, "Trade and barter on one side, we have a God-given mission here? Is that what you believe?"

"Implicitly." He swung round facing the bed, fighting the terrible battle all Englishmen of his type enter upon when called to acknowledge idealism. "Should I apologise? Is material gain essential to everything a man feels and thinks and needs? Great God, man, of course we have a mission! Did Cawnpore and Lucknow give you the impression these people could be left to themselves, to bloody-minded tyrants like Nana Sahib and the Ranee? Is this place, and every other place where we have a trading post and a missionary to be left to their dominion?"

"You'll need more than trained officers to prevent the same thing happening again. It isn't possible to uphold our kind of law by the Bible and sword, Roberts. God knows, it was difficult enough in my father's time, but today there are so many new factors. Empire building isn't a matter of occupation and annexation any longer. You have to take these people one by one and train them. As administrators, as doctors, as shipwrights, as ironmasters. You have to bring them sanitation and check the endemic killer diseases in their filthy towns and villages. You need roads, telegraph systems and, above all, railways. Mercenaries like us don't know a damned thing about any one of these bare necessities so what qualifies to deputise for God Almighty all over the world? Hand me that valise."

Roberts lifted the valise from the bench and set it on the bed. He said, tolerantly, "Why do I always let myself be drawn into this kind of discussion with you? Marryatt said you needed rest and we march at first light." He stood up stiffly, his back to the light, small, erect and indomitable, the way he had always appeared to Adam; Roberts, a man who, in thought and temperament, belonged more to the four-

15

teenth century than the nineteenth. He was five hundred years behind the times but lovable for all that.

"Then this is good-bye, Bobs?"

"If you mean what you say, it is."

"I mean it. This time I mean it." For a moment the claims exerted by many years' comradeship tempted him to confess about the necklace but he checked the impulse. Roberts would see the rubies as loot, and both of them had seen troopers and sepoys hanged for looting. For other reasons he left the valise unopened, rejecting the means of hammering his point home. Even given plenty of luck on Roberts' part it might be years before they met again. If seven years had not convinced Roberts that he was living in an age of steam and tremendous technical advances what could be achieved in the few minutes left to them? The heat went out of the day and out of their conflict of ideas. Roberts said, "It's going to be lonely without you, Adam."

"Not so lonely. Replacements will be coming in on every boat."

"Ah, yes, but what kind of replacements? The real business is finished. From now on it will be pigsticking, whist, bandit-hunting."

"Not for you, Bobs. Or for anyone else with a Victoria Cross."

"You'll write?"

"When I have something worth writing about."

"You're going home like that? Like a blind man?"

"I've had a dream, Bobs. A small one that might expand, but it required reconnaissance, of the kind our masters overlooked when they detailed me to block a beleaguered city with a single squadron. Study the ground. At least that's one thing the Army has taught me."

"The only thing, apart from how to ride, shoot and live rough and that won't avail you much at home."

"I think it will, given capital."

"And where will a stray like you find capital?"

Adam grinned. "I can smell it, and it's a sweeter smell than blood, Bobs."

He held out his left hand and Roberts shook it, lightly. It was typical of the man, Swann thought, that he made so light of handshakes and partings. At the low door he paused, turned, and saluted with comic gravity.

16

3

Surgeon-Major Marryatt had been optimistic. It was ten days before Adam Swann could shuffle round his quarters without leaning on the shoulder of an orderly, or his gap-toothed servant, Trooper Dawkins. But the interval of solitude was worth the price in stiffness, soreness, and the stifling atmosphere of the sick bay.

The first thing he did when he could crawl across the floor was to root out his sabretache and secure the necklace and sometimes, when he was unlikely to be disturbed, he would take it out and run it through his hands. The rich colour of the pigeon's blood rubies were atonement for his wasted years but he did not see them as another might, as insurance against penury or drudgery, but as a tacit promise of overhauling lost time, almost thirteen years of lost time, from the day of his eighteenth birthday, when, at his father's insistence, he had entered Addiscombe College as a cadet, to the final encounter with the casket-carrier on the plain outside Jhansi.

It seemed much longer than thirteen years for, looking back, he now saw that only the last few months had sped, from the moment a fugitive had ridden into the barracks with the news of the 19th Native Infantry's uprising at Berhampore, to the march on Jhansi and the storming of the Ranee's palace. The interval between, garrison duty in Ireland, riot-squad action in northern towns, his improbable Crimea interlude and, after reverting to Company service three years ago, endless sunsoaked days at a series of Indian stations, were but half-remembered, a trudge across a waterless desert, yet Roberts had been wrong in one sense. In addition to soldiering Adam Swann had wrung one other aptitude from the years and here, in comparative isolation, he had leisure to assess its potential. It was the habit of steady, objective thought, the product of conscious application of a kind almost unknown to professional officers. Men like Roberts and 'Circus' Howard had always thought of fakirs as savages, and dirty savages at that, but Swann had learned something from them, perhaps because contact with them had nurtured an intellectual curiosity he had had since he was a child roaming the Fells. It was a curiosity concerned with the nature of existence, the individual destiny of Lieutenant Adam Swann, having nothing whatever to do with orthodox religion. Such residual faith as he retained in the Jehovah of his boyhood he had thrown into the well at Cawnpore, for a Deity who ordained that kind of outrage did not belong in a pulpit of civilisation but beside the altars of Baal and Mithras. His curiosity was concerned with human activity, with the mechanics of everyday existence, with the slow, painfully garnered store of human knowledge. Alone among the officers of successive messes he not only read but studied accounts of Parliamentary debates printed in the three-months'-old copies of *The Times* that found their way into camp and had, whenever possible, supplemented their content with a range of technical journals so that his valise was stuffed with reading material his contemporaries would use to start a campfire. Novels, poetry and philosophy attracted him even less than theology. He was interested in facts and, beyond facts, statistics. It was now more than five years since he had set foot in England but he knew, approximately, what to expect when he did, and the prospect excited him in the way the promise of an attack on a fortified position would excite a man like Roberts. His intermittent spells of duty in the industrial north had done far more than familiarise him with the floodtide of technology. They had reconciled him, a countryman born, to the vast scenic and social changes that had followed what men were already calling the Industrial Revolution as it lapped over the shires in the wake of Stephenson's iron roads. He had paid more attention to this phenomenon than to any single aspect of the social scene, for he did not see the spread of railways as his contemporaries did – the wanton destruction of good hunting country at the instance of men who had never learned to sit a horse. Alone in his caste he saw it as the inevitable by-product of improved technology, steam power, and metal processing, and its challenge, even at this remove, was irresistible. For Swann's heroes were not those of Roberts, or men like Roberts. He saw the Havelocks, the Nicolsons, the Outrams and the Campbells as indomitable chawbacons. His awe was reserved for a man like Stephenson, unable to write his name until he was twenty, who had succeeded in forcing the greediest men in the world to finance his dreams. Stephenson, whose first passenger-carrying venture was launched when Swann was a child of five, dominated his imagination, but others had been canonised: Brunel, whose exploits he equated with those of Merlin; Hudson, the railway king; Watt, whose irresistible logic had revolutionised the mine and the factory, and other men whose articles of faith were set out in the manuals and blue books that found their way into Swann's eccentric maw. In barrack and bivouac he had thought about them and assimilation of their ideas, even at a distance, had created tensions in him that made him as lonely as a European marooned among headhunters.

And yet there was a barrier between him and them that had nothing to do with his training, or the narrow limits of a profession forced upon him by ancestral protocol. He recognised that barrier for what it was and for a time it baulked him, a genetic twist that was the inheritance of a long line of soldiers, an instinct of self-reliance that some would call pride and others, more accurately, a compound of obstinacy and conceit. Whatever it was it had fettered him, for he had known for a long time now that whatever he did would have to be done as his own master and it was this quirk in Swann's character that had checked his promotion. It had also been the means of keeping him in the Company's service as a mercenary.

The necklace could change all that, for he saw it as a watershed in his fortunes. Thirty stones, strung on a single thread, the largest as big as a bean, the smallest the equivalent of six months' pay and allowances in the field.

As the days passed, and word came of the departure of his regiment and the promise of a passage on the first westbound East Indiaman, he arrived, by slow stages, at a compromise with his ethics, or such ethics as had survived the shambles of the Mutiny. The Navy was awarded prize money while the pickings of the Army were, for some inscrutable reason, regarded as loot. But the rubies were not so much loot as treasure-trove, and as such should be shared equally between finder and Crown. He was not averse to this but, for the time being, the Crown could wait. The Crown might get its share over the years, if not in cash then in enterprise mounted by Adam Swann, lately in the service of the East India Company. It seemed to Adam it was better this way than to risk the rigmarole of a coroner's court for, given an impartial judgement, items of this kind had a habit of finding their way into the jewel caskets of the wives of prominent Company shareholders. No agony of soul was involved in the decision and no more than a rummage in his conscience. In this kind of game one made one's own rules, just as the Company had made theirs in the piping days of Clive and Warren Hastings.

He slit the lining of his valise, dropped the necklace inside, and sewed up the rent with twine. From now on the valise would perform a duty it had often performed in bivouac. It would serve as a holdall and a pillow.

Part One

Encounter:
Summer, 1858

1

Fugitive in a Crinoline

In the 'thirties and 'forties the river of enterprise had rolled due west from the slopes of the Pennines, engulfing Manchester and flowing on unchecked to empty its filth in the Mersey. Some of its stinking tributaries had forked north-west before the big city was overwhelmed and a good deal of the initial impetus had been absorbed in a triangle enclosed by Oldham, Burnley and Preston. The fate of Oldham, for instance, was typical of most Lancashire villages in this particular area. Almost overnight, or so it seemed to the older inhabitants, the closely knit community of farmworkers and cottage craftsmen had been absorbed, branded and delivered into bondage. In a year or so a dozen gaol-like factories were belching their bad breath to a sky that only a few years before had been washed clean by the soft rain of the Lake District not far to the north. Thousands of back-to-back two-room dens had been run up by the jerry-builders to house the operatives for the few hours they spent in them between interminable stints at loom and shuttle. Oldham was now called the biggest village in the world and its 'villagers', apart from the under-tens, and those too old or too broken to descend the steep streets to the mills, were absorbed in the task of unloading a gigantic flood of satins, sateens, fustians and sheetings on the markets of the world. Pending the passage of the Ten Hours Bill ten years before, the working population of Oldham had been even larger than it was today. For in that period, the hour of the first onslaught of the flood, children of five, four and even three had been taken on and their casualty rate beside the unfenced machinery had been written off as normal industrial wastage. Mostly they had worked in shifts and the foremen responsible for housing drafts of orphans and bastards recruited from country workhouses had been known to boast that their beds were never cold. One shift turned out, knuckling its bleared eyes, as the other reeled in. Meanwhile the community thrived and prospered. Or one section of it did.

But Oldham was only one among hundreds of villages that disappeared under the sulphurous pall that rolled down from the Pennines. The river of enterprise spared no single community within a thirty-mile radius of the city that some were already calling the new capital of the Empire. Like greased fingers running north, north-west and west from a sooty palm the scabrous clutch of the new, post-rural society reached out to Rochdale, Bury, Bolton and Wigan. Green spaces separating these country towns shrank to a minimum. The water in the streams about them turned grey and then black while the current, always sluggish, ceased almost to move at all. From the higher land to the north it was now possible to look down on that vast plain and see the city, not as a distant prospect, but as the site of a genie's bottle stationed somewhere about the terminus of the twenty-eight-year-old Liverpool–Manchester Railway, first in the world to carry passengers at the astounding speed of 31 miles per hour. The genie was unsleeping. Day and night he toiled for his indefatigable masters and the drifting grime he exhaled could be seen in the form of a gigantic mushroom, silvery grey and dun brown by day, jet black, shot with crimson, by night.

To the south, however, it was otherwise. Here the greater part of the Cheshire plain was green and gold, dotted with half-timbered farmhouses and neat rows of cottages linked by dust roads still bounded by hedges of hawthorn, elderberry and nodding cow-parsley. Cattle grazed here and nearby flocks of white geese strutted in charge of strident, red-cheeked children. Huge, creaking haywains, riding the gentle slopes like overloaded barges, moved across the fields at harvest time, and sometimes the sound of church bells, carried on a south-easterly, reached the line of merchants' houses marking the southern rim of the factory belt.

The line dividing these two worlds was a battle rampart broken by uneven gaps where the railway line crossed spongy open levels like the notorious Chat Moss. Its ramparts were the curving embankments thrown up by a hundred thousand Irish navvies and the little goose-minders would sometimes scream with excitement when one of the heavy trains moved snorting across the horizon. As yet the railway spurs had not probed south and the Cheshire plain dreamed on of its companies of archers recruited for London kings centuries before and of royal progresses that had once brought tumult to tidy market towns. The threat of engulfment remained, however, for the border town of Warrington had been wholly absorbed when the railway ran through and now, besides textiles, it was churning out a cascade of hardware and soap. The racket originating from the hardware factory was continuous but the soap factory advertised itself more subtly through the nostrils. When the wind swung to the north-westerly quarter the goose-children could smell it. It smelled like nothing within their experience.

Some of the Warrington merchants' wives had developed sensitive noses, their sensitivity running ahead of their husbands' bank balances. The menfolk, most of them less than a generation away from the midden, were indifferent to fumes of every variety but, as busy men, they were susceptible to nagging and a few had already succumbed to their wives' demands to better their living standards as well as their credit. So they packed up and moved, like a caravan of prosperous pioneers, across the county border and by the eighteen-fifties the northern rim of Cheshire was beginning to absorb the tide in a vastly different fashion from her sister county. It was getting a little of the gold whilst all the dross remained behind in Lancashire. Cheshiremen hoped it would stay that way but occasional visits to Warrington market did little to reassure them. There was always talk of new railways aimed at dreaming towns like Knutsford and Northwich, and the railway, taking in Chester, had already clawed its way as far as the Welsh coast. When it was completed the Irish Sea would be at every Lancastrian's disposal. At a statutory rate of one penny per mile.

In the meantime, however, Warrington, and its sister town Seddon Moss, boomed and grew, having even cheaper access to the Liverpool wharves than its overbearing neighbour Manchester. And its squalor kept just ahead of its prosperity, for Warrington and Seddon Moss elders were not afflicted by the evangelical zeal of certain leading Mancunians, being newer converts to the creed of muck and money and having their way to make in the world before they became the patrons of libraries, art galleries and soup-kitchens.

Structurally Seddon Moss had been unable to adapt to rapid expansion. The houses of the older town still stood in the centre, crowding together like a company of beleaguered veterans assailed by naked savages. Beyond them, in an ever-widening circle, the new streets of back-to-back dwellings moved out like the ripples of a cesspit, a hundred or more to a block and sharing, perhaps, six communal privys that gave off a stench in summer capable of vanquishing that of the soap-factory and in winter overflowed and covered the stone setts with ordure. Cheshire farmers noticed something else on market days. The inhabitants themselves were changing. Whereas, not so long ago, they would have been indistinguishable from working folk in Northwich and Middlewich, they now had the manners and appearance of an army of half-starved, semi-mutinous mercenaries living as best they could in the ruins of a pestilential citadel. Their faces had grown narrow and pinched and their eyes were the eyes of men and women who, at any time, and given the least provocation, would erupt and find pleasure in outrage. A proportion of them were not even whole but walked on twisted limbs, clubbed feet and with humped backs. Others lacked fingers and occasionally you would pass a man with an empty sleeve pinned to his shoulder, so that the country stallholders found them increasingly alien and quick to take offence, particularly if they thought they were being short-changed. Because of this, especially since the big strike and lockout at Rawlinson's, largest of the mills, a Seddon Moss market-day that had once been regarded by farmfolk as a weekly jaunt became a sally into an embattled area. Recalling the Manchester eruption of eleven years ago, when regular troops had been rushed in by train from London and Preston and several constables had been lynched, men wondered what might happen if Sam Rawlinson's obstinacy held out against his greed into the autumn and winter months, when bales of Georgian cotton cluttered every offloading bay and his operatives needed warmth as well as food. Bands of them were already roving the Cheshire hedgerows in search of berries and herbs and the kitchen gardens, hen-roosts and orchards of northernmost farms had been the scene of raids and forays. Mercifully, for the present, a brassy July sun beat upon the countryside. Under cloudless skies men could still hope and starving children were not obliged to stay indoors.

2

About seventy yards south of the house Sam had instructed his Manchester architect to raise an artificial knoll and crown it with a summerhouse. The summerhouse did not face the woods, as one might expect, but the monstrosity that Sam Rawlinson had tortured from the hunting lodge that had stood there for the last century and a half, a two-storey building of red Cheshire brick, with a portico supported by two truncated Doric columns and a façade of tall windows, the lower section opening on to a verandahed terrace.

The original hunting lodge, local men recalled, had been an inoffensive building, but Sam Rawlinson, after buying out the last defunct partner of Seddon Moss Mill, had set himself to amend that. The monster that resulted from a marriage of Sam's notions of domestic grandeur and the fumblings of an inexperienced architect was possibly the most eye-catching structure in the world, not excluding some of the new municipal townhalls that were being run up with cheap, ready-made materials made available by the new railway network.

The renovated Stannard Lodge, as it was marked on eighteenth-century maps, just escaped being a folly but was the poorer for it. Seddon Moss operatives, who sometimes walked the eight miles simply to gape at it, knew it by another name. They called it 'Scabs Castle', a name derived from a rumour that the new owner had obtained his start in life by leading a counter-revolutionary work force at the Rochdale mill where he had begun his career as an eight-year-old coal-comber and had progressed, through bale-breaking and furnaceman, into the lower grades of management.

Nobody in the Warrington area knew the facts of Sam's rise from the coal-comber to the mill owner but it had been achieved in a matter of thirty-five years. There was nothing very spectacular about that. In the decades leading up to the late eighteen-fifties the same rate of progress had been accomplished by hundreds of men, most of them cottagers' sons. The only thing singular about Sam Rawlinson was his willingness to leave production in the hands of a few, higher-than-average mechanics, and divide his tremendous vigour between administration and salesmanship. He had sold his first small mill at a handsome profit during a boom season and then ploughed everything he possessed or could borrow into Seddon Moss, a business that had been steadily running down owing to the reluctance of its elderly owner to replace the outworn plant.

That was in 1850 and in less than two years the decline of Seddon Moss Mill was halted and reversed, and the town had had to adjust to the impact of Sam Rawlinson's restless energy. He reorganised the mill from top to bottom, installed machinery that had not even been patented, signed on all the hands he could get, and went out after big oriental orders that called for quantity rather than quality. The home market he ignored, preferring to deal through his Liverpool brokers with customers who were too far off to complain in person or press claims for refunds.

He worked, on an average, fourteen hours a day, having no interests outside the mill apart from the embellishment of his new home. The word 'embellishment' played no part in his commercial life,

27

where he was concerned exclusively with facts and figures, but it featured largely in his domestic background and even his pliant young architect had been astonished when Sam told him to add a third storey to the Lodge, then decorate the south-facing frontage with four Gothic turrets. After that he added a castellated balustrade to the top of the portico, and then a row of arrow-slits to the buttresses between the windows, so that when it was finished the building looked like a top-heavy mediaeval fort balanced, none too securely, on a squashed red box. He then knocked twenty-eight per cent off the architect's fee and brought in a landscape gardener to cut back the encroaching timber, lay down an acre of lawn, excavate a large duckpond complete with an islet populated by roughcast herons, and raise the small hill so that he might have a convenient perch from which to survey his handiwork.

Nobody ever discovered whether it pleased him or not but in his limited spare time he went on looking at it as though it did. He had no friends, other than old Goldthorpe, the ground landlord of the area in which Seddon Moss Mill was situated, and even Goldthorpe, a notorious miser and rentier, had been heard to say that Rawlinson would dry, process, and sell the skin of a grape if he could find a market for the end product. Men of business in the area came to respect him, however, as by far the biggest employer of unskilled labour hereabouts. His small team of executives, locally known as 'The Strappers', tolerated him, if only because he could be absolutely relied upon to back them against the operatives on every occasion. In the men, women and boys who formed his labour force he inspired a compound of hate, derision and naked fear, but also a certain awe that one man, and him a widower without sons or local background, could have acquired so much power so quickly, and exercise it with such damnable attention to detail.

For although Sam Rawlinson rarely appeared on the factory floor he gave ample evidence of knowing everything that happened down there, and every word spoken that was relevant to his concerns. He might, indeed, have been watching them individually from the moment they arrived at six-thirty a.m., until they trooped out twelve to fourteen hours later. He knew when one of them was a minute late in arriving, or ten seconds early in shutting down. He knew to a fibre how much wastage occurred every day, how many breaks were detected on a particular machine every hour, and often such irrelevant data as which unwed operative was pregnant and who was the likely father. They hated his powers of concentration and they hated his unrelenting grasp of their personal lives but almost all of them, deep down, regarded him as a reliable provider, particularly after Seddon Moss had ridden out the last slump without resorting to short time, as had a majority of mills in the area.

Perhaps it was this certitude of regular employment that kept them so long from mutiny, and helped them to resist the exhortations of men like Cromaty and McShane to bluff the Gaffer into increasing the overtime rate by one penny an hour, and authorise a relief system for the ten-minute breakfast break, at present spent standing beside the chattering machines. In the end, however, the persuasions of a hard core of rebels prevailed and there was a ten-day walkout. Sam's reply had been a nine-week lockout, that had now lasted from May into July.

Sam Rawlinson's obstinacy seemed likely to outlast the heatwave. Indeed, its breaking-strain was linked to the thermometer for he reasoned that, whereas seven hundred operatives might well feel the pinch of privation in high summer, the nerve centre of his unruly mob would not be touched until rain fell on their slate-loose hovels, an earnest of what was in store for them in November and December.

He was now losing, at his own calculation, about a hundred pounds a week and that apart from orders that were going elsewhere, but although this appalling price exasperated him it did not daunt him. For one thing he could afford it. An overall loss of, say, two thousand pounds, would make no more than a dent in his invested capital. For another his commonsense, which he thought of himself as possessing in abundance, told him that in the long run the lockout would show a profit, for once the mill was working full-time again no man or group of men would dare to challenge him in the future. There would still be strikes and stoppages at neighbouring factories, so long as employers turned a blind eye to the engagement of men with truculent records, (a policy he consistently opposed at local federation meetings), but there would be no more penny-an-hour or breakfast-break deputations waiting upon him. Whenever the whisper circulated that one was about to assemble, the single men and girls would remember the penniless summer of '58, and the married men would heed wives with half-a-dozen bellies to fill. To walk through his mill now, to contemplate ten thousand pounds' worth of modern machinery as idle as his hands, was a depressing experience to a man who, in his teens, had worked a sixteen-hour-day for fourteen shillings a week. He found it, however, less irksome than living under the threat of extortion from troublemakers like Cromaty and

McShane, both of whom, he noted, had absented themselves from the deputation that had trudged out here two days ago, begging him to reopen on any terms short of a cutback in daily rates.

He knew millworkers and he flattered himself that he knew Sam Rawlinson. Under present circumstances acceptance of the deputation's terms would amount to a compromise and a compromise was half-way to surrender, perhaps all the way if one thought in terms of years rather than months. He could hold on, if necessary, until Christmas, and neither loss of orders nor the hint of violence that that bloodless old stick Goldthorpe had dropped when they had last met, could shake his nerve. He had studied the rules of the game of industrial bluff. During the '47 riots, that had spread north from the Midlands like a heath fire, erupting in every town within a day's ride of Manchester, he had been running a mill with less than seventy operatives, and although he kept his mill open he had heard some of his own hands sounding off at street corners during the troubles. But in the end he had seen those same men crawl back to work after the military had reinforced the police and the yeomanry. A few factories had been gutted, a certain amount of plant damaged, and acres of local palings had been torn up and used as weapons against batons and bayonets, but within hours of the North Western Railway depositing the Guards at the Manchester terminus there had been no more talk of 'Moscowing the town', whatever that meant. He had even had the sour satisfaction of erasing the names of street orators he recognised from his tally book.

As for the present upset, a short strike and an extended lockout, it was a personal not a national demonstration. Cromaty, McShane, and a few like them, had staked their reputations on wresting that penny-an-hour and that ten-minute breakfast break from him, and he knew what lay behind the demand. They were hoping to use these piddling concessions as a recruiting slogan for their newly-formed Spinners Alliance, a David pitting himself against the Goliath of the Local Federation and in this sense, or so Sam told himself, he was fighting everyone's battle. For if the Bible story repeated itself in Seddon Moss then God alone knew what price employers all over the country would pay in cash and lost working hours in the approaching winter.

So the Seddon Moss deputation had trudged the dusty road to Daresbury in vain, arriving and departing empty-bellied and empty-handed. It had been a rare pleasure to watch McEwan, his Scots gardener, hosing the half-moon flower-beds only a few yards from the

30

front steps while the men argued and pleaded. He had not given them so much as a drink of water and it must have been a leather-tongued sextet that trailed back to town, for all the streams on the plain were dry and every cottage was hoarding well water.

Meantime he had plenty to think about. Enforced idleness had given him an unlooked for opportunity to weigh every aspect of Matthew Goldthorpe's hint of a dynastic alliance, and the prospect of having Goldthorpe's poop of a son as the father of his grandchildren took priority over even such a matter as the shutdown of Seddon Moss Mill.

Up here in his summerhouse, with his back to the trees, he could choose a highway for his thoughts and march along it, shoulders squared, pugnacious jaw outthrust, prominent blue eyes—'marble' eyes his rivals called them—bulging balefully at his unlikely castle that always had the power of focusing his attention, if only because it represented proof that anything was attainable providing you wanted it enough.

He thought first of the bloodless Goldthorpe, reputedly the richest ground landlord between Salford and Birkenhead, and then, reluctantly, of Goldthorpe's son, Makepeace. What a damned silly name to christen a boy! What a gratuitous handicap to fasten upon a stripling due to walk into an income of several thousand a year once they trundled the old man away. *Makepeace!* Who wanted peace and, if peace was thrust upon a man, who wanted the odium of bringing it about? He remembered asking Goldthorpe what the devil had prompted him to penalise the boy at birth and the old man had told him that his son was named after the novelist, Thackeray, who was, it seemed, distantly related to Goldthorpe's hoity-toity wife. To Sam it was an inadequate explanation but he felt obliged to admit that it suited Goldthorpe's son and from here it was a short step to the contemplation of Makepeace Goldthorpe's loins.

It seemed unlikely, at first glance, that the boy would be capable of siring anything more aggressive than a jack-rabbit. He was thin, shambling, toothy and completely subdued by the prospect of his father's wealth. He had a moist handclasp, a wispy moustache, and a faint stammer but did physical disqualifications matter? Admittedly the prospect of grandsons was important but was that prospect limited to the womb of the one child his own wife had brought him and died, most inconsiderately, in the process? He was only forty-seven and would probably marry again when he could spare time. The lack of a wife over the past nineteen years had not troubled him overmuch. He spent very little time at home, retained the services of Mrs. Worrell, an excellent cook-housekeeper, and had access to any number of lusty operatives glad to satisfy his occasional needs for the price of a shilling. He had no regular mistress (the maintenance of one not only gave women grandiose ideas but invariably got about among the chapel people and was bad for business) but, by his own computation, he had probably sired half-a-dozen bastards. The claims of all had been silenced by a routine arrangement he had with Doig, his lawyer. Having satisfied himself that there was a chance of a claim being established, a small lump sum, and a statement exonerating his client from any further responsibility, disposed of the matter. Lately, on Doig's advice, Sam had taken care to find his fun in Manchester, among some other mill-owner's employees. It was, perhaps, an expensive way of going about things but Sam Rawlinson was not averse to spending money on himself. The arrow-slits and the four Gothic turrets embellishing Stannard Lodge proved that.

By now, however, with the prospect of finding a well britched husband for Henrietta, Sam's thoughts had been turning more and more to bringing order into his private life and there seemed to him no reason why he should not begin looking around for some healthy young woman who would get him a string of heirs to compensate for his wife's extreme carelessness in dying after producing a single child and that a daughter. As for Henrietta, she could make herself useful by marrying young Goldthorpe, or somebody like Goldthorpe. By so doing she would not only make fresh capital available but take out insurance in the matter of grandchildren.

He made a guess at Matthew Goldthorpe's pile. It was probably in the six figure bracket, even though most of it reposed in bricks and mortar of which half was property on the point of falling down. Not that that mattered. The real value lay in the sites and the Goldthorpes, who had been landowners about here for two generations, were known to own a great slice of the eastern sector of the town and to have pocketed upwards of twenty thousand when the railway came through twenty years before. On the face of it he was hardly likely to improve on Makepeace, particularly as Matthew also owned the strip of rubble-strewn land between his offloading bays and the railways goods yard. He wondered, remembering this, if Goldthorpe could be talked into making this over to him as a wedding pledge and decided that it was possible. As always, when he was assessing a problem, he identified with his opponent and on this occasion the result was encouraging. Matt Goldthorpe was copper-bottomed but he was also

32

greedy. Unlike Sam he did not think of himself as a rich man but continued to behave as though the odd sixpence represented the difference between a herring supper and going to bed on an empty stomach. The prospect of marrying into the family of the district's largest employer of labour obviously attracted him. Had it been otherwise nothing would have induced the close-fisted old buzzard to make the first approach. Deciding this Sam also made up his mind on the spot but in doing so gave a passing thought to the couple themselves. Makepeace, he knew, would marry a woman with two heads if his father gave the command, not because he was filial but because, endowed with his father's extreme fondness for money, the prospect of running contrary to its source, with younger brothers in the offing, was unthinkable. Apart from this, if he was a man at all, he would not find the prospect of marrying Henrietta displeasing, irrespective of any settlement Sam might make. Henrietta was a shapely, spirited girl, with her mother's refined features and his own clear skin and matchless health. With the minimum of assistance from Makepeace she could, he was sure, produce a flock of children and old Goldthorpe, a slave to tribal prejudice, would respond to that and be likely to observe the rules of primogeniture when it came to making his will. Sam did not know, neither did he care, how Henrietta would react to the bargain. Their relationship was humdrum. Most of his time had been spent at the mill, or drumming up orders, and because she was only a girl he had left her education, such as it was, to a succession of nursemaid-governesses. She could, they told him, tinkle the piano, sew a little, cook a little, and while away her time on other woman's pursuits, like pokerwork, crocheting and dressmaking. Unlike her father, she had been able to read and write since she was a toddler and no man in his senses would give a girl who promised to be pretty more than a minimal education.

Musing thus, it occurred to Sam that he knew less about her than he knew of some of his hands and he put this down to the fact that he had never recovered from the shock that she had not only had the gall to be the wrong sex but had, in arriving, killed his Irish wife, Cathy, thus depriving him of a chance to correct the error.

His memory, so accurate concerning matters of business, retained little of Cathy now. He saw her as a willowy girl who had caught his eye during a visit to the docks at Merseyside, one of innumerable refugees from the first of the Irish potato famines in the 'thirties. He found her sitting on a tin trunk looking extraordinarily composed in the midst of the dock turmoil and, for a reason that he could not, for

33

the very life of him, recall at this distance, she had made him laugh so that he had whisked her off and fed her with the intention of seducing her as soon as he had concluded his business with a Levantine skipper. But although she had eaten what had seemed to him an enormous amount of beef, cabbage and Lancashire cheese, she had laughed in his face when he had proposed she should settle the bill upstairs and had offered, instead, to wash his shirt that had been soiled by the Levantine's tarry cordage. He must have been in exceptionally high spirits on that particular trip—perhaps he got the better of the Levantine in the matter of freightage—for her impudence had made him laugh again and he proposed that she accompany him back to Warrington in his dogcart. Surprisingly she had agreed, and had even entertained him with sad Gaelic songs all the way home. Searching his memory for further fragments of the brief association he recalled now that Mrs. Worrell, his cook-housekeeper, had taken a liking to her, and it was probably the cook's remonstrances that had prevented him from turning her loose to fend for herself when she rejected his renewed advances with contemptuous good humour. Why, in God's name, had he decided to marry the girl? Had it been an impulse, related to the acquisition of Seddon Moss about that time and the need to establish himself among the conventional businessmen of a settled community? Had that snivelling priest who called on him to discuss the girl's future dented his self-sufficiency? Had he grown impatient with the need to go out and find a woman whenever he wanted one? Had he married out of fear of catching a venereal disease, or was it a subconscious groping after some form of permanence in the pattern of his life? He had never had time to find out. When, after a month or so she told him that she was pregnant, he was jubilant and when they told him that she was dead he was furious, feeling himself to have been the victim of a complicated practical joke of the kind the wild Irish were always playing on their betters. To an extent the experience had sobered him and he had gone his own way, using people and discarding them but following a policy of keeping his private frolics to a minimum. There remained, however, Henrietta, and suddenly, a little surprisingly, she was a capital asset.

He got up, stretched his clumsy limbs, slapped a midge or two, and stumped off towards the house, a tall, thickset, bull-necked man with thinning hair grey at the temples and the heavy florid features that go with sensuality and a refusal to suffer fools gladly.

Mrs. Worrell, as round as a bolster and crimson in the face after her exertions over the range in the airless kitchen, told him that Henrietta was somewhere about and he was to get out of her way if she was expected to prepare dinner for four at short notice. Alone among his seven hundred employees she could bully him, aware that a woman who could control staff, run a large, rambling house, and cook three wholesome meals a day was all but indispensable to a widower. Apart from that she was the only one among them that had known him when he was another man's servant and over the years they had adjusted to one another. He went out, across the hall and up the broad staircase, calling his daughter by name.

She answered from her quarters at the end of the corridor, an octagonal room representing one of the turrets in reverse and he went in without knocking.

She was standing in front of a full-length mirror trying on a new green dress and the sight of her, as she stood with her back to him absorbed in her task, gave him a moment to study her reflection and come to terms with her as a young woman, rather than a dumpy, imperious child. She was wrestling petulantly with the tough wire cage of a crinoline designed for a smaller waist and narrower buttocks. Her dilemma amused him but it also offered him a sliver of satisfaction, for he had no patience with this eternal preoccupation among both men and women for seventeen-inch waists that demanded the torture of whalebone corsets. When he put his arm around a woman he liked to feel flesh, not armour-plating, and he had always thought of the crinoline as a monstrous contrivance designed, he wouldn't wonder, to keep men at a safe distance. He said, tolerantly, "Where'd tha' buy that dam' silly thing, lass?" and she said, over her shoulder, "At Arrowsmith's, and it fitted when I tried it on. It's the first dress I've ever bought from a shop. Mrs. Worrell's niece sews for me and comes up time and again for fittings."

"Keep it that way," he said, "for tha'll get diddled every time tha' set foot in Ned Arrowsmith's premises."

She made no comment on this and when he crossed to the window she continued to ignore him. She was not, he reflected, in the least like other men's daughters, who fussed and fumed and fretted in a man's presence, even that of their fathers and brothers. She always treated him as though he was a casual acquaintance, or even a servant, and now that he thought about it she had always had some approximation of this attitude towards him, as though he was a useful piece of furniture, or a carriage horse awaiting her pleasure. It disconcerted him but deep down he admired her for at least it argued that she had inherited his independence and was unlikely to become anyone's fool. His mind returned again to Makepeace Goldthorpe and he thought 'By God, if anything does come of it there's no doubt who'll wear the britches!', and said, by way of a preamble, "Matt Goldthorpe and his son are supping here this evening."

"Mrs. Worrell told me. She said I was to help out with them."

"Aye, that's so." Her acceptance of the rarely demanded duty of hostess pleased him. She was, he decided, more like a man in her ability to grasp essentials without a lot of tiresome explanation and suddenly he warmed towards her, watching her movements in the mirror with an almost affectionate contempt.

"Eh, lass, let me lend a hand with that damned contraption. The neck of that birdcage needs stretching. It were made for a lass wi' nowt to tak' hold of." He lifted the wire over her head as she let fall the voluminous green folds, revealing her frilled pantalettes that he thought of as women's reach-me-downs and a corset that was laced so tightly that her chubby behind jutted beyond its rim like a ledge and pushed her rounded breasts half out of her camisole. He addressed himself to bending the master wire outward, giving the cage an overall extension of over an inch in circumference while she walked unconcernedly to the wardrobe and shrugged herself into a flannel gown.

The room, he noticed, was in disarray. Garments, packing paper and ribbons were strewn about and all the rugs were scuffed. Beyond the open door of the wardrobe he could see an array of dresses, cloaks and boots, and a compartment at the top full of hats. It occurred to him that he must have paid for all that clutter and also that Mrs. Worrell's niece was probably making a damned good thing out of Henrietta's patronage, but he didn't resent it. She was his property and there was no reason why he should object to reinvesting a little of his profits in one of his assets. He had not come here with the idea of sounding her out but now it seemed advisable to know where they stood in relation to Matt Goldthorpe's suggestion. Never having acquired the least finesse in the matter of striking bargains he went straight to the point.

"That son of Goldthorpe's, Makepeace, the eldest one. He's sweet on you, lass."

Her head came up sharply, trapping a ray of the afternoon sun in a cluster of copper ringlets. Before today, before he had begun to think about her as a marriageable woman, it would have taxed him to state the colour of her hair but now he saw it as one of her selling points. The new dress, and the carefully arranged clusters of ringlets worn over each ear, suggested that she was as interested in her personal appearance as all young women growing up out of reach of the looms, and it struck him that she might find a certain amount of satisfaction in what she saw in that long mirror. There was a word almost everybody about here used for a woman like her but momentarily it escaped him. Then it came to him, a word from over the Pennines. '*Gradely*'. Her sharp reaction to his mention of the Goldthorpes, however, had put him on guard so that he was not surprised when she said, "That Goldthorpe boy? The one with the droopy moustache who spits when he opens his mouth?"

He chuckled. "Nay, lass, his stammer's nowt to worry about. He'll get over that the minute he walks into Matt Goldthorpe's pile and he'll get pretty near all of it. The Goldthorpes think of themselves as gentry, and gentry don't divide the brass the way our folk do. It all goes to t'eldest lad."

She looked thoughtful for a moment. Then she said, carefully, "Is that why Mr. Goldthorpe is bringing Makepeace over here?"

"No," Sam said, "Goldthorpe's coming here to look you over himself, for I've never known Matt to buy a pig in a poke."

The colour that came to her face made him regret his choice of phrase. He had, as he himself would have put it, 'sounded out' far too many prospects not to sense undeclared opposition to a proposition and he now made a serious effort to improve his approach.

"You can leave the old 'un to me," he said. "All tha'll need to do is give t'lad a little encouragement. He's no oil-painting, I'll grant you that, and he's still fast under his father's thumb, but the old man won't make brittle bones from all I hear. When Makepeace walks into his father's brass he'll be t'best catch about here, tak' my word for it!"

She was staring at him now and the grimness of her expression puzzled him. "Makepeace is coming here to *propose* to me?"

He said, sharply, "Great God, it's not got as far as that yet! All I know is you've caught the boy's eye and he's mentioned as much to his father. That must mean business, otherwise I can't see young Makepeace screwing up that much nerve."

"We met at the Victory Ball in the Assembly Rooms last autumn,"

37

she said, slowly, "we danced together. Twice. Did his father tell you that?"

"No, he didn't, he just asked if you were spoken for, or likely to be."

"What did you say to that?"

"I said you weren't, and if any young spark came calling he'd do it through me or I'd kick his backside from here to the Mersey!"

He had an uncomfortable impression that he was being forced on to the defensive and made an effort to regain the initiative. "I say nowt to you capering round the Assembly Rooms," he growled, "so long as Mrs. Worrell was within call, but when it comes to a serious business of this kind I'll decide what's best for you, and don't get to thinking different."

"No," she said, in the same flat tone, "but don't you or that old miser Goldthorpe get any daft ideas about marrying me off to Makepeace or anyone like Makepeace! When I wed I'll wed a man, not a toad with a stutter and a clammy touch that makes me want to jump into the bathtub when he's had his paws on me. Now give me that cage and let me get dressed."

He was so astounded that for a moment he could do no more than put the frame into her outstretched hand. It was years since anyone had dismissed him in that tone of voice and the few who had had lived to regret it. He said, heaving his bulk away from the casement, "You can tak' your time with Goldthorpe but who and when you wed is something I'll decide, the same way as any man in my position would." A sudden suspicion crossed his mind and came near to frightening him. "If there's any other young buck who fancies his chance of walking into my money . . ." but she turned her back on him and stepped nimbly into the enlarged hoop so that he found himself not only hectoring a reflection but being interrupted by one.

"There's no one else! If it's any comfort to you I've never met a man I could marry," and somehow, because he entirely believed her, the sense of outrage left him and again he made shift to soften his approach.

"Listen here, lass," he said, so reasonably that his tone of voice surprised him, "I don't pretend to be gentry, and I'm not a man to hound a lass into wedlock for brass and nowt but brass, but it's time you realised you're in t'market and put a price on yourself. I hadn't decided on young Goldthorpe in particular. It was his father who made the approach. But if it's not Goldthorpe it will be someone in Goldthorpe's bracket, for in my book brass marries brass, make no mistake about that. It's no secret round here how much I can call on if I've a mind to, or that having no lads I'm likely to settle something substantial on you when we've picked our man. Keep young Makepeace on a string if you have to. Maybe that's the right game to play for a spell, but when he comes here tonight you'll be civil to him, and mighty civil to the old man, if only because he's my ground landlord. Dammit, I've got troubles enough, and you've no call to add to them so long as you expect me to pay for what's in that wardrobe!"

He paused then, half-hoping for some conciliatory word or gesture on her part, but none came. She clipped the cage about her, hitched it once or twice, and slowly drew the flounces of sprigged muslin level with her waist.

Deciding that nothing would be gained by pressing her any further at this stage he clumped as far as the threshold but here, feeling the honours remained with her, he turned and stood biting his underlip, finally adding, "After we've eaten, the old man will want to talk. When you get the nod from me tak' t'lad outside, do you hear?"

"They can hear in the kitchen," she said, and gave the bell of her skirt a pert little undulation that struck him as being the equivalent of a street urchin's gesture of derision. It was only then, notwithstanding her attitude throughout the interview, that he realised his daughter might prove as stubborn as the hard-core troublemakers who had absented themselves from the latest deputation.

4

The meal, a culinary success, did nothing to ease the tensions a malevolent set of circumstances had combined to exert on Sam Rawlinson throughout the hours leading up to the climax of a discouraging day.

There was the news that Joe Wilson, his overseer, brought him from the town about five, of operatives in a truculent mood and the certainty of the mass meeting hitherto dismissed as a bluff. There was Henrietta's hostile attitude towards him and his half-formed decision to accept Goldthorpe's offer of an alliance. There was the unexpected formality that the Goldthorpes, father and son, introduced into the house from the moment their coachman (Goldthorpe, too mean to employ a trained man, hired beery ostlers from the livery stable when he did not drive himself) deposited them on the front steps. And as if this was not enough to put a man off his meat and claret, there was his confoundedly constricting three-inch collar that he felt obliged to wear as an acknowledgement of the solemnity of the occasion.

One of the disadvantages of growing rich and moving up in society, he decided, was the necessity to encumber yourself with frock coats, stovepipe hats, punishing boots and, above all, that circlet of respectability about the neck that any well-ordered society would have reserved for felons.

Notwithstanding these preoccupations he set himself throughout the meal to dissipate the old man's gloom concerning the mood of the strikers, the Goldthorpes having passed knots of operatives making their way to the meeting. Makepeace, stuttering with glee that was the privilege, he supposed, of a man who did not have to deal with any opposition worse than defaulting tenants, had declared that the men had looked menacing and that one had shouted after the carriage, guessing its destination. Sam told them that Wilson had made his report and promised to ride out here again if there were further developments. He added that the police had been alerted and could call, if necessary, upon reinforcements from Manchester, but old Goldthorpe, damn him, went on to imply that he, Rawlinson, was putting the work forces of other employers in jeopardy by refusing to capitulate to the last deputation, and that the militants among them would now have plenty of brickbats to use at the meeting.

"You should ha' played for time, man, you should ha' promised to think it over," he muttered, scratching at his plate like a famished old cockerel. "If they were ready to go back on their demands it was a back-down, wasn't it? This lockout of yours is going to cost me a pretty penny before it's over. More than half of them live under my slates."

Had it not been necessary to mollify the old skinflint and divert attention from Henrietta's glacial detachment, he would have reminded Goldthorpe that he was fighting every employer's battle, and also that anyone living under a Goldthorpe roof was liable to get a wet shift when the dry spell ended. As it was he was obliged to go into the details of his long-term strategy. He was only partially relieved by Makepeace's enthusiastic espousal of his cause, dictated, no doubt, by that young man's determination to squirm into Henrietta's good graces. Listening to him endorsing the policy of implacability he could understand the lad's eagerness to demolish the barrier Henrietta had raised the moment she came floating down the stairs in that new green dress of hers. He was learning more than he had bargained for about his daughter when he had lounged into the house to discuss the prospect of marriage, never having realised she was so akin to him in temperament. She had, not beauty exactly, but a rare, eye-catching poise and prettiness in that decanter of a dress, and under it a figure likely to make a lustier man than Makepeace lick his lips. The last time he had looked at her consciously she had seemed no more than a fresh-complexioned schoolgirl, with a flat chest, an awkward legginess and a mop of coppery hair, and here she was ladling out sherry trifle like an artful and mature woman, trained to keep men guessing about what she looked like when she stepped out of that birdcage clamped to her waist. In the soft shine of the table-lamp her eyes looked as green as bottleglass, and her neck, short though it was, was perfectly proportioned to a pair of wide, down-sweeping shoulders. Sitting there, saying nothing, yet otherwise playing a hostess to perfection, she struck him as a study in pink and white and green that was the only cool and composed element in that airless room, and understandably that cold fish of a Makepeace did not know what the devil to make of her. As for the old man, he was senile enough to behave towards her with the circumspection he might have accorded a young duchess with money to invest in one of his shadier projects, and Sam decided that here, perhaps, was the sole rewarding aspect of the evening, the fact that his daughter had made a deep impression on the richest old badger in Seddon Moss. It was surely time to begin drawing up articles before Makepeace began to look elsewhere.

He said, pushing back his chair and clearing his throat, "Your father and I have some business to settle, lad. Take Henrietta a turn in the garden," and deliberately avoiding his daughter's eye he stood up and rang for the maid, at the same time offering his cigar case to Goldthorpe.

To his relief Henrietta also rose and grimaced in the old man's direction before gliding round the end of the table and floating decorously towards the French window that opened on to the terrace. He caught Goldthorpe watching her movements and the wintry smile on the old man's face helped to absorb the choler he felt that a chit of a girl could come so near holding him up to ransom. Impatient of the restraint he had had to exercise throughout the meal he discarded any attempt at a preamble and said, bluntly, "Well, Matt, now that you've met her . . .?"

"She's a bonnie lass," the old man said, carefully, "and a very civil one. She's not much to say for herself, but I'm not holding that against her. That's rare in a young woman these days. Does she ken why I'm over here?"

Leave your lad to do his own talking," Sam said. "At his age I wouldn't have wanted a spokesman for a lass like Henrietta."

It amused him that Goldthorpe had been so thoroughly deceived by his daughter's unrelenting glumness. No doubt Henrietta had hoped it would discourage them and here was the old man applauding it. Unexpectedly Sam felt the tensions easing and poured Goldthorpe a generous glass of port as they faced one another over the ruins of the meal. When the maid had reached the door with a tray of dishes he called, "Leave the rest, I'll ring when I'm ready," and turned back to Goldthorpe with a flourish. "We'll cut the cackle and get down to details," he said, biting on his cigar. "I intend to settle five hundred a year on her and I'll add another hundred when the first child shows up. More if it's a boy."

The old man's head came up sharply, disconcerted by his directness. Sam went on, without giving his opponent time to hedge, "But you can do me a favour in exchange. That strip of waste between my offloading bays and the railway siding—it could save me two hours' teamwork a day if I could run a brace of rails across it. I'm not expecting it for nowt. I'll pay a fair price for it."

The old man's head wobbled as though he had received a box on the ear. He shut his eyes, as if absorbing the smart, and his mouth, Sam thought, looked like a rockseam depressed at each extremity. He recognised the expression at once as Matt Goldthorpe's 'money-look', as much a feature of the local scenery as Scab's Castle. It pleased him to be able to summon it so effortlessly. Matt said, with a kind of groan, "Nay, I had plans to build two rows of cottages on that strip, Rawlinson."

"Aye," said Sam, indulgently, "happen you did, but then I had plans to go looking for a son-in-law among the shipwrights in Liverpool. Some of them are on the way to becoming gentry and there's not one who couldn't call up as much as you."

Goldthorpe blinked twice and Sam settled himself to wait, as for the next move of a doughty chess opponent. "Makepeace is shaping well," Goldthorpe said, noncommittally. "He thinks of little but work, or didn't until he took a fancy to your lass." Then, "Five hundred, you said?"

"Aye," said Sam, "subject to you selling that strip."

There was a longish pause. Through a blue haze of tobacco smoke

42

they measured one another's advantages, a matched pair, settling comfortably to the collar of avarice.

5

Twilight lingered in the open patches of lawn between summerhouse and copse and the air was heavy with the scent of roses and cloves. Makepeace and Henrietta walked decorously, two children given permission to absent themselves for a brief interval but without getting into mischief or soiling their Sunday clothes. It was very still out here. The only sounds that reached Henrietta was the whisper of her dress, (a dress she was already beginning to hate) and the plaintive squeak of Makepeace's new boots. Back in the house, in the presence of the older men, she had been protected against the sense of outrage that this pallid young man's suit represented, perhaps by easy accessibility to her own room, or by the nearness of Mrs. Worrell, her sole confidante, but out here she was vulnerable. She could not run far in this balloon of a gown and there was nowhere to run to in any case. Until this moment she had been conscious of any number of sensations concerning him but now he produced in her nothing but loathing, held in check by contempt for his timidity. As they moved down the slope, however, she sensed that he was not as timid as she had supposed. In the presence of his repulsive old father he was a quaking schoolboy, cringing under the rod. Released from that presence he acquired a kind of swagger that began to show in a strutting walk and the smug, proprietary glances he directed at her. He said, presently, "This is far enough, Henrietta," and caught her by the arm.

His touch, even through the elbow-length glove she wore, felt clammy and the prospect of being embraced by him threatened her like the onrush of a dragon with moist paws and foetid breath. She fell back on the only defence at her disposal, a counterfeit and conventional modesty, instilled into her by a succession of amateur governesses, withdrawing her hand and saying, *"Please, Makepeace! Behave!"*

It sounded very silly, a formal protest directed at a professional thief caught ransacking the family silver and, in a way, she felt herself beset by thieves, a trio of them, including among their number her own father. Their quarry, she realised, was not merely her freedom and future but the most private areas of her body. She was like someone trying to scramble to the summit of an icebound slope without much hope of avoiding a fatal tumble, arms and legs flailing, clothes ripped, and flesh bruised in a descent into—what? A lifetime in the company of this parody of a man, superintending his household, being pinched and patronised by that old miser back in the house, undressing and lying down in bed with Makepeace, and the sheer blankness rather than the unsavouriness of that prospect made her stomach contract within the confines of her tightly-laced corset.

He said, with a hint of bluster, "Behave? But I don't have to 'behave' any more, Henrietta. You know very well what they're discussing back there. You know why father and I are here tonight. You aren't saying your father hasn't mentioned it, are you?" He paused a moment and when she said nothing he drew a long, whistling breath. "I'm expected to propose marriage to you before we go in. Then there's to be a settlement and I'm to get 'The Clough' as a wedding present. We went and looked at it yesterday and found it very suitable. The tenant is getting his notice tomorrow."

What was there to say to that? He mentioned 'The Clough', a small, manor-type house they owned two miles north of the town, as though the prospect of sharing it with him would make any girl of her age swoon with ecstasy, and his very certitude had the power to divert her thoughts and check the panic advancing on her like a wall of sludge.

"When was all this decided? When and how?" she demanded and had the small satisfaction of seeing him look as disconcerted as had her father when she had challenged him that same afternoon.

"Why, soon after the Victory Ball," he said, with a hint of a stutter, "I made up my mind then, Henrietta."

"You made up *your* mind? Didn't it even occur to you to mention it to me?"

He seemed genuinely astonished. "Mention it? But how could I mention it? I had first to discuss it with father. How could I run contrary to him? I have no money. I get a weekly wage, like everyone else in his employ, but he'll make me a generous allowance as soon as we're married and you'll have money too. That's what they're talking about now."

It was astonishing how people like the Goldthorpes and her father were able to canalise everything that happened to them, or was likely to happen to them, into streams leading to that single reservoir. Birth, death, marriage, all manner of personal relationships, all human endeavours and aspirations, led back to that one word. Money. Nothing else counted. Nothing else was of the smallest importance. She said, desperately now, "But I don't love you, Makepeace. How could I? I hardly know you. We've met a few times, we've danced together twice. How could I make up my mind about anything as important as that at a moment's notice? Marriage . . . you and me, moving into a big house like 'The Clough' . . . living together, *always* . . .? It's something that any girl would have to . . . to . . . think about a long time, even a millhand!"

He laughed outright at this but there was relief in his laughter. He said, taking her hand again, "It isn't anything you have to decide, Henrietta. It's important, of course, far too important for someone like you to decide. You wouldn't know how, for that's a man's job and anyway, it hasn't been decided in a moment. I've been considering it ever since the Victory Ball, and so has my father and your father. And now it's arranged!" and his arm went round her waist with a firmness that surprised her.

The wave of panic touched her and broke over her so that she was too frightened and too breathless to find the strength to pull away from him a second time. She found herself groping for words as if they had been pieces of wreckage to keep her head above surface, but even in the tumult of the moment she had a horrid certainty that he assumed her to be overwhelmed by nothing more momentous than the majesty of the occasion, that and the vapourings that were reckoned obligatory on the part of an inexperienced girl receiving her first proposal of marriage. She said, despairingly, "*When* . . .?" but he seemed to take this as an invitation for both arms went round her and his face loomed over her, blotting out the light from the terrace. The scent of flowers in the half-moon beds were vanquished by the whiff of his breath, heavy with claret and a sourness that made her want to retch. She would have fought back with her knees if the arc of the crinoline had not made this impossible, and her right arm had not been pinioned by his left. There were only two avenues of resistance available, a left-handed downsweep of her fingernails across his cheek, or a simulated faint. She chose the latter as the easier to accomplish, buckling her knees so that she slipped below the level of his waistcoat. Then, before he could reach out and support her, she heard the steady drumming of hooves and the spatter of loose gravel and suddenly he was gone and she was on her knees on the grass, cocooned in yards of silk and muslin. Voices called distractedly from the drive and the terrace and she smelled the sharp whiff of a sweating horse. Behind her, as she rose, was a glow in the sky, yellowish

45

white and extraordinarily vivid, so that she thought for a moment she had indeed fainted. But then she saw that the horseman was Joe Wilson, her father's overseer, and that people, including Makepeace and old Matthew, were jostling round him where he had reined in opposite the dining-room windows.

Across the fifty-yard gap her father's voice reached her. "*Afire? Our* mill?" and then everyone began running back and forth, and she saw Makepeace glance towards the summerhouse and instinct prompted her to move out of the ribbon of light cast by the dining-room lamps and into the fringe of the copse where the ferns grew waist high. She heard him call twice but nobody came in pursuit and within minutes Goldthorpe's carriage came pounding through the stable arch and she watched the three men scramble in, and Joe Wilson wheel his sweating horse. Then, in a long, rambling clatter, they were gone.

She thought gratefully, 'It's a sign from heaven, it's God helping me to escape!' and without conscious thought her resolution was formed and she dodged round the summerhouse, avoiding the group of yammering servants gathering on the terrace as they stared up at the glow in the sky, and along the north side of the house to the conservatory door.

She went through it to the hall, up the stairs and along the passage to her room, still littered with her preparations for the dinner party. From the cupboard, where her dresses hung, she dragged out a small basket-trunk full of odds and ends and emptied them on the floor and after that the carpetbag holdall Mrs. Worrell had loaned her to carry discarded clothes to the needy. Recalling its purpose, and the patronage with which she had filled it, she thought of herself as far needier at this moment than the most impoverished family she had visited in the company of the curate, Mr. Burbage. She was deficient in many things, including advice, money and, above all, a plan, but there was no time to isolate any need beyond one to put distance between herself and Makepeace Goldthorpe. It did not occur to her to consider the prospect of staying on and defying her father, for no one had ever successfully defied Sam Rawlinson. A man who could hold a town to ransom through a long summer drought would make light of a locked bedroom door, or tears, or threats of suicide, or anything that she could do to divert him from the course he had decided. Men like Cromaty and McShane, the strike leaders back in the town, understood that and that was why they had put a torch to the mill and now, she supposed, they would all end their lives in gaol on that account. But Cromaty and McShane had offered her a loophole for in these circumstances he was unlikely to return to the house before morning and this gave her a minimum of eight hours to circle the town to the west, reach Lea Green, and catch a train to Liverpool where regular packet boats were said to leave for Ireland. She would be miles away, and perhaps even at sea, before a search could be mounted and it would be some time before anyone thought of asking Mrs. Worrell where she might have gone.

She wondered, as she began to stuff underclothes and toilet bag into the trunk, whether even Mrs. Worrell, the only person in her life who qualified as a confidante, would recall telling her those stories about her mother's family in Kerry. Her father, if he had ever heard of them, had surely forgotten them long ago. Months might elapse before inquiries could be pursued across the Irish Channel and at the moment she could only think in terms of hours. It struck her then that perhaps this flight was not a spontaneous idea after all and might have been dormant in her mind for a long time, or why else was the name and address of relatives she had never seen rooted in her memory? Uncle and Auntie O'Bannion. Shaun and Dympna O'Bannion. Briar Cottage, Ballynagall, County Kerry, Ireland. The words jingled like bells promising laughter and protection, so that she saw her unknown uncle as the traditional stage Irishman, with gap-toothed smile, and her aunt as a woman with a shawl over her head and kind, deepset eyes that would light up with pleasure when a fugitive niece came knocking on the door of Briar Cottage, Ballynagall.

When the basket-trunk was full, and fastened with a girdle, she began putting things into the holdall: shoes, a needlework bag, an extra pair of drawers, one or two pieces of trumpery jewellery, a nightgown, and a half-emptied box of toffees bought when she went into the town to collect the dress. On second thoughts, recalling that she liked toffees, she stuffed the tin under the girdle where it would be handy. Then she turned out her purse on the bed. There was a shilling and a few coppers, enough to buy a railway ticket from Lea Green to Liverpool but certainly insufficient for even a deck passage to Dublin. She put the small change back in her purse and the purse in her reticule and then, gathering up basket-trunk and holdall, she opened the door and listened.

The prattle of the maids rose from the hall via the stairwell. The staff would continue to relish the drama until Mrs. Worrell descended on them from somewhere, and Mrs. Worrell was surely to be avoided as the one person in the house with authority to detain her. For a few moments Henrietta hovered on the threshold, uncertain of her next move, but then something stirred around her calves and she heard the panting of Twitch, her liver and white spaniel, who must have been roused from his kitchen basket by the outcry and slipped up the backstairs to seek reassurance. The presence of Twitch was an added embarrassment. He was very attached to her and would certainly follow wherever she went. Standing there, shushing the dog, clutching the basket-trunk under one arm and the holdall in the other hand, her thoughts began to sort themselves out. She had to have more money. She had to reach the schoolroom and get her atlas (for who could find their way to Ballynagall without an atlas) and she had to reach the shrubbery bordering the drive without being seen. Money was the first priority and she thought she knew where she could find some. Taking brief advantage of a surge of the maids out on to the terrace, when someone shouted news of the crimson glow in the sky, she slipped downstairs and along the passage leading to her father's den.

In here a lamp still burned turned very low. It must have been overlooked during the panic exit of the men from the house. Twitch, scenting the excitement that engulfed the house, pranced along in her wake and she turned up the lamp in order to rummage in the drawers of the desk, recalling that Sam kept a cash-box there for paying out the domestic wages. Most of the drawers were locked but the one containing the cash-box was open and upending it she realised why. There was no coin of a higher value than a shilling and only two of those. The rest, perhaps about seven shillings in all, was made up of sixpences and coppers. She crammed the coins into her purse and leaving her bags under the window ran back along the passage to the schoolroom, still with the spaniel at her heels.

It was dark in here but she found the atlas by running her fingers along the bindings of the tattered school books on the shelf beside the fireplace. The dog was now whimpering with excitement and she hissed, pleading, "Be *quiet*, Twitch! For heaven's sake, be quiet!" and ran across the room, into the passage and straight against the yielding bosom of Martha Worrell.

The shock was so great that she cried out in alarm so that Martha Worrell's brawny arms went round her as she said, "I've been looking for you, child. You heard about the mill? Everyone's half off their heads, and you're to spend the night in my lodge . . .!" but Henrietta broke away, scudding down the passage to the den with Mrs. Worrell in breathless pursuit, until the sight of the luggage piled high on the desk stopped her dead. She hung on the doorpost a moment, gasping for breath. The passage was no more than ten yards long but Martha Worrell weighed seventeen stone. She said, at last, "Where do you think you're going? Who said to pack those things?" and Henrietta, her back against the window, stared back at her defiantly, as though the housekeeper was the agent of Makepeace Goldthorpe, commissioned to deliver her into bondage. She said, through her teeth, "You can't stop me, Martha. I won't stay, you hear? I'm going now, before they come back. They won't give me a thought with what's going on and when they do I'll be gone, I'll be safe in Ireland!"

Martha Worrell passed a hand half as big as a ham slowly across her brows.

"What *is* it, child? What's to do? For mercy's sake, what's scared you so? Those fools in the town won't bother wi' you . . ." and then, because she had known and handled Henrietta from the moment she was born, she sensed that it was not the riot in the town that had planted that stricken look on the girl's face but some other agency and that in some way it had to do with the ceremonial meal she had cooked for Sam Rawlinson's guests that evening. She said, with a flash of intuition, "Goldthorpe's son? Is it *him*?"

There was no help for it now. If she was to get clear in the time left to her Mrs. Worrell would have to be taken into her confidence.

"He's going to marry me. He says it's been arranged between his father and my father. He wasn't pretending, he couldn't have been. He's got a house, 'The Clough', over at High Barton . . ."

"You mean you knew nowt about it? Not until tonight?"

"Father mentioned it this afternoon but he only said Makepeace might come asking, he didn't say it was arranged . . . I *won't* marry him, Martha. They can't make me, can they?"

Martha Worrell had not kept house for Sam Rawlinson for twenty years without learning how to face facts. "Happen they'll try," she said, grimly, and felt the perspiration strike cold under her armpits.

"What else could I do to stop them? They'll keep on, they won't give up. I could see that tonight. It's to do with money, isn't it? *Isn't* it?"

The housekeeper cocked a shrewd eye at her, trying to gauge the difference between a tantrum and hysteria. Then she said, with a whistling sigh, "They'll try an' wear thee down, lass, if they've already got as far as that. Are you sure about 'The Clough'?"

"Makepeace was telling me when Joe Wilson galloped up shouting about the fire."

Mrs. Worrell glanced at the luggage on the desk.

"Eeee, but where did you think of going? Where is there to run to?"

"Ballynagall," Henrietta said, and Martha Worrell's escaping breath sounded like air forced from a split bellows.

"*Ballynagall?* Good life, child, those folk of your mother's haven't been heard of in years! They might be anywhere. They might even be dead! You can't go scampering off to Ballynagall just like that!"

"I can try, I won't stay here after tonight . . ."

The housekeeper made a despairing gesture. "Stop mithering, child. Let me think." She stood squarely against the door, hands clasped across her belly, broad, good-natured face crumpled in the effort of grappling with a string of imponderables.

From across the room, standing within the circle of lamplight, Henrietta divined sympathy and waited. Almost a minute ticked by. There was no sound now except the subdued panting of Twitch who had settled himself on the hearthrug, his attention divided between them.

"Ballynagall is nonsense," Martha said, at last, "leastways, it's nonsense the way you're going about it. I would have to write first, and then wait for an answer. But once your father got wind o' it he'd put a stop to that one way or another. Happen he's as set on that match as Matt Goldthorpe is. I had a notion he was, and maybe I should have warned you but I weren't sure, or not sure enough. It were brewing, that's all I knew for certain." The brooding expression faded and suddenly she looked obstinate and resolute. "But you're reet about one thing, lass. It's now or never, while there's such a to-do in t'town and there's nowt wrong wi' putting distance between yoursen and your father, if only to show your mettle. But *where*, that's the rub!" And suddenly she unclasped her hands so that they were free to slap her belly with satisfaction.

"Our Nelly, be God! Go to our Nelly, i' Garston!"

"The railwayman's wife?"

"Aye, Nelly's the one. She's more spunk nor the others."

"But won't that mean trouble for you if . . ."

"Nay, I'll say I sent you there for safety, and he'll not give it another thought. There'll be plenty to occupy his mind for a spell!"

Dramatically, instantaneously, the initiative passed to her, as though she was not the abettor but the fugitive. "Head for Lea Green and wait on t'first train that stops there. And when you get to Liverpool hire a fly at the station, it's nobbut a few miles. I'll write our Nelly a note saying I sent you on account o' the riots, and the hands throwing bricks at his windows. Tell Nelly my letter will be on your heels but someone'll have to tak' you to Lea Green and it'll have to be Enoch, for he's the only man left about here and that's a blessing. Enoch won't think it daft to be catching a train this hour o' the night. Have you got money?"

"About nine shillings. I took most of it from the cash-box."

She nodded fiercely. "I'll tell him about it. I'll say I couldn't see you go wi' nowt in your purse. But you'd best leave wi'out the girls seeing you. I'll find Enoch and harness the trap."

"May I take Twitch? Would your sister Nelly mind if I took Twitch?"

"You could tak' a zoo along to our Nelly's. The house is a fair tip, spilling over wi' spoiled children and spoiled animals, but the vittles won't be up to the kind you been used to, lass. Her man don't fetch home a sovereign a week and she was never a one to mak' do. Tell her I'll send money for board. Now drop that luggage out o' t'window and pick it up on the way round. I'll send Enoch down to the lodge wi' t'trap."

Henrietta turned her back to drop the bags out on to the gravel, but when she faced around Mrs. Worrell had already waddled as far as the door, so that the girl, with a little cry of dismay, ran across the room, threw her arms about her and kissed her perspiring cheek.

"Darling Martha! I made sure you'd stop me. Why are you doing this? Is it because you hate my father?"

Demonstrations of this kind embarrassed Mrs. Worrell and she shrugged herself free. "Nay, lass," she muttered, "there's far worse nor Sam Rawlinson around. Besides," her brown eyes half-closed as though searching the past, "it was kick out or go under where your father started from but nobody would have wed him to t'wrong lass! Makepeace Goldthorpe indeed! Sharing the bed of a lass I've raised. I'd see all of 'em burned first, along o' t'mill!"

She went out and a moment later Henrietta saw her beckon from the foot of the stairs. She whistled softly to Twitch, moving along to the front door that was standing wide open. Outside, at the den window, she paused to retrieve her bags and looking up at the face of the west turret noted how the glare in the northern sky had coloured it coral. She knew then, with certainty, that she would never see this ugly house again.

51

6

Beyond the copse that bordered the wilder section of the grounds the sky over Seddon Moss was bright orange laced with crimson, and the whiff of the burning mill, and who knew what else besides, was carried for miles on the soft currents of the night breeze. It could not have been mistaken for a bonfire smell for deep within it was the smell of the city, rank and sulphurous, the stink of a dozen factory chimneys out of hand.

The smell and the coral sky scared Enoch and it bothered the pony. Neither knew what to make of it and each, from time to time, lifted a head and snorted. They pushed on, however, beyond the fork of the dust road that led left-handed over the common towards Lea Green and the string of halts serving Cheshire folk living south of the factory belt. It was about here that Henrietta, on her rare excursions to Liverpool had seen the goose-children tending their flocks on the manorial waste but there was no one here now; just her, the scared pony, and Enoch, Mrs. Worrell's odd-job man, who had no roof to his mouth and was reckoned half an idiot.

Because, underneath her outward composure, she was just as frightened as man and beast, Henrietta decided to concentrate her thoughts on remembering how he had wandered up to the backdoor one winter's day, honking his willingness to sweep the drive free of snow in exchange for a drink and a bag of crusts. Henrietta had pitied him then and so, in her practical way, had Martha Worrell. She filled his belly, set him to work, and gave him a place to sleep, two planks laid along the rafters of the gardener's toolshed. Since then Enoch had been the gardener's drudge but the staff called him the Boffin Boy, for the 'boffin' was their name for where he slept. From time to time she had seen him at work in the yard and about the flower-beds, washing down setts, grooming the carriage horse, or hoeing and weeding under McEwan's direction. She had thought of him with compassion but genteel compassion, the kind one felt for blind beggars standing outside the Corn Exchange. Now, by a miracle, or series of miracles, he was her secret agent, helping her to escape from the clammy embraces of Makepeace Goldthorpe and she warmed towards him, wishing with all her heart that she could afford to reward him with a bright new shilling when he left her to await the train at Lea Green in obedience to Mrs. Worrell's instructions. But she could not afford such generosity. It would have to be a penny, or perhaps, if a train was due, two pennies.

About a mile down the track the last of the timber fell away and they began to cross a wide stretch of open moor. The glare in the sky remained constant on the right, where lay Seddon Moss, and over her shoulder Henrietta could see streaks of crimson in the blue-black fringe of horizon. She could contemplate the devastation without any feelings other than relief. Sam could build another mill. She had but one life and could not afford to share it with Makepeace.

Then it happened, suddenly and without the slightest warning if one discounted the interval of airlessness and oppressive silence that had endured since they emerged from the trees. A shaft of lightning forked across the whole width of the sky, its tongues leaping down on the glow in the north-east as though eager to join in such a bonus display. And within seconds of the glare thunder rolled from west to east, a long, long caravan of empty barrels trundled across the arch of the sky, pushing other barrels before them and trailing a string of laggards behind.

She was aware at once of the effect upon Enoch and the pony. Enoch began to honk, just like one of the geese that grazed here-abouts, and the pony stopped dead, bracing itself against the shafts so that the trap tilted violently and the basket-trunk, reposing on end against the box-seat, slithered over the edge and thumped down on to the road. Henrietta cried out and Enoch turned on her, mouth open, eyes almost starting out of his head, and then the whole countryside was brilliantly lit by a second flash, far more extensive than the first, and the thunder crashed down on them like a mountain avalanche, sealing them between walls of booming, thumping, ear-splitting sound that sent every thought but terror skittering across the moor for sanctuary.

This time the pony reared and although she could not hear Enoch's terrified honks on account of the thunder she knew that he was screaming, for his mouth was wide open and his tongue flickering like a snake's. He dropped the reins and threw both hands across his face and as the trap spun in a half-circle Henrietta lost her grip upon the rail and half-rolled over the shafts and down on her hands and knees in the road. The dog Twitch, who had been cowering beside the holdall, leapt after her, and when the third flash lit up the sky the pony was already tearing across the open moor, with Enoch hunched in the driving seat so that he looked like a mound of luggage rather than a boy.

It had all happened so quickly that Henrietta had no time to gesture or call out to him to stop. Before she rose upright, conscious of a smarting pain in her palms and knees, the trap was already fifty yards away and heading towards the main road at a prodigious pace. She saw it once again, silhouetted against the fourth flash, but then it looked infinitely far off, a speck on the empty landscape. Then, preceded by a few heavy drops, the rain began to fall in great, hissing sheets, solid water bucketing out of a world of darting flame and stunning uproar.

She acted solely on the promptings of instinct, trudging back along the road to retrieve her trunk but by the time she reached it she was dripping wet. She stood there for about a minute, water cascading over her head and streaming down her shoulders, so that her shawl stuck to her and small rivulets dribbled from its ends, losing themselves in the ridges and flounces of the crinoline. Then another blinding flash revealed the shepherd's hut built of cunningly-stacked stones and roofed with turf, no more than ten yards off the road and she ran to it, the dog yapping at her heels. There was no door but inside it was warm and dry, and, to an extent, the cacophony of the sky was shut off, as though ten thousand romping children had been banished to another part of the house. She lay on her side gasping and whimpering, the dog close against her breast, the basket-trunk under her head. And presently, while she still trembled, the storm rumbled and grumbled across the moor in the direction of Seddon Moss, and the rain settled to a steady downpour that fell on the turf roof as a shower of peas.

How long she lay like that, or whether or not she dozed, she could not have said but presently reason began to assert itself, its herald a fall in body temperature. The front of her, where the terrified Twitch crouched, was warm, but her back and shoulders grew cold under the dripping shawl and she realised, if she was to survive out here at all, she would have to make some attempt to help herself. She put no faith in Enoch returning to look for her. If he reached home at all he would be most likely to leap out of the trap and seek the shelter of his loft. He would not, perhaps, be questioned by Mrs. Worrell until morning and even then he would have the greatest difficulty in making known to her what had occurred. He might even lie about it, implying that he had seen her as far as Lea Green, and if this was so Mrs. Worrell would assume she caught a train, write her letter to Nelly, and sit back to await a reply. In these circumstances it might be days before she was missed.

The very bleakness of the situation injected courage into her but it was not the courage of desperation that had caused her to flee from the embraces of Makepeace Goldthorpe. She now saw her survival as a kind of apprenticeship in the craft of freedom, an ordeal set her by Providence to test her nerve and hardihood, and because she was Sam Rawlinson's daughter she began, albeit slowly, to take stock of her reserves. Putting aside the dog she carefully raised herself, finding that she could stand upright, her head all but touching the roof. She reached behind her and grappled with the first six hooks of the bodice and when the lowest of them did not respond to her blundering fingers she tore at the fastenings until the material parted and the skirt dropped away, settling itself at her feet. She unfastened the strap of the cage and her three petticoats, all as wet as the dress, fell by their own weight, and soon she was standing in camisole and linen pantalettes and it was at this stage that she made a pleasant discovery. Torrential as the rain had been it had not penetrated beyond the last petticoat and under the tent of the skirt the lower part of her was dry and warm. She went down on her knees again and loosened the strap of the basket-trunk. She had no recollection of what she had stuffed into it and now she made another welcome discovery, for her muff and braided mantle were there, together with two pairs of drawers and one pair of worsted stockings.

Everything that emerged from the trunk gave her infinitely more pleasure than she had experienced when the items had been acquired. There was a comb and silver-backed hairbrush, a square of flannel and a small piece of scented soap, and then, best of all, the tin of toffees, with heroes of the Crimea emblazoned on the outside. She crammed three toffees into her mouth and set about towelling herself with the mantle. The friction was exquisite. She could feel the blood flowing back into her numbed shoulders and the upper part of her arms and in less than five minutes she was glowing and the little hut began to take on a kind of cosiness, as though it accepted her as its new mistress. Outside the rain still fell but there was no urgency in the downpour. Inside with Twitch, already asleep and snoring gently, it was warm and dry and safe, and she found, to her surprise, that she did not care a rap whether Enoch returned or not. Methodically she settled herself crosslegged on a truss of bracken and began the process of wringing out her shawl and petticoats. She could do nothing with the dress and threw it, together with its cage, into the far corner. It did not occur to her that she had no spare skirt.

When the petticoats were as dry as she could get them she hooked them to protruding twigs in branches supporting the turf roof. Notwithstanding the storm the white glare in the east provided enough light to distinguish outlines even inside the hut that now looked like Mrs. Worrell's laundry-room on a Monday. The thought made her giggle, the first time she had giggled since her father had told her why the Goldthorpes were coming to supper. But that was already a thousand years ago.

Presently, having eaten the last of the toffees, she pulled both pairs of open-legged drawers over her head and wore them like two short nightdresses, with the free legs hanging like empty sleeves, and this made her giggle again. Then she put on her nightgown and over the gown her mantle, pulling it closely around her, turning up the fur collar and arranging the basket-trunk and her muff as a pillow. Twitch went on snoring and the rain went on drumming. Soon the two sounds fused into a steady rhythm and she slept.

2

The Black Dwarfs

HE would have thought that seven weeks' shipboard life, with nothing to do but stare at an empty ocean, would have enabled him to marshal his thoughts but in this respect he was disappointed. As the clipper rounded the Cape, and tackled the interminable haul up the coast, his imagination atrophied. He could isolate factors but they were unrelated to one another. The necklace represented capital, over and above the few hundred pounds he had saved from his pay and allowances, but he had no idea how much money it might yield or, indeed, what purpose that money would serve. He was free for the first time in his life but he had no idea what he would do with freedom. The predictability of service life had armoured him against uncertainties for thirteen years, and now he wondered if it was not too late to shed that armour and walk naked into the ring to compete with men who fought without benefit of lance, sabre and drill-book.

His confidence, he discovered, tended to shrink with every sunset, and it was not until the vessel had entered the Channel approaches that he formed any kind of plan concerning the immediate future. It was a very indeterminate plan, embracing what he recognised as obligations, arranged in order of precedence. There was his father, the Colonel, to be placated. There was the reconnaissance he had promised himself of industrial areas, from the shipyards of the north-east, to the cotton belt of Lancashire and the foundries of the Midlands. And there was the disposal of the necklace, without which he could not survive independently for more than a few idle months.

The clipper, they told him, had been diverted to Plymouth, in itself a damnable complication, for he had anticipated landing at Liverpool and disposing of the most important obligation at once. His father lived in retirement at Keswick, on the shores of Derwentwater, and Lakeland was a long way from Plymouth for a traveller encumbered with heavy luggage. Bluebooks, and accounts of Parliamentary debates in out-of-date copies of *The Times*, did not tell a man how to get from Plymouth to Derwentwater, but this was the least of his worries. What concerned him more was the necessity to confess to an ex-field-officer living on half-pay that his only son now possessed means to resign from the Service and take up some kind of commercial career. The old man, he supposed, would be humiliated to discover that a Swann, at the tail of generations of soldiers, was contemplating a break with family tradition at the late age of thirty-one, and was, moreover, proposing to finance it on loot. It was one aspect of the matter, however, that might conceivably be shelved, and he made up his mind that he would spend as brief an interval as was decently possible at home before ranging the country and assessing each opportunity as it presented itself. What he needed more urgently than capital was a confidant who could be trusted, but here the cost of his lost years was again apparent. All his confidants, save only Roberts, were dead. Where was he to find others in a land he had not seen in years and already seemed more alien to him than Bengal?

2

He had reckoned without the green, the great tide of green spilling down to the water's edge, and what the prospect could do to a man who had thought himself weatherproofed against sentiment and schoolbook patriotism.

He saw it for the first time a little after dawn, as the clipper shortened sail to double Rame Head and enter the Sound, a belt of green twenty miles wide and having within it a stupendous variety of shades, each capable of enlisting him in an army of a hundred generations of Englishmen making this particular shore. It tugged at his heart so compellingly that his eyes misted. It was not merely a rare and splendid spectacle but a new emotional dimension, with the power to move him as he had not been moved in a very long time. For years his eyes had been staring at landscapes compounded of greys and browns and soldier-scarlet, all under the glare of a white-hot sun. He had almost forgotten the existence of the word green, for green was a colour that had slipped away with his boyhood and early youth. He stood braced in the bows for more than an hour, marvelling and wondering how he could have forgotten this aspect of England. But now that he saw it again it impinged itself as something very comforting and there came to him, uninvited, a conviction that he would never willingly turn his back on it again.

That was the first miracle of his immediate return. The second was his encounter with Aaron Walker and to these two experiences he owed his re-entry into the stream of individual existence. He thought it strange, on looking back, that his meeting with Walker should have been prompted by curiosity on his part and suspicion on the part of the depot manager; strange, but laughable when one considered all that came of it, for he never saw the man but once. To Adam Swann the meeting was a key to every door he opened across the years. To Walker the encounter could have been no more than an incident in a busy day, superintending the arrival and departure of passengers at the Great Western terminus.

* * *

It was his second day ashore and he had crossed the city from his lodging alongside the boy trundling his trunks on a handbarrow. It was not his intention to stay in the Westcountry longer than it took him to reacclimatise his legs to dry land. Indeed, he only called at the station to despatch his trunks and buy a ticket for the north. The boy offloaded his kit outside a racklined cave labelled '*Left Luggage, Carriage Forward*', and a long-nosed clerk who came forward to receive it read the tags and announced, with gloomy satisfaction, that Keswick (he pronounced it 'Kes-wick') was not in his book. When Adam asked by what route his luggage, and later himself, could be transported there, the clerk consulted his book again and said that he supposed it would be via London, and then by one of the new L. & N.W. expresses, but all he could promise was transportation to Manchester or Liverpool. Then, because Adam's luggage was cluttering his counter and a small queue was assembling he became truculent, as though depositors had no business asking to be routed to places off the map.

Uncertainty had made Adam edgy. He said, impatiently, "Oh, for God's sake, man, you're supposed to run a railway ..." but then, at his elbow, a crisp voice said, "What's your difficulty, Tapscott?"

The voice had asperity, of the kind men like Havelock and Campbell would use to unravel a snarl-up in regimental transport, and Adam turned and looked at the towering figure of Aaron Walker, the depot superintendent, impressively authoritative in stovepipe hat,

59

blue frock coat, and fancy waistcoat festooned with a gold watch-chain. The clerk came to attention like a reprimanded private and explained, the superintendent listening patiently and politely. He said, "Get it on the three-fifteen to Fleetwood via Paddington and Manchester. Send the voucher to my office. The gentleman will be there to receive it," and to Adam, with a friendly nod, "I'll explain if you can spare a moment, sir. I can do it better with a map. Would you care to step along to my office?"

Adam followed the tall figure the length of the arcade, noticing as they went that not only employees but passengers made way for them, one or two bewhiskered men even touching their hats, as though hoping to be noticed. The superintendent wore his authority like his stovepipe, securely but without ostentation, and ushered Adam into a large, dingy room, dominated by an enormous desk, closing the door on an orchestra of escaping steam and human out-cry. Through a dirty window, Adam noted, the stationmaster could keep watch on his domain, a network of steel rails filling a space of several acres across which locomotives, large and small, coughed and shunted and nudged one another in a metallic ballet. But it was not the man or the view that engaged Adam's attention so much as an enormous map that covered half the facing wall and he saw it as the equivalent of a campaign progress chart, of the kind he had seen in regimental headquarters in India during the last eight-een months. The man intercepted his glance, smiling a slow proprie-tary smile. He said, "I'm obliged to know where my passengers can go and where they can't. The clerk was right, however. We can't route you to Keswick, not even indirectly," and he picked up a ruler, using it as Adam had seen his mathematics tutor use a black-board pointer.

The ruler was superfluous. The map spoke for itself. It was at once enormously complicated and excessively simple, with London as the hub of a skein of lines that ran north, north-east, north-west and south, like the warped spokes of a ruined waggon wheel. Every spoke sprouted innumerable spurs and some of the parent spurs smaller spurs. Here and there the hard outlines of the network tapered off into dotted lines representing, Adam assumed, projected railroads or railways in building. Every spoke and most of the spurs had a boldly-printed name, *North Kent, London & Brighton, South East-ern, Eastern Counties. The Essex & Suffolk* probed across the flat country to Harwich. *The Great Western* lunged at Bristol. The *Great Northern* shot off the map into Scotland. *The North Western* and its Midland progeny spilled across the heart of England into the cotton towns and the Wirral peninsula. He said, casually, "Would it be possible to buy a map like that?" and because he was still facing the wall he failed to note a hardening of the superintendent's expression, who said, sharply, "No, sir, I'm afraid not! That map is my stock-in-trade. What would yours be?"

Perhaps Adam's acceptance of the question, as one put in good faith by someone with little time to waste, disconcerted Walker but only for a second. He shifted his weight and cocked his head, at the same time studying his visitor's back with more than casual interest. Adam said, innocently, "I have to get to Keswick but not necessarily today. My concern is to get rid of my heavy luggage," and then he turned and met the ironic gaze of the man, his soldier's instinct telling him he was being assessed for other reasons than his ability to pay the fare. He said, uncomfortably, "How far can I go on the L. & N.W.? Or do I inquire again at London?"

The superintendent relaxed slightly but he did not drop his glance lower than Adam's chin. "I can give you any information they'll give you at Paddington about routes." Then, with the kind of jocular emphasis, that again reminded Adam of an usher, "Keswick? Fleetwood would be the best approach, and after that it would be by post-horse or hired fly, unless you made part of the trip on the new Kendal-Windermere track. Damnably difficult country up there. Too much water and too many mountains. Doesn't recommend itself to the stockholders, not even the sporting gentlemen looking for a flutter. No, after Fleetwood, it'll be a matter of livery stables."

It was clear then that by asking about the map he had, in some way, offended the man, and this puzzled him for up to the moment of entering the office he had been impressed by the superintendent's courtesy. He said, "I beg your pardon, Superintendent, I should have had better manners. Fleetwood, you said? Thank you," and turned on his heel but before he had moved a step the man said, with laughter in his voice, "Oh, come, it isn't your manners that are at fault, it's your tactics. I find them amateur and a military gentleman, specially selected by foxhunters and their lawyers, shouldn't want for tactical skill, should he? Sit you down. Have a cheroot. Then tell me who you are representing and we'll straighten it out somehow. We usually do, for if money can't buy a concession money plus stock can in nine cases out of ten."

To any other officer lately in the service of the East India

Company Walker's remarks would have been incomprehensible but to Adam Swann, primed on the Parliamentary columns of *The Times*, the superintendent's gibes had significance. Civilians had their wars and this man was clearly engaged in one somewhere along his routes. Adam turned back into the room, sat down, and accepted the proffered cheroot.

"You're right about the Service," he said, "but the fact is I'm a civilian now. I'm on discharge leave until the end of the month and I came ashore from the *Bombay City* yesterday."

Walker's wary expression did not waver. "You'll have to prove that," he said, biting on his cheroot, whereupon Adam took his discharge papers from one pocket and his ticket stub from another, placing them side by side on the desk and watching the man facing him knit his brows as he examined them.

"You mean you really are a bona-fide passenger for Keswick? You came in here independently?"

"I came in here at your invitation, Superintendent."

The superintendent threw up his head and laughed, and his hand reached out across the desk, the gesture of a genial extrovert who had never, in his entire life, been embarrassed.

"Damn me, I would have wagered a month's salary against one of those cigars you were a spy," he said, blandly. "I even gave those damned lawyers credit for trying a new approach." Then, suddenly, "But why *did* you want that map? What possible use could it be to you? We issue timetables."

"It's a long story," Adam said, "and I couldn't put more than half of it into words that would make sense to you."

"Try. If you succeed I'll give you the map."

"You mean that?"

"I scrap it and replace it every week. That one goes into the wastepaper basket the moment tomorrow's mail comes in with the latest amendments. You're thinking of investing in railway stock?"

"If I did it would be in my own branch."

"You came home to *build* a railway?"

"Not necessarily. I came home from a war that made no sense in order to engage in one that did, one in which I was required to use brains as well as brawn. My name is Swann, Adam Swann, and I'm the sixth Swann in line to hold a commission in the armed forces. It has taken me thirteen years to break with family tradition. It's not an easy thing to accomplish, Mr. . ."

"Walker, Aaron Walker, onetime railway architect under

Brunel, now shunted into this," and he spread a hand across the littered desk. "No, that isn't easy to accomplish, and I ought to know. My father was a parson, the third of his line, and he summoned the family doctor when I told him I intended to build railways. All the same, I wouldn't apprentice a son of mine to the trade now. In its heyday it was high adventure, particularly working under a genius like Brunel. Now it's a carcase torn by jackals. And I took you for one of 'em," and he laughed his booming laugh again. "Listen, Mr. Swann, I owe you an apology so here it is, plus some advice. Do something more original than build a railway. You look to me the kind of man who might, or why else should you have turned your back on India where the pickings now promise to be legal and substantial?"

"I helped to empty the well at Cawnpore."

Walker looked at him with a new interest. "That has a bearing on why you're here? But a man doesn't make money out of withdrawals, Mr. Swann."

"I should enjoy making money as much as the next man but it would have to be from some form of personal enterprise. India needs policing but I'm not a policeman. Maybe I have too much sympathy with the burglar or, at all events, with the burglar's motives. But even that isn't the whole truth."

"What is the whole truth, Mr. Swann?"

"Let's say I've had my fill of risking my skin to glorify buffoons, like that prize idiot Cardigan of the Light Brigade."

"You were in the Crimea as well as the Mutiny?"

"I saw the Light Brigade shot to pieces. I daresay I should have died with it if I hadn't had the luck to be riding a lamed horse that particular day. You could say I've had luck of a kind all along. Only two of my Addiscombe class survived the Mutiny, me and one other. But it can't last for ever and if I go down it'll be in my own cause. Does that earn me the map, Mr. Walker?"

The superintendent settled himself, shooting his long legs under the desk and tilting his chair. "Why take it for granted commercial warfare is less chancy? Or more civilised for that matter? I assure you it isn't, or not nowadays. The best times are behind us. It's a costermonger's scramble for money and power today. There's no idealism or personal initiative left in it. A thousand companies, most of them bucket shops, scrambling for concessions and for Johnny Raw's cash to squander. No cohesion. No unity of purpose. Just quick profits at the expense of the Crown, the public, and the other speculator over the hill. And speaking of hills, Mr. Swann, I'll give you something better than a map. Don't invest a penny in railways. Anything else you care to name but not railways. Why? Because all the main trunk routes are laid, and in less than ten years ninety-five per cent of the smaller lines will be carrying freight and passengers at a loss. All that's left for the gleaners is to build where no railway could possibly pay and that map will prove it. You obviously know something about it, so you might also remember Stephenson's Chat Moss? You watched Balaclava and I watched Chat Moss. It made my blood run cold. His reputation, and hundreds of thousands of speculators' cash, staked on the double track between Manchester and Liverpool, and there it was, disappearing into a bog overnight."

"Stephenson mastered Chat Moss."

"Men like Stephenson and Brunel are two in ten million, Mr. Swann. And in those days their backers were interested in something better than money. Do I make my point?"

Adam said, smiling, "You're making so many points that I'm beginning to wonder if I should re-enlist," and then, with an eagerness that made him feel a boy in this man's presence, "I've lain out there under the stars dreaming of people like you. Army life made a Crusoe out of me. I'm turned thirty but I've got ambition and a certain amount of capital to invest. If you were me, and wanted to start all over again, how would you begin, Mr. Walker?"

"That's putting a damnable responsibility on someone who mistook you for a lawyer's tout," Walker said, but tilted his chair forward and placed both elbows on the table, so that Adam, watching his expression, knew he would get an honest answer. Walker said, after a longish pause, "Forget steel, coal, cotton, wool, and everything else that gave us a headstart over the Continentals. Forget land too. British agriculture is marked down for death. I don't see you as a retailer, so what remains? Something where the years behind you aren't entirely wasted. Something where the lessons you learned in the field can be added to your capital."

"Go on."

"You're an ex-cavalryman and you must have specialist knowledge of horses. There's more future in horse-transport than the Cleverdicks would have you believe. The railways can solve all the big problems but none of the small ones. They can't in a group of islands threaded by rivers and broken up by stiff gradients and marshes like Chat Moss and the Fens. If I were you, Mr. Swann—

and I wish to God I were and starting all over again—I would spend the next week studying the *blank areas* of that map there. Then travel about and take a look at the goods yards of the most successful companies, and see merchandise piled in the rain on all their loading bays for want of a good dispersal system. Think about that, Mr. Swann. And here's a final piece of advice, to prove I'm a disinterested party. When you go north to Cumberland don't use my railway, except for your luggage. You've been away from your potential workshop a long time and you won't learn anything new about it staring out of a carriage window at cows. Get yourself a good horse—you can buy one at today's market for a handful of guineas— and take advantage of this wonderful weather we're having." He looked at the map. "Plymouth to Derwentwater. Say three-fifty miles, at around twenty miles a day, and as good a cross-section of the country as you'd find between any two points of the compass. Think about that too, Mr. Swann, and here is your homework, with my compliments."

He took the map from its clamps and folded it eight times, reducing it to a crackling package about eighteen inches long and half as broad. Somewhere a bell clanged and Aaron Walker glanced out of his peephole window. "That's the twelve-ten from Bristol, right on time and I have to meet it. There'll be a gaggle of directors aboard, all come to see how I waste my time 'downalong'. I have some difficulty convincing them I am not addicted to playing bowls on the Hoe, Mr. Swann."

They shook hands across the desk and Adam followed him out into the arcade. Nothing had changed out here. Sombre gentlemen in dark suits and tall hats, all the cares of commerce on their shoulders, dodged in and out of the platform barriers. Luggage trundled by on two- and four-wheel trolleys. Women in 'travelling' crinolines swished past, shaking their flounces to rid them of drifting smuts. The rumble of trucks, the intermittent hiss of escaping steam, the squeals of excited children soared like a multi-tongued prayer to the echoing canopy of the depot. With a lift of his hand Aaron Walker was swallowed up in a swarm of customers and underlings.

Adam drifted back to the luggage cave to claim the stub that the long-nosed clerk had been too busy to bring and recognising his man he looked worried. "Not had a minute, sir," he said, "but I got it right here tell the Gaffer," and he produced a voucher from his waistcoat pocket. "You can get your ticket at the booking-hall under the clock," he added, as though to ward off a possible reprimand, but Adam felt he could afford the luxury of a small joke.

"The luggage is going ahead," he said, "but I'm following. On horseback," and he thought he had never seen a man look more outraged. He went out into the June sunshine and boarded the nearest cab for the cattle market.

3

It was the most leisurely journey of his life and certainly the most instructive. As he moved north-east, sometimes taking as long as four days to cross from one county border to the next, a whole spread of England unfolded, so that he saw not merely their geographical features but the crafts and characters of the people rooted in successive hill-folds and river bottoms. His ear, always attuned to dialects, marked their speech idioms, vowel sounds, and habits, and sometimes even their professions were revealed to him in gait and gesture. As he watched them from an inn window overlooking some village green his sense of isolation fell away, leaving him tolerant, watchful and deeply at peace with himself, as though he had entered into a new and deeper kinship with all he remembered of childhood and boyhood, and all he had admired in Englishmen whose bones lay in shallow graves on the slopes of the Fedioukine Hills and the Causeway Heights, and in half-a-hundred squalid villages along the banks of the Ganges.

But this was by no means all he gained following Aaron Walker's eccentric advice. On still, midsummer nights, and again in the first hour after sunrise, he would sit crosslegged before his bivouac tent pitched in some woodland clearing, or beside some tumbling stream, sniffing, watching and listening to the life stirring about him, recalling the name of this bird or that, checking his memory against a flash of plumage among the June gorse, and slowly adjusting to the miracle of regeneration that the scenes and scents of the countryside presented. And as this healing process advanced the stench of putrefaction that had lingered in his nostrils since Cawnpore was exorcised by the scent of honeysuckle, and of a hundred hedgerow flowers for which he had no names. Soon this sense of liberation enlarged itself into an almost physical experience, so that to some extent he could analyse it, relating it to memories of a pastoral England that must have been hiding in his saddlebags all these years. It had to do, he supposed, with the casually bestowed legacies of Smollett and Goldsmith, Constable, Cotman and Crome, who gave a man a sense of belonging in the community of men who shod his horse and women who served him ale. But there was a wider, more restless community in the glades and along the verges where he unsaddled, a shy and puckish life-force that stirred and rustled and whistled and flitted whenever he and his mare were still.

There were so many Englands. On that first day's ride over the moor to Moretonhampstead he crossed a treeless tract that stretched as far as the eye could see and before the sun got up, drinking up the ground mist at a draught, he might have been clip-clopping across the clouds with only a distant tor for company. It was the best kind of weather for a jaunt of this kind, cool in the early mornings, when he sometimes urged the mare into a mile-consuming jog-trot, blazing hot at noon, when he sought the sanctuary of the woods, and cool again in the evening, when he would seek a pleasant spot for his bivouac, eat a cold supper, and listen to his thoughts. He was never lonely, as he had been during the voyage. Everywhere he went he met with a polite, impersonal welcome from cottagers, innkeepers, drovers and village craftsmen, who gave him directions and passed the time of day with the incurious civility of people whose lives had adjusted to the sweep of the centuries, whose traditions were habits before Angevin kings had brought a measure of security and stability into their fields and townships.

He first became aware of this on his third day out, when he was crossing Exeter on a market day and the grey towers of the cathedral were presiding over a weekly rout that had persisted among the huddle of shops and stalls and houses for time out of mind, and a much older England again asserted itself in Honiton, Taunton and Wells, all of which seemed to him to be enjoying the best of both worlds, the rich fat of a prosperous present, and the serenity of a settled past, for in all three places money was changing hands fast, the children looked fat and rosy, and time, doled out sparingly by the bells of thirteenth-century churches, had no power to accelerate the pace of the countryman's walk, or the speed with which he drove bargains with his neighbours.

On the seventh day he reined in a few miles beyond Bridgewater and looked over his shoulder at the field of Sedgemoor, recalling that these people had had their share of tribulation, and that the peace they took for granted had not been acquired without struggle and sacrifice, for it was in these dykes and withy clumps that Kirke and his dragoons had hunted men like coneys, slaughtering some and delivering others up to Jeffreys as human sacrifices to the bigotry of a London-based king. It crossed his mind then to wonder whether the clamour of battle would ever return to this sun-soaked plain, and whether Englishmen would continue to press for an extension of the basic liberties they had wrestled from Norman overlords, a greedy church, and the swarm of opportunists who, over successive centuries, had gravitated to the wealthiest city in the world. He had to admit that they looked more than capable of surviving down here among their hayricks and their sleek, cud-chewing cattle, but his confidence was shaken somewhat by witnessing, at a place called Radstock, west of Bath, a shift of coal-miners emerge from the pit and disperse to their cottage homes after a ten-hour stint in galleries far below the Mendips. He had not realised until then that they mined coal this far west, or that the stain of industrial expansion had spread so far beyond the Midland plain, the cotton belt and the woollen towns. The men, moving like stocky gnomes, looked exhausted and apathetic, but then he remembered that dramatic advances in the franchise were already being won from the central government by their counterparts in the Midlands and the North, and also that many vocal leaders were emerging from the ranks of that catalyst of independence, the good old British Puritan.

Through Bath, where he rested his mare for two days, then on over the uplands of the Cotswolds, through stone villages that looked as if they had been built to withstand annual hurricanes and an occasional earthquake, and on beyond Gloucester where he rode across the Vale of Evesham, rich with the promise of a bumper fruit harvest and populated by a brusquer, more matter-of-fact countryman than he had met further west.

It was half a day's ride beyond Worcester that he first saw the dun brown cloud on the north-eastern horizon, telling him that he was now approaching the cluster of towns at the junction of the four shires, shires that remained predominantly agricultural but ceded annual territory to the urban sprawl that constituted one of the main centres of national wealth.

He reined in here for a spell a few miles short of Stourbridge, and the process of assimilation was underlined for him by a sudden and rather poignant memory of young Paget, a chubby Worcestershire lad who had shared some of his vigils in the trenches before Sebastopol, and died soon after on the slopes of the Redan. The memory of Paget was very vivid here on his home ground, a pink-cheeked, fanciful youngster much given to spouting poetry, especially Gray and Wordsworth, a self-confessed hater of industrialisation and particularly averse to the spread of railways that bid fair, he declared, to ruin Worcestershire and Shropshire hunting. Paget, he recalled, had even invented a parable about it, involving the ransom this Midland heart of England had paid to what he called The Company of Black Dwarfs, changelings shown the door by the yeoman of the four shires and had then formed an alliance against them, with headquarters just across the Warwickshire border at what had been the village of Birmingham. Their aim, he vowed, was to extend their domination of every farm, field and coppice of the island kingdom, until the entire nation slaved and sweated under a sulphur-yellow pall lit by the glow of their furnaces.

It was an extravagant and prejudiced notion, but it had substance of a kind, and looking over his shoulder at the stationary mushroom cloud in the sky, he could share for a moment Paget's gloomy vision of the Black Dwarfs' master-plan—to filch a green acre there, to raise a brick breastwork there, to push their sooty picquet lines across fields yellow with charlock until their advance was stemmed by the mountain bastions of Wales, once more a final refuge for the original inhabitants of the island. For himself, however, he was prepared to compromise. From where he sat his horse on the last wooded bluffs of Worcestershire, and within sight of the town of Wolverhampton, the country fell away to a greyish plain of uniform flatness, where the theme of enterprise was marked out by the forking lines of the Severn Valley railway and the Oxford, Worcester and Wolverhampton line picked out in the puff clouds of two, slow-moving freight trains, one heading for the old England, the other into the heart of the new.

He sat there, his feet free of the stirrups, thinking of Aaron Walker's advice, pondering the multiplicity of products piled in those crawling waggons, and wondering what the volume of overland freight might be in the densely populated area on his right. The railways had their own door-to-door delivery services. He had seen some of their flat-topped drays, dragged by gigantic shire horses, moving ponderously along the few main roads he had crossed, but he would say that the service was slow and unpunctual, limited to roads that had gone into a terrible decline since the railways had killed off the coaching and packhorse companies. He took out his map and, dismounting, spread it on the grass verge, securing the corners by pebbles. Half-formed ideas began to shape in his mind and the most insistent of them was hitched to that parting remark of Walker about the open spaces between the lines criss-crossing the country. There were several to be spotted even here, where towns with populations of around forty thousand were almost two a penny. The great triangle between Worcester, Shrewsbury and Leominster; the squashed square staked out by Stratford, Spetchley, Droitwich and Birmingham itself; the hilly, untapped reservoir of central Wales where, he supposed, a railroad could never show a profit, and a closer study of the map showed him it was similar all over the east and south, and along most of the two hundred miles he had already travelled. Only in the north was the iron network dense and interwoven, where rails converged from the south and east towards the ruler-straight slash of Stephenson's pioneer line between Manchester and the coast. Here, as on the far side of the Pennines where lay the woollen towns, rail spurs projected in almost every direction, and even where they did not, dotted lines indicated that surveyors were already at work and the bickering between engineers, farming interests and foxhunters had begun.

He folded the map, replaced it in his saddlebag, and went down the gentle slope and across the plain to the southern suburbs of the city, the mare's shoes scuffling on sun-slippery setts, the bondsmen of the Black Dwarfs staring up at him curiously, as though they had never seen a man astride a horse.

The acrid atmosphere made him sneeze and the mare resented it too, for she flung up her head, as though eager to break into a canter and put bricks and mortar behind her. He pushed on through the city, tempted to follow the line of the Shrewsbury and Birmingham Railway to Shifnal and take a passing look at the King's Oak at Boscobel, but he thought better of it, reminding himself that he was here as prospector not sightseer. Thereafter he hugged the great trunk line of the London and North Western, that he might have been riding along had he not chanced to meet Aaron Walker.

Once the city was behind him there was more green country to be seen liberally dotted with farms and occasional coppices of elm, beech, lime and chestnut. But he had a sense of riding along a shrinking corridor, with pressures at either end, and the countrymen he met lacked the geniality of the men in the west, as though they were uncomfortably aware of the march of the Dwarfs.

At Stafford, and later at Crewe, he found the black army well entrenched but the next few stages took him on to the broad Cheshire plain where, although sliced in half by a main line, the countryman was still king. Up here were some of the neatest, cleanest and most prosperous-looking farms Adam had ever seen, and the men who inhabited them were clearly on the road to becoming gentry, for they sat thoroughbred horses arrogantly and wore well-cut broadcloth, with nothing in common with farmers south and west of the Cotswolds but the tan of the open air. It was a pleasant, settled country, likely to put up a sturdy resistance, or so he thought until, on his third day in Cheshire, he approached the northern border half way between Manchester and Liverpool and here, almost at a stride, he re-entered no-man's-land.

To the south the fields and copses spread away as far as the horizon but to the north, just beyond the railway, lowering sky banners told him the Dwarfs were in complete control of the landscape and there in such numbers that they could never be driven out.

It was evening then, a still, airless sunset, with every leaf drooping, the sun a flaming ball over the Wirral, and the smoke-stack of a tired, Liverpool-bound goods train shooting cotton volleys straight into the sky as it dragged itself east to west. He reined in where a dust road joined the metal road and studied his smaller ordnance map, thinking longingly of a draught of cool beer and perhaps the luxury of a hip bath in an inn. There was a town on the skyline, one of a line of towns that starred the father and mother of all railways, like a row of guard towers along Hadrian's Wall, and he had already seen sufficient of these towns to know that they promised little in the way of comfort. They were usually no more than vastly enlarged villages, where someone had converted a barn into a mill and then other mills had come and perhaps a small foundry. After that the jerrybuilders had swarmed in to run up their rows of back-to-back shanties along streets that often bore pastoral names but were, for all that, no more salubrious than the foetid alleys that ran inland from the wharves of Wapping and Rotherhithe. The mare was tired, however, both of them were hungry, and there was nowhere to bivouac, so Adam moved off down the macadamised road and straight into chaos.

4

The first indication that something unusual was happening in Seddon Moss was the number of men abroad, all surging in one direction towards an open space that did duty for a town Square. Their expressions were enough to alert him. He had seen looks of that kind in the days leading up to the first murders at Meerut, and there was a kind of loose discipline in the movement that made him think of the parade ground degradation of the 3rd Native Cavalry that had touched off the Mutiny, dragging from the massed ranks of sepoys the long, rumbling growl of *'Dohai! Dohai! Dohai!'*

Curiosity made him forget his fatigue and when a man at the door of a hovel glanced in his direction he reined in and asked what was happening. The man hesitated and then spat, viciously but not very accurately.

"If you're a stranger then give t'square a bloody wide berth. Lads mean to make an end of it but they've nowt agin anyone but Sam Rawlinson and ye c'n spread that as far as Manchester."

Adam swung himself out of the saddle. "I was looking for an inn, somewhere I can put up the horse and get a bite to eat. Is it a strike?"

The man looked him over carefully before answering. "Nay, a lockout," he said. "Sam Rawlinson's overstepped t'mark this time. There's men there as'll burn his bloody mill if they have their way, but that's daft. Burn t'mill and they'll fetch in troops an' yeomanry be railroad, same as they did last time, and them as they caught in the open are still blacklisted; if they haven't starved, or died in gaol long since."

Adam asked him how long the lockout had persisted and the man said, "Third month we're entering, and all over a penny an hour and a bloody breakfast break! Sam's daft and they're daft. There's nowt we coulden agree upon over a pint of ale."

A woman's querulous voice called from the dark interior of the house. "Who's there, Harry? Who's at t'door?"

"Nobbut a toff ridin' through," the man answered casually but the woman shouted, "Bolt t'door and come in out of it, like I warned!" and the man grinned toothily, indicating that orders of that kind carried more weight than the high-pitched voice of an orator Adam could already hear from the direction of the Square. He added, however, "Do like I say, man. Give bloody town a wide berth. There's a good enough inn no more than a ten-minute trot south, beyond the crossroads on the Warrington turnpike." Then he spat again and closed the door and Adam heard the bolt grate and the rumble of voices beyond.

He remembered the inn, a rundown establishment a hundred

yards or so up the dust road but he had passed it because it looked unsavoury. Now, he supposed, there was no help for it, for the mare's head was drooping and hunger gnawed at his belly. And yet he was reluctant to leave without hearing something of the men's grievances, and deciding whether the hagridden man at the door had mistaken a noisy demonstration touched off by boredom and the staleness of the day, for the certainty of a riot. Then he remembered the expression on the faces of the men and went on down the narrow street to the fringe of the crowd that now filled the small Square and was spilling into the approaches.

Here there was no mistaking the mood of the demonstrators, women as well as men and even groups of half-grown children, all chattering like magpies. The entire town was afoot, drawn to a loading bay on the far side of the space that was being used as a platform for the speakers. It was not long before Adam began to regret having failed to take the man's advice, if not for himself then for the sake of his mare whose manners were being sorely tried by the press. It was then about half past eight and not yet dusk, although the closeness of the atmosphere filled the Square with an unnatural yellow light as though the heavy sky, bent on coming to the meeting, was bearing down on the multitude and working upon the restlessness of every man, woman and child assembled there. A distant growl of thunder heightened this impression and a ripple of nervous anticipation ran through the crowd, producing a kind of sigh that was caught up by the strident voice of a wildly gesticulating orator.

No one molested him, but no sooner had he edged into the Square than he began looking for a way out, deciding that he was unjustified in exposing those about him to the risk of being trampled if the mare began to rear. Holding her on a close rein he edged his way along the southern face of the Square until he found a ramp that ran up towards the goods yard of the station. The crowd was thinner here and he could observe it individually. He had never seen so many misshapen people assembled in one place. At least half of the men and women about him seemed to be twisted or crippled, as though he had strayed into a world of the brothers Grimm, populated by the humpbacked, the lame, and the knock-kneed. On every face was the same sullen expression that he had noticed among the men on the outskirts of the town, but here he could smell their sweat and hear the whistle of their breath as they stumbled by in groups in an effort to come within earshot of their leaders' harangues. He saw two uniformed constables, whose faces were set and strained, and whose efforts to control the crowd seemed to be confined to packing as many people into the Square as it would hold, for they prodded the laggards into the main stream against which Adam now battled in his efforts to reach higher ground and cross the embankment to open country.

At the top of the ramp he saw that this was not possible. He was now in a cul-de-sac, sealed by a wire fence bordering the permanent way. A constable crossed over and asked if he was a member of the Yeomanry and when Adam said he was not, and that he had entered the town in search of an inn, the man said, "Any shakedown i' Seddon Moss will have its shutters up tonight, sir. There's nobbut a dozen of us, and what can we do now they've torn up the track? They knew we were expecting reinforcements down the line but somebody blabbed and Sam Rawlinson'll pay the piper if they don't get here in time." Then, with a bitterness that half-enlisted him with the demonstrators, he made a similar comment to the man whose wife's tongue had kept him off the streets. "To think it's come to this! 'Forty-two over again, and all on account of a penny an hour and a breakfast snap!"

"Are you expecting the Yeomanry?" Adam asked. "They're breaking no law holding a public meeting, are they?"

The man looked up at him sardonically. "Tha' don't know Sam Rawlinson's hands if you're banking on 'em listening to hot air and then goin' quietly to bed. They'll sack his mill if they have their way," and he looked balefully at the yellowish sky. "On'y one thing can save it now and that's a storm and a drenching all round."

They were interrupted by a full-throated roar that was echoed by a second roll of thunder and a flicker of lightning, followed by a third, much heavier peal. As the constable broke into a run, Adam saw the section of the crowd closest to him surge forward leaving the foot of the ramp almost clear. At the same moment a yellow streak of flame rose from the loading bays and ran the length of the piers. A stunted man came scrambling through the fence and ran past Adam shouting, in a gleeful, sing-song voice, "They've fired t'bales! They've fired bloody bales ...!" before disappearing round the corner at top speed. The mare began to tremble so Adam slid from the saddle and looped the reins to the fence post, running down the ramp to see if the nearest face of the Square was clear enough to make his way back by the route he had come. Mercifully it was, for now the crowd had split, one section surging across to the fire on the loading bays, the other and larger section moving diagonally across

74

the width of the Square towards a large oblong building opposite. Above the tumult he could hear the crash of glass and from the elevation of the ramp he saw smoke curling from several of the first-storey windows of the mill. Over on the left side of the Square a fire-bell clanged and through the smoke Adam could make out the tossing heads of stationary horses, apparently harnessed to an engine that was being prevented from moving towards either fire. He could even see the silhouette of the driver, arms upraised as in supplication, before he was dragged from the box and swallowed up in the crowd.

The frenzy of the spectacle kept him there for perhaps a minute, absorbing small, unrelated facets of the scene: a fat woman dragging a screaming child by the hand; a tall, scarecrow of a man scrambling on to a wall surrounding the building, a brand held above his head so that he looked like a figure in an allegorical painting; the wide, glittering arc cut by a metal object, probably a fireman's helmet, as it soared out of the group struggling round the engine. Then, like a frame for these pictures, came the steady lick of flames under the angled roof of the mill. He thought, grimly, 'My God, this is like Delhi all over again,' and ran the length of the ramp, untying the reins and dragging the horse round with the object of fighting his way out before the Yeomanry and police reinforcements waded into the mob. It was something he had seen once before, when the military had been called out to quell a bread riot at Hounslow during his first year of service. The memory of Englishmen trampling Englishmen still had the power to disgust after the passage of years marked by the Crimea and Cawnpore. The mare wheeled again, dragging at the rein and backing away from the intense glare and the uproar rising from the Square. With a curse he fumbled with the straps that enclosed his rolled boatcloak, dragging it free and blinding the horse with its folds. She quietened at once so that he was able to drag her down the ramp and along the unembattled face of the Square to the street by which he had entered the town. Here it was relatively deserted. He removed the cloak, tied it about his own shoulders, and lifted a foot to the stirrup. At that moment several things happened simultaneously.

Behind him part of the mill roof collapsed with a soft explosion and a million sparks soared, making the narrow street as light as day. Ahead of him, but as yet heard rather than seen, a group of horsemen thundered over the setts, the first coming into view while he stood with his hands on the pommel and one foot on the ground so that he paused before swinging himself into the saddle. Then, on

75

the blind side of the horse, a shambling little figure in clothes several sizes too large for him darted from the shadows and ran diagonally across the street towards the doorway of a shop. He was standing close against the wall immediately opposite the shop and another flicker of lightning lit up the scene in the greatest detail. He had time to take note of the first galloping horseman, a thickset man in a low-crowned beaver hat, who sat his horse awkwardly, as though unused to the saddle. The darting figure in the baggy clothes saw the horseman at the same time and he seemed to hover in the shop doorway. Then, with panic in every movement, he turned and ran back across the street, right into the path of the leading policeman, if policeman he was. A collision was not inevitable but the horseman made it so, swinging his horse hard left so that its shoulder struck the running figure a heavy glancing blow. Adam saw the man's hand shoot up and down, a short cudgel he was holding crashing down on the reeling figure with tremendous force, so that the crack of the wood on bone punctuated the uproar in the Square.

The force of the blow swept the victim inwards under the belly of the horse and then another flicker of lightning showed a feebly threshing ball, spurned by the rear hooves the width of the street and finally coming to rest against the wall of the shop.

By then the following horsemen were on the scene, about a dozen of them, some in uniform and some not, and behind them a reck-lessly-driven carriage containing two passengers, one elderly and sitting hunched on the box, the other young and standing upright, lashing the horse with a long switch. The cavalcade swept by in a confused mass, debouching at the Square where its arrival created re-newed uproar. In a moment the little street was empty except for Adam and the huddled figure under the window of the shop.

He went over and knelt on the greasy setts, turning the figure over and looking down at the face. It was a dead face, the face of a child about thirteen, wearing clothes that were obviously cutdowns, for sleeves and trouser legs were shortened to half their original length. The eyes, wide open, held an expression of terror, and thin trickles of blood ran from the nostrils and the corners of the mouth. Adam Swann had seen innumerable dead men before, slain in hot blood on a dozen contested fields, and had witnessed any number of execu-tions at Delhi and elsewhere, but this was different and he could only think of it as murder. This had occurred in an English street, and the butcher had not been a maddened sepoy, in the grip of terror, big-otry and prejudice but a middle-aged Englishman, at the head of

76

men representing the forces of order. He knelt there looking into the accusing eyes of the child and his gorge rose. The action was at one with everything ugly he had noted passing through the territory of the Black Dwarfs. It was pitiless, pitiable, obscene. It had the power to stir him as no scene of carnage apart from the well at Cawnpore had stirred him, for there was nothing inevitable about it, as of one blind force colliding with another. It was a single, decisive gesture, proclaiming the terrible arrogance of the propertied against the weak and dispossessed, and in a way it fused with the terrible indignation he and Roberts and every other mercenary had experienced in their fighting advance along the Ganges.

He took a handkerchief and wiped the face clean. Then he straightened the grotesquely clothed limbs and looked over his shoulder in the direction of the wild outcry behind him. It was futile to seek justice there or, for that matter, anywhere else in the area. Judging by the fury of the crowd, and the storming approach of the horsemen, there might be many such deaths before dawn, and with the arrival of police reinforcements and the Yeomanry the fire-raisers would be hunted from street to street as he had once hunted sepoys. The prospect, together with the dead boy at his feet, made escape from this foul place imperative. He hoisted himself into the saddle and turned the mare's head towards open country, and as he went he swore an oath. If, in the time left to him, he involved himself in commerce of any kind, then he would throw away the book of rules that clearly governed its practitioners in places like Seddon Moss. He would write new rules, embracing an entirely different set of values, of the kind that he had always supposed were acceptable in Western communities that were making some kind of attempt to emerge from the Middle Ages. There would be no reciprocal hatreds of this kind, no cut and thrust regulated by profits on one side and mob rule on the other. In his ledgers, if he ever came to keep any, the life of the child wearing his father's cutdown corduroys would count for more than a penny an hour and a breakfast break.

He crossed the railway line and headed back to the fork in the road where the dust track joined the turnpike, and as he coaxed the tired horse into a trot the thunder crashed overhead and the first heavy raindrops fell like pellets. He thought of them striking the upturned face of the child under the wall of the shuttered shop and no longer felt hunger in his belly.

3

Pillion-ride

THEY saw one another at the same moment, Adam topping the last fold of the moor with the rising sun at his back, Henrietta standing in a shallow pool, her head turned sideways as she struggled to free her copper hair of the husks sown in it during the night. Perhaps he had the minimal advantage. When the level of his eyes rose above the heather rim south of the shepherd's hut they fastened on the one incongruity present in the view, the momentary glimpse of a pair of neat buttocks, enclosed in white pantalettes as she straightened herself after completing a perfunctory wash.

He never afterwards forgot this unconventional introduction for on that particular morning he felt himself to be in need of laughter, and the prospect of a girl washing herself in a puddle on a deserted moor was not only unexpected but droll.

He called, cheerily, "Hullo there!" but the little figure in the pantalettes whirled and fled back into the hut at such speed that he wondered, for a moment, if he had imagined her. Then he went on down the gentle slope to the hut, reining in outside the entrance and calling, in the tone of voice one might use to coax a child, "Hi! You in there! Don't be scared. Can you tell me if this road spans the railway?"

Seconds elapsed before a dishevelled, copper-coloured head peeped from the hut like a turtle from its shell and he saw then that what he had mistaken for a half-dressed urchin was a young woman and that she was blushing but looked more indignant than frightened.

"Go away!" she said, severely. "I'm not dressed. The road leads to Lea Green and there's sure to be a bridge. There are bridges for all the halts along the line."

The girl interested him. Her accents were not those of a gooseminder, or a shepherd's daughter, but of someone at pains to overlay a strong, Northcountry brogue with a spurious gentility, and this made him wonder why a girl like that should be making her toilet in

78

a puddle after, as appeared evident, spending the night in a turf-roofed hut on the open moor. He said, trying to keep the laughter from his voice, "Are you lost? Did you get caught in that storm last night?" and she replied, primly, "I'm not in the least lost. I live near here. I . . . er . . . I had an accident."

"What kind of accident?"

"I was thrown from a trap when the horse was frightened by lightning." She had now withdrawn her head and was addressing him through the wall of the hut.

"Are you hurt?"

"No!" The voice was petulant now, a child thoroughly exasperated by grown-up nosiness, "I took shelter, that's all." Then, with the merest hint of appeal, "Would you be going to Lea Green?"

"I'm going that way," Adam said, "then across the county to Cumberland."

There was a long silence before she said, pleadingly, "Could I ride behind you?"

"Why not?" he said, grinning.

"Wait then, let me get dressed, but ride away and I'll call when I'm ready."

He chuckled at this but humoured her, squeezing the mare's flanks so that she retreated as far as the hillock. The sun began to siphon moisture from the moor, so that the hut was soon rooted in vapour and presently she called, "Turn your back," and he swung round watching, over his shoulder, her undignified exit on all fours, draped in what seemed to be a green tent so voluminous that she had to support its folds with both hands. Her coppery hair hung down in tangled hanks but she had done what she could to dress it with a piece of ribbon tied in a bow. The dress she was wearing looked as if it had been put through a mangle.

"It's awful," she said, surveying herself, "I must have been crazy to run away in this. Wherever I go, I'll be noticed. Then they'll catch me and send me back. I'm hungry too. I've only had those toffees."

He looked at her closely, liking what he saw: a small, indomitable figure, enveloped in a green dress that had, he supposed, begun life as a crinoline but now looked ridiculous draped about her and held in damp handfuls about her hips. Her face was the face of a pretty, imperious child but she had a woman's figure and there was maturity of a kind in the way she planted her feet and stood her ground, as though to counter mockery.

79

"You ran away? You mean from that riot in the town?"

"No, from that toad Makepeace."

"Makepeace?"

"Makepeace Goldthorpe."

He was at a loss what to make of her. She looked like a genteel girl who had lost her way in a thunderstorm on the way home from a soirée or dance, but her assumption that he should know all about the encounter with Makepeace Goldthorpe, whoever he was, reduced her to the status of a child, and a spoiled child at that. Alone up here, and enveloped in the ruin of a cageless crinoline, she did not seem in the least afraid of him and he supposed this was due to ignorance, or a privileged background that would encourage her to take his respect for granted. He said, with a smile, "I'm a stranger, I rode into the middle of that riot last night and decided to make a detour. Is Makepeace Goldthorpe anything to do with that shoddy little town over the hill?"

She looked confused and then, rather charmingly, revealed a pair of enormous dimples in a smile. "I *am* a goose," she said, "I thought everyone about here would know the Goldthorpes. They own most of Seddon Moss, all but the mill that is, and my father owns that. The mill beside the railroad."

He stared at her unbelievingly. "You're Sam Rawlinson's daughter?"

She said, sharply, "If you're a stranger ..." but he interrupted, impatiently, "Yes, I am, but I heard about Sam Rawlinson and his lockout last night, before the real trouble started. How long have you been out here alone?"

"All night," she said, "since the storm began."

"Then you won't know your father's mill was burned down?"

"I knew they were setting it afire. Father's overseer rode up and told him, and they all rushed off in Goldthorpe's carriage. That was the last I saw of them." The dimples went out. "That's the last I *mean* to see of them!"

"Why?"

She hesitated, her eyes travelling the full length of him, from his mudsplashed boots to the crown of his hard hat. "That's none of your business," she said. Not rudely but firmly.

"It's my business if you hope to ride behind me as far as Lea Green."

She frowned and hitched her dress and then, quite suddenly, the dimples came out again.

"All right," she said, cheerfully, "I'll tell you, so long as you promise to keep it a secret. Makepeace wants to marry me and my father wants it too. I think he's hoping to get something out of it, land or free rent or something, for he usually does. It was arranged before anyone said a word to me, and after supper last night Makepeace proposed—well, sort of proposed."

"How old are you, Miss Rawlinson?"

"Eighteen. But that doesn't mean they can make me, does it?"

"Perhaps not. Your father, what's he like? To look at, I mean?"

"Why do you ask that?"

"I think I saw him last night. He was helping to drive the mob away from the fire engine. They were fighting in the streets."

The news did not appear to concern her overmuch. "I guessed they might be. Was my father hurt?"

"Not that I know of, but one person was killed. A boy ... he was ... trampled by horses, just as I was leaving." She received this news with equal indifference.

"They're mad," she said, "the whole lot of them. There's been trouble all summer and I'm right sick of it. I shall be glad to get away, apart from escaping from Makepeace. Sam—my father—is a big, redfaced man. He always looks as if he's in a temper but usually he isn't, or only when things go wrong at the mill. He's better than lots of fathers. He doesn't whip me, like Sarah Hebditch's father does, and he doesn't fuss about where I am and what I'm at. But when I marry I'll marry someone I choose. Even if they fetch me back I won't change my mind about that."

There was no gainsaying her description of her father or, for that matter, of Makepeace. A big, redfaced man, who looked angry. It fitted Adam's recollection of the leading horseman, just as the word 'toad' would apply to the pallid young man driving the chaise. He said, "Who knows about you running away?"

"Mrs. Worrell, the housekeeper. She said I was to go to her sister's at Garston and I was trying to catch a Liverpool train when the pony bolted. I was soaked through and Enoch, the Boffin Boy, didn't come back for me. I didn't think he would. He'd be too scared."

"Was Enoch driving?"

"Yes, but he's half-witted and can't speak very well. He's got no roof to his mouth and he'll pretend he left me at the station until Mrs. Worrell drags it out of him, and she won't have a chance for a spell

81

if the mill is burned, like you say. Everything will be in an uproar so I'll be in Liverpool before they find I'm gone."

He said, gently, "I don't think you will, Miss Rawlinson. The rioters tore up the track and it'll be at least a day before the trains can get through. I think you'd best let me take you home again."

She reacted violently, clutching the green rags about her and stepping back until checked by the wall of the hut.

"I *won't* go back. Whatever happens I've got to get to Garston, and stay away long enough to show Sam I mean what I say. Don't you understand? Anything could happen now. If the mill is burned down my father won't have any money, and maybe old Goldthorpe won't let Makepeace marry me. It was only father's money that made him agree to it."

"And Makepeace?"

"Oh, he likes pawing me but he wouldn't dare to do that unless his father said he could. He couldn't do a thing except stand around and stammer if his father wasn't right behind him." Her head came up, sharply. "I'll *walk* to Lea Green. It isn't far and I've got money for my fare."

Her defiance touched him. Life in the garrison towns had left him with a conception of women as two races inhabiting widely separated worlds. One was the delicate girl, who tinkled the piano, did a little crocheting and poker-work, fainted at the sight of blood, and lived her life, both before and after marriage, in a genteel seraglio, and her opposite, the doxy, who might or might not be a common prostitute but who was, in either case as coarse minded as a ranker and could usually drink and swear like one. The girl standing before him did not approximate to either class. Whilst she obviously came from a good home he could not imagine a woman of her type would make light of spending a night alone in a moorland hut. He said, finally, "Won't your mother be anxious about you?" and she told him, unsentimentally, that her mother had died when she was born. "There's only Mrs. Worrell," she added, "and she'll think I'm safe at her sister's by now."

It was a difficult dilemma for a man whose life had been lived exclusively in the company of men, for while he did not pay much account to her schoolgirlish rejection of Makepeace, he was reluctant to return her bag and baggage into the keeping of a man who, if his deduction was accurate, had ridden over a child with as little compunction as he would a cat. A man of this kind would have no scruples in using a pretty daughter to further his own ends, and the

more he thought about this the less inclined he was to do Sam Rawlinson a service of any kind. He might be mistaken, of course, in
which case he had no business conveying the girl as far as Lea Green.
To do more might be to compound a felony, for he was not in the
least sure how English law would view a case of this kind. It might
even come under the heading of abduction.

The girl switched his thoughts, giving him time to ponder the
problem. "I'm starving," she said, "have you got anything to eat in
those saddlebags?"

He whistled the mare and she ambled over, the girl lifting a hand
to stroke her muzzle. While he was unstrapping the bag and taking
out a portion of bread and cold fowl he had bought at the hedgerow
inn, she went on, "You've asked me a lot of questions. Now it's my
turn. Who are you? And why are you riding a horse all the way to
Cumberland?"

"My name is Swann," he said, "Adam Swann. I've been away
from England for a long time and I'm riding north to visit my
father and aunt. They live at a town called Keswick, near Derwentwater."

She accepted his bread and chicken wing without thanks and
munched away with relish, seemingly concerned with little else than
to satisfy her hunger. She might, he thought, be a rich man's daughter but it was obvious no one had tried to make a lady out of her.
Her strong, white teeth tore into the meat and she continued to talk
with her mouth full.

"Where did you come *from*? From Birmingham?"

"Now how could a man be set ashore at Birmingham? Didn't
they teach you any geography?"

She did not appear to resent his banter. "Not much," she said,
cheerfully. "I've had lots of governesses but they didn't harp on anything except sewing and deportment."

"Deportment?" He laughed outright. "What kind of deportment?"

"Oh, silly things," she said, "like walking with a book on your
head, and not accepting a gentleman's chair straight off."

He had often heard of girls being taught to acquire a good carriage
by parading up and down with a book balanced on their heads but
the prohibition concerning the offer of a seat was new to him. "What
the devil has not accepting a seat got to do with deportment?" he
demanded, and she said, with a sidelong smile that was the exact
equivalent of a schoolboy grin, "You never heard of that? It's in

83

the book. 'The chair is still warm from the gentleman's person'!"

His laugh rang across the moor. He found some aspects of her exquisitely droll. She was like a mischievous peasant child, masquerading as the daughter of a duke in an unlikely pastoral play, and she seemed to have a flair for mummery. Everything she did or said had about it a touch of saltiness, together with a lack of artifice that reminded him of children he had seen playing outside the barrack gates in faraway places. In some ways she seemed to have the mental age of about twelve and yet, behind her artlessness, was the buoyancy of a street urchin that one might have looked for in the boy her father had ridden over the night before. Presently, still munching, she went into the hut and returned carrying a basket-trunk.

"If you were thrown from that trap last night how do you come to have luggage?" he asked, and she said, with a shrug, "I was lucky. This fell off at the same time when the pony reared," and rummaged among the contents until she found a blue, tattered book.

"What's that?"

"An atlas. I took it because I thought I would have to find my way to Ireland. I've got relations in Ireland I've never seen. Mrs. Worrell, the housekeeper, told me about them and I was going to them at first. That was before I found out she was willing to help me." She thumbed through the pages. "Birmingham . . . that's right, there's no sea at Birmingham. Have you ridden all the way from London then?"

"From Plymouth."

"Plymouth?" Her long slender finger went to tracing the coast-line and the lunatic quality of this encounter impressed itself upon him. Six in the morning on an open moor; a pretty, vivacious girl of eighteen washing herself in a pool of rainwater whilst in flight from a bridegroom selected by a father who rode over children in the street. He had a sense of being caught up in a pattern of improbabilities that were ready to engulf him as completely as had the John Company up to the moment of his finding the necklace, and with this came a desperate and irrational need to confide in somebody, even the daughter of Sam Rawlinson.

He said, "Plymouth is in Devonshire. I intended to travel north by Great Western and North Western as far as Fleetwood but I changed my mind. I bought the mare and decided to ride and take a look around on the way. I'm glad I did. The place has changed a good deal in seven years."

"You've been away all that time?" and when he nodded, "For heaven's sake, *where*?"

"India mostly, and more than a year in the Crimea."

This enthralled her. "Then you must be a soldier? That's marvellous—look!" and she held up an empty toffee tin decorated on all sides by pop-eyed portraits of Raglan, Cardigan, Lucan and the French general Bosquet. She looked at him hopefully.

"Did you see the Charge of the Light Brigade?"

"Yes," he said, smiling at her enthusiasm, "I might have been killed in it if my horse hadn't gone lame at the start and fallen behind."

"*My stars!*" she said, with unfeigned admiration. "*And* the Mutiny?"

"I served through that, but how would a girl like you know about the Sepoy Mutiny when you can't even find Plymouth on the map?"

"Oh," she said, gaily, "that's easy. I used to read all the newspaper reports aloud to Mrs. Worrell. She had a nephew in the Crimea and was very proud of him but Mrs. Worrell can't read, although she can scribble a bit. I like reading. I've read all sorts." She threw away the chicken bone and clasped her knees. "Tell me some of your adventures. I've never actually talked to anyone who was there, although some of the Foot Guards attended the Victory Ball where I met Makepeace. I thought they looked fetching in their uniforms. Why aren't you in uniform?"

"Because I'm no longer a soldier."

"You mean you were wounded?"

"No, I just gave up being a soldier."

She seem astonished and dismayed. "Why? Why did you do that?"

"For all kinds of reasons, far too many to explain now if you still want a lift to Lea Green."

"Then you *will* take me?"

"I'll take you but if we run into your father, or anyone else looking for you, I just found you wandering on the moor. I don't know you or why you came to be there, is that clear?"

"Of course." She said it lightly, as though it was something to be taken for granted, but the doubting smile she flashed at him was a warning of some kind. There was something about her that he still couldn't fathom, a sardonic secretiveness, implying she had already taken his measure, even if he had not taken hers. She said, bunching her absurd draperies, "May I call you Adam?"

85

"If you like. What's your given name, Miss Rawlinson?"

"Henrietta."

"Very well, Henrietta. The first thing we'll have to do is to cover you up with something. Shouldn't that thing you're wearing have a cage?"

"Yes, it's in there, but how could I sit a horse with that on? Why don't I just bunch the skirt and petticoats and sit astride?"

"With your pantalettes showing? Good God, child, we should have a crowd behind us from the moment we passed houses. Here, wrap this cloak round you and sit side-saddle. It'll be uncomfortable but I can't think of a better way."

"This is fun," she said, a child on holiday again. "Do you know, Adam, I dreamed something like this would happen?" and she draped the boatcloak about her shoulders so that its folds enveloped her with plenty to spare. He told her to stand on a rock, brought the mare alongside, mounted and helped her settle herself on the rump, her arms about his waist. Contact with her gave him satisfaction and he noted once again the unusual elegance of her hands. They were, he thought, the one aristocratic aspect she possessed, apart from a self-confidence as emphatic as Lord Cardigan's.

2

Their bivouac was under a small spread of Spanish chestnuts on what was probably the most westerly fold of the Pennines. The map called it a forest, the Forest of Bowland, but there were few trees hereabouts, apart from the clump that crowned the spur of a slope rising behind them to a height of about two hundred feet and sown with boulders all the way to the summit.

To the west, far beyond the winding waggon track they had followed from Preston, lay the sea, and the air up here had a whiff of salt that blended pleasantly with the summer scents of parched fern, rock moss, peat and flowering gorse. Away in the distance one or two farms lay huddled in rocky gullies, little blobs of greyish white against a gold and olive background, but the dust-road was empty of traffic, for one macadamised road followed the coast towards Lancaster and the other, several miles to the east, ran due north from Clitheroe. As fugitives they had chosen the older, packhorse route that lay half-way between.

The enormity of what he had done might have worried him if he had thought about it but he continued to hold it off, busying his mind with the routine chores of a trek across a sparsely-populated wilderness, and was now engaged in trapping a rabbit for it was time, to his way of thinking, that she had a hot meal and he preferred to avoid farms and inns.

There was water to drink from the dozens of moorland streams they had crossed and once, to her delight, he had cornered a cow in the angle of a drystone wall and taken a pannikin of milk from her. For shelter they had his tiny bivouac tent, now given over to her and Twitch, while he slept within call, wrapped in the cloak that covered her by day. Interested glances had been directed at them as they passed through villages and one small town but nobody had challenged them and this was not really surprising. A man and woman riding pillion, with a dog at their heels, was commonplace and curiosity, such as it was, was confined to the basket-trunk balanced on his pommel and the fact that Henrietta was wrapped in a boatcloak, notwithstanding the continuing spell of dry weather. Perhaps, thought Adam, people took her for an invalid and left it at that. Now, he supposed, there was no other course but to deliver her into Aunt Charlotte's keeping and await developments, although what might result from this madcap ride he could not imagine. At best, he thought, an undignified wrangle with her father. At worst, a court case, with himself in the dock on a charge of enticing a minor away from her legal guardians. He didn't know and didn't much care. His respect for conventions had been blunted by years of rough living, and he preferred to follow his soldier's nose until presented with a direct challenge. It was a long time before he was able to adjust to Western civilisation. Henrietta Rawlinson was the first of many to recognise and exploit the fact.

He had taken her along, he told himself, from motives of curiosity and compassion after the Lea Green stationmaster had informed him that trains were unlikely to run either way for forty-eight hours. The same man told him something of what had occurred in Seddon Moss the previous night. The town, he said, enjoying this unlooked-for chance to broadcast calamitous news, was still in a turmoil. Four rioters had been killed and any number arrested. Police had converged on the area from Liverpool and Manchester, and there had been outbreaks of looting during which two constables had been injured. When Adam asked if he could hire a trap or dogcart to drive as far as Garston, he was told this was out of the question.

87

Every posting horse in the district had been commandeered by the Yeomanry, who had been put on an alert in anticipation of further outbreaks in Warrington and elsewhere.

"A police inspector told me it were like 'Forty-two all over again," he said, importantly, as though it wasn't everybody in whom police inspectors confided, "but tha'd be too young to recall that, sir." Adam said he was, gave him a shilling and returned to the gorse thicket where he had hidden Henrietta.

He was not surprised when she told him she would prefer to walk down the line to Liverpool than return home. He was adjusting to her obstinacy but had made his own decision regarding her when he learned that Mrs. Worrell's sister was not expecting her. They did not even discuss her future until they were in open country again, and frying bacon over a fire he kindled under a hazel bank. He said, "If I hand you over to my Aunt Charlotte will you promise to abide by her decision?"

"What's your Aunt Charlotte like?" she asked, guardedly, and he said he could not give her an up-to-date answer, not having seen her for years, but recalled that she had a reputation for observing the proprieties and wore corsets that made an embrace with her a painful experience. She laughed at that but said it wasn't enough to go upon. When had he last seen Aunt Charlotte?

"When I was fifteen. Her sister Agatha kept house for the Colonel in those days and Charlotte, the eldest of the Swanns, ran a Dame's school. She'll probably give you a thrashing, me the rough edge of her tongue, and return you to Seddon Moss as soon as you've had a bath and a hot meal," he added.

"And your father?"

"Ah, the Colonel," he said, and she noticed the lines of his face softened, "he'd never lift anything but his hat to a woman. He'll spoil you worse than your father has," and he looked at her intently where she sat out of range of the smoke, fondling the spaniel's ears. "He'd have a reason to do that, I imagine."

"What reason?"

"You're approximately the size, build and colouring of my mother. I know that because he has a portrait of her made when she was a year or so older than you. I remembered it the moment I saw you peep out of that shepherd's hut. She was French and she died when I was six."

"How did your father come to marry a French lady, Adam?"

"He met her in France, in a little town called Perpignan, when he

88

came over the Pyrenees with the Old Duke. Romantic it might have
been but not wise. She never adapted to England."

Her eyes opened wide, as he noticed they usually did whenever
he mentioned soldiers. "You mean your father actually *knew* the
Duke of Wellington? You aren't teasing?"

"Well, I won't swear to him knowing him," Adam said, smiling,
"because he wasn't a colonel then. He was a cornet in the Sixteenth
—the Sixteenth Light Dragoons, and helped chase the French all the
way from Lisbon."

"Then he must be terribly old, Adam."

"Why? It's not all that long ago. His first action was Busaco, in
1810, and he was only twenty at the time."

"Then he's sixty-eight."

"Your mental arithmetic is better than your geography. Have some
more bacon."

She accepted a brittle rasher, nibbling it as though it was a toothsome biscuit. Presently she said, without looking at him, "Adam,
may I ask you something?"

"Ask away."

"What made you stop being a soldier?"

"I was bored with it."

"How could a soldier ever get bored?"

"Nine-tenths of soldiering is dull. The rest is terrifying."

"I'm sure you weren't scared."

"Indeed I was, many times. Scared and . . ." he broke off and
stood up, scooping a handful of soil from the bank and using it to
damp the fire.

"This has no bearing on what is to happen to you," he said,
gruffly. "That's what we should be discussing."

"We don't have to," she said, "for there's nothing to discuss. I'm
coming with you and I'll do whatever your aunt thinks best. What
were you going to say?"

He had been tempted to tell her something of the well at Cawnpore
but thought better of it. Instead he said, lightly, "I had a fancy to
become my own master and make money, like Sam Rawlinson," but
she replied, sulkily, "I do wish you'd stop treating me like a child,
Adam! I'm not a child, and you don't think I am really."

"You behave like one most of the time."

"For wanting my independence and being ready to fight for it?
Isn't that just what you're doing? Isn't that why you're here instead
of India?"

He looked disconcerted for a moment and then smiled. He had, she decided, a very nice smile. He looked years younger when he used it. "That's a fair point," he admitted and then, in what she had already learned to think of as his boot-and-saddle manner, "We can make five miles before sundown and had best do it. As long as we're this close to the main line we'll meet people and one of them might be your father."

* * *

From then on he said little but the silence, and the increasing distance they put between themselves and Seddon Moss, oiled their relationship, so that soon it seemed to him they had been travelling companions a long time, a hardbitten man of thirty-one, a hoyden of eighteen, an over-burdened horse and a dog moving slowly across the parched landscape between the Pennines and the sea. It was when they reached the site of their first overnight camp that he saw a change in her, noticing that she was subdued and perhaps secretly scared by the finality of her flight.

He pitched the tent and lit a fire between stones, setting his billy-can to boil on a tripod of sticks for tea brewed from a packet he carried in his saddlebags. She had come to look upon his saddlebags as a transportable bran tub, of the kind seen at chapel bazaars where one could expect to find all manner of things. So far she had seen him handle a piece of cold mutton wrapped in oiled paper, a needle and thread he had used to sew up the trailing hem of her green dress, a homemade but very effective tinder box, all kinds of homespun items that she supposed campaigners stowed in their kit. She was impressed by his dexterity, of the kind she associated with Mrs. Worrell at work in her kitchen. Nothing seemed to fuss or harass him. He lifted her down, pitched the tent, unsaddled and haltered the mare, lit the fire and set about cooking their rations as though this gipsy life was the way everybody travelled. It was only when he told her to crawl into the tent that she asked "But where will you sleep?"

"Under the hedge. Where else?"

"But supposing it rains?"

He looked at the sky. "It won't rain."

That was the way of him. He was a superior being, knowing everything and fearing nothing, cool, deft, self-sufficient, gathering to himself the apparatus of survival as he went along. He was handsome, too, in a dark and rather forbidding way, with strong features surprisingly innocent of whiskers, heavy, arching brows, and a skin tanned the colour of tobacco. She liked the easy way he moved his big, loose-jointed limbs and his quick smile, even though it had the patronage of all male smiles, implying that the sharpest woman in the world was half an idiot. It was curious, she thought, that she did not resent this, as she had in other men. But then he was a soldier thoroughly accustomed to fending for himself and judging anyone who could not a milksop or sluggard. She had always admired soldiers, not only because they looked fierce and resplendent in their scarlet uniforms and tall busbys, but because they were so far removed from all other men in her experience, foxy-faced merchants like the Goldthorpes, brutes like her father's overseer, pallid, round-shouldered clerks in mill and counting-house, and slow-moving artisans like McEwan, gardener at the Lodge. Soldiers were clearly men who could impose their will on anyone, who could and did mould circumstances to their pleasure and like Adam they were almost invariably big, handsome creatures who could whisk a girl off her feet and march across country carrying her like a prize. Lying there under the taut canvas of his little tent she wondered what it would be like to have him behave in this way towards her and the fancy, improbable as it was, made her shiver with fear and delight, for nothing remotely like this had ever happened to her, despite the licence she had enjoyed under Sam's roof. There had been half-a-dozen swift embraces under the mistletoe at Christmas parties, and the occasion when Sarah Hebditch's blond brother, Edward, had held her more closely than was *de rigeur* during a waltz at the Assembly Rooms. She had liked that at the time and had even fancied herself half in love with Edward, but now she realised it must have been nonsense, because Edward Hebditch was less than half a man compared with Adam Swann, who could sleep soundly in a hedge and order the rain clouds out of the sky.

This feeling of reverence, that was something entirely new to her, began to enlarge itself during the second day's ride. Physical contact with him, as she sat perched on her bunched petticoats, one arm about his waist, the other hooked in his belt, produced a glow that had nothing to do with the clammy heat generated by the folds of the cloak. It seemed to pulse through her from her toes to the roots of her hair, compensating for the almost unbearable ache in her buttocks caused by her cramped position on the rump of the mare. He must have been aware of her discomfort, however, for he pitched camp long before sundown, telling her to watch the fire while he and Twitch went over the hill to try for a rabbit, and presently he returned

91

carrying one by the ears and she watched him skin and joint it at twice the speed of the kitchenmaids at home. She said, as he put it into the billycan, seasoning the stew with herbs from a packet produced from the lucky dip of a saddlebag, "You don't need money and houses and servants. You could manage wherever you happened to be, Adam," and he said, carelessly, "Any fool could live off this kind of country in summer. Besides, there's no competition. It's very different when you have to share a route with ten thousand other thieves."

She found it very difficult to imagine him in any other capacity. "But what will you *do*, Adam? For a living, I mean. Or are you rich, and won't have to work at anything?"

"I'll tell you if you're interested, but after supper. I'm famished, and I'll wager you are, so scout around for some more firewood. Why should I work like a black when I've got a camp-follower?" and delighted at last to be of some service to him she scrambled up and poked about the copse until she had a nosebag full of faggots but was deflated when he told her that some of them were chestnut and wouldn't burn well. Despite this, the rabbit stew was excellent, one of the most appetising she had ever tasted, and when the pan was scoured and set on its tripod for tea, he showed her Aaron Walker's map and told her something of the kind of enterprise he hoped to launch after he had paid his duty visit, got her off his hands, and gone about the business of buying teams and recruiting waggoners.

She was disappointed by the ordinariness of the project and unable to keep disapproval from her voice. "You mean be a *carrier*? Humping boxes and cotton bales from place to place?" but he laughed at her crestfallen expression.

"I certainly don't intend doing my own driving, if that's what you're afraid of and I shan't limit myself to cotton. The railroad system in the cotton belt is good and all the important centres are linked but down south, and in places like Wales and the West country, there are any number of little manufactories miles from the nearest railhead. I've got what I think is a good idea. I'm going to have three services, light, heavy and medium, and they're going to be fast and run to a schedule, like the railways. I'm going to have a crest or a trademark that everyone in the country gets to know and all the waggons will display it and be painted in the same colours, and the men who drive them will wear a distinctive uniform, like the commissariat in the army. Whenever one of my vehicles goes by you'll say, 'Ah, there goes a Swann delivery.' I shall recruit the right kind of men, work out the shortest and fastest routes and in time I could be known all over the country."

"Like Pear's soap," she suggested and he laughed.

"That's right, like Pear's soap."

The project began to sparkle a little under the elbow-grease of his enthusiasm so that she could regard it as a somewhat more exciting endeavour than those men practised in Seddon Moss. With him directing it, there was at least a hint of adventure here, enough to prompt her to inquire thoughtfully, "Did you save money while you were abroad? Enough to buy a fleet of horses and waggons, and hire all those men?"

"They don't pay soldiers on that scale," he told her, "but I can raise it, one way or another. What I'm concerned about is giving it an individual stamp, something that makes an impact on tightfisted merchants like your father, and that old miser Goldthorpe. Those are the kind of men I mean to go after. I want to hit on something that makes them associate me with the business of transporting their products from one county to another. I've been cudgelling my brains for days but nothing has recommended itself. Suppose you think about it?"

His tone was jocular, so that she knew he was patronising her again and this put her on her mettle. She said, unexpectedly, "You've got an easy name to say and an easy one to remember. *Swann.* Everyone likes swans. No one takes a swan for granted. People stop whatever they're doing and say 'Look! A swan!' "

For the very first time in their acquaintance he looked at her as though she was an adult.

"Have you thought of something already?"

"You'll only laugh at it."

"Try me!" and he sounded serious.

She said, blushing, "The *name* is what people will remember. You could use it as . . . well . . . as a trademark. A swan on wheels."

She said it very diffidently and was therefore quite unprepared for his exuberant and immediate reaction. In a bound he had cleared the camp fire, thrown his arms about her and kissed her on both cheeks. Then he held her off at arm's length, eyes alight with excitement, jaw out-thrust, looking very boyish and ardent.

"By God, that's capital! That's *precisely* the kind of inspiration I've been looking for ever since that stationmaster put the idea into my head! A Swann! *A Swann on Wheels!* Wait—" and he lunged over to where his saddle rested on a bough and picked up a square leather satchel of the kind she had seen strapped to the swordbelts of the cavalry officers who attended the Victory Ball. Then he was back again and taking a notebook from the pouch found a blank page and began to draw, his pencil flying over the paper with such precision that she found herself thinking, 'He can draw pictures faster than a drawing master and more lifelike ones I wouldn't wonder,' and was so interested that she quite forgot the burning spots on her cheeks where he had planted his kisses.

He said, handing the book to her, "Is that what you had in mind?"

It was far more precise than anything she had had in mind. He had sketched an arrogant-looking swan in full sail down a river and superimposed on the facing wing was a large wheel, like the wheel of a gun carriage with each spoke outlined.

"Why, Adam, that's marvellous! Where did you learn to draw like that?"

"To the devil with the drawing, I can do better than that on a drawing board. What colour should it be? And what about background?"

"Well, all the swans I've ever seen are white," she said, "and on the side of a van it would show up best on black canvas, wouldn't it?"

She thought then that he was going to embrace her again and so he might have done if she hadn't raised the notebook in defence. As it was, he snatched it back, crying, "Better and better!" and fell to shading in the background until the swan on wheels stood out in sharp relief and the broad-bladed spokes had each a name— '*London*', '*Birmingham*', '*Manchester*' and '*Leeds*'. It was such a distinctive trademark that she began to feel smug about having invented it. "Why, I can see it," she told him, "stencilled on the hood of a waggon. You're quite right, Adam. It *is* something people will remember. It has a kind of—well—*difference* about it, like the lion and the unicorn."

"Henrietta," he said, "you're your father's daughter in spite of yourself and I'm going to keep in close touch with you when I set up for I might need that head of yours." Then, his smile giving way to a contemplative expression, "You mentioned capital just now. Can you keep a secret? From everyone?"

She assured him that she could. In fact she knew she wasn't at all good at keeping secrets, especially important ones, but she would have promised him anything at that moment. He replaced the notebook in the pouch (telling her in passing that it was called a *sabretache*) and probed in its depths for what looked like a small sachet of sailcloth, double-stitched along the folds. He took his claspknife, cut the thread and drew out the most breathtaking string of jewels she had ever seen or expected to see, a necklace composed exclusively of rubies, a handful of rubies, some as large as a small egg, down to several the size of peas. Each jewel was cut so that it trapped the slanting rays of the setting sun filtering through the leaves above their heads.

"Why, Adam," she said, ecstatically, "it's lovely, the loveliest thing I've ever seen! Could I . . . *hold* it?"

"You can wear it but only for a moment and if that sounds ungracious it's because the necklace represents all the hope I have of hitching the swan to a dray." And then came a moment she was to remember all her life. He moved behind her, held the necklace before her eyes, and snapped the filigree catch into its socket. Her fingertips came up to caress the largest jewel, the ruby hanging at the full extent of the loop, while he sat back on his heels and said, "I daresay it looks better on you than it did on the scraggy neck of that damned Ranee. Do you know anything about the value of jewels?"

"Nothing at all, but I'm sure these are the kind the Queen might wear, aren't they?"

"I hope so," he said, lightly, "but if they are I shall have to sell them at about a tenth of their real value, and think myself lucky into the bargain."

"You mean you stole them?"

She said it as though she was not much concerned if he had robbed a coach to get them.

"Would it matter to you if I had?"

She considered this. "No," she said, stubbornly, "after what you've done for me it wouldn't matter a bit. I'd still be grateful and glad you rode up to that hut when you did."

"Then set your mind at rest. I didn't steal them, at least, not in the sense you mean. I stuck my nose in them when I was unhorsed during a brush at a place called Jhansi," and he told her briefly about the encounter with the horseman carrying the casket.

"You think of them as belonging to you, then?"

"Why not? I could have left them lying where they were, in which case a medical orderly, or a burial party would have pocketed them. I could have handed them into the paymaster, when they would have been impounded, locked up in a safe somewhere, and then found their way to the Company directors. Neither course recommended itself to me at the time and it doesn't now. I risked my life a thousand times to protect the John Company's investments and came out of it with three hundred pounds after seven years of far rougher living than we're experiencing now."

"What will you do with it? I mean, *how* will you turn it into money?"

"Old soldiers have ways and means," he said, evasively, "but now I'm going to put it to bed again. If you wear it a moment longer you won't care to part with it."

She reached behind her and unfastened the clasp. It was only when she was returning it to him, and he was carefully retying the severed threads of the canvas wrapping, that she understood the stupendous compliment he had paid her by trusting her with such a secret and this was ample compensation for parting with such a prize. She said, shyly, "Why did you tell me, Adam?"

"Why not? I don't care to be under an obligation to anyone, and your idea of the swan on wheels was worth money to me. It's as hard to put a value on that as on the rubies, but we'll see. And now, Henrietta, it's high time you tucked yourself up in that tent. We've a long ride ahead of us tomorrow. If the weather holds we might get beyond Kendal and then we're almost home."

The mention of his home reawakened her anxiety for the future so that she said, her lip trembling, "What's to become of me, Adam?"

He looked at her then with tolerance and sympathy devoid of patronage.

"Don't worry," he said, "I've been in far worse scrapes and come out of them. Aunt Charlotte will think of something. She's had a great deal of experience with flighty young women."

His tone was casual but when she had crawled into the little tent and he had laced the entrance, extinguished the fire, and rolled himself in his cloak, he remembered that involuntary quiver of the lip. He lay looking up at the stars for a long time, contemplating the chain of circumstances that had saddled him with such an unlikely companion near the end of his journey. He had ceased to think of her as a nuisance, a truant child, even the self-willed daughter of a man who could bludgeon a terrified boy to death. He saw her now as a new factor in a vastly complicated puzzle he had set himself to solve the moment he regained consciousness after the brush at Jhansi. Somehow, like it or not, she was closely involved with him, not so much as a woman but as a comrade and this, for some reason he did not fully understand, pleased and comforted him. His relationship with women had been those of all professional wanderers. From time to time he had hired the services of a garrison moll, or one or other of the nautch girls introduced into overseas stations and tolerated by the authorities. They had brought him physical relief but little pleasure, certainly none in retrospect. Only one did he recall with any tenderness, a fifteen-year-old Circassian, who must have been little more than a child when her parents sold her to the trade in Scutari. Her trained stealth, and her pathetic eagerness to please, had touched him, so that he had given her enough money to buy the clothes and gewgaws that would enable her to hoist herself several rungs up the ladder of her profession. Henrietta Rawlinson had no kind of kinship with girls like that and almost as little with the sisters and nieces of serving officers, who came out husband-hunting on the autumn bride-boat, as the pagoda-shakers had learned to regard it. She seemed, in fact, to have no destiny beyond latching on to him, and making his complicated life more complicated on the strength of a town riot and a chance encounter on a deserted moor. He already accepted this and perhaps it had a bearing on the confidence he had reposed in her by showing her the necklace. She was like a stray mongrel, looking to him for scraps and a dry place to sleep. Socially, the association was preposterous and yet, in another way, it had about it an element of inevitability crystallised in that remarkable idea she had produced so effortlessly. *Swann. Swann. A Swann-on-Wheels.* It was apt yet outrageously simple, knitting together all the loose threads that had emerged from Aaron Walker's advice, giving it shape, substance and purpose. Close by an owl hooted and the north-westerly breeze came soughing in from the Firth, rustling the leaves overhead and causing the near extinct embers of the camp fire to glow like the rubies. He fell asleep, still wondering about her.

*   *   *

His guess concerning the reception she was likely to get from the Colonel was accurate enough. The moment the old man's eye rested on her Adam saw him glance up at the oval portrait of the woman over the open hearth. The facial similarity was quite remarkable and it occurred to him then that this might have played a part in his decision to bring her along against the dictates of common sense. They had the same lively, greenish eyes, the same broad cheekbones and slightly pendulous cheeks curving to a small, obstinate chin, the same pert nose, offset by a generous mouth. Even their hairstyles, separated by close on half a century, had similarities. His mother had worn a straight fringe and curl clusters bunched over the ears, and although

Henrietta's hair was in disarray (despite frantic attempts to tidy it during an interval in the summerhouse while he announced her) it seemed to him that it had the same coppery sheen where it swept down on either side of the wide parting to ringlets bunched on the temples.

The old man, advancing stiffly, exclaimed, in wonder, "My poor child . . ." and seemed, in that instant, to shed forty years, so that Adam saw him briefly as he must have appeared to little Monique d'Auberon in the spring of 1813, when a torrent of victorious young Englishmen had poured through the passes of the Pyrenees to fight their first battle on French soil and break all the hearts in Haute-Garonne. The encounter touched him. It was well worth the tempest of Aunt Charlotte's wrath and the flailing she gave him with her tongue.

4

Bride-in-Waiting

IT had required an effort to nerve himself to admit that he had not
arrived alone and that in the summerhouse, desperately attempting
to make herself presentable, was a girl of eighteen who had fled a
respectable home and been escorted over a hundred miles of track
and fellside by a soldier, returning from places where this kind of
conduct would arouse no special comment. That was how Charlotte Swann saw it, once he had admitted the facts, and that was how
she expressed it, in terms that made his ears burn. Not that his conduct surprised her, for he was a man and she regarded all men as
irresponsible fools unlikely to advance far beyond the mental age of
a child.

She was a formidable-looking woman distinguished by Swann
height, hawk nose and thinly compressed lips. She was not only tall
but impressively upholstered and when she was roused, as now, she
could summon the voice of a rough-riding sergeant drilling a squadron of recruits.

"In the *summerhouse!* You hid the little goose in the summerhouse? *Unfed? Unwatered?* And wearing the rags she travelled here
on the rump of that jaded brute you stabled so conscientiously?" She
flung round on the Colonel. "You know I've always thought you a
fool, Edward, but you and that foreign gel you married succeeded in
breeding a bigger one, and there he stands, with his silly mouth agape.
He's taken close on a month to get here when he might have made
the journey in thirty-six hours, at a fraction of the expense and without abducting a young woman en route!"

"Dammit, Aunt Charlotte, I haven't laid a finger on the girl. All I
did was to help her on her way."

"She's ruined just the same," boomed his aunt, "as any young
woman would be who had travelled unchaperoned four days and
four nights in the company of a man with no more sense of fitness
than a Turk! Didn't *that* ever occur to you? Didn't it strike you that
the only course open to you was to take her to those relatives of hers
at Garston?" and before either Adam or his father could comment

she had sailed out of the house and down between beds of lupins, sunflowers and delphiniums to the shed facing the ruffled surface of the lake. The Colonel said, ruefully, "She's right, boy. You do seem to have got yourself into a rare scrape," but then, with a humorous lift of his shaggy, white brows, "Is she pretty? But that's a damfool question. She must be, or a Swann wouldn't have carried her this far."

Adam said bluntly, "Nobody could convey that young woman a single yard against her will and Aunt Charlotte will find that out soon enough. I daresay you'll think her pretty enough for to my mind she's rather like mother, facially at all events. She's more buxom and round about three inches broader in the beam I'd say, but that stood her in good stead. A hundred mile trek on the rump of that mare must have been punishing . . ."

He broke off, hearing voices on the garden path and said, hastily, "Let's leave them to sort themselves out after the introductions. I've a great deal to tell you about past and future, and something to add that won't please you, I daresay, but I've made my decision and here it is. I've resigned from Company service and dropped the idea of buying my way into a regular regiment. I'm done with soldiering," and he paused, expecting the old man to look outraged, or at least unbelieving, for he recalled that the old fellow was proud of the family's military tradition. All he did, however, was shrug his shoulders.

"You're over thirty, I can't dictate to you. Had a notion you wouldn't renew your contract after you wrote to me about that shambles at Cawnpore." His light blue eyes narrowed and he looked, for a moment, older than his years. "We heard about that here, of course. I remember having the same revulsion after the sack of Badajoz, and again after San Sebastian, where my own regiment ran amok. Sickened me at the time. Never wanted to see another shot fired. But I forgot it as soon as we found ourselves billeted among civilised folk. I daresay you'll have second thoughts, and a long furlough is what you need now. Stay here for a spell. It's the best kind of country for idling, and that mare you arrived on must be a corker if you've ridden her three hundred odd miles and two up over the final stages. Do a bit of fishing in the lake while she's out to grass."

Adam said, regretfully, "I've got other plans, sir, and the means of putting them into effect if I'm lucky. I intend starting up in business as soon as I've seen that girl settled. I haven't told Aunt Charlotte the full facts. There was another reason for getting her clear of the district. Her father is a bully and a scoundrel. I wouldn't make him

100

custodian to a sick cat after what I saw him do in the filthy little town he rules like an oriental despot. The truth is there's no knowing what might become of her if she was sent back before things quietened down. All I want is for Aunt Charlotte to care for her until I can get legal advice on that and a number of other matters. Will you do that for me, take her on trust for the time being?" But before the old man could assent Henrietta came creeping in on the heels of Aunt Charlotte, whose indignation appeared to have been stoked up by the girl's appearance. She presented her rather as though she was a barrister submitting irrefutable proof of male idiocy to a court of adjudicators.

"*Look* at her, Edward! Just *look* at her! Half-naked and she hasn't been near soap and hot water for a week!" She whirled on the grinning Adam. "How *dare* you treat a decent young woman as though she was a drab in one of your infamous garrison towns . . ." but here the drooping Henrietta perked up and protested, "Oh, please, Miss Swann! Adam was very kind and considerate . . ." and Adam had the satisfaction of seeing some of his aunt's asperity diverted elsewhere for she snapped, "Hold your tongue and listen to me! I'm not interested in the reasons that prompted you to run away from home and attach yourself to this freebooting nephew of mine, but from now on you'll do what *I* say, and my first instructions are that you shall take a hot bath, eat a Christian meal at a table, and go to bed while we decide what's to be done with you. In the morning you will sit down and write a letter to your father at my dictation and after that, when every stitch you are wearing has been laundered and aired, we shall see, you hear me?"

"Yes, ma'am," said Henrietta, so dutifully that Adam laughed as he watched his aunt half-propel her out of the room and into the hall where their steps went clattering up the stairs towards Aunt Charlotte's quarters, presumably with the intention of finding something to wear whilst the washtub was being prepared.

He saw very little of her throughout the next few days and when he inquired cautiously of his aunt what had become of her, Charlotte answered that she was recuperating from the exertions of her journey, and that this was hardly to be wondered at after the way she had been treated, first by her father, then by an even bigger fool masquerading as a White Knight. Somehow she managed to imply that he had hauled the girl from bed and dragged her across two counties in order to be ravished and that in some way his father was an abettor.

On the fourth day he saw them returning from a shopping expedition to Keswick. A still subdued Henrietta then appeared at table wearing a sprigged muslin gown, a lace cap, and little black slippers, and on the day after that she tried (but failed) to hold a whispered conversation with him whilst Aunt Charlotte's back was turned. She seemed so chastened as to be a different person from the little devil who had talked him into bringing her here, and he wondered whether her subjection was due to fear of being returned home, a resolution to keep the promise made to him that she would abide by his aunt's decision, or domination by his aunt's forthright personality.

Perhaps it was a combination of all three. When they met during meals he confined himself to general conversation. Even had he wanted private conversation with her, however, this would have been difficult, for Aunt Charlotte was clearly compensating for four days and four nights unchaperoned association with him and kept the girl close to her whenever Adam was about the house. Partly because of this, and partly because he had privately decided to make an effort to get to know his father rather better, Adam spent most of his time riding or walking along the margins of the lake in the Colonel's company. He found the effort rewarding.

They had never been close. During his childhood, and throughout the early part of his boyhood, the Colonel had been serving in distant parts of the Crown dominions and they had met infrequently on furlough. After that Adam had been away at school, and later, when he entered the Company's service as a cadet, they were separated by hundreds of miles, even when his father was home-based. He had thought of him, in the years after he had sailed for India, as a withdrawn, rather disappointed man, whose youth had been sacrificed to the long, dragging war in the Peninsula followed by the now almost legendary Waterloo campaign, where two fingers of his right hand had been severed by a French cuirassier. After that, he supposed, his father's life had been blighted by the death of the little French girl whom he married in the first year of the peace. He soon discovered, however, that the old man had mellowed over the last few years and was no more than politely interested in the professional side of Adam's life, declaring that his own martial experience was now as dated as Agincourt. Since retirement he had developed a variety of unlikely interests, chief among them landscape gardening and painting watercolours, and sometimes he would set his easel at Friar's Crag, or under the falls at Lodore, trying to capture the shifting shadows on the fells, or changing sky patterns over the broad expanse of the lake. He said, when Adam caught him at work one morning, "If I had my time over again, boy, I'd learn to paint properly and count the world well lost. I've derived more satisfaction out of this than anything else I've ever done, except maybe to raise prize vegetables, or plant those borders in the garden. I'm no damned good, mind you. Any fool could tell you that but I don't have to sell 'em. Just look at those shadows creeping across the underside of Falcon Crag, and that sun throwing diamonds about in the spray where that water comes over that drop. Marvellous, all of it! Something else painting did for me. Taught me to make use of my left hand, and that was something the regiment never did. Went through the last twenty years of my service holding a sabre like a damned crochet-hook in what Johnny left of this one," and he held up his maimed hand, now crippled with arthritis as well as minus an index and middle finger.

The old man's allusion to diamonds gave Adam's conscience a twinge and he toyed with the notion of explaining how he came by the necklace but decided against it. He now thought himself a fool to have confided in the girl and he was by no means sure whether the old man would accept his theory that the necklace qualified as prize-money. He did not want his entire future imperilled by a prize-court that might order its restoration now that the Mutiny was over. Instead he said, "Do you ever look back on your life as wasted, sir? The way I've come to look on mine so far?" and the Colonel said gruffly that he was damned if he did, for his years in the Peninsula had been shared with innumerable jolly companions and that it had "been a pleasure to beat the dust out of Johnny Frenchman's hairy knapsacks all the way from Lisbon to Toulouse." From his next remark, however, Adam gathered that they might not be so far apart after all, for he went on to say, "That war of mine was cleanly fought. I never hated the French. They were damned good soldiers most of the time and could cover the ground faster than we could and on shorter rations. Apart from that we were better led, which is more than one can say of you fellows in the Crimea. The Duke had brains and I don't need to tell you that's rare in high command." He laid down his brush and arched his eyebrows in a way that warned Adam he was about to ask a direct question. "Just what kind of business are you hankering after? Anything to do with horses?"

"It might well be; draught horses."

"Draught horses? Is there a living in that?"

"I think there is, the way I hope to go about it."

"But you don't care to discuss it with me?"

"Not yet. Later on I'll be glad to."

The old man accepted this gracefully but went on, "Then how about that wench you brought here? Is she involved in your plans, boy?"

"I'm afraid not," said Adam, smiling, "and if Aunt Charlotte says otherwise she's twisting her facts to fit feminine theory."

The old man, he thought, looked nonplussed but all he said was, "She *is* like your mother. Or like her when I first set eyes on her, serving vin blanc and mincepies to men who had ridden a thousand miles on salt beef and small beer." Then, as if Adam had challenged him, "Mind, I never regretted marrying her. I was damned proud of her everywhere I went, here and overseas. She kept her looks and her figure, and that's more than you can say of most women who reach thirty. Pity she didn't live to see you in uniform. I'll tell you something. She always hoped to fill a dozen British uniforms, don't ask me why. Her people welcomed us as liberators from poor old Boney. Come to that, I would have liked a big, jolly family myself but now it'll be up to you, unless the Swanns have fired their final shot. Can't imagine it, somehow. We've always been in a fight somewhere. I'd give that a thought, boy," and suddenly embarrassed by having said more than he intended he picked up his brush and set to work furiously on his half-finished watercolour.

Adam walked home unable to decide whether his father's remarks had been designed to urge him to return to the army or to supply a lonely old man with grandchildren. He was still pondering this when he saw a cab in the stableyard and a man in a coaching cape, obviously a hackney driver, adjusting his nag's nosebag. The man gave him a salute but before he could inquire what he was doing there Aunt Charlotte called softly from the kitchen window and he noted at once that something had stripped her of her birthright, the assumption of authority in whatever company she happened to find herself. She looked, he thought, very put out and her voice faltered as she said, "That man is here! That *dreadful* father of hers! He's taking her away, Adam. He has a paper, a legal paper . . ." and then, to his considerable astonishment, she burst into tears.

He went through the kitchen into the hall, expecting to find them in the drawing room but the room was empty. Then he heard a despairing cry from the stairhead, "Adam!" followed by the growl of Rawlinson, as though he was threatening a dog.

Glancing up he saw Rawlinson descending the stairs and the man's arrogance struck him as singular for he trod the stairs as if he was a

landlord evicting a tenant. Henrietta appeared behind him, one hand
on the bannister, the other holding her ridiculous basket-trunk. He
called up, sharply, "Go back to your room, Henrietta!" but Sam said,
with a grim smile, "Ah'm giving bloody orders today young feller-
me-lad. Get in t'cab, lass, and let's have no more o' this damned nonsense or I'll peel the hide off you the minute we get home. I'll not be
long wi' His Lordship." He came down into the hall, facing Adam
with his feet planted apart and a not unfriendly grin on his florid face.
Henrietta made no move to obey either order but stood her ground
at the head of the stairs.

Adam said, at length, "I suppose I owe you some kind of explanation, Rawlinson. We'll talk in here," and without waiting for
assent turned on his heel, led the way into his father's study, and
stood aside holding the door open.

He might have been mistaken but it seemed to him that some of
the truculence ebbed from Sam who nevertheless darted a glance left
and right, as though suspecting an ambush. He came in, however,
saying as Adam shut the door, "Ah'm not playing blind man's buff,
lad. Ah've taken legal advice."

"No doubt," Adam said, "but so have I, Mr. Rawlinson. Take a
seat and stop trying to frighten me, as you seem to frighten everybody else."

His tone must have disconcerted the millowner for he at once re-
verted to bluster. "Now listen here, don't gammon me into believing
you've got a leg to stand on in this how-de-do! Nobody gave you the
right to entice my lass up here and hide her away, as if she were t'
parson's daughter in t' family way! I could have the police on you and
that housekeeper of yours, and anyone else who's had a hand in t'
business, but that's not my way, or not yet any road! Bring it into
court and I'd spoil the girl's prospects, so we'll take it on trust that
she's still the maid she swears she is and send in the bill if she isn't!
Meantime she's coming wi' me and if you say no to that I'll have the
uniformed branch up here and press charges."

"What charges?"

Rawlinson slowly relaxed, eyeing his man as he had eyed a thous-
and millhands and commercial prospects and seeing nothing specifically formidable in his opponent.

"I don't have to tell you what charges," he said. "You're not the
boy I reckoned to find back o' this silly business. You're old enough
to know the law takes a serious view of tempting a girl of her age
away from home. Aye, and there's more to it than that. The lass was

engaged to be married. Did she let that slip, when she was riding behind you all the way from Lea Green?"

"She told me you were trying to force her into an objectionable marriage. I understand that was why she ran away."

"Well, that's neither here nor there!" said Sam, calmly. "The point is, do I take her along as she is, and say nowt if it turns out she's telling the truth, and there's been no more than a kiss and I daresay a fumble under a haystack? Or do I drive out of here and come back within the hour wi' two constables and a warrant? Suit yoursen, lad, but I'll tell you straight, Ah'm not falling over meself to make public issue of it. No man would in t' circumstances, with a marriageable daughter on his hands. But I will, by God, if you force me to it!"

Adam said, mildly, "Fetch the police if you care to, Rawlinson. You lay your charge and I'll lay mine. I saw you storm into the Square the night of the riot. I saw all manner of things on that occasion, your mill set alight for one, and you ride down and kill a child for another. I don't suppose that's generally known, not even in Seddon Moss. There was far too much commotion when it happened and the boy might have come by fatal injuries in a dozen ways. But you and I know he didn't. He tried to get out of your path but you swerved and beat him over the head with that cudgel you were carrying. You were wearing a low-crowned beaver and riding a skewbald hack. I could identify you and I could identify the horse, so let's stop trying to browbeat one another. If your daughter wants to stop here she's very welcome. For my part I think you would be wise to let her."

The man had nerve. He was obliged to admit that. By the time Adam had finished there was no truculence in his expression and the heavy jaw had certainly sagged an inch or so but there was no fear there either, just a clouded look, as though his sharp wits were already assessing new factors in what had seemed a straightforward situation. He sat quite still, knees apart and hands resting on his thighs, a man who had long since learned how to adjust to an unexpected realignment of circumstances.

He said, finally, "Your word against mine, Swann. And mine counts for something down there. Ask anyone. Ask the police who helped me round up those fire-raisers that night."

"I don't doubt that. But a manslaughter charge would be heard at an Assize Court, away in Manchester or Liverpool, and there, I daresay, we should start abreast, Rawlinson. Then again, there might have been other witnesses and I might have their names and addresses. It was my first look at Seddon Moss and any judge and jury would be obliged to admit I have no axe to grind. I didn't even run against your daughter until the next day. If there are other witnesses, local witnesses, maybe some of them would be prepared to elaborate once they saw you in the dock. Put it this way, I'll wager you a pound to a penny there are a hundred spinners in Seddon Moss ready to swear your life away, with or without a bribe."

Sam said, almost genially, "That horse won't run," and Adam had the impression that his tactics had increased his stature in Rawlinson's eyes. "Nay," he went on, "that's a nonstarter and I'll tell thee why. Happen you could make things awkward for me, but a conviction on manslaughter, on your say-so or anyone else's is nowt but bluff. Think on it, lad. A man sees his mill going up in smoke, and ten score fools doing a clog dance round t'bloody fire engine. So he oversets whatever stands in his way, acting i' name o' law and order, mind. A man tries to grab my bridle and gets his skull broken for his pains. That's nowt to do wi' manslaughter. It's just dam' bad luck on t'grabber's part."

"It wasn't a man though, and he made no grab at your bridle. It was a child and he was running for his life when I saw him."

"Who's to swear to that, apart from you? Happen others did see it but if they spoke up they'd never work again in the cotton belt."

"Where does that leave us, Rawlinson?"

"I'll tell thee," Sam said, sitting back in his chair, "you wi' means to make it tiresome for me to build a new mill, and sign on operatives to run it. Now I'm a man o' sense, so if you're that much struck on my lass you can keep her and be damned to you both!" He looked about him with interest. "You've got a snug place up here, wi' a nice view an' all. Folk don't settle in places like this unless they've got money put by."

His cynicism might have outraged some men but he was addressing one who had spent years in countries where it was not in the least unusual for fathers to put a cash price on their daughters.

Adam said, "How about this young man who was bidding for her before I came along? Grimthorpe or Gawthorpe or some such name?"

"Times have changed," Sam said, cheerfully. "Mill warn't fully insured and that means I shall have to dip into capital to get started again. I'll call no bluff about Goldthorpe's boy. He's gone cold on t'lass and I can't say I blame him."

"Then why all this hullabaloo to get her back?"

Sam shrugged and scratched his nose and Adam found it difficult to withhold a certain grudging admiration for the man. He was so sharp, and so completely unprincipled. It was like doing business in a Calcutta bazaar.

"She's a goodlooking lass," he said, "pretty enough to make you whisk her from under my nose, so why should you be the only one interested? There's plenty of men as well britched as you who would look twice and then again at Henrietta. As for me, I'll be in debt to the bank, I daresay, before I'm warmest man in Seddon Moss again. But not for long. You can be damned sure o' that, lad."

"Good God, man," exclaimed Adam, "we're not in the Levant. Are you suggesting I should buy your daughter, even if I wanted to?"

"Did I mention money?"

"You implied it."

"Eh, you're taking a rare lot for granted," said Sam, patiently. "I'm not a man to take money for my flesh and blood but I wouldn't throw it away, either, not on a girl who runs contrary to me the way she's set on doing. Maybe I'm wrong about that. Maybe it's just a girl's foolishness, and she'll grow out of it as soon as a lad wi' more to him than yon Makepeace throws his hat in the ring. I can't be sure as to *that* but there's one thing I am sure about. She either gets in that cab and comes of her own free will, or kisses goodbye to me and my pile, living or dead. As for you an' me, lad, I'll make a fair offer—no charges amounting to running off wi' a minor, so long as you don't show in my part of the world while the Magistrates' Court is sortin' out that riot. Ordinarily, mind you, I'd want that in writing, but I've done business wi' your kind before. A handshake would satisfy me." He paused, hesitated, and then, taking the bit between his teeth, went on with rather less assurance. "I'll add something to that and then shut t'book on it. Tim Garvin, that lad who I say as grabbed my bridle, and you says as didn't, were wearin' his dad's jacket an' corduroys. It were bosky an' my eyesight's not what it was. So what's it to be? A stand-up fight, or do I write that lass off as spoiled stock and go about takin' another wife and startin' all over again? It's been in my mind for long enough now. A man in my position is a damn sight safer wi' lads than a lass who'll never learn which side her bread's buttered. And that, I reckon, is about the middle and both ends of it."

"I'm not sure it is, Rawlinson."

"Speak up, then. We'll not meet again unless it's in court, and if it comes to that you'll find me a hard man to best."

"You may find it difficult to believe but I took Henrietta along because she seemed to me in as much danger as any other youngster running wild in that stinking little town of yours. My first inclination was to take her to that place she was heading for but that wasn't practicable. When I got to know her better I grew fond of her, although not in the way you seem to think. I liked her gall and her determination to escape from your clutches. We were four days and three nights on the road, but all that time I never thought of her as much more than a scared child and I treated her like one. Do you believe that now that you've spoken to her?"

Sam looked at him unblinkingly. "Aye," he said, at length, "happen I do. Gentlefolk have queer notions sometimes about what don't concern 'em." Then, "Does that mean you don't give a damn what becomes of her and are holding me to ransom for the fun of it?"

"No, there's more to it than that." He got up and went into the hall, anticipating that Henrietta had disobeyed him to the extent of remaining on the landing but surprised to find her crouched on the lowest stair, her basket-trunk on her knees. She looked, he thought, nearer nine than eighteen, a child about to be chastised for stealing jam. Her eyes were red and her hair as disordered as when she had first arrived. It occurred to him that she might have been listening at the keyhole.

He said, "Come in and join us, Henrietta. Your father has put a proposition to me and I want to hear what you have to say about it. Leave your luggage for the time being."

She got up and followed him across the hall, making a wide circuit round her father's chair so that he thought of a spaniel skirting a mastiff. Inside the room she stood as far away from her father as possible and her timidity must have irritated Sam for he growled, "Come, lass, there's no need to behave that way in front o' company. Have I ever laid a hand on you? Not that you haven't asked for it times enough."

She said, surprisingly, "Stop treating me like a child. Both of you. *Stop* it!" and then turning to Adam, "He said if I didn't go he'd get the police here and clap you and the Colonel and Aunt Charlotte in prison. You've been kind to me, all of you, and I couldn't let him do a thing like that . . ." and she stopped, biting her lip.

"There's no question of that, Henrietta. You can go or stay, whichever you prefer, but if you stay your father will have nothing more to do with you. It's a matter for you to decide."

"Aye, that's the size of . . ." growled Sam, but Adam broke out, saying, "Oh, for God's sake, man! Let *her* decide. It's her life! She isn't one of your damned millhands!" and when Sam clamped his jaw shut, "Well, Henrietta?"

"I'll stay," she said. "I couldn't go back now, not after what's happened. Aunt Charlotte said I could work for my keep, and that's what I'll do so long as he goes away and leaves you alone." She turned to Sam. "Now tear up that paper you showed Aunt Charlotte and go back where you belong."

Sam scratched his nose. He did not enjoy being bullied but the experience was novel and interested him. He was seeing her for the first time, a Rawlinson with her defences down, and in a curious way it shamed him. He had never thought to see a child of his so vulnerable.

"Talk to him," he said, gruffly, "he'll tell you I've no choice."

"Makepeace has backed down," said Adam.

Her eyes showed no more than a flicker of interest, "Makepeace never mattered one way or the other," she said. "He knows very well I'd never have married him."

"Will you marry me, Henrietta?"

They heard the breath go out of her and her right hand groped behind her, as though to reinforce the grip the other had upon the curtains. Sam said, jumping up, "God damn it, man, only a minute ago you said . . ."

"It doesn't matter what I said, I'm asking Henrietta and in your presence. Let her decide. Will you marry me, Henrietta?"

Sam subsided again, now so far out of his depth that he felt he knew what it was like to drown. There was a long silence in the room. The pendulum of the French clock on the mantelpiece spun but its tick was inaudible under its glass dome. A trapped bluebottle buzzed in one of the recesses and outside, far across the lake, they could hear the soft plash of oars and the creak of rowlocks. She said, finally, "You know that would be the most wonderful thing that could happen to me. But it doesn't have to happen just because of him and that paper."

"Oh, to hell wi' bloody paper!" shouted Sam, unable, as a plain-speaking Northerner, to endure a spectacle of pathos a moment longer. "Say you'll wed the man and be done with it, or climb in yon cab and let's get off home!" but the outburst left her unmoved. She went on, in a voice just above a whisper, "Of course I'll marry him, but only if he really wants me to. I can't imagine wanting to marry anyone else."

For some reason the admission restored to Sam enough confidence

110

to resume his bluff. He said, heartily, "Well, damn good luck to you, and happen I'll beat you to it." Then to Adam, "This is a daft way to get a daughter off your hands. I'm not even sure of your name. Did I hear right? Was it Swann?"

"You heard right."

He was regarding Henrietta so intently that he had almost forgotten Rawlinson. A small part of his mind kept insisting that, even a few moments ago, it would never have occurred to him to resolve the situation with such finality. But he was glad, somehow, that it had been so resolved. He could not have given adequate expression to any of the half-hidden reasons that had urged him to propose marriage in that melodramatic way, but he did not regret the offer. In some way it had invested her with a dignity that reduced her uncouth father to the status of what he was, an oversized guttersnipe. He heard Rawlinson erupt again and turned to see him once more on his feet, very red about the face and neck. He heard him say, with emphasis but without rancour, "Nowt from me, lass . . . not a pennypiece, d'ye hear? I'll be starting out all over again . . ." but she paid him no attention, remaining there motionless against the window, framed in the soft, afternoon light, and Adam crossed to her, addressing Sam over his shoulder. "Leave her to me, Rawlinson. Stand by your bargain and there's no more to be said."

But there was, one more thing, if only to give expression to Sam Rawlinson's bewilderment. He looked at his daughter, then at the tall, sunburned man towering over her, then back at Henrietta. "Damn it," he said, shaking his head, "what kind of chap are you?" and lifted his hand, letting it fall in a gesture that underlined his incomprehension. He never had understood the irrational impulses that governed the behaviour of a class he dismissed, collectively, as 'the gentry', for those impulses did not seem to spring from anything within his own experience. The few he had met, and set himself to bargain with, were as alien to him as Turks or Russians, and even more unpredictable, and as always when facing a situation that could not be resolved in terms of hard cash, his inclination was to turn his back on it. "Let it rest then," he growled, "but go back on me, come my way making trouble about that lad Garvin, and you'll wish you hadn't. By God, you'll wish you hadn't, lad!" Then taking his hat, he stumped out of the house and a moment later they heard him clip-clopping away in his cab towards Keswick.

*   *   *

111

He said, at length, "Do you want me to call Aunt Charlotte?" and she made a swift, negative gesture, relinquished her grip on the curtain and slowly subsided on to the window seat.

"*Why?*" she said. "Why like that, Adam? Was it the one way to be rid of him?"

He smiled at that. "If it was then it worked. I thought he was bluffing but it seems he wasn't. Well, he's gone, Henrietta. I hope you realise you've seen the last of Sam Rawlinson."

"What did he mean—about that boy, Garvin?"

"I'll tell you another time. It was the main reason I took you along with me, though I don't think I realised as much at the time."

"Tell me now, Adam. There's so much I don't understand and I've got to begin understanding."

He told her. It wasn't easy to explain why and how he regarded her father as a man who should be facing an Assize judge on a more serious charge than inciting a riot but she didn't seem particularly shocked, or even surprised. "He's like that," she said, "all of them down there are like that. Money and property is the only thing that makes any sense to them. That's what's so different about people like you and the Colonel." She went on, thoughtfully, "If you go forward with that haulage and made a million pounds out of it, it wouldn't alter you, not inside." And then, looking at him with a kind of desperate challenge, "What you said—about marrying me. I know it was said for him, to get rid of him, to stop him making trouble, but if . . ."

She stopped and he saw tears welling. Here was a chance to withdraw if he wanted withdrawal. He had only to say something soothing and walk out of here, free to go about his business and hand her over into his aunt's keeping, but although he was tempted something checked him and it had to do with the maturity she had assumed during the confrontation. She had reason to complain. It was time somebody began treating her like a human being and put an end to this cynical use of her as a counter in a whole range of issues, from the death of Tim Garvin to her father's mendacity, and his own involvement that he was still at a loss to understand. He lifted her up, tilted her chin and kissed her softly on the mouth, saying, "Find Aunt Charlotte. Tell her what happened, what we've decided upon."

"I daren't, Adam. She'll be even angrier than Sam. She'll think I meant something like this to happen . . ."

"She won't think anything of the kind. She's been expecting it to happen ever since I brought you home."

"We'll tell her together then."

112

"No. I'm going south right away. I've wasted enough time and if I'm brought into it there'll be endless talk of money and family matters. There's something important I must do, before we get married."

She looked up at him sharply. "Dispose of that necklace?"

"Yes. A man can't get married and set up in business on three hundred and that's all I possess at the moment."

She said, incuriously, "Where will we live, Adam?"

"London. I couldn't operate a business of that kind from anywhere else."

"I've never been to London."

"I'll show you the sights, once I've done what I have to do."

"You haven't told anyone else about those rubies?"

"No one."

"Not even your father?"

"No, he wouldn't approve."

She was silent a moment, finger in her mouth, very childlike again. But when she spoke it was clear that she had his measure. "Very well, Adam. I'll tell your aunt and the Colonel what happened. Go right away. Go this moment before they start asking questions."

He said, gratefully, "That's more than I deserve, but I'll make it up to you, Henrietta," and he kissed her, this time boisterously. "I'll not be away long, a week or so maybe. You'll need to buy things. Tell Aunt Charlotte to take you up to Carlisle and charge whatever you get to me." He paused, eager for solitude but sensing that it was almost indecent to abandon her so abruptly. "Is there anything else?"

"No," she said, carefully, "except to say thank you, Adam."

She went out, closing the door softly and he heard her climbing the stairs. He stood there alone for a moment feeling absurdly inadequate, as though, in some strange manner, their rôles had been reversed and that the initiative had passed to her. Then he went out, across the hall and through the kitchen quarters to the stableyard.

2

She wore successive states of mind like layers of petticoats picked up and put on at random, so that it was a matter of chance which one was innermost and which would show when she hitched her skirt.

The choice was regulated, of course, by mood but the factors that dictated the mood were beyond her control, so that she was never in

113

the least sure how she would regard the future when she woke up or how it would appear when she blew out her candle and lay watching the moonbeams on the ceiling of the little room over the porch that she had been told to call her own.

That was how she regarded the Colonel's house now, as a home quite unlike the turreted lodge on the plain that already seemed to belong to her childhood. The house was home, Aunt Charlotte was her Aunt Charlotte, and the old man was more of a father than Sam had ever been. Especially since the day before yesterday when, in response to an appeal by Aunt Charlotte (for once eager to concede her inadequacy) she had recoiled from Henrietta's shy approach on the subject of what was expected of her as a bride.

"Good life, child," she exclaimed, "how should I know? I was never a bride, and never sought to be one!" but then, meeting Henrietta's startled gaze, "You were raised by a man and I daresay you're as ignorant as I am. I *hope* you are, at all events. I'll ... I'll speak to the Colonel. It isn't a subject I care to broach to a man but better him than that hulking son of his!" and she bustled away leaving Henrietta with a strong impression that her innocent question had outraged the old lady.

It set her thinking, however, of what little she knew of the vaunted secrets of marriage and of snippets of information that had come her way in the last few years via kitchen tittle-tattle and speculative conversations with her best friend, Sarah Hebditch.

There was that curious affair of Agnes, the kitchen-maid, and Amos, the pigman, solved—she was not quite certain how—by Mrs. Worrell's intervention, after Agnes had come to her blubbering and confessed that "Amos had put it across her when she was tiddly and now she was fair ruined". As it turned out she wasn't, for Mrs. Worrell saw to it that Amos married her on pain of dismissal without a character. Months later, her girth having been stealthily observed during the interval, Agnes became the mother of a bouncing boy. In itself the incident had done little but confirm Sarah Hebditch's assurance that unborn babies lived in their mother's stomachs, and that it obviously took two to make one, but neither she nor Sarah were clear about what it was Amos the pigman had put across or what precise part potato wine, to which Agnes was known to be partial, had played in the scandal.

From then on, however, Henrietta was alerted and her presence on the edge of a teeming mill town had inevitably introduced her to the seamier side of life that came to her partly through the prattle of loose-tongued servants, partly through her own powers of observation and deduction. Sarah was fortunate in having brothers whereas Henrietta, having none, had a stroke of luck in catching a fleeting glimpse of a traditional rite among the millgirls of what was locally known as a 'sunning'. A 'sunning', she learned later, was an uproarious practical joke involving male operatives once it was known that they had celebrated their fourteenth birthday, and consisted of a pounce by all the older women in order to debritch and upend the victim, presumably to speculate upon his potentialities.

Avenues of this kind did not offer the curious more than a few hints but between them, shortly before they were seventeen, she and Sarah had hammered out a possible sequence of events. Their difficulty lay in confirming it and this they had never succeeded in doing. On the whole they were inclined to doubt the sum total of their conclusions, feeling that there was, within their calculations, a gross element of error, for the thing itself, viewed objectively, seemed a physical impossibility and they therefore concluded that somewhere along the line they had been misled or hoodwinked.

It was in the hope of qualifying for more information in this particular sphere that Henrietta had approached Aunt Charlotte but the plan miscarried in two ways. Not only did it cause the old lady acute embarrassment, it introduced into Henrietta a nagging doubt that she was not equipped to marry anyone, much less a hulking, experienced man of the world like Adam Swann, and this she found extremely vexing for it did a good deal to tarnish the pleasures of anticipation that had been hers ever since the project had proved acceptable to her future in-laws.

This was the point where her state of mind began to change almost hour by hour. There were secure moments, when she felt safe and snug in this rural retreat, triumphant moments when she could contemplate the future with a satisfaction that was close to smugness, and doubting moments, when she wondered, unhappily, just what it was about marriage that made old women furtive and younger women apprehensive, as though it entailed, besides orange blossoms, a ring, a trousseau and a change of name, a mysterious and frightening ritual capable of driving weak-minded brides out of their minds, a possibility introduced by one of Sarah's garbled stories about a cousin whose wedding she had attended as a bridesmaid.

Recollection of this quite blunted the edge of her delight in an overnight shopping expedition to buy her trousseau in Carlisle but on the day following she accepted the Colonel's invitation to accompany him on a sketching expedition to Friar's Crag. It was here, sitting on a log beside the gentle old man, that she was at least able to learn what marriage might have to offer under ideal conditions, that is, between two people who were attracted to one another. She got no more than a few useful hints it is true, for the old man spoke solely out of a sense of duty. But his very reticence and good humour helped to allay the worst of her fears, even if it did next-to-nothing to dispel her doubts, particularly the doubt that had run her most promising conversations with Sarah Hebditch into a series of cul-de-sacs.

He said, by way of a preamble, "Charlotte tells me your mother died the day you were born. Is that so, m'dear?" and she said it was, adding helpfully that she had approached Aunt Charlotte for the purpose of discussing the kind of things mothers would be likely to discuss on the approach of a daughter's wedding. It was, as it happened, a felicitous approach, for it at once broke down the barrier of reserve between them and even made him chuckle. He said, laying down his brush, "That was a sensible thing to do, m'dear. Many gels wouldn't have had the brains or the spirit!" and he basked for the moment in the lively recollection of his sister's red face when she had implored his assistance. It was the first time in his experience that she had ever confessed to helplessness.

"Well," he said, with no more than a trace of diffidence, "suppose we clear the ground. How much do you know? Gel of your age and liveliness must know something." She told him what she knew and without much embarrassment, for he listened politely and encouraged her with a smiling nod or two when she recounted the predicament of Agnes the kitchenmaid, and how that had been put right by Mrs. Worrell, the housekeeper. It was only when she went on to relay Sarah's dolorous story, of the bride who was shocked into madness, that he said, with a snort, "Dam' lot o' nonsense! Never heard such balderdash! Don't believe a word of it and you mustn't either, you hear?" His emphatic reaction, however, made clarification more necessary than ever. She said, desperately, "But why should anybody invent a story like that, Colonel? And why is everyone so secretive about babies and how women have them?" and he replied, with a vigorous shake of the head, "Damned if I know now that you speak of it. Wasn't always so. When I was your age people didn't hush it up the way they do now. Perfectly natural process. Man fancies a woman, marries her, and they have children . . ." but then his basic honesty compelled him to admit that he wasn't getting anywhere and he said, a little grumpily, "I don't know why I should be expected to tell you things a girl ought to know at your age. That's something for the man you're about to marry I should say, but I'll tell you this, if it'll do anything to settle your mind. There's deficiencies in that boy of mine: He's impulsive, harebrained, and never did take kindly to discipline, but he's good-hearted, and not a man to ride roughshod over a woman. More the opposite, I'd say, if you handle him right." He gave her a keen glance and when she still appeared troubled he took her hand in his maimed one and went on, "I'll add something to that, Henrietta, and you can credit it to my Monique, twenty-five years dead and no more than a memory to me, but a very pleasant one when I look at you. A wife's first duty as I see it is to put a sparkle in a man's eye, and everything follows from that, with a lot less fuss than many folk, including preachers, moralists and dry old sticks like Aunt Charlotte, would have you believe! Now my eyes tell *me* you're head over heels in love with that lad of mine. That's a fact, isn't it?"

"Oh, indeed it is," said Henrietta, without a blush, "but I'm not in the least sure he's in love with me."

"Nonsense," said the old man, "he more or less abducted you and proposed marriage to you, didn't he?"

"I think," said Henrietta, "that that was due to his kind-heartedness."

The Colonel thought a moment. It seemed to him that there was a good deal of truth in this and his instinct warned him that it was no time to fob her off with flattery. He said, at length, "See here, he must have taken a rare fancy to you, for he's turned thirty and never yet given a thought to settling down. Be that as it may, a girl like you shouldn't have much trouble heaping fuel on the fire, if you follow me."

She did, more or less, remembering fleetingly how his hands had played over her when he had crushed her in that initial embrace and with this came a recollection that the sensation produced in her by his kisses had been the precise opposite to that induced by the clammy touch of Makepeace Goldthorpe. She would have liked very much to have improved the occasion by appealing to the old man for more specific instructions but she hesitated to trespass on his patience. She said, carefully, "There's a word in the Bible that one of my governesses said was meant to describe marriage. But, like everyone else, she wouldn't explain properly, or maybe she didn't understand herself. It was 'knew'. It said Adam '*knew* his wife'. Is that what you mean, that when you love somebody you know them,

117

every part of them?" and was surprised to see him regarding her with beaming approval. "Upon my soul," he said, "you've got more damn sense in that pretty head of yours than any of the flibberti-gibbets I've seen about since I went on half-pay! Gaudy creatures, most of 'em, whispering and giggling together, and twirling their parasols like catherine-wheels every time a man tips his hat to them. You've got *sense*. That's precisely what I'm getting at, and the word was written down at a time when English men and women weren't so damned concerned with airs and graces, or giving fancy names to everything, even things about the house. A woman *knows* a man and a man *knows* a woman once they're alone, with one another's arms about them, and the satisfaction that comes of it is the middle and both ends of choosing a partner and raising a family." He looked at her keenly again, "You mean to have a family, I hope?"

"Why, naturally," said Henrietta, feeling more composed than at any time since she had adjusted to the reality of Adam's act of libera-tion in the library, "and I'll tell you a secret. If I can help it, Col-onel, they'll be soldiers like you and Adam were, or at least soldiers' wives, for I wouldn't care to see my sons spend their lives money-grubbing the way Sam Rawlinson and all his cronies do. I should want to be proud of them when I was your age."

"Amen to that!" said the old man, "and I hope I'm spared to see 'em all in uniform!"

*   *   *

That same night, after she had undressed and was about to slip her nightgown over her head, her instinct prompted her to do something it had never occurred to her to do before, to stand naked in front of the mirror and assess herself as an agent for, as the Colonel had ex-pressed it, "putting a sparkle in a man's eye". Mystified as she still was about the ultimate expressions of affection between a husband and wife, she yet sensed she had made definite progress towards ex-posing the most jealously guarded secret of the mystique, and the very act of standing there by candlelight, trying to imagine how he would be likely to regard her in the unlikely event of him ever seeing her without clothes, introduced a glow to all areas of her body, that seemed to emanate from a sharp but by no means unpleasant pricking sensation under the heart. She even noticed, or thought she noticed, subtle physical changes in her appearance. Her colour was high and there was no necessity to bite her lips to increase their redness, a prac-tice she had indulged in more than once before the mirror in the ladies' room at the Assembly Rooms during a soirée. She saw herself now as the equivalent of one of those daring reproductions of a Grecian statue, glimpsed in the catalogue of the Great Exhibition her father had left lying about the house, and the thought returned to her that she equated more with the classical conception of a perfect form than with the kind of girl men were supposed to prefer, willowy wasp-waisted women, who threatened to keel over in a gust of wind. Despite this, however, she decided she liked what she saw. Her skin was very white, and entirely without blemishes if one overlooked the incongruous triangle of hair where her thighs met, and according to Mrs. Worrell (whom she had consulted in alarm when it first began to appear), every adult in the world was afflicted by that. Her shoulders sloped away in the classical manner, her breasts were firm and nicely rounded, her stomach flat and her legs shapely, with slim ankles and long feet that matched hands of which she had always been proud. She reached up, untied the ribbon that bound her hair and watched her copper ringlets cascade over her shoulders. The movement, that produced a ripple of shadow, excited her so that she whirled round to see the effect at the back. Released from her stays, her waist now appeared to her at least two inches thicker than it should have been, and drew attention to the pronounced chubbiness of her bottom. She said, aloud, "I'll just have to refuse second helpings," and skittishly she girdled herself with her ribbon, frowning when the loop seemed almost wide enough to wriggle through. Then for no reason at all, she felt ashamed of gazing at herself without clothes in such an immodest manner, and bundled herself into her nightgown, blew out the candle and scrambled into bed, wondering what had prompted her to do such a thing and deciding it must have something to do with all those doubts and uncertainties, partially stilled by the old man's patient and patently honest advice. Her mind returned to those whispered confidences she had exchanged with Sarah Hebditch on the subject of men as they were reputed to behave once they had you alone in a bedroom like this, and the glow she had carried upstairs began to subside, making room for doubts. The debris of hints over the years began to form a pattern in her mind and although it was blurred and indistinct it was yet definite enough to frighten. And then, like the comforting wink of a light in the dark, she remembered what the Colonel had said about his son's kindheartedness, of which she had so much proof since he had first ridden over the fold in the moor. Whatever awaited her was unlikely to prove hurtful and shameful. He might scold her, and treat her condes-

119

cendingly, he might even bully her as he had been inclined to do on their way over the fells. But he was incapable of being cruel and dominating in the way she sensed Makepeace would have been. On this thought, greatly comforted, she slept.

Part Two

The Cygnet Years:
1858 - 1861

1

Cicerone

JOSH AVERY was his quarry, for Josh was the only man of his acquaintance who had been shrewd enough, or ruthless enough, to show a profit on the years he had devoted to the service of the East India Company; a cool, cynical rascal, who had not only seduced his colonel's wife, and thus precipitated a resounding regimental scandal, but had, it was rumoured, done it on the proceeds of a substantial bribe given him by the Nizam for unofficial military support in a palace plot. This, however, had never been proved and Avery forestalled an inquiry by resigning his commission and going off home, the simpering colonel's wife in tow. Rumours reaching the garrison towns since insisted that the Nizam's bribe had consisted of a handful of diamonds and that Avery had put his capital to very good account.

Adam remembered him vividly. No one who ever got to know Joshua Avery really well subsequently forgot him. Adam had seen him, but privately, as a kind of pocket Talleyrand, using his musical, low-pitched voice to beguile not merely silly, bored women, like Kitty Sullivan, but bankers and others who should have known better, bazaar merchants, martinet-visionaries like Roberts, and even men who were seeking the Imperial Holy Grail and hoping to bring it home to Windsor on their retirement. A slightly-built man, with greenish eyes set in an almost triangular face, hard cheekbones, a pallor that had defied any number of tropical summers, and a small, thin-lipped mouth from which no ill-considered word had ever made its escape.

* * *

Avery had written offering him luncheon at a raffish eating-house off Drury Lane, where he had booked an alcove, curtained off from the gilded dining-hall, a place full of diners who were, so far as Adam could discern, either actors, or courtesans, together with a sprinkling of city merchants, who somehow contrived to wear a wolfish air of brigandage in a way that made piracy a semi-respectable calling.

After so many years away from the capital, Adam found himself fascinated by the London scene as it moved at a gallop towards the end of a dynamic decade. Disproportionate changes appeared to have taken place during the seven years he had been overseas and he sensed that this had a bearing on the proliferation of the railways. The London he recalled as a youth had been a sprawling, half-rural community, with its grass roots still embedded in the era of Brummel, Fox, Pitt, and to a degree, in that of Johnson and Hogarth, but that was past. It was now a frenetic, impersonal city, erupting before the eye with an extraordinary variety of enterprises, and the emphasis on money and conformity rather than on style. One had only to walk down the Strand and poke about in the labyrinth of streets linking that thoroughfare with the Thames, to note the sharp contrasts between those who were emerging as the new masters, those who served them, and a majority that had been left far behind in the race.

There had always been the London poor, thousands of mutilated beggars and barefoot urchins, the streetwalker, the huckster and the artisan only one rung above this flotsam. Removed from this swarm there had been the town dandy, and the man of means, spanking along in an eye-catching phaeton, or picking his way along the crowded pavements in an ensemble that would keep any one of the derelicts fed and housed for a twelvemonth. But now the traditional contrasts were muted as society fragmented into a hundred rather than a dozen segments. The fop, and the man of fashion, were still to be seen, but soberly-dressed businessmen predominated and these, Adam noticed, occupied a series of social plateaux, all the way down the scale from the steeple-hatted city gent, puffing his cheroot while he struck his bargains, to the hurrying clerk in threadbare worsted, who was probably feeding a family on what his employer paid a head waiter for a single meal.

Money, and the hundred-thousand ventures chasing money, was in the soot-encrusted air, and above the never-ending clatter of grinding wheels and scurrying feet one could almost listen to the comfortable rustle of bankers' drafts and the steady chink-chink of small change. Everywhere ratty old buildings of the last century were being torn down and replaced by warehouses and tall, narrow-fronted dwellings with four storeys and a basement area. The new, stylishly painted shops were beset by customers, the pavements were thronged, and the traffic jams in streets that had been designed to carry market-carts and a carriage or two, reminded Adam of the clubbed approaches to a bridge in the path of an advancing army. Contemplating it all he thought, 'I'm only just in time it seems. If I had left it much longer the door would have been slammed in my face' and he turned in at the eating-house, giving Avery's name and noting the servility it earned him.

Avery arrived late, passing between any number of jovial, back-slapping friends in their patent boots, tight, strap-over trousers, blue frock coats with gilt buttons the size of catherine-wheels and canary yellow waistcoats slung with the inevitable cross-cable chain and fobs. Watching him, and recalling the hardbitten Avery of bygone days, Adam wondered whether he had committed too much of his own story on paper, but once they were settled over their porter he was soon reassured, for Avery drew the alcove curtains, leaned forward and became, for a moment, the old campaigner, saying: "I wouldn't have wagered a shilling you had the wits to take a leaf out of my book. Swann. You brought the loot with you, I hope?" and when Adam looked hesitant, "Oh, easy man, I never come in here unless I'm doing business. Every lackey is in somebody's pay but I know each of them and each of them knows me," whereupon Adam dipped into his pocket and dangled the necklace just beyond Avery's reach.

He saw Avery's eyes light up for a second and then they were hooded. "You'd trust a man of my reputation with something as genuine as that? Well, I find that flattering, but don't expect me to return the compliment."

Adam said, with a shrug, "What choice do I have? I'm not such a fool as to sniff my way about London, hawking it to the highest bidder, whereas we all know where you went to butter your bread. The only difference between us is that I faced odds of fifty to one to get this. All you did was to involve two or three hundred other poor devils in somebody else's quarrel, stand back, and get paid for the lot of them."

It had never been possible to snub Avery. He said, quietly, "Let me handle it, fondle it," and Adam passed the necklace across reluctantly. Everyone in the Company's service knew about Josh Avery's lust for stones.

"Before I value it what is it you're seeking, Swann? A cash transaction? An advance at around ten per cent? Or a straight sale on commission?"

"That would depend on you. I need as much capital as that will produce. I'll pay commission, of course, and a heavy commission at that, for it can't be helped. Are you equipped to value it?"

Avery took out a glass and screwed it firmly into his eye. Then, having come prepared, he ran the necklace stone by stone along a metal gauge of the kind Adam had seen the goldsmiths use in the bazaars. Perhaps a minute passed before he said, "I'll not attempt a bluff, Swann. It's worth ten times what you'd get for it, and around five times as much as I could squeeze out of it the way I shall have to go about it."

"I expected that," Adam said.

A gleam of humour showed in Avery's green eyes. "Cards on the table, old comrade-in-arms. Even I couldn't sell it as a necklace. The stones would have to be recut and disposed of separately. They'd lose a carat or two in the process."

"I expected that, too."

"Then let's consider. Thirty stones, varying considerably in size and quality. These big ones eight-to-six carats, the smaller ones three-to-five. All Burmese rubies, by the way, none of your Ceylon gewgaws." He looked intently at nothing just beyond Adam's head, whistled a stave and then went on, "Say an average of a hundred a stone in my kind of market, and that's the only market open to us in the circumstances. Three thousand pounds, less ten per cent."

"Twenty-nine hundred," said Adam. "I'm keeping one stone back."

"Oh, come now, there are less expensive souvenirs of your wasted years with the John Company."

"I'm getting married shortly and I want one of the medium-sized stones made up into a ring."

Avery looked shocked. "Married, you say? Good God man, you can't afford to do that yet, not even if I drop my commission to eight per cent for old times' sake. But perhaps she brings a dowry and that's why you aren't haggling?"

"She brings me the clothes she stands up in and even those were bought with my money."

Avery said, curiously, "I was surprised to get your letter but knowing you its contents made sense. However, you're not a man I would have thought to see hooked on that particular bait. Dear old Roberts, maybe, or 'Circus' Howard, or any of the young bucks who rode into battle carrying lockets and hair rings. But not you, Swann. Deep down I had the impression we had more in common than any two of them. Was I so wrong?"

"You were half right," said Adam.

"How many of our Addiscombe class survived the Mutiny?"

"Only Roberts, and he's been badly bitten by the Imperial bug. You'll hear more of him if he survives, but let's stay with the business on hand, Josh."

"Don't be so damned greedy. Thirty Burmese rubies are worth lingering over. Why do you need capital? Is it to buy your way into a crack regiment?"

"Far from it. I'm done with soldiering. I resigned and came home to take a bite at your cherry, Josh."

He noticed then that curiosity, of the kind that made Avery as untypical as himself, had been aroused in the man and also, notwithstanding the prospect of financial gain, that it would have to be satisfied before he could enlist Avery as his agent. Even so it was not like trusting a civilian. Avery was a scoundrel but there existed between them the bond of shared experiences under fire, and it struck Adam that it might be to his advantage to put that bond to the test. He said, "I've got a dream, Josh. Not your kind of dream, to set up as a gentleman for at thirty plus I know myself better than that. Six months of it and sheer ennui would drive me back into the army. I need action but not the kind of action I was trained for. A very great deal has been happening over here in the last ten years and I want to participate. Fortunes are being made every day by men with less initiative than we needed to survive in the field. Does that answer your question?"

"Only partly. What's the substance of your dream, Swann?"

Adam told him, as much but no more than was necessary, and Avery did not miss a word although, with those heavily-lidded eyes, he might have been dozing. He said, pocketing the necklace, "Well, at least it's original, but I couldn't say more than that, Adam."

"I think you could if you cared to. You've been home long enough to get acclimatised."

"I'm marginally involved in a variety of businesses but I'm not such a fool as to practise one. That would mean breaking my two golden rules, rising before noon and accepting personal responsibility. In short, I finance but I never operate. I leave that to people like you, people who dream dreams. However, it is true that I'm in a

127

position to give you good advice. Will you listen, or do you prefer to make your own mistakes?"

"I've made one reconnaissance and I intend making another before I take the plunge. There's something you could tell me at once. Assuming you advance three thousand, do I buy a rundown established business, or do I set up independently?"

"Nobody sells a business that is making money. Start one of your own but play for big stakes from the day you open. Three thousand, plus what you must have saved, isn't a fortune for the caper you have in mind, but it's enough if you go about it the right way. You wouldn't take kindly to a bona fide partner, I can see that, but you'll need a backer, someone with close contacts among the men you'll have to tout as a carrier."

"You'd be prepared to back me?"

"Perhaps, but don't let's keep it personal at this stage. My view is you'll need guidance, and I could supply that if I had a mind to. You'll need many other things—agents all over the country, upwards of fifty reliable drivers, and as many vehicles, coach-built by someone with a reputation at stake. You'll need good horseflesh, for the coach roads have gone to hell since the railroads were built, and that means a number of strategically-placed depots, with good stabling available. Damn it, I could sit here all day giving you free advice on any one of these matters but you know me. I don't give advice, not even to old comrades-in-arms, I sell it. That's my business."

"Then take first things first. Can you dispose of that necklace on the terms you mentioned?"

Avery said, thoughtfully, "I can do a lot better than that, Swann, depending upon how far you trust me."

"Say the width of this table, Josh."

"That's far enough." Avery rang the bell, a waiter appeared and he issued orders for a meal. As soon as the waiter had disappeared he went on: "There were rules in our kind of warfare. Sometimes our opponents didn't observe them but we had to, for political and fancy reasons. The war you're so eager to join in is played without rules, except a few loose ones between the parties investing and the parties who do the spending and earning. You remember the Thugs in the North and Central plains? They sacrificed men to the god Kali. Over here two older gods share a six-day week, Mammon and Moloch. Jehovah still collects his dues on Sunday, but on the stroke of midnight his temple doors are slammed, everyone gets off their knees and goes back to Thuggery. You do business on that principle and it isn't easy to accept at first."

"I rode a horse from Plymouth to Lakeland, passing through a lot of country and keeping my eyes open so I'll accept it. But sooner or later there will have to be rules. It'll be that or French-style revolution, in my opinion."

"Oh, they'll bend rather than break if they have to. The holy Joes, men like Shaftesbury and Gladstone are already drafting legislation. Factory Acts, fenced machinery, compulsory education, even an extended franchise. But that won't do more than enlarge the free-for-all and multiply your labour difficulties. Mammon will still work a six-day week. What you saw in the Midlands and North is a phase in the switch from an agricultural to an industrial economy, but that isn't what I'm talking about. I daresay you think you can handle men, Swann, but you haven't satisfied me yet that you can handle money. If you could you wouldn't be here, falling over yourself to accept three thousand for something that deserves a place in the Tower of London alongside the Crown Jewels. The flower of the flock at all events, for I've never seen a ruby as large or as perfect as that big one. Maybe you should keep that in reserve. So here's a proposition. I'll give you a banker's draft for three thousand and we'll see what use you make of it. A year would be long enough, for by then you'll either amount to something or you'll have gone bankrupt. If that happens don't look to me to bail you out. The partnership I bought for a song was owned by someone like you, who came home determined to climb on the haywain, fell off, and broke his neck. On the other hand, there's a certain promise about you, Swann. The way I look at it is this—you're alive, and all the others save Roberts are dead, so it must follow that you're either exceptionally lucky or exceptionally quickwitted. I'll gamble on you being both."

"Am I to infer from that you want to put your own money up?"

Avery smiled and Adam thought of an old dog-fox sitting well to windward, and watching the pack stream by on a false scent. "No, my friend. I wouldn't invest sixpence in transport by road, rail or canal. For every transport venture that shows a profit ten stockholders throw themselves out of windows come quarter day. But I'll cheerfully invest *your* money in it, being the difference between what I pay and what I get paid for twenty-nine rubies, won from the Ranee of Jhansi in all but single combat. How does that strike you?"

"As playing the hand you played in Bengal," said Adam, "winner take all."

"Ah," said Avery, "but I've learned since then, and two years is a long apprenticeship in Pam's London. You never saw me take the risks in the field that I take every day in the city. Now you were once a death-or-glory boy, Swann. You even tagged on to Cardigan's charge at Balaclava but I won't hold that against you. I like that kind of man out ahead of me. He draws the fire and what have I got to lose but time?" He paused, thumbs hooked in the armpits of his canary yellow waistcoat. "You like my proposition?"

"So long as it isn't committed to paper."

Avery smiled and nodded three times and Adam recalled that, although continuously interesting, he had never been liked, except by the troopers who always admired a showman. "I stopped putting things on paper when I resigned my commission," he said, "but now and again I like to shake hands."

They shook hands. It was a strange and rather casual beginning.

2

Looking back on that exploratory period in later years Adam always saw it as a feat of mountaineering attempted by an amateur.

The first base camp was his initial decision and then followed the long, toilsome advance. Later on, once he was fully committed and had his second wind, the foothills were accounted for at a good, steady pace, each successive summit representing an encounter, and what resulted from those encounters.

There was his chance meeting with Aaron Walker in the depot at Plymouth; the long ride across England; the witnessing of the riot that gave him an insight into the latent menace of the relationship between master and man and then, most improbably, Henrietta Rawlinson's flash of inspiration concerning the naming of the enterprise.

After that came his loose arrangement with Avery and all that emerged from that, so that he came to see this as the scramble that carried him, breathless but optimistic, to the peak. And it was here, again improbably, he came face to face with Saul Keate.

Keate, perhaps more than anyone else, was his catalyst, for it was Keate who was instrumental in recruiting and training his original labour force. Josh Avery's lazy patronage was to prove of great and lasting value to him in a variety of spheres, but no one aspect of it was as rewarding as his contemptuous gift of ex-sergeant Keate.

He met Keate on his final day in London, but all the preceding days, including three Sundays, were spent in affrays planned by Avery but executed without benefit of his chaperonage. For here Avery was as good as his word, generous with introductions and information but remaining very much in the background and only appearing from time to time, like the daemon in a pantomime.

Despite this Adam could have gone further and fared much worse, for Avery's passport into the world of the men of Moloch and Mammon was not his flamboyance and surface charm, and not even his nerve or his access to capital although he used all these weapons. At a much deeper level it was his memory for trivia that put him on such good terms with a wide cross-section of men, without whom Adam might have floundered for months without achieving very much.

Avery directed him first to Blunderstone, a coach builder who made drays and waggons for some of London's most prosperous breweries and here, in the waggonmaster's yard off Galleywall Road, he invested a third of his promised capital in a fleet of waggons, placing his orders on the strength of Blunderstone's designs for one-horse and two-horse vehicles, of the kind in general use for the transport of light and heavy goods over provincial roads. To Adam's amazement the coach-builder was able to promise delivery within eight weeks of signing the contract.

From here he was passed on to McSawney's stables, where he spent a day inspecting cart horses of every breed and crossbreed, heeding the advice of McSawney's nagsmen but, in the main, making his own decisions. He left McSawney's having spent another five hundred pounds' worth of Avery's money on a string of haulage animals capable of transporting the baggage train of a battalion over terrain where no metalled roads existed. The beasts he chose, Clydesdales for the heavy work, Cleveland Bays for lighter, faster routes, were probably the best available in Europe. The Clydesdales particularly inspired confidence. The smallest of them stood seventeen hands, weighed two thousand pounds and was capable, he was told, of hauling a full load twenty miles a day if harnessed to the type of dray Blunderstone was making to his specification. His cavalryman's eye was attracted to the Percherons and Suffolk Punches but he chose the two alternative breeds as most likely to serve a purpose that was becoming more clearly defined every day after discussions with wholesalers to whom Avery introduced him, usually by letter.

These letters amused but slightly embarrassed Adam, representing him as a man well-established in the haulage business, and invariably referring to him as '... *my good friend Swann, owner and managing director of Swann-on-Wheels, Ltd., a concern I have no hesitation in recommending as highly competitive in rates and time schedules.*' The wholesalers, who seemed to have many dealings with Avery and his associates, accepted this introduction at its face value, and by keeping his wits about him Adam was able to learn a good deal about likely competitors, notably the main line railways, whose rates seemed to him high and whose service was accepted as being notoriously unpunctual.

In the course of his expeditions in and about the city, and an occasional visit to the wharves above and below London Bridge, Adam came to the conclusion that, although railways now linked the capital with every main centre of industry south of Tyneside, the policy decisions of almost every important manufacturer in the country were made within hailing distance of London Wall. Here were based the distributors of all the clamorous enterprises that had quadrupled their output under the impetus of steam, and although most of them might have originated in places like Seddon Moss, in one or other of the pottery towns, in the Yorkshire dales, or the coalfields of the North-East and Midlands, the newcomers lost no time in acquiring the brashness of the London-born merchant, and were quick to adopt his contempt for provincials. He met Staffordshire men who would never have admitted to walking two hundred miles south-east in search of work after the riots of '48, and Manchester men who might have been among those who fled from the yeomanry sabres at Peterloo but had since learned to look upon their northern kinsfolk as chawbacons. He heard a Batley man mangling his vowels in an unsuccessful attempt to conceal a strong Yorkshire accent and correct the odd idiom that slipped out when boasting of how much shoddy he had shipped to the Orient last month. They were all, it seemed, disenchanted with the provinces and spoke of their home towns, if at all, as an absentee bishop in the last century would have referred to rural pocket-livings that enabled him to drive a coach and four through his fashionable diocese. Every one of them had an office or a warehouse hereabouts, the steel men of Sheffield, the wool barons of Bradford, the more important spinners of Rochdale and

132

Oldham, the leather men of Leicester. Here, eating themselves to death in fashionable chophouses, were Dubliners, Glaswegians, Lancastrians, Geordies and Welshmen, merchants with thriving businesses on Mersey and Tyne, and Midlanders building their mock-Georgian houses in Kensington and Bayswater on the proceeds of factories that were fouling the skies over Walsall and Dudley. There were spare men, gross men, sober men and men whose clothes and breath reeked of the taproom. There were men who were open-handed and others who, like Rawlinson, would have taken pride in skinning a grape for a profit. There were men who spent their time impressing others that they were on Christian-name terms with the cousin of an earl, and others who made a cult of vulgarity and could have been hobnobbing with Sam Rawlinson the day before yesterday. Three things they had in common, an impressive display of whiskers and energy, and an insatiable greed, but it was greed that made the more socially ambitious among them as ruthless as a starving fox in a hen-run. To Adam Swann this had advantages. Transport rates quoted at a penny a hundredweight below the current average ensured their civility from the moment he entered their offices, and not one of them demanded credentials after glancing at one of Avery's larded introductions.

*　　*　　*

He had taken lodgings in a small hotel kept by an ex-butler in a clean little street off the Gray's Inn Road, returning there each evening too tired to do more than enter up his day-book, eat a simple dinner and go to bed, but he found, to his surprise, that sleep did not come as easily as it had after a day in the saddle and that, in the last afterglow of the sunset, his thoughts would return not to the debts he had incurred during the day but to Henrietta, some three hundred miles to the north-west.

At this hour, when the city clamour was muted, he wondered if she thought of him too and their madcap association seemed, at this distance, as improbable as a runaway match in one of Mr. Mudie's chain-library romances. And yet, reviewing it objectively, he discovered that he had no regrets and few anxieties concerning her, for the truth was he sometimes thought of her with amused tenderness that made him half understand what had encouraged him to make such a leap in the dark at a time when he was likely to need every penny he possessed. Then the essential rightness of her place in the new pattern of his life would reassert itself, and he would see a cer-

133

tain inevitability in the chain of events that had occurred since that first glimpse of her on the moor, and find himself smiling at something she had said, or one of the expressions that chased another from her face. And with this came a kind of certitude that they were, in many ways, a matched pair, striking out together in search of change and adventure.

He was particularly aware of this the night Avery appeared at his lodging shortly after supper and talked him into a night on the town. He remembered enough of Avery's reputation to know that this meant no more or no less than a visit to some of the capital's houses of pleasure, and so it proved, for after an hour's drinking and parading in Cremorne Gardens, they went on to Kate Hamilton's notorious establishment in Princes Street, Leicester Square, described by Josh as "the safest and most exclusive whorehouse in Europe". "Kate," he said, "not only employs girls selected and groomed for elegance, but subjects them to regular medical inspection. She numbers crowned heads among her regulars."

They might, indeed, have been paying a call on a foreign potentate. To pass the portals of the house required the scrutiny of two commissionaires, after which they were inspected by a third through a peephole. Once inside, a dark passage led them into the most ornate and brilliantly-lit salon Adam had ever seen. Mirrors covered the walls and between immense chandeliers were insets of ceiling glass. At the far end sat Kate herself, enormously fat and strikingly ugly but none the less enthroned like a queen, her half-naked handmaidens grouped about her, and, here and there, occupying couches covered in sky-blue, crimson or black satin.

The impact of this vulgar splendour was so striking that it was a moment before Adam noticed that every woman in the salon save Kate was dressed in a single, diaphanous gown that revealed, in the greatest detail, figures calculated to appeal to every conceivable taste. The girls, all of them young and attractive, and a few possessing great beauty, were heavily rouged and carmined but their bearing, obviously imposed on them by what he assumed the parlour equivalent of a drill-sergeant, struck him as comic in such a setting. It was as though they were not whores at all but priestesses, here to perform some kind of mystic rite rather than cater for the extravagant whims and perversions of Kate's customers, and when he and Avery sat down to a supper of oysters and devilled kidneys it was served them by two of these goddesses, who introduced themselves gravely as 'Olympia' and 'Flavia'. Olympia was a brunette and Adam judged her to be about Henrietta's age, but his girl, Flavia, was a well-upholstered blonde, with blue eyes and smooth, slightly pendulous cheeks. She was foreign and spoke English with a guttural accent that he took to be Dutch or German. Avery, as a regular patron, was at once recognised by Olympia, and acknowledged her decorous greeting with a friendly slap on her thinly-veiled bottom, after which he ordered champagne and the girls sat with them, sustaining a conversation that would have been acceptable at a tea-party on a vicarage lawn. As they ate supper, however, the place slowly filled with gentlemen of fashion and Avery, sardonically amused, pointed out some of the notabilities, who included an important foreign diplomat and two members of Parliament. He talked to Adam as though the girls were sempstresses' dummies, telling him that about half of Kate's women were imported from the Continent and others, just emerging from the trainee stage, were youngsters from the provinces, some of them no more than fifteen, who had been enticed to London by advertisements appearing in journals that were Sunday reading in pious homes and promised service with a good family and the prospect of Continental travel.

"Most of them get their trip abroad if they come up to scratch," he said, "for Kate has an exchange system with French and Belgian houses. Many of the clients here have a preference for foreigners, and this promotes a two-way traffic across the Channel. Flavia comes from Rotterdam, I believe. That's so, isn't it, my dear?"

Flavia said it was so and poured the champagne, Avery disclosing it was four times the price of the best one could buy at a city merchant's, and that, although this was generally known, it was not resented.

"Kate's overheads are prohibitive," he said. "She not only has to pay for these fittings and all this gaslight but for a network of provincial procurers and also for police protection. Everything in London is damnably expensive just now but nothing more so than feather-bedded vice."

Adam was interested by all he saw about him and admitted that the food was better than any he had eaten in London but when Avery, with a yawn, told Olympia he was ready to retire to the private apartments, Adam had little inclination to follow his example and admitted as much. Avery said, lightly, "Ah, I was forgetting. You're to become a bridegroom in a week or so. We shall probably see more of you in due course." Then he and his partner passed up the gilded staircase, along the brilliantly lit gallery and out of sight.

Adam's girl, Flavia, looked so bewildered that he felt obliged to explain Avery's cynical comment, saying, "It's true I'm getting married soon but that isn't the reason. I came here as a sightseer but you won't lose on that account." He saw her glance uneasily in the direction of the dais as she said, in her deep, guttural voice, "I do not please you, m'sieu? Why do I not please you? Be so good as to tell me. It is important that I should know."

"You please me well enough," he said, amiably, "but why should that matter to you? Madam has been paid the admission money, and I shall pay you whether we go upstairs or not."

"Madam misses nothing," the girl said nervously. "Last week Niobe was sent away for the same reason. Madam will not keep the rejected, m'sieu."

Adam said, suddenly, "How old are you, Flavia?" and she said she was twenty-five, and had been working in London for two years. "This is a good place," she went on, "the very best in London, but I have not yet saved enough money to return home. Like you, m'sieu, I have plans. I hope to marry as soon as I return to Rotterdam." Then, pleadingly, "Will you please follow your friend? For appearances' sake?"

He said, cheerfully, "Certainly, for I wouldn't like you to lose your situation on my account," and got up, cursing Avery for involving him in such a situation.

Flavia led the way up the broad staircase and into a cubicle off the long passage, and even this confined space was oppressively overlit and enclosed in wall mirrors and ceiling glass. There was no furniture in it but a bed and washbasin, and the only section of wall free of mirrors was hung with a crudely-drawn picture of a cherubic girl glancing roguishly down on them whilst in the act of shedding her drawers.

The combination of Flavia's uneasiness, and the torrid vulgarity of the apartment, produced in him a sensation of disgust and this surprised him very much, for he had never thought to feel squeamish in a whorehouse. He wondered, vaguely, if this was something else that might be credited to Henrietta's account, and reacting to this felt half-inclined to accommodate the girl, if only to establish his independence. But then he realised that the reason went beyond that, and had to do with a deeper and more private distaste for the idiotic trappings of the house. He thought, sourly, 'Good God, there must be a more adult way of satisfying a purely physical need. It's months since I had a woman, and this poor creature is at least clean and personable, but I'll be damned if I need titillating, like an old badger past his prime,' and he said, as she began pulling her gown over her head, "It's nothing personal, you understand? Do you smoke?" and he offered her a cheroot, watching her rescue a little of her dignity as she sat on the edge of the bed exhaling little puffs of smoke. He said, for something to say, "What will you and your fiancé do when you marry? Will you set up in business in Rotterdam?"

"In Aachen," she told him. "He is a baker there and would be his own master. But he has no money. It is therefore important that I bring a dowry."

Suddenly he was ready to pay tribute to the girl's placid acceptance of realities and laid a sovereign on the washstand. "For your *dot*, mademoiselle," and she looked confused, saying, "But this is not necessary, m'sieu. We are paid a percentage of the house fee, and sometimes a gratuity. But only when the gentleman is pleased with the service."

Her attitude increased his impatience with the place, with all its absurd, sybaritic trappings, that somehow reduced the association of men and women to an obscene formula. To take her now in this bed, to watch himself sweating over her in half-a-dozen angled reflections, struck him as an act of a fool or a pervert, so that it suddenly became imperative to breathe fresh air and he went out and down the stairs, leaving her to stare after him with her puzzled expression, one hand fumbling with the fastening of her dress, the other covering his sovereign, as though he might think better of the impulse.

He passed out into the street and made his way down the Haymarket to the Strand. Out here, with a night breeze blowing upriver, he could contemplate the general rather than the particular, wondering at the stresses that created a demand for places like Kate Hamilton's, and asking himself if a girl like Henrietta would be aware they existed in every city in Europe. It was odd, he decided, that men reckoned mature and successful in so many technical spheres should find it necessary to siphon their lust into the indifferent bodies of girls like Flavia and Olympia, who were reduced to borrowing exotic names in order to heighten the illusion of adventure. Most of them, unlike himself, had a home, a wife and a largish family, and yet, if their wives had advanced a single step towards acquiring the techniques of a spreadeagled harlot, they would be outraged. Why should this be so, when the words of the marriage service spoken in all churches they attended each Sunday acknowledged the needs of human beings to seek comfort in one another? Kate Hamilton,

Flavia, and the starvelings of the Black Dwarf country, were all at one, evidence of a signal failure on the part of Western Man to match his technical achievements with self-knowledge and a real, rather than fraudulent, civilisation. Everything was topsy-turvey, every facet of this hustle into the future demanded a double-standard of values. It was practised in bed and in all the counting houses he had visited. It was present in the concept of Empire and in the conclaves of lawgivers at Westminster. One followed certain courses for gain or personal gratification but never, not even privately, admitted the truth concerning motives. Instead one groped for other, more specious reasons for worshipping money and machines, and clung to them, come what may, and for a brief moment he was able to stand back and contemplate the monstrous folly of it all, not only the mirrors and couches of Kate Hamilton's shrine, but all that nourished it, the warehouses, the moored barges clustered in the Thames tideway, the helter-skelter scramble of every living soul down there to accumulate metal tokens representing an entirely fictitious security and independence. Then, slowly coming to terms with himself, he admitted his own purely voluntary involvement in the chaos, thinking, 'And who the devil am I to question it? I stole jewels and travelled thousands of miles to make my grab, and there's only two reservations so far as I'm concerned. I'll make it with dignity and, so long as it doesn't involve detours, observing some kind of standards as regards the use I make of people.'

The resolve brought him reassurance so that he buttoned his coat against the keen breeze and strode down towards the Law Courts, turning away from the river towards his lodging.

3

Avery appeared unannounced the following evening, just as Adam was finishing supper. His mood, Adam sensed, was tetchy, and he seemed for once a little unsure of himself. When the table was cleared, and they were alone in the sitting room, he laid a banker's draft on the table. It made payable to Adam Swann the sum of three thousand, five hundred guineas. In spite of himself and a suspicion that enthusiasm of any kind irritated Avery, Adam could not conceal his gratification.

"This is getting on a thousand more than I expected, Josh. Your estimate was three thousand pounds, not guineas!"

"I'm sharpish but I'm not a thief," he muttered, but Adam said, clapping him on the shoulder, "You're a rum chap, Josh. I'm only trying to express gratitude and not solely on account of the draft. I could have wasted months exploring the ground on my own," but here he stopped, seeing in Avery's expression a positive distaste to have his patronage acknowledged.

"We struck a bargain," he said, "and it's turned out to my advantage as much as yours, so stop prancing about like a child emptying a Christmas stocking!"

"I'll say thank you whether you like it or not, Josh. How much did you get for the stones?"

Avery's head came up sharply and for a moment he looked deadly. "Now what the devil is that to you? Your share was more than you expected, so leave it at that, man."

"I'll do that readily enough," said Adam, puzzled by the ex-cavalryman's touchiness, "so long as you tell me if you disposed of all the rubies or some of them. Remember I made a condition that one three-carat stone was to be held back when the necklace was broken up but I won't hold you to that if you were up against stiff opposition and I'll wager you were."

Their eyes met at that and Avery's looked troubled. He said, finally, "I'll tell you something, Swann, something I freely admit I didn't intend telling you when I came here. I kept one stone back. As a matter of fact I kept every stone back. Twenty-nine of them are still in my bank and they'll stay there until you find you need more capital, as you will sooner or later. God help me, what does an eel like me *do* when he runs into an honest fool, with some kind of claim on his past?"

Adam shrugged. "That's for you to ask yourself, Josh."

"Yes it is, and I've been asking it ever since you gave me a fortune in precious stones to dispose of, taking my integrity on trust. Well, I've come up with some kind of answer, and I'll tell you what that man does, Swann. He's persuaded to play the sentimental fool himself unless he's a thoroughgoing blackguard, and I never was that, or not the kind those time-servers in India thought me."

"I never did. Razor-sharp, maybe, but not a scoundrel. Perhaps because I took your troopers' opinion into account, and they always thought well of you. Maybe you remember that."

"I remember, damn it," Avery said, "and I daresay it's cost me the easiest money I'm ever likely to pocket. You did yourself a rare good turn reserving judgement on me, that day they drummed me out, Swann. If it had been one of the others, Roberts, or one of those popinjays who prattled about the honour of the regiment, he could have gone hang and be damned to him. But no, it had to be you, someone else who didn't fit. Well then, here's the aperitif, and we'll discuss the main course in a moment," and he laid a small leather box on the table, turned his back, and went over to the window.

The lid of the box opened by a spring and inside, on a bed of blue velvet, was a golden ring, slender at the waist but flattening to a broad shank, encrusted with small diamonds. The centre stone, the only one of real value, was a medium-sized ruby taken, Adam guessed, from the centre of the necklace. It was handsomely set and looked as if it had rested there ever since it was mined. But then something diverted Adam's eye from the stone and looking closely at the shank he saw that a clever craftsman had inscribed there an insignia, or rather two insignias. On either side of the mount, each facing inwards, a swan had been engraved, and when he held the ring to the lamp he saw that in place of each facing wing was a wheel.

He said, quietly, "I don't give a damn what you've done with those stones, or what you plan to do with them, Avery. This is a gesture on your part I'll remember all my life." And then, "This draft, it's a personal advance, isn't it? You've made no attempt to sell that necklace, have you?"

"I'm well secured so long as I've got rubies of that quality. Did I pretend they weren't worth ten times that sum, even on our kind of market?"

"No, you didn't, Josh, but there's more to it than that."

"Yes, there is. More than you know."

Avery spun on his heels and stood with his back to the light so that his pale, triangular face was no longer disfigured by pock craters and the scar that ran diagonally across his forehead. He said, with a grin, "I've had a thousand field comrades, men I sometimes respected but would never have sought out in civilian life. Since then I've had a hundred associates, some I could trust at a pinch. But one thing I've never had, someone of my own generation I could call a friend. Maybe it was thinking on that that encouraged me to play the fool over those rubies and your harebrained enterprise. I don't know and may never know, but time could tell me. Here it is then, I averaged those stones at five carats apiece. A Burmese ruby of five carats fetches three hundred guineas in any saleroom, even a backstage auction. I knew that as soon as I took a good look at them, so work it out for yourself. To you, to me, to Hatton Garden, that necklace is worth at least nine thousand guineas. Subtract three hundred for the one I had made up for the dowerless bride, and about seven hundred for recutting wastage. You still have a stake of nearly nine thousand pounds."

"Less three thousand five hundred of your advance. I can be prickly too."

"There's no condition attached to that advance, except an interest rate of five per cent, payable half-yearly."

"And the balance?"

"Keep it in reserve. You still don't know what you're up against. A long spell of frost, a series of mishaps, an alliance of pilferers among your waggoners, or a single crooked depot manager in the pay of a competitor—any one of these things could cripple you. If you think big, as I'm urging you to, you're going to need every penny of that capital, and I'm likely to prove a better custodian than you. What do you say to that, Johnny Raw?"

Adam was silent a moment. Then he said, "I'll say be damned to you unless you agree to take half of the balance, for I'll not be under that much of an obligation to anyone. If you won't do that then come in as a full partner. Take your choice. Fourteen and a half Burmese rubies or a half-share of the profits. Let's see how much of a gambler you really are."

"You said you wanted independence."

"I did and I do, but I could work with you if you stayed in the background. To my way of thinking it would double my chances, me as roving field manager, you sitting right here in London."

"Swann and Avery? Something of a pun, eh?"

He lounged over, hands in pockets. "You're feeling your way now, and open to good advice, but later on, once you settle to the collar, you could be as obstinate as a pack mule. Very well, so be it, and we'll drink to it while we're still on speaking terms."

He poured two glasses of port and they spun a coin for the twenty-ninth stone. Adam called heads and won. "Lucky as ever," Avery said, "but I made allowances for that. Anyone else would have lost that necklace between here and Jhansi. That makes you senior partner, I suppose?"

"To the tune of three hundred guineas. Not enough margin to hamstring a man like you, Josh."

They sipped their port in silence as dusk stole into the room. Pres-

141

ently Avery said, "Let's stop assessing one another's potential and talk strategy. We'll need a depot, with good stabling and a warehouse. The bread and butter money is right here, within easy reach of the docks, Covent Garden, Smithfield, Billingsgate. When you've taken the road those four areas alone could keep your light traffic moving." He took out a map and spread it on the table. It was a large-scale map of the capital and its environs, with the Thames writhing a course clear across the centre creases, all the way from Chertsey to Woolwich. "Somewhere in this rectangle, that's our pitch," Avery said, and pencilled a square bounded by Rotherhithe, Whitechapel, Ludgate Hill and the Abbey. "North of the river would be ideal, for there we should be in the direct line of goods flowing south-east, but the kind of premises we're looking for would be hard to find and the rent would come too high. It will have to be somewhere south, west of the Surrey Docks, east of the Waterloo Road. Will that wife of yours adapt to that kind of neighbourhood?"

"She won't have to," said Adam. "I've taken a short lease on a small place in the country."

"How deep in the country?"

"Deep enough. I shouldn't care to spend the brief periods I'm likely to be home in a district where I couldn't get a canter and breathe pure air. It's near Addiscombe, within a stone's throw of the old Academy. You probably remember it as good riding country."

"Now it is," Avery said, "but don't deceive yourself. This city is expanding north, south, east and west, at the rate of more than a mile a year."

"I can always move out ahead of it."

"Aye, and get further and further from your main field of operations. We've both seen campaigns lost that way."

"London isn't my stamping-ground, Josh, and never will be. I chose this business for the elbow room it offers. If I didn't think I could leave the hub, and know you were available, I wouldn't have agreed to a partnership."

"I'm agreeable," Avery said, "for you can browse among your hawthorn and honeysuckle for my part. To live anywhere out of town is a kind of death to me. My father was a country parson, and even now the sound of church bells drives me to the bottle! However, talking of parsons reminds me of Keate."

"Who is Keate?"

"The best recruiting-sergeant I could enlist on your behalf. He's calling for you now. Take my word for it, you'll get along famously. You're both Puritans."

"What's his function?"

"Anything you care to call it. Waggonmaster, yard gaffer, even bodyguard. He worked for me for a spell, and I should have liked to have kept him, but some of my dealings ran contrary to his moral principles. Keate is strong on principles and a dedicated family man into the bargain. Yes, I see you and Keate harmonising."

"I don't need one man, I need fifty."

"Keate will find you the men you want, and if he recommends them sign them on, without indulging in any fancy notions concerning their suitability. Keate knows his business. He spent fifteen years as a commissariat N.C.O., and a further ten in charge of Drury & Dagenham's brewery deliveries. That was before he forswore the Daemon Drink and took to preaching. I had the devil's own job to find him again and when I did it wasn't easy to persuade him to work for any friend of mine."

"He sounds a prig."

"Oh, he's an insufferable prig, but then, you're something of a prig yourself, Adam."

There was a knock at the front door and they heard the landlady answering it. Avery said, "That'll be Keate. Punctuality itself. I'll see myself out, via the back if you've no objection. I prefer you and Keate to step off on the right foot," and he stuffed the map into his pocket and left the room, so that Adam wondered, briefly, if they had entered into a business partnership or had been indulging in a bout of mess buffoonery. Always, he was to find, it was to be this way with Joshua Avery. The value of his seemingly casual judgements were sometimes hidden for as long as a year, or even two years. It was so in the matter of Saul Keate, servant of Christ, amateur philanthropist, and waggonmaster extraordinary.

143

2

Novitiate

THE four-wheeler set them down at the junction of the Borough High
Street and Old Kent Road and they walked north to London Bridge,
then east into Tooley Street.

It was a Saturday night exploration of the south bank in the company of not so much a man as a Presence, and Adam had been
aware of this during the cab ride. Now, taking lengthy strides to
keep pace with the gigantic Keate, he had a sense of accompanying
a celestial ambassador on a tour of Tartarus, and of receiving considered judgements on everything they saw down there among the
sulphur clouds.

He had always thought of himself as being above average height
and strongly made, but beside Keate he felt puny, for Keate stood
six foot five inches in his socks and his breadth was equally impressive, the two features combining to give his grizzled head, with
its countryman's red cheeks and mournful eyes, a slightly incongruous look, as though God, suddenly appalled by the majesty of His
handiwork, had decided to spare lesser men the menace of a head to
match.

When Keate first introduced himself, enclosing Adam's hand in
one approaching the size of a mattock blade, Adam thought at once
of a Cromwellian troop-captain, the kind of man of whom the Pro-
tector had once written, '. . . give me the men who know what they
fight for and love what they know', a warrior who would dash among
the Amalekites shouting Isaiah into the wind and oversetting Cava-
liers like ninepins. Now, as they elbowed their way through a Saturday night Bacchanalian riot, this impression enlarged itself. He
would not have been much surprised had Keate gravely excused himself, taken hold of a handy beam or shutter, and cleared the streets
before resuming his commentary on the shortcomings of modern
Babylon.

Avery had obviously told the giant a good deal more about the
project than he had indicated, for Keate was in possession of all

relevant details, even such matters as the type of waggon and draught horses Adam had ordered from Blunderstone's and McSawney's. It was also obvious that he approved of the enterprise and Avery had been right about the man's undoubted experience in transport, for Keate told him he had been in the business one way or another since childhood. He had served his apprenticeship as a drayboy and had graduated to the post of coachman on the famous 'Wonder', that achieved the record run between London and Shrewsbury, a run of 158 miles, at an average speed of twelve miles per hour. He had then served a term as driver with George Shillibeer, who operated the three-horse omnibus service running between Paddington and Marble Arch and could talk informatively of the various attempts to promote a practical steam-carriage omnibus service in the capital, notably the original Trevithick model, that had attained an average speed of fifteen miles per hour between London and Windsor twenty years before.

All this, however, concerned his profession, and Saul Keate was far from being absorbed in the pursuit of his daily bread. Most of his nervous energy, Adam gathered, was directed towards soul-saving, and by looking about him Adam realised that it was a task likely to sap the patience and initiative of even such a man as Keate.

He had anticipated revelry on a lively scale when Keate proposed they should walk from London Bridge to Greenwich marshes, before looking in on his home at Rotherhithe, and discussing terms of engagement, but the scene far exceeded his expectations. Avery, however, had not exaggerated Keate's moral rectitude or the prejudices it inspired, and it soon became evident that he was not a man to be signed on or rejected at the whim of a prospective employer. He reserved the right, as a freeborn Englishman certain of a place in Paradise, to comment freely, and ask as many questions as he answered, and as they went along Adam realised that this tour of the South Bank was a kind of examination to which Keate was submitting him, in order to discover his fitness as a hirer of labour.

Tooley Street, that headed them down into Southwark and round the south bend of the Thames to the docks, was lined with naphtha-lit stalls, and studded with taverns and beer-houses. Both stalls and taverns were doing thriving trade, for hordes of ragged women surrounded the street vendors and the drinking shops were crammed with men, many of whom were already fighting drunk. In the space of a hundred yards Adam saw three broils and five arrests. The uproar was continuous and deafening and the turmoil in the less well-lit sections was reminiscent of an Eastern street riot. In the long funnel between the tall warehouses sweating police, operating in groups of four based on two-horse vans, were engaged on every side, mostly with men and women too far gone in drink to put up more than a token resistance. The major fights they avoided if possible and Adam did not blame them. Had hucksters, street-traders and revellers made common cause against them the scattered detachments would have been overwhelmed at once.

"They do their best, poor fellows," said Keate, "but they achieve very little. Nothing can be done down here until Parliament limits the hours the taverns may remain open, and the age and sex of the poor wretches The Trade exploits. For most of these people Saturday night is a brief escape from the weekly drudgery of up to a hundred hours' toil. So long as they have a few pence in their pocket they'll make the most of it. The curious thing is, Mr. Swann, it ceases on the last stroke of midnight, when police reinforcements are sent into the Borough, not to save life and property but to ensure the sanctity of the Sabbath. A curious concession to Almighty God, is it not? Six days of debauchery and unbridled licence, with rich profits flowing into the pockets of the brewers, then one day set aside for Our Father."

"You actually live among this?" Adam asked, "a man of your convictions?" and the giant turned reproachful eyes on him, saying, "But of course, Mr. Swann. Where else could I do His bidding? Further on, when we get as far as the coal wharves, you will understand, perhaps. That's where the street Arabs can be found about this time, and I have a certain proposition to put to you concerning a few of the most promising of them. We shall see, Mr. Swann. I think, somehow, that I may be of some service to you, so that you may be of some service to Him."

He spoke as though a carrier service was very small beer measured against the larger enterprise of salvaging humanity, and Adam wondered if, by dispatching him on this evangelical tour, Avery had been exercising his eccentric sense of humour. For the time being, however, he kept his thoughts to himself, commenting, "Mr. Avery gave me to understand you could find me some drivers. I shan't need them for a month or so, but good waggoners are always in demand, and I should be prepared to advance retaining fees if we found the right type of man. Is that at all likely in this stew?"

"I keep a register," Keate said, "with the name and lodging of some of the experienced waggoners hereabouts. We shall consult it.

I have no doubt but that I can find you the men you require, and some of them might be willing to work outside London. However, I would be uncommonly obliged to you if you could spare an hour to look at my boys, for it is there we should seek the roots of a long-term enterprise, such as I am given to understand you have in mind."

He spoke, Adam thought, a stilted, half-Biblical English, entirely out of keeping with his background, and with hardly a trace of accent. He said, cautiously, "I take it you are a self-educated man, Mr. Keate?" and Keate said that he was, having taught himself to read at the age of nineteen (George Stephenson's literate age, Adam reflected) and to write legibly a year or so later. Since then, he added modestly, he had studied some of the social prophets, including Bentham, Owen, Ruskin and even Carlyle, so that Adam's respect for this huge, bumbling carter-coachman began to increase. Keate, he reflected, was an embodiment of the popular doctrine of self-help, and his portentous earnestness and obvious sincerity, something of a counter-poise to the appalling squalor around them. He thought, with a certain satisfaction, 'The double standard works among men like him, as well as with greedy merchants and class-conscious churchmen. With a couple of thousand men like Keate I could fight my way from here to Cathay if I had to,' and he said, "What induced a man like you to enlist, Mr. Keate?"

"Curiosity, sir," Keate replied, promptly, and with the wisp of a smile, "and it was more than satisfied in the Crimea. I took my discharge in '55 but by then, of course, I had made the Surrender, and realised my work was here. It is of little use, Mr. Swann, sending Christian missionaries among the heathen when one encounters this kind of thing on one's own doorstep," and he pointed to a screaming crone, blouse open and drooping breasts bare, being frog-marched along the pavement between two bearded police officers.

"I've thought the same for some time now," said Adam, and they passed into the relative peace of Southwark, heading down towards the river, with the docks on their right and the Thames making another of its loops, this time round the Isle of Dogs, made famous all over the English-speaking world by Dickens' 'Oliver Twist'. It looked, thought Adam, a foul, unsavoury place, and a fit breeding-ground for any number of Fagins.

It was about here that they came, unexpectedly so far as Adam was concerned, on the first of Keate's boys, a filthy little urchin with bare, mud-encrusted legs, who was engrossed in the task of emptying a bucket of mud dredged from the foreshore and extracting from the

147

liquid mess a few knobs of coal that had fallen from a collier's barge. In the last glow of the orange sunset Adam watched him with interest and Keate said, "One of the coal gleaners. There are hundreds of them hereabouts living on what they dredge up and sell for a ha'penny a bag. They are some of the few on friendly terms with Jack Frost. In a hard winter their prices rise by as much as two hundred per cent."

"Where the devil do they sleep?" Adam asked, and Keate pointed to a long row of hogsheads flanking the quay wall. Looking more closely Adam saw that about a dozen of the hogsheads were occupied by children, some sitting up, others sleeping under pieces of sacking.

"Don't the local authorities accept any kind of responsibility for these waifs?"

"Yes, indeed, if approached by parents who are unable to feed or house them," said Keate, "but these are survivors of the baby-farm scandal. They either do the best they can or go into the workhouse, to be farmed out to manufacturers as slaves. Mostly they prefer their independence, insecure as it is. They not only feed better on average over the year but they have the whole Borough in which to dodge the police. It's a hard life, no doubt, but no harder than working under a foreman's strap in the match or paper factories."

"But isn't there legislation against that kind of exploitation?"

"Yes, there is, in Shaftesbury's Bill, but who is there to enforce it properly? No one is interested in teaching them a trade, and that brings me to my point. When your freight line is established how will the waggons operate over a long-distance haul? With a single carter, responsible for delivery only?"

"Why not? Loading and unloading would be the responsibility of consignor and consignee, that's the usual practice, isn't it?"

"Yes, it is," said Keate, "but what I have in mind is to enroll a carefully-selected group of boys as trainee drivers, each under the supervision of a responsible waggoner. Given food, clothing, and a place to sleep, a majority are industrious little rascals, as you can see, and all are quick learners. Down here, living on their wits, they have developed the self-sufficiency one looks for among trained infantrymen. They can even be taught self-respect and become useful, God-fearing citizens, providing one has the patience. It is not so difficult as one might imagine, providing one catches them early enough. But now that you've seen them, come along home with me, sir, and I can introduce you to my own small family," and he gave the little coalsorter a coin and led the way up the wharfside entry and across the main artery into a maze of streets of terrace houses, all leaning one upon the other as if, deprived of mutual support, they would collapse in a cloud of yellow dust.

Keate's house, in a block of back-to-back dwellings built under the shadow of the wall marking the entrance to Brunel's tunnel, was recognisable even at a distance. Its curtains were clean and its step scoured free of soot. Its front door, opening on the pavement, had a polished brass knocker and the room on which this door opened, perhaps twelve feet by ten, was lit by an oil lamp and scrupulously clean. There was a Turkey rug on the floor and a few pottery ornaments and the walls were hung with texts, each embodying a quotation from the Sermon on the Mount.

Mrs. Keate, summoned from the adjoining kitchen, whence issued a rich smell of baking, was obviously a fit partner for the evangelist, for she was almost as generously built and it astonished Adam that all three of them could be accommodated in the low-ceilinged room and still avoid collision. Keate addressed his wife as Martha but she took no such liberties with him, referring to him as 'Mr. Keate', dropping Adam a curtsey that was like the dip of a circus elephant. For all her size she was obviously subservient to her husband, making no comment when he peremptorily ordered tea but disappearing into the scullery after carefully closing the connecting door. While Keate was unearthing his register Adam looked about him, sensing that Keate's family were in bed but not asleep, immediately above them. Every now and again he heard a subdued giggle, followed by a shushing sound and a light scuffle.

"How large is your family, Mr. Keate?" he asked, and Keate seemed uncertain, for he did a sum on his fingers and finally announced that the house sheltered eleven, including himself and Mrs. Keate. Then he corrected himself and said it was twelve, for he had forgotten Joseph, the baby, asleep in a laundry basket under the scullery table.

Adam could not disguise his astonishment. "You rear ten children? In this little house?" and Keate smiled, saying gently, "Well no, Mr. Swann. I cannot claim to rearing more than two, Matthew and Joseph, my own boys. The others live here until I find places for them."

The last of Adam's misgivings based on the man's unction disappeared. "You mean, the other eight are boys like that coal-puddler we saw down at the wharf? They share the room above with your own lad?"

Keate said, with a kind of defensiveness, "What else can a man do? There are eight here, but there are one hundred thousand on the streets of London. They want for space, of course, but we manage somehow. Fortunately there is a stable in the area out back. We eat out there, in relays."

"Where the devil do they all come from?"

"A variety of places. Some from homes where the parents have died or have been taken sick and laid off. Some whose fathers are on the treadmill or picking oakum, but a majority are children born out of wedlock and sold to baby-farmers, who abandon them as soon as the parent's back is turned. You might regard them as the more fortunate, for every year hundreds of farmed-out children die of neglect and starvation, and a few are deliberately murdered."

"Good God," exclaimed Adam, "it's as bad as India."

"It's far worse," Keate said, "for England has had the benefit of the Light."

"How old are they?"

"Most of them couldn't tell you. Ned, the biggest, is around eleven I would say. We could start him straightaway, and perhaps two or three of the others by the time your waggons are on the road. But perhaps I am presuming?"

"You're not presuming," said Adam, grimly. "May I see the children?"

"Why, certainly. They should be asleep but I'm afraid they're not. Martha has her hands full when I'm not around at sundown," and he motioned Adam to the ladder that led up to a trapdoor, as in a stable loft.

Adam went up carefully, for the ladder was old and rotten, and reaching the top lifted the trapdoor and stuck his head above floor level. The entire floor space was occupied by boys sleeping head to toe and the urchin closest to him gave him a grin, winked, and said, equably, "Wotcher, Guv'nor!" There was no furniture and Adam noted that the bedclothes consisted of a few patched blankets, eked out with pieces of sailcloth and potato sacks. He closed the trap and came down.

"How do you feed that number of children if you're out of employment?"

"I've been a saving man," Keate said, "I had a little put by and I draw a few shillings from the mission when money is available. As I say, we manage."

The thing that struck Adam most forcibly was the man's cheerful acceptance of so vast a responsibility, as though there was nothing remarkable about accommodating eight dockside waifs and two of his own children in a four-roomed hovel. One had the impression that, had someone suddenly presented Keate with a barn, the first thing he would have done would have been to scoop up every urchin within easy walking distance, trusting in his Old Testament God to fill innumerable bellies in the morning. He said, "Have you ever heard of the Underground Railway in the United States, Keate?" and Keate said that he had, and understood it to be some kind of organisation for the rescue and redemption of runaway plantation slaves. He did not, however, see the connection. He was not a particularly quickwitted man. Perhaps there was no room for quick wits in a body that housed so large a heart.

"It came to mind when I looked in that dormitory of yours," Adam said. "You're right, of course. Those children can't be rescued by charity, not even charity on your scale. If I agreed to take a steady flow of them as van boys, and make sure they were trained in the care of horses and vehicles, would you be my adjutant? That would be an incidental office, of course. What I really had in mind was to make you my waggonmaster. I could pay you two pounds a week and make a regular contribution towards that orphanage you have up there. If the boys were coming straight into my service that would be in my interest as well as yours. Perhaps, when we were properly organised, we could enlarge your premises somewhat. Does a proposition along those lines appeal to you?"

For the first time since they had met Keate shed his formal demeanour. His pink cheeks became pinker and for a moment he looked, most improbably, embarrassed. Then, as Martha Keate appeared with the tray, he bowed his head. "It is more than I hoped when Mr. Avery brought me word of you, Mr. Swann. Do you place much reliance in the power of prayer, sir?"

"None whatever," said Adam promptly, but Keate did not flinch. He said, carefully, "Some men don't. God gives them other means of forming judgements. How do you form your judgements, Mr. Swann?"

"By instinct usually. That's what's guiding me as regards you, Keate."

"It could work that way," Keate said, and left it at that.

Martha began to pour the tea and suddenly the giant's head came up. He was over his moment of embarrassment and looked Adam

151

in the eye. "You won't regret the impulse," he said, "for if I pledge my loyalty to a man it's his for good. Those boys up there, I'll not gammon you about them. We'll get our failure rate, but it won't be striking, I can promise you that." And then, with an air of having disposed of preliminaries he opened his register, an exercise book filled with his round, childish scrawl. "How many vehicles will you be putting on the road in the first instance?" and when Adam told him round about thirty he said, running his huge hand over his chin, "Any fool can handle a one-horse waggon in open country. Its different managing a team hauling a loaded, fixed-axle dray. That needs patience and sobriety, and I can't promise you more than ten sober men, Mr. Swann, or not yet. We'll do our best, however, but it might help if I had some inkling as regards areas of operation. Are you that far advanced with your plans, sir?"

"Not by a long chalk. But when they've been decided upon I'll see that you get copies of schedules, together with maps. There is one other thing you should know. Mr. Avery will be acting as my backer and London agent but I shall be responsible for the actual running of the business."

"And I would be responsible to you alone, Mr. Swann?"

"Yes, and so would the waggoners and boys. Mr. Avery's concern begins and ends with consignors, and only that in the metropolis."

"I'm your man, Mr. Swann. Now sup your tea, sir, before it goes cold. Martha, get Mr. Swann a cab from the mews. I'll sift this book for a labour force and on Monday I'll run down the men and engage them, provisionally, at a rate of one pound a week plus two shillings a night out-of-town allowance. Would that be satisfactory to begin with?"

"Perfectly. I'll leave that side of it entirely to you until I return to London. Did Mr. Avery mention I was to be married before then?"

"No, sir, he did not, but I should like to drink the health of you and your good lady, Mr. Swann," and Keate raised his cup, bringing to this simple act the deliberation he brought to every gesture he made and every word he uttered. It was the first time Adam could recall his health, or anybody else's health, being drunk in tea, and it seemed a fitting end to one of the most interesting and instructive evenings he had ever spent. He took out the box containing the ring and snapped it open. "Mr. Avery's wedding gift to my fiancée," he said. "The swan on wheels is to be our trademark. It was my fiancée's fancy and I intend stencilling it on all our vans. Does that strike you as frivolous?"

"Indeed not," said Keate, "quite the contrary. Every reputable enterprise should have a readily recognisable trademark. Our own is a case in point, recognisable the world over," but Adam had not yet quite adjusted to Keate and wrinkled his brow so that Keate, with one of his childlike smiles, said "You asked me a moment ago if I was out of regular employment, sir. I'm not. I never am, but now I have two trademarks. A swan on wheels and a cross."

Mrs. Keate returned to announce that a cab was waiting under the tunnel embankment at the end of the road. She dropped Adam another elephantine curtsey and they went out into the street. Darkness had fallen now but the carnival still had an hour to run and its subdued roar could still be heard from the direction of the river. Keate walked him as far as the four-wheeler, its side lamps winking from the shadow of the tunnel approach. Adam said good-bye, shook hands and scrambled into the musty interior, but he did not tell Keate he had left five guineas on the tea-tray, having placed it there less as an advance in wages than as conscience money.

2

Pride sustained her up to the last moment, the moment when he reached down among the well-wishers and rose-petal throwers, grasped her hand bearing the wedding ring his mother had worn, and hoisted her into the waggonette as if she had been a prize, won on a storming day. Then pride slipped away, leaving a vacuum that was more frightening and bewildering than anything in her experience, so that she sought most desperately to fill it with memories in which he played little part, for they belonged to the pleasant days spent in the old house in the company of Aunt Charlotte and the gentle old man whom she had come to love.

Memories were less fickle than pride. They sustained her as far as Thirlmere, where, she sensed, he made shift to strike a bargain with his shyness that had taken refuge, now that they were man and wife, in a stolid withdrawal without parallel in their association. Indeed, it seemed to her that he was back in the world whence had come all those incomprehensible letters about a man called Avery, and another called Keate, and a third called Blunderstone and a fourth who sold cart-horses, people who clearly took precedence over herself and everyone else in the sanctuary he had found for her and was now compelling her to leave.

She had not missed him so much as she anticipated or, for that matter, so much as she felt she should have missed him. In a sense the Colonel had taken his place, petting and flattering her, as his son had never done, and probably never would even though it seemed to her she had forgone a courtship. Meantime, Aunt Charlotte had embarked upon a rampage that roared through the house like a gale, engulfing them all in flurries of dress lengths and linen, in cartons, packages, appointments and expeditions. Notwithstanding the excitement it generated, she was glad to leave the old lady to continue her planning alone, and creep into the comforting presence of the Colonel. At his request, she would seat herself under the portrait of the little French lady who had thrown flowers under his mare's hooves and later (it seemed hardly possible) presented him with that long, lunging, impulsive young man who had ridden over the crest of Seddon Moor, seen her standing in her pantalettes, and whisked her out of one life and into another.

She found that she had no fear whatsoever of the Colonel and it was hard to believe that anyone could have feared him, even when he was young and fierce and flourishing that great sabre of his that hung over the hearth. All the fire had gone from him, quenched perhaps by the caresses of that pretty little thing in the oval picture, or perhaps by her early death. Sometimes he would tell her stories, and sometimes he would read to her from a book written by a French soldier, who had been young when he was young but had fought on the other side, and had any number of adventures in distant corners of Europe. It was this Frenchman, indeed, who helped to build the bridge between them, for when she repeated that she wished Adam had remained a soldier, and hoped for soldier sons, he had looked at her speculatively and said, in that slippered voice of his, "You really wish that, my dear? Then stick to your guns and I'll load for you!" Then, as though catching himself in a rôle he had long since renounced, he added, seriously for him, "You'll have a say concerning the children, no doubt, but don't quarrel with this business of his. It means more to him than family tradition, and he's done his duty by that. Come to that, he's showing more nerve than any one of us did in the past."

"Now how can you say that?" she demanded, darting a glance of approval at a brace of cockhatted Swanns whose portraits occupied

154

panels on either side of the window seat, "Adam is only starting a carrier's business, and while I daresay that's clever of him, considering he's had no business experience, it isn't the kind of thing one associates with bravery, is it?"

"There are many kinds of courage, my dear," he said, gently, "make up your mind to that," but she replied, "Tell me then, for I want very much to be a good wife to him, and could be if only I ..." but there she stopped, for even in his tolerant presence it was difficult to admit that she considered all tradesmen and all businessmen louts or misers, like her father and the Goldthorpes, and everything they did dull, mucky and degrading. She would have liked very much to have said this, for she sensed that he shared her point of view, but it seemed disloyal to his son so she concluded, lamely, "... if only he had stayed here and given me time to get used to him."

This had the same effect upon the Colonel as some of her remarks had upon Adam, for he laughed and then converted the laugh into a cough that became a real cough and gave him a moment to compose himself.

He said, breathlessly, "Oh, come now, my dear, you can't expect him to waste time courting a girl as pretty as you," and then, more seriously, "You admitted you were in love with him, and frankly I was delighted to hear it, and so was Charlotte. However, I daresay we could persuade him to wait a little. Suppose I asked Aunt Charlotte to help you compose a letter ..." but he got no further, for she realised that he was teasing her and told him that he should be ashamed of himself, and that if she was in mind to delay the marriage she had no need to consult Aunt Charlotte or anyone else, and in any case had no intention of giving Adam an opportunity to back down on his proposal. In support of this she quoted a girl she knew in Seddon Moss, who had tried those tactics and had ended up attending her beau's wedding as a bridesmaid.

It was this kind of relationship, easy, warm, and gay, and soon she began to use the old man as a mooring post for her emotions, bringing him not only her hopes, fears, and doubts, but also Adam's letters, that she declared were not love-letters at all but business reports that might have been composed for a mill-overseer. He was able to reassure her, saying, "That's an aspect of Adam you'll have to adjust to, my dear. The boy was away from home for seven years this last time and we only had seven letters from him and those read like a page out of this book, only less comprehensively set down. For all that he's affectionate and I'll vouch for it. His mother was, and he's got French blood in his veins, that offsets the Swann stodginess."

"You're the least stodgy man I ever met," she said, but he replied, shaking his head, "Don't deceive yourself, my dear. The Swanns have been suet puddings for generations. Ten out of every dozen went straight into the army from school, and those who survived became potterers, like me. But Adam, he's either a throwback to some thieving archer, or the end product of his mother's line, tradesmen to a man. Thank your stars that it is so. It means you won't have to sit at home waiting for notes like these from Walcheren, or Alexandria, or Bombay. Neither are you likely to find yourself a widow at twenty-five, or nursing a legless hulk through the prime of life. Think on that, Henrietta and take comfort from it. Keep glory where it belongs, between the covers of a book, like Baron de Marbot's."

His advice was at one with the house and in the weeks of waiting for Adam to return, something of this peace entered into her as the dry spell ended in a succession of rainy, gusty days that sent the cloud masses scudding over the fells, dappling the surface of the lake and stripping the first of the leaves from the oaks and chestnuts. She loved the house and she loved the setting, and the interval became a period of quiet fragrance that came to her on the scent of stocks in the borders, and linseed in the dark corners of the stairs, and lavender in her trousseau in the chest of drawers Aunt Charlotte had given her. This place was home to her, the only real home she had ever known and she wondered, sometimes fearfully, if she would ever be clever enough to make one like it elsewhere.

3

He came home in late September bringing gifts for the Colonel, for Aunt Charlotte, and even for the cook-housekeeper, but none for her, so that she was secretly very piqued, and only partially consoled by the reflection that her wedding-dress and trousseau, purchased by Aunt Charlotte, had been paid for with his money.

His manner towards her was something different again. She would have expected him to be either patronising, in the way that all males were patronising, clumsily devoted, or just plain shy, but he was neither one of these things. He behaved towards her rather as he did towards the spaniel Twitch, administering an absent-minded pat

156

when she got under his feet but otherwise taking her for granted. He seemed fit enough, for all his stay in the smoky city, but would talk of little but his projects and the encounters he had had down there among the hard-cash men. The Colonel, she noticed, was now taking both him and his enterprise more seriously, and they would discuss all manner of technical details concerning horses and haulage rates and manufactories, as though she wasn't there, but she had no time to sulk, for soon Aunt Charlotte introduced another gale into the house with the arrival of the carrier's cart bringing her wedding gown from Carlisle, and there were fittings and fidgetings without number in her room, in Aunt Charlotte's, and in the sewing room where a seamstress from Keswick had been installed.

It was not until she had paraded in front of the full-length mirror that she was able to share in the general turmoil, for what she saw reflected there did a little to restore her confidence, and she thought she could hold her own with any bride in the country under that cascade of lace and satin, with its chic little Plantagenet circlet supporting a Honiton lace veil embroidered with true-lover's knots, and elbow-length lace mittens, and satin shoes to complete an ensemble that promised to stun the senses of any young groom, even one whose head was buzzing with subjects like the thickness of waggon-wheels and the distance between East Coast herring sheds and the nearest railhead.

After a dress rehearsal, with the seamstress standing in for the rector, and the gardener for the groom, she had her photograph taken, a novel and interesting experience involving two visits to the studio, and a great deal of posing and arranging on the part of a little man who kept reappearing from under a curtain of black felt. She had her own picture taken first and then Adam joined her, disappointingly dressed in broadcloth, and was posed with one hand on her shoulder and the other on a bamboo table supporting a potted fern, whilst she sat on a red plush chair with the folds of her finery arranged about her and her hands anchored to an ivory-bound prayer book and a fan.

The result, finished in sepia, was daunting. Adam looked like a wicked, eighteenth-century squire, his mouth puckered in a tight, sly grin, as though contemptuous of the proceedings, whereas she came out looking expressionless, as though she had been asleep with her eyes open. She remembered then that it was said to be very unlucky for the bride to wear her wedding gown in the groom's presence before the actual ceremony but when she mentioned this in the presence of the seamstress the Keswick woman said that superstition only applied to the actual wedding day, not to preceding days, that wedding photographs were now de rigueur, and as they consumed so much time it was necessary they should be disposed of in advance.

Then the house began to fill with strangers and she wished with all her heart that she had been able to have at least one person there from her side of the family, not Sam, for she was done with him, but Mrs. Worrell or, better still, her bosom friend Sarah Hebditch, to whom she had written, recounting her astounding adventures. A second cousin of Adam's (a born sniveller, needing a smart box on the ear) was found for bridesmaid and tricked out in sky-blue silk, with a matching poke bonnet and criss-cross white boots, and one of the Colonel's cronies, an overblown old major, late of the Royal Horse Artillery, was found for best man. And so, Aunt Charlotte assured her breathlessly, everything was settled, and so it seemed to be, except for any active participation on the part of the groom, who somehow managed to avoid involvement in the whirlwind that engulfed them all during those last few days in the old house by the lake.

She went through the actual ceremony in a kind of daze, as though she was watching somebody else married and watching, withal, from a great distance or perhaps through a spyglass like the one hanging beside the Colonel's sabre. She made her responses and heard the intermittent drone of the rector's voice, and then Adam's booming (but still casual) *"I will"*, preparatory to slipping his mother's ring on her finger and kissing her chastely on the brow. Only a few odd impressions were trapped, the size of his hand and the firmness of his touch, the sudden and disconcerting hiccough contributed by the artillery major standing just beyond Adam, and the seemingly vast crowd of strangers who scrambled over the graves to get a closer look at her when she emerged on the porch. The experience, tremendous as it was, remained secondhand and somehow removed, even when jolly speeches were made and healths proposed at the wedding breakfast back at the house. It was not until she went upstairs to change into her smart little travelling costume that she felt, not married exactly but at least sold, consigned, and awaiting her stick-on labels, and this frightened her so much that she would have wept had it not been for the presence of the seamstress, who had stayed on to help her change for the road journey to Windermere, where they were stopping overnight, and the subsequent rail and road journey to London.

Face to face with the imminence of this terrifying odyssey, as she was helped into her watered-silk tartan dress, green velvet hussar jacket that fitted like a sheath, and green tasselled pill-box that tied under the chin and was worn at a military angle, she wished with all her heart that she had accepted Aunt Charlotte's offer to make a two-day stay at home, before plunging into the unknown. As always, however, the sight of herself in the mirror raised her spirits and she swung this way and that while the seamstress fluffed out her five petticoats, converting the tartan into a semi-crinoline but a crinoline in which she could at least sit comfortably during the waggonette drive to Windermere.

*   *   *

The astonishing thing was they seemed to have nothing to talk about. They had exhausted their stock of wedding-day small talk long before they drew level with the lower slopes of Helvellyn and with Thirlmere behind them, and the two horses keeping up their level, mile-consuming trot, even the memories of those serene, rooted days in the old house were not mellow enough to hold panic at bay, so that presently, despite the most determined efforts to prevent it, one tear and then two welled up, spilled over, and splashed down on the revers of the little green jacket. The gulp that accompanied them brought him up short, bellowing, in that cavalry-man's voice of his, *"Whoa! Whoa there!"* as he pulled off the road on to a grass verge, with Rydal Fell and Grasmere just ahead, and still some ten miles of open road before she could hope for privacy.

He said, in that same offhand tone, "We'll give them a breather. Care to stretch your legs?" and when, unwilling to trust herself to speak, she shook her head, increasing the angle of her pill-box by another three degrees, he whistled a few bars of a jaunty tune and, with a show of heartiness she judged to be false, slapped his knees and said, "Now there's a fool you've married, Henrietta! He even overlooked his gift to the bride but no harm done, I remember where I put it. I meant to give it to you when we got back from the church. Try it on, and if it doesn't fit we'll get a watchmaker to adjust it first thing in the morning," and he groped in his side pocket and brought out a package about the size of a cotton reel.

Her absurd little pill-box was now in danger of slipping off altogether as she fumbled nervously at the seals, making such heavy work of removing the wrapping that he took it from her and stripped it away, revealing a little red box that opened at the touch of a spring.

She caught her breath as the lid popped up and the afternoon sun, stealing like a nosey neighbour between two peaks in the west, lighted upon the loveliest ring she had ever seen, a piece of jewellery almost as arresting as that necklace he had shown her the night they bivouacked under the Pennines. Then, unaccountably, necklace and ring fused in her mind, as she realised that he had remembered her London present after all, and had been withholding it until now, when she stood in such need of a boost, and the understanding of this brought a great gush of relief, for she saw it not as a gift that any woman below the rank of duchess would be happy to accept, but as an indication that he was not indifferent to her terrible uncertainty and nervous exhaustion.

She looked at the ring, then at him, and then at the ring, and the inadequacy of anything she could say robbed her of the ability to say anything at all, but he didn't seem to expect an acknowledgement, for suddenly he looked boyish and the cloud of indifference he had trailed since his bustling return from London fell away, exposing him as the jolly companion he had been up to the moment Sam came blustering into the house and trapped him into making the alliance binding and final.

It was good to see him like this again for it gave her access to him in a way she had very much missed since his proposal. Suddenly the weight of her multiple anxieties was lightened and replaced with a queer but rather pleasurable sensation in the pit of her stomach, of the kind she had felt as a child when something stupendous was about to happen.

He said, gently, "It's one of the string I showed you. I got rather more than I hoped for the others and Avery, the man who advanced the money, was kind enough to have this one made up when I told him I was to be married," and when she still said nothing he lifted her hand and slipped the ring down the third finger until it rested, rather snugly, on his mother's ring. Then he turned her palm so that the sunlight danced across the facets of the ruby like a live and laughing thing.

She found her voice at last. "It's wonderful, quite wonderful . . . ! I'd forgotten all about the necklace, but even if I hadn't I'd never have dreamed ... Oh, *Adam*, I'm such a *greenhorn*, and everyone's been so kind and so generous, and I never seem to know the right words to say to let them know I realise it. You, and the Colonel, Aunt Charlotte, and all those other people who didn't even know me, but especially you, Adam, who started it all and now *this*—why, like I said, a queen would be proud to wear it!"

"A queen did," he reminded her, adding, "one way and another I seem to be putting those stones to better use than the Ranee. But you haven't noticed something. Turn it round, look at it closely."

She edged it round her finger, relieved to find that it was a close fit and that she wouldn't be called upon to part with it again, and then, with a yelp of delight, "The *swan*! The swan on wheels! Why, Adam, it's . . . it's marvellous of you to remember that, it makes me . . . well . . . *belong*, if you understand?"

"If you don't belong now," he said, chuckling, "that parson was an imposter and you're hopelessly compromised," and then he took her in his arms and kissed her just as the Keswick coach topped the rise and came bowling down on them with three outside passengers and a four-chinned-coachman, who raised his whip in acknowledgement of the spectacle of a young couple embracing on the box of a wagonette. Then the outside travellers raised a ragged cheer, and Adam, not a whit abashed by an audience, lifted his hand but without releasing his grip on her shoulders, so that she cried out, "For heaven's sake, Adam . . .! They'll carry the news into Keswick, and everyone there will guess it was us!" but she felt happy and secure none the less, for now he was the knight of Seddon Moor again, and she was riding behind him like a princess in a fairy tale, instead of a distracted girl lost in a maze of ignorance and self-doubt.

4

Not that she was done with doubts.

They drove into Windermere just after seven, having rested the horses in Ambleside, a few miles short of their destination. He set her down at 'The Glades', putting her in charge of a poker-faced housekeeper and telling her he was going to drive on to the livery stable before checking on their train out of Windermere in the morning.

She envied him his easy familiarity with the demands of a journey. He seemed to know precisely where to go for information, and what choice to select from a bewildering variety of alternatives in any given situation. He not only carried the name of every town in England in his head but knew the most direct route to it, how many people lived there, and how far it was in measured miles to the next village. He knew about money and clothes and rents and horses and wars and riots. He knew, she suspected, far more than she did about kissing. There was nothing, it seemed, that he did not know, and when the housekeeper ordered the staggering porter to carry their trunks up the stairs, and along a passage to a scrupulously clean but starkly unfamiliar room overlooking the lake, she was reminded of so much that she didn't know, and how dependent she was, from here on, on his patience and protection. Then the housekeeper dropped a curtsey and left, and the porter dawdled about arranging their luggage in little pyramids, so that she realised he was awaiting his tip and she had no idea how much to give him and fell back on the rôle of the grand lady, saying, loftily, "Mr. Swann will attend to you when he returns from the livery stables," so that he left with a slovenly salute and she thought, '*Swann!* Mr. Swann! It slipped out like that and it's my name now, and that's something that hadn't even occurred to me! *Swann. Mrs.* Swann. Mrs. *Henrietta* Swann—no, Mrs. *Adam* Swann . . .!' and suddenly she giggled and hitching skirt and petti-coats bounced on the broad double bed in a swirl of recklessness, thinking. 'It's no use pretending, for the more I pretend the bigger the fool I shall make of myself! He's kind, and he surely knows I'm in that much of a tizzy, so he'll make allowances, the way he pretended not to notice I was terrified out of my wits when he stopped and gave me this wonderful ring.' But here a malicious little guttersnipe popped up and reminded her that this neutral approach might serve her well enough in daylight but that the sun was already low over the lake, so she went on, even more recklessly, 'When it's dark I'll just tell him how scared I am, without making any bones about it, and he'll laugh I daresay, but I don't mind that, for no one can blame him for laughing and anyway when he laughs he looks much nearer my age, and not nearly half as old again, and a man who has been everywhere and done everything and must know that I haven't the least idea what is expected of me.' And having, as it were, packaged her doubts into one clumsily-tied parcel, she realised she was hungry and thirsty and dirty, and took off her pill-box, jacket and mittens and put them away in the wardrobe, after which she drank two glasses of water from the night-table carafe and washed her face and hands at the washstand.

She was in the process of unpacking her night-bag to take out her brushes and nightgown when she noted a half-concealed wallpapered door where the roof sloped away in the corner furthest from the bed,

162

and discovered it led to another room with a single truckle bed, a chair and another washstand and ewer. The discovery comforted her, for at least it was somewhere to hide while she was struggling with corsets that had required the combined services of Aunt Charlotte and seamstress to fasten that morning, and the thought made her ponder the advantages of travelling with a ladies' maid, who could at least smooth away this kind of difficulty. Then he came stomping in, saying he had ordered dinner and that their train would take them beyond Kendal in the morning to a point where they could hire a fly to Burnley, and then another train would take them to the North Western depot. He said, slipping his arm round her waist, "Imagine that, Henrietta! By this time tomorrow you'll be running into London, and the day after that you'll be giving orders in 'The Spinney'. That's no more than a temporary base, mind you, for I don't fancy making free with someone else's staff, furniture, plate and linen, but it will tide us over until we find a place of our own. Do you want to change, or will you dine as you are?"

"I can't wait to change," she said, "for I'm starving. I was too nervous to do more than peck at all that lovely food Aunt Charlotte prepared for us. Is this a good hotel, Adam? By your standards, I mean, for I've never stayed in a hotel in the whole of my life, and I really don't know how to behave, so you mustn't mind showing me that ... and, well, everything. I don't mean to remain the little fool that I am."

She expected him to laugh at that but he didn't. Instead he put a hand on her shoulder and said, "You're very far from being a fool, my dear. A fool hasn't the sense to admit being at a loss and watch, or ask for advice. I knew that much about you within ten minutes of meeting you out on that moor, so don't ever be afraid of me, do you understand? And here's something else, since we both seem to be ripe for confession. You doubtless see me as someone very sure of himself but I can assure you I'm not. Oh, yes, I've travelled half across the world, but I'm more of a stranger in England than you are, and what's more to the point I'm a Johnny Raw in the rôle of a husband! Now let's eat, and take a glass or two of claret to keep our courage up," and he armed her out of the room and down the stairs towards a delicious smell of roast duck that made her feel hungrier than she had ever been in her life, not excluding the morning she awoke to find herself alone on Seddon Moor.

She never did decide whether it was over-indulgence on her part or a shrewdly managed plot on his, whether the wine was an exceptionally high quality table claret, of the kind she had sipped in minute quantities at the Colonel's table, or something with more body to it, like one of the French wines Sam served his occasional guests, declaring it "no fit tipple for a bit of a lass". Whatever it was it not only crowned the day but passed into family legend, surviving as a joke that lasted them down the years.

She ate her gourmand's meal and after the first brimming glass of the 'claret', the room assumed new and splendid dimensions, so that the sense of detachment that had persisted during the wedding returned, but with a significant difference, inasmuch as colours were heightened and every sound seemed anxious to whisper a mellow and excessively convivial message, the soft chink of the cutlery, the tuneful rattle of the plates, and above all the intimate rise and fall of his voice, as he entertained her with reminiscences, selected for their diverting qualities and having little in common with the dashing aspects of military life as portrayed in journals and newspapers her father left lying about the house during the Crimean War and the Sepoy Mutiny.

Everything conspired to sustain her in this uplifted mood, gay to the point of being coquettish when he urged her to recharge her glass, or try a little more of this or that. It was an altogether splendid occasion, contriving, as by magic, to set the seal of maturity on her new status. His kindness extended to smoothing away the minor embarrassments that might, had he been less discerning, have punctured the balloon of conceit that enclosed her when she stayed his hand as he proposed a fourth glass of that delicious wine. By that time they had arrived at the savoury and her corsets, laced with the object of concealing the fact that she was not as wasp-waisted as fashion decreed, began to emit a series of danger signals in the form of flushes that touched her cheeks like the pulse of a winter fire, and were accompanied by a terrible desire to belch that had somehow to be converted into a volley of restrained hiccoughs.

In addition to this, as time went on, she became conscious of an urgent need to excuse herself for a few moments, but for the life of her could hit upon no idea how to fulfil such a simple need and wondered, unhappily, if there was a recognised formula for it on these occasions.

Apparently there was. Suddenly and mercifully he rose, saying, "I'll go up for your shawl, and you can join me on the terrace, my dear. A meal like that calls for a good cigar." Then, with a casualness that dispensed with the need to blush (if a blush at this stage would have been noticed) he added, "The ladies' retiring room is through that door under the staircase," and made her a little bow, just as if they had been playing charades at a Christmas party.

She could have hugged him then for sheer gratitude but there were more urgent matters to attend to. She swept out of the room ahead of him and found the ladies' room just where he had indicated, spending rather more than ten minutes closeted there, for she had trouble reaching under her petticoats and locating the bow that secured the tapes of her corsets. The relief that followed the initial tug was bliss, as though an area of her body had been denied the gross pleasures of the evening and now came scampering to join the rest of her, like a child released from lessons. She gave a half-dozen ecstatic sighs and then a whole series of hiccoughs, so unrestrained that she began to wonder if she was well on the way to being tipsy but decided that if she was it was his doing, and that in any event it was such a pleasant sensation that she could understand why so many people made a habit of it. She moved over to the mirror on feet that seemed not to touch the ground and decided that the pinkness of her cheeks, far from being an embarrassment, emphasised the sparkle of her eyes and healthy glow of her complexion. There had never been a time when her reflection had not brought her satisfaction but tonight she looked her very best and somehow, in what way she could not have said, more grown-up, at least twenty-one. She thought, gratefully, remembering his friendly reassurances just before they went down to dinner, 'He really is the most amiable man in the world, and not in the least frightening, as I had begun to believe up to the moment he noticed I was snivelling and gave me this wonderful ring. In a way he's almost as kind as the Colonel, so long as one faces up to things, and doesn't wilt or whine, and I think I've learned that much about him already. He'd lose patience if he found himself married to what he would call a "twitterer", and behave towards me as he did when he thought me a child, and took me along for no other reason than to spite Sam for killing that boy. The fantod type wouldn't suit him at all, but I've never been like that, and am never likely to be!' and she winked at her reflection and swept out into the hall with her head high, carried along on a tide of claret and a resolve to put her theories concerning him to the test.

The moon was up, riding high above the long wooded island in the centre of the lake, and although the setting lacked the intimacy of Derwentwater it was still very beautiful and she was sorry to be leaving it and returning to the cities again, for after nearly three months away from Seddon Moss she never wanted to see a factory stack again and told him so as they walked arm in arm along the terrace to a little gate that access to the footpath following this part of the shore.

He said, "You'll find no stacks where I'm taking you. It's almost as rural as this and at least a dozen miles from London Stone. There are plenty of other houses there, of course, for they've started building a good class of property in the area, and we might look at them when I have time. The house I've rented is set back from a country road, connecting two main highways, and the back of it looks over farmland. The owner told me the wood is full of bluebells in the Spring. You'll like it well down there, Henrietta, and so shall I when I'm home."

"Will you be away a great deal, Adam?" she asked, and rather enjoyed the pang that followed his admission that he would, for it showed she was already learning to miss him and this, she felt, was precisely how a brand new wife should feel.

"I'll be travelling all over the country and even when I'm not I shall be at the London depot all day." His tone became serious, "I've staked everything I possess in this venture and I mean to succeed. You don't want to be married to a pauper, do you? You'll be a little lonely at first, I daresay, but you'll have a house to manage, with a staff of three I took over with the lease. A cook-housekeeper, a kitchenmaid-cum-parlourmaid, and a handyman gardener. And then you'll drive and ride, for I mean to teach you both."

They had reached the lake where a wall overlooking the shallows had been provided with a rustic seat. He stopped and looked down at her, with one of his quizzical smiles. "There are villages within walking distance, so I daresay you'll attend church and enlist in the Good-Works brigade. There's sure to be one, there always is in those kind of places. Didn't you busy yourself making waistcoats for the heathen in Seddon Moss?"

She told him she had participated in ventures organised by curates that had been dominated by severe old ladies with very strict notions of propriety, and a nasty habit of reporting upon the behaviour of the younger set to parents. "They soon stopped complaining about me to Sam," she said, "for he didn't take at all kindly to that kind of thing," and he said, genially, "In a way that old devil spoiled you. Well, I don't intend to!" and he whirled her round and kissed her in a way that differed from any previous approach on his part, possessively and masterfully, as though he was demonstrating his ownership.

The kiss did not alarm her. Instead it seemed to light the fuses of a row of sky-rockets, planted by the good cheer inside her, and with the tapes of her corset trailing they had, as it were, freedom to soar, so that she found herself responding to the kiss in a way that she hoped he would attribute to the wine. Then, quite suddenly, caution caught up with her, and she dropped her hands on her lap, offering him a passive face, for she remembered that ardour was a man's prerogative and nothing she had ever heard or read implied the contrary. She would have been surprised had it been light enough to see his expression as he drew back, saying, with impatience, "Henrietta, you're still afraid of me, in spite of what I said, and all that wine."

"Why, of course I am, and why not? Nobody ever held me or kissed me that way before and that's a fact, Adam!"

The wine must have had some effect on him. After all, he had accounted for two-thirds of a bottle, as well as a generous tot of brandy, so that her protest, for he interpreted it as such, exasperated him, reminding him of what he thought of as the absurd inadequacy of women's education in the West. When she had come sailing out on to the terrace with head held high, and positive jauntiness in her step, the wine had seemed to have done his work for him but now it struck him that the crust of that damned modesty pie they baked their women in over here was thicker than he had suspected.

She was sitting demurely, chin lowered and hands on lap, as though expecting a rebuke, possibly for drinking more than she could accommodate or, more likely, for giving rein to her instincts. More than anything else her dutiful posture told him that postponement would not help either one of them in this chancy business of adjusting to one another.

He said, taking her hand, "Listen, Henrietta, we're man and wife now. Tell me precisely what that means to you? I'm sorry if it embarrasses you but I have to know, for your sake as much as mine. What *does* marriage mean to you?"

It was, she thought, a very odd question from a husband of a few hours, but was glad he had asked it here in the dark, before the door of their room closed on them and she had to answer in lamplight.

She said, deliberately, "Well, for one thing it surely means it's perfectly proper for you to kiss me any way you choose. I'm not such a booby as to be ignorant of that, Adam."

"That's right," he said, with a certain amount of relief, "and at first you liked being kissed. But then, because you thought it was proper for me but not for you, you didn't."

She had always been impressed by his powers of perception but never more so. "If you know that is so, then why are you making me blush by asking me?"

"Because I have to hear you admit it so that I can tell you you're wrong. Whoever taught you that it was improper for a girl to return a kiss hasn't the least notion of what marriage is about, even if they've been married for years. I can't take pleasure in kissing you, unless you want to be kissed, and show me you do the way you did just a moment ago. That isn't wrong between a man and woman, Henrietta, not even if they're unmarried, if they really care for one another."

This did astonish her, for it suggested a licence to kiss almost any man in that abandoned way but she let it pass, for the conversation promised to be very instructive indeed, and far more rewarding than discussing the topic with Sarah Hebditch.

"What else?" she said, "what else does marriage mean? I know, of course, that it almost always means babies but I don't believe any longer you get babies by kissing. Oh, you can laugh"—and he was laughing—"but I did believe that before I found out about Agnes and the pigman!"

"Agnes and the who?"

"The pigman," and she recounted the story she had told the Colonel at Friar's Crag. He seemed more amused than his father and said, when she had finished, "But didn't *anybody* give you straightforward advice about this kind of thing? That housekeeper, Mrs. Warlow or Wotton, or whatever she was called? Or Aunt Charlotte, while I was away?"

"No," she said resentfully, "neither one of them. I did ask Aunt Charlotte but she fobbed me off. I can't say I was surprised about that, for after all she's a spinster." It occurred to her then to admit to the indeterminate conversation she had had with the Colonel but thought that could wait.

He said, "Well, I should have taken it kindly if she had made the effort but as she didn't it's left to me, and because you're the person you are I suppose I'm luckier than most bridegrooms in this day and age. What I'm really trying to say is this, my dear. We've undertaken to spend the rest of our lives together, to share the same bed and maybe raise a family, so you should get it into your pretty head here and now that love isn't—or shouldn't be—a male prerogative, and only a lot of fashionable taboos persuade people that it is! One other thing. Those strictures aren't observed among the so-called heathen. In fact, most heathens I know would find them incomprehensible. Do you believe that, Henrietta?"

"I do if you say so. You wouldn't start telling me lies on my wedding day, would you?" and she looked up at him mildly.

"No," he said, laughing again, "I most certainly wouldn't. In fact, I'm beginning to believe I should find it difficult to gammon you in any way at all, but here's something else while I think of it. Don't be upset if I laugh at you, because I've just decided that's one of the reasons I married you. As long as you go on being as frank as you are I just have to laugh once in a while. Now where were we?"

"You were telling me about 'taboos'. What *is* a taboo, Adam?"

In a way he was beginning to enjoy himself, although not at all in the way a man might be expected to on his wedding night. He said, "It's a Polynesian word meaning 'forbidden', and how it got into our language I can't say, but I wish it hadn't because it's being sadly overworked. What I'm trying to say is really quite simple and it amounts to this. To be an experience worth having love has to be shared, and there's nothing shameful or shameless about it, if only because it's as natural—well—as wading into that dinner you ate tonight because you were hungry. Damn it all, if men stopped needing women, and women stopped needing men, everything would soon come to a full stop. Isn't that obvious?"

"You mean by that just *any* man and *any* woman?"

"Well, say a majority. The Colonel was very much in love with my mother and she with him, and even your father must have been attracted to your mother, or how did she get him as far as the church? Now nothing I've said so far is very startling, is it? And most of it can't even be new to you. You must have thought about it, and talked it over with other girls before you ran into me."

"Oh, yes," she said, eagerly, "I did that, but we'd get so far and started asking but then, well, the people we asked told us we weren't even to think of such things. Was that because of taboos?"

Her ingenuousness, he decided, was one of the most endearing things he had ever encountered and suddenly he decided that without it she would be as unrewarding as all those discussions she had had with her friends.

"Yes," he said, "taboos of one sort or another were behind it. Now kiss me again as if you had never heard of the damned word."

She was not quite so artless as he had supposed. She lifted both hands, took his face between them, and kissed him warmly and firmly on the mouth, and although it was no more than an experimental salute, the softness and submissiveness of her lips encouraged him to enlarge the embrace to an extent when she was all but enfolded by him. Then, telling himself she was an industrious learner, he let his left hand slip from her shoulder and run the length of her body until it was stayed by what seemed to be the point of a broad-bladed spear, striking a downward course through the folds of her dress and petticoats. He was so astonished by this unexpected phenomenon that he exclaimed, "Good God, what's that?" and she said, with a giggle, "The rim of my corset. I untied it after I'd eaten so much," and this, because it was so thoroughly characteristic of her, made him shout with laughter.

He said, when he had done, "But isn't it very uncomfortable?" and when she said that it was, but it was a cross she had to bear because she had an eighteen-and-a-half-inch waist, and that was almost an inch above average, he said, still holding her close, "Listen to me. I don't give a rap if your waist is twenty inches. You don't have to go about in a cuirass in order to indulge me or anyone else. It can't be healthy for you English girls to lace yourselves up in that fashion. That's just another piece of nonsense they've foisted on you over here," and then, suddenly reminding himself that it had probably been the most exacting day of her life, "Come along home. You must be tired out with all the excitement and travel and that enormous dinner you ate. Our train isn't until midday, so you can sleep on if you want to," and he hoisted her to her feet and they walked up the winding path towards the terrace lights, his arm about her, her head on his shoulder.

*   *   *

It may have been the stimulus of this conversation, begun so casually on the seat beside the lake, or it may have had to do with the tensions released by the wine, but their wedding night was something each of them was able to look back on as a less dramatic climax than either one of them had anticipated up to the moment of entering their room.

170

The table-lamp was burning on a low wick, the curtains had been pulled, and the coverlet turned down. There was even a small coal fire in the high grate, so that the room looked much cosier than when she had first entered it.

Standing before the window with his back to her as she loosed the ribbons of her pill-box and slipped out of the green hussar jacket, he said, "I'll sleep on that truckle bed, Henrietta, and we'll breakfast up here at eight," but she said, surprisingly, "No Adam, stay here with me. I... I'd prefer that, I really would," and when he turned, saying, "You're sure? You mean that? Or is it just because you think it's expected of you?" she replied, firmly, "Not in the least, Adam. I love you very much, and I want to be a good wife to you. Always." Then, as he still seemed hesitant, "Unhook me at the top, for I can't reach," and turned her back so that he unfastened the row of tiny hooks of the bodice and when that was done, and she had shrugged herself half out of it, he kissed her shoulders and neck as they stood there for a moment, with her weight resting lightly against him. Then to the wonder of both of them, the initiative passed to her, for she reached up and pulled his hands down, holding them over her breasts and his touch must have gone some way to banishing taboos that lingered, for a moment later the five petticoats lay in a tumbled heap on the rug and the gaping corset, miraculously released from its central hook, joined them there and she was standing in her cotton shift and a pair of frilled pantalettes, not unlike those she had been wearing when he first saw her standing in the puddle.

He said, "We're going to be very good for one another. You believe that now, don't you?" but she had had enough talking and turned in his embrace, her arms encircling his neck and her small, compact body pressed to his with all her strength. There seemed nothing to say that was capable of expressing the sudden tenderness he felt for her at that particular moment, so he kissed her eyes and mouth and hair, not only in response to the mounting desire he felt for her but with a kind of deliberation and compassion. It crossed his mind then that this was as new an experience for him as for her. Innocence was something he had never encountered, and now that he did it made his occasional sallies seem arid, so that he could not, on any account, accord her the kind of treatment both parties took for granted in a hired transaction and said, gently, "Go to sleep now. We've got the whole of our lives before us ..." But she replied, seeming to guess what was passing through his mind, "I'm your wife, Adam, and I want to give you something, not just because you've

171

given me so much but because—well, because I'm not the least bit afraid any more. Look I'll prove to you I'm not . . ." and she pulled her chemise over her head and began to fumble with her stockings. He reached out and extinguished the light, appraising her body in the glow of the fire, and thinking he had never looked at a woman who held out more promise, not only of physical fulfilment but something more difficult to define: solace, perhaps, or an end to a deep, personal loneliness that he had mistaken until this moment for a compound of pride and self-sufficiency. He said, more to himself than her, "I know now why I wanted you," and passed into the dressing room where he shed his clothes without haste, still half-inclined to leave her, and wondering whether her professed eagerness was a form of hysteria of which it would be churlish to take advantage.

She was not hiding under the coverlet but standing where he had left her on the hearthrug and he noticed that she had even removed her hair ribbons, so that her breasts were half-masked by tresses that reached almost to her waist, trapping within them a few gleams of firelight.

She met his gaze so frankly that he thought, 'I hope to God I can be gentle with her', and then, 'Who was I to question her experience or lack of it? She's not the only one who needs help . . .' and he began to praise her with his hands, first cupping her breasts and kissing them, then caressing every part of her body.

He was surprised not so much by her initial passivity as by his own restraint, that came to him easily and naturally until the moment when he raised his hands to her face and kissed her mouth that was the one part of her that was not passive and inclined him to lift her and hold her cradled like a child for a moment before lowering her, less patiently, to the bed. Then, in a matter of seconds, it seemed, he entered her with the minimum of difficulty, finding in her pathetic attempts to accommodate him a measure of pride and satisfaction that he had never encountered in the arms of a trained harlot, for she came to him gladly as a person and not as an instrument, and this, in his experience, was unique.

He said presently, when they were still, "If I hurt you it was because . . ." but she shook her head, almost defiantly, and when he made a slight movement to withdraw she clung to him so that gladness swept through him and he buried his lips in her hair, lifting his hand to stroke her cheek and wondering how he could express his relief and gratitude in words that she would find acceptable. Then it came to him that words of any kind were superfluous, and her refusal to be parted from him spoke for itself, telling him that she had clearly expected something infinitely more devastating than this, and was herself savouring a kind of triumph that she had succeeded in conjuring from him a temperance that she had suspected would have no permanent rôle in this kind of encounter.

*   *   *

She lay there for what seemed to her a very long time, listening to her own heartbeats and to his, and waiting until she was quite sure he was asleep before she eased herself half free from his sprawling embrace, and could turn her head and look at him in the light of the coals rustling in the grate. He looked, she thought, very boyish lying still like that, with his dark hair tumbled on the pillow, and his lips parted showing a glimpse of strong teeth, each of them big, square and dependable like the rest of his features. She studied him critically and with a ground swell of amusement that was based, she suspected, in his recent antics, for suddenly and very surprisingly she no longer thought of him as her senior by some twelve years but an approximate contemporary, like Sarah Hebditch. And it was thinking of Sarah that reminded her she was now in triumphant possession of the secret that had eluded her for so long, and she wondered very much why it had been swaddled in so much secrecy and whispering and shushing and head-nodding, for in a way it was very close to what she had expected and had somehow half-known, although no one had ever hinted that it was so richly rewarding in the sense that it swept you out of the eternity of childhood and on to a plane where you were no longer entirely dependent on the whims of adults, especially male adults. It could even become (with a little practice) an excessively pleasant experience but she was not, at the moment, assessing it from a physical standpoint but rather what it meant in terms of status within the confidence of a male, particularly a lusty, well-disposed, tolerant male like the one asleep beside her and beginning to snore. It provided answers to a whole range of related questions that had puzzled her, concerning the way strange men looked at her, and where Sam got to when he departed in his Sunday broadcloth on business engagements to areas where his kind of business was rarely conducted, and the popularity among Seddon Moss males of the pantomime posters outside the Hippodrome depicting smiling young women with thighs as thick as hams and bosoms like the flying buttresses of the new town hall. It had a good deal to do, she supposed, with all manner of other things, women's fashions, saucy jokes, and unmentionable words, and even went some way to explaining Make-peace Goldthorpe's desire to marry her.

It was at this point that she related what had occurred to her current position as Mrs. Adam Swann, and she wondered how much part her looks and figure had played in his initial championship that had developed, in less than three months, from an uncle-niece relationship to the pair of them lying side by side in a double bed, without benefit of nightdress and nightgown. She was by no means sure, even now, how much this could be credited to the impact she had made upon him as a woman rather than a stray, and was content to leave it in abeyance for want of further evidence. There could be no doubt, however, that he found her more satisfactory as a mate than he had looked for little more than an hour ago and this, regarded in isolation, was a perfectly splendid development, for it surely followed that she possessed the ability, properly deployed, to keep him interested in the years ahead.

Then she had another, more generous thought, and this brought her added satisfaction, for until now their relationship had seemed to her very lop-sided, all give on his part, all take on hers. It was very gratifying to reflect that at any time he came seeking kisses she was licensed to give him not merely her lips but a body of which she was properly proud, and in which he evidently delighted. This not only gave her a sense of permanence but a taste of something she had always envied men, glorious independence.

A rustle of coals interrupted her reverie and she eased herself out of his grasp and then out of bed, to creep round the room, retrieve her scattered clothes, and pile them on a rocker chair by the window. He continued to snore softly and suppressing a giggle, she slipped into the dressing room, groped her way to the washstand and sponged herself, taking the greatest care to do it without splashing. Then she went back into the main room and peered about for her nightdress, recalling that it had been lying on the coverlet when they came in. She found it at last and was in the act of slipping it over her head when an owl in a copper beech close by hooted and for some reason this released the giggle so that she glanced nervously at his pillow, or rather her pillow and thought, as she edged herself back into bed, 'To think of the hours I spent embroidering this négligé and he never even saw me wear it before he went to sleep. I wish now I'd done something more practical, like knit him a pair of socks.'

A kind of proprietary smugness stole over her and she felt for his hand, lifting it very carefully and bringing it to rest under her breast.

His warmth and stillness was like a balm, healing the harassments and anxieties of the long, eventful day. In such warm and cosy proximity with him she could contemplate the physical aspects of the tremendous occurrence, remembering not only his conversation about that South Sea island word—what was it again?—'typhoos' or 'taroos'—but also her discussion with the Colonel concerning the biblical verb, 'to know'. Well, she certainly knew him now and he knew her, without any reservations whatever and presently, blushing in the dark, she was able to ponder the mechanics of the ritual with the objectivity she could bring to the purchase of a new dress or a bonnet. She had to admit, at this stage, that the preliminaries and the aftermath had been both congenial and gratifying but as to the act itself she had certain reservations. It was not that it had proved as painful as he seemed to anticipate but it certainly qualified as startling, and there had been a moment, she recalled, when she had had to make a great effort to master panic. Something told her, however, that this was linked to its novelty, and that knowing precisely what to expect was surely more than half-way to acceptance. She supposed now that she would have a baby and the prospect, far from scaring her, only added to her sense of achievement. Taken all round it had been a stupendous day for getting on in the world, and she supposed men must feel rather like this when they had won a battle or secured a rich contract. As though to assure herself that she was indeed sleeping upon the field she settled herself more comfortably within his listless embrace and lifted his heavy hand to her lips. Then, with a sigh almost loud enough to wake him, she slept.

3

The Big City

HE had come to terms with the big city, with its stink, its squalor, its
grime, its sulphurous smoke, its nonstop groundswell of greed and
noise and muddle, and one reason why he had been able to do this
was the unique observation post he had secured for himself in those
first frenetic months.

Avery had found them a depot, a large, tumbledown area in the
centre of a seething rectangle formed by the Old Kent Road, Tooley
Street, Tower Road and the river itself. It was not the most salubrious base he could have picked on the south of the river but it had
the great advantage of being cheap and central. It had started out in
life, several centuries ago, as a nunnery, and the chapel tower, three
storeys high, still remained, a forlorn witness to God and his angels
among a vast clutter of sheds, stables and ashstrewn yard wholly
given over to Moloch. It was here, in a strange octagonal chamber
than had been the nunnery belfry, that Adam had his office, maintained his logbooks and account ledgers, and hung his wall-maps
and all the data gathered in the journeys he made in his first eighteen
months in England.

The belfry, his eyrie as he called it, had an impressive view, even
when the smoke pall shrouded all the one-storey buildings around.
From his desk he could look between other buildings at the sluggish
Thames, the Tower itself, the wharves and barge traffic, the London
Docks, and even the western edge of the Surrey Commercial Docks
further east. He could see the smoke puffs of the Bricklayer's Arms
goods depot, a large tannery, a biscuit factory, a match factory and,
passing between these points down the arteries that linked them, the
ebb and flow of wheeled traffic and the scurrying, doll-like figures
of draymen, hawkers, urchins, clerks and dockers, and the more deliberate passage of the paunched gentlemen who held this multitude
in thrall.

Up here, forty feet above the apparatus of his own adventure, he
had leisure to dream, to take a detached view of his endeavours

and what it meant in terms of his future and Henrietta's and the child she would bear him soon, but it was not often that his dreams were personalised or localised. More often they probed across the river to the shires where hedgerows were still green, where trees stood, where the pace of life was still as leisurely as it had been in Tudor times, and every now and again, when a ship went down with the tide, he would follow it in his fancy, rounding the North Foreland and sailing to distant shores he had seen and to others he had not and probably never would now that his anchor was down. Yet it intrigued him to reflect that he was now an active participant in this gigantic and ever-expanding business, that it really mattered to him how much tonnage of manufactories were gathered here to be transported to every corner of the world and also that, as this imperial venture grew and grew, so would his own concerns, and those of the sixty-odd men and boys who looked to him for their wages every Saturday.

It gave him a feeling of contributing that he had never had as a mercenary, and for the very first time in his life he felt a glow of self-justification, of being who he was and where he was. In a subtle way this certainty began to enlarge him as an individual, so that his personality flowered under the triple pulse of power, responsibility and risk. He shed much of his barrack-square brusqueness and shyness, involving himself in the destinies of underlings in a way that had never been possible in squadron or regiment. For he was now committed, deeply committed, and so, in a sense, was the least of Saul Keate's vanboys moving to and fro down there on the greasy cobblestones between warehouse, stable and waggon park. One and all, he told himself, they would sink or swim with him, and an understanding of this not only reinforced his confidence in himself but endowed him with tolerance and patience and put a curb on his temper.

Everybody about him noticed this broadening and deepening of his character. Not only Henrietta, bustling about her little house in Shirley twelve miles to the south-west, but hardbitten men like Josh Avery, and dedicated men like Keate, and all the crusty old carters and snotty-nosed urchins Keate had recruited on his behalf. Paternalism not only grew on him but suited him. Little by little they began to trust both him and his judgements, and he secretly basked in that trust.

*   *   *

The depot had been other things besides a nunnery. At some time in its existence it had served as a brewery and then as a knacker's yard, and later still a livery stable. There was no form about its design, for every trade had left its stamp upon the place, a labyrinth within a labyrinth, a slum hemmed in by slums. It was surrounded by a long, clapboard fence with double gates on two sides, and a central yard enclosed by a tumbledown warehouse cut up into sections, a waggon park on the north side, where vehicles not in use or in the course of repair were housed, innumerable sheds and dumps and tackrooms and lofts and finally, in somewhat better heart, the stables themselves, where there was always activity, even at night and on Sundays.

It was still very much a London enterprise, although plans to expand as far north as Berwick, and as far west as Truro, were in train and awaiting the drying out of the roads. The delay in launching out had chafed him during the initial stage but now he saw that Avery's advice and Keate's doubts had been justified. There was so much to do, so much to hire and buy, so much to be committed to memory and to paper. Avery had said, when he had displayed his original wall maps, "Good. From the beginning I urged you to think in guineas instead of sixpences—now I'll add a rider to that. For God's sake, don't go off at half-cock! You're facing stiff competition, not only in the haulage field but from the railways. You've got to prospect your areas one by one, and plot your rates and routes down to the last penny and the last half-mile. The potential is there awaiting you but you have to be able to give a service that no one else is prepared to give, you have to be in a position to guarantee punctuality and intact delivery of every product the country is putting on the home and overseas market. The name Swann has got to be synonymous with speed and reliability. Ensure that and you can build a reputation in six months and once it's there you'll be your own best advertisement, providing you can make good your promises. Merchants will seek you out, their pockets stuffed with lading bills."

Keate's comments had been more restrained, perhaps because, unlike Avery, he had lived his life thinking in terms of halfpennies. Keate, warned of the projected expansion and the establishment of depots right across the country, had demurred on the grounds of equipment and staff, for it already seemed to him that this strange, impulsive man had taken an excessively large bite at the cake and would need a decade to digest it. He had hummed and hawed over the difficulties of finding enough men who could be trusted to operate efficiently and honestly at such distances, and the number of horses and waggons needed to establish links between the source areas and the nearest railheads. It seemed to him a prodigious undertaking, almost like the exploitation of a sub-continent, and because of this he urged consolidation before serious thought was given to the kind of expansion Adam had in mind.

He hinted at the necessity of farrier and veterinary services. He told gloomy stories of cracked axles and lost lynch pins, of bad debts, bad roads and bad characters among the waggoners, few of whom he could vouch for except as masters of their craft. But in the end, after the first year's trading figures were shown him, he capitulated, and perhaps even his imagination was stirred by the vastness of the project, a criss-cross of light and heavy waggon routes embracing thirty counties, a caravanserai equipped to serve the great gridiron that now linked every sizeable town in the country. He said, when he had studied the maps, "So be it, Mr. Swann, and God be with you. I'm your man now and so is Tybalt. We'll find enough waggoners if they are there to be found."

Tybalt, the chief clerk, was the most important of Keate's protégés. He and Keate were fellow workers in the Lord's vineyard, inasmuch as they both attended the same Thameside Mission Hall, and were equally obsessed with the necessity to work their passage across Jordan and past the barriers of the Celestial City. Tybalt was as small and insignificant as Keate was huge and impressive. Standing beside his friend the top of Tybalt's bald head barely reached Keate's shoulder and whereas Keate had a chest like a beer barrel, Tybalt, viewed from the neck down, could be mistaken for one of the urchins who skylarked in and about the stables, or danced a jig on the end of one of the knotted ropes at the tailboards of the waggons. Yet Tybalt, with domed head, parchment pallor, and rimless eyeglasses, could perform prodigies of mental arithmetic, so that Adam came to depend upon him to a very great extent, recognising in the man the same quality of conscientiousness exhibited by Keate, and also something of the gambler that was absent in his friend. Adam would sometimes look down on this strange pair as they paced the yard, debating some problem that concerned him or their personal salvation, and his imagination, heated by the stresses of the adventure, would encourage him to see them as a talkative David and an attentive Goliath acting in concert. He would tell himself, with a grin, that St. Peter would be a jackass to refuse either admission, for, whereas Saul Keate could be relied upon to quell any repetition of a Satanic revolt, the finances of Paradise could have no better auditor than Andrew Tybalt.

It was strange that a busy man, with a wife and future family to

179

support, and every penny he possessed locked up in a single, complex project, should indulge in fancies of this kind but it was an aspect of the new Adam Swann who, in his secret heart, believed himself a match for anything that awaited him in a war far more demanding than any he had engaged in so far. Admittedly the pace was killing, and the day-to-day risks sometimes terrifying, but as his own master he was in a position to weigh risks as he had never been able to do in the field. It was this, perhaps, that enabled him to mount that first exploratory campaign with joyful gusto, advancing across an unfamiliar terrain with the aid of talents he had never been called upon to employ as a soldier.

One such talent, he discovered, was an instinctive discernment of a man's potential worth, and it came into play when Keate asked him to inspect a mob of waggoners assembled in the yard.

They stood in a sullen rank, thickset, ruffianly, blear-eyed men, dredged up from the murky pool of London's unemployed coachmen and guards, rendered obsolete by the march of the railroad that had, in a matter of ten to fifteen years pulled them from their perches on the box-seats of their Telegraphs and Tantivys, and left them to rot in idleness after they had grown to manhood thinking of themselves as an élite.

It was an aspect of the railway boom that he had never thought about, the genocide of a class of men who had once been the best paid and most pampered professionals in England, pocketing their substantial tips with the air of men conferring a favour on passengers, grossly flattered by young bucks with incomes of five thousand a year, and fawned upon by armies of innkeepers, ostlers and barmaids along the metalled highroads that ran out of London in every direction. For these were the men who had whirled passengers the one hundred and fifty-eight miles to Shrewsbury in fourteen hours, forty-five minutes, to Birmingham in twelve hours at eleven miles per hour plus, or from the 'Bull and Mouth', at St. Martins-le-Grand, the two hundred and seventy miles to Newcastle in a matter of thirty hours, including stops. These same men, and their four-horse equipages, had been the wonder of their time, a race apart, as dissolute and dependable as the toughest infantry at the peak of training, yet here they were lining up for haulage jobs in their late forties and early fifties, traditional truculence undispelled by their desperate need to earn a living the only way they knew.

He talked at length to one of them, a man named Blubb, who had driven a four-in-hand at seventeen, and later taken the overnight coach to and from Newark through ten winters of storm, snow and flood without a single accident to blot his record. It was from Blubb that Adam learned that these derelicts had one thing in common, an unremitting hatred of the innovation that had dispossessed them which they referred to as 'the gridiron' or 'the tea-kettle', and could hardly bring themselves to mention without the blasphemy for which they had once been famous. Blubb said, bluntly, "You'd never have got the half of us here, guv, if it hadn't got about you was ready to challenge the bloody gridiron. We'll serve any man who does that, who holds out agin 'em, as Chaplin and Horne should ha' done. Now there's a brace as can roast in hell for my money. Time was when they stabled fifteen hundred apiece o' the best leaders and wheelers in creation, but what did they do after the bloody gridiron pushed as far as Brum? Went into partnership with 'em, and invested all the blunt we made for 'em in bloody railroad stock, while the likes of us were turned off to beg or starve or drive omnibus short stages, if we could fit ourselves for lad's work! Now you're signing us on to hump baggage behind carthorses, and there's some here who would ha' cried shame at driving 'pickaxe' or 'unicorn' a dozen years ago."

"It's regular work," Adam said, "and there's no shame in that," but the old coachman was unrepentant.

"We'll do it, Mr. Swann, but I'll have you know one thing. It's not because it's that or starve, but because it's a pleasure to serve a man who can still smell out a good bit of horseflesh when he sees it, and'll risk his shirt beating the bleeders at their own game! I'm not such a fool, mind, as to think we could ever compete for the passenger traffic, but we can still beat 'em in the haulage field, no matter how far they spread. I'll take the job, and I'll get through to places they can't, and in weather hazards they stinking tea-kettles couden face, and you'll find most of these brandy-faced devils over there in like mind, for it'll prove we're still flesh and blood, and not waitin' on smoke and clatter for our meat and drink."

It says a good deal for the widening of Adam's mental horizons that he recognised at a glance how he could harness this thunderous truculence to his advantage, for his business was at once a direct challenge to the railroad, and an answer to its deficiences. He also saw the implacability of men like Blubb as the nucleus for an esprit de corps that might, with skill and patience, be injected into the enterprise. Against Avery's advice he signed on every ex-coach-and-four driver who applied, promising them thirty shillings a week basic plus overnight allowances. It was his first independent decision and he never regretted it, despite the warning from Keate that some of these rejects drank to excess and carried themselves, on occasion, as if they were still passing the ribbons to a nobleman to drive a coach over a level stretch at a shilling a mile. Mixing with them, listening to their breezy reminiscences of the great days of the coaching era, he soon picked up their jargon, and perhaps it was this that encouraged him to view them as he would have viewed a newly-raised regiment of troopers high in potential but without battle experience.

As time went on his ideas about them crystallised and he introduced a uniform consisting of blue reefer jacket, leather breeches, yellow gaiters and low-crowned hat with a band bearing the Swann insignia over the brim. To Keate's astonishment (for he and Tybalt thought of each of these men as earmarked for hell) the uniform was a success, restoring to them a little of their pride, and elevating Adam to a pinnacle alongside the former coach proprietors, like Chaplin and Sherman, and this, as Tybalt warned him, was surely premature, for according to his ledgers twice as much money was going out as came in from the short-haul contracts they depended upon in the early days of the venture.

Tybalt was right, of course. Recruitment was the least of Adam's worries. The dominant worry was always finance, for out of his starting capital of about four thousand he had laid out four-fifths in equipment, and that without opening a single branch depot. The staggering total of the initial outlay took his breath away when Tybalt brought him the figures on the last day of the old year, before they had earned a penny, or secured more than promises in the way of long-term contracts. His order with Blunderstone for the heavy drays and the light vans, that he thought of as his men-o'-war and pinnaces, cost him a little under two thousand four hundred pounds, and his middle-aged Clydesdales, bought in at a cut rate of thirty pounds per beast, accounted for a further one thousand three hundred. For the lighter Cleveland Bays he had to call on another draft on Avery, and when he had bought his harness he had less than three hundred in his account, including his own savings.

The first month of the new year was a testing time. Somehow a wage-bill of round about seventy pounds a week had to be found, plus an additional twenty for forage, farriers and harness fitters. It was Tybalt who staved off disaster by securing an unexpectedly large contract from the tannery where he had worked and the directors, attracted by a low quotation, paid out a quarter's advance. After that Keate came in with a short-haul contract between the docks and the nearby match factory, and then, but with agonising slowness, Avery's nebulous business contacts began to bear fruit, and a series of regular runs were established between a group of small manufactories south of the river, mostly wholesalers who needed daily transport to and from the docks to keep their warehouses from becoming choked.

It was this that drew Adam's attention to the fact that very few of these smaller firms had transport systems of their own, finding it cheaper to rely on outside haulage. Immediate advantage was taken of this so that the Spring trading figures showed a small excess of income over expenditure. Keate went on worrying and so, but silently, did Adam. Only Avery never wavered, and when his advice was sought would reiterate his counsel to 'think in guineas', and urge his partner to drive his staff to breaking point in order to maintain Swann's reputation for punctuality. He also advised Adam to keep the vision of expansion well in view. Only thus, he would declare, could a raw amateur hope to capture the heavy hauls between isolated shire areas and railheads that served the sources of raw material so vital to the manufactories. He advanced another argument in support of an invasion to the north and west, basing it on the rapid expansion of the cities, where local populations were increasing at the fantastic rate of a thousand families a week.

He would say, rolling the eternal cheroot between his lips, "They've all got to be fed, man. They can't work a twelve-hour day on broth and potato scrapings. They need meat, milk and vegetables, and every back-to-back street of hutches these damned jerry-builders run up reduces the homegrown yield within local delivery distance of the mills and furnaces. These places were still growing their own food a few years ago, and every pint of milk they sold off the streets came from a cow within ten minutes' walk of where it was sold, but not now. Go see for yourself. Some of these new towns shelter a hundred thousand hands, and nothing but a few cabbages grow within miles of 'em."

"How about the railway companies' spur lines?" Adam argued, partly against himself, for he had never forgotten Aaron Walker's advice concerning the empty squares of the gridiron. "Most of the big companies are laying down branch lines to every country town within twenty miles of an industrial centre. Come up to the eyrie and look at my railway map."

Avery said, hunching his shoulders in that suit-yourself gesture that was characteristic of him, "I don't give a fig for your railway map, notwithstanding the trouble you take to keep it up-to-date. That map is all but complete now. The main line Exeter-Truro extension was the last big thrust. From now on all the little fish will be gobbled up by the pikes. I'll make a wager with you. I've got fifty guineas here that says twenty years from now every railway in the country will come under one of six sets of Directors, and don't let that Bible-thumping Keate persuade you otherwise. Pike aren't interested in tiddlers once they've cornered every yard of permanent way between here and John-o'-Groats. They prefer red meat, and they won't go looking for that in hopfields and turnip patches. Some of these country districts won't get a branch line within the lifetime of the people who live there but people do live there, more than two-thirds of the nation still live there, and to continue doing so they'll be obliged to export nine-tenths of their produce to the cities. Study maps by all means, but not that railway chart hanging in your office. Make maps of your own, and trace 'em over with the rail network that already exists."

It was this conversation that induced Adam to devote most of that Spring and Summer to what he was to look back upon as a railway odyssey. It took him over every railway between the Carlisle-Berwick-Newcastle track in the north, and Brunel's broad-gauge track in the west. In the course of these journeys he left the rail-way in order to make any number of exploratory trips into the rural areas separating the triangles and rectangles and oblongs of what coachman Blubb called "the bleedin' gridiron they've laid on the country". And wherever he rode or walked in these months he carried a red leather day-book that became, for as long as he lived, a ready reckoner in terms of distances, road surfaces, river crossings, gra-dients and, above all, accessibility to railroads built or in building. And this in turn related to the crafts and practices and natural wealth of every district he visited, so that when at last he returned home it was not, as Henrietta had hoped, to take a holiday, but to closet him-self in his den at the top of the house and translate the day-book data into a gigantic section map that ultimately covered seven of the eight octagonal walls of his office, with the eighth reserved for the faded map Aaron Walker had given him the day he came ashore from the clipper.

It was this enormous map, more than any knowledge gained in his wanderings, that fired his imagination in a way it had not been fired since his encounter with the disenchanted railway superintendent. For this was his own creation, owing nothing to Walker, or Keate, or the ledger-bound Tybalt, or even Avery, whose advice had sped him on his pilgrimage. He saw it as a blueprint for the entire future of 'Swann-on-Wheels', indicating, as well as the line of flight in the first stage of a migration into the shires, its likely breeding grounds stationed as far apart as the Welsh coast and the Norfolk-Lincoln border, the Isle of Wight and the slopes of the Cheviots in the far north. Into each sub-section went its yield, actual and potential, a miscellany of everything from fish to filbert, butter to butterscotch, slate to sheep, chalk to china clay. It was much more than a map. It was a private encyclopaedia of almost every human activity that went on in remote areas so that when, years later, business cronies met over their chops, and somebody would mention a village or a valley and ask, in the way of Victorians, 'what it was good for', someone would say, with friendly irony, "Ask Swann. He flies over it twice a week," and the gibe, or variation of it, found its way into the glossary of city small-talk.

* * *

But that was much later. For the time being Swann's flights were limited to a quadrilateral staked out by Maidstone, Windsor, Uxbridge and West Ham, and his insignia, the swan with waggon wheels where wings should have been, had never been seen a day's haul beyond London, or talked of either, unless one recalls the prattle of a girl riding pillion behind a man who plucked her from a puddle on a moor years before.

* * *

He thought of his territory as an ambitious farmer thinks of his meadows and again like a farmer he gave each parcel of land a name that might have remained a nickname had he not, in a moment of mischief, entered those names on the company's maps. After that neither he nor anyone in his employ ever thought of the territories by any other title.

He went about it in a methodical way, first tracing out the borders of the sections, then relating each of them to the districts on either side, particularly those areas where local crafts were practised, or areas that were known for the production of a special crop, a mineral, or even a delicacy. Then, having marked the nearest railhead and made allowances for natural barriers that promised to keep the railways at bay, he ringed twelve separate stamping grounds, each with its provincial capital where the local base would be established.

He then went to work tracing waggon routes between the bases and the extremities of each section, and feedback routes from capital to railhead, after which he listed the local products of all the sub-areas in all the main sections, relating each to its likely needs in terms of transport equipment. This part of his survey, of course, was largely guesswork but it was inspired guesswork. By now he not only knew what specialist goods every shire in the country produced, but also the probable markets for those goods in the nearest distribution centres and, above all, in the capital itself.

His arithmetic was sketchy, but his mapwork was as precise as an old maid's crocheting. When he had finished he carried the sections to the largest room in the house, pushed back the furniture and pinned the sections together so that he could get a clear idea of how much of England and Wales was at his disposal. He was surprised to discover that, in terms of area, it was more than half, and in order to be quite clear on this point he shaded the areas that lay outside his sections.

It was at this point that he began to see his territory in terms of a family and reminding himself that every member of a family has a name, and sometimes a diminutive, he amused himself christening them, beginning with the 'Western Wedge', with its capital, south of centre, at Exeter, and its frontiers at Bristol and the tip of the Cornish peninsula. Down here, in untapped areas north and south of the arteries represented by the Bristol and Exeter, the South-Western extension, the South Devon, and the recently opened Cornwall line to Truro, there must exist a potential, especially as there was only one important lateral railroad, the Exeter and Bideford. It was typical, perhaps, of all the sections, inasmuch as it had main line railways but very few spurs to the country towns, and the rich agricultural districts no longer linked by coach services of the kind once served by men like Blubb. For here was an obvious anomaly. The railroad had killed coaching but although, where a railroad ran, goods and passengers could now pass from one main depot to another at ten times the speed of traffic in previous generations, the maps proved beyond doubt that whole areas of the country were withering, and that life in some of the holes in the gridiron had slowed to the pace of a Tudor peasant.

He remembered riding out along one of these highways northwest of Abergavenny near the end of his odyssey, and meeting no living soul until he came across a tramp trudging along the crown of the road. He had stopped to talk to the wayfarer, commenting on the emptiness of the road, and the tramp had replied, in his sing-song

Welsh, that he now had the highway to himself and was right glad of it, for he could never have walked so blithely along a main road when coaches were plentiful.

"Covered in dust, I was, or spattered with mud, and running up the hedge for my life efferry few minutes," he said. "Giff you a lick wi' their Short Tommies they would, the bastards, soon as look at you, if you didn't get out of their road."

Chats with Blubb had made Adam familiar with coaching slang and he knew that the 'Short Tommy' was a heavy whip used by the more brutal of the coachmen to get the maximum effort from their teams. He said, chuckling, "Come, now, you're lying in one respect. The Short Tommy wasn't used by top-class coaching men. They had to nurse their teams, didn't they?" but the tramp assuming that half-furtive, half-knowing look characteristic of his race, replied, "Were iss it you've been all these years, sir? Before the railroads came competition wass cruel among they ole devils. Drive one another into a ditch they would, and gallop on laughing, with the outside passengers egging them on, you know? Glad to God I am they'm gone from yer, leaving the roads to the likes of me. Walked five mile from last night's camp I 'ave, and you're the first I've seen today and the last as'll cross my path before noon, I wouldn't wonder."

Adam gave him a sixpence for his information and rode on, but now, studying Mountain Square, he remembered him vividly, and drew speculative pencil lines from the proposed capital, that was in fact Abergavenny. to the railway tracks running west to Fishguard, north to Chester, and over Brunel's bridge to Holyhead. It was a pity, he thought, that they had spanned the Menai Strait. In the absence of the bridge he would have had almost the whole of Wales as a monopoly.

From Chester to the Humber, and again from Harrogate to Preston, the territory was shaded, a great, industrial wedge where railways proliferated near their original breeding ground. There would be nothing here but short, unprofitable hauls. Every millowner in a fair way of business had his own transport, and even if he had not it was no more than a mile or so to the nearest branch line. North of the Cotton Belt, however, was far more promising territory. Here were the familiar fells and lakes encompassing a district reaching south from the line he had drawn between Allendale and Whitehaven, with its capital at Appleby. The roads he knew were bad in this untamed area, christened the 'North-Western Polygon', but the profits, hauling coal, fish, sheep, dairy produce, slate, granite and possibly cotton from the Lancashire railheads, should be correspondingly high, as they promised to be in the Border Triangle between Berwick, Carlisle and the outskirts of Newcastle. There was a main line linking Newcastle with Carlisle and the triangle he had marked out here was bisected by the Border Counties Railroad, but with a base at Hexham these might serve his purposes admirably, for all the areas between were untapped and likely to remain so.

It was different again down the east coast, where he had traced a huge, coastal crescent and divided it, almost equally, into three subsections, naming them 'Crescent North', 'Crescent Centre' and 'Crescent South'. Crescent North had its apex at Redcar, its base at Market Weighton, and its coastal capital at Whitby. To the north was the father and mother of all railways, the Stockton-Darlington, and the area was now traversed by three other lines, the Hull and Bridlington, the Hull and Holderness, and the Malton and Driffield, but there was ample room to manoeuvre in between, and in the east and north of this area agriculture was still the dominant industry.

It was the same with 'Crescent Central', a great swathe between Humber and Wash, running through the eastern outskirts of Doncaster and Newark to Spalding. Here, so his memoranda told him, grew wheat and barley and potatoes. Fine cattle were raised on the farms and in the north there were iron foundries. The Great Northern ran north from Peterborough to Boston, then north-east to Gainsborough, and the Eastern Counties served a string of inland towns, but a huge stretch of coastline had no spurs at all and it seemed to Adam, already prospecting for customers, that there might be prospects of a regular fish run inland from Grimsby and smaller ports.

'Crescent South' lay north of a straight line drawn from Spalding to Yarmouth, with its capital at Norwich. It was served, to some extent, by the Eastern Counties and the East Anglian, the latter still in the process of construction, but there were wide areas of the plain where the railroad was no more than a puff of smoke on the horizon, and apart from agricultural potential there was a well-established wool and silk trade, practised, he recalled, by the descendants of French and Dutch Protestants who had sought a refuge here two centuries before.

Below this again was an area he named 'The Bonus', an improbably large triangle, enclosed by Yarmouth, Chesterford and Southend, where it touched the widest sector of the Thames Estuary. Its freedom from railways had puzzled him at first until he remembered it as a region of broad, slow-moving waterways and marshy ground, of the kind under-capitalised companies avoided when they could. Clear across it the Eastern Counties ran from London to the mouth of the Stour, but there were very few spurs serving the districts either side of the line, and he remembered that a large proportion of the food eaten by Londoners was grown on the Suffolk and Essex farms.

He was now close to his base but down here, in the south-eastern corner of the island, he discounted the bread-and-butter hauls that continued to preoccupy townsmen like Keate and Avery. From the highest reaches of the Thames, clear across country to Portsmouth, he had drawn his 'Kentish Triangle', enclosing some of the richest soil in the land, with its immense variety of products. He made Tonbridge his capital, following a close study of the rail tracks dominated by the South-Eastern running down to Folkestone and Dover, the choice being dictated by the junction of the North Kent to Maidstone, and the two spurs of the main line running south to Hastings and north-east to Canterbury and Ramsgate. There would be other spurs, no doubt, (one to Sheerness was already started) but the pattern of population, and the prolix commercial activities in this section, was more promising than anywhere in the country. Hops and fruit, he thought, would be his main standby, but it occurred to him that he might contract with the military and naval depots that abounded hereabouts, for Keate told him that the Government sometimes put their haulage out to tender, and it crossed his mind that there was talk of laying up the type of warship that had carried him to India and the Crimea, and replacing it with a fleet of ironclads. Most people, of course, would dismiss this as a fantasy but not Adam Swann. In the England he had prospected since his return anything seemed possible.

The circle was almost complete now. From Portsmouth, north to Aylesbury, lay the eastern border of his last big section, a gigantic square west of the capital, running through Oxford to Cheltenham, then south-west via Bristol to the coast at Bridport, where it joined the eastern boundary of the Western Wedge.

Railways were plentiful about here. To the north ran the broadgauge line of the Great Western and its ancillaries, and below it the main line of its great competitor, the South Western, already in being as far as Salisbury, now nearing completion beyond Yeovil. The Wilts Dorset and Weymouth ran south-west out of Westbury, and the Salisbury and Yeovil Extension from Salisbury itself where he meant to establish a base. Spurlines, complete or nearing completion, linked many of the areas in between but by no means all. There was still plenty of room to manoeuvre inside the frame and his little red book told him that here were possibilities of great variety, including the transport of Portland stone and all manner of local handicrafts and industries of which gloves, lace, tiles and chalk were but four. Wheat, barley and cider apples grew down here in profusion. Sheep were raised on the Dorset downs and Hampshire plain, and someone had told him that half the milk that went into London's puddings came from Wiltshire, although he did not believe this, any more than he believed that Wiltshire had a monopoly in bacon, or Somerset in cheese. His surveys had been too detailed to prejudice him in favour of any one area as regards agriculture. It flourished, despite the technological revolution, in every county, having few dominant centres, as had cotton, wool, steel and coal.

It was this thought that led him to give names to three sub-sections, where he meant to set up depots, and because they were small and scattered he thought of them as postscripts to the master map. There was the Isle of Wight, so far without a railroad, and what he thought of as 'The Pickings', two areas that had somehow been bypassed, although each was within a day's ride of highly industrialised centres. He did not know what he would make of the Isle of Wight (he christened it 'Tom Tiddler's Land'), save that its base should be Newport, but in the other areas his plans were beginning to mature. One was a long, isosceles triangle, pointing west of a line drawn between Sheffield and Derby, to an apex at Buxton, and he fixed the capital at Ashbourne. The other, away to the south-west, was a longer, narrower triangle, enclosing Worcester, Gloucester and Shrewsbury, that he had noted during his ride north from Plymouth. There was no knowing what could be hauled in and around The Pickings, for they seemed to have slipped through the net of the gridiron and their potential was impressive. Here was the heart of the high quality porcelain trade, as well as the richest fruit-growing district in the country. He meant to have his share of both.

* * *

He was still crouched there, his mind sifting the revenue potential of herrings, tomatoes, fleeces, graphite and rootcrops, when Henrietta found him and frowned to note the furniture had been pushed against the walls, the rugs scuffled, and every inch of floor space littered with what she could only think of as an untidy exercise in map-making. She stood back from the threshold, one foot on the

Cornish peninsula, the other on the knob of Norfolk, and exclaimed, "Really, Adam! Why can't you do whatever you're doing in the den?" and he said, vaguely, "Because there isn't space there to make a pattern of it and see it as a whole. Well, it's finished, or as good as finished. We've got the whole damned island sewn up, and as soon as the roads harden I'll be launching out in twelve different directions."

His enthusiasm puzzled her. Almost eighteen months had passed since she rode beside him down the winding road from Keswick to Ambleside, and he had kissed her in view of all the outside passengers of a passing coach, but since then, once he had settled her in the little rented house on the Kent-Surrey border, she had lost him to a mistress who lived out there under the smoke pall, someone who seemed able to exert an influence on him that she could never hope to match, for she was able to send him scurrying all over the country, to reappear at intervals with homecoming gifts, a Paisley shawl, a box of shortbread, or a model of the Eddystone lighthouse in crystal. It was not, she reflected, that he was in any way debilitated by his wanderings. He invariably reappeared in high good humour, and would seize her and use her with the vigour and dispatch of a returning Crusader, but although she had little to complain of in this direction, there was an aspect of their marriage that bothered her. Once as it were, having disposed of her doubts that he still found her personable, he would become distrait, even while she was still in his arms. There was no doubt in her mind where he was on these occasions. He was away prospecting some dingy town like Seddon Moss, or crossing some vast, rural waste, so that in this sense he was not so different from men like her father and old Matt Goldthorpe, his mind almost exclusively concerned with making his mark and setting his stamp on the world and also, she had to concede, making the money that kept them fed, clothed and housed. She was realistic enough to understand the necessity for this but it was a pity, she thought, that a man whose lightest touch could make her knees tremble, should spend so much of his time away from home. She was sufficiently inexperienced, on the occasion of his unexpected reappearance late one night, to mention this, not plaintively but in words that evidently led him to the wrong conclusion, for he said, with a laugh, "You miss me then? Well, it's handsome of you to admit it," and before she had the least opportunity to be more specific he had addressed himself to her with renewed enthusiasm, so that she wondered where he stored so much energy, and if all husbands were as

191

easily satisfied with this purely passive rôle in a mate. It did not occur to her then or later that he had already come to certain conclusions concerning any other rôle she might play in his life.

On the map-making occasion, however, when he had been at home rather longer than usual, she made another attempt to penetrate the armour of his self-sufficiency, saying, in the little girl's voice she had come to employ when she hoped to beguile him, "Adam, dearest, I . . . I wanted to ask you something, something *important*."

That worked. He looked up at her sharply, scrambled to his feet and said, "You're feeling well? Doctor Groom is satisfied, isn't he?"

"Perfectly well," she said, encouraged by the note of anxiety in his voice, "I never felt better in my life, now that dreadful sickness has stopped."

"That's good," he said, "that's as it should be," dismissing the subject with relief, for her pregnancy was the one thing that had the power to interpose between him and his obsession. "Suppose we go for a drive? Would you like that before dinner?"

"I would have liked it very much this morning, when you were shut up for hours on end," she said, pretending to sulk, "but now I want to talk. I never seem to get the chance any more."

The protest interested him. She was not, he reflected, the least like the wives and sisters he had squired in India. Nor was she a placid buffer for her husband, like the self-effacing Mrs. Keate. Taken all round she was the same girl he had carried pillion from Seddon Moss to Keswick, a wilful, endearing, bull-headed little baggage, who never quite abandoned her attempts to achieve some kind of equality, and this at a time when equality between the sexes had never been less fashionable. Not that this displeased him or even ruffled him, for he had never been a man to endure pretensions of this kind. On the whole (but in the wariest way) he applauded her independence, reminding himself that it was this that had attracted him from the outset. Since then, of course, she had enlarged her hold upon his affections, a little every day and night they spent together, but he still had the greatest difficulty in taking her seriously, was still inclined to think of her as a mascot rather than a woman who would present him with a child in a little over two months. She had retained the ability to make him laugh and he thought of her, he supposed, as a toy but a very engaging toy and one that was, moreover, strongly put together. This was just as well for he had never learned the art of cosseting women. During those first days with her he had, or so it seemed in retrospect, made some kind of effort to gentle her, but he soon discovered that she had no wish to be gentled, and that deep down in her, held slightly in check by a few second-hand notions of propriety, was a generous dash of her father, to which was added, he supposed, the sensuality of the Celt. It made, he felt, for an undemanding marriage, and sometimes, when she was sleeping in his arms, he would congratulate himself on his good sense and good luck. He had neither the leisure nor the inclination to woo a woman, no mind to be steered by one and certainly no stomach to bully one, as it seemed to him most wives were bullied under a cloak of sentimentality.

He said, tolerantly, as he raked in his maps, "What is it you want to talk about?" and she replied, reverting to the child again, "Can't you guess? Haven't you the least idea, Adam?"

"I daresay I could but I'm not going to try. Tell me if there's anything you want, and there is something, for it didn't take me long to adapt to your tactics."

She did not resent her bluff being called. Their relationship was like this, jocular, matter-of-fact, not in the least like she had imagined it would be during that period of waiting at Derwentwater.

"You won't explode?"

"Have I ever exploded?"

"No," she said, "you're very kind to me, Adam, and I do appreciate it, but there *is* something needed to make me—well—the happiest woman in England."

"Ah," he said, still humouring her, "then you don't need to tell me what this is. To have me sell up and put on a uniform again."

"Indeed no," she said, seriously, "I did want that but it's very clear you enjoy what you're doing, and I wouldn't presume to suggest anything to the contrary. I'd like—I'd like a house of my own, *really* my own. An *old* house. A *real* house. Somewhere I could—well—however can I put it, so that you won't think me quite stupid? Somewhere to *begin*!"

She had certainly succeeded in surprising him now and the fact that she had gave her a certain inner satisfaction, for he was a man she very rarely surprised.

"Begin what exactly?"

"Why, a family—*your* kind of family, what else?"

Suddenly he remembered and remembering he understood. It had to do, he supposed, with this curious obsession she had, not so much with soldiers but with tradition, with belonging to a caste that seemed to her to possess stability and dignity, of a kind lacking in the families clustered round the chimney stacks along the Manchester-Liverpool railroad, a caste of which the archetype was the Colonel, whose ways were predictable and whose watchword was continuity, and perhaps it was not altogether remarkable that the seed of a filibuster like Sam Rawlinson should find the need for roots and permanence and predictability necessary to her peace of mind. To a degree the same urge prompted half the merchants he met in his comings and goings about the city and the industrial belts, as though these men, whom he had at first mistaken for the missionaries of the new iron age, were only innovators by chance. They wanted nothing better, once they were buttressed by wealth, than to sink back into a pastoral England of green fields and lush pastures and petty squires discussing crops and cattle with a race of bucolic peasants. It was an interesting thought for it had, in a way, a direct bearing on his own concerns and made him, in one sense, even more isolated than he had felt in the mess. Hardly one of them, he thought, man or woman, was more than half aware of what was happening around him, or how utterly and finally the impact of men like Stephenson, Brunel, Watt, Crompton and Arkwright had changed the traditional pattern of the nation's tapestry.

They had passed through the garden door to the small enclosure at the back of the house. From here the winter fields sloped gently away towards the Kentish border, a patchwork of green and red and russet, studded with clumps of elms and oaks where, in summer, cattle browsed in the shade. On the horizon the long village of Wickham ran along the skyline, and the top of Shirley church spire could be seen to the right. He said, carefully, "If that's what you want I daresay we could make Trowbridge an offer for this place. I can understand your not caring to put too much of yourself into rented property," but she said, eagerly, "Oh, no, Adam, you haven't understood. It's not just that this place doesn't belong to us, it's because it's almost new. When I was a little girl . . ." and she stopped, biting her lip.

He was sure then that she was going to confirm his thesis and prompted her. "Go on."

"Oh it sounds very silly, I suppose, seeing that I was raised in a place like Seddon Moss, and have a dreadful, money-grubbing father like Sam, but it's there just the same."

"What's there? Tell me in your own words if you can."

"A kind of longing for starting something and—well—being someone who counted, and that means living in a house covered with creeper, with old furniture inside, and drawers that smell of lavender. Oh, you can smile, and I know I'm not putting it very clearly, but it isn't so different from what you're so set on doing."

"Oh, yes, it is. It's as different as it can be."

"No, no it isn't! It's not wanting to be grand, or anything of that kind, but making something *lasting* out of money instead of . . . well, *more* money, if you see what I mean."

Her naïveté touched him even though there was no real bridge between his dreams and hers. He already belonged to an established line, and everything he had done since returning to base had been concerned with the breaking of new ground and identifying with the new century rather than the old. He had never taken pride in his lineage, or in the Swann military tradition, thinking of both as anachronisms that discouraged a man from meeting the challenges of his own generation. And yet, because of his father and background, he understood its pull, and was prepared to tolerate it in a girl, although he might well have despised it in a man younger than his father.

He said, putting his hands on her shoulders, and drawing her to him, "Very well, we'll start looking for such a place when I'm well launched, and providing we can afford it. But that boy of yours, if it is a boy and not a girl as I'm half-persuaded, comes into the business when I feel like putting my feet up. I'll go part way with you. There's no sense in creating something if you can't hope to pass it on to your children. You see, I've got my own notions about continuity, and they seem to me more realistic than yours. Meantime make the best of this overnight stop, for I'm likely to need every penny I possess until this time next year. You'll have your child by May, and that'll give you plenty to think about while I'm away setting up provincial depots."

She knew him well enough by now to understand that he would keep this half-promise if he could and although, to some extent, it satisfied her as a first step, she was dismayed by the prospect of him being away again throughout the best months of the year.

"Are you going to be travelling *all* spring and summer?" she demanded, but he was not willing to commit himself about this and only said, bending to kiss the top of her head, "I'll go wherever I'm needed to safeguard the money I've already invested. And it's not just on my account. I've got a responsibility to all the men I employ, and to all those urchins that idiot Keate landed me with," and when she said, carelessly, "Pooh, I wouldn't worry my head about them, for if they don't draw wages from you they'll have to draw them from somebody," he realised that there was, after all, a considerable gulf between his outlook and hers. Like Sam, she was unable to think of an employee as anything more than a piece of animated equipment, like one of Sam's machines, or one of his own carthorses.

4

Whim of a Carriage-Horse

AN old place, with creeper-covered walls, and something left behind of long-dead families.

In spite of his initial impatience it insinuated itself and sometimes, between bursts of energy that ate up the last days of winter and early spring, he found himself returning to the fanciful notion. But then, with May Day as the target date for launching the first batch of depots, it was buried under the avalanche of hopes, fears and figures that attended the approach of the expansion, especially as this seemed likely to coincide (and with maddening exactitude) with the birth of his child. The prospect would almost surely have escaped out of his consciousness had it not been for Dancer, the elderly carriage-horse that he bought for their rig during the last stages of Henrietta's pregnancy, for he judged the cob rented with the house too inexperienced for sedate drives along the deep wooded lanes towards Cudham and Westerham and Keston; Dancer, a dappled grey with a long, sad face, an old warrior who had his own notions of country seats, with creeper-clad walls, and his own way of making his passengers aware of them.

*   *   *

Henrietta's health during the last months had been a source of satisfaction to herself and old Doctor Groom who attended her. She had cause enough to pout at her waistline now and sometimes, when she was waddling about the bedroom, she would pause a moment to wonder why she had worried so much on this account in what she already thought of as her 'silly days'. She looked, she declared, as thick as one of Farmer Still's elms, and even a new French crinoline could not disguise the fact, for under stern instructions from both husband and doctor she had laid aside her corsets and some of her petticoats with them, having more than enough weight to drag about the house.

Whenever she looked at herself in the mirror she bewailed her lack

197

of inches and smallness of bone, reasoning that a tall, willowy woman could get through a pregnancy without changing herself into a penguin. It was a relief, she told herself more than once, that Adam was so preoccupied with his work and was, moreover, the kind of husband who saw nothing shocking in her appearance, and could even joke about it in that rather coarse campfire way of his. His attitude not only made the sacrifice of her figure bearable but also helped to batten the hatches on fear for although in the main she accepted the reassurances of old Doctor Groom, fear was never absent from her mind, not on account of the fact that she would soon bring forth, but because her size surely implied that the child inside her must be enormous, at least ten pounds by her reckoning, and quite definitely male. It might even be twins and sometimes, in her calmer moments, she wondered how she and Adam would view the sudden arrival of a brace of sons and whether, in that case, they could have one apiece, the elder earmarked for the army, his brother a predestined cygnet on wheels.

During those final weeks he showed her more tenderness than she had expected, even returning home each evening well before dusk, and keeping her near him on Sundays. She appreciated this very much although she did not mention it and when, one sunny April afternoon, he came home an hour after luncheon, proposing to take her for a drive, she was delighted, for the cob's unreliability had kept her housebound for almost a month.

He said, "We'll try that grey, Dancer. He'll be quiet enough at his age. I bought him at that auction over in Beckenham. They tried to tell me he was twelve but he's sixteen if he's a day, and that's really why I bid for him. You'll need something that ambles along when Mandrake takes you and the baby out while I'm away. He's called Dancer and the nagsman said he came from somewhere round here. Wouldn't surprise me to learn he had begun life in the Company's riding-school down the road."

She remembered then how it came that they had settled here when they moved south. The East India Officers' College, where he had been trained a dozen years ago, was only a few minutes' walk nearer Croydon, and she suspected that he had always had an attachment for the district, with its miles of open heath, stony hills, and old woods of beech, oak, chestnut and elm. He would never admit to this, of course, for he hated to be thought of as a man who lived in the past. It was not often, in fact, that she could get him to talk about the Light Brigade, or the excitements of the Sepoy Rebellion. He much preferred to gossip about his waggons and his contracts and the odd characters he encountered in that stale old yard beside the Thames. Perhaps, she thought, he would be more communicative about his real adventures when he had a son for an audience, for men would talk to men about that kind of thing but always assumed it curdled the blood of a woman. And thinking this she sighed, as she always did when she remembered how gladly he had exchanged scarlet and gold braid for topper, frock coat and the strapover trousers of the city uniform. He had had his way over that, of course, but there was another battle looming that she was resolved to win. The young man who seemed so impatient to view the world was going to wear scarlet whether his father liked it or not. She had quite made up her mind about that.

Their route took them up the long slope of a dust road that wound its way between gorse-studded hills, then down the sharp descent of the Spout Hill towards the open country beyond Addington. He drove very soberly, holding the grey closely in hand, and the little carriage was so comfortably sprung, and so well-cushioned, that behind the box-seat she seemed to be floating into the sunset. He said, over his shoulder, "Make the most of it, my dear. I'm not risking an outing even behind an old stager like this when you're nearer your time. Are you quite comfortable back there?"

Very comfortable, she told him, admiring his straight back and the military way he held himself when handling the reins. It was the most perfect kind of evening for late April, with the sun sinking like a great, burnished plate behind streamers of heliotrope cloud, and the scent of honeysuckle coming from the hedgerows. They turned off the main road just beyond a hamlet, crossed a shallow watersplash, and entered a straight narrow lane that ran between a park wall and a piece of woodland overgrown with rhododendrons. Beyond the low bank on the left she could see great drifts of bluebells in the bud, and their scent, the most country scent in the world, seemed to linger in the hollow like bonfire smoke.

Then, almost imperceptibly, Dancer lengthened his stride and began to trot so that Adam said, "By George, he's lively. It must be spring," and then, but without urgency, "Whoa, there! *Whoa*, you old badger!" But Dancer had no disposition to whoa, and broke into a loping canter and then, as they rattled round a bend in the lane, into a long, uneven gallop.

She saw at once that he was alarmed. He braced himself against the rail, bunching the reins and throwing a harassed glance over his

199

shoulder before addressing himself wholly to the task of checking the horse but his anxiety did not communicate itself to her until she was assailed by the first pain. It advanced on her slowly, brought on by the first yards of jolting, but its final pounce was swift and devastating, so that she set her teeth and pushed her feet down into the well of the carriage, taking a frantic grip on the rail of the seat. Then, quite suddenly, she was deluged in pain, and a wild cry broke from her, so that he swung half-round and at the moment of his turning a cock pheasant, startled by her yell, blundered out of the covert, soared and flew a diagonal course across the lane under Dancer's nose.

It was all he needed, apparently, to defy the bit and settle to a mad, weaving dash towards a huddle of buildings at the junction of the lane and a private drive marked by a pair of stone pillars topped by enormous stone balls. With ears laid back he seemed almost to fly over the ground, so that she was flung first to one side and then to the other, and all the time the great waves of pain crashed over her like breakers.

She thought then that she was going to die, for surely no one could survive such an experience and live. She opened her mouth to scream but whether or not the sound reached him she never knew for, obeying some mad instinct, the horse suddenly checked its stride and swung left between the pillars, dragging the carriage round in a quarter circle and bringing its nearside rear wheel into violent collision with a pillar. Then, as the pain subsided, she was conscious of a number of things; of a man with white hair running out of an enclosure behind the buildings to the right, of a tumbling stream and a slowly-turning mill-wheel, of Adam standing up on the box-seat and cursing at the top of his voice and of the carriage coming to an uncertain halt just inside the drive. Then the pain was gone, leaving her limp and exhausted, so that she could only listen, half-hearing, to the brief conversational exchange between Adam and the miller, the latter saying, in tones of wonder, "Christ A' Mighty, it's Dancer! It's Dancer found his way home again ..." but Adam cut in with, "Where's the nearest doctor? My wife is expecting a child and a thing like this could ..." but she did not hear if he shared her conviction that she was dying, for he leapt down and keeping the reins in his hand edged the man towards the railing enclosing the mill and here they had begun a consultation when the second wave of pain rushed upon her and she cried out in anticipation of the torment it promised.

The next thing she remembered was being carried bodily from

the carriage and over the threshold of a building that seemed, improbably, about twenty times as large as the mill, but she could not be sure for a haze surrounded it and now she hoped fervently that she would die and be done with it, for every nerve in her body was twanging and quivering like violin strings under the blundering fingers of an amateur. The intervals between the waves of pain became shorter and her body reacted in a kind of mad and defiant despair. This seemed to her to continue indefinitely, and the contest was so absorbing that she hardly noticed the presence of a fat woman bobbing in and out of her limited range as she threshed and twisted on a couch or pallet. She noticed one or two other things, irrelevant things, like a moulded ceiling high above her, a latticed window pane from which, unaccountably, daylight had departed and a yellow half-moon could be glimpsed, and then the sound of heavy boots and male voices and after that, with a sense of relief surpassing anything within her experience, came a gradual receding of the storm of agony until it was no more than a whisper. The lull was accompanied by a lassitude like that immediately prefacing a deep sleep and she yielded to it gratefully.

2

His experience of women in labour was wider than might have been supposed. As a dismounted lancer he had been attached, for a time, to the regimental surgeon of the Horse Guards outside Sebastopol, and had been present on several occasions when the major had delivered some of the canteen women who had followed the army to the Crimea. Later, at Cawnpore and elsewhere, he had been billeted near the married quarters when the wives of resident officers had been brought to bed, usually of children who did not survive long in that climate and under those primitive conditions. This was why he was able to assess the situation even before the collision with the gatepost and the appalling possibilities had brought him to his feet so that he could throw his whole weight on the reins, boots braced against the splash-board. It must have had some effect upon Dancer for the grey faltered after swinging round in that unpredictable quarter-circle, and then Adam saw the miller run across the drive and grab Dancer's noseband, bringing the lathered horse to a standstill. He understood then what had led up to the incident. Dancer had recognised the lane as the approach to stables he had occupied for years before being put up to auction. It was nobody's fault, not even Dancer's, for who could have predicted that his first outing with a new owner would lead him here? But in the meantime it was quite clear, even to the miller, that Henrietta was now in labour. That fool of a doctor must have muddled the dates, or perhaps the fright and jolting had induced a premature birth. There was no profit debating this now. Something had to be done at once and the old, instinctive disciplines of the battle-field returned to him as he said, sharply, "Where *are* we? Where is this place?" and the miller said, "Tis 'Tryst', the Collinwood seat, zir, but they'm all gone, Everybody but me and the missus. I got a key tho', I could tak' the lady there. It'd be best, for there ain't room to swing a cat in my cottage an' the mill's fair cluttered on account o' yesterday's flood. Wait on, zir, I'll fetch missus."

He seemed, thank God, a reliable fellow, with more than his share of commonsense, and was back in a moment with his mountainous wife and the four of them went on up the long drive between two rows of magnificent copper beeches to a large, rambling house built in a deep hollow between two arrowheads of woodland crowning a spur of brushwood and full-grown oaks and beeches. Somehow, be-tween them, they lifted her from the carriage and followed the miller's wife into a hall, where everything was draped in white sheets, and then on and into a room with low-silled latticed windows and a beau-tifully moulded ceiling.

The name Collinwood struck a chord in his memory. He had known a Collinwood in the Crimea, a hulking chap with a stammer, and he would have asked the miller more about the owners of the place had not Henrietta, at that moment, emerged from what he thought of as a coma and begun to scream again. He said, breath-lessly, "Where can I get a doctor? Is there a village near?" but the fat woman said, "Ned'll tell'ee but it'll be over'n done with be the time he gets yer. You'd best ride for him tho', and leave the lamb to me!"

She sounded efficient but less subservient than the miller, and he watched her for a few seconds making up some kind of bed on a divan with sheets dragged from the shrouded furniture, while the man pulled a table alongside the couch and busied himself lighting and trimming an oil-lamp shaped like a shell. Henrietta had stopped yelling now and was looking up at him with eyes that registered no kind of recognition but a kind of mute accusation that made him feel like a jackal. He said, "What's that doctor's name, and where's the village?" and the man said, "Birtles. He'll be home now to supper. Tis the square house on the right as you enter Twyforde Green. It'll tak' ten minutes behind Dancer if the hubcap bain't knocked off."

"Damn the carriage," Adam said, "I'll ride the grey. Don't worry, I'm ex-cavalry, and if that crazy beast wants to break his neck here's his chance!"

He had Dancer out of the shafts in thirty seconds and in thirty more was galloping down the incline, using a cane snatched from a window-box to supplement the hammering of his heels. The horse, once he had discovered he had a master, moved in long, easy strides, confirming Adam's guess that he had been a good hunter in his time, and it was only when they came in view of a broad street that Adam realised he had guessed the direction to take on leaving the mill. He was, he reflected, very fortunate in the people he met that evening. The doctor was a gaunt, uncommunicative Scot, incapable of being ruffled by any fresh emergency life had in store for him. Leaving his untasted soup he picked up his bag, shouted a command to his housekeeper, and steered Adam out the front door to climb into a trap that a groom led out from the stableyard. The groom was given Dancer to stable and Adam jumped up beside the doctor who was already moving off, as though he regarded husbands as excess baggage. The only remark he made during the drive was "From Shirley? Old Groom's patient, nae doot!"

Adam confirmed the guess, adding that the child had not been expected for nearly a month, and that Dancer had landed them at the Collinwood place. The village doctor said nothing to this and Adam was left in no doubt that he thought of both him and his wife as a couple of fools but was too well grounded in human fallibility to comment. Just as they were getting down Doctor Birtles permitted himself the luxury of one more remark. He said, "If there's any delay dinna get under ma feet. But maybe it'll be over, for that Michelmore woman has had eleven children and I didnae deliver six of them."

They went in then but at the door of the drawing-room Mrs. Michelmore blocked his entrance. "Tis all done with," she said, phlegmatically, "and 'er was luckier'n 'er deserved if it's the first. You too, Mister," and she nodded at Doctor Birtles, who ignored her and passed inside.

Adam was left to stand there gaping, watching the woman wipe her hands on a greasy apron.

"You mean, she's *had* the child? She's all right?"

"She's well enough. The doctor will zee to 'er. My man'll tak' you back to the mill to wet the babby's head."

"Can't I see her?"

"Nay," the woman said, "you can't, or not for a spell," and suddenly she called her husband in a querulous voice, and a sheepish Michelmore emerged from a room at the end of the hall and shuffled forward, grinning. Then the woman retired, shutting the door behind her and Adam, passing a hand across his brow, said, "I'm uncommonly obliged to you both. To your wife especially. Could a thing like that happen so quickly?"

"Why, damme, zir," the man said, equably, "I've seen it happen in half the time. She's a bonnie girl, or so Ellen says. And so's your daughter, zir."

"Daughter?"

"Didden the Missus tell 'ee?"

"No," said Adam, and suddenly he wanted to laugh, wondering what Henrietta thought about it, and if she would care a row of beans now that it was over. He knew how he felt, mildly proud and foolishly elated, and then he told himself it was damnable to gloat after those awful yells of hers, and wondered what he would say to her when they let him into a room full of a stranger's shrouded chattels.

The miller said, as though this was a matter solely for women's jurisdiction, "Missus tells me you'll be staying overnight at the mill while she bides up yer. Will you come on down with me, and let me drink your health and the babby's?"

"I'd consider it a pleasure to drink yours and your wife's," Adam said, "for I'm hanged if I know how I could have managed without you. This place, 'Tryst' you called it, I can't help feeling we're taking a gross liberty making free with it. Are you the caretaker?"

"Aye, for as long as there's no tenant," the miller said, "but they Collinwoods won't be back. The last of this branch of the family died two months since, Sir Mark Collinwood 'ee was, you might have heard of him. In Parlyment for a spell, then made a rare name for himself building East Indiamen on the Medway. He never owned this place, o' course, it's been in the Conyer family for time out of mind."

"Will it be going back to them now? I shall have to notify them if my wife stays here until she's well enough to be driven home."

"God bless you, zir," said Michelmore, with a smile, "there's no call to worry on that account. They've got four thousand acres in one place or another, and they'll let this place again soon as it suits 'em. When the agent comes I'll tell how it all come about and that'll be that. Mr. Phillips is a reasonable man, and any Christian would have been obliged to see you out of your difficulty. The Conyers are my landlords, and Mr. Phillips will be calling on account o' the flood damage I suffered when the leat broke."

They went down the drive and Adam looked back, seeing the house squatting between the two dark spurs of woodland, moonlight casting long shadows across the pantiled roof. It looked, he thought, like a self-indulgent old man, snuggling under the blankets, with the silvered chimney-pots showing as a few tufts of hair above the counterpane.

The miller produced a cask of home-brewed beer and solemnly pledged "the little maid's health and happiness", and then fetched a saddle of mutton and pickles, and Adam was surprised to discover that he had an appetite. While he was eating he mentioned Collinwood of the 15th Hussars, whom he had known in the Crimea, and Michelmore said that would be Mad Jack, one of the Collinwood cousins, who had often visited here as a boy. "He were nigh drowned in my leat," he added. "I were never surprised to learn he come through the war unharmed," and this encouraged Adam to admit that he too was at Balaclava, and had afterwards served in the Mutiny. The miller was greatly impressed but then, like Henrietta, deflated by Adam's confession that he had left the army to become a haulier.

He showed Henrietta's automatic respect for uniformed men, and the same prejudice against a gentleman going into trade. "Be there any future in wheeled traffic nowadays, zir?" he asked doubtfully. "They railways be everywhere, baint they?" and Adam said, "Half of them will be bankrupt five years from now, and those that aren't will have been absorbed into a few big lines. There's a fortune waiting for someone who establishes a fast and reliable service, and I've taken it into my head to be that man," but the miller remained unconvinced and there was no doubt in Adam's mind that he had lost caste in his eyes. It was odd how every craftsman, artisan and soil-tiller in the country continued to regard money-making as a degrading occupation for a man qualified to serve in the armed forces, and he wondered if this stemmed from the inarticulate pride that the lowest-paid labourer in the land was beginning to feel in the haphazard acquisition of a vast overseas Empire. Milieu had little to do with it. Their feelings were shared by Henrietta and by Roberts, away on the North West Frontier, and even, to some extent, by un-

205

imaginative men like Keate and Tybalt. Only a few eccentrics seemed to have come to terms with the England that had emerged from the establishment of a communications system that consolidated the unique achievements of the inventors and engineers.

Then the Scots doctor appeared, announcing that his patient was sleeping and was not to be disturbed until morning, that Mrs. Michelmore would feed her and watch over her, that the child was "bonnie and round about seven pounds" and that he would send his groom back with the carriage horse before breakfast. He then departed, without stating his fee, promising to call again tomorrow, depending upon his commitments.

It was then past ten o'clock and Adam wondered briefly what he should do about notifying his household staff, and the Bermondsey yard, that he was stranded in the depth of the Kentish countryside, but in the absence of any means to send a message he turned in, sleeping in the room over the mill-wheel where Michelmore had raised his large family, long since dispersed. Just before he slept he wondered at the improbability of it all, his first child, a daughter, making her debut as casually as a gipsy's child born under the hedge. There was, he thought, something looming about it and whatever it was had to do with that sprawling house crouching under the lee of the woods. The significance of it eluded him and so he dismissed it, rolling in his blankets and sleeping the sleep of a trooper who has stumbled on a comfortable billet after a gruelling day in the saddle.

*　　*　　*

The settled, timeless atmosphere of the place grew upon her, helping her compose her mind and relax her body. They had moved her into a more comfortable bed in a room above the one where the child had been delivered and at first she did not question the unfamiliarity of her surroundings, for somehow they were not strange at all, but comfortable, comforting and reassuring.

It was obviously a remote, very 'countrified' house, enjoying a close communion with everything she thought of as traditional and pastoral. From the great bed, with its luxurious bolsters and lavender-scented sheets, she could see an oblong of sky scored by the spreading branches of old trees, and trailers of wisteria that had crept over the window sill. From first light until dusk the birds whistled and quarrelled under the eaves, and when Mrs. Michelmore, a staunch advocate of fresh air, opened the casement the scent of wild flowers came from the coppice beyond the lawn.

She needed a period of repose, not only to banish the rapidly receding memory of the pain she had endured but also to adjust to the disappointment of having produced a daughter, but this proved easier than she had anticipated, for Adam, cockahoop over the accuracy of his prophecy, was more than satisfied with the mite whose brick-red face and clownish tuft of hair had startled her when Mrs. Michelmore had introduced them. She had fed the child, finding the experience interesting if uncomfortable, but as time went on she was able to adjust to this too and concentrate her thoughts, idle, far-ranging thoughts centred on the place she was in, and how she came to be there. Soon a kind of pattern began to emerge from the freakish incident, and with this came a curiously compelling sense of belonging, so that she began to think of the house as a home in the sense she had never thought of Scab's Castle, the Shirley lodge, or even that sanctuary house on the shores of Derwentwater.

The current of life, having once decided to wash her from the Cheshire plain, had now assumed dramatic control of her destiny and was sweeping her along at a tremendous pace, first away out of Sam's reach and into the arms of a great, hulking husband, then down the full length of England to the capital, and finally here, into a stranger's cosy, well-appointed home and into motherhood. Who could say where it would take her next?

She discovered other things lying here, luxuriating and husbanding her strength, among them an objectivity towards the man who had been responsible for all these adventures. Right up until the moment he had driven her out on what was to be a mere evening jaunt in a carriage, he had been her master but now, unaccountably, she had been promoted, or had promoted herself, to a position of near equality, so that when he came in and stood beside the bed looking awkward and bashful, she could laugh inwardly at him, as he had so often laughed openly at her. And with this came a conviction that men were monstrously conceited bluffers, assuming a superiority that was quite spurious, and trading on it, even the most amiable of them like Adam Swann, for when their conceits were stripped away they were really little more than gawky boys, with nothing much to say for themselves. They stood around coughing and patting and twisting their mouths into counterfeit smiles and then, like overgrown children dismissed to play, scampered about their own concerns. She supposed now that they had always been rather like this

207

and it had been the way of the world from the time when a woman lay on skins in a cave, the man made his insignificant contribution to the complicated process of reproduction, after which he scampered away to hunt bears in the undemanding company of other men.

She had never had these kinds of thoughts before and discovered they had the power to inflate her ego to a point she would have thought very presumptuous less than a week ago. She was able to think through the entire process of reproduction, from the moment of being clutched and crushed and gasped over, to the moment when she heard the first squawk of the child who now lay at her breast and seemed, in its single-minded absorption, to underwrite the importance of women and the comparative irrelevance of men. For the very milk that the child sucked down did not have to be tapped or even paid for by a man. It was there for the asking, for all who had need of it.

When she felt stronger and able to take a less detached interest in things, she asked Mrs. Michelmore to tell her about the house and the people who had lived in it and discovered, to her surprise, that the miller's wife had a romantic streak in an otherwise practical nature, for she gaily recounted the story of the man who had built it centuries ago, another miller called Conyer, who had owned the most prosperous mill for miles around at a village two or three miles upstream, in the days of Queen Elizabeth. Miles Conyer, the first of his line, had fallen in love with a certain Marion Cecil, whose father was the gentleman owning Cecil Court, a great house on the Westerham road beyond Twyforde Green. There was no hope, however, that Miles's suit would be welcomed by Marion's family, for they were known to have enriched themselves by the acquisition of church lands and were a forceful, thrustful family, but Miles, it appeared, was a man with Adam's belief in his own infallibility. Far from despairing, he set himself to convince Marion Cecil that he was worth waiting for. He sold his mill, invested the proceeds in a well-found privateer, and embarked on a series of rewarding raids along the Netherlands coastline, and then down as far as Cape St. Vincent, where his vessel picked up a lame duck of the Indies Treasure Fleet. In three years he was one of the richest men in Kent. He did not, however, risk his own skin in any more ventures, preferring the counting-house to the gun-deck. During the time he was amassing his fortune he maintained regular trysts with Marion on the very site of the house he subsequently built, and that was how it had acquired its name, the Cecils subsequently welcoming him into the family as a man likely to enlist friends in their intrigues at the court of the first Stuart.

Henrietta, intrigued by the story, learned no more than the bare bones from the miller's wife, who had completely abandoned her husband in order to act as nurse and cook. She filled in the details during a courtesy visit by Mr. Phillips, Conyer's agent, who had already been seen by Adam, currently rushing between 'Tryst', his Shirley home, and the Thameside yard in an attempt to keep to the target date for the expansion and Phillips, a gentle, elderly bachelor, seemed captivated by his chance tenant, calling a second time and bringing her a nosegay of spring flowers, together with a silver rattle for the child. It was Mr. Phillips who took tea with her on the first afternoon she was downstairs and he acted as her guide around the house and the fifty acres enclosed by the long wall under which Dancer had bolted.

Everything Henrietta saw enchanted her; the broad, curving staircase, with its balustrade made from the timbers of Miles Conyer's first privateer, the minstrel gallery over the hall where, so Phillips said, Conyer's son entertained guests with his own madrigals (one of which had survived down to this day), the long, wainscotted passage leading to a chamber Phillips called the 'Muniment Room', whatever that meant, the portraits of seventeenth- and eighteenth-century Conyers by Lely and Kneller, as predatory-looking a bunch as one could find today up in the Lancashire cotton belt, the Dutch garden where tulips and weeds fought one another for living-space, the great rhododendron banks climbing behind each wing into the woods crowding the slope and forming a convenient windbreak to the north-east. There was the cubby-hole behind one of the fireplaces that Phillips said was a priest's hole, although he did not explain how such a feature came to be included in the country seat of a family of militant Protestants and, above all, the Conyer crest in stone over the front porch, a shield bisected by a St. Andrew's cross with a variety of unidentifiable birds and fishes in the spaces. It was, Mr. Phillips admitted, a rather suspect coat-of-arms, for this branch of the Conyers were never ennobled but its presence, merging into the mellow brick-work of the long façade, was additional proof of the ex-miller's enterprise.

Henrietta did not know, of course, that old Collinwood's sudden death had converted 'Tryst' into an expensive white elephant, for such of the Conyers who possessed the means or inclination to occupy the place were serving in various parts of the colonies and the agent had instructions to find a tenant for a period of five years, after which the situation was to be reviewed. He mentioned this just as he was leaving, saying that he had an appointment with a prospect that very evening. It was this parting remark, perhaps, that made Henrietta very thoughtful over her broth and beefsteak, eaten under the sullen glare of a Jacobite Conyer who had died of drink in Rome after a curious incident Mr. Phillips referred to as 'The Fifteen'.

* * *

He came about noon the next day, bringing a new day dress she had ordered in anticipation of regaining her normal figure. It was, he thought merrily, a very fetching dress, its tight waistcoat bodice featuring pagoda sleeves finished with what he had been told were known as 'engageantes'. The crinoline skirt displayed multiple flounces and there was a trimmed bonnet to match but it was not the new ensemble that engaged her attention when he displayed it on its wire hanger. He said, "I've seen Doctor Birtles and he tells me you can travel home tomorrow. I'll send Mandrake over to fetch you and the baby early afternoon. Be ready because he's due to meet me at Croydon before six," but then noticed that her expression clouded, and that she made that familiar, appealing grimace that he had first noticed when he tried to abandon her at the wayside station of Lea Green during the earliest stage of their escape from Seddon Moss.

He said, "You want to come home, don't you?" and she replied, devastatingly, "I *am* home, Adam. I'm more at home here than I've ever been anywhere in my life." Then, as he raised his eyebrows, "Oh, I daresay it sounds silly but it's true, it's true, Adam! I *love* this house, and I love this garden. I belong here and I never want to leave it."

He said, reasonably, "Come now, that's nonsense, Henrietta. It really is, and you must see that it is. I know that I said you should live in an old house eventually but I didn't mean now, and I certainly didn't mean a place of this size. It's not only the upkeep, it's the distance from London. Shirley was bad enough, and I hoped to move closer in when the lease ran out, but this is more than twenty miles out and in bad weather it could take me two hours to get into Croydon. Quite apart from that I couldn't afford to buy 'Tryst', even if I called off the expansion and pledged every penny I possessed."

"Oh, but you don't have to buy it, it's for rent. Mr. Phillips, the agent, told me so only yesterday. They want a tenant for five years

210

and after that you could almost surely get it renewed if you wanted to."

"No," he said, "it's quite mad!" but she went on, obstinately, "Why is it mad? Your friend Avery is always telling you to think in guineas and not sixpences, and if I understand that rightly it means pretending to everyone that you're richer than you are. In the meantime you'd have somewhere peaceful and lovely to come to whenever you were tired, somewhere for your children to grow up and give me what I want and need, a home to love as well as a husband." Suddenly she became very earnest. "You'd never ever regret taking it, Adam, I promise you. It isn't because baby was born here, and everyone has been so friendly and helpful, it . . . it's something I feel but can't properly explain, I mean . . . how there comes to *be* a house here, and the man who built it, and how like you he was in the way he went about it!"

She paused for a moment trying to assess whether her outburst had made any impression, whether he regarded it as anything more than an exhibition of what people called 'post-pregnancy fantods'. He looked astonished but there was no sign of the indulgent smile he sometimes used when she made more modest demands on his pocket and patience. Instead there was a hesitant, rather speculative gleam in his eye as he ranged, hand in pockets, along the façade of the house, looking about him with the air of a man seeking an escape from her importunities.

She held her breath when he stopped, turned and looked up at the roof and then, pivoting slowly on his heel, took in the full length of the house, from the muniment room in the west to the little gargoyle perched below the twisted chimney pot of the eastern wing where it jutted out, as though it was one of Miles Conyer's afterthoughts. He came back to her.

"How much do they want per annum? Did you ask Phillips? Or didn't it occur to you that the old rascal was hard at work selling you something?"

She threw up her head as though he had offered a personal insult. "No, it didn't and I don't think he was. He told me because I asked about the history of 'Tryst'. He was just being kind and polite, in a way you couldn't understand."

He said, goodhumouredly, "There now, I don't want to upset you. You shouldn't work yourself up in a state at a time like this. Come down off that high horse and don't resort to snivelling, because it doesn't fool me any more than your other little tricks, although I never seem able to convince you of that, do I?" and he threw his arms around her and kissed her, saying, "Come right out with it if you must. I'll accept the fact that you're taken with the place, and that you made up your mind to bully me into taking it the moment you heard it was in the market. But what's this nonsense about me and that pirate who built it three centuries ago? What the devil have people like the Conyers and me got in common?"

"A lot more than you think. He was someone else who wouldn't take no for an answer, who thought he was capable of anything and proved it. That's why I know 'Tryst' is right for you, apart from what I think about it. You'll succeed here, far more than if you buy or rent some ordinary little place. Besides," here she pouted again, "how long do you spend at home anyhow?"

A male thought occurred to him. With a place like this on her hands her mind was likely to be so occupied that she would make fewer demands on his time than she had been making of late. There was also something to be said for her theory that it would bring prestige to the enterprise. Every successful city man was a snob, and the more money a man was seen to be making the more emphasis rivals placed on his social background. He could imagine the impact his tenancy of a grand house like this might make in and around London Bridge, and on the Manchester and Birmingham exchanges. "That Swann feller—the haulier with the strange device. Must be doing well. Bought himself a country estate they tell me. Up and coming man I should say . . ." and again he thought how much of the father had rubbed off on the daughter.

He said, finally, "Look here, Henrietta, there might be certain advantages but it depends entirely on what Phillips hopes to get in the way of a rental. I'll not be held to ransom because you see yourself as lady of the manor. And it'll mean me spending more time in London, for I can't be expected to come back here every night of the week. I should spend half my time travelling. When it comes down to it, it's a question of asking yourself which you prefer most, a place in the country, or a lodger for a husband."

"You know that isn't true," she said, spiritedly, "and it's unkind to imply it. Of course I'd sooner have you than a house, any kind of house, but I can have both if all you say about the future of Swann-on-Wheels is true, and not just the kind of talk men use to convince themselves that what they are doing is right. I don't want this place if you don't. Why don't you explore it, as I have ? All I'm saying is it's the kind of place a successful man of business ought to be looking for if he means to raise a family."

He said, "Don't threaten me with any more children for a spell. We haven't even found a name for the first one yet. Have you got any more bright ideas? That last list sounded pretentious to me, especially 'Patience'. Patience, indeed, when she was practically born behind a carriage horse! Put your thinking cap on for she'll have to be christened in a week or two."

He went off then and she saw by the way he moved that he was embarking on one of his exploratory probes, of the kind that had already taken him from one end of the country to the other. She thought, gleefully, 'He'll have it! That shot about thinking in guineas went home!' and addressed herself to the less important problem of finding a name for the baby.

* * *

He explored the outside first, moving up the grassy incline above the Dutch garden and taking the path that led through the rhododendron clumps until he could look down on the house from the wooded eminence that rose to a height of a hundred feet.When he had seen it in moonlight he had thought of it as an old man, composing himself for sleep, but now it looked very feminine, a cheerful, broad-beamed matron of about forty-five, with a spread of handsome children and a hearty husband who still appreciated what she had to offer on the table and between the sheets. There was vitality down there harnessed to a settled habit of mind, as though something of old Conyer's restlessness had been built into the place and was still trying to get out after three centuries of sun, rain and wind. The colours appealed to him, the cider-apple redness of mellowed brick and pantiles, the chocolate brown of the cross-timbers and the yellowish white of the chimneys, with their long, graceful twirls, more like the work of a pastry-cook than a mason. And beyond, where the double row of copper beeches ran down to the lane, there were great patches of bluebells that had been budding the evening he brought her here but were now in flower, as were the primroses under the hedges either side of the drive. Away to the left, half-hidden in a wooded hollow, he could see a blur of buildings that was Twyforde Green and between here and the village the river ran across level fields and coppices on its way to join a broader stream that would carry it to the Channel nearly forty miles to the south. Behind him, running the whole length of the escarpment that

213

sheltered the house, were trees that had taken root the time the Kentishmen marched on London under Tyler and Ball, some of the older oaks towering to a height of a five-storey building, others gaining in spread what they lost in height. The place had a settled, civilised look that recommended itself to him as the end product of centuries of conservation and commonsense. It was planned, ordered and deeply rooted, and although it promised comfort the pursuit of ease was not its mainspring. The merchant impulse in Henrietta had detected something that he had missed. The house was redolent of achievement and endeavour on the part of a long line of Englishmen, all of whom knew what they wanted and meant to get it, come what may.

He moved over to the balustrade that overlooked the stableyard and went down a flight of shallow terraces to the kitchen quarters. Here was a range large enough to roast a buck, and the ironmongery that would attend the endeavour. There were several still rooms and pantries floored with blue slate, and an ornate pump beside a stone-lined well covered with an iron grating. Three jerks on the handle brought water gushing into the wooden trough and he thought, 'That's a spring in the slope above and will keep the house bone dry in winter, for the well will drain every gallon that slips through the spread of roots beyond the yard', and he passed on through rooms with which he was half-familiar until he came to the little sewing chamber off the drawing-room, where the baby lay in a cot under the window.

He looked down at her, surprised at the power she had to enchant now that she looked like a real baby instead of the puckered, squalling bundle they had shown him the morning he returned here after his night at the mill. The tuft of hair was receding and under it was a glint of gold so that he thought, 'She'll be fair, like her grandfather, not blackpolled like me, and there's not much of her mother's mulishness about her so far as I can see. I wouldn't wonder if she isn't a withdrawn little thing, who lets her mother put upon her', and he reached down, lifting the tiny fist and noting the perfect formation of fingernails that reminded him of forget-me-not petals. The fingers uncoiled and made a feint at his thumb and two unwinking blue eyes looked up at him with the solemnity of an old bishop pronouncing a blessing.

He stood there conjuring with names, an avalanche of names but none of them seemed apt. There were the usual biblical names, Judith and Ruth and Rachel and Rebecca, and a string of maiden-aunt names, like those of his father's sisters, Emma, Harriet, Martha, Ann and Charlotte. There were fashionable names like Florence, and royal names, like Adelaide and Victoria, and names that were supposed to set the owner an example, like Faith and Charity, and the one Henrietta had suggested, Patience. Patience might have suited her, but now, because of the circumstances of her arrival, it had an ironic ring. He wanted something that symbolised feminine qualities and Eve was an obvious choice, but then he had another thought and a very arresting one. There was that child's body he had lifted from the well at Cawnpore just as dusk was falling, and a single bright star hung in the sky, witness to the ghoulish task that he and Roberts were performing on that sombre occasion. He recalled that the presence of the star had seemed to him a kind of requiem and now, looking down at his own child, he remembered that a solitary star had hung low over the woods when he set off on that mad gallop for the doctor. *Stella.* She should be Stella. To him at least it represented renewal and suddenly he was resolved upon it, whether Henrietta approved or not. He replaced the hand under the coverlet and went upstairs, ranging along the corridors, glancing into the bedrooms, and wondering how much of the furniture was Collinwoods' and how much went with the house. In a row of intercommunicating attics, he saw a huge cistern, presumably installed with the object of building a modern plumbing system, and made a mental note to pursue inquiries in this direction, but now his examination was no more than cursory. He had made up his mind and was already casting around for a formula that would save his face. Ordinarily he was not a man to bother about such niceties but with Henrietta it was always advisable to take this kind of precaution.

She said, when he rejoined her, "Well, what do you think?" and he replied, "Stella. We'll call her Stella. It's an easy name and she's going to have starry eyes." Then, before she could exclaim, "As for the house, it's more intelligently planned than I supposed, and there's pasture here for half-a-dozen horses. I'll see Phillips before I go up to town in the morning and find out what he's asking. More I don't promise. Let's have supper."

His nonchalance did not deceive her but she was wise enough to let the subject drop. All she did, in the way of bolting the door on him, was to slip a message to the miller's wife to get word to Phillips to be available the following day until noon. She had no need to do more than hint at the reason. Ellen Michelmore was already her sworn ally.

215

5

Assignation with Shires

On her account he had missed his target date. It was hopeless, in view of all that followed that eventful evening drive across the Kentish border, to adhere to his plans to break out into even a few of the mapped-out territories, yet some good came of it. She was still, if unwillingly, mascot and talisman of Swann-on-Wheels.

If this was her function the rôle of Tybalt, the old-maidish clerk Keate had introduced into the business, was that of power-house, for it was Tybalt who collected and scrutinised the county almanacks, Tybalt who hit upon the idea of compiling a list of potential customers from Berwick to Fishguard, across the empty pockets of the west to the sheep farms of Dorset, then eastward to where the South Eastern Railway ran almost within sight of 'Tryst'. More important still, Tybalt put into practice Adam's own notion of consolidating this vast amount of information and relating it to all the data reposing between the covers of the red travelling diary.

Tybalt, a man who did not indulge in frivolities, called his apparatus 'The System' but Adam, always inclined to romanticise commerce, soon found another name for the ungainly object they built to make the information readily available. He called this aidememoire 'Frankenstein', for that is how it looked to him when it was complete, a method of fact-assimilation that seemed to him, when he consulted it and got an unexpected answer, to combine the logic of Solomon and the willingness of the Genie of Aladdin's lamp.

The almanack survey came first, for without it Frankenstein would never have been invented. Adam estimated that he had lost six weeks' leeway on account of Stella and her mother's infatuation with 'Tryst', but the time sacrificed was not wasted. It was put to good use by Tybalt and Keate, and led to all manner of changes and adjustments in the original plan, not least the introduction of some medium-sized waggons that he came to call frigates, because they were handier than the drays and possessed twice the carrying

216

capacity of the one-horse pinnaces. He invested another five hundred pounds in frigates and teams to pull them, and because their design was his, and had been disowned by Blunderstone the coach-builder, he took a proper pride in their arrival in the yard, a fleet of handsome, high-sprung, canopied waggons that would stand up to any amount of hard usage on country roads but were yet light enough to come within a mile or two of the records set up by coaches like the Bagshot to Staines 'Quicksilver' and the Leicester to Nottingham 'Lark'. For in the territory they were designed to exploit the emphasis would be on light merchandise rather than on the heavy hauls requiring three-horse drays.

Tybalt came to him with the almanack idea on his first day back at the yard, soon after he had signed his five-year lease and despatched Henrietta, gibbering with glee, about the business of packing their belongings for transport into rural Kent. The clerk appeared in his office carrying a stack of grubby, paper-bound books that looked like an assortment of railway timetables, and when Adam asked if they were Bradshaw guides Tybalt replied, "No, sir, almanacks, *county* almanacks. I have been accumulating them by post and I have a conviction that a great deal might be learned from them."

Tybalt addressed everybody in this fashion, rarely using a short word or an idiom if he could avoid it, and Adam formed a theory that it was a habit he had developed a long time ago in order to compensate for his insignificant appearance and lack of inches. The clerk went on to explain that every county in England now had its own almanack and that, whereas this had been so in the earliest days of the century, the scope and format of these brochures had been greatly enlarged by the spread of railways. Nowadays, he said, they were not issued for the benefit of the man of means travelling across unfamiliar country but offered information that was needed by the penny-a-mile, fare-paying passenger, and the commercial traveller humping his skip up and down the country. Most of them contained classified lists of local business houses, summaries relating to agricultural yields, commentaries on local monuments, road-systems, geological strata, the personnel of county notabilities and, indeed, everything relevant to a specific shire.

"I have no doubt, sir," he went on earnestly, "that some of the facts published here have already found their way into your diary but nothing can be lost by verification. It was with this in mind that I compiled a detailed list of all the established businesses in two of the five areas under review for expansion. I chose, for reasons I will

217

explain, the er ... the 'Western Wedge', and the 'Southern Square'."

Adam smiled when Tybalt mentioned the two territories by nickname, knowing that he would have preferred to call them what they were named on the ordnance maps.

"It sounds as if you have been putting my absence to good use, Tybalt," he said. "Let's see what you extracted from those almanacks," but he was quite unprepared for the spate of information written on a sheaf of foolscap sheets covered with Tybalt's copperplate handwriting.

It was astounding how much information Tybalt had milked from the pages of dry-as-dust guides issued by Hampshire, Wiltshire, Dorset, Devon, Somerset and Cornwall. Here was everything that mattered, set down in precise, alphabetical order. The cereal, fruit, and dairy areas in the Hampshire plain, the milk-processing plants and bacon-curing factories further west, the cider apple output, the fish tonnage landed at a string of points between Poole and Mevagissey, the flower-growing districts and tin mines of the Cornish peninsula, and a couple of pages devoted to the china clay industry and the staple product of beef on which Adam realised he must depend in most isolated districts. It was all there, with the names and addresses of men involved in each industry, and Adam's sole doubt concerning the indispensability of the breakdown rested on the belief that many of these producers must have established their own transport links with the nearest railhead. Tybalt, however, had foreseen this and said, with a tincture of superiority, "I did not include the front-rank men, sir. Producers in a fair way of business would have their own carts and carters, but if you succeed in establishing a faster and more reliable service, linked to goods trains running over the main lines, you could soon under-cut monopolists in most areas. Look at it this way, Mr. Swann. 'A' has his own transport and 'B', in a much smaller way of business, depends on local markets, with no chance of selling in Covent Garden, Billingsgate, or the like. With our service, timed to the minute if I might emphasise that, sir, 'B' 's products will be in London before 'A' 's, and 'A' will come knocking on your door the moment he is aware of this."

The logic made instant appeal to him and it seemed to him that Tybalt should be given credit for some very original thinking.

"I've gone over this ground very thoroughly and made what I thought an exhaustive survey," he admitted, "but it's a very inadequate one compared to yours. I discounted the smaller men, assuming that everything they produce would find its way on to the stalls of local markets. But how could we possibly make personal contact with all these smallholders and cottage craftsmen? It would take a team of men a two-year canvass, wouldn't it?"

"By direct approach it would, Mr. Swann, so there remains the postal service. To break new ground in any of these counties would mean a postal canvass, stating our rates and schedules and that, of course, is what I had in mind when I compiled the list."

"You can't undertake a job of that size. Are you saying we should sign on some junior clerks?"

"Why, yes, sir, but not from outside. There are two or three of Mr. Keate's vanboys who could be taught something more useful than swinging on a tailboard rope. I ... er ... took the liberty of discussing the matter with the waggonmaster. He has at least one lad I can lick into shape, and two or three others who have expressed a desire to improve their education."

"Damn it all, man, none of those urchins have ever been near a school. Hardly one of them can write his own name. Why not advertise for a couple of trained clerks and start 'em off at a pound a week?"

"If you have no objections, sir," said Tybalt, huffily, "I prefer to train youngsters in my own methods."

"Very well. Get Keate to assign them to you from today. How can I argue with you when you produced a scheme as good as this? But wait a minute, come over here with me and take a look at the maps. To begin with, why did you choose those particular areas?"

"They were two of the five earmarked for expansion. The other three, if you recall, sir, were The Polygon, north of the cotton belt, The Mountain Square in Wales, and The Bonus embracing, I take it, the Essex and Suffolk coast."

"Have you done a breakdown on all those areas?"

"Yes, sir, and I suggest we should find a substitute for the last of them. That is, if you still intend to open four depots instead of three, as I believe Mr. Keate prefers. He has had no success in finding a waggonmaster for that east coast area, although the lists show the potential is there. The fact is, it is too near London and we're likely to meet stiff competition."

Adam conceded this but added that there was another good reason for a switch. "You'll have heard I've just settled myself in north-west Kent? I've made some useful contacts through the agent

219

and the solicitors I've been dealing with. We'll shelve The Bonus for the time being and set up a depot at Tonbridge to serve the Kentish Triangle. I daresay, once we're established, we shall need a sub-depot at Horsham or thereabouts. You've studied these maps, Tybalt?"

Tybalt said he had used the maps extensively when compiling his lists and had no quarrel with their boundaries, or the siting of depots. Together they searched the areas again, applying a slide rule to the distances between individual producers and the nearest railheads and making detailed notes on contours and river obstacles that would have a bearing on time schedules. It was this task, a complicated one involving a good deal of guesswork, that was directly responsible for the birth of Frankenstein.

He was calculating the distance between Bristol and Bridport, the dividing line between the Southern Square and the Western Wedge, when it struck him that there must be an easier way of arriving at a figure equating time, distance and the quality of available roads. He said, suddenly, "What we need, Tybalt, what we must have, if we're to make full use of your almanack material, is some kind of ready reckoner, something that helps us to make on-the-spot decisions by comparison. Can you dredge something more from that dome of yours before we start the canvass?"

Tybalt admitted readily that he could not, having already wasted a great deal of time checking distances and railway timetables when they were planning their suburban runs in and around the capital.

"An index is what we need," Adam said, "but it has to be one that doesn't involve trotting to and fro between ledgers, invoices, maps and Bradshaws. What we want is something we can use to give us an approximate answer to any one set of queries. Go and clear the ground for that canvass in the areas we've selected and steal those boys of Keate's while you're about it. I'll think of something, if I have to walk round this belfry all night."

And this, in fact, was what occurred, for the dawn mists were over the Thames when he descended the spiral staircase from his eyrie, peeled off jacket and shirt, and washed under the stable pump, to the astonishment of the night-duty stableman, one of Keate's elderly derelicts, who came out of the hay store and stopped to stare at his employer spluttering under the jet. He said, disapprovingly, "Lord ha' mercy, Mr. Swann. I 'eard splashing an' woulder bet it was one o' they loafers who'd climbed the fence to steal forage. I was just gonner fetch my scatter-shot gun," but Adam said, cheerfully, "I've been working overtime, Hoskins. Now I'm going down to London Bridge station for coffee and a bacon sandwich. Throw me a clean horse cloth, there's a good fellow!" Hoskins handed him the cloth and watched him towel himself, pondering the caprices of the gentry who, with money in the bank, preferred to work through the night within close range of a stinking tannery when they might have been home in bed with wife or light-o'-love. He said, "Any special instructions for Mr. Keate when I go orf dooty, sir?" and Adam said, "None for Mr. Keate but a word to Mr. Tybalt. Tell him I've invented the ready reckoner. No more than that—'Mr. Swann has invented the ready reckoner'. And by the time I'm back make sure the carpenter is available. I've got a special job for him."

The carpenter, a part-time employee responsible for running repairs on the short-haul waggons, was awaiting him when he returned and so was Tybalt and Keate, both hoping to be introduced to Frankenstein. It meant very little to them on the drawing board but the carpenter grasped the idea readily enough and undertook to assemble a prototype by noon, providing he wasn't disturbed.

It was really no more than a large, slabsided frame mounted on a turntable, and the idea had developed from Adam's comparison between a terrestrial globe and Mercator's projection. It had four faces, each fitted with spring clamps capable of holding smaller frames, and each frame could be lifted out to expose one below. The faces were designed to provide a summary of the four component factors of a long haul, the type of goods likely to be handled in a specific area; the roads and natural hazards within that area; the equipment and personnel available at any one base; and, finally, the time schedules of goods trains running over the railways in the territory under review. The whole thing was designed to spin according to requirements, and there was a set of frames on each face relevant to the area concerned. By standing beside it, and spinning it in full circle, it would be possible (providing his calculations were correct and the material on the frames up-to-date) to reduce the nature and weight of a haul to a formula in relation to distance travelled, time consumed, type of waggon and team employed, and the flow of goods traffic across the twelve areas on the master map.

Tybalt was captivated by it, declaring that once the result of a canvass was analysed Frankenstein would prove invaluable to the person charged with the task of arriving at an estimate. Unable to wait for the carpenter's prototype he persuaded Keate to give him details of equipment and personnel likely to be allocated to Exeter, capital of the Western Wedge. Then he set about calculating the profits of a ghost haul from Moretonhampstead, in the railway-free fringe of Dartmoor, to the Exeter goods sidings. Soon he had enlisted Adam in a trial run of two frigates, each carrying a load of milk churns consigned for Bristol. The result, they found, was very encouraging. They could do the run at a competitive price and still have the milk aboard an eastbound goods train within two hours of loading. Another two hours, with wholesalers to meet it, would see it arrive at Bristol dairies. The prospect of such a swift passage between cow and customer impressed him, giving him the impetus to begin work on a Western Wedge canvass that same day.

In the event it was by no means as simple as he had supposed. The summarised material required to fill forty-eight frames demanded concentrated research that kept Adam office-bound for ten days at a stretch, and even when it was assembled, and indexed for easy reference, scores of minor adjustments were seen to be necessary. By the time Frankenstein was ready to spin he was desperate for fresh air and exercise, and with the new target date fixed for July 1st, he took time off to prospect the Kentish Triangle on horseback, basing himself at 'Tryst' in order to superintend his domestic upheaval but paying far more attention to a follow-up of Tybalt's postal canvass of the area.

Replies were coming in now, first in a steady trickle, later in a stream amounting to an overall result of around forty per cent of the whole. Browsing through them, and preparing quotations, Adam had indisputable evidence of the blight that had struck the national road haulage system since the completion of a mainline railway system within the last few years. Short-run haulage was booming, as his own London returns proved, but medium and long-distance transport had undergone a dramatic decline. In many rural areas no regular waggon service for heavy goods or produce existed, so that he sometimes wondered how all these teeming cities were fed and how difficult it must be for some of the locally-based craftsmen to seek markets beyond their doorsteps. It was as though, with the arrival of the gridiron, the British had been segregated into categories of first, second and third class citizens, like the passengers they whirled from one end of the country to the other. At one end of the scale were big manufacturers, city merchants and well-established tradesmen, who could transport products at a speed undreamed of only twenty years before. At the other end was an agriculture drained of its labour force and communities living in small towns and villages that were as isolated as Crusoes if they happened to live far from the main arteries of the railroad companies. Spurs were entirely dependent upon population. The big companies saw no reason to waste mainline profits by opening up cross-country lines to serve a limited or scattered community.

It was a state of affairs, however, of which he had no reason to complain. With something like eight hundred contracts written into his ledgers he was tempted to take an even bigger gamble, by opening eight or ten depots, instead of confining himself, for the time being, to four. He held back, however, inhibited partly by staffing problems, partly by a reluctance to put more strain on the shoulders of the indefatigable Tybalt and his apprentice clerks.

Avery seldom appeared in the yard more than once a week. The partnership that existed between them was absurdly loose and, in actual fact, Adam was never really clear as to the extent of his reserves, for they had nothing in writing and their financial arrangements continued to rest on mutual confidence, apart from the fixed rate of interest for the two initial advances.

His books told him that the necklace had so far yielded him a little over five thousand pounds but he could never make up his mind whether this was wholly or partly Avery's money, or how many of the stones representing their reserve capital had been disposed of by his intermediary. It seemed to him a very weak link in what was becoming a solid chain of enterprise but when he raised the matter, suggesting that they should have a proper agreement drawn up, Avery flatly declined to enter into any such arrangement, pointing out that the less lawyers knew about the source of the money the better. Adam, he said, could draw on his account if he needed fresh capital at any time, and Avery expressed himself wholly in favour of more and more expansion. Aware that inquiries concerning the source of capital might be awkward, and might even put the whole venture in jeopardy, Adam followed his advice and let this side of the business drift. In this respect, he told himself, he was in the fashion. Every day now he crossed paths with merchants in a very big way of business, who blithely borrowed what seemed to him astronomical sums from banking houses and from one another in order to invest in all kinds of dubious ventures, both here and in faraway places where men like Roberts were opening up new and apparently limitless markets

2

Adam Swann was probably the first city merchant to institute what later generations of businessmen learned to call the weekly conference of heads of departments.

It grew out of need to correlate the day-to-day work of Keate, responsible for personnel and rolling stock, Tybalt, immersed in his gigantic canvass, as well as the income and outgoings of the parent yard, Blubb, the ex-coachman, who was a kind of quasi-sergeant-major of the London waggoners and their apprentices, and himself, as the man who had elected to drive this unlikely team across half England.

Tybalt, he discovered, he could trust to complete any task set him and they were in almost hourly contact with one another, usually through a booming speaking-tube that connected the belfry with the counting-house near the weighbridge. Keate, who was inclined to be over-conscientious, was obsessed with the shortage of reliable carters, men he felt he could personally recommend to an employer who had lived up to all his initial promises and was now absorbing most of the local waifs who could be lured into regular employment. It was by no means easy, he told Adam, to find men who could be trusted out of his sight in places as far away as Salisbury, Exeter, Abergavenny and Maidstone, and it was essential, as he saw his duty, to put such men as consented to serve in the provinces in charge of thoroughly trustworthy depot managers, who could be relied upon to resist the temptation to 'shoulder' goods, as men like Blubb had once 'shouldered' passengers, that is to say, carry them intermediate distances on a coach-run and pocket the fares. Such men were difficult to find and of those interviewed only a few signed on to undergo a period of training at Headquarters.

It sometimes seemed to Adam, vetting all the applicants, that there were now only two kinds of Englishmen. Humourless, Bible-educated evangelists, like Keate and Tybalt, who although hard-working and scrupulously honest, allowed their judgements to be clouded by moral prejudices, and hard-drinking, hard-swearing rascals like Blubb, who could be relied upon to do a good day's work but were usually of an extremely independent turn of mind. Even the waggoners and their apprentices tended to drift into one or other of these two camps, mutually contemptuous of one another, and united only by their loyalty to the man who filled their weekly wage-packet. Among the coachmen there was a minority of Holy Joes, enlisted by Keate or Tybalt from the lowest strata of the mission hall congregations, but the majority were men of Blubb's stamp, who had known better days, and were not slow to remind younger colleagues that they had once conveyed belted earls over the turnpike roads at fifteen miles an hour and were now reduced to humping goods from one district to another at an average rate of under ten.

He had almost given up hope of finding men with managerial propensities, who were neither preachers nor crusty old drunkards, with a hatred of everything associated with the railroad. Then, out of the blue, John Catesby presented himself, and Adam discovered an entirely new type of artisan who seemed to him a direct product of the new age, a man who was equipped to meet its brassy challenge and prepared to fight hard to enlarge his precarious foothold in society.

Catesby was frank from the outset. He was partially self-educated and both conscious and proud of his essential place in a world where a man's labour was all he had to sell. He demanded a guarantee of six months' employment, subject to Adam's satisfaction and expressed a preference for piece-time rates against the basic wage and out-of-town overnight allowance. He was a tall, ravaged Lancastrian, who had spent his childhood in the mill before the Ten Hour Act went some way towards the abolition of juvenile slavery, and his experiences there had left an indelible mark upon him. His truculence, however, unlike Blubb's, stemmed not from a distrust of mechanisation (of which he wholly approved) but from a hatred of exploitation of the majority by the lucky few, men like Sam Rawlinson, who had made the grade and were now hard at work forgetting how their success had been achieved.

Adam, liking his outspokenness, encouraged him to talk about the *laissez-faire* relationship between labour and capital that men like Palmerston championed, declaring it to be the only road to riches for master and man. Catesby, risking the job he had come seeking, denied this doctrine, saying that it was the best prescription he knew for a French-style revolution, and could only be made to work for both parties if the labour forces of the country organised themselves into guilds or unions, like the craftsmen among their mediaeval forefathers. "As it is," he said, "the only safeguard the majority has against enslavement is the presence in Westminster of a

225

humanist minority, led by Lord Shaftesbury, and he has to fight vested interests every inch of the way, even for such obvious improvements as fenced-in machinery. I'm not quoting from an anarchist's pamphlet, Mr. Swann. I've slaved under the overseer's strap in one of their damned mills, a mite of nine, working a twelve-hour day, and being beaten black and blue if he nodded off and was lucky enough to fall backwards and not face foremost into the cogs! I've seen folk treated as no plantation owner in the cotton fields would treat blacks he valued as property, and this is a Christian country! I'll admit to another thing and you can make what you like of it. I've done time in one of their stinking gaols for rioting in Bolton before I were twenty, and I wouldn't be telling you that if it hadn't got around that you were a good man to work for, who pays over the odds hourly rates, and don't treat men like cattle."

Adam made one of his swift, intuitive decisions. "I'm looking for a man to open up northern territory," he said, "and I prefer local men if I can find them. My base up there, in what I call the Polygon, will be Appleby. It's a biggish area, and virgin ground so far as I'm concerned, well north of the cotton belt but within reach of the rail network, with a south-western limit at Preston. In that kind of country, where there are still hundreds of towns and villages by-passed by the North Western, I hope to carry manufactured goods in and farm produce out. If there's enough work for them I'll send in a couple of men-o'-war—flat drays—to haul graphite, lead, slate and marble, but for the moment it will be lighter vehicles, perhaps half-a-dozen to begin with. Are you a married man, Catesby?"

"Yes, with two grown children, a boy and a girl. The boy, Tam, is unemployed, and we live in one room and a cubbyhole off the Jamaica Road. Could I take the boy along as a waggoner?"

"Providing Mr. Keate approves him," Adam said. "It would do your family good to breathe clean air again. I'm offering forty shillings a week but if you want piece rates it would depend on what we haul once we get started."

Catesby said, knitting his brow, "I'll take the basic for the first twelvemonth, Mr. Swann. If I increase the turnover we could come to a new arrangement, mebbe. You won't find me wanting. I'm not one of these scabs forever bellyaching about the privileges of capital and selling the boss short on labour."

"I'm sure you're not," Adam said, "and as for that spell in gaol I regard it as a recommendation. I've seen what goes on up there, and I sometimes wonder why we still send our missionaries to Papua and Calabar."

They shook hands on it and within twenty-four hours Catesby was travelling north to hunt up a yard and stabling in Appleby, with the promise of getting his first waggons within a fortnight. Before he went Tybalt gave him a rundown on the results of the canvass in northern Lancashire, western Yorkshire, and the Lakeland area, Catesby undertaking to make personal contact with the farmers and small manufacturers who had asked for quotations.

The engagement of Catesby began a small run of luck in an area that had caused the maximum anxiety, the enlistment of reliable men as base managers. Within a week two other vacancies were filled, the Mountain Square and the Kentish Triangle, the first by a thoughtful, middle-aged Welshman, who seemed to lack the gregariousness and garrulity of his race, the other by Blubb, himself a Kentishman, who surprised everyone by applying for the Tonbridge vacancy, where he had innumerable contacts among the old coaching and mail-carrying fraternity. Adam gave him a trial on the strength of this, for he had an intimate knowledge of the roads and the contract situation down there was already well advanced.

For roughly the same reasons he engaged the Welshman, Lovell, who had travelled the Mountain Square as a packman. Lovell spoke Welsh and this seemed to Adam an essential qualification for a manager based in Abergavenny, and concerned almost exclusively with the farming fraternities in the Principality. Lovell, it seemed, had no great admiration for his countrymen, placing small trust in their promises represented by the canvass.

"I'll be satisfied when I see the colour of their money," he said. "It's a rare place for bad debts and no Englishman could collect them."

Lovell and Blubb left for their depots in the second week of June, Blubb actually driving one of the fully-loaded three-horse drays allocated to Maidstone. He voiced an ultimate grumble when he saw the stablemen harnessing a third Clydesdale in front of the two wheelers.

"Time an' agin I've spat at men driving 'unicorn'," he growled, heaving himself on to the box, "and here I am doing it, be Christ!"

Keate, overhearing him, reproved him for taking the Lord's name in vain but Blubb, who habitually called his immediate superior 'Creepin' Jesus', was unabashed. He said, giving his whip a crack that could be heard across the yard, "I got no bloody call to pay lip

227

service to the bleedin' pulpit. I once pulled a bishop out of a bog when we overturned the old Tally-Ho, just short of Canterbury. Saved 'is bleedin' neck I did, an' what did I get? '*Arf* a guinea? Not on yer life. 'E makes straight for the gaffer, 'fore he got the mud orf 'is gaiters, accusing me o' reckless drivin'!" He moved off, blowing out his purple cheeks and Adam, watching him go, wondered if he had made a wise choice. The following day Hamlet Ratcliffe presented himself, asking for the Exeter vacancy and of the four depot managers he seemed, at first acquaintance, the most engaging.

Ratcliffe had never sat behind a horse in his life but he was familiar with a variety of Westcountry trades, having been trained as an auctioneer in Barnstaple and had never lost his North Devon burr during his ten unsuccessful years in the capital. Like Catesby and Blubb he had endured hard times, the firm that had tempted him east having recently gone bankrupt. "I daresay I could get a billet hereabouts," he said, "for I know the trade, Mr. Swann, but I'm zick o' the bliddy vogs and clatter, and zo is the missis. The streets yerabouts was paaved wi' gold, so they told me backalong. All I zeed zince I took the Great Western out o' Bristol is zoot. Youm offering me a starter of vorty shillin', ten short o' what I was paid up under St. Paul's, but the missis says I'll live to spend me wages downalong, whereas up yer I'll be carried out in a box bevore I'm vifty."

Adam said he entertained high hopes of the westcountry, for it seemed to him unlikely that the uplands of Devon, and the territory north of the new line to Truro, would ever be exploited by railways. Ratcliffe agreed, reminding him that not so long ago the West had a bigger population than any area of the British Isles outside London. "Tidden zo no more o' course," he added, sadly, "on account o' they bliddy savages up north. What's us cummin' tu, I wonder, wi' volk crowdin' into they ole factories? Time was when us lived well enough on the land, and tiz the land us'll vall back on come a new slump or any fresh trouble wi' they ole French."

He spoke as if the chapter of the Napoleonic wars had been closed the day before yesterday but Tybalt, who talked to him about agricultural prospects in the area, gave him a favourable report and said he considered him fitted for the job. So Ratcliffe departed ahead of his small fleet of waggons, having secured premises in advance by telegraphing an old friend who ran the 'White Hart', in the shadow of Exeter Cathedral.

For the first time in weeks Adam was able to sit back and relax for a spell. Musing over the juxtaposition of the names of those signed on to preside over three of the depots—Catesby, Lovell and Ratcliffe—he was reminded of a piece of doggerel he had learned at school, concerning the intimates of the last Yorkist king and repeated, chuckling,

> " The Cat, the Rat, and Lovell the dog
> Ruled all England under a hog."

It seemed to him some kind of omen, and these days he was very much alive to portents.

3

Before the leaves fell she was pregnant again and proud of it, having made up her mind to waste no time founding the line of swaggering sons she had long since resolved to launch upon the world now that she had persuaded him to provide an impressive background for a race of warriors.

She had sensed that he was a somewhat reluctant partner in this enterprise and had even gone so far as to doubt the wisdom of deliberately increasing their family so rapidly, but by then she was taking his measure more accurately than he had taken hers, or was ever to take it.

He had his waggon teams, proliferating all over the country, and she had her own obsession, and it seemed to her a more dignified ambition than that of humping other people's packages and milk churns over hill and dale. She had almost forgotten her indirect part in the origins of the venture, and when she saw one of his waggons it was not often she recalled it was she who had suggested the insignia that now made the name Swann prominent in newspaper advertisements and was becoming known, she supposed, to almost everyone associated with the transportation of goods. The engraved ring was there to remind her but she did not often wear it about here for fear of losing it in a flower bed. Gracefully, and without acrimony she bowed herself out of that part of his life, and he soon ceased to tell her anything about the business unless it was a comic incident, like the ex-coachman Blubb's capture of a pilferer he caught running from an unattended waggon with a ham under his arm, or how the northern manager, Catesby, unaware of their relationship with Sam, had actually hauled one of his boilers into Rochdale where the new Rawlinson mill had replaced the Seddon Moss ruin.

She had both her husband's and father's ability to concentrate on what she thought of as essentials. 'Tryst' was one, and her enchantment with it grew day by day through the long dry summer. Another was her resolve to produce children in whom she could take pride. A third, of course, was how to handle him both as man and husband.

The mirror assured her she had not only regained her original shape, with no more than a trifling addition to her waistline, but had taken on a kind of glow that showed in her fresh complexion and an access of vitality that warmed her blood down here in sun and country air. Adam had remarked on it when he came back from his first tour of inspection in the north and west, a tour that kept him from home for a month. She had missed him, of course, but not as much as before, for who could be lonely or feel neglected in a house and grounds of these dimensions, and under the flattering tutelage of Ellen Michelmore, who guided all her decisions regarding furnishing, provisioning, engagement of staff, and a hundred other matters?

She now had a cook, a parlourmaid, a kitchenmaid, and a sewing-woman, in addition to a gardener, a gardener's boy, and a handyman who did inside and outside work. Ellen, who had ordered her husband to sell the flooded mill and take up residence in the largest of the lodges, was her major-domo and would stand no nonsense from a staff that had intimidated Henrietta because they asked so many questions that she was unable to answer, and in a dialect she could not always understand, but she soon learned to retreat into the shadow of her dear Ellen, who never presumed and was as efficient as Mrs. Worrell had been in house management but treated her as though she was a fragile and superior being, and not a tiresome twelve-year-old. Under Ellen, who had seen service in a Hertfordshire country mansion, she learned to make and receive calls, to compose prim little invitations and shopping lists at her writing bureau, to take solemn carriage rides in the calash, to pretend to an interest in what the gardener raised in the hothouse, to cut and arrange flowers, and even to scold the girls, although she took care to keep clear of Mrs. Hitchens, the cook, with whom Ellen maintained a feud.

It was, she supposed, as close to the life of a fairytale princess as one could expect here on earth, and most of Henrietta's fantasies could be traced back to princesses in fairytale books drooping over castle battlements and wearing conical hats with billowing veils and gold slippers the size and shape of chisels.

But this was only her outward life and she accepted it (though gratefully) as a just reward for someone who had had the courage to run away from home in a thunderstorm, and had later displayed the sense to hold fast to a prince's coat-tails. As to her relationship with the prince, for some time now she was, despite progress, not as sure of herself as she would have liked, for she had discovered that he possessed three identities and she had never decided which was the real one, or, for that matter, which she preferred.

There was the paternal and bountiful Adam, who was such a generous provider, even though he continued to treat her as if she was a wilful girl about seventeen, and had a disconcerting trick of giving her so much of her own way that she was dismayed when he pulled her up with a jolt, the way he would check the restive horses he liked to ride. Then there was the absent-minded, almost elderly Adam, who mooned about during the week-ends as though he begrudged the time spent in her company and was homesick for his stableyard, his lading bills, and all those hobbledehoys with whom he had surrounded himself. And finally there was the hearty, bottom-pinching Adam who came striding into the house, swung her off her feet in a first, crushing embrace and, as like as not, whisked her upstairs before she had digested her supper and lost no time at all demonstrating that he had few regrets about saddling himself with a wife who, as he was not slow to point out, would ruin them with her extravagances and fashionable fads. In fact, his personal approach to her seemed to depend on a variety of imponderables so that in some ways, now that his business was launched, it was like getting married all over again to someone she had known a long time ago. His mood was dictated, she discovered, by things wholly outside her control; how much money he was making or losing; what difficulties he had encountered in what she thought of as a jungle where men struggled with one another for spoils with weapons used by her father and the Goldthorpes. It depended also on whether he had just solved a problem or was in the process of solving one, on how long they had been separated, on his appetite, on all manner of things that needed to be considered in advance, so that the period immediately preceding a homecoming was always an anxious one, needing time on her part to step out of the rôle of lady of the manor and back into that of the silly little goose she had been the night he

231

set her down at that Windermere hotel, plied her with claret, and initiated her into the mysteries of her new status. For this, so her instinct told her, was how he preferred her on these occasions, not the grown woman she had become but the girl he had carried pillion across the fells, someone he could indulge and dominate but who was expected, none the less, to enter into the spirit and practise of his frolics.

She did not learn this, of course, by any means other than trial and error, but she learned it well and in this respect at least—or so she told herself—she was probably unique among the married women of her acquaintance.

A staging-post in their relationship was reached one damp September evening, about six months after they had settled at 'Tryst' when he appeared late at night, after she had abandoned hope of his return and gone upstairs to bed. She had only partially undressed when it occurred to her to try on her newest day dress, in which she hoped to set tongues clacking at the next of Mrs. Roydon's At Homes, for it was the very latest fashion, known as the 'Corsage Postillion', with buttons down the front as far as the hemline, two short basques at the back, and sashed at one with the bodice. The bow was enormous and had to be carefully fluffed out, leaving trailing ends when tied at the back.

He came stamping in out of the wet and she was not even aware of his arrival until he burst into the bedroom, reached over her shoulders as she stood before the mirror and pulled her against his mud-splashed topcoat so that she reacted with a squeak of protest, shouting, "*Mind*, Adam! *Please*, my bow ...!" and was dismayed by the dramatic change in his expression and the way he skipped back, locking his hands behind him and looking just like her father in one of his moods when things were going badly at the mill.

He said, in a tone of voice he had never used before, not even when he was ordering Sam out of the house, "Listen to me! I don't give a damn what sort of airs you give yourself downstairs in my absence, but don't ape the lady of the manor in the bedroom, do you hear?"

She said, momentarily at a loss for words, "Adam, I didn't mean ... I only said ... well, you're muddy and I ... I didn't expect you!"

"What the devil has that got to do with it? Is it too much to expect you to show you're pleased to see me?" and went past her into his dressing room, slamming the door.

It was the nearest they had ever come to an open quarrel and it had the power to make her feel sick. Suddenly she decided that she looked at least thirty in the dress and fumbled impatiently at the buttons, shrugging herself out of it and standing beside the great Conyer fourposter in her shift, with a finger in her mouth, like a child deprived of a lollipop and hovering on the edge of tears.

Through the closed door she could hear him hurling his boots about and presently, listening very carefully, the steady rasp of his razor on the day's bristles. She sat on the edge of the bed thinking hard, trying with all her might to equate his flash of ill-humour with the breezy affection he had demonstrated when he entered the room, and in the contrast she thought she discerned one of the really basic characteristics of the male animal, not merely a craving to be acknowledged as a superior being, for whom all clocks were expected to stop, but a creature likely to become unmanageable if the most casual overture on his part had to await its turn in the appointed routines of life. And then this thought carried her deeper into the male mind, so that she remembered other times he had returned after a brief absence, and demonstrated a kind of impatience that made normal communication between them almost impossible until he had her to himself up here and spreadeagled in that bed. After that, she reflected, he was always the excessively amiable man she had married, who would tease her and bring out some trinket he had bought on his travels and then, for a spell, everything would go smoothly and predictably until he rode away again towards that saucer of dark sky to the north-east.

It was very odd, she thought, that physical contact was of such tremendous importance to men. Women could communicate in all kinds of other ways, with glances and smiles and tosses of the head, with rustlings and hints from the armoury of artifice, but a man, especially a big, vigorous, decisive man like him, had to be granted that romp between the sheets before he could be expected to behave like a civilised being and not a servant under notice.

She got up, nodded encouragement at her reflection in the mirror, tapped on his door, and said, very softly, "Adam? *Dearest?* I'm very sorry. I do apologise. Will you come out now?"

The door opened at once and revealed him standing on the threshold, still scowling but with his glumness half-concealed under a coating of lather. She held out her arms and with a mere pretence of reluctance he laid aside his razor, wiped one half of his face and strode back into the room, taking her in what began as a very restrained embrace but soon enlarged itself, so that blobs of soap

233

transferred themselves to her cheek and ear. He said, with a grin, "Here, let me wipe that off," but she clung to him, saying, "No, no, don't bother! First *tell* me something, something I ought to know by now, for you surely couldn't imagine I wasn't pleased to see you and to have you hold me like this again?"

"You didn't show much enthusiasm," he said, and then. "Was it because of the mud? Or because I surprised you?"

"It wasn't for either reason, not really," she said, "and that brings me to what I've always wanted to know but . . . well . . . could never bring myself to find out. People who love one another, people like you and me, is it right that . . . well . . . that the man should always begin it, and the woman just . . . well . . . wait?"

The question both amused and interested him, as abstract lines of inquiry on her part often did. He said, chuckling, "Well, now, the man is usually reckoned the hunter, and I believe most men are embarrassed if the rôle is reversed."

She was encouraged by this to be more precise. "I'm not concerned with most men. How is it with *you*?"

"That depends entirely on you," he said, "as I've told you before, the first night we shared a bed if I remember rightly. A good marriage should be mutually rewarding. It's just a European fashion to pretend otherwise."

"Then it's wrong to . . . well . . . to pretend not to take pleasure in it; *your* sort of pleasure I mean?"

He came as close to blushing as she had ever seen and then he laughed at himself and ran his hand over her head. But she wasn't in the least embarrassed now, for her curiosity had reached a point where it had to be satisfied and she was not even prepared to make a concession to his dignity.

"Well?"

"I'm not at all sure how to answer that. You use the word 'pretend'. How much have you 'pretended' in that respect since that first occasion at Windermere?"

She said, calmly, "I've always pretended, Adam. In spite of all you said that night."

He looked baffled then and his arm dropped from her shoulder. "You're saying all that's happened between us has been the performance of a duty on your part?"

"Oh, no!" she said, emphatically, "I don't mean that in the least! I've often tried to forget all I heard on the subject of loving before I married but it isn't easy. It really isn't, Adam. What I mean is, a

234

person like me can't help feeling that to ... well ... to join in turns her into a certain sort of woman and that would be quite dreadful wouldn't it?"

He said, reaching up to brush the soapflakes from her cheek, "I'll tell you something, Hetty, something I should have made very clear a long time ago. I've always half-realised I didn't succeed in removing all those tomfool prejudices they pump into so-called civilised women when they're about to be married, so that many brides find themselves pregnant without really understanding why. I should have given it more thought, I suppose, but it's not too late, particularly as you've been honest enough to raise the subject. A man's pleasure in a woman is regulated to a very great extent by the pleasure she derives from him. At least, that's what they think in the East and that's how it seems to me. It's for that reason, I suppose, that I never cared very much for what you call 'a certain sort of woman'. Your instinct isn't at fault, either. You put me out of temper a moment since but thank God you've got a damned sight more commonsense than the majority of women seem to have over here. A man and wife ought to be able to talk freely to one another, the way we're doing now. That's surely one of the rare privileges of marriage, and as for that sense of shame you feel when I run my hands over you, peel it off with that shift and behave just as your pretty little body tells you to and I'll love you the better for it. Do you follow me, or would you like me to be more explicit?"

She said, levelly, "I understand perfectly, and thank you for listening and explaining. I'm sure most husbands wouldn't," and he replied, chuckling, "I'm sure they wouldn't. Some would have given you a sound spanking themselves, and others would have sent you back to your father for one. However, that's their loss. They should have taken as much time as I did looking for the right kind of wife!" and with that he took her in his arms and covered her face with kisses, after which, without any assistance from her, he pulled her shift over her head and extended the range of his embrace to every area of her body. Finally, seeming to begrudge the brief interval it occupied him to tumble out of his own clothes, he took possession of her with a wholeheartedness that made all his previous demands experimental, for there was a new element present and in a way she only half-comprehended while she composed herself to sleep within his embrace, she saw herself for the first time as a wife rather than a junior consort.

*　　　*　　　*

235

She never made the same mistake again. Whenever she had warning of his return after more than a day's absence, she would slip out of the house without telling anyone where she was going and make her way up the rhododendron path to the top of the wooded hillock behind the house as though in performance of a rite. Here, she would slough off her dignity like a petticoat, and consciously think herself into the kind of woman she knew he expected to greet him as soon as he crossed the threshold, and once they were alone there was no necessity to think about anything at all but enjoy to the full the licence he had bestowed upon her and this, she discovered, offered a secret bonus. In the mood she was able to induce he was never able to deny her anything, however fanciful.

She had made all manner of discoveries about herself since the day he came jogging over the rim of the moor south of Seddon Moss but this was by far the most important of them.

6

Death of a German

ADAM SWANN could never recall a time, not even as a schoolboy, when food held more than a passing interest for him. Having inherited an excellent digestion from forebears conditioned to hard tack and whatever they could freeboot from the alien fields they traversed over the centuries, he seldom noticed what he was eating and would sometimes forget to eat regularly, making do on whatever came to hand in a local eating-house or tavern. Tybalt, cursed with a delicate digestion, envied his employer's supreme indifference to victuals, but would shake his head and prophesy internal troubles in middle age when, during the midday break, Adam would refuse to stop work and dismiss the clerk while he spent the interval in his eyrie. When this happened the faithful Tybalt would perform one of his daily rituals, laying *The Times*, the *Morning Post* and other newspapers on Adam's desk before seeking his own meal. For this was the hour that Mr. Swann was known to study the day's news, fortified, more often than not, by a tankard of porter and a cheroot.

He had learned, over the last three years, how vital it was to keep a close watch on the home newsfront and in the closely-printed columns of the London journals he would often detect trends that had a direct or indirect bearing on his business. A new foundry was being opened here, a new railway spur there. The last wooden battleship was being laid up, the first ironclad launched. The 'Great Eastern', Brunel's masterpiece, looked like being a costly failure. An Anglo-French trade treaty had been signed. There had been severe flooding again in the Severn Valley. Canal barges were lowering their rates in the never-ending battle with the railroads. Dickens was denouncing pirate publishers in the United States for reprinting his stories and paying him no royalties. The painter Millais, having finally deprived that pompous chap Ruskin of his beautiful wife, was now putting Effie on canvas and exhibiting her at the Academy, to the delight of every tittle-tattler in town.

237

He had a retentive memory for this kind of trivia and it made him welcome in mixed company, and yet, for a man who had travelled halfway across the world and back again, he took little interest in foreign affairs, for he was one of those Englishmen who found it difficult to take a serious view of anything the foreigners did or said, subconsciously equating their public occasions with the cries of children at play. This was how he thought of Garibaldi's much-trumpeted liberation of Italy that autumn, and later the succession of the dour old Wilhelm I to the throne of Prussia. It did not and could not concern him or, for that matter, his country, for more than ever nowadays he had a sense of being in the swim of London affairs, whereas he continued to think of Germans, Frenchmen, Turks and Spaniards as splashing about in the shallows. It was an insular conceit, no doubt, but not a singular one. His views were shared by most of the men he met and trafficked with in the city, or during his regular forays into the provinces, and were based, perhaps, on the evidence of his eyes. From his belfry he could watch the vast volume of shipping coming and going on the Thames tideway, and the forest of masts in the adjacent docks. *The Times* told him that Britain was now carrying three-quarters of the world's seaborne trade, and his own business went booming along like one of the tall East Indiamen breaking its own record in the grain race from the far side of the world. It was thus not surprising that he took no note of the secession of South Carolina from the American Union in the last days of the old year, or raised an eyebrow over the decision of five other southern states to follow her example in the first month of 1861. There was no reason why he should. He carried little or no cotton in his waggons, and the significance of what was happening in America entirely escaped him until it was pushed under his nose by no other person than his father-in-law, Sam Rawlinson, now of Rochdale, and in a bigger way of business than he had been when they last exchanged views.

He rarely gave a thought to Sam these days, whereas Henrietta would often go out of her way to avoid mentioning him, as though he was someone whose portrait had been turned to the wall. If he had thought about it Adam might have regarded this as unforgiving on Henrietta's part, for Sam had made no move to molest her from the moment he marched out of the Colonel's library and climbed into his cab shortly before her marriage. Adam bore him no malice. Time and events had clouded his memory of the boy who died under Sam's horse the night of the riot, so that he had been amused rather than irritated by Catesby's innocent gaff in transporting a boiler on the

238

millowner's behalf. He did write to Catesby, explaining the relationship, and making one or two sardonic remarks about Rawlinson's character, but the account went through the ledgers and it even pleased him to think he had lifted five pounds, ten shillings from his father-in-law for a nine-mile haul performed by a three-horse team in two hours, door to door.

He was therefore much surprised, in the first week of February, to receive a letter from Catesby reporting that Sam had not only written demanding a quotation for transporting roofing slates from the Upper Polygon to Rochdale, but had added a postscript to the effect that his son-in-law would be welcome if he cared to call at the mill when he was in the district. Adam, who had been planning to make a trip north within the next week or so, deemed it wise to say nothing of this to Henrietta, deciding that he would take the old devil at his word and prospect the ground before taking his wife into his confidence. Then he forgot about it, busying himself with preparatory moves to open a branch in the Isle of Wight, designated 'Tom Tiddler's Ground' on the master map, and after that a breakdown by himself, Tybalt, Keate, and their mutual friend, Frankenstein, of possibilities of launching the service in the Border Triangle. He did not know what he would make of the Isle of Wight, but a Scotsman called Fraser, who had run a carrier service in the north-east, was selling up and offering teams and waggons at what Keate declared a knockdown price. Avery, consulted on the prospect of moving north to the Border, gave his approval but added that he had never yet met a Scotsman or a Yorkshireman who would sell anything worth having at bargain price.

Then the Colonel wrote saying that Aunt Charlotte was down with chronic bronchitis, and he feared she would not survive the winter, so Adam decided to go north at once, with the triple object of seeing what Fraser had to sell in the way of teams and goodwill, paying a call on his father and aunt, and studying Catesby's methods at firsthand, for he had been astonished by the turnover from the Polygon after Catesby had demanded three-horse instead of two-horse men-o'-war, and had also broken into the short-haul market in the cotton-belt itself, for when planning the Polygon Adam had assumed the railways would monopolise transport in southern Lancashire.

He travelled up from Euston in one of the L. & N.W. smokers, hauled by one of the new Crewe locomotives at what seemed to him a prodigious speed, and Catesby met him at the depot, driving him to

Salford where a yard had been rented to handle the traffic north of the Manchester–Liverpool line. Adam was impressed by what he saw. Catesby already had five one-horse pinnaces operating in this area, mostly concerned with the distribution of bolts of manufactured fabrics and hardware to small towns on the western edge of the Pennines, but his main efforts were directed towards developing a system of transporting heavy machinery to out-of-the-way mills in the north and east of the county, where the delays in the goods yards caused men like Rawlinson, regarding time as money, to find alternative means of getting their raw materials from the Manchester depots to their premises. Here, in the extreme southern section of his beat, Catesby had a dozen men stationed.

He said, "It's largely on account of machines being sent out of the foundries in sections light enough to manhandle. Time was when their kind of equipment was built up in a single unit, needing an eight or ten-horse team to drag them off the sidings. Nowadays most mill-owners can assemble their own machinery, and there is a steady demand for spare parts that are needed within hours unless the whole output is to be halted on account of a defective crank or flywheel. I had the advantage of knowing the trade, and that brandy-faced chap Rawlinson has been a missionary on your behalf, Mr. Swann. I made him one quick delivery and he's told all his cronies for miles around."

Adam was not surprised that Catesby, despite knowledge that Sam was his father-in-law, should nonetheless refer to him as 'that brandy-faced chap', for this was Catesby's way. He was impressed, however, by Rawlinson's apparent eagerness to boost Swann-on-Wheels, and said, "Knowing my father-in-law, I'm persuaded our rates must be well below those of competitors. That old rascal wouldn't patronise us out of sentiment. I'll call and see him when I've finished my business in Hexham and Keswick. You've made a fine start up here, Catesby, and I'd like to thank you. You can go on piece-work rates now if you prefer. If not, I suggest you work on a commission basis."

Catesby, a true Northerner, seemed embarrassed by praise, grunting something to the effect that 'this could be worked out as time went on', but adding offhandedly that he was encouraged by the initial figures. Then, becoming thoughtful, he went on, "Things are changing up here, Mr. Swann. Some mill-owners are finding themselves obliged to co-operate with their hands in a way that would have been impossible a few years ago. There's even talk of an operatives' union among the lads." He glanced shrewdly at Adam under

240

grey brows. "How would you respond to the introduction of that kind of bargaining factor in all the basic trades?"

"I'm hanged if I know," said Adam, lightly, "but it can't concern me, can it? I transport goods, I don't manufacture them."

"You employ men," Catesby said, obstinately. "You must have well over a hundred on your pay-roll at this moment."

"I can't see a scattered gang of waggoners forming a union but if they ever did, and a level-headed chap like you was behind it, I'm sure we could arrive at some mutually satisfactory arrangement."

For the first time since they had met Catesby relaxed his defensive attitude, saying, with emphasis, "Then you can depend on me, Mr. Swann, for I know how to distinguish between a good gaffer and a jumped-up swab. Your kind will always get the best out of a working man and that cuts both ways, although few employers can bring themselves to believe it," and then it was Adam's turn to feel embarrassed.

He travelled north-east, taking the North Western to Leeds, the Leeds and Northern as far as Darlington, and then on through the network of the Newcastle and Carlisle to Hexham, crossing country with which he was unfamiliar. He passed the journey making notes in his daybook, having at last learned the trick of writing legibly in fast-moving trains. It seemed to him, up here among so many inter-related lines, that the prospects of road-haulage were barren, and he was also confirmed in his earlier prejudice that the industrialised belt enclosed by Harrogate, Redcar, Newcastle and Allendale, at the north-eastern tip of the Polygon, could not support an independent service unless he was lucky enough to find another Catesby. This was not the case, however, in the territory marked out as the Border Triangle. Here, apart from the coastal line, and the new Border Counties Company, the land was ripe for exploitation, and when he met the Scots haulier Fraser at Hexham he saw at once that Keate's guess had been accurate, and that Fraser's stock was indeed a bargain, nine medium-sized waggons good for another two years' work, and twenty-three heavy crossbreds, much inferior to his own Clydesdales and Cleveland Bays, but not the broken-down crocks he had expected to find in the stables of a man who was selling up.

"Why are you selling the business?" he asked bluntly, and Fraser said because he had no head for paperwork, and that was what every business demanded of its owner nowadays on account of competition from London-based railways. He was, Adam thought, an open-air man, who had probably enjoyed travelling the roads when it was no more than a matter of moving from town to town at his own pace, but the complexities of the railway age, and the price they had put upon speed, had broken the rhythm of his life and he was ready to work for someone else if he could find a younger man to employ him.

"Would you consider staying on as my area manager?" Adam asked, and the man seemed astonished.

"You're intending to take over the runs as well as the stock? Up here? In border country, that's as foreign to you as London is to me?"

"That's the point," Adam said. "I prefer to employ local men."

Fraser considered. "There'll be no paper-work?"

"Some, but most of it is handled by Headquarters. You could make hauls yourself if you felt inclined."

"Aye, I'd like that fine," Fraser said, thoughtfully, "for snow and rain never bothered me like being stuck in an office. My father was a chapman, a pedlar that is, and my mother another's daughter, so wandering the roads is bred in blood and bone. How much time would I be expected to spend in the yard?"

"That depends on your turnover. I pay two pounds ten shillings a week for a foreman waggoner but later on, if the work merits it, I can get you a clerk. The point is, you've already broken the ground up here but I'm getting your goodwill thrown in for the price of your waggons, teams and stabling. Would you like time to think it over?"

"No, I wouldna'," the man said, "for there's no' so much 'goodwill' as ye call it. Give me the price I'm asking for the stock and I'll stay as manager and find carters who can be trusted to pass an alehouse without haltering."

And so it was settled, and during his crosscountry journey to Keswick Adam reflected that he had been very lucky in a trade he had entered as a raw amateur, for here he was opening his fifth sub-depot, and four were already paying off, two of them handsomely. By next spring he would have waggons and teams in all twelve of the territories, and Swann-on-Wheels would be on the way to becoming a household word, like Pear's Soap and Bryant & May's matches. But then he wondered if he would lose something he valued by overexpansion, reflecting that enjoyment of the past two years had been derived from the opportunities offered of learning at first-hand what happened to a rural society when it took off its smock and populated ten thousand factories and foundries in a single generation. He was deeply interested, and always had been, in people like Keate and Tybalt and Catesby, and this new man, Fraser, not as individuals

242

but as segments of the new society, and this, he supposed, had a bearing on his conception of England, English traditions, English values and England's comparatively new preoccupation with the acquisition of an overseas empire. Throughout the whole of his youth it was this last aspect of national life with which he had been concerned, and against which, he recalled, he had rebelled.

The train of thought led him on to contemplate England and the English in the abstract. The evangelical zeal and rooted urbanism of Keate and Tybalt was only one facet of the race. Cutting a furrow of their own were the men like Catesby, uncompromising in their conception of human dignity, and ready, if necessary, to fight and starve for what they regarded as basic human rights. Then again there were the Blubbs and the Frasers, clinging stubbornly to an England that had begun to wither the day Stephenson laid the first yard of rail along the old Stockton–Darlington line, and there were many other segments that he had taken for granted, the Robertses and the Averys and men of Rawlinson's stamp, who were to be found in their hundreds in Threadneedle Street and on the Manchester Exchange. Thinking of Sam led him to ponder the impact the new iron age had had upon Englishwomen. Most of the men who had made fortunes in a matter of years seemed to have felt obligated to consign their womenfolk to a national seraglio, where they spent their lives whispering, gossiping and parading a succession of French fashions, so that unless one was almost brutally frank with them (as he sometimes felt he had been with Henrietta), they turned themselves into mindless little dolls before they were twenty-five.

His thoughts, thus diverted, dwelt upon Henrietta for the remainder of the journey, wondering how much nervous energy he would have to expend in the years ahead teaching her that marriage was much more than an exchange of one set of shibboleths for another, and that he had no fancy to spawn a family of red-coated martinets of the kind he had seen dancing attendance on dolts like Raglan in the Crimea, or copies of Roberts, with his romantic imperial visions. Surely that part of the English tradition was as dead as Blubb's Tally-Ho coach, and Fraser's three-mile-an-hour package deliveries. It would be more rewarding, he thought, to raise a spread of pretty daughters, and spend one's declining years teaching them to put a proper price on themselves as the consorts of a new generation of husbands, the enriched sons of artisans and mechanics.

243

The Colonel met him at the gate and told him at once that Charlotte was on her deathbed and that he appreciated his act in turning aside to pay what would surely prove a final visit. The old man looked frail himself, Adam thought, and wondered how he would fare up here alone when the prop of his sister's stronger personality had been knocked away. The redoubtable old lady seemed to him smaller and less formidable than he remembered. She could still converse, he found, but in an urgent whisper, that involved a whistle like the approach of a far-off train, and when he took her hand, and told her about her great-niece Stella, he detected a softening of the rigid lines of her face and a momentary gleam in an eye that had silenced so many noisy children when she ran her dame's school and done battle with those who disturbed her brother's peace.

He sat there wondering what he should tell her of an enterprise he knew she thought of as vulgar, and unbecoming, but he need not have bothered. She soon demonstrated that she was more interested in Henrietta than in his concerns, and this he found puzzling, for the old besom had bullied the girl mercilessly when she was on hand. She now atoned, however, saying, in that insistent whisper, "Took a rare fancy to that gel. She's a better wife than you deserve, and she'll prove it before she's done with you. She's got a will of her own and you might have done worse, boy. Have you realised that yet?"

He said, smiling, that he had, and that nobody need remind him Henrietta had a will of her own, for she had talked him into hanging a millstone round his neck in the form of a country estate that he could only visit one day in ten.

"That was the right thing to do," Charlotte said, with a tiny splutter of malice. "It offsets having a husband in trade. It's a pity your child was a girl. Henrietta told me she wanted boys, to carry on the family tradition."

"That was just her way of enlisting you," Adam said, but his aunt wheezed, "She's plenty of time. There's another due, isn't there? I hope she'll be luckier this time." She stopped, rallying her small stock of breath for what emerged as the first direct appeal he could ever recall her making, to him or to anyone else. "Listen, boy, I've done my best for your father all the time you were abroad. Will you do something for me? Will you make me a promise that if that child of hers is a boy you'll have the grace and good sense to let him take up a commission? I don't ask this for myself, or on account of the family but for her. She . . . she wrote to me on the subject."

"She *wrote* to you? Henrietta did?"

The old lady withdrew her hand and opened a gaol of a handbag that stood on the night table, taking out a letter addressed in what Adam recognised as Henrietta's round, babyish hand. "Read it," she ordered.

It occurred to Adam then that it was strange he should have been thinking of this obsession of Henrietta's on the way over here, and the letter, a short and simple one that had obviously cost Henrietta some trouble to compose, touched him when he thought of her sitting at that bureau of hers, with her tongue curling between her lips, as she struggled to put her thoughts on paper and enlist an ally.

"My dearest Aunt Charlotte," she had written, "Adam tells me he is going to visit you and I'm glad because it is time he did and I wish I was with him because I shall never forget how kind you were to me that time he brought me home and I was so much in need of friends. I am expecting again in early June, and I don't have to tell you how glad I am, for you remember I so wanted a family of boys. I love little Stella, of course, and she is going to be pretty, but I did very much want a boy and shall weep if I have another girl in June. Adam is away from home a great deal but he seems to like what he is doing and I do love him very much, Aunt Charlotte, even though I am still sorry he gave over being a soldier like the Colonel and all the other Swanns. However, I do mean to make a soldier out of this one whatever he says and I am sure you approve and so will the Colonel. My best love to you, dear Aunt Charlotte, and to Adam's father, and I hope your bronkitis is gone when the weather gets better. Your loving niece, Henrietta."

He did not say what was in his mind, finding it difficult to tell her that he knew Henrietta far better than she did, and that this appeal was no more than a crafty backdoor approach to achieve what had, indeed, already been achieved, a confrontation on the importance of family tradition. It passed through his mind that here was an unlikely alliance, an old woman, rooted in a tradition that went back across the three centuries, and the vanity of a girl who wrinkled her nose at realities that had been meat and drink to her father and probably a long string of Rawlinsons. But the old lady was now looking at him intently and he said, with a shrug, "Very well, since you both seem so bound to family precedent I'll give him the option, providing he wants it. You'll live another twenty years and be on hand to greet some pimply lad when he struts into the house in his scarlet and gold. There'll be no question of buying him a commission by then. He'll have to show some aptitude for soldiering," and she said, "Poof! As if a Swann would lack it!" and then dropped off to sleep, so that he felt some small satisfaction in bringing her a composure she had probably lacked since the arrival of that extremely artful letter.

He said, when the Colonel and he were at supper, "Don't think of staying up here alone if she goes, sir. Henrietta would like you to make your home with us and I should like it too. There's room enough in all conscience, and you'll find our part of Kent very much to your taste. Henrietta rides now and it would be pleasant to think of you squiring her round the countryside when I'm away."

The old man seemed attracted by the proposal, for he cleared his throat, saying, "She really does remind me of your mother, boy," and his glance shifted to the portrait of the little French woman over the fireplace. He went on, "Something almost piratical about the way we Swanns do our courting. I came across your mother in a pastry-cook's on what I thought of, until then, as enemy soil. Never had second thoughts about her nor her about me. Then you have to scoop a wife from some Godforsaken moor, and apart from the colour of her eyes they're as alike as two peas. It doesn't end there, either. There was that tale of your great-grandfather, who served under that damned scoundrel Cumberland. He married the orphan of one of the MacDonalds who had fought at Culloden. Had to resign his commission on that account I'm told, for he could hardly stand by while The Butcher hunted his wife's kin up and down the glens. Maybe our true rôle is pacification through marriage."

"Henrietta would enjoy that story about great-grandfather," said Adam. "It has the correct romantic touch and doesn't necessarily have to be true. Will you pack up and come south if you have to?"

"Aye," said the old man, "gladly. You two and your children are all I've got now."

*　　*　　*

He rode post to Windermere and travelled down to the Rochdale area where he sent his card along to the gaunt new mill, already aiming one more plume of smoke at the blameless sky. A message was brought to him within the hour and he walked up the hill to an off-loading siding where Sam awaited him in one of the bays, square jaw set, legs planted astride, as though poised to repulse any new attempt

upon his dignity as a local overlord. In spite of his stance Adam
noticed he had mellowed, and that his aggressive attitude was a pose.
There was an aura of conciliation about him and a flabbiness that
had not been there when he had come storming into the house to reclaim his daughter two and a half years before.

They shook hands and he conducted Adam into an office under a
squeaking hoist that continued its laborious work of transferring
bales from handtruck to platform all the time they were below. He
was friendly enough, however, and called for brandy to drink the
health of his granddaughter, of whose existence, Adam soon discovered, he was aware. He also seemed to have kept silent watch on
their movements over the period.

"Lass is settling to t'collar, I hope," he said, as though Henrietta
had been a filly of dubious reputation, and Adam said she was well
on the way to becoming the fashion-setter in the district, and was
costing him, one way and another, more than he cared to admit.

"Nay, tha'll have to put a stop to that, lad," Sam said, seriously,
"and it can be done at her age. Wi' strap if necessary. But then, I'm
a fair one to brag, for you'll ha' heard I were fool enow to marry
again?"

"No," said Adam, "I hadn't, and I'm sure it will be news to Henrietta. Congratulations, from both of us."

"Tha' can spare me that," Sam said, glumly, "for I thowt as I
knew women but discovered I didn't, no more'n a bit of a lad. I picked
a fair tartar second time round. Henrietta's mother was stiffnecked
but our Hilda, she's ahead of her by a mile or more. Mind, she's a
gradely lass, and a comfort to a man night times at my time o' life,
but there's no putting on her. We had our picture took by a chap
who set up his studio hereabouts," and he opened a drawer in his
desk and extracted, not without pride, a photograph of man and wife,
set in a gilded, oval mount with the obligatory palm-tree growing
beside the table at which Sam was sitting.

The new Mrs. Rawlinson looked about thirty and well able to
take care of herself. She had abundant hair, a robust, tightly-cor-
setted figure, and a proprietary air, indicated by the presence of one
muscular arm resting possessively on Sam's shoulder, as though holding him there until the police arrived, "Ah kept this one by if you
care to take it, and show it t'lass," he said and then, with a snort,
"Fee, lad, there's no dam' sense in father and daughter going to their
graves wi'out a friendly nod to one another. I'll own I were wrong
about you, for I took you for a popinjay, wi' nowt about him but

swank and a way wi' the lasses. I've kept my eye on that venture o' yours and it's got around you give value for money. Are you ready to let bygones be bygones, and handle my stuff?"

"I'll haul anyone's goods who pays on the nail," Adam said, and the reply must have pleased Sam for he smacked his thigh and exclaimed, "That's how I'd like to hear a son o' mine talk! I'm reet glad now Henrietta gave yon Goldthorpe the go-by. When I were in deep water, after t'mill were burned down, I soon found the difference between friends and vampires. Goldthorpe had the gall to offer me a loan at nine per cent. Think on it! Nine per cent! Come to finish I got what I needed at half the rate, and I'm in a fair way to setting up again, as you can see from where you sit, lad."

Adam acknowledged this but queried Rawlinson's motives in offering him a road haulage contract. "You have the rail here," he said, "and while we can make cheaper and quicker hauls to the north the bulk of your exports must go direct to Liverpool, by freight train."

"Ah'm not concerned about what goes out," said Sam, gloomily, "it's t'raw material Ah'm bothered about. You'll have heard about the carry-on in the plantations no doubt?"

"I've heard there might be war between the states."

"*Might?* Nay, lad, it's not just a bit of a shindig, that'll sort itself out in a week or two. Six months from now no more than a trickle o' cotton will come out of the Carolinas and Georgia, so how in hell are we to keep wheels turning in the Belt?"

For the first time since he had read of the dispute between the states Adam gave the matter serious thought. "If you knew it was coming," he asked, "why didn't you buy in bulk, the moment Lincoln was elected President?" but Sam said, blankly, "Nay, do you still think I'm that much of a fool, lad? I *have* bought, but not from the Liverpool men. They're alive to it down there, and the scramble for bales began the moment word came of Carolina's secession. I bought in bulk, and chartered ships to bring it in and offload at Whitehaven. Why Whitehaven? Because if it came in to Liverpool it would start a run, and how could I trust the shipowners not to sell to others, and blackmail me into paying three times the wholesale? Nay, I were two jumps ahead of all of 'em. There's two cargoes up there awaiting my collection at this moment, and your waggons can hump 'em in any time you've a mind to, subject to a fair rate per ton, mind. That's what you and I should settle before we part company. No damn sense at all in letting money pass out of the family."

"Won't the war with the North compel the planters to export all they can pick?"

"Aye, they'll try, no doubt, but there's talk now of a blockade, and if that happens all Lancashire is for the bankruptcy court, lad."

"Given those two shipments, how long could you hold out?"

"A year, or more with what I've hoarded," Sam said, so they agreed the rates there and then, with the minimum of bargaining. Sam urged him to come home to dinner and try Hilda Rawlinson's cooking, but Adam had wasted enough time already and was impatient to acquaint Catesby with the details of the deal and the Border Triangle situation, and then return to London to get things moving. Sam saw him as far as the station, and even went so far as to give him a paternal pat on the shoulder when the branch line train slid into the platform. He said, as they shook hands, "Will you gammon Henrietta into calling a truce, and sending me a picture of the little lass?" and Adam said he would do his best and mentioned that Henrietta expected her second child within a few months. The news delighted Rawlinson, who said, pursing his thick lips, "Eee, that's the style, lad! Put 'em to bed and give 'em plenty to think on!"

He watched the solid figure dwindle as the train gathered speed, thinking, 'The old man might be a coarse brute, but he's human somehow, and all of a piece with the landscape.'

3

The travelling diary was still in use but its function as a record had been superseded by a much fatter book, a book almost as thick as a Bible, with brown leather covers and a thousand ruled sheets.

Into this book went not only facts and figures relevant to the 1860–61 expansion, but a distillation of all Adam Swann's thoughts concerning the eight unexploited territories, together with a record of the teams he maintained, the men he signed on, and the nature of goods hauled. He did not make entries concerning income and expenditure. That was Tybalt's province and the clerk guarded it jealously. Adam's book was not a ledger in that sense. It was more of a private Domesday Book, used for the purpose of clarifying ideas before he was ready to share them with anyone, even his sleeping partner, Avery.

The book still exists, hundreds of pages covered with Swann's neat, angular handwriting, and one very early entry, dated June 1st, 1861, relates to his first inroad into Tom Tiddler's Ground. It is a laconic entry and reads, '*June 1. House removal to Ventnor, I. of W. Blubb's haul as far as Lymington, then on by collier to Yarmouth. Blubb's teams turned back. Four horses hired the far side.*'

The entry signified both an extension of territory and a deviation in the established pattern of his business up to that date. For this was the first house removal Swann-on-Wheels had undertaken, and concerned the transfer of the chattels of a naval captain who, on retiring, had elected to leave the Medway area for a clifftop home where he could enjoy an uninterrupted view of Channel shipping.

Tybalt's quotation was cut to the bone, not only because the old seaman was tightfisted, and had rejected estimates submitted by other carriers, but because Adam suddenly came to realise that there might be money in house-removals, more commonplace now than even ten years before. Twenty years ago it was rare for a man to move out of the county where he was rooted, but now people were more restless, as if rail travel had given them a taste for migrating and they were reluctant to settle anywhere until they were too old to be bothered.

In terms of time and cash the firm lost money on the removal, but it gave Adam a chance to prospect the Isle of Wight and ended in the establishment of a base at Newport, equipped with four one-horse vans and an Islander, a young mail-driver called Dockett, in charge of the four men established there. Because, so far, nothing heavier than pinnaces were based there, and because the island seemed, more or less, to be self-supporting, the branch specialised in house removals from the outset. By the end of the year it was showing a profit.

The incident remained fixed in Adam's mind for another reason. The following day, 2nd June, Henrietta gave birth to his son Alexander, and although she produced a boy weighing well over eight pounds she was spared a repetition of the ordeal that had accompanied Stella's arrival, or so she assured him when he went in to congratulate her after the doctor had given his reluctant assent.

He never recalled seeing her more cock-a-hoop but the child made a different impression on him. His daughter, he remembered, had looked alert and wise even at this stage, but the boy, with his square face, uncomprehending eyes, and utter indifference to everything but his mother's breast, seemed to his father a miniature parody of all the stolid, whisky-swilling regulars Adam had met in barrack messes from Deal to Allahabad. He looked also as though he would never open his mouth except to eat, drink or utter a platitude, would execute every order he received to the letter, no matter how stupid or out-of-date it was, and would never, under any circumstances whatever, show a spark of initiative. 'A rare plodder if ever I saw one' thought Adam but said, dutifully, "Well, my dear, it looks as if you've got your soldier," and Henrietta, unconscious of irony, cooed, "Oh, but he's beautiful, beautiful! And he's going to be as strong as a bull and as bold as a lion."

They chatted awhile about the impending arrival of the Colonel, Aunt Charlotte having died a month ago, but she was not really interested in anyone but the child at her breast and soon he excused himself, looking in the nursery where Ellen Michelmore was preparing Stella for her morning outing. He said, for something to say, "Mrs. Swann seems to have got through this last business fairly comfortably," but Ellen replied, tartly, "It's never that comfortable, sir. If men had the babies I wager you'd hear them roar from here to Sevenoaks."

Because he wanted to be on hand to settle the Colonel into his quarters Adam had stayed at home and for a moment thought of taking Stella a ride on his saddle bow, but then reflected that she was still too young for this kind of excursion, and he would have to wait upon the pleasure for a spell. A cautious, exploratory relationship was already developing between father and daughter, and whenever he was about the house he was conscious of the child watching him with her serious blue eyes. She was, he decided, an extraordinarily attractive child, with a curiously adult air of deliberation about everything she did, and a developing ear for words that she sometimes seemed to be rehearsing before translating to sound. He said, squatting on his hams, "Has Ellen told you you've got a brother?", and suddenly, for the first time, the child smiled, holding out her arms to him so that he said, eagerly, "I'll take her. We'll walk up to the crest and back," and he swung Stella out of her pen, carrying her down the broad staircase and into the sunshine that was flooding the face of the old house.

It was full summer out here, with the woods humming with sound, and the smell of parched grass and wildflowers coming from the thickets. The gardener and his boy were at work on some delphinium beds in the lawn but Adam had never cared for cultivated flowers and said, "Come, I'll show you some real flowers," and hoisting her on his shoulder took the path through the rhododendrons and up to the

251

spot where he had stood overlooking the house the day he had decided to lease it.

He had, if he was frank, no regrets about that decision. Henrietta, without knowing it, must have been acting in all their interests, for it was surely a wonderful place to spend the eternity of childhood and would encourage in the least imaginative a sense of belonging in a community that was safe and rooted. Where the timber fell away, and the drop to the stableyard was steep, all manner of plants had seeded themselves among the moss and bracken. On a stretch of stone wall built, he supposed, by the original Conyer to guard against a landslide, he saw herb robert, toadflax, wandering trumpets of convolvulus, bright red campion, stitchwort, the tall dragonfly spires of rosebay willowherb, and dozens of other wildflowers. Nearer to hand stood a single foxglove as tall as himself and sporting a hundred mottled bells. He saw the child's eyes stray to the flower and would have picked it but remembering it was poisonous, said, very articulately, "It's a foxglove, my love. Papa's favourite wild-flower. *Fox—glove!*", and Stella arranged her lips and echoed, with remarkable clarity, *"Fox—glove!"* It was the first identifiable word he had heard her speak and it seemed to him a miracle, performed for his benefit. He set her down with her back to the wall, and finding that she could stand fairly steadily retreated a few yards into the wood, saying, "Walk, Stella. Walk to Papa!" The child braced herself, hands thrust back against the wall and then, pushing herself off, stumbled towards him, her fat little legs working like pistons. She reached him without a stumble and he said, triumphantly, "Splendid! Absolutely splendid! You've walked and you've talked, all in five minutes!", and swung her up to his shoulder again, thinking as he did so, 'Henrietta can have her boys, any amount of them. I'll settle for this one, for she's really mine' and with a light heart he went down the winding path to the forecourt where old Michelmore, who had swapped the profession of miller for that of groom and coach-man, was awaiting him, holding the mare that had carried him the length of England and he had never disposed of, for somehow she had a place in the complicated pattern of his life over the last three years.

It was late August when he opened up the Crescents territory, finding a Yorkshireman named Wadsworth to supervise the east coast segments, based on Whitby, Newark, Spalding and Norwich, with a control centre at Boston, where they leased a yard within sight of the Stump.

It was a huge slice of territory to manage but Wadsworth, who had driven locomotives until he was involved in an accident that had left him lame, was familiar with every mile of it, and Adam thought himself fortunate to engage a man as intelligent and dependable. Wadsworth was a widower, and the father of a boy in his early twenties who was serving as a fireman on the Eastern Counties. He also had a daughter who kept house for him and was capable, during her father's absences, of taking his place in the Boston yard, exercising an amiable despotism over the waggoners, stablemen and, on occasion, customers, who were not averse to a little sharp practice, for up here were some of the most penny-pinching hagglers in the country, men who would spend half-an-hour debating the difference between threepence and fourpence on the transport of a bag of hops.

He soon learned to trust Wadsworth and respect his judgement but he never succeeded in making a friend of him, as he did his brisk, buxom daughter, Edith. With his penchant for fanciful nicknames, he always thought of Edith as Boadicea, having first encountered her driving a two-horse frigate, her red woollen skirt tucked up above her knees, her weight thrown back on the reins as she scolded the team. She looked, he thought, like one of the Iceni riding out to do battle with the Romans.

There was a great deal to do up here and he spent the tail-end of the summer coming and going, assessing what the territory required in terms of men, waggons, teams and premises. The first hauls were almost wholly agricultural, sugar beet, potatoes, Norwich turkeys, great round cheeses and baskets of fish out of Hull, but later Wadsworth secured two iron ore contracts in and out of Middlesbrough. Within three months they were under a full spread of canvas, so that the Crescents began to overhaul the Polygon where, as Rawlinson had predicted, a crippling blight had set in following the tightening of the Federal blockade of the cotton states.

More and more during these busy weeks he felt himself drawn to

Edith Wadsworth, partly by reason of her abundant commonsense and close involvement in his concerns but also, in a way that disturbed him slightly, by the positive energy reposing in her strong, supple body, so that he caught himself thinking of her as a woman capable of bringing him something more than loyal and imaginative service in a stableyard. And this was odd, he decided, for he now thought of himself as a man of settled habits of mind and body, and he wondered if the strong impression she made on him could be traced to the way she looked at him and addressed him, rather than to his appraisal of her trim figure and cheerful good looks. She had a way of assessing him with a cool, steady gaze, as though she too was seeing him as a person outside his function as her father's employer, and sometimes, feeling defensive on this account, he would challenge her but with laughter in his voice. He said to her once, "You've got more initiative than half the men I employ. Have you ever wished you'd been born a man?", and she replied, with a candour he had learned to expect from her, "Do I look like one to you, Mr. Swann?"

"No," he said, laughing, "I can't say that you do, but it puzzles me why some likely young chap hasn't snapped you up long ago. How old are you?"

"That's a saucy question to put to a girl," she said, with an answering smile. "You wouldn't have asked it of one of those fragile ninnies, who wouldn't appear in public unless she was fenced in by hoops and a dozen petticoats, and had taken the shine off her nose. However, I'm used to it, for the lads don't think of me as a woman, maybe because I'll not stand for their nonsense. I'm twenty-four. Well on the way to the shelf."

"Don't believe it. Men up here don't marry the ninnies, although they enjoy flirting with them. I'll call in one day, and find you fussing over your trousseau like any other girl. It won't please me, for I'm hanged if I know where I should find a deputy manager."

"Ah," she said, gaily, "that's my cross. No one can ever replace me but everyone takes me for granted." Then, out of the corner of her eye, she saw a carter dragging a crate from a tailboard and bawled, in a voice that carried as far as the Stump, "Careful, you fool! That's soft fruit you're handling, not gravel!"

She skipped across the yard and laid hold of one end of the heavy crate, bracing one clogged foot against the wheel-rims so that the breeze, lifting her skirt, offered him a glimpse of sturdy thighs and then, as she shifted her weight forward, of a chubby behind under a pair of short cotton drawers. He chuckled, reflecting that if the spread of the territory north and south of Boston led to her father's frequent absences, he had no need to worry over a lack of supervision here.

They managed to get The Bonus area (based on Harwich, and running inland from Yarmouth and Southend as far as Chesterford) off to a slow start by late autumn, but this was all that could be achieved until spring, for the Southern Square, comprising Hampshire, Wiltshire and part of Dorset and Gloucestershire, was still to be opened up, as were the two smaller areas marked on the master map as The Pickings, one hinged on Worcester, the other enclosed by Sheffield, Derby and Buxton.

Of the twelve territories, however, he now had nine well established and of these three were showing a good profit, and four others were producing promising returns. Only two, the Western Wedge and the Mountain Square, were disappointing, for there was strong local competition in Devon and Cornwall among farmers too conservative to entrust their produce to a stranger, whereas in Wales the roads were atrocious and played havoc with Lovell's time-schedules.

As autumn ended, the third autumn since he had made his first haul into the London suburbs, he decided to spend a few days in each of these territories, discussing with Ratcliffe and Lovell, the area managers, what could be done to improve the turnover, but it was not to be, for suddenly trouble flared up in the Polygon and he found himself faced with a problem no one could have foreseen when he approved Catesby's sally into the cotton belt.

*　　*　　*

It began with a letter from a firm called Higginbottom, big spinners owning a string of mills not far from Seddon Moss. One of the directors wrote informing him that his manager in the district had refused to handle goods north of the Manchester-Liverpool line, even though a verbal agreement had been arrived at and the first of the deliveries made. Thinking there must be some misunderstanding Adam telegraphed Catesby at the Salford depot and the manager replied the same day. The telegram read: '*Will you wait for a report or come north?*', a message that Adam found so unsatisfactory that he decided to postpone his trip to the west and go north at once.

A sullen, uncommunicative Catesby met him at London Road and Adam could get very little out of him until he agreed to eat lunch at a restaurant Catesby patronised in the Shambles, one of the few remaining quarters of the old Manchester that had resisted the march of King Cotton. When they were seated over their beefsteaks he could

255

contain himself no longer and said, flourishing Higginbottom's letter, "Look here, Catesby, all I want from you is whether or not Higginbottom's letter is true? What's behind this confounded mystery?"

"You could say no more than a principle, Mr. Swann. I asked you to come because I backed you to uphold it." Catesby glanced at the letter and handed it back. "It's quite true. I did break the contract, if you can call a verbal agreement a contract. I refused to handle their bales, just as they say."

"Why! Do you suspect them of short-changing us?"

"Nay," Catesby said, with a grin, "nowt like that, but those bales they want us to haul came in by a Confederate blockade-runner. Every cent they make on them in a city starved of cotton helps those bloody plantation-owners maintain slavery. Aye, and kill men trying to stop it."

"You mean it's that kind of principle? A political principle?"

"Not political, Mr. Swann. Human, for it concerns every man, black, white or yellow, who earns bread by the sweat of his brow. I take it you don't approve of slavery as an institution? Well, no more do I, nor any one of the operatives up here, not even those with empty bellies. What's more they've proved it. I'd like you to meet someone who's in the thick o' this fight. That's another reason I got you up here."

"Wait a minute," said Adam. "Before we get involved with a third party, tell me this. If we don't haul those bales someone else will, is that so?"

"To be sure they will," said Catesby, "but what's that to do wi' it? We make a stand alongside others who have refused to touch them, never mind the greedy bastards calling themselves Christians, who can square their consciences by the road you just pointed. There's plenty paying lip service to the North, who are telling each other t'bloody bales might as well be used now they're in the country."

"I'm not sure that isn't a sane point of view," Adam said but Catesby suddenly looked as if he was having some difficulty keeping his temper and when he spoke his voice had the bitterness Adam had noticed on the first occasion they met. He said, with an effort, "Listen here, Mr. Swann. I told you when you signed me on that I knew the folk up here. Well, I thowt I did, but in a way I were wrong, for while it's as true now as it was years ago that Lancashire has its share o' scabs ready to work men like the blacks on those plantations, it's also true that a majority of folk are ready to put principle

256

before the next meal and the roof over their heads! If it wasn't so there wouldn't be folk like Johnny Biglow, yonder."

He pointed to a balding man sitting at a table across the aisle and as he did the man half-rose and Adam realised that he had been awaiting the summons. Catesby, however, motioned him to stay where he was.

"You ever set foot in the States, Mr. Swann?" and when Adam shook his head, "Well, I did, soon after I come out of gaol that time. I worked a schooner in and out of Savannah and New Orleans, and I watched slave auctions on the levees. I saw a man sold upriver from his wife, and the wife parted from children. It's not pretty, Mr. Swann. You ever hear what Lincoln said on the subject?"

"No."

"He said the same thing as I'm saying now—'If I ever get a chance to hit that, then by God I'll hit it hard'!"

"Perhaps, but isn't the war being fought to preserve the Union? The North hasn't freed the slaves yet."

"They'll get round to it, and if it falls to me to do what I can to help then I'll do it, and to hell wi' your bloody wages if need be."

He made a sign to the bald man who shambled over, moving like a wrestler in the ring, knees bent and hands hanging loose. He seated himself beside Catesby and the latter said, "This is my gaffer, Johnny. Him I were telling you about. He's had a belly-aching letter from that scab Higginbottom."

There was nothing apologetic about the way Biglow eyed Adam, looking him over as he might an opponent in the ring. He said nothing, however, except a long, dubious "Ahhh", and then grinned, showing a row of broken teeth. Catesby said, "Johnny and I worked at t'same loom as nippers. He were in clink wi' me too, time o' the riots. But now he's on a different tack and legal as near as dammit. He's organiser for six thousand hands in mills along the Manchester–Liverpool line, and it were him who started t'collection."

"What collection?"

"The money we've sent over. Upwards of two thousand, and more coming."

"You've collected two thousand pounds for the North?"

"It's gone to Washington for the wounded. There's a woman there name o' Barton, who tags on to the Federal troops with ambulances."

"Who subscribed it?" Adam asked, and Biglow said, "Who but the Lancashire field-hands, Mr. Swann? And most of 'em laid off at that."

257

"You collected two thousand pounds from among unemployed cotton operatives?"

"Why not? It's their cause in t'long run. We had a rally in St. Peter's Square, and went round with the hat. But that's nobbut the start of it. We got a headquarters now and full-time collectors."

"Willard and Slade," Catesby added, naming two of the Polygon's waggoners. "And there's another thing I'd best mention, since you've been civil enough to listen. Headquarters for the Washington Ambulance Fund is your yard."

The two men waited for him to absorb this and when he did, without comment, they looked relieved. He said, at length, "You're an impudent devil, Catesby, and you take a hell of a lot of liberties, but I don't see why I should subscribe since you're using my premises rent free, and have already cost me a contract. What do you expect me to to do about Higginbottom? Send him a copy of *Uncle Tom's Cabin*?"

"You might do worse," Biglow said, and then, to Catesby, "Heard from your lad, Jack?"

"Aye," said Catesby, "a week since. He's in a unit they're forming of volunteers from overseas, Germans mostly, he tells me."

"Your son is out there fighting?"

"He's done none so far, and wasn't welcomed as he reckoned on. However, after the whipping the North got at Bull Run, they weren't so particular, so I daresay he'll see his share before it's over."

It seemed strange that one of his own overseers had to bring him up to date on a war being fought three thousand miles away, and to hear someone talk of Bull Run as though it had been Balaclava. He had read brief reports of the early fighting but, until that moment, it had not impinged on his mind as a war in which Englishmen would be likely to take sides, especially those who looked to cotton for a livelihood. But now that he did think about it it seemed logical, and certainly characteristic of Catesby to identify himself with what was happening out there; characteristic and somehow touching. He said, presently, "If there's no work in the area move your teams north," and to Biglow, "I'll take it up with Higginbottom, and since the Salford yard is likely to be empty during the cotton famine you might as well use it." He took out a sovereign and laid it on the table.

"That's not a subscription, Catesby. It's a reminder to keep me informed about everything that goes on up here. And in the States too if you get further word from your boy. I'm still professionally interested in wars. From a safe distance, that is."

258

He nodded to Biglow and went out into the street but Catesby did not follow him. He was learning about Swann.

* * *

There was an hour to wait for a train so he retraced his steps down the station approach and poked about until he found a post office, buying one of the new, franked letter-cards, and taking it across to the rest beside the post-box. With the watery ink and half-crossed nib supplied he wrote, 'To Messrs. Higginbottom, Dawley Mills, Nr. Warrington. Sirs, Reference your letter, dated 3rd November, alleging breach of contract. My manager informs me the arrangement was verbal, and I am satisfied that this was the case. You may therefore regard it as cancelled but thank you for drawing the matter to my attention. Faithfully, Adam Swann. Man. Dir. Swann-on-Wheels Carrier Service.'

He blotted it, dropped it in the box, and went up the hill to the station entrance. In a way, it was as final a committal as turning his back on India.

5

It was the Catesby–Higginbottom incident that was instrumental in broadening his mind. It caused him to take an outward as well as his habitual inward look at men and their affairs.

Until then the narrowness of his horizons as soldier and mercenary, and later, the deep concentration demanded by the business, had encouraged insularity, perhaps a certain amount of intolerance with things that did not have much relevance to him, or to England. Now, with the example of starving cotton operatives in the forefront of his mind, he began to take a lively interest in all foreign news items, particularly in the fratricidal war being waged in Virginia and the Mississippi Valley. He watched, with some concern, the international crisis that followed the removal by a Federal warship of the Southern emissaries from the fancied security of the British vessel Trent that seemed, at one time, likely to bring Britain into the war on the side of the Confederates. When it became known that the Prince Consort had risen from his sick-bed to persuade Palmerston to tone down his reply, and enable the North to withdraw without too much loss of face, his opinion of the tall, gloomy German soared, so that he kept an eye on the Windsor bulletins concerning Albert's illness.

The alliance between the young Coburger and his pop-eyed, trivial wife, had always interested Adam. He was far from being a blind worshipper of royalty, and had enjoyed the spate of bar-room stories of the Queen's frantic dependence on her husband, reflecting that they might well be true. After all, Victoria was a Hanoverian, and her ancestors had been a sensual tribe, but he thought the royal relationship must be based on something more substantial than that, for he was old enough to have heard stories of the Queen's irresponsibility and political naïveté before Albert took her in hand. He remembered the change in climate concerning the Prince once his genuine enthusiasm for the sciences had inspired the Great Exhibition, providing the country with such an impressive advertisement. Now it was being said that the Consort was working himself into the grave, that his Teutonic obsession with thoroughness, and his insistence on personal involvement in State affairs, kept him at his desk from first light until dusk, and also that he was having parental trouble with the Prince of Wales, said to take after his disreputable great-uncles.

It was probably Prince Albert's deliberate and much-publicised identification with the new machine age that stimulated Adam's interest in him, setting him apart from the Court, and from the hardcase professionals, like Palmerston and Lord John Russell. Almost alone among their generation, or so it seemed to Adam, he and Albert were utterly impatient with past traditions and present conceits, each seeking a way to establish a working partnership between master and man, and the means of increasing the nation's lead in technology and social reform, that would surely succeed the doctrine of *laissez-faire*, so dear to men like Palmerston. For *laissez-faire*, as Adam saw it, and as he believed the German saw it, properly belonged in the last century, or the century before that. There was surely something more to life than making and investing money, and using brute force and chicanery to secure new overseas markets. Identification with a great industrial democracy like modern Britain should offer an experience to be shared on equal terms by intelligent adventurers like Avery, sober, earnest men like Keate and Tybalt, the harassed and dispossessed, like Blubb and the carrier Fraser, and even incipient revolutionaries like Catesby and his friend Johnny Biglow. The lead, he supposed, could only come from the top, from someone like Prince Albert of Saxe-Coburg and, at a lower level, from men like himself.

It was thoughts such as these that exercised his mind one frosty night in mid-December of that year as he sat late in his eyrie, looking down on the necklace of lights marking the broad curve of the Thames.

Below him the yard was still and empty, save where the duty stable-man and watchman pottered among the sprawl of sheds. Hours ago Keate, Tybalt and all their minions had departed, wishing him good night, but before he left Tybalt had laid before him a breakdown of their progress up to the end of November, 1861, comprising the outlay and expenditure involved in three years' trading and expansion.

It was compiled in the form of a graph, climbing slowly upward to the point of the July breakout, dipping as he had invested in more teams, drivers and premises, and then rising again to within an inch of the edge of the paper where it levelled off, before showing a final dip that represented his latest ventures in the Border Triangle and Tom Tiddler's Ground.

He would have been hard to please if the graph, and the figures it represented, had not induced a glow of satisfaction. Despite a heavy financial outlay, and a weekly wage and fodder bill topping three hundred pounds, he was making money fast, particularly in the older established areas, like the London suburbs and the Kentish Triangle, and it occurred to him that he had been extremely fortunate in his choice of executives. Keate and Tybalt were now as deeply involved in the success of the venture as he was himself, and between them they had enlisted the personal loyalty of a majority of waggoners and vanboys, particularly those in the latter group Keate had gathered in from the banks of the Thames. In the provinces he could depend utterly upon Catesby, Fraser in the Border Triangle, and Wadsworth and his daughter, Edith, in the Crescents.

Looking at the list of bases and personnel his eye paused on the name 'Wadsworth' and he thought again of the lasting impression the girl had made on him. He had met many young women during his jaunts about the country but none remained in his mind as a personality like Edith Wadsworth, with her buxom good looks, nut-brown hair, and gay self-confidence or, for want of a better word, thrust, and now that he had decided to award Christmas bonuses it seemed just that he should include her, as though she had been a base manager in fact as well as fancy.

The list was long and likely to prove expensive but he did not begrudge the demands it would make upon his bank account. Keate and Tybalt were earmarked for ten pounds, as were Wadsworth and

Catesby. Below them, underwritten for eight pounds, came Blubb, at Maidstone, Ratcliffe, still waging an uphill fight in the far west, the Welshman, Bryn Lovell, at Abergavenny, and Fraser in the far north. The newcomers, yet to prove their worth, were represented by Vicary, manager in The Bonus, and Dockett, in Tom Tiddler's Ground, who were to receive five pounds apiece.

There remained Edith and he was by no means sure how to express his appreciation of her unpaid services as deputy when Wadsworth's work took him out of the Boston area. A gift of money might be misconstrued, but a trinket, or a gown accompanied by a letter of acknowledgement would be appreciated. He exchanged pencil for pen, took a sheet of paper embossed with the Swann device, and wrote, 'Dear Miss Wadsworth; I am enclosing a draft for ten pounds in respect of your father who may or may not be on hand. Give it to him with my compliments, and thanks for all his work in establishing us in such a vast stretch of territory. In due course, as I have told him already, I will pursue the original plan to split the area into three—north, central and south, and whilst he will retain overall authority, I hope to engage two sub-managers, leaving him based on Boston as now. In the meantime, aware of the very real contribution you personally have made in the area, I am sending you a Christmas gift under separate cover, to arrive within the next two or three days. My warmest regards to you for the festive season and the new year. I remain, very sincerely, Adam Swann.'

He read the letter through and it seemed too formal to harmonise with their relationship, so he added a postscript: 'I expect to be in Boston in late January or early February, and look forward very much to seeing you again. I don't feel obliged (in view of what I observed on the last visit) to ask you to keep the carters up to their work and safeguard our reputation for undamaged deliveries!'

He made out the other drafts, stamped the envelopes and then, looking at the clock, noted it was coming up to eleven. Shrugging himself into his topcoat and muffler he extinguished the lamp and descended the spiral staircase to the yard gates.

When he remained overnight in London he used a hotel in Norfolk Street, and on occasions like this, when the night was free of fog, he would compensate for his hours spent at the desk by walking the distance across London Bridge, down Cannon Street to Ludgate Circus, into Fleet Street and on past the Law Courts to the Strand. Tonight, because the frosty air invigorated him, he took pleasure in the walk and arriving at the junction of Norfolk Street decided to extend it, moving on down the Strand and past Charing Cross into the Mall.

As the moon rose its pale light subdued the yellow glow of the gas lamps, set at regular intervals along the thoroughfare. Traffic was very light, a few roysterers driving to or from the stews in Covent Garden, handbarrows and a dray or two, making overnight deliveries to restaurants and hotels, and every few paces a beggar or a perfumed drab, wan and hesitant in the guttering lamplight. Two or three women accosted him halfheartedly but he moved on, minding them no more than the grind of traffic, or the acrid whiff of horse manure awaiting collection by the scavengers.

Once in the Mall, with the spectacular façade of Carlton House on his right and St. James's Park, still under frost, to his left, he went on down towards the Palace, intending to make his way back to his hotel via Victoria, but as he approached the railings of the Palace a smart, gaily-painted equipage dashed out of the double gates and the elegance of the coachman told him that it was not one of the ordinary mail vans, for whom everyone else was expected to make way, but one of the vehicles from the royal mews. He was watching it disappear, wondering a little at its reckless speed, when he saw an officer of the Grenadier Guards making his rounds of the sentries, and his professional eye registered something unusual about the man's uniform so that he looked at him carefully, noting the crepe band tied above the elbow of the right arm.

The significance of this was not immediately apparent, not even when the lieutenant stopped outside a sentry box and the sentry slapped the butt of his weapon, the sound echoing in the frosty air. Then a police constable confronted him, a friendly, full-bearded officer who half-hesitated, as though he was finding his night patrol tedious and sought contact with another night-prowler. He said, in a respectful tone prompted by the quality of Adam's braided topcoat and calf-length boots, "Very sad news, sir. Her Majesty is going to be might put out over this," and Adam said, with the eagerness accorded any sensational news-item, however shocking, "The Prince Consort? Is he dead?" and the man nodded, gravely and deliberately, as though it was his duty to put the worst possible face on such a national calamity.

"You saw the mail dashing off to catch the boat train? I thought there might be a special edition on sale but it's too late, I imagine. The papers will make hay out of it in the morning, I wouldn't wonder. Did you ever see His Royal Highness, sir?"

"No," Adam said, "I never did," and at once the man expanded, saying proudly, "I did, often enough. I was a stone's-throw from here, as a youngster, of course, when that lunatic took a pot shot at 'em. And now he's gone, and him only forty-two." He leaned towards Adam conspiratorially. "Typhoid, they say, and it don't say much for the doctors, does it? If they can't cure *him* how would the rest of us fare, I wonder?"

The man was not unsympathetic but a generous part of him was already responding to the enormity of the occasion and Adam supposed, by the time the winter's sun rose over the city, that this would be true of millions of Englishmen. There would be an orgy of mourning, of crêpe hangings, with black-bordered newspapers, flags at half-mast, and pulpit eulogies without number. But he remembered a time when these same Londoners had begrudged Albert his Parliamentary grant for, although the Queen's husband, he was yet a foreigner, with foreign notions about how to conduct himself. They had even sneered at his Hyde Park exhibition until it had proved such a thumping success, and it was only dogged persistence that had won their respect, although never their affection. He said, suddenly, "What did *you* make of him, constable?" and the officer, stroking his beard, said, "Oh, he wasn't at all a bad sort for a foreigner. And Queen Vic must have liked him, for they've a rare tribe of children." It was, Adam supposed, as kindly an epitaph as a foreigner could look for this side of the Channel.

He said good night to the policeman and crossed the gardens towards the Horse Guards. With him, consciously assembled, went a hotchpotch of history, for he remembered that the amiable, whoring Charles the Second had walked these same paths with his spaniels, and that, within a couple of hundred yards, was the spot where his father's head had been hacked off by a masked butcher's assistant. The place reeked of history. From close by, Charles' brother James, had fled his capital throwing the Great Seal into the Thames, to be recovered by a waterman, and then, as the next century wore on, a workable compromise between king, grandees, country squires and people had been hammered out and labelled 'Democracy'. Yet it had never deserved that name until the Chartist mobs had scared the Government into extending the franchise, and the new iron age had dawned, driving the Blubbs and the Frasers from the roads, and filling vast areas of a green countryside with filthy, urban sprawl. He supposed now that there would be a State funeral, like the funeral of the old Duke that his father had travelled all the way from Keswick to attend ten years ago, and as he remembered this he had a sense of crossing a watershed that was both national and personal for the Duke and his peers were mostly dead and buried under the new civilisation that the German Prince and a few like him had traced out, often in the teeth of reaction. Now there would be more changes, thousands of changes, proliferating with the years, and if he lived out his normal span he would doubtless play a part in some of them, but change would soon leave him behind. His two children would be a year or two younger than Albert when the century drew to a close, and by then who knew what kind of England would have emerged, or how close the rest of the world had come to overhauling her?

The inevitable drab emerged from the belt of shadow between two gas lamps. "Hello, Mister ... *hey, Mister* ...!" one of the twenty thousand said to be making a living on the London streets, the streets of the capital of the world. He walked on into Whitehall and crossed it, heading for the Strand. Bengy Hall's gigantic clock at Westminster struck the first stroke of midnight and the reverberations of the ponderous strokes followed him as he drew level with Charing Cross. There was a kind of fatalism in the long, booming sounds and they seemed to have a message for him but what it was he could not tell. Perhaps it was a lap bell, warning him that he still had a long way to travel. Or maybe a knell for the earnest humourless man, now lying dead. He reached the corner of Norfolk Street and hurried down it, suddenly eager for his hot toddy and sleep.

Part Three

Cob at Large:
1862 - 1863

1

Swann Treble

WHEN, towards the end of the nineteen-fifties, Algy Swann, four times married and the father of nine children (five of them legitimate) saw fit to make public his denial of the rumour that he and two of his most powerful rivals were merging, a good deal appeared in the press concerning the origins of Swann-on-Wheels Limited, and Algy, smiling over it, promptly commissioned an official history of the firm, then within a year or so of its centenary.

It was a shrewd move, for a book of this kind, tracing the history of Swann-on-Wheels through nearly ten decades of national and international hurly-burly, bestowed upon the enterprise that accolade of antiquity so dear to the heart of every English tradesman, as proclaimed by foundation dates adorning the premises of ten thousand businesses up and down the country. Algy, as it happened, did not sell, but the book put a higher value on his principal asset. For even men who make their millions on the telephone, without knowing more than a dozen of their five thousand employees by name, like to think they are buying history as well as stock-in-trade and goodwill. It flatters the least romantic among them to reflect that they are now the masters of something that has resisted the buffets of time, and it offers a challenge to late arrivals bent on grafting a chromium-plated personality on a venture that is more of an institution than a going concern, as though they were buying the Monument, or the Tower of London, with licence to demolish and redesign the one, and open the other as a self-service store, selling their own brands of margarine and quick-mix baking powder.

The book that resulted from the researches of two hacks, however, made only tolerable reading, for it skipped nimbly across the earliest years of the enterprise and dwelt lovingly on the dawn of the motor-age, and yesterday's post-war boom, when Swann's wheels, eight and ten to a vehicle, could be numbered in thousands. It did not probe deeply into the subtle stresses of the first, post-expansion period, years that saw the completion of the British gridiron, for its

269

authors had no reason to regard 1862-4 as the watershed Adam had predicted that December night when he stood in the Mall and learned from a policeman that the Prince Consort had succumbed to typhoid fever. This period came under the vague, general heading of *'Early Beginnings—the Age of the Horse'*, and at least three incidents that went some way to making Adam Swann a national figure were not mentioned. There was no reference, for example, to Hamlet Ratcliffe's spectacular feat in the west, or Blubb's bloody brush with Fenians in the east. Neither was mention made of how Bryn Lovell, in the Mountain Square, brought off the Swann treble in a remote Welsh valley, in the very last days of that eventful year, and this despite the fact that all three occurrences found their way into newspapers that printed Gladstone's speeches verbatim. For how could these things be known to a couple of hired hacks (with one eye on the money to be made out of a TV soap-opera) when the names of Ratcliffe, Blubb and Lovell were no more than entries in an account book, handed to them by Algy Swann when they were halfway through their chore? In this way, perhaps, historical keys fall through the pockets of time. Adam Swann should have written his own history, instead of confining himself to casual jottings in the daybook he kept in his eyrie.

* * *

Hamlet Ratcliffe, sometime auctioneer who had taken the post Adam offered him as manager of the Western Wedge had not succeeded in making good the promises given shortly before returning to his native Devon in the vanguard of Swann's provincial missionaries. Hamlet was an amiable man, too amiable perhaps for the initial prejudice he encountered, but Adam had not completely misjudged him. He was loyal, hardworking and honest, and had he succeeded to a branch already established by a younger, more thrustful man like Vicary (who soon had a virtual monopoly in the section marked on the map as The Bonus) he would have been an excellent choice. He knew his Devon and his Devonians, and proved as much by getting plenty of short-haul work in the base area on both sides of the Exe Estuary; but he failed lamentably to attract business further west and north, where the majority of hauls were commissioned by agriculturalists, and the goods carried by road were almost exclusively produce of one sort or another.

Ratcliffe was under no illusion as to the reasons for his failure. Most of the prosperous farmers, that is to say, men cultivating four hundred acres or over, were committed to locally-based carriers. Others had made satisfactory arrangements with the two main railroad companies operating in the west and others again, among whom were many of the smallholders, made do with their own transport, a cart or a haywain, pressed into service for the collection and delivery of milk churns and the transport of goods and cattle to local markets. Thus, one way and another, Tybalt's canvass of the area yielded almost nothing in the way of long-term contracts. It was difficult to convince men of this type that speed was money in their pockets, for down here speed was not and never would be a feature in the pattern of their daily lives. The farmers had adjusted to the pace of herds coming in from pasture, and to the slow but predictable rhythms of the seasons. Deliberation was bred in their blood and bone. They were as fond of money as the next man but they did not need it so urgently as the men of the cities, for the means of continuity reposed in the soil, the timber, the thatch, the leather, the very clothes they wore on their backs, providing they were prepared to work fourteen hours a day in their meadows and byres. It needed a more persuasive man than Hamlet Ratcliffe to convince them that he could lighten their burdens and increase their turnover by hauling cheap manufactured goods in and carting produce out, but rooted conservatism was the least of his worries. In the two populous cities, and the three dozen thriving towns in his territory, near access to the railways had already been achieved. Exeter and Plymouth were both situated astride main lines and so, for that matter, were towns in the southern half of Cornwall. The North Devon line ran clear across his territory to Bideford where, as a native, he might have looked for some support, and three great slices of his domain, Exmoor to the north, Dartmoor and Bodmin Moor to the west, were sparsely settled and did not boast of a single good road, so that large areas were completely isolated in severe weather.

All these factors—prejudice, conservatism, established local opposition, bad roads, rough terrain, all these were obvious handicaps to him, and he took cognisance of them, severally and collectively, and yet, because he was an inward-looking man, he knew that they were not the basic causes of his failure. The real cause was closer to home, reposing not in his circumstances but in his temperament and record, boy and man.

Nobody, from the moment he had trotted round his father's farm in the wake of a string of lumbering, Jan Riddish brothers, had paid much attention to Hamlet, or judged him capable of anything in the way of personal achievement. About the farm he had always been referred to as The Runt, for what other label could his parents give a son measuring a shade over five feet, when his shortest brother, Abel, was an inch over six? And it was not merely a matter of inches. His brothers were hulking, musclebound peasants, capable, so it was said, of balancing carts on their bellies and pointing them to the sky. Each was a slow, purposeful man, dedicated to the soil, and beside them, scuttling about the South Molton holding, Hamlet looked like a timid terrier who had strayed among oxen or, more accurately, perhaps, a rosy little cider apple lost among pumpkins. Not only did he fail to grow, his complexion was proof against the North Devon sun and wind. His skin did not ripen and coarsen after puberty but remained, even at fifty, as smooth and pink as a girl's, and it was on account of these physical disparities that his father decided that Hamlet should wear a collar and 'work clean', apprenticing him at the age of twelve as clerk to a corn-chandler.

It was the first of his failures. He remained perched on a stool (from which he was obliged to leap down to the floor) through the remainder of his boyhood, then drifted through a succession of indoor jobs, counter-jumping jobs mostly, but made his mark nowhere, and the reason for this was that he was always at war with himself, a very small man with big ideas that would inflate in each new environment until they were pricked by his own inadequacies.

When he was twenty-two he met and married Augusta Bickford, youngest daughter of a Tiverton undertaker, and here, at last, he found the one person in the world who would accept him at his own valuation, believing him to possess not merely brains and initiative but, beneath a cherubic exterior, a hard and unrelenting masculinity.

There was a reason for this too. When Hamlet appeared Augusta was twenty-eight, the very last of the seven Bickford girls who sat stitching shrouds for their father until somebody spoke for them. Agnes, the last to go, had been married four years when Hamlet proposed and Augusta, speechless with relief, enfolded him in an embrace before he was halfway through his proposal. In a sense she had never relaxed her hold. As though fearful that one day he would escape, and she would find herself back at the shroud bench, she invested her entire emotional capital in him, inflating his confidence like a nonstop bellows, and dismissing all his failures with the statement, "Twadden gude enuff vor 'ee, 'Amlet." When any of the Bickfords or the Ratcliffes pointed out that it was time Hamlet chose a trade and stuck to it, Augusta would shake her head and say, "No, that ole job—twadden gude enuff for 'Amlet," and leave it at that. Her loyalty sustained him wherever he went and remained untarnished when even Hamlet himself was beginning to entertain secret doubts about their future. He would have doubted long before had he not mastered a trick of convincing strangers, for at least a month, that he was a man of ideas and even Adam Swann, reckoned an excellent judge of character, had been deceived at the first interview. Now, with the Western Wedge lagging far behind newer territories, he became reluctantly convinced that, so long as the area was managed by Hamlet Ratcliffe, it would be restricted to short hauls in and around Exeter, and in the spring of 1862 he made a decision. Unless Ratcliffe could land a few contracts necessitating the use of two-horse frigates he would have to go and his territory be joined to the Southern Square, booming along under the hand of a Bristolian called Abbot, reckoned a slave driver by his teamsters.

The decision, conveyed to Hamlet by letter, was the worst jolt in a lifetime of disappointments and for once the level of his mercury failed to respond to Augusta's boost. When she said, "Dorn 'ee mind, midear, twadden gude enuff for 'ee," he exposed in sudden flash of temper, a Hamlet she had not encountered in getting on for thirty years of marriage, for he said, rounding on her, "Dorn 'ee talk so daft, Mother! This is the best billet I ever had an' a bliddy zight better than I'll ever have, now we'm both over the hill. You know it an' *I* know it, zo us'd best make up our minds to *do* something!" and when she said, meekly, "Do what midear?" he roared, "How do I know? But *something*! Something as'll make 'em all zit up an' taake notice! I'll keep this billet if I . . . if I 'ave to ketch the Bamfylde Lion zingle 'anded!"

She accepted this, of course, as a figure of speech.

Indeed, that was what it was at the time, for Hamlet had used the phenomenon to give vent to his exasperation and sense of personal inadequacy. It was, to both of them, the ultimate in derring-do, and yet, no sooner had he uttered the words, than they translated themselves into the kind of resolve that must have been slumbering in Hamlet since he was a child under his brothers' blundering feet. In a single phrase, it summed up everything he thought himself capable of achieving and from here, to a man drugged on Augusta's faith and his own optimism, it was but a short step to believing such a feat to be entirely possible.

To catch the Bamfylde Lion singlehanded. That would rattle them.

That would have everybody out in the street cheering and would not only make him world-famous but would provide Swann-on-Wheels with a magnificent advertisement. For who, in his senses, could neglect an opportunity of doing business with a man who attracted publicity wherever he went? And here, as it transpired, he was not deceived, for in a way, and without being aware of it, the imagination of Hamlet Ratcliffe had leaped a century, straight into a world where a single bizarre feat was enough to fix a man so firmly in the public eye that he remained linked to that feat for all time. Perhaps, after all, he was half-aware of this and of the importance of what he had said, for presently, adjusting to his mood, Augusta set the seal upon his declaration, saying, "Well, 'Amlet, if you *zay* you'll do it you will, and there tiz, midear. How will 'ee go about it?"

With a stir of inner excitement that acted upon him like a quart of cider on an empty stomach he knew how he would go about it. The properties, and a means of employing them, came tumbling into his brain. Recognition, adulation, public acknowledgement of Hamlet Ratcliffe as a superman that had capriciously evaded him for half-a-century, were out there awaiting him, and he even knew where—in the thickets and river bottoms north-west of the farm where he had been born. He marched out of the house and set about the business of mounting his safari.

Visitors to Devon during the last month had heard of the Bam-fylde Lion but most of them dismissed it as a local hoax, a reference to a mythical beast approximating the unicorn or the dodo, but this was an error on their part. The Bamfylde Lion was real enough, a circus animal that had gone astray when the horse-box that had been conveying it from Barnstaple to Exeter had overturned a mile or so west of South Molton. At the time of Hamlet's boast the Bamfylde Lion was a twenty-seven-day wonder, for that was the period it had been at liberty.

Hamlet had taken a keen interest in the incident, partly because he came from the area where it was at large, but also because, to his great satisfaction, the Two Rivers Carrier Service, his principal rival in the eastern half of the territory, had been held responsible for the escape, the lion having been left behind by a travelling circus after a breakdown at Barnstaple and later sent on under private charter.

The story of its escape, stripped of local embellishments, was simple. The driver had been drunk and had neglected to fix the brake shoes before descending a steep hill. The van had then run away and overturned in the ditch, where the doors had burst open and the lion had walked out, disappearing into the rough country north of the road before the concussed carter had been rescued.

In the period that followed there had been numerous sightings and local hue and cry, with parties of armed farmers and constables beating the area day by day but so far without success. Then claims for slaughtered livestock began to be filed but in this kind of country they were difficult to check, and everyone accepted the fact that isolated farmers would make the most of such a unique opportunity. Half-devoured carcases were said to be found as far north as Lynton, and as far west as Swimbridge, and Hamlet had followed all these reports with great thoroughness. Now, taking out his map, he marked down the most reliable sightings and drew a square enclosing an area of about twenty square miles, centred on the village of Filleigh. In his way, and at least in theory, he was an exceptionally painstaking man. He took the trouble to read about lions in an encyclopaedia and discovered that they were not, as a rule, in the habit of wandering vast distances but usually stayed within a comparatively small area, providing food could be found and food would be plentiful up there, with any number of sheep, heifers and ponies grazing on unfenced hillsides. He knew the country well. It consisted of a succession of steep, scrub-covered hills watered by innumerable streams seeking the river Bray. There were woods in all the river bottoms and to the north, where the pastures fell away to join the Exmoor plateau, there were no real roads and very few inhabitants.

Having satisfied himself as to the approximate position of the fugitive he put the next stage of his plan into operation, posting down to the Exe water meadows to interview the lion's owner, Mr. Begbie, of Begbie's Menageries, who was detained in Exeter by the Lord Lieutenant's warrant forbidding the outfit to move on to its next booking.

Mr. Begbie was a very worried man. He had long since exhausted the local potential and, apart from a shower of claims, had already been obliged to cancel a string of Somerset dates so that his employees, a rough lot as Hamlet noted, were now verging on mutiny. Hamlet went straight to the point. Buttonholing Mr. Begbie in his tent he said, unequivocally, "I'm Sou'-Molton born and bred, and I reckon I know just where that lion o' yours be. With help from you I could nail 'un. Do us do business, or dorn us?"

The trick of impressing people on first acquaintance worked on Mr. Begbie as effectively as it had worked on a succession of astute businessmen to whom Hamlet had made imaginative proposals. He said, sourly, "What's at back of it? The reward?" but Hamlet dismissed this sordid suggestion with a grandiloquent gesture. "No it baint," he said, "Tis what you might call an adver-*tise*-ment for my waggon service, Swann-on-Wheels. Mebbe you've heard of it?" Mr. Begbie had not but this did not check his mounting interest in this apple-cheeked Tom Thumb. He said, "Well, it's worth twenty pound to me to lay ahold o' Dante. For one thing, I'm stuck here an' losing all my bookings. For another I'll lose some o' my best acts if I don't stir myself soon. And in the meantime Beetriss is pining."

Hamlet knew all about Beatrice, the pining lioness, and it crossed his mind how Augusta might react in similar circumstances. Beatrice was, in fact, the mainspring of his plan, and now it occurred to him that Mr. Begbie, the Lord Lieutenant, the police, and all the farmers like his heavy-footed brothers, must have been extremely stupid not to have thought up a similar plan within an hour of Dante's escape. Authoritatively he spread out his map. "Lookit here," he said, briskly, "the Bamfylde Clump is within a mile or two o' where that beast o' yours first ran loose. He's still around make no mistake, for here's fower places where he's been spotted, an' none of 'em more'n two mile apart. Tis rough country thereabouts. full o' gullies and suchlike. He could bide there a twelvemonth without anyone comin' within a hundred yards of him. To my mind he's in one o' two places. High Bray, north o' Charles Bottom, where the woods run right down to the river; or higher up in they thickets below Heasley Mill. You lend me that mate of his for a day or two and I'll undertake to vetch un back and I won't charge 'ee neither. I won't even claim that there reward. What's more I'll use me own transport!"

It seemed to Mr. Begbie an extraordinarily generous offer and his heart warmed towards the little man. He was cautious, however, for the use of the lioness could conceivably make a bad situation worse. He said, carefully, "You'll have to take Dan'l with you. Dan'l's their trainer, and if he can get within range o' Dante that lion'll come to him like a dog to a whistle." He lowered his voice and glanced at the tent flap. "Truth is, Mr. Whatsisname, Dante's getting on, and all these stories concerning his rampaging are libels. Dante never bit no one, not even when he was a cub. He wouldn't know how."

"I'm very glad to hear that," said Hamlet, and he was, although, by now, he would have persisted if Mr. Begbie had told him Dante was accustomed to a diet of Christians.

It astonished everyone but Hamlet how speedily and smoothly

the operation was mounted. Within two hours he was jogging along the road from Cowley Bridge to Crediton, with the morose Dan'l seated on the box beside him. His vehicle, the largest in the yard, was a two-horse cattle van, high boarded and roofed with a thick wire mesh, and for the purpose of the decoy the box had been divided into two equal parts by the erection of another strip of wire mesh, fastened to the sides by enormous staples and lengths of rope. Beatrice seemed snug enough in her straw and slept most of the journey. Either Mr. Begbie was correct, and she was low in spirit on account of Dante's absence, or she was as tame as a marmalade cat. From his perch above Hamlet could both smell her and listen to her soft, fluttering snores, but she gave them no kind of trouble. By dusk they had reached Eggesford, where Hamlet obtained a change of horses for a down payment of three pounds, half of which was to be refunded on the return journey.

They kept moving through the mild spring night and about sunrise were entering South Molton. They ate a frugal breakfast at an inn and within an hour were turning off the main Barnstaple turnpike at Castle Hill, taking a winding road through a forest of wild rhododendrons until they came to a crossroads that marked the descent into the Bray valley at Charles Bottom.

Hamlet had long abandoned attempts to get his companion to talk but now that they were approaching the first sphere of operations it was necessary to make a plan so he said, "We'll try the river bank first. The track's rough but it'll serve, for the weather's been dry for a month. When us get to that slope go up an' whistle, and if us dorn have no luck we'll move east towards Heasley." He wetted his finger and raised it, adding, "Us is lucky. The wind's in the west, and if that bliddy lion is in the woods he'll scent her, worn he?"

Daniel conceded that this was possible but his long face and lugubrious expression proclaimed that he did not share Hamlet's confidence in the operation. They stopped in a flat water-meadow between the edge of the wood and the tumbling Bray, and here Hamlet turned the waggon so that its rear faced the trees. Then, while Daniel moved up towards the trees, uttering a series of piercing whistles he lowered the platform and took a leg of mutton from the tool box.

For the first time since Daniel had led her into the van the lioness showed a flicker of interest in proceedings. She yawned, stretched herself and sniffed the mesh but Daniel had already fed her and she

277

soon relapsed into somnolence. Hamlet said, gently, "Dornee worry, midear, us'll zoon have un back to 'ee." He had decided that he not only liked lions but had a way with them.

By now Daniel had disappeared although, from time to time, Hamlet could hear his whistles coming from somewhere near the crest of the wood. He climbed back on the box and composed himself to wait, luxuriating in the mild sunshine, strong for this time of year, and watching an otter run across the meadow and disappear in a patch of wild iris growing beside the stream.

It was very quiet and peaceful. Odd moments of his childhood returned to him like shy, kindly guests and presently, having been awake and abroad for something like twenty-four hours, he dozed.

It was the soft rush of heron's wings that awakened him and he started up as the bird crossed the river from the woods. Then, from the far side of the meadow, other birds shot up and he supposed they must have been alarmed by Daniel returning through the undergrowth. But when he rubbed his eyes and looked that way it was not Daniel. It was Dante, creeping out of the brushwood, like an exhausted St. Bernard returning from an unsuccessful search for a missing mountaineer, and the impression was heightened by the fact that the lion still wore his broad leather collar. He moved with great uncertainty, as if tipsy, and when he was clear of the bushes he actually staggered to the left, recovering himself with an effort. It was impossible to be afraid of him. He looked as if he would be grateful for a small lamb chop, to say nothing of the great leg of mutton awaiting him, and suddenly Hamlet found himself trembling from head to foot, but certainly not from fear of being trapped in a water-meadow with two lions, one of them at large. What was occurring before his eyes was suddenly clear to him for here, in the guise of an exhausted half-starved circus lion, was the consummation of everything he had believed about himself for fifty years, and everything Augusta had believed with him. Here, less than fifty yards away, was self-justification on a scale that even he had never anticipated, and the certainty of this brought tears to his eyes and a stammer to his tongue. He said, hoarsely, "Cccome on, Dante. Come on home, midear, us worn hurt 'ee," and then, when Dante stopped a few yards short of the waggon, "Why you poor ole toad! You'm not on'y starved, you'm in tatters!"

Then he noticed Beatrice, a few feet below him. She was standing poised like an alerted whippet, her wrinkled nose pointing towards her mate. For perhaps half a minute she stood thus and then, with-

out the slightest warning, she threw up her head and uttered a roar
that sent every bird within half-a-mile soaring and startled Hamlet so
much that he all but fell from the box. He had a horrid fear then,
not of being devoured by a lion but of seeing yet another splendid
opportunity escape him, this time on account of the horses. For they
too had been badly startled by Beatrice's sudden roar, and backed
clumsily against the crossbar of the span, preparatory to bolting
headlong into the river. Their caracole gave him about two seconds
in which to act. Leaping down from the box he ran around and
threw his entire weight on the bridles, hanging on as the team plunged
and reared, and Beatrice roared again, and Daniel came running out
of the woods adding his high-pitched whistle to the uproar. Hamlet
was so involved now that he was unable to see precisely what happened but Daniel must have known his business for when, having
been flung this way and that with his feet clear of the ground, Hamlet
was able to look again, Dante was already in the outer section of the
waggon, with his teeth buried in the meat, and the trainer had upended the heavy platform and was slamming home the bolts. Between
them, and with considerable difficulty, they managed to quieten the
horses and walk the waggon across the soft ground to the track, and
here began, for Hamlet, a triumphant progress down the valleys of
the Bray, the Taw, and the Exe.

At every village and town people behaved precisely as he had
expected them to behave. They came out of their doors shouting and
gesticulating and soon word of the waggon's approach ran far ahead,
so that little deputations awaited them at every crossroads. Throughout it all he conducted himself modestly, saying, in response to the
plaudits, "All it needed was a bit o' thinking on," but nobody believed him, and he would not have expected them to, so that he
was not much surprised when, on entering the parish of St. David's
north of the city, the Mayor was there to greet him and beside him
clutching a nosegay, was Augusta, her eyes glittering with half-
shed tears.

Soon all the Westcountry newspapers were printing the story and
he was able to read of himself in the most extravagant terms. One
called him, 'Hamlet Ratcliffe. Lion Tamer Extraordinary', and another, 'The Man Who Brought Devon's Reign of Terror to An
End'. He thought this extravagant, for surely anyone could see
that Dante was as harmless (when caged, of course) as a jack rabbit,
but when they made him a presentation a day or so later, and when
the Mayor, in the course of a windy speech, spoke of him as 'a true

279

son of Devon', he went out of his way to ensure that Swann-on-Wheels received a share of the credit, saying, in response, "It weren't nothing but a job for my boss in London. He reckons to haul anything and deliver on time, and that's more than you can say for others, baint it? 'Two Rivers' to name no names." His rivals could have sued him for saying that in public but they did not. The newspapers had already printed the story of Fred Slater, the carter who had originally mislaid Dante, and there were rumours that he was to be prosecuted when he came out of the infirmary. However it was, the incident turned the tide in Hamlet's favour and he was astonished by the flow of inquiries and commissions that resulted from this one burst of publicity. Within a month he was using two-horse frigates, and a month after that, on long runs across the Tamar, he was hauling loads of hides and fleeces and sandstone building blocks on men-o'-war, harnessed unicorn. Adam Swann wrote him a congratulatory letter and the only person who made no kind of fuss was Augusta, for it did not seem to her at all remarkable that Hamlet should have done precisely what he said he would do. After all, he had rescued her from a lifetime of shroud-stitching, and it was time somebody else acknowledged his qualifications as a knight-errant.

From then on the Western Wedge began to thrive and within two years its returns were standing third on Tybalt's charts. Adam, chuckling over the framed picture of Hamlet Ratcliffe standing beside a sleek, well-fed Dante (the photograph had been taken at his insistence some weeks later) had no more thoughts of replacing his manager for somehow, in establishing himself in his own estimation, Hamlet had confirmed Adam in at least two areas. One was his penchant of picking lieutenants and the other was that press advertising was all very well so long as it was boosted by a news item that the public wanted to read. He had ample confirmation of this within the next few months.

2

Ratcliffe's exploit as a lion catcher, and the publicity it attracted to the firm, were enough to get things moving in the west but because the story had comic undertones the London newspapers reported it with that touch of patronage inherent in all their accounts of occurrences in the provinces. It was otherwise with Blubb's swashbuckling contribution to the publicity drive, for his exploit was performed less than forty miles of the capital and touched on kindred topics that were beginning to bedevil British politics, the Irish Home Rule issue, and the militancy of the newly-formed Republican group calling themselves Fenians.

Coastal England, Adam reflected, seldom lacked a fashionable bogeyman. Over the centuries there had been the Papists, the Jacobites, the French, the Spanish, the Dutch and the slave-raiding Barbary Rovers. Now the popular child-scarer seemed to be the Fenian, whom the public, fed on a strong diet of Parliamentary debate supplemented by travellers' tales of outrage beyond the Dublin Pale, had come to regard as homegrown French Revolutionaries, hellbent on arson and murder.

In fact the Fenians of the 'sixties were very small beer indeed, currently no more than a nuisance value to Government, police and informers. It was therefore singular that they should have been instrumental in giving the firm a tremendous boost, and inflating one of its depot managers, no other than Timothy Blubb, into a Kentish hero. For in most respects Blubb, obese, surly and now entering his own sixties, was an even more unlikely knight-errant than Hamlet Ratcliffe.

To the surprise of everyone at the yard, particularly Messrs. Tybalt and Keate who regarded him as a foul-mouthed old ruffian, Blubb had prospered as an outpost commander of Swann-on-Wheels. His network of acquaintances, that included innkeepers, ostlers, chambermaids, barmaids, tramps, carriers, railwaymen, merchants, longshoremen and at least a score of ex-goalbirds and gipsies, had given him immense advantages over the other base managers, and his position as Swann's manager in the Kentish Triangle had done a great deal to restore to him his self-respect as a professional of the open road.

Down at his base he became a man to be reckoned with, and as his hold upon road traffic was enlarged he soon emerged as a man of substance, for he had not forgotten the tricks of the coaching trade and was known to accept gratuities from merchants who wanted goods shifted in a hurry at a cut rate. Adam was far from being unaware of Blubb's sideline, but was prepared to wink at it, so long as the monthly returns in the Triangle doubled themselves every six months. If Blubb lined his own pocket by undercutting a rival service then he also landed more contracts than any other manager in the network. The military contract, entered into with the army ordnance depot at Deal in the first months of that year, was only one example of Blubb's salesmanship and perspicacity, for to get it he bluffed his way into the barracks one morning and emerged, slightly the worse for drink, with a short-term contract to haul small arms and ball cartridge ammunition from a Government arsenal near Maidstone to Deal, Folkestone, Hythe and several smaller military establishments that lay within his territory. It was, as Adam saw at a glance, a very profitable contract. Nobody ever haggled over the spending of Government money and by the summer of 1862 regular consignments of stores were moving out of Maidstone in two-horse frigates, usually over the old coach road between county town and coast, and because some of the loads included gunpowder, carried at transporter's risk, the rates sometimes ran as high as 160/- a ton.

No official secrecy was involved in the journeys, but Blubb, at Adam's insistence, selected his most reliable waggoners for the runs, remembering that not long ago, during a haul up in the Midlands, a spark from a clay pipe had blown another carrier's convoy sky high, killing waggoners and teams, and half-demolishing an inn where the drivers had stopped to refresh themselves. Blubb, a two-quart man, accepted the logic of his employer's instructions and whenever arms were carried the frigates were in charge of two brothers called Arscott, both of them Baptists and teetotallers into the bargain.

It was from one of these drivers that Blubb received a hint that other people, who would seem to have no connection whatever with the transportation of Government property, were showing a lively interest in the consignments and being a naturally suspicious man at once took upon himself the responsibility of personal investigation.

In more than thirty years as a coachguard and coachman, Blubb had outfaced every hazard that could overtake a traveller. In his time he had been snowbound, fogbound and awash, as well as being involved, one way or another, in collisions, runaway incidents, oversets, and at least one highway robbery when he and all his inside passengers were stopped by a couple of footpads near Retford. But adventures of this kind were now reckoned part of the lost tradition of the road. Breakdowns still occurred, even to slow-moving goods convoys, and occasionally there was pilfering at the depot or at an inn, where waggoners risked instant dismissal by leaving their vehicles unattended.

It was pilfering, possibly on an organised scale, that he had in mind when he travelled down to the Ashford area to question Job Arscott, the waggoner, but what he learned encouraged him to take the matter more seriously. Arscott, it seemed, had been questioned concerning the nature of his load by a well-dressed woman who spoke with an unfamiliar accent, and when the waggoner had refused her offer of cheese and porter at an inn where he was changing teams she had followed him, at a distance, almost as far as Deal. This, in itself, was odd and would seem to preclude Blubb's theory of a decoy, the usual method of tavern-thieves, especially as Arscott had seen the same chaise in the inn yard on his return journey. To Blubb it smacked more of a spying foray by a rival haulage firm, and he went on to the inn without much hope of finding the agent in residence. He was therefore considerably surprised when, on entering the yard, he recognised her by Arscott's description, talking to a man wearing a riding cloak and sidearms, an unusual feature of a horseman's outfit since the decline of the coaching era.

It was the man's short, businesslike sword, the traveller's hanger of a past age, that alerted him more than the woman who was, as Arscott had described, a handsome, saucy wench, who made very free with herself, as he learned from Blossom, horsekeeper at the 'George'. Blossom, an old coaching crony, told him she called herself Mrs. O'Connell, and that she was as Irish as the name suggested for her brogue was so rich he had difficulty in following the orders she gave him. She was, Blossom went on, 'a tolerably flighty madam', who had entertained a number of men during her stay at the inn and had made several excursions in a hired chaise. The man she was talking to had visited her on Monday and afterwards ridden away towards the coast on a piebald cob. Blossom also confirmed that Mrs. O'Connell had made approaches to Arscott the previous Monday but attributed this to her readiness to gossip with anyone, even a middle-aged Bible-puncher like Job Arscott.

Blubb at once made up his mind to pursue his inquiries further and booked a room at the 'George', choosing one with a window that overlooked the livery stable, and it was not long before he saw Mrs. O'Connell set off on another expedition, noticing that she handled the ribbons like an expert and went spanking down the Deal turnpike in a way that recalled the reckless driving of women who had consorted with the racing bucks a generation ago.

He made up his mind there and then to follow her and discover, if possible what she was up to, but by the time he got his trap clear of the yard she was a mile ahead and he did not catch sight of the chaise until it was turning into a sideroad beyond the hamlet of Mersham Hatch, five miles nearer the coast.

He reined in at the junction, watching his quarry bump along the unsurfaced track and disappear behind a clump of trees straddling the lane but was perplexed when it failed to reappear on the far side, where the country was open. At that moment, while he was still undecided what to do, a little knot of horsemen cantered up from the direction of Deal and turned off down the same track, and he noticed that one of them was the tall, swashbuckling fellow he had seen talking to Mrs. O'Connell in the inn yard.

Blubb was wise in the ways of the world, especially the world of the gentry. If the man with sidearms had been alone he would have accepted the coincidence as evidence of an assignation of a certain nature and would, moreover, have been prepared to wager a guinea that the young buck was not Mr. O'Connell. But a man was unlikely to share a tryst with a pretty woman with half-a-dozen other young sparks. Whatever was intended down there under the trees had nothing to do with romance.

Thoughtfully he turned his trap and walked the horse back to the inn and was stationed at his window when the chaise came rattling over the cobbles, the dashing Mrs. O'Connell perched on the driving seat and looking, he thought, extremely pleased with herself.

By now he was thoroughly intrigued. In some way that woman, and those hurrying horsemen he had seen, were planning something outside the law, and he had a strong suspicion that whatever it was it had to do with his consignments of arms and ammunition to Deal.

He went about forming his conclusions in his slow, methodical way, giving each factor the isolated speculation he had once applied to the hazards of getting his coach from 'The Bell', Islington, to Newark in under eleven hours, irrespective of weather. There was the woman herself, skittish and yet, in a flamboyant way, mysterious and devious. There was the raffish-looking cavalier with the hanger, who had managed to assemble a group of companions out of nowhere in just over the hour. There was the meeting between these parties under cover and clear of the main road. There was the woman's approach to Arscott, and the fact that she had followed him on the road to Deal. Finally, there was another arms run scheduled for Friday over the same route, with a change of teams due in the same inn where Mrs. O'Connell was a guest. It all added to something but for a long time Blubb was at a loss to know what. Then he remembered that the woman was Irish, and a long way from home, and poked among his memories for what he remembered about the Irish. They were good judges of horseflesh, he recalled, and inclined to indulge in ceaseless chatter when they travelled his coaches as outside passengers. It was this that gave him his idea.

He found Blossom, handed the ostler a shilling and said, with a wink, "I got two more o' those in these 'ere britches that tells me you're going to set me up with that pretty widder," and when Blossom, biting on the shilling, said that Blubb was too long in the tooth for that kind of frolic, he said, "Mebbe, but I got me reasons, tho' I've no call to tell an ole ruin like you wot they be. Just you set me up like I said. Tell her I'm the best-known whip south o' the Thames, and down on me luck just now. Do that and there'll be more money in it for you as soon as my gaffer gets here tomorrer," for he had decided that he had reached a stage where he should confide in Swann before acting on a plan already taking shape in his mind. In the meantime, however, he said nothing to anybody but went into the supper-room and ordered a roast served with three vegetables and a tankard of Kentish-brewed beer.

Before his plate was clean Mrs. O'Connell came in and before he was halfway through his second tankard she crossed over to him and asked if he had a reliable map about him saying she intended visiting friends at a place called Dymchurch the following day and was unsure of her road.

He found her ploy crude, in that she went out of her way to flatter him and his like, declaring that it was a crying shame that coaches had been ousted by 'that stinking tea-kettle'. Blossom, he reflected, must have primed her very well, for she plied him with a score of questions concerning his former calling, and it was some time before he could let slip that he was now employed by a carrier service called Swann-on-Wheels hauling military stores from the Maidstone arsenal to Deal barracks. She sparkled a little at this, he noted, so he went on to tell her that he was awaiting Friday's convoy, and was charged with taking over from the Maidstone waggoner when the teams were changed at the halfway mark. That, as he had hoped, proved her excuse to break off their chat and after he had accepted a third tankard of ale 'to drink to the good old days', she left him, went up to her room, reappeared in a blue riding habit and crossed the yard calling for Blossom. Ten minutes after that she came posting out of the stableyard on the best riding horse the inn possessed. He watched her out of sight and then, reserving his own room and one other, took the road for Ashford.

Adam was sceptical when he arrived in response to his manager's cryptic telegraph, but it did not require a great deal of persuasion on Blubb's part to half-convince him that some kind of attempt on the next consignment by Fenians, or some kindred body, was a possibility. When Blubb declared that in his view it was a certainty, he said, "Very well then. Our obvious course is to pass the information to the constabulary. I imagine they'll make thorough inquiries concerning this Mrs. O'Connell, and that might save you and I making damned fools of ourselves," but Blubb said, obstinately, "Aye, you can do that if you've a mind to, but if it was me I'd look to the advantages you could wring out of this kind o' lark. Ketch 'em redhanded ourselves, that's my fancy!"

"Come, now, you can't be serious, Blubb," protested Adam, but Blubb said he was, and the risk of failure was minimal. "Send the waggon on as usual, wi' both they Arscotts aboard. Offload the stuff inside the stable, when we change teams at noon on Friday, stow the pair of us under the canvas and see wot comes of it down at that crossroads beyond Mersham 'Atch. Why, damme, we could wing two of 'em before they got the tailboard down. Then, mebbe, the Arscotts could take a shot at 'em before they run for it."

The prospect of a brush of this kind appealed to the man of action in him but Adam said, doubtfully, "I'm not saying it couldn't be done, Blubb, but I've no right to risk your neck in this kind of scrape." Blubb said, almost passionately, "Lookit here, gaffer, it's my neck, and to my way o' thinking it'll pay off handsome. Not on'y to you, but to me, on account o' the blood money the Guvverment hands out to anyone who fetches home a footpad dead or alive. It woulden surprise me if there ain't ten pund apiece on they Irishers. You take the credit an' I'll take the money. There's not much risk, neither. I woulden show my arse to no Paddy alive, and there won't be no more than five of 'em, if that. They're taking enough risk as it is gallopin' about in a bunch in country where they'm seen an' noted by the locals. Tidden as if it were London, where 'arf the dam' population is Irish." And then, almost wheedling, "Look at it from my standpoint. It means little enough to you to get your name in the papers, tho' you won't dispute that it'd do the business a power o' good in passing, but me—well—I was somebody once, when you was no more'n a gleam in your dad's eye. I was looked up to an' thought well of by the swells. There weren't one of 'em who wouldn't have parted wi' silver to take the ribbons from Tim Blubb, driving the Telegraph or the Tally-Ho up the Great North Road, or down the Brighton Turnpike. Those days are gone, I'll own, and I'm getting up along now, but I've a fancy to be spoke well of again before I drop the whip in the bracket. Let's *do* it, Governor, without calling the bloody sodgers in. For if we do then mark my words they'll botch it, and they Irishers'll get clear away and try their luck on some other road Fishguard or Liverpool way."

It was impossible, Adam thought, to resist the old rogue and also, to an extent, to look at the situation through his eyes. He was old and fat and gross but at this moment, with a man's job ahead of him, he was suddenly Tim Blubb again, flattered and petted by all the inside passengers, and God's gift to every tavern trollop along the routes he travelled. He said, chuckling, "You really back yourself to bring this off, Blubb?"

"Aye, I do that. Providing you'll stand by me, and you a trained man wi' firearms, no doubt."

"Can you use a pistol if you have to?"

"I can use my old blunderbuss," Blub said. "I once put a handful of rusty nails into the arse of a likely lad who tried to stop the old Wellington at Stamford one dark night. That was when I was riding guard tho'."

"And forty years ago, no doubt," said Adam.

"Wot of it? I'd still back myself against Irishers. They can sit a horse well enough but they're no great shakes at standin' and facin' fire from the glimpse I got of 'em. Besides, if we ambush 'em, we'll have the edge on 'em, won't we?"

"I certainly hope so," said Adam, "for you've talked me into it, Blubb, and if there is blood money to be earned you're welcome to it. I'll settle for the free advertisement."

*   *   *

It occurred to him, as they went about their preparations, that Blubb would have made an excellent troop sergeant. He was bold but deliberate, foreseeing all manner of contingencies and taking it upon himself to order the entire ambush, down to the last detail. They took the Arscott twins into their confidence and it was arranged that one should travel down to Ashford as driver while the other lay concealed in the back with a pistol and a cudgel. When, soon after noon, the waggon came into the inn yard, Adam and Blubb were awaiting it concealed in the stable loft. Twelve boxes of ball cartridges and two stand of arms were offloaded and left in charge of the ostler, Blossom, bewildered by all this secrecy but bribed into silence by a handful of silver. Adam and Blubb then joined Reuben Arscott in the back and his brother Job laced them in, leaving one corner loose to serve

287

as a spyhole. Adam had a pair of single-shot pistols and Blubb an old-fashioned blunderbuss, of the kind he had carried as a guard. It was not his own for he had no time to fetch that, but one he borrowed from a local crony and although Adam watched him load it with nails and scrap metal, and prime and charge it with the greatest care, it did not look a very serviceable weapon to use against a gang of wild Irishmen. Whilst they were going about their preparations Adam speculated aloud on the reason for a raid of this kind, so far from the centre of Fenian activities, but Blubb had already made up his mind about that.

"They need a regular supply of arms for the mischief they'm planning over there," he said, "but there's a deal more'n that. The more shindig they stir up over here the more they'll get gabbed about. Being Irishers they'm divided among 'emselves, you see, and this lot is the livelier section, bent on showing the others up. Me, I never driven in Ireland, tho' I talked to men as did. This kind of business is still commonplace over there, I'm told, for some of 'em are savages, and all of 'em spoilin' fer a fight."

As the waggon rolled out of the yard and turned south on the coastal road Adam had a moment's misgiving. It seemed to him quite absurd that he should have allowed a man of Blubb's disposition to embroil him in something that was clearly a task for the Crown forces, but as they jolted south the old instincts of the seasoned campaigner returned to him, and he thought how Roberts and 'Circus' Howard would have relished the occasion. By the time they reached Mersham Hatch he would not have been anywhere else but here, with Blubb nursing his absurd weapon and Arscott, tense and silent nearer the box, where he could communicate in whispers with his brother.

The road seemed almost deserted, a fly or two speeding towards London and one knife-grinder's trap, with the owner fast asleep in the June sunshine. Then, as they approached the crossroads, Adam noticed a closed cab of a kind not often seen on the roads nowadays and it looked unattended, with the horse cropping the grass verge twenty yards down the sideroad that Blubb told him led, by a roundabout route, to Dymchurch on the coast. He would not have been surprised to see a knot of men lounging close by but the sight of the driverless vehicle directed his attention to that side of the road, where the hedgerows were high, and he did not see the Irish woman standing by a milestone on their side of the road. Blubb saw her, however, pinching his arm as she stepped forward, and then everything happened with a rush that might have overwhelmed them had not the driver on the box pulled hard over to the centre of the road so that the waggon swung round at a wide angle blocking both routes.

Adam's attention, notwithstanding his glance at the woman through the chink in the curtains, had never really left the supposedly empty cab in the side road and this was just as well. Suddenly its offside door was flung open and two men bundled out brandishing pistols. At the same time, out of the corner of his eye, he saw three others leap over the nearside hedge of the turnpike, one making for the horses' heads, the others running round to the back of the waggon.

Blubb's blunderbuss went off with a fearful roar that stunned the eardrums and the interior of the waggon was full of smoke. The driver fired at the man holding the horses' heads but the ball missed its mark and must have clipped one of the animals for the team began to plunge, and after that it was difficult to see what was happening for around them, in and out the smoke, figures were running and crying out, and the woman screamed as one of the attackers reeled against her, clutching at her dress and slithering to his knees on the road.

Adam fired one pistol, aiming at the two running figures who had jumped from the cab but then, not caring to be penned in such a confined space, he burst through the back flaps and jumped down, Arscott following on his heels. A ball whistled past his ear and he heard it smack into the wooden frame of the wagon as, running round to the front, he saw Blubb standing on the box, flailing down at a tall, wiry-looking assailant with the stock of his blunderbuss.

It was an utterly improbable posture for a man so gross and blubberly as the ex-coachman. He looked like a grotesque clockwork toy going through its routine, arms rising and falling with a kind of jerky precision. Then, as the man fell against the shafts, the scene changed utterly, with nothing happening around the waggon but a combined rush in the direction of the sideroad, where a sixth man suddenly appeared, mounted on a bay horse and leading others. Within seconds the woman and four of the men were galloping away towards a copse in the first fold of the hill, and suddenly there was silence, the dust and smoke settling to reveal the scene of the encounter. Adam saw Blubb scramble down, his little piggy eyes shining with excitement as he rolled his man on his back and looked down at his shattered skull. Another man, greyhaired and much older than the lean fellow, lay spreadeagled near the tailboard, a pistol clutched in his hand. He, too, was dead, with a ball through his heart and a smear of blood already showing through his topcoat.

Blubb shouted, triumphantly, "Two of 'em, Governor! And one o' they others was winged, for they had to help him mount," and he sucked his bleeding thumb where the blunderbuss had backfired and a piece of metal had laid open the joint.

It was like clearing up after a skirmish on the road to Jhansi. They heaved the two dead men into the waggon and turned the horses back towards Ashford. One of the Arscotts mounted the box of the abandoned cab and followed them, Blubb recognising the equipage as a vehicle hired from a livery stable at Deal. Blubb said, dolefully, "I smashed the stock o' this blunderbuss. Smashed clean to bits it is. He had a thickish skull I reckon, but that's common enough among Irishers." His tone of voice, and the fact that he made no attempt to boast of the success of the ambush or the part he had played in it afforded Adam a brief glimpse of the man Blubb had been in his prime. He thought 'He doesn't belong in this century at all. He's a Hogarth character and in another decade or so, if he survives, he'll turn into Falstaff.' Then, without warning, the driver Arscott was sick, so that they pulled up and waited. He said, humbly, "I never seen a man killed before, sir." Adam took the reins and sent him back to join his brother in the cab. At a slow walk the little cavalcade drove back along the road to Ashford.

3

There was no blood money. The authorities were embarrassed at the prospect of holding a double inquest on two unknown Irishmen who had tried, unsuccessfully, to rob Her Majesty of the consignment of arms and ammunition. But after the inquest, when the coroner pronounced 'killed in the execution of a felony on the high-road' there was a dispute as to who should foot the bill for the funerals. Nobody came forward to claim the bodies and the woman and her four companions were never seen again. It was said they had got away by sea from Dymchurch, where a brig sailed within an hour or so of the battle at Mersham Cross.

There was, however, a great deal of publicity and Blubb, like Ratcliffe before him, achieved a passing notoriety and was drunk for almost a week. This time the impact on the firm was national rather than local. Catesby heard about it away up in the north and Edith

Wadsworth wrote saucily from the east, saying she was interested to learn that Adam had exchanged the rôle of haulier for that of thieftaker. City men discussed it, some of them sarcastically, and Henrietta, finding in it proof that the soldier in Adam was not dormant introduced it into her sedate conversation at her monthly 'At Home', an event that Adam declined to attend.

But all this, the publicity resulting from Ratcliffe's feat in the west, and Blubb's in the south-east, was no more than an overture. The real breakthrough into national recognition was made in a remote Welsh valley, six months later, where Bryn Lovell, manager of the Mountain Square, suddenly found himself invested with the halo of Glendower.

4

The blight of the second iron age was upon this country too but its taint, although glaringly obvious, was not as overriding as in the cotton belt and the potteries. In the north the volcanoes of wealth had erupted and afterwards been levelled off and built upon, so that the factories and the dormitories of those who served them were now so thick upon the ground that the pastoral heritage of the areas had been all but obliterated. Something at once more subtle and more sinister had occurred down here, along the southern face of the Mountain Square. The desolation was not absolute because the outward manifestations of the sickness were scabrous. Instead of falling on the land like a bludgeon its ravages were wayward, sometimes almost casual, as though the valleys had been probed with sooty fingers that left triangular islets of greenery isolated on some of the spurs. Away in the distance the grape blue line of the mountains still stood like the deserted ramparts of a Promised Land, near enough to be seen but, in all other respects, as remote as the mountains of the moon. For up there beyond the skyline was beauty, emptiness and worklessness, and only a small minority of rebels, self-outlawed from a land of tips and fouled streams, fought an ancestral battle with tools that were not unlike those used by the tamed but were employed against more elemental forces, wind and granite and an eternity of soft, seeping rain.

Most of the older pits were sited along the ancient river beds, their skeletal apparatus pitched in the narrow valleys seamed by row upon row of tiny, terraced houses, some of which seemed to have begun life at the top of the hillsides, slithered halfway down, and were now crowding upon the remains of earlier settlements, as though they wanted nothing more than to push them down the shafts and fall on top of them. The conical tips about here were high and crowned with a crust of brittle slurry that, in dry weather, could be broken by the touch of an iron-shod boot but was more often soft and moulded, particularly after winter rains converted the tips into gigantic black sponges. Sometimes, when shifts were coming or going, it looked as though nothing but a multitude of plodding, greyish beetles lived down there, insects trained to the toot of the whistle so that they surged up or down the hills in obedience to some blind, primeval impulse. The railway had reached this far a long time ago, running out spurs from the Newport–Abergavenny–Hereford line as it dropped down to link up with the South Wales railroad. Trucks, full and empty, moved ceaselessly along these spurs, and more branch lines were building as coal was clawed from newer, smaller pits higher up the slopes, and in valleys where, even yet, green predominated over black and slate grey.

Llangatwg was such a pit, north of the Abergavenny–Merthyr Tydfil road, still only two years old, and as yet without a rail to call its own, discounting the narrow gauge laid down by the owners when the pit first opened. For to link Llangatwg to a main siding was proving an expensive business, not only on account of the gradient but because of a freakish rock-seam that ran diagonally across the projected course and converted the approach into a series of ridges that were the despair of the engineers. They had persisted, however, in the way of railway builders, and were now only a mile or so short of the pithead. They might, with luck, have made the connection by the end of the year had not heavy snow fallen, causing a suspension of work. On the second day they called in their teams and paid them off to kick their heels for a week or two. It was hopeless to excavate under conditions of hard frost, and no coal had come down in the last forty-eight hours for the narrow-gauge line was soon obliterated by drifts that built up between the ridges and the levelled tipping ground at the top was already full of freshly-mined coal.

Work ceased for the engineers but not for the miners. Fifteen hundred feet below the mountain the weather was the same all the year round, and men and ponies continued to use the main roads and galleries heedless of the snow, just as they were indifferent, in high summer, to the airlessness of the narrow valley, or the rain bucketing from the rock ledges in spring and autumn. There was even a certain eagerness among the men coming on shift from the town below to seek the shelter of the pit after the long, stumbling slither up the slope to work, whereas men coming off shift, spilling from the cage like schoolboys, still found the energy to toboggan down the ridges to their homes.

*　　*　　*

The day shift had been below an hour or more when it happened. Men trundling tubs across the level stretch from grading screens to where a line of trucks stood frozen to the rails, heard a muffled boom and then a long, hissing sigh, as though the mountain had belched and turned in its sleep, and soon the pithead was like a squat magnet attracting everything on two legs for half-a-mile around, and the sustained wail of the siren brought awareness of disaster to night-shift men and womenfolk in the town below, so that the long slope was streaked with running, stumbling figures churning the clean snow into yellow slush as they clawed their way upwards.

Men looking like frenzied gnomes darted in and out of the sheds, shouting to one another that the lower level main road was flooded roof-high, and when the few who had escaped the avalanche of solid water were lifted out and counted it was found that eighty-seven men and boys were missing, perhaps half of them already drowned and the rest, in the more distant galleries, as good as dead, unless, by some miracle, the water could be pumped from the road and shaft, and the rescue teams could make a thorough search against the checkers' lists.

News of this kind, news of men and boys whose lives hang upon a thread attached to some imponderable shift of circumstances outside the range of men above ground, is not circulated by means of the printed word, or doled out in verbal driblets by some desperately worried official, juggling with words at the window of a besieged office. It circulates freely, accurately, and almost instantaneously within a closed community, where almost every living soul is involved in the tragedy, and even those who are not find themselves sucked into the vortex by the currents weaving about them.

It is as though each new scrap of information is scribbled on a scrap of paper and tossed above the crowd where it is caught and broadcast over a square mile. A lampman at the foot of the shaft tells of a half-drowned miner gasping out that the water roofed above the first dip in the main road, sealing in the shift a hundred yards or so deeper in the mountain. A checker, who was one of the last up, says that the cage cannot descend below the second level because there must, by now, be twenty foot of water in the shaft. A third man brings news that the supplementary shaft further down the slope is also flooded, and so the news circulates, passed from mouth to mouth in a matter of seconds, and officials, checking names of the missing against known casualties, recruiting rescue teams and gauging the sucking power of the pump, have no need to keep watchers informed of progress.

It was by some such means that Bryn Lovell heard about it and was able, even at a distance, to estimate the chances of eighty-seven entombed men, and it was a conviction that he could make a unique contribution that sent him scurrying over from Abergavenny and ploughing up the slope to the pit yard where, by now, some three thousand men and women were standing about the pithead.

He was a strange, sombre man, a misfit in the community in that he was aloof and very solitary, seemingly without the need for the solace of wife, children or even a friend, and lacking the sense of humour that saves the isolated Celt from self-destruction before he attains middle-age. He was considered, by the few who knew him to be an educated man, with any amount of book learning under his thatch but this was only half true. Although he had taught himself to read with a primer when he was in his early twenties, he had read but two kinds of books, those dealing with social history and those concerned with moral philosophy, and perhaps it was what he dredged from these humourless tomes that made him walk alone, conjuring with the theories advanced by their erudite authors. He was tall and spare, with thinning grey hair, and a slight stoop. He was also near-sighted, and wore a pair of steel-framed spectacles that had served his father through two decades of the eighteenth century, and were now pressed into service by his son who was a frugal man and saw no reason to buy a new pair. He subscribed to no religious cult, his evenings with his books having taught him to distrust all creeds, but he was a man of great integrity and none of those with whom he did business held out for a piece of paper pledging Lovell to abide by his quotations or schedules.

Here in the Mountain Square Lovell had got off to a slow start but he was now firmly established in the north and centre of the Square and was, to Adam's gratification, making steady progress in short-haul work within an area well-served by rail. He had established a string of reliable agents along the South Wales main line and Swann-on-Wheels pinnaces and frigates were beginning to be seen in all the upper valleys, where they carried a great variety of goods, everything from pit-props to cabbages. Taken all round Adam Swann had reason to consider Bryn Lovell the most reliable of his provincial managers, equating him, in terms of enterprise, with Catesby in the north, and in terms of reliability with a man like Wadsworth in the Crescents.

When Lovell arrived at the pit he went straight to the engine-house where he spent five minutes staring at the pump. He knew something about pit machinery, for his father and uncles had worked for a man who made pumps and winding gear in the early days of the boom, and Bryn had spent his boyhood in and about the machine shops. He recognised the pump at once as an old Boulton and Watt product, of a kind that had superseded the Newcomen pump some thirty years ago, and it shocked him to find such a museum piece in a new pit. It straddled the engine house like a giant bellows, sucking and wheezing and gurgling, as though protesting against the strain placed upon it. He would say, at a guess, that it was capable of keeping the level of the water constant in the flooded shaft and road but no more than that.

When he had done with looking he asked a furnaceman how it came to be there, and why a new pit like Llangatwg was not equipped with modern apparatus. The man said, breathlessly, that it had been bought second-hand from an old, worked-out pit lower down the valley. Lovell went out of the shed, crossed the yard and shouldered his way through the crowd into the pit manager's office, where a group of men in topcoats were standing round a stocky figure studying a plan of the workings. He did not bother to introduce himself but said, firmly but politely, "Who is the owner of the mine? Would it be one of you gentlemen?"

They looked at him, surprised that a layman, and a stranger at that, could ask such a question at a time like this. Then the man holding the plan grunted, "I'm pit-manager. Gaffer isn't here yet. Who the hell are you?"

"My name is Lovell," Bryn said, still politely. "I'm Abergavenny manager for Swann-on-Wheels, the hauliers, but there's no point in wasting time. I know a way to get those men out alive. If you're prepared to listen I'll talk. If not then I must go and find the owner."

The men gaped at him, their protests checked by his air of authority. Then Dowlais, the manager, said, "Never heard o' you or your business, but if you've anything useful to say for Christ's sake say it. I'll listen."

"That pump can't do more than keep the water level," Bryn said. "What's more, if you go on working it like that its boiler will burst and then the water will flood all your levels. It's a very old pump and ought never to have been installed in the first place."

Dowlais took his pipe from his mouth, stared hard at Lovell and then spat at the stove. "You've got no call to say things like that," he said, "even if they're true. What the hell do you mean, barging in here and lecturing me about the bloody pump?" He had been on the point of ordering Lovell from the premises but the man's unwinking gaze made him think twice about it so he went on, in a surly tone: "Not that you're talking twaddle. We could clear that shaft and road in twenty-four hours if we had a Shannon pump, but where the hell are we to lay hands on one? You got a Shannon pump in your pocket?"

One of the men standing by tittered but Lovell's expression did not change. He said, in the same level voice, "I know where I can find a Shannon pump. With a cleared line down below I could get it into Llangatwg before dark. There's a Shannon pump consigned for Steepcote Colliery waiting at Merthyr. It's lying on a siding now. If I were you I should commandeer it. I wouldn't waste time getting the owner's permission, for he doesn't even know it's arrived yet. It's two days early, on account of me hauling the casing to the railhead three days ahead of schedule."

It was a long speech for a man of Lovell's temperament and it embarrassed him. Suddenly the men surrounding him formed themselves into a respectful circle while Dowlais the manager, looked almost exalted. He moved forward a pace and caught Lovell by the arm. *"You just hauled the casing of a Shannon pump to Abergavenny?* You saw it stowed into a wagon and sent on to Merthyr?"

"Yes," said Lovell, fastidiously extricating himself from the manager's grip, "but that was two days since. The pump is dismantled, of course, and would have to be hauled up here and assembled."

The flush of excitement in Dowlais' face faded. He said, with a bitter oath, *"How?* How could a thing as heavy as that be hauled up and set to work? Bloody narrow gauge is frozen solid. We can't even get a hundredweight of coal down much less something weighing four tons up."

"I'll get it here if you'll make a place for it and start it working. You've got men here who could assemble it. It's very simple."

"Damn it, I could assemble it myself," Dowlais said, his voice shooting off key, "and Steepcote's directors wouldn't give a curse about me borrowing it. No colliery would at a time like this, wi' nigh on a hundred men holed up in the galleries east of that dip." He paused. "How could you get it up? You mean you've got waggons and teams down in the town?"

"No," Bryn said, "I haven't got any waggons and no teams of my own nearer than Abergavenny. But I could assemble them by the time the Shannon was here, for I know to a decimal point what haulage gear you have about here. It's part of my business to know a thing like that."

"Aye, it would be, it would be," Dowlais said, thoughtfully, and then, suddenly erupting, "Get about it, man! Get drays and teams assembled at the halt platform ready to load up, and leave that bloody Shannon and the railway company to me. Thomas—Rudlipp —Morgan, run and tell Trevor Davies to clear his line and keep it clear. Stop every train running between Abergavenny and Merthyr both ways, and make him find a driver and fireman to run a light engine and two flat cars along to Merthyr depot the minute you get down there. Tell him you've Steepcote's permission to load that Shannon and bring it back here, and two of you go along and see it's done, d'ye hear me? Corder, Powlett—tell the linesman and deputy to come in here. I'll want all those trucks of ours heaved off the rails to leave it clear for offloading. I'll want the shed over the new shaft stripped clean to house the pump. I'll want any damn number o' things. . . ."

"You'll want every man and woman standing out there to dig the track free of snow for the horses to get up the gradient," Lovell said. "See that they spread the snow evenly each side of the track. That way I've some kind of platform to work on." And then, with a nod, he turned on his heel and walked out as men ran before him and past him on their various errands and the crowd parted to let them through, as though their urgency represented the first seeds of hope planted in that place since the siren had summoned them there.

5

Mercifully the sky remained clear and no further snow threatened, but towards the middle of the afternoon the wind got up, blowing down from the mountains and raising a spume of powdered snow on the surface of the drifts. It was an easterly that cut to the bone but nobody heeded it. Down the length of the mile-long narrow gauge a thousand men and women scooped and shovelled, laying bare the sleepers and digging deep into the hard snow between them with spades and hearth shovels and scraps of board and sometimes their bare hands. They worked tirelessly and in almost complete silence, so that soon the track lay exposed the whole of its length, with sand and gravel making a fairly level path all the way from the main line halt to the first of the loading bays. Over to the right, where the winding gear of the new shaft was silhouetted against the sky, men were making a second path, not broad enough for a waggon, for these had been Lovell's instructions, but wide enough for the passage of a horse or a string of horses, one yoked behind the other. The shed at the end of the path was stripped clean, its contents flung out into the snow, and when Dowlais was satisfied that all that could be achieved pending the arrival of the pump had been done he stumped the length of the track, asking for an Abergavenny haulier called Lovell, and learning that he was below awaiting the special goods train that Stationmaster Davies had dispatched on his own responsibility.

Down here was tremulous expectancy, in great contrast to the active, feverish atmosphere higher up the slope. Men, women and children stood about, blowing on their hands, stamping their feet, and every now and again each of them glanced up the line, hoping to be the first to spot the smoke of Trevor Davies' special, carrying the miraculous Shannon, as it came trundling round the bend. Dowlais, striding through them, found Lovell supervising the work of removing the wheels from two drays borrowed from a brewery, and when Dowlais realised what he was doing he said, wonderingly, "What are you about, man? You can't get the pump up that mountain without wheels, can you?" but Lovell said, in the same quiet tone, that he could not get it up there on wheels, and was converting the linked drays into a large sled that could be dragged over levelled stretches of packed snow on either side of the track. Harnessed to this a string of horses, one ahead of the other, would have some hope of finding a sure footing in the gravel between the sleepers.

Dowlais knew then that he had been far luckier than he deserved, than any man in his situation deserved. This politely-spoken Abergavenny haulier was a genius, a genius of improvisation, and no other kind of genius would have been the slightest use to the men trapped in the pit. Dowlais' practical training came hurrying to his

298

rescue, so that he was able to accept the man's thesis at once and consider its implications. He said, speculatively, "How many horses will you need, Lovell? Remember that gradient is one-in-six," and Bryn replied, "I've had offers of fifty but I can't use more than ten. They'll have to work in a string and a string of ten will be hard to keep in line. I've already selected the ten strongest. They'll do it, I hope, properly managed."

"You'll stay and supervise?"

"I wouldn't trust anyone else to do it. A generation ago people in the valleys knew something of horses. But since then you've done your hauling by rail."

Dowlais said nothing to that. His own life, as surely as the lives of the men in the flooded galleries, depended upon this quiet, forceful stranger. If the men and boys could be taken out alive, he still had a chance. If they were already dead he was finished anyway, not because dismissal would surely follow but because no man in the valleys could carry that load of guilt and survive.

A ripple of excitement culminating in a ragged cheer announced the first sighting of Trevor Davies' Special and as the engine and its two flat cars rattled round the wide curve in the line it was seen that the raid upon the Merthyr goods yard had been successful. Two tarpaulin-covered humps on the cars proclaimed the presence of the pump and within seconds of the train sliding into the halt a hundred pairs of hands were stripping away the fastenings and exposing the green casing of the Shannon in four, straw-filled crates, each as tall as a man.

Down here on the platform the snow was no great hindrance. Men slipped and slithered, and one fell on the line breaking his leg, but the crates, eased from their clamps on the cars, glided across the platform and down the ramp to the point where the dismantled drays had been laid, two cumbersome rafts bolted together at twenty points, and stripped of every protuberance that could be removed with hammer, screwdriver or wrench.

Lovell himself backed the first of the horses into the single shafts, a great broadchested Shire, the only horse present that would have caught his eye at an auction. Then, with a volley of shouts, a snapping of leather and the pleasant jingle of metal, nine other horses were added to the string, so that children prancing in the snow forgot their grief and terror for a moment and stared wide-eyed at the cavalcade, seeing perhaps a sledge made ready for a winter journey by a warrior king, Llewellyn, or Arthur himself.

299

Lashing the crates dead centre of the sledge proved tricky but Lovell, not to be hurried, instructed the carpenters to screw a set of clamps either side of the centreboard and then, as an additional safeguard, he used some fifty yards of rope threaded through the iron loops on the leading edges of the drays. Dusk was falling when the strange cavalcade moved off across level ground to the foot of the narrow-gauge track. Breath hung on the frost laden air and lanterns were lit to illuminate the scene round the point of departure where Lovell set about marshalling the team in a dead straight line before calling Dowlais to ask if he could recommend a reliable man to take the bridle of the leader.

"My place is with the wheeler," he explained, "for that's where things can go wrong. One false step from that Shire and the sledge will slip sideways, and God knows how we should get it back on course if it happened halfway up."

Dowlais said, "Ted Hughes is your man then. You don't need me, I'll go ahead and collect a team to assemble the pump overnight. With luck we could have her working by morning." He did not add what was in his mind, that even if the Shannon was as good as he anticipated, twenty-four hours would elapse before it pumped shaft and road free of water. By then the men would have been entombed for thirty-six hours. He looked back halfway up the slope and saw, as in a scene painted by Brueghel, the long string of bobbing lanterns around the double-blob that was Lovell's sledge.

Lovell placed a man on either side of each horse, twenty men in all, with himself astride the line holding the wheeler's bridle. Others he told off to space themselves back from the rails all the way up the slope, with instructions to keep the snow untrodden on each side of the track. If it once turned to slush under their feet, he said, a straight course was out of the question and all hope of an ascent would be forfeited.

When everything was ready he gave the command and the long line moved off, passing smoothly over the first two hundred yards where the gradient was no more than one in ten. Then, when they were level with one of the rock flaws that had tormented the railway engineers, the team faltered and the ungainly vehicle began to lurch, left, then right, then left again. For five seconds the enterprise hung in the balance as he threw his whole weight forward, as though to drag the wheeler up the slope, and suddenly they were back on course, moving at the rate of perhaps a mile an hour, with a score of men pushing, or trying to push, and two files strung out along the ad-

300

vance, each man holding a wedge to jam under the backboards if the horses floundered and the sledge began to slip.

At the halfway mark, at a word from Lovell, they dropped in their wedges and the horses took the strain, their hooves flailing madly in the gravel and skidding from the glacial surfaces of the sleepers. For a moment it was touch and go but once more, after a moment's breather, they started upward again, the crowd of struggling men in the rear growing every moment as more and more came streaming down from the pithead.

A rumour that soon became fact ran among them as they heaved and struggled in the wake of the sledge. Bummy Watkins, seventeen years old, had emerged half an hour ago, bobbing out of the black water in the shaft like a man returning from the dead. Incredulously they heard that he had swum the dip, twenty yards or more under water, surfacing half-drowned among a swirl of props floating on the scummy surface. The feat was a miracle and one that only Bummy could have performed, for he was reckoned the strongest swimmer in the Valley, but he would have drowned for all that if, beyond the dip, he had not had the luck to surface directly under a spot where roof subsidence gave him head clearance. Then, understanding precisely where he was, he had dived again and this time he had made the shaft, attracting the attention of a safety inspector who was perched there taking soundings. He was too chilled and exhausted to tell them much but the news he brought out was enough to sustain hope. At least fifty-one of the missing men were alive and clear of the water level. There was no gas down there and although some of the men were injured they could hold out if enough water was pumped out to enable them to wade as far as the shaft. Dowlais, hearing Bummy's story first-hand, went out to the loading platform and stared down at the long, bobbing line of lanterns, now, he estimated, within four hundred yards.

"We'll save 'em yet," he told the linesman. "We'll save every one alive down there but we couldn't have, we couldn't have done a damn thing without that man Lovell." He resisted the temptation to join the scurrying groups, now racing down the steepest section of the hill towards the crawling sledge. His place was here, briefing the men who would install and operate the Shannon pump before daylight crossed the rim of the mountain. For this at least he could promise, if only the Shannon could be brought to level ground.

They were about two hundred yards from the crest when the leading horse stumbled and its follower, throwing its weight on its haunches, sent a shudder down the whole line so that once more there was recoil and the sickening, horrifying zig-zag, left, right, left again as the cry went up for the wedges.

They held her for more than a minute, muscle contending with gravity, iron-shod boots skittering for a purchase on the damnably slippery surface. Lovell, scrambling out of the line, stumbled the full course, remarshalling the team, steadying each horse and each man with word or gesture. Then they were off again, moving now by inches, and five minutes later he knew they would do it for the leader, breasting the crest and finding a firm foothold on level ground, exerted his full weight for the first time since setting off and this straightened the line and doubled the pace as horse after horse came floundering over the rim.

Lovell dragged himself clear, saying nothing about a crushed toe where a hoof had descended on it a hundred yards back but feeling very little pain from the injury for his legs were numb from the knees down. In the confusion of whirling across flat ground to the new pumphouse, and the excitement of offloading and unwrapping the sections, he lost Dowlais but made no effort to seek him out. The man, he thought, would be working to a schedule reduced to seconds. He would have no time to spare for civilities.

For a few moments he watched men clawing the sections from the crates and then limped across to the manager's office, where cocoa was being brewed in a great soup tureen. Someone handed him a mug and he sipped it gratefully. Sensation returned to his feet and he sat down on the floor, pulling off boot and sock to find that both were bloody and the nail of his great toe was askew. As the wound began to throb he took out his handkerchief, bound it round the toe and then replaced sock and boot, wondering where he could find someone to remove the nail and apply a proper bandage. Then, despite the persistent throb, a great drowsiness stole over him and he rested his aching back against the timber walls, his chin touching his breast.

He was still there at four o'clock in the morning when Dowlais, satisfied that the Shannon would be pumping within three hours, came stamping in for cocoa and almost fell over the man asleep, his feet to the fire. He said, wonderingly, "For Christ's sake . . .!" and bent to wake him but then changed his mind and left again, throwing his reefer over the lower half of Lovell's body and leaving instructions that when he awakened he was to be sent across to the pump house.

302

But Lovell did not receive the message. He slept on for another two hours and was overlooked in the turmoil that accompanied the first plunge of the new pump, and the wild cheering that greeted the news that it was a corker, and would reduce the flood to a string of puddles in no time at all. He pottered around for a while and then, after giving the teamsters instructions to return the horses and drays to their owners, he went limping down the slope into the town and boarded the first train for Abergavenny. He knew, somehow, that they would get through in time. And unlike his colleagues, Ratcliffe and Blubb, self-advertisement debased him.

It was four days after that, when the whole country was aware that fifty-one of the missing eighty-seven had been brought out alive after the installation of a Shannon pump, dragged up the hillside by ten dray horses and any number of Welshmen, that Dowlais ran him to earth in his shabby little lean-to at the Abergavenny yard.

He said, with a northcountry oath that sounded foreign in this area, "Don't you realise the whole bloody shift would have been down there yet if you hadn't told me about that pump, and hauled it up there practically singlehanded? I don't give a damn whether you like it or not, a full report including your name has gone in to the owners, and you'll be well paid for your trouble. Aye, and for your brains."

He glanced around, noting a billhead on the desk flap bearing a curious trademark, a swan with wheels where its wings should have been. "This boss of yours in London," he said, "what's his name, and where can I reach him?" and when Lovell told him, "He ought to know what kind of chap he's got down here, running his tin-pot waggon service!"

But then Bryn Lovell surprised him again, saying, with dignity, "The fact that you seem to be unaware of the service is your loss, Dowlais. Swann-on-Wheels is established now in all parts of the country. It has a good reputation, both as regards rates of haulage and delivery on time, sometimes ahead of time. If that hadn't been so that pump would have been scattered about the goods yard yonder, instead of where it is, drying out your ill-found pit. Remember to put that into your report to the owners."

Dowlais was not offended. He stuck his short pipe in his mouth and said, equably, "And so I shall, man. Every damn word of it. And while I'm here I'll take the liberty of pocketing some of these billheads and drum up some Valley trade on your behalf. You deserve that if nowt else! How many waggons has your firm got based about here?''

Lovell told him a dozen, two three-horse-men-o'-war, four two-horse frigates, and half-a-dozen pinnaces for local deliveries. Dowlais said, grimly, "You'll soon need a dam' sight more if I have owt to do wi' it!" and then left. Like Lovell he was a man of few words.

*   *   *

The story leaked out in driblets. Down here there was no trumpet blast of publicity, as in the case of Ratcliffe's lion-catching exploit, or Blubb's brush with the Fenians, but the impact was more lasting and productive. The people of the Valleys, Adam found, had retentive memories. No man who had witnessed or taken part in that haul over the snow ever forgot it, or the man who made it possible, so that whenever Lovell appeared in the district people referred to him as 'Swann's man', and what he had accomplished with someone else's drays, and someone else's horses, attached itself to his employer's trademark rather than to himself. Soon the insignia was familiar all over the southern part of the Mountain Square. When waggons were needed it was the sign rather than the man who sprang to mind, even among prosaic men, who had once been content to let their goods hang about railway sidings during complicated cross-country deliveries. They would say, when consigning merchandise here, there and everywhere, "Get it on the rail ..." and then, "No ... send it by road. That Swann-on-Wheels joker, who stole the pump from Steepcote's, time o' the Llangatwg disaster," so that ripples of that struggle up the narrow gauge moved out across the Principality and beyond, finally reaching Tybalt, in the Bermondsey yard. He would say, pushing up his spectacles, "My word! Lovell is a trier, Mr. Swann. Here's another contract from the collieries. Do you suppose he's found a way to undercut the railways on short hauls from dock to pithead?" And Adam would reply that one could never be sure what was to be expected from Lovell or Ratcliffe, or from that old drunkard Blubb, and this would sometimes set him thinking on the nature of a race that could produce, out of the hat as it were, three such eccentrics, each such a contrast in character and temperament but having some qualities in common; courage, ingenuity, and a streak of obstinacy, that set them apart from the ordinary run of mankind.

2

Study in Soot

NEITHER Henrietta nor Ellen Michelmore, the miller's wife now installed as housekeeper at 'Tryst', had ever heard of the Baroness Lehzen, or of the crisis at Windsor shortly after the young Queen's accession that was caused by the German governess's reluctance to abdicate her rôle. And yet, by the spring of 1863, when the Swanns had been settled at 'Tryst' for three years, an almost exactly similar situation developed between a young woman who saw herself as lady bountiful of the district, and an astute peasant, herself the mother of a string of married daughters and the disappointed wife of an amiable rustic.

Ellen Michelmore, in whose sagging body burned a flame of ambition rare in a woman of her circumstances, behind whose pale, expressionless eyes lurked a brain as sharp as a pin, lost no time at all in exploiting her stroke of luck at being the only person on hand to deliver Henrietta Swann's first child. It was this that had gained her the confidence of man and wife and once she was elevated to the rôle of housekeeper, and had satisfied herself that Adam Swann, obsessed by his business concerns, spared hardly a thought to his domestic background, she set about translating that confidence into indispensability. In a few months she was recognised by all as the force to be reckoned with at 'Tryst'. Within two years, when Henrietta's second child Alexander was still in long clothes, she was accepted, in all but fact, as the mistress of the place, Henrietta having become entirely dependent on the seventeen-stone villager, who issued most of the orders and vetted all the servants, engaging those who were likely to pay her deference and dismissing applicants who promised to resist dictatorship.

She achieved all this by a skilful mixture of bluff, stealth and flattery, together with a single-mindedness that Baroness Lehzen herself might have envied. Towards Adam she was careful to display the utmost respect, and when she could kept clear of him, for her instinct told her that he was a man not easily gulled. Her efforts were

305

therefore directed exclusively towards Henrietta, concerning whom, within a month or two of the commencement of their association, she made a number of interesting and profitable discoveries.

She discovered, for instance, that what Adam tolerated as immaturity and inexperience in his wife was really part of her inheritance as the product of a penniless Irish immigrant, and a man who had started out in life as a coal-comber in the furnace of a Lancashire cotton mill. Adam had seen, indeed he still saw, Henrietta's quaint obsession with scarlet-clad Empire builders as a romantic fancy for the traditional trappings of military pomp, of the kind put to good account by the manufacturers of the tin of toffees she had packed in her basket trunk the night she ran away from home. Ellen Michelmore, having served time as a scullerymaid among the newly-rich in a country house in Hertfordshire, recognised it as something more significant, the terrible yearning on the part of an upstart to be absorbed into what she thought of as something deeply rooted in the social pattern of the nation, an impulse as hard and thrusting as her husband's apparent need to look for his reputation in the matrix of the new age.

Ellen was not, of course, alone in this assumption regarding her employer. Every member of the staff at 'Tryst' flattered themselves that they could distinguish between the 'real' gentry and one of themselves, who had made a fortunate marriage. They did not hold this against the missis. The least generous of them begrudged her her luck and the others, a majority, accepted the situation as confirmation that their folklore was spun from fact and that, from time to time, a Cinderella did watch a pumpkin turn into a coach and marry the Prince. There was nothing in the fairytale to suggest, however, that, once installed in the palace, Cinderella was eager to move over for one of the Ugly Sisters, and this was precisely what was occurring before their eyes. Everybody for miles around was aware that Ellen Michelmore was disposed, if permitted, to give herself intolerable airs, but not until now had the locals taken her pretensions at all seriously. With the new missis entirely under her sway this was something they were obliged to do and those who continued to snigger were soon identified, sent packing and replaced with the housekeeper's nominees. Steadily, month by month, and sometimes, it appeared, day by day, the influence of the miller's wife became more absolute and no one understood, in precise terms, how this subtle miracle was achieved. But Ellen knew, and hugged herself in the knowledge.

Ellen Michelmore made other discoveries about the twenty-two-year-old girl of whom she learned to speak (but did not think) as 'the pore lamb', as though Henrietta had been the ailing heroine of a tragic tale in one of the weekly magazines, or even a subject for one of Mr. Tennyson's gloomier poems. In addition to her longing to be absorbed into the class, of whom the old Colonel was a fair sample, her mistress was, Ellen decided, a lazy, shiftless girl who was inclined, at the least excuse, to leave the mechanics of day-to-day living in more experienced hands and retreat into fantasy. Her complete lack of practical experience in the field of housewifery was, in fact, one of Ellen's trump cards, and she played it remorselessly, even going so far as to proclaim to anyone who would listen that she was 'takin' the pore lamb in hand', or 'teachin' young missis 'ow to conduct 'erself, 'ome an' abroad'. Ellen Michelmore's notions of how a person in Henrietta's situation should conduct herself were based upon her observations, through the green baize door, of the large household where she had served part of her childhood and most of her youth as scullerymaid, kitchenmaid, still-room maid and ultimately, for three blissful months before marriage, as parlourmaid. Her tuition hinged upon the simple precept that no 'real lady' ever soiled her hands with work, or made a single decision concerning the ordering of the house without first consulting the departmental expert, via the housekeeper. There were, however, certain matters that she was privileged, indeed obliged, to attend to, including the issuing of invitations to her monthly 'At Home', an occasional croquet party and, of course, the visiting of the sick and aged in the surrounding villages. These duties, in her opinion, were more than enough to occupy the mind of the lady of the manor, leaving her no leisure to participate in such mundane rituals as the preparation of menus, the weekly check of linen, the training of young servants, and the replenishment of household stores. In the odd, unoccupied moments between visiting, entertaining and 'resting' on the sofa, she could, if she felt disposed, do a little flower arranging, sew a little, picnic, or play with the children, so long as she confined this to regulated hours that did not conflict with the syllabus of the plummy-voiced governess Ellen had engaged. That was all, apart, of course, from keeping the master happy on the rare occasions he was at home, and as regards this Ellen was very particular, for it was not lost upon her that her mistress wilted at the knees the moment Adam embraced her. This suited her very well. It meant that, during his brief visits, she was free to run 'Tryst' the way she would have run it herself had she enjoyed Cinderella luck when she was seven stones instead of seventeen, or had possessed the looks and figure that had secured, for this chit of a girl, the good fortune of attracting the roving eye of a gentleman.

In this way, moving stealthily from covert to covert, Ellen Michelmore soon had the entire ménage safely in hand. The comfort and security that had eluded her in life was now within her grasp, and she felt she could look forward to an uninterrupted reign of cushioned privilege that would have seemed an impossible dream before that horse Dancer had taken it into his head to deposit a man and wife on her doorstep. In the whole of her calculations Ellen made but one minor error. She did not, it seems, make allowance for the effect a life of idleness might have upon Henrietta, once she had come downstairs after her second confinement and was looking about for a means of passing the time during Adam's follow-up expansion period, when he was away three weeks out of four.

It was this miscalculation, one that anyone might have made, that led to an incident that ruined the whole enterprise, exposing her expectations as fantasies of the kind her mistress indulged in concerning gentility and her future rôle as the mother of heroes. For the fact of the matter was, as time went on, and Adam became more and more absorbed in business that swept him from one end of the country to the other, Henrietta grew insufferably bored and her boredom, unable to digest a nonstop diet of fantasy, induced in her a petulance that was wholly uncharacteristic. 'At Homes', where she entertained, or was entertained by, a succession of tittle-tattling old trouts, were not frequent enough to absorb the energy she accumulated during the periods Adam was away and neither, it seemed, was sick-visiting, an occasional croquet party, sewing, flower-arranging, and an hour or so a day spent in baby-talk with Stella and Alexander. Slowly, and reluctantly, she came to realise that life at 'Tryst' was not all it had promised to be, that there were times when she yearned to cook a little, scrub a little, even flirt a little, but she had not yet arrived at the point where she would admit, even to herself, that the colours were beginning to fade and she felt as unsettled as she had been at Scab's Castle before flashpoint.

She tried, most desperately, to fill her days, without disregarding dear Ellen's persistent advice as to how the gently born should fill them, and in a way she half-succeeded by romanticising at a remove, that is to say, becoming a devoted subscriber to Mr. Mudie's Select Library.

Until then she had hardly ever opened a book, for she was not endowed with the ability to sit still for more than ten minutes, but with so much time on her hands books began to play an important part in her life, so that she developed a taste for all Mr. Mudie's currently popular authoresses, beginning with Miss Charlotte Yonge, and moving thence to Mrs. Henry Wood, Mrs. Oliphant, and Miss Braddon. The book that obsessed her beyond all others was Mrs. Henry Wood's *East Lynne*, that still had the entire country in tears, although it had been published about the time of her marriage and had since had many imitators. She also subscribed to a number of popular magazines, including the improving *Monthly Packet*, containing romantic stories by other lady novelists, notably the mysterious 'Ouida' (Henrietta was never sure how to pronounce the name) who also wrote for *Bentley's Miscellany*, and seemed, to Henrietta, to be excessively daring and was said by some to possess a dangerously heated imagination.

It was curious that a young woman like Henrietta, whose experience of life was, she would judge, broad by the standards of other young wives she met, should derive such deep satisfaction from the cautious adventures of heroines she would have dismissed as 'touch-me-notters' had she met them in person. But she did, for somehow, or so it seemed to her, these women, particularly the newly-married among them, were courted and won by far more unpredictable males than Adam, inasmuch as one never quite knew, until turning the page, how their menfolk would react to a given set of circumstances. With Adam one did know and that, she thought was sometimes very tiresome.

The heroine who enslaved Henrietta's imagination the moment *East Lynne* came into her hands was Lady Isobel, whom she regarded, within certain limits, to be her own parallel, for Mr. Carlyle, Isobel's husband, obviously loved her dearly but was very much wrapped up in his business and, again like Adam, inclined to leave her to her own devices most of the time. Possibly alone among Mrs. Henry Wood's subscribers Henrietta Swann was not surprised when Isobel ran away with the wicked Captain Levison. She was clearly at a loss to know what else to do with herself and sometimes, although not very seriously, Henrietta wished that a less caddish and more timid Captain Levison would make some improper advances to her so that she could experience the satisfaction of being sought after by someone other than her husband, who, notwithstanding the illuminating discussions concerning the relative rôles of husband and wife, persisted in treating her like an enlarged edition of Stella, his three-year-old daughter.

Sometimes, particularly when she was riding her cob Stocky around the park or down the towpath of the river as far as the village, she would find herself yearning to participate in some tremendous adventure of the kind that Adam seemed to have had in plenty but to have taken very lightly, but then she would tell herself that she was not so much in need of this kind of stimulus as a boost of a more personal nature, of being the very core, for instance, of some man's world and for rather longer, she would hope, than it took Adam to satisfy his storming impatience the moment they were alone.

Not that she had the least quarrel with the demands he made upon her. Indeed, she wished he was on hand to make them more often, although perhaps in a more restrained manner for gradually, under his gay tutelage, she had rid herself of those feelings of guilt she had experienced during moments of intimacy in the past and had learned to accept his boisterous advances as a welcome bonus of marriage to a man who came and went like a Jack-in-a-box.

She had hopes, that spring, of being pregnant again, and producing another son who would grow up to join the Navy, and perhaps engage in a friendly rivalry with Alexander of the Household Cavalry, but when it proved a false alarm she felt cheated and was sufficiently self-analytical to understand why. Deep in her consciousness she still saw her main function in life as the mother of a tribe of big, lusty men, who campaigned in the furthest corners of the globe, and came home loaded with honours and clanking with medals. She was aware that Adam thought this obsession of hers ridiculous but it was not ridiculous to her, remaining the one focal point of her dreams and, as such, the only aspect of her that survived the time when she was a fifteen-year-old, reading stirring tales of the Crimea and the Mutiny in newspapers that Sam brought into the house. It therefore qualified as nostalgia and it was very easy to indulge in nostalgic dreams when she was alone so much, and had her being in a place like 'Tryst', with its whispering stairs, its overgrown coverts, and its subtle garden scents. It gave her a sense of living a life within a life, of identifying not only with the heroines of Miss Yonge and Mrs. Wood, but with all the heroines of poetry, and perhaps the most haunting of these was that unfortunate Lady of Shallott, whose brief, tragic career had been graphically illustrated in one of her magazines. There was a special reason for this, of course. A mile or so down the river, at a point where the stream broadened after threading its course through a belt of timber, there was a small wooded islet, and whenever she passed it she would glance across just to make sure that Lancelot was not in view, and to satisfy herself that no battlemented tower showed above the willows that grew down to the water's-edge.

These kinds of fancies, of course, were forgotten the moment Adam returned from his Bermondsey headquarters, or from one of his visits to those areas he called by outlandish names, 'The Crescents', 'The Polygon', 'The Western Wedge', and the like. Then, as though she was deliberately stepping out of the Middle Ages into a life of stir, bustle and laughter, she would become Henrietta Swann again, or even Henrietta Rawlinson, the girl a real Lancelot had kidnapped, married with a mere pretence of wooing, saddled with a house and a couple of children, and now liked to treat as though she was his toy to be taken from the cupboard and tossed about with a kind of exultant glee, against the time when he had more urgent matters on hand.

It was very disconcerting to sit on such a seesaw and one morning, in March of that year, when the noise of birds in the wisteria outside the window awakened them simultaneously, she opened her heart to him, telling him that she ached with loneliness when he was away, and asking him if it was not possible, now that he was well established, to spend more of his time at home. He was not angry or irritated, as she feared he might be, but sat up in bed, yawned, and looked down at her indulgently.

"Now why tell me that," he said, tolerantly. "You're happy here, aren't you? You've got the house and the children and the Colonel for company, and it's what you wanted, isn't it? Because if it isn't and you would sooner move nearer London, we'll move and the devil take the tail-end of the lease. It was what I originally intended, to live much closer in. If I did I could get home two weeks out of three, and every night when I was in town."

The prospect of being deprived of her foothold in the world of the real gentry dismayed her so that she said, hastily, "Oh no, dearest. I *love* this place, and so does Stella and the Colonel, and so will Alex when he grows a little older. I wouldn't like to live in a city but . . . well . . . it would be *nice* if you were here to enjoy it more often."

"Enjoy you or the background?" he said, with one of his infuriating grins and she said, impatiently, "You know perfectly well what I mean! Why won't you stop treating me as if I was a ninny?"

"Oh, come now," he said, though still amiably, "if I talked business to you you'd yawn your pretty head off and I can't say as I'd blame you. Being immersed in a job like mine is one thing. To have to listen to second-accounts of it, and supply the dutiful 'Really, dears?' and 'How splendids!' every so often, is quite another. Besides," he continued, passing his hand across her rumpled hair, "it wouldn't be you, Henrietta. It wouldn't be the little scapegrace I married. I'm satisfied with you as you are and by now that ought to be obvious to you."

"But we're not talking about *your* satisfaction," she protested, "we began talking about mine, and I don't mean by that I want more things and clothes and friends, but more of you."

"That brings us back to the original question," he said, and she was encouraged to see that he was no longer teasing her but at least moderately interested. "If you enjoy being a wife to me, and you're still bewitched by the house, what the devil have you got to complain of?" Then, with that knack of his he had for rooting among her secret thoughts, "Are you trying to tell me you were disappointed that you weren't having a third child? I suppose I understand that if you were. Children to you are what a new branch is to me, and that isn't as silly as it sounds. It's fulfilling a purpose, creating something, and you've never made a secret about wanting a thumping great family." He paused again and she saw that he was now regarding her with a kind of speculative interest. "That's unusual too, come to think of it. Most women of your age would only pretend to be pleased if they found themselves pregnant a third time in four years. Did you know that?"

"I often suspected it," she said, her humour restored by the fact that at least he had stopped talking down to her, "they bill and coo too obviously, and start boasting as soon as the men have left the room."

He laughed at that and she reflected that she invariably made him laugh when she spoke her thoughts aloud. But she had no intention of letting him turn the conversation aside, as he usually did when she was advancing a point of view, and went on, "Honestly, Adam, I'm at a loss to know why you married me at all. Men—or your kind of man—could get along very well without a wife, and you actually did for years. You've got your business, and clearly get a tremendous amount of pleasure out of building it up, and well . . . as for the shameless way you use me up here, there are those other kinds of women, that nobody mentions but anyone with a hap'orth of sense

312

knows about. Of course, you spoil little Stella, but you're not really a family man. If I had a dozen children I'm sure you would mix up their names when you came back after one of your tours."

She had him interested now and experienced a certain satisfaction at her own cleverness. He said, seriously, "I've asked myself that many a time, Henrietta," and her glow of self-satisfaction faded. "As you say, I've done precisely what I set out to do, founded something vital and constantly developing, and I never even thought about marrying until I was turned thirty. But for all that I did, didn't I? And without second thought when it came to the crunch."

Her vanity began to steal back, re-entering a room from which it had just been banished and recalled by an indulgent parent. She said, "Well?" and when he said nothing, "Come now, it's not fair to leave it like that! You've often half-told me but never properly, never in a way that I can think about when you aren't there."

She touched him then, as she often could with her impish ways and little spurts of rebellion. He kissed her on the mouth and kicking the bedclothes clear with his heels ran his hand the length of her body, so that she knew this promising conversation might as well not have been started. She did not care either, or not that much, for suddenly his towering masculinity impinged itself on her in the way it invariably did when they were alone in this great bedroom, with its ghosts of innumerable earthy Conyers, none of whom had bothered to debate the abstracts of marriage. She said, stroking his chin, "Oh, fiddlesticks, you can tell me later. Tell me something else. Why don't you grow whiskers, like other men? I thought of it when I went to that fête over at Kynaston House, for there wasn't a man there who wasn't stroking his mutton-chops, or twirling his moustaches. I said to myself, 'How horrid it must be to be kissed by someone with hair all over his face'. Apart from those bristles of yours before you've done shaving, of course."

He said, with tremendous emphasis, *"Why, that's it, Henrietta!!* That's your answer! That's why I married you."

She was genuinely astonished. "Because I never complained of your bristles?"

He said, laughing, "Good God, no, woman. Because you were a nice shape in and out of corsets; because you were fresh and pretty; because you never could stop being a little rascal ready to run away in the middle of the night if you didn't get your own way, but mainly, because you can make me laugh without even trying!", and he seized her and emphasised his approval with a powerful smack on her

313

behind that developed into a wrestling match and came near to depositing them on the floor. He said, when they were breathless, "Wait ... *wait* ...! You asked me a question and it deserves a serious answer. I don't grow a beard because everybody else grows one without knowing why. Or if they did they've forgotten."

"How's that? No, really, I'm interested."

"It's to do with this soldier measles that you and everyone else seems to have caught. We were innocent of whiskers, the whole damned lot of us, until the winter before Sebastopol, when shaving in redoubts was a penance. That was the time photography started, remember? Or were you too young? The patriotic gentlemen at home saw pictures of Raglan's heroes looking like rustics, and suddenly— hey presto—beards were in vogue! Now, of course, they daren't shave them off for fear of losing their authority. Ask any barber and he'll tell you the same!"

She was kneeling above him now and suddenly, almost involuntarily, she was moved to express her extreme satisfaction with him. "Oh, Adam," she cried, "Adam, darling, I do love you! You're so *different*, so—so *unstuffy*, if you see what I mean! Times like this, when we can talk and shut everyone else out, I think myself the luckiest woman alive!"

"I'm delighted to hear it," he said, "for maybe you are." He swung his long legs from the bed, sniffing the morning air with obvious relish. "Suppose we go down, saddle up, and ride over the heath? It's a rare day for a gallop, and nobody will be stirring yet. Would you like that, Mrs. Swann?"

"Yes," she said, eagerly, "I'd like that better than anything," and skipped out of bed a child again, forgetting that she had awakened in such a self-questioning mood, or that he had said very little to resolve the terrible restlessness she felt all the time he was absent. Their marriage was like that, she supposed, a kind of rollicking, tomboyish game they had learned to play with each other, and from which, a little unreasonably to her way of thinking, he could withdraw at will, leaving her to play by herself. And yet, when he was there, and her cheeks were tingling with the scratches inflicted by his bristles, nothing but a deep feeling of thankfulness for his being found its way into a brain that she sometimes thought must be as immature as he had always declared it to be. But she didn't care, not in his presence, and certainly not on a morning like this. She went singing to the clothes closet and yanked out her riding habit, the waisted velvet jacket with big buttons, tight sleeves and wide revers, and the voluminous blue skirt that hitched up at the right to give freedom to a leg hooked over the saddle-horn. He had not yet seen her in this outfit and while he was in his dressing-room, splashing himself, she perched the little hat with its curled ostrich feather on her head, lifting her nightgown to her thighs and prancing back and forth in front of the mirror. He heard her giggling and called, "Hurry now, before Stella catches us and begs to come along."

2

Sometimes her trivial conversations and pouting complaints planted a seed in his mind that would enlarge itself and emerge as an idea that he thought of as his own. It was so in this case for, a day or so later, when he announced that he would be gone for a few days, he suddenly suggested she might occupy herself by arranging a supper dance on the occasion of her approaching birthday.

It was unusual for him to suggest anything of this kind. Such entertaining as she did was of her own or Ellen's ordering, and he very seldom brought guests to the house, telling her that the people with whom he did business were dull dogs outside their counting houses, and he had no mind to inflict them on her. There were several families, however, whom they had met at church, and who had paid calls in his absence, and until then she had always assumed he would dismiss them one and all as 'twitterers', a favourite word of his for the kind of people who left cards, went in for charity fêtes, and made a solemn round of 'At Homes'.

She had made some kind of place for herself in this parochial society but had never aspired to giving anything as grand as a supper-dance that would require, she supposed, a great deal of organising, and the hiring of musicians. She saw his suggestion, however, as a challenge and decided to meet it, saying, "I'd like that, Adam, but on two conditions. One is that you'll promise faithfully not to make a fool of me by staying away, the other that I have new hangings for the double room, for the fire smokes horribly and the furnishings are quite black. It needs a new carpet but we won't want a carpet for dancing and I can get someone to wax the floor."

"Well, that's your concern," he said, carelessly, already in a hustling mood. "Buy what you need, so long as it isn't too fancy, and I promise to be home for your birthday. I'm only going as far as

315

Crescent South and looking in on The Bonus on the way down."

She went about the preparations with the greatest enthusiasm, sending out fourteen invitations to families who she knew had sons and daughters who would enliven the occasion, for so far nearly all her visitors had been couples of another generation. The response startled her. Everyone accepted, and the final tally was thirty, of whom nearly half were people of her own age, or younger.

Under Ellen's eye she pretended to supervise the cleaning and clearance of the big double room west of the porch, where there would be ample space for the polka and even, at a pinch, a set of lancers. Above it, the minstrel gallery added by the Conyer who had composed his own madrigals, was cleared out to make room for two fiddlers and flautist, promised by the rector, Mr. Bascomb, who earned an invitation on that account. The floor coverings were removed, an accumulation of dust banished, and the maids told off to beeswax the pine floor, after which Henrietta drove into Croydon to spend a pleasant day selecting brocade in a shade of sunflower yellow for the new curtains, and a length of green, bobble-fringed silk for a mantelshelf drape that Ellen arranged in carefully regimented folds.

All other work about the house was scamped and the staff responded nobly to her appeals, so that the days flew and every morning she awakened with a renewed flutter of excitement and sense of having overlooked any number of essentials. Among them, not recollected until forty-eight hours before he was due to return, was the rogue chimney, for when Ellen lit a trial fire in the grate dense clouds of smoke threatened to leave a layer of soot over the new curtains and asphyxiate the guests into the bargain if a fire was lit on the night.

Ellen dried her tears by promising to get hold of Millward, the sweep, within the hour, explaining that at this season of the year a fire was essential, and that the chimney needed a thorough scraping. To her certain knowledge, she added, it had not been swept in seven years.

Millward appeared that same afternoon and Henrietta thought she had never made the acquaintance of a dirtier or more brutalised man, not even among the town rowdies of Seddon Moss. It was difficult to judge his age under so much grime, and he might have been anything from forty to sixty. As well as masking his features and coating all other exposed areas of his body, soot had apparently taken residence in his windpipe. Every time he inhaled he whistled and his

316

slurred speech emerged as a sustained hiss that was sometimes difficult to interpret. He took a close look at the chimney with which, he
said, he was familiar, having climbed it himself when he was an
apprentice during the tenancy of the last Conyer occupant.

"Rare blessing you sent for me an' no other," he wheezed. "I
know that chimbley of old, and she's a reg'lar tartar, M'm. She goes
up a matter o' twenty feet, turns sharp left level wi' the first floor, goes
on another ten feet, and comes aht under the woods where the stack
ketches the downdraught when the wind's in the west. She'll smoke
then, no matter what, but not nearly ser bad, not when I done wi'
her. But that level stretch is fair choked, and'll need to be dug out
be the sackfull. After that I dunno, tho' we'd best cross our fingers
fer a shift in the wind, in which case she'll burn sweet an' free."

There seemed nothing to do but pray for a change of wind and
commission Mr. Millward to get about his business with despatch,
but once she had given the order she realised there was more to sweeping a chimney than that, for Ellen said that every item of furniture
would have to be covered with dust sheets, and Millward said he
would have to go back to the town for his two apprentices, Jake and
Luke, the liveliest lads in the trade, who could scale any chimney,
including the episcopal ones at the Archbishop's Palace, where boys
had been known to stay lost for days before being hauled out through
the roof or broken out through a bedchamber wall.

Henrietta was vaguely familiar with the trade, having seen the
flues cleaned by grimy urchins at Scab's Castle, but she had not
realised until then that the architects of old houses had gone to such
extraordinary lengths to dispose of smoke, designing exits that were
as intricate as a maze. She packed Millward off and set the girls to
work hanging dustsheets over the windows, untacking the carefully
arranged mantelshelf drape, and covering furniture too heavy to
be carried into the hall.

Millward appeared with his apprentices very early the next morning and Henrietta, roused by the clatter, jumped from bed and
dressed herself hurriedly, for she did not trust Millward to have a
care for her furniture, taking him to be a man likely to put clean
chimneys before disordered rooms and ruined furnishings.

She bolted her breakfast and was on the scene before eight, when
the sweep and his team had been at work for more than two hours.
The quantity of soot that came down appalled her. She would never
have believed that so much could accumulate in one chimney but
she noticed that Millward himself, for all his knowledgeable airs,

took no part in the actual work, but stood about drinking Ellen's home-brewed beer and paying lugubrious compliments to the maids, who seemed to regard him as a fruity character who might, if flattered, attend their weddings and ensure marital bliss with a traditional sweep's kiss.

Henrietta was less impressed by him. She said, anxiously, "How long do you think you will be? I've got a supper-dance here the day after tomorrow and this room will have to be scoured when you've carted all that mess away."

Millward said that it didn't do to hurry these things and that his gloomy prophecies had been proved correct. The horizontal section of the flue was packed with soot and young Luke was now halfway along it, passing his bags back to Jake, the senior apprentice, who was stationed at the top of the main shaft.

Presently Jake emerged, a bag slung round his neck, and Henrietta gave a yelp of horror. He was like nothing human and did not even resemble a monster. The only feature that reconciled him to the human species was his bloodshot eyes that rolled upward as he said, addressing the sweep, "Bin waitin' 'arf-hour an' Luke ain't passed no more back. You reckon he's stuck?"

"How do I know, you idle little bastard," the sweep said, aiming a blow at him that Jake expertly dodged, "get on up agin and find out. Holler for 'im, and make sure I 'ear you do it!" and then, as Jake re-entered the chimney, Millward remembered that he was in the presence of the lady of the house and wheezed, "Beg pardon M'm, but you've got to chivvy 'em all the time. They'll work, but on'y if they're kept to it. I've known boys sit in one o' those chimbleys 'till you lit a fire under 'em!"

Perhaps because she had gobbled her breakfast, or because the sight of Jake was difficult to put out of mind, Henrietta felt sick and retired to her sewing-room to wait. She was still there, sipping a cup of tea Ellen had brought her, when she heard a frightful uproar from the direction of the double room, followed by a series of indeterminate thuds that seemed to come from above her head. She ran into the hall and across to the big room to find both Jake and his master hauling on a length of rope that went straight up the chimney. Man and boy, she noticed, seemed very excited, and Ellen was on the verge of hysterics, wringing her hands, moaning, and chewing her lips. She cried out, as Henrietta appeared, "Don't stay, M'm, there's trouble, bad trouble! That boy's stuck fast ..." but at that moment Jake shouted, "He's coming! Watch out, missus!" and dropped his hold on the rope to run under the canopy of the fireplace that was blotted out by a flurry of soot, reducing visibility in the room to inches.

Her first thought was that her wonderful supper-dance was ruined. They could never make the room spick and span again in the time left to them and she could have shrieked with vexation, but then, as the cloud of soot began to disperse, dismay was succeeded by horror, for the thing that shot out of the chimney and sent Jake staggering was a boy, a human being, with arms, legs and a great sooty blob for a head, and from where she stood, over by the window, he looked as though he might well be dead.

Ellen let out a shriek and the master sweep began to prance and curse as Jake fell on his knees beside his fellow apprentice, and began a rhythmic cradling movement that amounted to a sustained rocking on his part, but after a minute or so he looked up at Millward and said chokingly, "E's gorne, Mr. Millward! We was too late! I carn't do nothing', nothin'!" and at once began to blubber.

The master sweep dragged him aside and lifted the inert child by his ankles, shaking him as though he had been a sack but then Henrietta, rooted to the spot and speechless with terror, saw that the boy's ankles had a rope knotted to them, and that this was the rope Millward and Jake had been hauling on when she came in.

The realisation that the apprentice had been pulled from the level flue like a cork from a bottle, and had then fallen something like twenty feet down the vertical flue, struck her as the most dreadful experience she had ever contemplated and instinctively, as she partially regained her faculties and ran forward to assist the sweep in his frantic attempt to resuscitate the boy, she realised how Adam would react to such an occurrence, for he had never forgotten that boy Tim Garvin who was ridden down and bludgeoned the night of the riot. She screamed, *"Stop it!* Stop that, you dreadful man! Ellen, fetch your husband, get a doctor ... get water ... *do* something, except shake him like that," and then, as though he too had entered the room via the chimney, Adam was standing there in his riding clothes, crop in one hand, gauntlets in the other with his hat with the silver buckle still on his head. It was like a scene re-created out of a terrible nightmare and, unable to adjust to it, her knees buckled and she fainted.

319

He was much earlier than he had anticipated, remembering how insistent she had been about him returning in time. At the Croydon livery stables, where he kept his gig, he decided to ride the rest of the distance, hiring a chestnut mare that caught his eye. She exceeded expectations and he was turning into the drive in just over an hour of leaving the train.

He looked out for little Stella as he topped the rise but she was not to be seen. Instead, at the entrance of the yard, stood a dogcart with a dejected pony between the shafts, and as he passed it he noted the words, 'J. Millward, Sweep', painted on the backboard.

He paid no particular attention to it but as he was unsaddling the horse he became aware of a stir at the rear of the house and scurrying to and from the kitchen where the pump was clanking. He thought it odd that no one ran out to greet him, and that Ellen's husband, now the groom, was not to be found. He went in through the stableyard door where one of the maids, wheyfaced, and seemingly half out of her wits, was jerking away at the pump handle, and letting the water swill over the edge of the trough. She went on pumping even when he shouted at her. Then he heard his wife's voice raised in violent protest, and ran through the hall and into the double-room, where he saw Henrietta disputing possession of what appeared to be a bag of soot with a squat, bowlegged man evidently J. Millward. Beside them were the Michelmores, both looking as if they had seen a spectre.

For a few seconds he stood gaping, unable to comprehend what could have happened, but then he saw that what he had mistaken for a bag of soot was a boy with a rope tied to his ankles, and blood clotting on raw areas of flesh on knees and elbows that were ringed with soot. He understood then, at least in part, what must have occurred, and it had the power to enrage him in a way that nothing had since he helped to empty the well at Cawnpore, for he had read Lord Shaftesbury's recent appeal to the Lords concerning the usage of chimney sweeps, and the evidence cited had sickened him. Now, he realised, fresh evidence was being accumulated, and that on his own hearthrug, and shame galvanised him into action. He seized the sweep by the shoulder and swung him round, and at that moment Henrietta pitched forward on her knees and bowed her head, just as if she had been shot in the back.

Her fall made no immediate impression on him and he had forgotten she was there when Ellen intervened, wailing some gibberish about the boy being stuck in the chimney. That made him look more closely at the body on the floor and he saw at once the boy must have been dead for some time, for his limbs were rigid and his mouth, half full with soot, was wide open, as though he had died in the act of screaming.

The man said, in a voice that quavered, "Best lad I ever 'ad. If on'y . . ." but he was unable to finish whatever he had been going to say for Adam dropped crop and gloves, swung his fist, and sent him spinning across the width of the room with a tremendous buffet on the point of the jaw.

Millward would have fallen had he not cannoned against the shrouded garden door and clutched at the dust sheets suspended there so that for a moment he seemed to hang, like a bloated spider framed in the aperture. Then, slowly, he half-subsided and his hand shot up to his face as he said, feebly, "You got no call to do that, you got no right to hit . . ." but before he could complete his protest Adam struck him again twice more and this time he did go down, the first blow striking him in the belly, the second stretching him senseless on the floor.

The primitive violence of the assault did something to sober Adam and the haze that floated in front of his eyes shredded away, so that he was belatedly aware there were others in the room besides himself, the sweep, and the dead boy in the hearth. Henrietta was still crouching near the door, with Ellen fussing about her trying to make her sip from an enamel mug, and beyond the bundle of rags in the hearth was another boy, with rolled-up trews revealing thin, spindly shins, who was obviously in a state of shock for he was scrabbling at the granite slabs of the fireplace as though, if he pushed hard enough, they would part and enable him to escape into the open. The sight of the terrified child restored some kind of sanity to Adam, so that he spun round on Ellen, shouting "Get her out of here! Give me that mug," and Ellen said, reproachfully, "It's brandy for Mrs. Swann, sir, she's fainted . . ." but he roared, "I don't give a damn, give it to me! Get her out of here, and come straight back, do you hear?", and she passed him the mug and took Henrietta by her shoulders, dragging her from the room.

He went over to the whimpering boy, thrusting the mug towards him.

"Drink it," he said, "drink it and go through to the kitchen. Ask

321

the girls to send all the men in here," and the boy Jake, responding automatically to the voice of authority, took the mug and gulped down several mouthfuls of spirit, his hands shaking so violently that the mug rattled against his teeth.

Over by the window the master sweep stirred and the movement deflected Adam's attention from the boy who suddenly darted past him and out, fleet as a scared cat. Adam crossed the room and prodded the sweep, with his boot. "Get up," he growled, "get up, man, before I kick you to death!", and the man rose unsteadily to his feet, glaring at Adam with bleared, resentful eyes, and passing the back of his hand to and fro across his bleeding mouth.

"I didden kill 'im," he mumbled. "It was that flue o' yours. Missus says to scrape it, but how could I know he'd git stuck wivaht even 'ollerin' back, like 'ee's trained to?"

Suddenly the mere sight of the man began to act on his self-control like a wrench so that he knew, if he looked at him a moment longer, he would strangle him. He flung open the garden door, grabbed Millward by his collar, and dragged him on to the terrace, and as the sweep writhed in his grasp he remembered the water butt in the yard. They arrived there together at a run and with a single heave he swung Millward clear of the ground and dropped him bodily into the vat.

"Wash the blood off your hands then get out of here before I break every bone in your body!" he said. "Don't show yourself here again or, by God, I'll see you get ten years for this!"

"There's my other boy an' gear ..." Millward spluttered, not daring to make any attempt to climb out of the vat, but Adam said, "The boy stays here and I'll bury your gear with the one you've just killed. I'll give you ten seconds to get in that trap of yours and out of my sight ..." but the man made no further attempt to remonstrate, projecting himself out of the tub, crossing the yard and leaping into the trap, where he grabbed the reins and laid his whip across the pony's back. In something under the time limit he was out of sight behind the first of the copper beeches.

Michelmore came out, the one person in the house, it seemed, in command of himself. He said, bitterly, "I would have stopped it if I'd known, sir, Leastways, I would have warned Mrs. Swann. She couldn't have realised. ... Ellen should ha' told her," and then, seeing Adam's expression, he fell silent.

Adam said, "See to that other boy. Get him washed, fed and bedded down in one of the lofts. Then go for the doctor, he's a magistrate and will have to be told anyway. If he's out on his rounds find him, wherever he is, but before you leave find the gardener and send him to me," and he went along the terrace thinking how quiet everything had gone, so quiet that he could hear rooks cawing in the elms, and the swish of the gardener's billhook in the spinney.

The big room was empty save for the corpse under the chimney canopy. Soot was everywhere, lying in a pyramid in the grate, smeared on the dust sheets, and even marking the imprint of Millward's hands where he had clutched the door coverings. Its acrid smell filled the room and made his eyes smart. He knelt by the boy and satisfied himself that he was dead before lifting him clear of the fireplace and laying him on the sheet covering the chaise longue. Then he went across the hall and into Henrietta's little sewing room behind the dining-room, finding her sitting with her hands in her lap, and on her face the crumpled, bewildered expression of one who has just witnessed something incomprehensible.

"You knew that man was sending his boys up that chimney? You were there when they went up?"

She said, tonelessly, "They were up there when I arrived. One of them came out while I was there but the sweep made him climb back to help the other."

"You let him do that? You *knew* there was a boy stuck up there and let them drag him out with a rope?"

"I . . . I went away . . . I felt sick."

"No doubt," he said, grimly, and then, in an impersonal voice that was foreign to her, "I'm fetching soap, water and a nightshirt. We're going to wash him and lay him out before the doctor comes. Just the two of us, Henrietta, Find an apron or something," and turned on his heel.

Her cry reached him as he was halfway across the threshold. "Adam, I *couldn't*!", and he turned back, staring at her as though she had been an insolent servant. "You will, though, or I'll serve you as I served Millward."

"But why, Adam? Why? It wasn't me who . . ."

"You could have stopped it. You're mistress here, or supposed to be, and you'll do it if I have to drag you there by your hair. Find an apron and gloves," and he went into the hall leaving the door open.

She had the impulse to run, to dart across the paddock to the woods, or up the rhododendron path behind the house and on to the moor, anywhere that offered a refuge from his cold rage, and the

323

prospect of stripping and washing that obscene little corpse in the room across the hall. But she knew that wherever she ran he would pursue her and catch her, and that in the end it would be done in the way he wanted it done, and that he would accept no excuse and no substitute, not even if she died at the task. She dragged herself up, crossed to the chest of drawers and found an apron and a pair of gardening gloves. By the time she had them on he was back with a bucket in one hand and a steaming kettle in the other. Under his arm he had a bundle and she recognised one of her nightdresses by its embroidered collar and lace-edge wristbands.

In the big room the soot had settled but the atmosphere still reeked and she watched him fling open the garden doors. Then, averting her eyes, she joined him beside the couch where he set down his pail and filled it from the kettle. Methodically he began to strip away the filthy rags that covered the child's emaciated body, exposing wide areas of flesh that were only a shade paler than the face, feet and hands. She noticed too that each elbow and kneecap was crowned with an inflamed sore, and that not only the mouth but the eyes and nostrils were choked with soot.

Mechanically, at a nod from him, she dipped one of the cloths in the bucket and tried to remove some of the filth from the loins, while he performed the same task on the chest and shoulders. Slowly the horror of what she was doing began to recede and in its place came pity, but mostly pity for herself at being involved in such a task. Once, when revulsion reached a certain point, she flung down the cloth and turned away, retching, but he said, in the same toneless voice, "Finish it, or you walk out of this house today and never come back."

It astounded her that he could threaten her like that, that he could behave to her as Millward had treated the boy Jake when he had crept from the chimney, whining that he had lost contact with his fellow-apprentice. And then, in a freakish way, she accepted his tyranny, for it went some way towards extricating her from a crushing load of guilt, and as she became aware of this she began to work more attentively, removing layer after layer of grime from other chimneys than her own, and pausing every now and again to wring water from the cloths. When the water in the bucket was quite black he threw it out, replenishing it from the kettle.

After about ten minutes Ellen crept in, her mouth forming a hard line as she realised what they were about. She said, in a whisper, "Dawson and the boy were in the spinney. They'm coming now," and when he made no answer: "Mrs. Swann should go and lay down, sir. It's been a rare shock for her."

Henrietta thought then that he was going to strike Ellen across the face and braced herself against the blow that would send the house-keeper reeling but then he locked one hand over the other, saying, "Take a cloth and help. There's something here you should see, the pair of you." He made room for her and Henrietta stood aside too, following the direction of his pointing finger towards the boy's groin. She saw then that all was not as it should be, for a cluster of seamed scars showed in the crutch. Adam said, in something like a recog-nisable voice, "He's not only bowlegged and a hunchback, he's also a eunuch. He's probably been at the trade since he was five or six. That's a scrotal affliction caused by soot and known as chimney-sweep's cancer. The only treatment for it is the knife. Slip this gown over him while I lift him. Take the other side, Henrietta."

She was past all thought of rebellion. There was implacability in every word he uttered, as though to question it would be to invite the prospect of being throttled and laid beside the child on the couch. Both she and Ellen accepted this and responded to it, so that between them, with him raising the body, they managed to shroud it in her nightgown. She noticed that, small as it was, the robe was too big for him. A foot or more of it had to be tucked under the feet. Then mercifully, he took another sheet from one of the chairs and covered the body, including the face.

"Take her away now," he said to Ellen, "but don't either of you leave the house. You'll have questions to answer, both of you, when the magistrate gets here." They crept from the room, supporting one another like a pair of ageing drunkards and leaving him to his penance.

4

The enterprise was a vast, angled web with its threads running out across innumerable half-deserted turnpikes, dust roads, tracks and streams, spanned by mediaeval packhorse bridges, and rail bridges hardly settled on their redbrick piles, leading to city, town, hamlet and nearly a thousand miles of indented coastline. The coastline was the frame that extended up to the far north-west, along Hadrian's wall, down to the South Foreland, then west to the knob of the

325

Cornish peninsula, but half-a-hundred shorter, lateral threads linked the country in between.

His waggons, more than three hundred of them, followed the routes of derelict coaches now mouldering in outhouses and henruns, out across shire, spurline, river, marsh, across cities old and new, and down the narrow twisting streets of many an ancient market town and village. Yet, one way or another, each of those threads led back to where he sat in his truncated belfry above the Thames, and at every terminal were men answerable to him and him alone, for somehow, over the cygnet years, his zest and self-confidence had run out along the threads to sustain them, and now it was difficult to imagine an alternative dynamo that would keep the wheels turning, or enlist among them much more than a grudging servitude.

This was how they saw it and this was how he had always seen it, a huge, ever-expanding web, with himself as the master spinner, and in the spring of 1863, when the last of his waggons had rolled to their allotted territories, it had seemed a time for self-congratulation, for he had no need of reassurance that his steadfastness and vitality had confounded the Jeremiahs, and that when they doubted now their voices were muted and their warnings qualified. It was even, perhaps, time for retrenchment and consolidation, words that, until then, he had never used, for to him they signified a licensed idleness. In the years ahead there would, so he told himself, be ample time for further expansion, for encroachment into faraway areas like the Highlands where a boy could still grow to manhood without seeing a locomotive, or in Ireland where, despite political turmoil, haulage markets were wide open for the man with ideas and capital to invest. He thought of this as he trotted along the Kentish lanes with his wife's twenty-fourth birthday present in his pocket, warming himself at the glow of his own achievements. And then a thirteen-year-old child called Luke Dobbs came plummeting down his chimney, crashing on to his hearthrug and through the nerve-centre of his ethos.

It would be unrewarding to look for logic in his reaction. Logic, although playing a rôle in his tactics, had no place in his strategy as man or merchant. For four years now his strategy had been based upon certain concepts, and in the main they were concepts at odds with his time. He subscribed neither to Palmerston's *laissez-faire*, nor the simple zealotry of evangelicals like Keate and Tybalt. Philanthropy, as such, made no direct appeal to him, and neither did the militancy of reformers like Catesby, although he made allowances for all these creeds. He saw his own and his nation's destiny in terms of an adjustable balance, labour in one scale, capital in the other, and at centre nothing but an amalgam of commonsense, human dignity, and administrative efficiency. But Luke Dobbs, crashing feet first down the chimney, destroyed that equilibrium, and for the time being indeed, for a long time to come, he was without a formula and at war with himself in search of one.

Perhaps the most salutary aspect of the incident was the sense of isolation it introduced. He had observed and counted the blood money of commercial imperialism at Cawnpore and Lucknow, and had witnessed, on the setts of Seddon Moss, the vicious recoil of the age, but on these occasions the impact had shocked without shaming, for he had been able to seek sanctuary in self-righteousness, merely shrugging and telling himself, 'Not this way. Not for me and my concerns.' But this was no longer possible. Luke Dobbs had been crushed and suffocated in his chimney, and at the instance, if indirectly, of his own wife, who thus demonstrated that she valued her soft furnishings above the flesh and bones of children. This involved not only him but his whole concept of civilisation, as though the world he had chosen was not a place of commerce at all but a carnival of lunatics dancing a carmagnole on the bones of the underprivileged.

A thing like this, taking place in broad daylight, and inside a Christian home, made nonsense of every word that dripped from every pulpit in the land, and every pious platitude that issued from the mouths of lawgivers at Westminster. It reduced to obscenity the popular music-hall ditties extolling the land of the free, and a theology that sent missionaries to win heathen souls. For while the savage slew and sometimes ate his adversary, he did it in obedience to ritual or hunger. Savages did not feed their fires with the children of the vanquished.

*   *   *

When the little coffin had been trundled away, when the coroner had tongue-lashed the mastersweep and revoked his licence, when all the messages had been sent to all Henrietta's guests informing them that there would be no supper-party at 'Tryst', he would have thought that the tide of self-disgust would recede but it did not, and one reason why it did not led back to the smallness of the stir about him. For the unspeakable death of Luke Dobbs occasioned less local newspaper comment than Ratcliffe's lion-catching exploit, or Blubb's brush with the Fenians, and seemed to make no more than a dent in the armoured complacency of his staff and intimates. He could have understood this in the case of his father, or the coachman Blubb, who were men of the eighteenth and not the nineteenth century. He could even accept it in the Keates and Tybalts, having personal access to Jehovah who had assured them that, given time, he would reward the just and punish the wicked. But there were others, among them his wife and neighbours, and the doctor who had certified the death of the boy, who seemed to accept Luke Dobbs' murder as nothing more than an embarrassing mischance, that could occur in the best regulated household and could be forgotten now that the corpse had been hustled out of sight, the room tidied, the sweep reprimanded, and a report sent to swell the postbag of the good Lord Shaftesbury, currently canvassing an Act of Parliament aimed at extending the life span of chimney sweeps.

That Adam Swann was unable to follow their example was his misfortune and evidence, possibly, of his eccentricity. At first his morbid preoccupation with the fate of Luke Dobbs passed almost unnoticed. Then, in ones and twos, people began to remark on it, and it was seen that, in the breaking and recasting of his mould of thought, his character had undergone a dramatic change, and that his judgements, formerly so concise and original were becoming clouded. What was worse, his absorption with his enterprise changed to a self-absorption that led him to spend his time mooning about the woods and heaths, and writing letters to newspapers and cranks, who were campaigning for all kinds of obscure causes, of which the elimination of the trade of flueboy was but one.

At first, individually and collectively, they tried to humour him, and when this failed, to argue the case with him but they had little success. Sometimes he would listen to them and then, without comment, set out on one of his solitary walks but more often, the moment they touched upon the subject, he would urge them to mind their own damned business and they would go away shaking their heads, wondering why such a commonplace occurrence should make such a deep impression on a man who had seen service in Bengal and the Crimea. They hoped, fervently, that his withdrawn mood did not indicate the onrush of religious mania, and that soon, seeing his leaderless business in a trough, he would pull himself together and attend to more important matters.

He was well aware, of course, that they were talking about him, and that when he continued to drift about the house, silent and all but unapproachable, his father, his wife and his sleeping partner

Avery had taken counsel together, but he neither knew nor cared what conclusion they had reached or what course, if any, had been decided upon.

It was some time after that that Avery made his direct approach and got short shrift for his pains, being told, sharply, to let the matter rest and take charge at the yard for a spell.

Then Tybalt sought him out on the excuse of discussing some new contracts Catesby had sent down, and when these had been referred to Tybalt touched, somewhat hesitantly, upon the death of Luke Dobbs, saying that Adam had no reason to take it so much to heart for, from the facts Tybalt had gathered, the boy had been dead before he had arrived on the scene. Adam stared him down so menacingly that the little man began to shuffle. "And how in hell does that absolve me?" he demanded. "It happened in my house, and it was my wife who stood by and let that scoundrel Millward drive the other boy back into the chimney!" Tybalt almost said something to the effect that the ladies would have their places kept spick and span, but, fortunately for him, he bit on it and reminded his employer that a bill was likely to pass Parliament forbidding the practice, and that in the meantime any number of matters were waiting his personal attention in the yard. "We miss your drive more than I can say," he said, earnestly. "Mr. Keate sent his compliments, and hopes to have the pleasure of discussing an applicant for the Derbyshire base as soon as possible."

"Tell him to do nothing," Adam said, "for I doubt if I shall go ahead in The Pickings. I might even contract," and Tybalt left feeling less secure than he had felt for a long time. It seemed to him incomprehensible that the future of a thriving concern like Swann-on-Wheels could rest upon the fate of a thirteen-year-old chimney sweep. He was a kindly man, who devoted most of his spare time to good works of one sort or another, but he did not think the death of one chimney sweep should be allowed to clog the wheels of commerce. It was Tybalt's experience that foundlings had always been expendable. One saved the souls of some but the workers in the vineyard were few and he supposed a majority must find their own way home in the dark.

The next approach was made by the Colonel but his decision to intervene was urged upon him by what he considered a protracted and largely pointless quarrel between a son he respected and a daughter-in-law he had come to cherish. It was Henrietta, in fact, who asked him to try, declaring indignantly that Adam seemed to

329

blame her for the whole sorry business and this, she felt, was the ultimate in unreason.

The old man came upon his son one evening when he was standing in front of the fatal chimneypiece, having just caught a disconcerting glimpse of himself in the mirror that hung there. What he saw dismayed him. The face was haggard and the eyes sombre, the eyes of a man who had not slept soundly in a long time, and even in his present, self-punitive mood this struck him as incongruous. He thought, wretchedly, 'God damn it, I didn't feel this badly at Cawnpore, and nothing like so helpless when her father rode over that boy at Seddon Moss. What the devil is it, then? Are they all of a piece? Is that poor devil of a chimney sweep no more than a reminder of the monstrous hypocrisy we practise about here? Because if so it's high time I left hauling to somebody else and set about making my voice heard at Westminster alongside Shaftesbury, and the few like him,' and then the Colonel came in, saying, in his gentle, woman's voice, "There's no logic in blaming her, boy. She was no more responsible for what happened than I was, for I was about the house at the time, tho' I'm not pretending I would have stopped it. Lads have been cleaning chimneys ever since they've had chimneys."

"Not my chimneys," growled Adam, and then, as he decided the Colonel was here as her envoy, "Let Henrietta speak for herself if she's anything to say. She's mistress here in my absence, and one glance at that man Millward should have been enough to induce her to send him packing."

"Very well," the Colonel said, mildly, "then tell her so, and put it all out of mind. It's done now and can't be undone, and there are your children to consider into the bargain."

"My children! Good Christ, don't you realise I find it difficult to look at them without being aware of the gulf between cossetted brats like that and a majority of children in this day and age? Sometimes I think Catesby is right. If people like us don't bestir ourselves we'll soon have a Paris-style revolution on our hands, and a damned good thing too, for I know where you'd find me if it did happen!"

It occurred to the Colonel then, and for the first time in years, that this tall, scowling son of his was only half an Englishman, and that this must be the French half of him talking. As someone who had grown to manhood in the period when a mob reigned in Paris, who had seen at first hand the cruelty and social chaos that attended revolutions, the remark had the power to shock him. He said, stiffly, "We don't incline to that in England, boy. When collision-course threatens we legislate. Soon enough we'll legislate about this, the way we already have about the children in the factories and coalmines," but Adam said, bitterly, "Aye, we'll do that! In twenty years, forty years! And meantime helpless little devils like Luke Dobbs will choke to death in flues, and when they don't answer a hail will be dragged out feet first by a rope, or have a fire lit under them! God damn it, don't you *feel* any blood on your hands? You fought your way from Lisbon to Paris alongside boys like that apprentice, but that was half-a-century ago. Even so, did you treat them as he was treated, to keep them up to their duty?"

"No," the Colonel said, "I never did, for that wasn't my way. But others did. I've seen men flogged senseless for a trivial act of insubordination, and others hanged for looting on enemy soil. But that kind of ordinance has been expunged from Queen's Regulations, as I said it would be at the time. However, I didn't come here to discuss social reform but your responsibilities as husband and father and employer of labour. Pull yourself together, man, and begin by telling Henrietta that you don't identify her with that brute Millward."

"In a way, I do."

The Colonel lifted his shoulders. "Then you're more of a fool than I took you for," he said, and left, closing the door quietly behind him.

It was, he supposed, reasonable advice, and despite his denial it must have made some kind of impact on him, for that night, for the first time since Luke Dobbs had been carted away, he came out of the bedroom along the corridor that he had been occupying and went to her.

She was sitting up in bed reading one of her trashy novels and looked, he thought, small and pathetic under that vast canopy. She glanced up hopefully, throwing her book aside, and for a moment he thought she was going to cry. Then, apparently deciding that he had not come here in search of tears, she forced a smile and he thought, fleetingly, 'Damn it, the old man is right. It hasn't touched her. She blames anybody but herself and that's her way. She's Sam Rawlinson's daughter all right, and her mental age is ten,' and suddenly he felt a terrible need to commune with a woman whose thoughts and actions and responses were not at the mercy of her emotions, who was capable of helping him to get this thing into focus. She said, chirpily, "Don't let's sulk, Adam. It's so silly letting something like this come between us. Surely you understand how dreadful it was for

331

me at the time, and how much I would have given to prevent it, but how was I to know . . ."

He cut her short with a gesture that expressed not so much impatience as a kind of hopelessness, although she saw it as an impulse more characteristic of him, and obligingly wriggled over to her side of the bed. She waited until he turned out the lamp before indulging herself in the luxury of a suppressed giggle, reflecting that she must have been a fool to imagine that a man as lusty as he could sulk indefinitely. But later, when he had turned away, and seemed to be sleeping, she wasn't sure that it was as uncomplicated as it seemed, for he had used her in a way that was strange to her, absentmindedly, and entirely without that affectionate boisterousness to which she had grown accustomed and which she took for granted. It was as though he was performing a duty urged upon him by his loins, and was in a hurry to accomplish it and retreat within himself once again, and because of this, or perhaps because her mind was still preoccupied with the long, smouldering quarrel, she took no pleasure in him, despite all her efforts to please. Then she found comfort in the reflection that he had his pride and this, no doubt, was his way of capitulating without too much loss of face. Reconciliation, she supposed, would have to be accomplished in stages, spaced over a week or two, and so long as she kept her mouth shut, and went to work on him with her body, she was confident it could be achieved without much bother. At all events, even this was better than having him skulking out of her reach, and in the moment before sleeping she felt grateful to the dear old Colonel for his intervention. Men were an odd lot and he was more odd than most, shunning her and turning the house topsy-turvy because of an accident involving the death of someone who was not even a relation. It was almost as though little Alexander had choked in the chimney, and she was the one who had ordered him to climb it. Thinking this she gave a little shudder and then, as was her way with all unpleasant thoughts, she shooed it out of mind and slept.

*   *   *

He did not sleep. Her body had done nothing to release the tensions in him for they were not physical tensions and even had they been she, at the time, would have been an imperfect instrument for the purpose. Presently, into his mind, unbidden but persistent, the longing for an adult confidant returned, someone who could attempt to answer some of the questions he had been asking himself since he had stood looking down at the bundle of rags on the hearthrug, and he remembered Edith Wadsworth, whose commonsense he always appreciated when he went into the Crescents. The thought of her brought him a tincture of relief and he wondered, vaguely, what she would make of it, whether she would be likely to think him the sentimental ass that Avery thought him, or the enigma he must seem to a man like Tybalt. He did not know but, as he lay there pondering, it seemed to him essential that he should find out, for here at least was something more positive than mooning about like a man with a permanent hangover.

At the first glimmer of light he slipped out of bed and along the corridor to the room where he had left his clothes. No one was astir when he went down the backstairs to the yard and saddled the bay mare he had hired at Croydon three weeks ago. When she was ready he led her through the arch and across the grass verge, the sound of her hooves muffled in dew-soaked grass. Beyond the first copper beeches he mounted and rode on down the long winding drive. The early morning air was rich with the scent of hawthorn and an enormous hare, alerted by the clink of iron on gravel, bounded from a tussock near the gate and went scudding across the road to the ash coppice opposite. The sense of oppression that had weighed so heavily upon him began to lift, slightly but appreciably. He filled his lungs and spurred the mare into a trot.

3

Riverside Confessional

HE had the devil's own job to find her and by the time he did the whole of his eastern system was aware that he was seeking her. This did not worry him at all and he had, in fact, been slightly amused by young Rookwood's knowing look when he told him Miss Wadsworth was unlikely to be found at her base in the Crescent Central, having moved north a fortnight ago to relieve her father in the sector above.

"She might be at Whitby, sir," he said, managing to convey the impression that he was aware of his employer's real reasons for going north, and that whatever business was transacted between them would be unlikely to involve the counting-house staff.

"How the devil do you keep track of all these local movements?" he asked, noting the youngster's perception, and Rookwood, maintaining his poker face, said that Mr. Tybalt had introduced a map system by which clerks were required to record information of this kind with flags, marked with the names of base managers.

"It saves a lot of crossed mail," he added, and for the first time in a month Adam experienced a flicker of interest in the business, and asked Rookwood to show him the map. Studying the back of his head, as the boy rolled back the covers, Adam remembered that Rookwood was one of Keate's originals, an impudent, rollicking pink-faced urchin, who seemed always to be enjoying a secret joke of the kind he was relishing at this moment. Adam saw him then as a prototype of Dickens' Artful Dodger, and his fellow-clerk, Willie Vetch, as Charley Bates. He said, briefly, "Right, Rookwood, tell Mr. Tybalt my whereabouts and that I wholly approve of this map. Can't imagine why I didn't think of it years ago."

"Are you likely to be in the north long, sir?" Rookwood asked. "Mr. Tybalt is sure to want to know."

"A week at least, but only a day in the Crescents. Tell him I shall probably move across to the Polygon to see Mr. Catesby, and then down to the Southern Square and home. I'll keep in touch by telegram." He paused and went on, "Tell him I'll tackle the backlog the minute I return. That'll cheer him up."

"Yes, sir," said the boy, saluting, "he's ... er ... been rather low lately, sir, and so has Mr. Keate."

He took a cab to Kings Cross, buying a ticket for York and musing, as he waited for the train to start, how much tittle-tattle must circulate in the yard concerning the confidence he reposed in Edith Wadsworth and whether, in fact, serious-minded men like Tybalt and Keate put Rookwood's construction on it. He thought not, for he was known to have his favourites among the managers, and had made no secret of the fact that he extended more trust in the Wadsworths, Catesby and Bryn Lovell than in men like Fraser, in the Border Triangle, Abbott in the Square, or Ratcliffe in the West.

He felt more cheerful already and it occurred to him that he had been a fool to potter about at home all this time, as though his presence within range of that chimney could bring Luke Dodds back to life. Contentedly, he watched the northern suburbs slide past, as the great Sturrock locomotive settled to the run and then, more relaxed than he had been for a long time, he slept, to be nudged awake by the guard at York. He made inquiries concerning the cross-country journey to Whitby, eating lunch in the station restaurant whilst awaiting the York and Scarborough train, and learning that he would have to change to the Pickering-Whitby spur about halfway. The sun was setting as he leaned from the window and sniffed the sea but a disappointment awaited him here, for when he called in at the yard, and asked the depot-manager if Miss Wadsworth was about, he learned that she had taken an empty frigate to Yarm, and was then going on to Richmond, one of the drivers on the dairy run there having broken a leg and damaged his vehicle.

"I don't think she'll come back this way, sir," the man added. "She said something about taking the repaired waggon back to Crescent Centre. It's one of theirs, you see, that was on loan to us up here."

Adam considered. He was not tired, having slept at least five hours in the two trains, and it was a mild night, with a full moon rising over the bay. He said, "Is there a livery stable handy?" and the manager said there was, Baverstock's, in the adjoining street, where he could hire a hack and ride on a stage if he was so minded.

Even when he was on legitimate business Adam Swann travelled light and the luggage he carried could be accommodated in a saddle-bag. He went down to Baverstock's and hired a piebald gelding, telling them who he was, and promising to leave the animal at Yarm or Richmond, depending upon where he overtook the waggon. Then filling his pocket flask with brandy, he set out, crossing a tract of unfamiliar country and heading due east over the old coach road to Guisborough, a stage of around fifteen miles.

He thought, as he jogged along, that many would regard this expedition the ultimate in idiocy, a man in his mid-thirties, with a wife, a young family, and a business employing three hundred waggons and as many men, riding through the night in pursuit of a girl before whom he proposed laying self-doubts concerning the death of a chimney sweep. And yet, in another way it did not seem in the least ridiculous but an instinctive groping for a friend, whose advice was likely to be unprejudiced. For years now, ever since he had become so absorbed in the enterprise, he had not felt the need for friendly counsel. Avery, when they first set up their partnership had admitted to such a need, but he had not used Adam's availability and they had never been more than business associates. The Colonel had always been at hand, with his quiet courtesy and restrained affection, but the Colonel's world was dead, and the old man had never adjusted to the new age and a fresh set of values. Henrietta, in this particular sense, had been a disappointment, for he still found it impossible to treat her as anything more than a mascot, with her stupid prejudice against his involvement in trade, and her obsession with the make-believe rôle of Lady of Tryst.

Out here, alone in the bright moonlight, with the whiff of the sea competing with the tang of heather, he was able, at long last, to separate Henrietta from the recent turmoil on his doorstep and modify his irritation concerning her. He saw now that he had behaved illogically and impulsively. He did not regret having compelled her to help him wash that corpse, for this had obliged her to face life as it was lived, and not as she liked to pretend in her story-stocked mind, but it was manifestly unjust to blame her for positive inadequacies. She had had no education and no upbringing, and if she was spoiled from the moment he had married her then it was he who had done the spoiling. The fact was, he thought, he had come to regard her more as a mistress than a wife, and so long as he continued to do so she would remain one, able to beguile his idle hours, and relieve him of the necessity of hunting up a woman every so often, as men like Avery preferred to do, and in this rôle at least she had been an unexpected success. But this surely ran contrary to all a man should seek in a wife. He had demolished her false modesty and enabled her natural high spirits to find an outlet whenever he was on hand to summon them, but he had failed in encouraging her to mature and this, he supposed, was the real cause of her blindness as regards what he thought of as essentials.

His thoughts passed from the particular to the general, and he began to thaw at the prospect of remounting the helter-skelter of competitive business that had now taken too firm a grip on his imagination to be discarded like a shirt. Moneymaking, and the risks attending were well enough, and most of his contemporaries seemed to find complete fulfilment in it, but something important was still missing and if he was unable to say what it was perhaps a down-to-earth woman like Edith Wadsworth could tell him.

Guisborough was fast asleep when he rode in but there was a light at the livery stable the Whitby manager had recommended, so he handed over the piebald and arranged to call for a replacement at seven. The ostler directed him to an inn where he ate bread and cheese and drank a pint of beer before seeking his bed.

Six hours later he was on his way again, following the deserted road almost due east to Marton before turning south-east across open country until he struck one of the great loops of the Tees, where birds sung in thickets beside the shallow, fast-running stream, and a clear sky promised another warm day. Soon he was jogging down the main street of Yarm, recalling that Blubb, driving the Thirsk 'Telegraph', had changed teams here during his fast night-runs to Stockton, and also that it was here, of all places, that his boyhood hero Stephenson had persuaded hard-fisted merchants to invest money in the Stockton-Darlington line, the Adam of every railroad in the world.

It was market-day in Yarm and the main street was thronged with carts and carters, but the elusive Edith Wadsworth was not among them, and a carrier's agent told him she had set out at first light with the original frigate and two dapple greys, leaving the waggon she had hauled from Whitby as a replacement. He thought, distractedly, 'Damn the woman, it's almost as though she's evading me', and left his second horse with the agent, choosing a frisky young chestnut that had been left with him overnight from a Richmond stable.

"You can turn her in when you catch up with Miss Wadsworth," the agent said. "She'll be nowt but a mile short o' Richmond by then. Follow the byroad to Scorton Cross, then the line of the Swale that'll be fordable anywhere in this dry spell. If you miss her she'll be offloading at a mill called Forsythe's, under the castle walls."

COB AT LARGE: 1862–1863

He set off in sweltering heat, glad to seek the shelter of the trees where they arched over the road. The mare, pestered by flies, threw her head about but once they reached the Swale, and she had slaked her thirst, she kept up a steady trot until the fantastic pile of Richmond Castle showed above the line of the trees. It was here, dismounting to offsaddle for ten minutes while he washed in the river, that he heard through the closeset timber on his right, the thin sound of a reed pipe playing an air on a scale of five notes, and as an accompaniment the slow, gritty grind of waggon wheels descending a hill, with brake-shoes applied.

It seemed to him a very relevant sound in that setting, and although he would not have thought that a person of Edith Wadsworth's disposition would have lightened her journey with a tune on a hand-whittled reed, he knew, with a curious certainty, that it would be her waggon that came round the bend in the track. He hitched the chestnut to a tree and took his place beside a willow, chuckling in anticipation of the shock she would get when he hailed her, and when the waggon was still fifty yards off he had leisure to study her, sitting relaxed on the high seat, reins looped over her shoulder, skirt hitched to the knee, feet encased in a pair of clogs and the pipe at her lips, so that she looked more like an illustration in Piers Ploughman than the practical woman he had seen bullying waggoners in the Boston yard.

She was, he thought, an even bonnier girl than he remembered. Her skin was tanned by sun and wind and her arms, bare below the elbow, were a mass of freckles. Her thick chestnut hair, falling to her shoulders, was restrained by a single strand of green ribbon.

He called, "Hi, there! Would you like company as far as Richmond?", and she dropped the pipe and made a grab at the reins, bringing the dapple greys to a sharp halt and looking across at him with an expression that indicated surprise certainly, but not the degree of astonishment he would have expected. Then colour rushed to her cheeks and she seemed, for a moment, almost embarrassed. He saw her glance down at her threadbare skirt and clogs and then, with a toss of her head that set her curls jostling, her independence reasserted itself. "*You?* Playing highwayman right up here? Who on earth told you I was this far afield?"

"Oh, we keep an eye on you at H.Q.," he said, "but I had a devil of a job to run you down. It's taken the services of three trains and three hired hacks, and I was in the saddle half the night. Have you got anything to eat in that waggon?"

"Of course I have," she said, with a touch of her northcountry asperity, "you don't imagine I'd haul a waggon across North Riding and over the Humber on an empty stomach, do you?"

"They have inns in most towns," he said, unhitching the chestnut, and she replied, "Aye, they have, and all of them full of thieves and twice-warmed victuals. I cook for myself when I'm travelling. Will cheese and beer do, or will you be wanting a hot meal?"

He had intended tying the chestnut to the tailboard and jogging along beside her as far as Richmond but now he changed his mind, hobbling the mare after leading her over to a stretch of turf growing beside the Swale.

"If you can provide something more substantial then I could do justice to it," he said, "and those greys of yours could do with a cooling off. Let's camp here, where there's shade and water."

"You're the gaffer," she said gaily, and swung herself down, going to the tool-kit compartment and taking out a wicker basket.

"Light a fire," she said, "but in that open patch. It's been dry hereabouts, and it won't help our reputation to start a heath blaze."

"I've got twelve years' campaigning behind me," he said, "so don't address me as though I was a townsman," and she replied, with a laugh, "I was quite forgetting. You think like a townsman, and I always picture you as one."

It was extraordinary, he thought, how easily they adjusted to one another, and how little use she had for the flirtatious chitter-chatter that even working-class girls were beginning to cultivate, in imitation of the weekly magazine heroines. There was no restraint in her manner and no coyness either. He was just a man who paid her and her father for a job of work, and was therefore entitled to good service but no deference. In five minutes he had a fire going and in five more she had bread, bacon and eggs sizzling in a frying pan she had produced from somewhere. A tin kettle was filled and edged on to the improvised grate, and while she was busy he led the waggon under the trees, unbuckling the harness and turning the greys out to graze alongside the mare. She had, in that hamper of hers, everything necessary for a picnic—tin plates, enamel mugs, tea, a screw of salt, a couple of two-pronged forks, and even a phial of olive oil. "Dripping melts on the road," she said, "and the food tastes second-hand, no matter how hard you scour the pan. I like a fry-up now and again when I'm travelling, but more often I brew tea and live off bread and cheese."

He said, as they began to eat, "How often do you make lonely hauls like this, and how far afield do you go? They said at Whitby that this was an emergency on account of an accident."

"I made that the excuse," she said, with a smile, "for I had a fancy to see the North Riding in late spring again. It seems a lifetime since I was up here," and then, more seriously, "It's my country and I love it. We come from here originally, a village near Middleham. Father shifted to Doncaster when Mother died, but I grew up around here. You couldn't lose me in this part of Yorkshire. You can keep West Riding, the manufactories are fast spoiling it."

"They're spoiling most places," he said, suddenly remembering what had brought him here. "That's partly why I sought you out, Edith. I needed someone to talk things over with. Have you the patience to listen?"

"What kind of things?" she said, and when he hesitated, "Oh, I've heard talk, for you don't only run a carrier service, you live in a grapevine."

"What exactly did you hear?"

"That you were thinking of selling out and finding an easier way of making a living. Is it true?"

He knew the answer was important to her and said at once, "No, it isn't. It's true I've not been near the yard for a month, and I suppose that's why rumours are flying, but I never thought of selling out, not seriously. I've got a lot of satisfaction out of what we've built here in the last few years: Until a month ago, that is."

"Is what happened to do with your wife?"

He noticed that she was looking at him steadily and that her eyes, the colour of the sea a long way from land, seemed to be assessing his state of mind with a kind of doubtful objectivity, as though she had certain notions about how he regarded her, and was examining their portent in her shrewd, uncluttered brain.

"Not specially," he said, "although Henrietta is involved. You'd best hear it from the beginning and form your own judgements. I came a long way to pick your brains as the one person in the network I could depend upon to give unbiased advice."

He told her then, holding nothing back, how his pride and self-sufficiency had been shattered by a black bundle in his hearth, with its mouth full of soot. He told her how the death of Luke Dodds had become inseparably linked in his mind with the pressures bearing on every British man, woman and child who lacked the means, the will, or the education to escape the cogs of the complicated machine fed with Christian ethics, and how, to his mind, the fabric of a traditional set of values had been discarded, and the rough pastoral justice Englishmen had been at such pains to win was being set aside, in favour of a code based upon money and a man's ability to make it anyway he liked.

"Something's gone wrong somewhere," he said, "and for the life of me I can't say what or where. In my father's day they hanged children for stealing five shillings, and the old and sick were at the mercy of circumstance, but charity was there, and a sense of responsibility among the so-called quality. Today charity, real charity that is, is as clammy as a frog's belly, and the only responsibility merchants accept is to make enough money to ape the squires of a century ago. That child Dobbs was a foundling and his fate isn't in the least uncommon. The same kind of thing happens in the cotton belt, in all your Yorkshire wool towns, in the Potteries, and even among rural communities that used to take a pride in sharing one another's troubles. I've seen it all travelling around and it's gone sour on me. That child's death was no more than a match to a bonfire, a bonfire of a number of experiences—my father-in-law killing another child in haste to save his mill; the murder of those miners at Llangatwg when it took no more than Lovell's brains to save others by the skin of their teeth; those urchins Keate rescued from the dockside, no more than a sprinkling of the thousands one sees in London streets every day. Damn it, a man ought to be aware of what's happening, and then do something to make others aware of it! Suppose ..."

She had been listening intently but now, interrupting him, she said, "You mean on the lines of Shaftesbury's campaigns? Getting elected to Parliament? Making windy speeches?"

"Not necessarily."

"You could buy a newspaper. That would give you a platform to launch a crank's crusade."

"Does a social conscience make a man a crank to your way of thinking?"

"No," she said, equably, "far from it. I used the word because that's how the majority of people, occupied with the business of filling their bellies and keeping a roof over their heads, see a man of means who takes up a cause."

"Is Shaftesbury a crank? He's devoted his entire life to checking the exploitation of five-year-olds by bastards like that sweep."

She smiled, not cynically exactly but with resignation. "Shaftes-

341

bury is a kind of saint. You aren't, and never could be."

"You don't have to tell me that," he said, disappointed at the line she was taking, "but the self-disgust I've felt at being on the wrong side is real enough."

"Oh, I don't doubt that. Knowing you I wouldn't have expected anything else, Adam."

He said, thoughtfully, "I'm damned if I'd mind being thought a crank if I was listened to by a vocal section of the public. As a matter of fact, it did occur to me to turn over the business to Avery, and stand as a radical for one of the London boroughs."

"That wouldn't help at all," she said. "In the first place, to win a seat at all would cost you far more than you could afford. In the second place, not being the holy sort, you'd lose your sense of purpose and throw away the chance you already possess of making your point."

"What chance is that?"

She looked at him severely. "Why, this service, lad! This thing you've conjured out of nothing!"

Suddenly she began to speak with emphasis and conviction, addressing him as though he had been a stupid child, stuck on a slateful of sums and getting a string of wrong answers. "Do you discount your influence on the commercial ethics of the country at this very moment? Do you think you can employ three hundred men, including Keate's vanboys, without setting an example, good or bad, to others? Good God, man, didn't it ever occur to you that you're unique in the trade, that men like my father look up to you, and work over the odds for you, without looking for another sixpence in the wage packets every Saturday?"

"No," he said, sincerely, "I didn't know that. I thought myself a businessman, competing with other businessmen and much the same as them except that I'm more open to new ideas than they are."

"That's precisely what I'm saying," she said, "for there isn't a man working for the network, from the Border down to the Wedge, who hasn't directly benefited from these 'new ideas', as you put it. Oh, I don't mean your routes and schedules, and all the mere mechanics of the service. I'm talking about your *approach* to the people who work for you, and that's original in all conscience! Ask Catesby! Ask Lovell, over in Wales! Ask any of the waggoners in the Crescents how they would feel if you dropped the reins. They believe in you as I do and take a pride in their work—or most of them do—because they know that you know they exist, and are more than a pair of hands standing beside a machine in one of those damned factories. You're known as a good gaffer everywhere your waggons roll, and here you are proposing to go join a debating society, or turn evangelist and snuffle round with a hymnbook and blankets for the poor! That isn't a man's work, of the kind you've been doing this five years. With some of them it's no more than a means of catching Peter's eye at the Gate. Your ideas are your own, and they're based on a sound set of rules. This mood, brought about by that boy who died in your chimney, doesn't surprise me. It's what I would have looked for in a man of your parts, but for God's sake don't let compassion make a fool of you. That would be a score for all the mastersweeps and millowners and sweatshop bullies who get the last ounce out of their people and take out their insurance in church every Sunday."

It was as though he had suddenly ceased to breathe stale, unprofitable air. He understood then that his instinct had not been at fault in going to such pains to seek her out and also that, whatever he did from here on, would be done with the assurance that had been a feature in the early days, when he had taken conscious pleasure in backing his own judgement. He got up and went down to the water's edge, watching the strong current break on the stones and eddy, like his gloomy thoughts, into the pools under the cutaway. The sun danced on ten thousand ripples and bubbles and peace lurked under every wavering shadow.

He heard her stowing the gear in the tool box and the greys being snapped back into harness. Then she was standing beside the fire, covering the embers with earth and he crossed to her and said, briefly, "That was worth the journey, Edith. Thank you, my dear," and taking her hand raised it and kissed it, so that she looked quite bewildered for a moment before withdrawing it, saying, "That's a nice gesture, Adam, but it isn't necessary. You would have arrived at the same conclusions yourself if you hadn't been in your usual tearing hurry. You'll ride alongside as far as Richmond?"

"I'll ride beside you," he said, and unhaltering the chestnut, hitched her and scrambled over the tailboard and through the curtains to the box. They rode the two miles into town in silence.

343

2

When she had shed her load, and met him by appointment outside the livery stable he said, "I'll be crossing the Pennines into the Polygon, for I might as well go back to work from here. Where will you turn off?" She told him at the turnpike above Ripon, for she had calls to make on the way down. He said, in a way that forestalled discussion, "I'll travel that far with you, and turn in the mare at Ripon. Then I'll go down the Great Northern and find a connection with the North Western. I can sleep the night under the waggon, it's dry and I'm well enough used to it."

Whatever she might have thought of this proposal she kept to herself and it was not until they were out on the open moor again, crossing a tract of wild, unsettled moorland cut about by innumerable streams, that she emerged from her shell again, pointing with the whip to a square outcrop of stone on their right, all that was left, she told him, of Middleham Castle, once the seat of the great Neville family. "Full of ghosts, is Wensleydale, and one of them royal."

"Who was that?" he asked, sensing that the spell of this countryside, with its open sky, chattering rivers, and vast, elemental loneliness, was in her bones. She replied, lightly, "Ah, now, there's a tomfool question from a man who has earned the Queen's shilling. The last king we had. The last *real* king, that is. Richard, the one libelled by that liar Shakespeare, and others who shall be nameless. King Dick spent the happiest days of his life hereabouts and fell in love for good measure."

"He was a blackhearted scoundrel, none the less, on a par with my father-in-law and the sweep Millward, wasn't he?"

"Stuff and nonsense," she said, "you've swallowed all that stinking fish they left lying about. I don't know as he murdered his nephews, but I do know he loved England and died for it. Which is more than can be said of any of the misers and weaklings who succeeded him."

Her jocular assessment of history interested him. He saw it as another facet of her character and now that he thought about it it was not so unlikely that she should reveal herself as a champion of Crouchback. He remembered that the man had been respected up here, and his habit of driving himself and his adherents was in keeping with her own drive and self-sufficiency. "Tell me more about him," he said.

She told him then of Richard of York's associations with the area, how, as a sickly boy, he had been sent up here to train in the profession of arms, and had made himself not only the equal but the superior of all the other lads farmed out to learn their trade under the warlike Nevilles.

"He was nine when he arrived at Middleham, and thirteen when he left," she said, "but he was a man for all that." She gave him a steady, sidelong glance. "Your kind of man I like to think."

"You said he fell in love. It must have been calf love?"

"Why? Children grew up earlier in those days. The more privileged they were the less they were coddled. That younger Neville girl, Anne, had a tiresome time of it. She was chased from pillar to post, in and out of sanctuary, and then disguised as a kitchenmaid when he eventually found her and married her."

"Aye," he said, indulgently, "I remember. She was a widow too, for he killed her husband at Tewkesbury, didn't he?"

"Oh, he might have, in battle," she said, carelessly, "but it was only a marriage arranged by the French woman, Margaret. Anne had no say in it."

"Did she have in choosing her second husband?"

"No, but I like to think she preferred him to the son of an idiot. They both spent the happiest years of their life up here, and came back as soon as they could. I don't fancy a man like that would stifle his nephews with a bolster. It's not in character, somehow."

"That's Yorkist prejudice," he said, jokingly, but she flashed back, "Oh, no it isn't! The Yorkist kings were always prepared to fight for their crown, like the Stuarts. That German line we've been saddled with since are a poor lot. Look at our present Majesty, making a cult out of mourning."

"If you had lost your man I daresay we should find you in mourning!"

She gave him another of her keen glances. "It so happened I did," she said.

It was absurd, he told himself, but he experienced a pang of jealousy. It had never once occurred to him that she had been deeply attached to anyone. She always gave him the impression that she despised most men, and would be unlikely to surrender to one incapable of dominating her. 'But maybe he did', he thought, admitting to a positive curiosity about her past, 'Maybe he was some surly, six-foot Yorkshire lad, who walloped her regularly, and this forthrightness of hers is a northcountry version of Victoria's lamentations'. "Well," he said, as she readdressed herself to the team, "you can't leave it there. I'll be making guesses for the rest of my life."

She said, noncommittally, "Matt was a sailor, mate and part-owner of a brig. A lad to be reckoned with was Matt Hornby. We were to be married the day he was home from a coaling run up to Leith. But his brig was lost off Holy Isle and he drowned, along with the rest of them."

"How old were you then?"

"Rising twenty."

"What was he like, Edith?"

"Like you in build. Big, strongly-made and with ideas of his own."

She seemed unwilling to vouchsafe more information and as they went creaking over the moor he thought about Matt Hornby, picturing him stumping ashore in jersey and sea boots, and sweeping her off her feet as she ran to greet him. It seemed an improbable picture. The only aspect of it that struck him as plausible was her silent battle to come to terms with the wreck of her hopes, and without knowing why this brought her closer. He said, suddenly, "They know where I am back in London and I got the impression they gossip about us. Will that annoy your father if he gets to hear of it?"

"Father and I go our own way," she said, with a shrug, and then, "This marriage of yours; it seems a rum thing to fight about, a dead chimneysweep. Or maybe you didn't tell me the full facts."

"Now what the devil am I to make of that?"

"Whatever you like. I can give you the kind of advice you came looking for because I know what is important to you. But I'm not qualified to judge you as a husband, and I've never set eyes on your wife."

"Then why confuse the two issues?"

"It isn't me that's confusing them. Wasn't that one reason you came looking for me?"

He said, thoughtfully, "I wouldn't care to have to hide things from you, Edith. What do you want to know, exactly?"

"As much as you care to tell me."

He told her than of the circumstances in which he and Henrietta had met and married, of the successful and unsuccessful aspects of the match, and the difficulty he had reconciling his domestic life with

346

the demands of his business. He tried to do Henrietta justice, and made no attempt to excuse his own shortcomings, but admitted he was close to abandoning hope of finding in Henrietta the kind of maturity he had hoped for when she settled down and became the mother of two children. "I was thinking during the ride over here that this is more my fault than hers," he concluded, "that I've spoiled her."

"Aye, I'd already decided that," she said, "but it was none of my business. They say she costs you upwards of four hundred a year in ribbons and bonnets, but having started on that tack you'll have to abide by it, unless you want a scold on your hands."

"And I daresay you think I'm begging further trouble settling her in a place the size of 'Tryst'?" he said, but she replied, surprisingly, "No, I don't. I should want that if I was in her place. It's fitting you should live in style, fitting for both of you," and when he asked why she said that, having launched something new in the way of an enterprise, he was a natural inheritor of the kind of home the adventurers in the past had made for themselves out of the proceeds of piracies. "There are two changes I'd make if I was in your shoes," she went on, "and the most obvious is to own your own acres. People like the Nevilles and Conyers have had their day. This one belongs to people like you, able to make their own way in the world. Most of the men who succeed in business build themselves a town house within a carriage drive of their counting houses, but that isn't for you. Having found yourself a home why pay rent for it? No Yorkshireman would invest hard-earned brass in property he couldn't lay title to."

"That's worth thinking about. What was the other changes you had in mind?"

"You'll think them even more presumptuous." She gave a tug on the reins and sat back, facing him squarely. "Where the devil were your brains to install a young wife in a house of that size, saddle her with a couple of children, and then surround her with a flock of hangers-on to make certain she lived in idleness."

"Oh, come now," he protested, " 'Tryst' has forty rooms . . ."

"That castle yonder had more, and the lord was away to the wars and about his state business most of the year. But you aren't such a fool as to think his wife spent her time drooping over the battlements watching the road against his return? She had servants, yes, but she also had the ordering of them. You've got an ignorant peasant installed in your house, usurping both your wife's place and yours, but that isn't the worst of it. You've got any number of girls and lads to fetch and carry for her, and I daresay some drudge to answer a bell and put coal on the fire. You've got a cook who helps herself to the best cut of roast before it finds its way to your table, and a bit of a lass to wipe the children's noses when they need wiping, and teach them their A.B.C. Your wife turns up her nose at trade, you say. Well, that's neither here nor there, because a man like you wouldn't take kindly to nagging in that area, but how is she to fill her days if she's nowt to do but worry about her waistline, and try on a new bonnet while she's waiting for you to come home and 'pleasure her with your boots on' as the saying goes? Lady Cicely Neville kept her own keys and linen, supervised the salting, bottling and pickling for five hundred retainers, and was glad to put her feet up at the end o' the day."

"Good God," he said, "Henrietta's had no kind of training in that field!" but she said, glowering, "She can set about getting some, can't she? She's young and healthy and northcountry born, and if she doesn't use up her energy that way she'll get into mischief one way or another, or turn into one o' those wilts who spends her time on a sofa pretending to be delicate. You came here seeking advice of one sort or another but here's some you didn't ask for. Sack that housekeeper, sack half the staff, tell your doll of a wife she's responsible for the way the place is run down to the last detail, and tan her backside every time she lets you down. She'll love you the more for it if she's from over the Pennines, for the Lancastrians might be fools wi' their brass but there's few of 'em who don't thrive on hard work. There now, I've spent myself talking sense into you, so jump down and go about your business, leaving me to go about mine!"

He gave a great guffaw of laughter and his appreciation of her, demanding physical expression, induced him to throw his arm round her shoulder and kiss her on the mouth. She accepted the kiss for what it was, an impulsive gesture of goodwill, but beneath her show of impatience with him there must have been turmoil of a sort, for when he proposed, half-seriously, that she shifted down to The Bonus in order to be handy as a counsellor, she said, very sharply, "Nay, I'll stay where I am, thank you!"

"Why?"

"There's no telling what might happen next time you come sharing your troubles. For my part that is, to say nothing of yours."

The remark was intended to convey more than it said but somehow he missed the hint, saying, "You're not telling me a person as level-headed as you would be bothered by gossip?"

She hesitated a moment, as though considering his artlessness, but then, regarding him stolidly, replied, "For a man of business, Adam Swann, you can be damned thickheaded. If I was persuaded things were past mending between you and your wife it would come easily to me to send you home with something better than talk to remember me by. It's not from want of inclination, I'll tell you that. But you're a family man at heart, and a man who needs to keep his home life as tidy as his accounts, so it wouldn't be in your interests or mine in the long run. However, I'll not tempt Providence by spending a night under the stars with you, so ride on ahead into Ripon and be done with it."

"You'd prefer that?"

"Ay, I would. I had a man of my own once, and there's times when I fancy another. You don't want it spelt any clearer, do you?"

"No," he said, laughing, "and I take it as a great compliment, Edith," and reaching behind him for saddle and bridle swung himself down from the seat.

She followed more slowly, standing off and watching him as he tightened the girths and slipped the irons down the leathers. He did not notice that the sparkle had left her as she stood looking down on the road, her freckled forearm resting on the edge of the tailboard, but when he had adjusted his saddlebag, and was raising a foot to the stirrup, she called, sharply, "One minute, lad . . .!" and held out her arms. He left the mare standing and embraced her and she said, as their lips parted, "Good luck, lad!" and broke from him, moving quickly round to the step and hoisting herself back on the seat. He stood irresolute for a moment, wondering whether she was the kind of person who was able to make light of a roll in the hay and deciding, glumly, that she was not. Against her inclination she had given him good advice and it was incumbent upon him to accept it. He mounted and turned the chestnut's head off the road and on to a moorland bridle path that made a bowstring for the wide arc of the Ripon road.

He had looked for torpor in the cotton belt, where he knew most of the looms were silent now that the bales to feed them arrived in a trickle from blockade-runners and a few fast-sailing privateers, like the Liverpool-built *Alabama* there had been so much fuss about. Lassitude, and an all-round slackening-off maybe, but not this, not a plague that hung over the huddle of towns like a new Black Death that would ultimately carry off half the population and reduce King Cotton to beggary.

The clearest evidence of what was happening was all around him before he had ridden a hundred yards from Exchange Station. The army of workless, sullen, listless, and mostly in rags, stood about at street corners, many of them looking as if they had not eaten a good meal in months. Mendicants, old and young, were everywhere, and down near the Cathedral he passed a soup-kitchen around which pallid children were being marshalled into queues, too dispirited to rattle their cups and pannikins.

Further out the blight was even more obvious. For the first time in his experience the sky overhead was high and clear, and the smell of the great city was not the familiar reek of smoke, but the sour odour of decay under a burning sun, a smell that made him think of alleys and hovels in places like Lucknow and Allahabad.

He went first to his father-in-law in Rochdale, finding Sam submerged in the general gloom, and this despite the fact that his chimney was one of the few still sending up a plume of smoke.

"Aye, but it's a desperate business, lad," said Sam, when Adam commented on the slump. "You'll ask me summat I can't tell you if you ask how it's likely to finish. In bankruptcy all round as like as not, and half-a-million on parish relief. Ah'm still running but I'll be silent come autumn, this road. Living on me fat, you might say, for I saw this a mile off, and stocked up, as well as hoisting my rates. But nine mills out of ten are on quarter-time, and thirty shut bloody gates long since. None of us bargained for a war running to years, and that's a fact. A twel'month, or half as long again mebbe, but there's no sign of it finishing yet, or any one o' the plantation ports opening up and shipping over."

"It always amazed me why you people crammed all your eggs in the one basket," Adam said. "Why the hell didn't you diversify when you had the chance?" but Sam reacted to this as if he had uttered a blasphemy. "Busy oursen wi' owt but cotton? And city well on t'road to becoming capital o' the country? Nay, lad, don't talk that way up here, not even now. We would have had Parliament sitting up here if those damned fools could have settled their quarrel wi'out cutting one another's throats and ours into t'bargain!"

"How are you going to manage when your stocks are gone?" he asked and Sam said he supposed he would have to enter the frantic scramble for Liverpool contraband. That, or shutting down and sitting it out like his competitors. "It'll be making itself felt on your freight line, no doubt?" he asked, but Adam said he could only answer this when he had seen Catesby. After giving Sam family news he excused himself, taking a cab back to the city and out to the Salford depot.

Catesby also looked grim, admitting that town haulage had fallen off to nothing, and that all the waggons in the Polygon were idle. Farmers north of the belt had a surplus but the demand for it among town wholesalers had kept pace with the catastrophic decline in wages. "I've got ten men-o'-war and a dozen frigates here and in the Appleby depot that haven't been harnessed up in a month," he said. "Couldn't you use them elsewhere? Fraser in the Triangle is paying his way, and the Mountain Square has gone ahead since Lovell hauled that Shannon pump to the mine."

Adam said, "They've both got their full quota, and if they need more teams they'll put in a demand for them." Then, "I saw a soup-kitchen ladling out stew on the way over. What kind of relief organisation have the city fathers established?"

Catesby, surprisingly, admitted that it was a better one than he would have anticipated, but grossly overburdened.

"It's a queer thing," he said, "but real trouble brings out the best i' folk, even the hardfisted among 'em. We've raised enough funds to fill a hundred thousand saucepans a day, but it's hard to find meat and fresh vegetables wi'out paying famine prices for the stock and greens. Not much is coming into the Belt from the north or the Cheshire farms. The railways have cut their regular goods runs, and I don't have to tell you overland haulage on that scale sends the market-garden prices rocketing."

Adam said, thoughtfully, "Are you in touch with the soup-kitchen?" and Catesby, looking at him shrewdly, replied, "Aye, I am that. I'm on t'committee. But why do you ask?"

"I've got an idea and I'd like your comments on it. Suppose there were stockmen and market-gardeners willing to sell second-quality produce at cut rates, instead of feeding it back to their animals, or trying to market it locally?"

"I could name a score," Catesby said, "but funds still wouldn't run to bringing it in. You can't fill half-a-million bellies twice a week on small change, gaffer."

"You could make it go further if the haulage was free."

"Use those laid-up waggons? You'd authorise that? They're longish hauls, and rough roads at that. It would take a year off the life of every waggon and team, wi' nowt coming back into the till."

"It would pay off in the long run. The war over there can't last forever."

Catesby began to calculate aloud.

"Twenty waggons, hauling free of charge to the kitchens already dishing out. It could mean the difference between a square meal a day and a bowl of thin stew twice a week. But make no mistake, gaffer. Folk you'd be helping to feed aren't those who could make it up to you when t'mills were running full time again."

"I daresay not," said Adam, "but it'll get around, the same as it did in Lovell's area. Where's the profit in waggons standing idle and teams out to grass? See what you can arrange while I'm up at Appleby. I've telegraphed to Fraser to cross over and meet me there from the Hexham depot."

"Aye, I'll do that," Catesby said thoughtfully, and then, with a grin, "Happen they'll put a handle to your name before you've done."

"I don't know about that," said Adam, "but Lovell's brains in Wales and Ratcliffe's high jinks in the West taught me the value of getting talked about. If this war drags on indefinitely everyone about here will forget we run a service. Free hauls will help to keep us in mind. How's that boy of yours, the one serving with the Massachussetts regiment?"

"Not heard in weeks," Catesby told him. "The last letter was one I sent on, telling about a big battle they had at a place I can't call to mind."

"Sharpsburg," Adam reminded him, "and I daresay you'll have heard since that Lincoln issued the emancipation act?"

"Aye," Catesby said, "and to my mind he should ha' done that at the start of it."

"That chap knows what he's about," said Adam, "and you can

352

back him to win. See to those waggons, I'll look in the day after tomorrow."

But it was a different Catesby he found on his return, two days later. He came in from the north, passing a trio of his own waggons loaded with potatoes and green vegetables on the outskirts of Bolton, and knowing Catesby's preoccupation with the troubles of the under-privileged, he would have expected to find him setting up new feed-ing centres. He was not to be found in his office, however, and a waggoner told him the manager could be located in a tavern near the docks, a place called 'The Three Tuns', patronised by the canal bargees.

Catesby was there sure enough, and at first glance it occurred to Adam that he was drunk. He sat leaning against the wall, his long legs thrust under a bench on which stood an array of tankards and three or four tots that had contained whisky chasers. The liquor had done nothing to lift his spirits. He groped in his pocket and pulled out two folded sheets of coarse paper, handing them over without comment. One, covered with a childish, pencilled scrawl, was from his son Tam, and was headed '*14th Dec. Fredericksburg*'. It had been written in two parts, for halfway down the page there was a break and the following date was 9th May, when young Catesby, now with a Pennsylvania Regiment, was back in Washington as a convalescent.

The letter, written with what looked like a carpenter's pencil, was surprisingly literate for a lad of twenty, whose schooling had been limited to a couple of years at a penny-a-week Church school. It read: '*We got into a stand-up fight here before Christmas but I got no chance to rite because we were whipped by Johnny crost the river an lost more than half our mates trying to get up to there guns on some hills behind the town. I'm no jeneral but it seemed daft to me to send us bekos Johnny had any amount of guns there and I was lucky to get off in one piece. I did tho and ever since I been helping get the wounded away and our jeneral Burnside has been sacked an a new one called Hooker put in for another go when the ground hardens up. I'll rite more when I gets a chanct but this it to say Im still givin as good as I get. Your lovin son, Tam.*'

The second half of the sheet was laboriously compiled, and told how Tam Catesby had taken part in the new general's advance to a place called Chancellorsville, where the famous rebel General Stonewall Jackson had been killed, but the Federal forces had again been defeated. In the withdrawal the boy had been shot through the

353

thigh and said he was lucky to have reached Washington, where the wounded were 'thick as flies on a dead dog along the Irwell'. He went on to say he was getting good nursing, and that his father was not to worry, for it looked as if he would be on rear duty when he rejoined his unit.

Adam then read the second letter that was written in a firm hand, and signed by a man calling himself *'Walt Whitman'*. Its message was brief. Whitman, whoever he was, had written, *'Sir, I found this letter on going through your son's kit and it seemed right I should send it on, together with the sad news that your son died under an amputation here early today (21st May), his leg wound having mortified and an amputation being the only way open to the surgeons to try and save his life. This is a very terrible war, sir, and the suffering on both sides is grievous, but for our part we mean to go on to a finish that I pray may not be too far in the future. If you write me at this hospital I will try and send on some small personal effects of Private Catesby but they may take a long time arriving. Meantime, sir, I know the President and all our people here would wish me to thank you for having shared our national sorrow and assisted in our great cause, also to tell you that I kissed your boy for you before we laid him to rest with his comrades in Arlington Soldiers' Cemetery.'*

What was there to say? Catesby had taken the news badly, as though it seemed never to have occurred to him that soldiers were killed in wars and something told Adam that, although he had not heard from his boy in months, he had never worried much. All the usual platitudes, 'died in a good cause', 'fought for something worth fighting for', seemed far too banal to utter, for Catesby had not only loved the boy but had been proud of him, as though, by crossing the Atlantic, and joining the Federal army, Tam had embraced his father's crusade for human dignity everywhere. And now he was dead, his blood poisoned by a neglected wound, and the corpse was tucked away in an alien patch of ground three thousand miles away. There was some kind of link here, Adam thought, with Tim Garvin who had died under Rawlinson's horse beside the Liverpool line, with the trapped miners Lovell's enterprise had been unable to save, and with the bundle of sooty rags in the hearth at 'Tryst'. It was always these poor devils who bore the brunt of the battle and suddenly, as never before, Adam Swann identified not only with the silent Catesby, but with all the Catesby's determination to demolish the pyramids of privilege and avarice that straddled the lost farmlands of the Western World.

He said, touching the manager's shoulder, "You're wishing it had been you, John," and Catesby, raising himself said, "Aye, I am that! He had another fifty years to fight. I'm nearly done."

"You'll live to see changes for all that, and your boy helped them forward." Then, seeing that little he could say would revive the fighter in the man until Catesby had had time to absorb the blow, "I passed three of our waggons on the way in. You didn't waste any time getting them rolling. Will you write H.Q. when every laid-off team is at work?"

"Aye, I'll do that," Catesby said, thickly, and with a tremendous effort roused himself, stood up and offered his hand. Adam shook it, thinking that, with deputies like him and Lovell and Edith Wadsworth, he was better placed to take some hand in reshaping the times than in getting himself elected as a legislator. He went out and caught a street-car to London Road, boarding the express for Derby and then a slow train for Ashbourne, his next port of call.

*　　*　　*

He was away from home longer than he had anticipated, spending two more days in the Northern Pickings, a broadly-based triangle betwen the West Riding, Derby and Buxton, where Godsall, a young ex-ensign recently installed by Avery, had made a promising start hauling cheap manufactured goods, mostly tinware, and was breaking new ground with the transport of roof tiles, earthenware, and high-quality porcelain that rated a higher fee than any other type of goods, except explosives.

He took a liking to Godsall, a man of good family who, like himself, had turned his back on a military career in favour of trade but had had the good sense to do it much earlier than Adam. Godsall had served in China under Napier, and had 'seen the light', as he jokingly expressed it, in the course of a pointless war in a bad cause. He was a lively young man, with plenty of ambition, and because they had both been under fire Adam found he could communicate with him more freely than with civilians. Godsall said, "After storming the Taku Forts I decided that if I was to risk my neck and live rough there was no reason to pay for the privilege. My father was supplementing my pay and allowances to the tune of a hundred a year, but he didn't take kindly to my resigning a commission. He and my sisters are appalled by my going into trade. They talk about me as if I was dead."

"Don't lose sleep over that," Adam told him. "I made the same decision after the Mutiny and in five years I haven't reconciled my wife to the word 'merchant'. You're making headway up here. When Blubb down in the Kentish Triangle, is too old and too soused for the work, would you consider taking over the Tonbridge depot? It's more profitable than this will ever be, and the prospects for you would be that much better."

"Better wait and see how I shape, Mr. Swann," Godsall said, and Adam, approving his caution, passed down into the other Pickings, based on Worcester, then on into the Southern Square, where the enterprising but unlikeable Abbott was handling a fleet of nearly thirty waggons based on Salisbury, and collecting the milk piped into the capital along the South-Western every morning.

From here, having settled to the collar again, he found his way back to the headquarters, not caring for the stench of London after the clean air of the uplands but reflecting that he had seldom made a more rewarding journey. He was surprised, on entering the Bermondsey yard, to see his own yellow gig standing outside Tybalt's office, and as he approached the Colonel came out of the counting-house, his old face lighting up as he saw his son. Then the expression of pleasure faded and was replaced by a look of uncertainty, as he said, with obvious relief, "Well, thank God you've shown up at last, boy! They told me you might be hard to find," and Adam, scenting more trouble, said, "Anything wrong at home?"

"Not wrong exactly," the Colonel said, evasively, "but there could have been if I hadn't taken a hand." He looked round carefully. "We'd best talk, boy, and when I've had my say no word of it is to reach Henrietta about me waylaying you. That way she'll think she's kept her silly secret, and good luck to her. Where can we go?"

Adam led the way up the belfry stairs and threw open a window. "This is as good as any place," he said, grimly, "for I've reconciled myself to camping here until I'm as old and evasive as you."

4

Skirmish on Shallott

WHEN Henrietta opened her eyes shortly before eight and found him gone she was reassured rather than otherwise. His abrupt disappearance at once suggested a return to familiar habits and this was confirmed as soon as she had checked his room and stables and satisfied herself that his travelling bag and the livery horse were missing. Her spirits soared when, by the evening post, a note from Tybalt reached her, announcing that he was off on one of his far-ranging trips and would be absent for about a week. Gleefully she sought out the Colonel, saying, "I'm not really surprised. It was time he came out of his sulk and he was almost himself again last night. This surely means he's decided to put that dreadful business behind him." And then, rather resentfully, "Why do you suppose he took it so much to heart? Sometimes he almost made me feel as though I had a hand in killing the poor little wretch."

The old man rubbed his nose thoughtfully. He had grown very fond of his daughter-in-law since he had made his home with her but he did not credit her with the ability to read his son's mind or, indeed, to do anything beyond amuse him for an hour or two. In that respect, he mused, she wasn't in the least like the shrewd little brunette he had courted half-a-century ago, for Monique had been an inward-looking person with a Frenchwoman's intuitive knowledge of men and male inconsistencies. He said, guardedly, "Ah—um—well, he's half-French, remember, and we must make allowances for that. The French are a rum lot, with any amount of rum ideas. I recall that even the dull-witted among 'em was half a politician and he's very far from being dull, m'dear. Got a damned sight more brains than any Swann I ever heard of and I daresay I should have spotted that when he was a half-grown lad and put him to a profession where there was a use for 'em. Made a lawyer of him, maybe, or a parson, although that was always reserved for the fool of the family in my day."

She laughed at that, kissed him, and skipped away to spend an idle hour with the children's governess, a gossipy little spinster only

357

a year or so older than herself. Later that day, when supper was done, he passed her room on his way to his own and heard her singing so that he thought, with a twinkle, 'Maybe she has learned how to handle him after all, for they shared the same bed again last night. It isn't so hard to guess what sent him briskly about his business at crack of dawn for she's a pretty, saucy little pigeon when she sets herself to please', and suddenly, for the first time in years, he warmed himself for a moment at a physical memory of Monique, with her little rounded limbs and soft, luminous skin, and begrudged the years they had been separated before her death in early middle age.

Her high spirits, and a sense of release, carried her on into the next day, as though to compensate for a month under the cloud of his displeasure. By mid-afternoon, with a heat haze lying over the river valley, she had ridden off through the woods that ran the length of the eastern border of the estate, stretching almost to the river above the islet that she thought of as Shallott.

It was cooler down here and the water was so low that the stream could be forded anywhere, so she crossed over and walked her placid cob along a screen of pollarded willows that lined the towpath until she came to the ox-bow where the head of the islet pointed upstream, its spur piled with the flotsam of spring floods. Down here, with grain fields on each bank, spring was in pell-mell retreat from summer. The cuckoo honked his monotonous notes, and wild iris grew in great clumps among the reeds. A vole dived and swam along the bank, its progress marked by a rippling 'V', and finches flirted tirelessly in the thickets. On the far bank, where the woods thinned out, the glades were carpeted with bluebells and the river breeze, soft as a child's kiss, riffled the surface of the pools.

She had reined in here, on a stretch of path where it ran between two ranks of trees, when she heard a heavy splash that seemed to come from the blind side of the islet. A moment later a blond head bobbed round the spur, moving into midstream towards a pool that was never less than five feet in depth. Then, peering through the foliage, she recognised the swimmer as Miles Manaton, youngest of the Manaton tribe at Twyforde Court, three miles downriver. The sun, slanting through the willows, glinted in his long fair hair and the wisps of that absurd Sir Walter Raleigh beard he was trying to grow, but then, as he turned on his back to float with the current, she saw that he was naked and giggling she backed away to a point where she could overlook the pool without fear of being seen.

She knew Miles slightly, having met him at the croquet parties old

Mrs. Halberton had given the previous summer. He was, she recalled, a lieutenant in the Royal Horse Artillery, and on the last occasion they had met he had appeared in his splendid uniform, with frogged jacket, strap-over trousers with a broad red stripe and plumed busby with scaled brass chinstrap. Some of the young women had declared themselves on the point of swooning and had clustered around him in a swarm, one of them even venturing to finger the gold wire of his epaulette. She had thought him very conceited then, and had made a point of demonstrating her failure to be impressed, and he must have noticed this for, later on, when they were all sipping tea and talking nonsense on Mrs. Halberton's lawn, their eyes had met for a moment and he had smiled. He was, she supposed, a handsome man if you cared for the dandified type. He had a narrow head, curling hair, regular features, a slim, boyish figure in a uniform that would flatter any figure, and a pale complexion, a great contrast to Adam's tan that turned almost mahogany after a day in the sun. Now she saw that the rest of Miles' body was as pale as his face, so pale that it looked almost feminine floating there in clear water between the browns and greens of the foliage.

The spectacle interested her without embarrassing her. She had seen but one man mother-naked and he was not in the least like this but altogether harder, tauter and more sinewy, with bunches of knotted muscles and a chest that was like a black mat. Miles Manaton's chest was as smooth and white as her own, and even his pubic hair was no more than a tuft of golden down. She took her time, watching him enjoy himself cavorting in the pool and then, with another giggle, she turned the cob and headed him upstream a hundred yards or so, cocking an ear meantime for the sound of splashing, and promising herself that when it ceased she would ride down again and let him know that he had been spied upon for this, she thought, would surely puncture his insufferable conceit.

She gave him ten minutes and then rode out into a more open section of the bank, urging the cob into the shallows and letting him drink. In the event, however, it was he who surprised her, for suddenly he called in a cheerful voice and she saw him standing on the tip of the islet in a shirt, a pair of breeches and his elegant, calf-length boots. Even in this unconventional dress he looked far more of a man than when he had been naked and certainly more masterful, for although he was fair there was something Byronic about the way his shirt flared open at the neck, and the trick he had of standing with legs planted astride and hands resting on hips.

He called, "Hello, there! It's Mrs. Swann, isn't it?" and shaded his eyes against the sun so that she called back, "Yes, Mr. Manaton. And when you go swimming again put a notice on the towpath!"

She thought that would take the bounce out of him but it did nothing of the kind. He threw back his head and laughed, calling, "You're a regular Peeping Tom!" and it was almost as though he had said, "How lucky you are! That's a rare privilege, I can tell you!" so that suddenly she found herself blushing.

He shouted, cupping his hands, "Ride on over. Take the narrow part of the channel, it's no more than a foot deep," and when she hesitated, "This is a wonderful place. I used to come here a lot as a boy!"

The statement did a little to reassure her. He was, she thought, still a boy, and therefore likely to be manageable, so she started across the twenty-yard strip that divided the islet from the path.

He came to greet her, a pleasant smile on his woman's mouth, and droplets still glistening in his beard. She said, for something to say, "I often come by here and I've always wanted to cross. It looked a romantic place, as if there ought to be a castle on it."

"Oh, but there is," he said, and when she looked astonished. "Well, not a castle, exactly, but a bower. It was a place people used to fish but that was before your time."

He talked, she thought, as though she was a little girl and his half-grown beard gave him the right to patronise her.

"Get down," he went on, almost as an order, "and I'll show you. We'll tether the cob."

She was not in the least sure about getting down but to refuse would be to give him the advantage and he had already taken far too much for granted, as though she was one of those young idiots who had flattered him at the croquet party. With a man of his type, she thought, it simply would not do to stand on ceremony and the obvious way to draw level was to avoid giving him the impression that she took him seriously. She said, "Hold the bridle, then," slipped her stirrup foot free, hooked her leg over the horn, and slid to the ground, managing to elude his attempt to catch her. He said, looping the cob's reins round a thorn tree, "It's in here, under the trees. One of your predecessors built it, years ago. Then old Wilson Conyer patched it up, for he used to come here after the trout."

He led the way over a little path that passed between a small grove of sycamores and horse chestnuts to the far side of the islet, where

360

there was a clearing forming a rough square. In the middle of it, ten yards from the bank, was a drystone structure with a shingle roof and a stone floor. It had an open fireplace and one or two items of rustic furniture, including a chair, a bench, and a rush table with one leg missing. Ferns peeped through the walls and the flags were slippery with moss but inside it was cool and secluded. The word 'bower' described it exactly.

He stood back, smiling, whilst she examined it, noting the rest of his clothes piled on the bench. The coat and stock were neatly folded, as though by a woman. He must, she thought, be a very fastidious young man, again in contrast to Adam, who scattered his clothes everywhere.

"I'm glad it was you," he said, "for I wanted to get to know you better. I was very put out when you called the supper party off. I came over specially from Deal and was looking forward to it." She remembered then that the Manatons had been invited and coloured at the recollection of those gruff cancellation notes Adam had sent out. Feeling some explanation to be necessary she said, "You heard what happened, I imagine? I was very much upset at the time. Everyone at 'Tryst' was, for it was a dreadful thing to happen on one's own doorstep."

"Yes," he said, making it very clear that he regarded the death of a chimney sweep a social inconvenience rather than a calamity, "I daresay it put you all to a great deal of trouble. But why not call the party on again now that I'm home on a month's furlough?"

"That's quite impossible," she said. "For one thing my birthday has gone by and for another my husband is away."

His expression of interest in this announcement made her regret having made it and it occurred to her then that perhaps, after all, she was a little short of experience in handling brash young officers who did not seem to be the least embarrassed when they were observed swimming in the nude in somebody else's stream. Most people, she supposed, including his own mother, would consider it very improper for a married woman to be here in his company, even though it was broad daylight and he was the trespasser. Then she remembered that, in all the time she had known him, Adam had never exhibited a spark of jealousy, and also that he had no patience at all with the fiddle-faddle that polite society hedged about young married and single women. The thought gave her confidence so that she said, carefully, "I'm not in the least sure I ought to stay talking to you after you had the impudence to go swimming in our reach without so much as a pair of cotton drawers. Why didn't you make sure the towpath was empty? Anyone at all might have seen you."

"Yes," he said, looking at her gravely, "they might at that. Even Mrs. Halberton," and at that she had to laugh for Mrs. Halberton was acknowledged the self-elected arbitress of social proprieties in the district. "I hope you won't tell her," he added, and she replied, "How could I? Without starting a scandal?"

"Well that's handsome of you, Mrs. Swann, but I can't say I'm really surprised by your attitude."

"You think I make a habit of watching men go swimming?"

"No," he said, seriously, "what I meant is that you're obviously a person who shares my impatience with conventions. There's far too many of them nowadays and they're becoming an insufferable bore to everyone young enough to enjoy life."

"Now that's very curious," she said, "for my husband is always saying precisely the same, and has done, ever since we married." She noticed that his eyebrows lifted in a quizzical way so she went on, hurriedly, "What I mean is, Mr. Swann has travelled a great deal and served in two wars, so that that kind of thing doesn't bother him overmuch."

"I'm glad to hear it," Miles said, "for it means you could help me to pass the time very agreeably while I'm on leave, providing you've nothing better to do, of course," and before giving her a chance to protest, "I usually take my furloughs during the hunting season, and go out six days a week. This is the first summer I've been home since I was commissioned and frankly I'm finding it dull."

She was not absolutely sure what niche a gunner occupied in the complicated military hierarchy but she was aware that it was higher than most. She said, "I wanted my husband to remain in the army. He was a lieutenant in the East India Company, the 'John Company' he always calls it. I believe you're in the Royal Horse Artillery, aren't you?"

"Yes, I am," he said, proudly, "and I'll wager you are the only woman of your age in the district who would know as much. As a matter of fact," he went on, "I got the impression at that croquet party that you didn't approve of me and wouldn't have cared two straws which regiment I served. I take it as a compliment that you not only found out but also remembered."

It struck her, with a kind of wonder, that everything one said to Miles Manaton was construed by him into some kind of compliment and attempting to alter this state of affairs she said, quickly,

"Pray don't jump to conclusions, Mr. Manaton. I've been interested in military matters ever since the Crimea and in your case I recognised the badge. I can tell you most things about soldiering, and even which regiment takes precedence over others. I know, for instance, that all you regular officers look down on the Indian army and that the Guards look down on you."

The laugh that greeted this was not conventional. It ran clear across the river, starting a moorhen out of the reeds. "You're too sharp for me, Mrs. Swann," he said, "and I promise upon my honour not to tease you again." Then, standing back a pace, he looked her up and down in what many women would have considered an almost indecent fashion, and would have made her blush if he had not added, with obvious sincerity, "You can't imagine what a relief it is to chat to a very pretty woman who treats you as though you were a brother, and doesn't take refuge in meaningless chatter. It used to be fun with my sisters, but they've suddenly grown up, and put on the most ridiculous airs, whereas every so-called 'eligible' my mother introduces into the house acts like a doll wound up by mamma and likely to run down at any moment."

She found that she liked this line of talk for it made her feel very much at ease. "I know what you mean," she said, "and I'm sure Adam would, but you can hardly include me in the eligible class, can you, Mr. Manaton?" expecting him to laugh again.

He did not, however, but dropped his gaze, appearing, to her considerable astonishment, somewhat confused. Then, turning away and looking across the river, he said, sombrely, "No, unfortunately not, Mrs. Swann, and I'll risk offending you by saying that I consider your husband a very fortunate fellow indeed. Among the most fortunate in the county!"

Who could avoid being flattered by this from a man like him, she asked herself. She had noted his bored acceptance of the adulation he had received from all the unmarried girls at the party, some of them pretty, but there was something almost abject in the way he propped himself against the doorpost and avoided her eye, as though her presence subjected him to a deep emotional strain. Whether this was so or not the certainty of his interest in her as a woman rather than a neighbour excited her. It was a long time since she had regarded herself as anything much more than a man's plaything, and while this satisfied her vanity it was pleasant to learn that a man existed, and a young and handsome man at that, who regarded her as a person in her own right. She was still cautious, however, and

363

said, "I don't think you should say that to me in these circumstances," but was careful to keep coquetry from her voice. "After all, Mr. Manaton, there must be a great number of unattached girls about here who would be very flattered by any attention you paid them."

"I daresay," he replied, with a boy's surliness, "but not one among them with a thought in her head except what the Empress Eugénie is wearing, and a whiff or two of local scandal." Suddenly he faced her with what she could not help but regard as an air of desperation. "You must have realised that I've been very much aware of you, ever since we met at Mrs. Halberton's."

"I'm aware of nothing of the kind," she said, truthfully. "How could I be? We've never met again until this moment."

"That's so," he said, smiling now, "but I've watched you walking and riding about here none the less, and often been tempted to hail you, for you were always alone." His engaging smile faded and he looked at her with a new kind of interest. *"Why* are you always alone? Isn't your husband concerned about you roving the countryside afoot and on horseback, without an escort?"

She said, smiling, "To tell the truth I don't think he knows, for he's away so often about his business. But if he did I think he would trust me to look out for myself."

"Aye," he said, giving her another of his appreciative scrutinies, "and I'd wager you could if it came to the pinch. Your husband runs a transport service, doesn't he? Surely that's a rum thing for a gentleman to do, especially a man who rode in Cardigan's charge. I'm not the only one to remark on it. It puzzles a majority about here. Did you know that, Mrs. Swann?"

"Yes," she said, calmly. "I knew it. It doesn't do to be in trade with some folk but Adam says it will soon be accepted, even by county families like yours. He says it's quite silly to pretend otherwise. That was why he didn't give a fig for family tradition."

"What tradition was that?"

"Why the Swann tradition," she said, proudly. "A Swann has served in every major war since Crécy, or so the Colonel, my father-in-law, tells me. He fought under the Grand Old Duke, and was wounded at Waterloo. He gets invited to the Waterloo dinner every June, and *his* father fought under Lord Cornwallis, in America. When America was a colony, of course."

He smiled, rather condescendingly she thought, offered her his hand and led the way out of the bower into the sunshine. "You really are an intriguing person, Mrs. Swann. Here's your husband running a freight service all over the country, and getting his name into all the newspapers, and all you can talk of is his family's military tradition."

"I can't help that," she said, equably, "it's the way I'm made."

"But what on earth does your husband think about it? About your attitude to trade I mean?"

"Oh, he just laughs at it and goes about his own business no matter what me and the Colonel say to the contrary but he has made me a promise and I mean to see that he keeps it."

"What promise is that? Or is it a secret?"

"No, it's no secret. He's promised me our son Alexander shall take up a commission in a good regiment as soon as he's done with school. It would have been Stella, of course, but she turned out to be a girl."

"Were you very disappointed?"

"At the time I was, but I got over it as soon as Alex was born and I mean to have other sons. After all, I'm only twenty-four."

Her artlessness had the power to silence him. It was so unlike the simulated ingenuousness of garrison town wives to which he was accustomed, or the rather tiresome naïveté of the kind of girls Mrs. Halberton invited to her croquet parties. Suddenly, and quite definitely, she began to interest him for it occurred to him that a woman who could talk so frankly to a man she hardly knew might well prove a very easy conquest inasmuch as her mind did not run along the rigidly prescribed lines of current fashion. Already he had half made up his mind to try his luck, partly because this promised to be an excessively dull furlough but mostly because Miles Manaton was a man who regarded every pretty woman he encountered as a challenge. He was not especially ruttish, and rarely consorted with the professional drabs who infested the barracks and overseas stations where he had served, but for all that he was a very dedicated womaniser, using women as a kind of diet to feed an insatiable ego that had been his principal characteristic ever since he had discovered, at the age of about three, how strikingly beautiful he was, and how natural it was that his sisters, and all the old trouts in married quarters should go out of their way to spoil him. He could never have enough flattery. Without it, even for a day, he was like an addict deprived of his opium. The act of physically possessing a woman meant very little to him, but her homage, even for the few sweaty moments she was beneath him, meant everything, for he assessed each conquest in the way a miser assesses a bargain or a piece of gold. At twenty-six he had already accumulated a sizeable hoard, beginning with an adolescent encounter with a besotted young governess, and ending a month or so before he began this furlough, with the wife of his military tailor in Canterbury. He had sired a number of children here and overseas but he thought of them not as children but as proofs of his infallibility with women, all kinds of women, from housemaids and milkmaids to the wives of elderly officers and busy merchants. What was even more unusual than his tally, however, was his adroitness in evading the consequences of nonstop lechery. He operated like a skilled fencer, first estimating the ability of his opponent to defend herself, then deciding upon an approach, then moving into attack, and finally skipping back out of range and usually out of sight, for none of his affairs engaged him sufficiently to hold his attention for more than a month. Once heavily engaged, however, it became a point of honour with him not to desist until the quarry had either capitulated or made it absolutely clear to him that she never would. In the latter case he would drift away and take his revenge by dropping hints among colleagues concerning the woman's character and here again he was almost unique among men who made a practice of seduction. He had never, in the whole of his life, been troubled by a single twinge of conscience.

There was a kind of scale in his armoury of tactics and its pitch was dictated by the overture. If the prospect looked easy he could be wildly passionate but if there was likely to be opposition he could simulate the despairing, lovesick youth better than any professional actor performing at Drury Lane. Sometimes, according to the quarry's mood, it was necessary to compromise, alternating rapidly between paroxysms of desire and transports of despair, and occasionally he had to resort to a less direct approach, seeming to seek a soulmate rather than a bedmate, a woman equipped to solace his loneliness and be an older sister to him. There was even a fourth approach, the one he decided upon now, and that was to reverse the tide of flattery, feeding it back to the woman who, he had decided, was not simply bored, as in the cases of most wives he had seduced, but dwarfed by a dominant partner, and perhaps on the point of having her individuality extinguished altogether.

When he encountered such a person his wealth of experience told him precisely how to act. He would gently isolate his victim from her background and then, almost inadvertently, display her to herself as an earthbound goddess whose celestial qualities had been churlishly overlooked by her partner. This, he found, was almost certain to bring her back to him again and again, until the moment arrived when he could dart in like a bullfighter and end the contest at a blow. He walked back to the tethered cob in Henrietta's wake, planning his moves like a pickpocket. She was very pretty. She was very vain. She was neglected. She was virtually subdued by that lout of a husband, who was so deficient in commonsense as to throw up a military career (even a pinchpenny one among sepoys) to become not a merchant but a hawker, whose income depended upon what he was given to lug about the country in a cart. Moreover, the poor fool was not only absent from home most of the time but allowed his wife to range the countryside like a ripe little milkmaid or cattle-herder, ready to be ravished behind the nearest haystack by the first man who happened along. The conquest of Henrietta Swann, he decided, would be swift and complete.

2

They had parted on a promise that she would meet him again in a day or so but that this time he would come mounted and give her a lesson in horsemanship. Adam, he acknowledged, had taught her to manage a quiet cob, but there was more to horsemastership than that and obviously poor Mr. Swann was far too busy with his important concerns to have time to give her the necessary instruction. He would be happy, he said, to teach her something of dressage, and was prepared to bring along a well mannered hunter from his father's stable for her pleasure.

She said nothing to anyone at 'Tryst' about the encounter for she already thought of it as a safe, stimulating flirtation, of the kind many of Mr. Mudie's heroines indulged in from time to time, without getting themselves fatally enmeshed like poor Lady Isobel, in *East Lynne*. For that, she decided firmly, was not for her. She was not even physically attracted to Miles, having had a unique opportunity to look him over without benefit of uniform. She thought of him, indeed, as a handsome, rather silly boy, who was, it seemed, as lonely as she had been on occasion and who had, in passing, been almost ruined by the fussy attentions of women, among them his domineering old mother and her three plain daughters. She could, she felt, safely show him a little sisterly affection in return for the personal enlargement his attentions had brought her. She might even let him kiss her, providing he went about it reverently and modestly, and then she would let him know that she was quite unable to return his love, and this offered a mutual bonus for, whereas she was badly in need of a boost, he needed to be shown that there were still women about who were proof against his charms. All men, of course, were egotists, but the egotism of Miles Manaton was exceptional and deflating it, by means of a series of gentle pinpricks, offered a welcome break in a flattish routine until Adam came cantering home with all that chimney sweep nonsense out of mind. There was really no comparison between being swept off her feet and tossed about by a real man like Adam Swann, and flattered and petted by a self-inflated masher like Miles Manaton, but Adam's lack of jealousy had always irritated her a little, and it could do no harm, and might even do some good, if he learned, in a roundabout way, that other men not only thought her pretty but in possession of a full set of wits.

It was a rather smug Henrietta who stretched herself out in the big double bed that night and before she slept she had resolved upon setting out for the towpath the following afternoon, and discovering whether he had kept his promise about giving her a riding lesson on one of his father's hunters, known to be thoroughbreds.

He was there sitting on his own mare, a dainty little bay, with expensive-looking accoutrements and holding another horse by the leading rein. Moreover, he was wearing the undress uniform of the Royal Horse Artillery, and looked far more manly than he had in ruffled shirt and breeches or, for that matter, flat on his back in the pool. They spent a pleasant, restrained afternoon. He was, she had to admit, a superb horseman and possessed the patience to teach her to jump over a log, which was something Adam had never been able to do. They rode up across the moor and down into the adjacent river valley, and all the time he was gracious and polite and talked to her about army life, recounting a number of amusing anecdotes about his superior officers and their feuding wives. She went home thinking she might have misjudged him, for he was really a most agreeable companion, and seemed to have set aside his outrageous conceit for her benefit, or perhaps because he already realised it failed to impress her.

It was a Monday when she had first crossed to the islet and by the following Saturday they had enjoyed three similar expeditions, all unremarkable in every way, save that she seemed, by then, to have tamed him completely, for he began to behave towards her with a reverence that she found delightful to contemplate. Nobody had ever shown her the least deference in the past and the sensation it imparted encouraged her to reward him with any number of soft words and expansive smiles, and even the licence of half an embrace each time he helped her mount and dismount. Once, she noticed, as she leaned her weight on him momentarily, he gave a kind of groan, as though he had a stomach ache, but she thought it impolite to comment and when they parted, and she set off through the wood for home, she glanced over her shoulder and saw him standing there, a lonely, disconsolate figure, holding the reins of the two horses, and staring after her as though she was one of Mrs. Henry Wood's heroines who had just rejected his advances.

It was, she decided, a very engaging game and perhaps a rather one-sided one but that was no reason at all to end it, for a young man with his looks and prospects could hardly expect to go through life without finding an occasional dose of castor oil on his silver spoon.

She expected that Adam would be home in a day or so and then, of course, this nonsense would have to stop, but in the meantime they had another assignation, having agreed to meet on foot, for the horses were due to be shod and he had suggested she might like to try her hand at fishing. She proposed riding her cob as far as the islet but he said, quickly, "No, Mrs. Swann, don't bring the horse, for the best place to try for trout is that gravel bed near the narrow part of the channel, and if the cob is tethered close by they won't bite. I'll look out for you our side of the footbridge, and carry you over the stream, for the river's no more than a trickle," and to this she agreed, reflecting gleefully that it might put a strain on him to have her in his arms for a few seconds.

She dressed very carefully, choosing a wide-brimmed straw hat, a white muslin dress sprigged with forget-me-nots, a cross-over fichu to cover her shoulders, and a pair of white slippers for the ground was bone dry and the distance across the paddock not above half-a-mile.

She left the house carrying a flower basket and gardening gloves, having no intention of being questioned by Ellen as to why she was setting out in flimsy garments and indoor footwear. She idled along one of the lower flower beds and then, when the gardener's back was turned, hid basket and gloves behind the raspberry canes, walked down the blind side of the wall enclosing the kitchen garden, and darted across the few yards of greensward to the wood. She was sure nobody had observed her leave but she was wrong. The Colonel had been watching her from his sitting-room window ever since she passed out of doors, and when he noticed the unconventional manner of her departure he put down his paint brush, rubbed his nose, and went downstairs to collect his field glasses.

In point of fact, Henrietta's behaviour during the last few days had puzzled him. Although he could understand her rather secretive high spirits now that Adam had returned to work and written two cheerful if noncommittal letters home, he was at a loss to know why his daughter-in-law should go out of her way to advertise to everyone about her that she was so confoundedly cock-a-hoop. It showed in the sparkle that never left her eye, in her glibness when he asked her what kind of day she had spent and, above all, in her restlessness, that had her glancing at the clock every so often, as though Adam might appear at any moment when she knew quite well that he was in the north. Then there were her regular disappearances on that cob of hers, and the fact that she always took an identical route, through the paddock copse and down to the river, where she crossed the footbridge and could be seen for a moment through a gap in the trees passing along the towpath before being lost to view behind the willows.

He was very far from being a suspicious man but she was guileless enough to arouse any man's suspicions and as the days passed he began to wonder what mischief she could be engaged upon, and why she went about it with a mixture of nonchalance and secrecy. He was not seriously worried, however, until he witnessed that casual stroll along the borders and sudden dart for cover. To pretend to be gardening, and then pursue her usual course on foot and wearing house slippers seemed to him nonsensical. He trained his glass on the gap and waited, finding a fixed point and holding the brass cylinder steady by resting it on the window-ledge. In this way, he recalled, he had once saved his life, spotting an ambush laid by that wily old rascal Soult on the French side of the Adige. In five minutes she reappeared, walking briskly, as though she had a definite purpose in mind and he made his decision. If she was up to anything likely to introduce fresh discord into the house he was going to do his best to scotch it while Adam was still at a distance. That chimney-sweep business had made everybody miserable, and life had taught him to value domestic tranquillity above every other state of mind.

He went into the stableyard and summoned Michelmore, telling him to saddle the skewbald and saying that he fancied an hour's ride in the woods. Michelmore, who had been enjoying a nap in the tack-room, took his time about saddling up, and helping the old fellow on to the mounting block. Then, looking up at the sky, he prophesied rain within the hour, and this interested the Colonel who fancied himself as a weather prophet, so that they got into an argument, the Colonel declaring that the thunder heard earlier in the afternoon was well to the west, and that whilst Surrey might get a storm Kent would not. Michelmore, declaring that he, as a Kentishman, qualified as the better judge, persisted in his point of view, pointing out that birds were flying low and there was cloud across the river, and for some minutes the Colonel forgot the purpose behind his ride and only recollected it on seeing Henrietta's basket half-hidden in the raspberry canes. Then, telling himself that his ability to concentrate was deteriorating, he turned the skewbald towards the trees and was riding through them when the first local thunder pealed out and the horse nodded his head, as though signifying agreement with Michelmore.

3

They had not been fishing ten minutes before the first of the heavy raindrops fell and Miles, glancing up, said there would be a heavy thunder-storm in a matter of minutes and that they had best take shelter in the bower on the far side of the islet. He was right. Moments later thunder crashed out and rain began to fall in vertical sheets, so that they abandoned their gear and ran for it.

Looking back on the incident, as she sometimes did in the years ahead, Henrietta fancied that Miles Manaton must have had influence with the Devil to be able to summon up a storm out of a clear sky, for here, within hailing distance of the towpath, he would have been obliged to take no for an answer, and she could have put a term to any persistence on his part by recrossing the ford at the expense of a ruined pair of slippers. On the left bank, however, where the bower was situated, the channel was deeper and timber ran right down to the water. There was no path here and the sycamores and horse-chestnuts behind the building completely screened anyone using it.

She followed him without hesitation, however, for now the rain was heavy and although the islet was no more than fifty yards wide her fichu was sticking to her shoulders when she ran across the threshold and into his outstretched arms.

She thought then that he was merely taking sly advantage of their dash for cover and when he kissed her on the cheek she did not resent it, but only said, mildly, "Now, Miles, do behave yourself, rain or no rain," but his grip on her tightened, and then he was kissing her mouth, so that she had to exert all her strength to break from him. She was at a loss to find words to express her displeasure and sought a moment's respite wrestling with the damp ribbons under her chin, and taking off her crumpled hat. Then, as she straightened herself after placing it on the bench, she saw that he was staring at her in a strange disquieting way. His eyes were hard, and his woman's mouth was set in a prim, downcurving line, as though he found her resistance insulting.

She said, "Why are you looking at me like that?" and he replied, levelly, "Because you practice one set of rules and pretend to another! How long do you expect a man to dance on the end of your bonnet string, Henrietta?"

His arrogance amused her, so that for a moment she forgot to be frightened at his tone of voice, or the way his insolent glance played over her, from her slippers to the crown of her head. It was a baleful, menacing glance. He might even have been measuring his distance with something repellent. She said, at last, "*What* set of rules? If you think you can just . . . just *grab* me, and kiss me without so much as a by-your-leave, you're very much mistaken, Miles Manaton! If you had asked for a kiss I might have said yes, but I'm not one of those silly creatures who would think it a great privilege if you raised your hat to them in public!" and she turned her back on him, half-inclined to march off into the hissing rain but deciding that this would leave him with the honours, particularly as she would have to wade the stream to regain the towpath.

He was checked for a moment reassessing the situation. In his career as master-masher Manaton had met with any number of temporary rebuffs but he had usually anticipated them. Women, in his experience, could be divided into three categories, the genuinely innocent, those who used innocence like a fan or twirling parasol, and those who, when it came to the point, enjoyed both chase and kill. He had slotted Henrietta Swann into the last category, deciding that she was a basically sensual little pigeon, and that once firmly within his embrace she would stay there with no more than a murmur or two of protest. His sharp observation told him, however, that her indignation was genuine, so that it followed he had made an error of judgement, and that she really belonged in the second group, flirting with innocence, and prepared to retreat into it until she had regained the initiative. It was difficult to hurry this kind of courtship and unfortunately there was not much time left, for his furlough expired in a day or so, and her husband might appear on the scene at any moment, so that both factors contributed to the course he decided upon, a feigned withdrawal under a mantle of resentment, with the object of putting her in the wrong, and giving him a chance to make a second storming approach. He looked at the rain gratefully, hoping the thunder would roll and the lightning flash, for it was his experience that most women were upset by thunder-storms.

He said, glumly but reasonably, "I'm sorry, Henrietta I didn't mean that. But you must realise you have given me reason to hope."

He did not think of this as a fiction and in a sense it was not, for she had made no play of convention, or even modesty, during their association. She had ridden with him all over the neighbourhood, and had been seen by any number of local folk. She had listened to and laughed at stories most men would have hesitated to recount to a young married woman. But it seems she did not regard it in this light at all for she said, though less emphatically, "No woman likes to be . . . well, *pounced* on in that way. I'm sure I don't, anyway. I've enjoyed meeting you, Miles, and it's been very agreeable, so why did you have to do that and spoil things?"

He now began to doubt if Henrietta belonged to any one group for surely, by now, anyone but a half-wit would have had an inkling as to how such a relationship would end, so he went off on a fresh tack, saying; "You'll catch a bad cold if you stand there under those drips with that fichu sticking to you. Take it off, you're dry underneath," and when she hesitated, "Good heavens, Henrietta, you don't think I'd harm you? I'm terribly in love with you."

It says much for Miles Manaton's technique that this was accepted at face value and that his confession, spoken without benefit of faltering voice or heavy sigh but as a statement of fact, made a direct appeal to her emotions. It was a speech right out of the books of Miss Yonge and Mrs. Henry Wood, and nothing remotely like it had come her way in the past. Makepeace Goldthorpe had wanted to marry her for cash, and Adam, over the years, had shown her a great deal of affection, but he had never once admitted to being in love with her, and suddenly she felt ashamed of having encouraged him to that extent.

She said, turning back from the door, "Undo the knot, for I can't reach it," and presented her back to him, with the innocent object of getting rid of the fichu and wringing it out. It did not occur to her that he would regard this as unconditional capitulation, and even when he had loosened the knot, and the ends of the fichu were freed, she felt no sense of alarm, for she now saw him as an unhappy bewildered boy, who could be kept in check by a few gentle pats and a gentle kiss on the cheek and brow. Then as the fichu fell away, his arms shot round her and locked under her breasts, and his mouth was close against her neck and she understood she had entirely misjudged him, not only as a lover but as a man. His grip told her that he was beyond pleading with, and also that she was neatly trapped and would be very fortunate to escape from this encounter without staking everything she valued on the outcome of the next few minutes. Her first impulse was to scream and kick at his shins but then she realised that she could never put up more than a token struggle, and that the only possible alternative would be to employ the kind of tactics he had used in getting her into this kind of situation. She fought down her panic and said, "I'm so frightened, Miles. If my husband ever found out ..." and then stopped to see what advantage she had gained, if any.

It was appreciable. He was familiar with this last-minute, pre-surrender bleat, accepting it as the small change of victory. He said, "Why should he, until it's too late for him to get you back?" and then, as his hands slipped over her breasts, she thought of Lady Isobel's fate, and it seemed to her so credible that it came storming right out of the printed page, so that she thought she would faint on the spot. She managed to hold on, deciding that if that happened there was no doubt at all how a man of Miles Manaton's character would act. In less than a minute he would have her stripped and in one minute more past and present would have retreated out of sight, leaving nothing but an appallingly bleak future, for her instincts were serving her well enough now, and she had no doubt that he was absolutely ruthless as regards women, ruthless, cruel and without scruple of any kind.

It was this, perhaps, that restored to her a measure of courage and cunning, so that she was able to say, leaning her full weight on him, "I daren't go back there afterwards, Miles. If you want me so much then let's run away. Now. At once!" and before he could find a suitable reply to this she turned in his embrace and began showering him with kisses so that he thought, fleetingly, "Why, damn it. I

374

wasn't wrong at all! She's no more than a genteel whore posing as a virtuous wife," and her proposal that he should abduct her seemed as specious as all her other artifices, something that could be forgotten as soon as the rain had stopped drumming on the roof.

He would say one thing for her, however. She certainly knew how to rouse a man, and that husband of hers must have taught her a trick or two, for she was now kissing strumpet fashion, and using her thighs and fingers like a trained mistress coaxing her lover into a giving mood. It would not have surprised him very much if she had not broken off the embrace in order to tear off her clothes and suddenly he wanted to laugh, not only in triumph but at her terrible impatience that was feeding his vanity in a way he would not have thought possible a moment ago. He said, breathlessly, "Wait ... over here ..." and lifted her on to the broad wooden bench, flattening her and groping under the folds of her flimsy dress, with the intention of securing a grip on the waistband of her drawers, but then a strange thing happened. In the very moment he hooked his fingers under the tape a great red bubble soared and burst in front of his eyes, and he fell sideways, striking his temple a sharp blow on a projecting edge of the stone wall.

It occurred to him, vaguely, that the bower had been struck by lightning, and that he and she and everything about them had gone up in a puff of smoke but then, his vision clearing somewhat, he saw her standing over him, with her copper hair a disordered mop, and her eyes fixed on him with a look that was as close to hate as he had ever seen in the eyes of a woman. The expression communicated something to him and his hand shot up to the crown of his head, coming away wet and sticky, and then he noticed that she was holding a triangular piece of stone, of the kind that were laid one upon the other to form the wall, and he half-recognised the relationship between her expression, the piece of stone, and the sudden enlargement of his head. Even so he rejected the idea that she could have struck him and the notion of a thunderbolt returned to him to add to the imponderables.

Then, but still through a reddish haze, he saw her move swiftly across the floor and make a grab at her hat and fichu, and it was this evasive movement that restored him to something like full conciousness, so that he let out a wild bellow of rage and flung himself forward just as she reached the entrance of the bower.

He almost caught her. His fingers hooked in the neckband of her dress and there was a long ripping sound as the material parted all the way down to the waistband, exposing the criss-cross lacing of her corset. The jerk delayed her flight for a second or so, pulling her sideways against the doorpost, and it was while he was straightening himself for a renewed pounce that a second blow, far more painful than the first, struck him in the groin, doubling him up like a jack-knife and bringing him to his knees with a yelp of agony.

He knew then there was no question at all of her innocence, and that she had not struck him on the head in panic but because his head had offered the easiest target when he had been reaching for her drawers. This second blow, deliberately aimed at his crotch, was a calculated one, and minutes passed before he realised she was no longer there to pay the price for such a terrible outrage. He crawled round in a half-circle and sat with his back against the post, rocking himself to and fro and trying to decide which area of pain claimed the most attention, his bleeding skull, his grazed temple or his violated genitals. Then, to his disgust, he vomited, bowing his head to the floor. He was crouched there, like a wounded animal, when the Colonel came in and stood looking down at him.

4

When he emerged from the wood and made for the footbridge, it was already raining hard and the Colonel had half a mind to retreat under the trees and wait for it to stop. Then it occurred to him that she would be soaked through in a matter of minutes, and probably very frightened out here alone in a thunder-storm, so he rode over the bridge and turned downstream towards the line of willows, now masked by a curtain of rain that was bucketing down on him and running into his boots. He did not mind a wetting but he began to be very worried about Henrietta, and urged the skewbald into a trot until he drew level with the ox-bow that he had painted more than once, for a variety of wild flowers grew here and over on the islet he could sometimes see waterbirds too shy to nest along the open reaches. She could, he reasoned, have gone but one way, straight down the towpath, but he could only guess her destination. It was probably Twyforde Green, the village two miles downstream, or possibly the side road halfway along that led, ultimately, to Mrs. Halberton's place, at Broad Oak. Then it struck him that her manner of departure precluded both possibilities. If she had been going as far as Twyforde Green she would have taken the cob, whereas, if she had intended visiting Olivia Halberton, there would have been no secrecy about her departure. The more he considered it the more disturbed he became. There was a man in it somewhere, and the fact that there was did not surprise him, for he had often questioned his son's wisdom in leaving a spirited girl like Henrietta unchaperoned for weeks at a stretch. She was probably enjoying a flirtation with one of the young bucks around here, for it explained her archness, her frequent disappearances and, above all, the way she had quit the house that afternoon. He thought, glumly, 'Well, I daresay there's very little to it. She's plenty of commonsense at bottom but if Adam should hear of it the whole damned house will be in an uproar again,' and he turned up his collar and crammed his hat over his eyes, with the intention of seeking her somewhere between here and Twyforde Green. Then, as he kicked the skewbald's flanks, he saw her, or someone very like her, a dishevelled figure with skirts bundled up, running from the trees and into the river less than fifty yards from where he sat his horse.

Even at that short distance it was difficult to be sure, for the bank was obscured by the threshing rain and the woman splashing through the ford, now thigh deep, looked like an animated scarecrow, her clothes in tatters. The moment she saw him she altered course, and a few seconds later was clawing at his stirrup and shouting up at him, but what she said he was unable to hear, for just then thunder went crashing across the valley and she loosed her hold on his leathers and pressed both hands to her head. He dropped out of the saddle and looped the reins round his forearm, for the skewbald was showing signs of restlessness under the impact of the thunder and Henrietta's jostling. She shouted in his ear, "I've killed him. ... he's over there ... a hut beyond the trees!" and with that a little of his half-forgotten battle experience returned to him and he made the first decisive move of the afternoon, shouting, "Take the horse! Go home! Get away from here Henrietta!" and when she stared at him uncomprehending, and continued to dither, he bent, grabbed her foot, thrust it into the stirrup and propelled her into the saddle where she slumped forward, clutching the skewbald's mane, the tatters of her dress trailing across its haunches to the ground.

He pulled the horse round and gave it a thump so that it began to canter back along the towpath and was soon lost to sight in the blurred landscape. Then, as the rain slackened and settled to a moderate downpour, he sloshed across the ford and found a path that

377

led through the trees to a stone building on the far side of the islet. He thought, dismally, 'She's hysterical. Can't be true! She couldn't kill a chicken . . .' but then he remembered the state of her clothes, and the fact that she had been half-crazy with terror and running like a hare when he had spotted her, and the recollection made him sniper-wary so that he made a circuit of the building, fetching up at a point where he could look through the doorway without being seen.

A man was there, a young man wearing fashionable clothes, and he noted with relief that whilst he might well be injured he was far from dead, for he was crawling across the floor like someone in an advanced stage of intoxication and suddenly he checked the movement to vomit. Fascinated, and still extremely puzzled, the Colonel edged closer until he was standing in the doorway, glancing around for some discarded weapon but seeing none, and presently the young man wiped his mouth and stood up, very unsteadily, so that the Colonel saw a deep gash on the crown of his head, and a streak of blood from a superficial cut on his temple that had run down under the ear and stained his collar. He was still standing in the doorway when the man saw him and glowered, as though he was a trespasser, but he said nothing, seemingly preoccupied with a third hurt in the area of his groin that he began to massage very gingerly, swearing and muttering under his breath. The Colonel had the impression that he had seen the fellow before but he couldn't be sure so he said, in a parade-ground voice that he hadn't used in twenty years, "What the devil has been going on in here? What sent my daughter-in-law flying across the river half-naked, and half out of her wits, hey?" and the man made an effort to pull himself together, seating himself very carefully on the bench and saying, "She's mad! Mad as a hatter! She tried to brain me with that stone—there—under your feet with my blood on it!" The Colonel glanced down and saw a triangular piece of stone that might have weighed a couple of pounds. It was lightly spotted with blood and the stain caused him to look more closely at the pulpy swelling on the crown of the young man's head. Aspects of this unlikely affair began to form a pattern as he said, noncommittally, "Ah, that's as may be," but he thought, with approval, 'She might have looked helpless but it seems she can take care of herself if she has to,' and then, because his chivalry was instinctive, and not the fashionable abstract of a later generation, he growled, "Would it be too much to ask what you did to provoke her? Was it for stripping the clothes from her back, and forcing

378

yourself on the girl like a wild beast?" but when Manaton made no reply his temper hissed up like a Congreve rocket and he stepped closer, saying, "Speak up, lad, for if that's the case I won't wait upon the Magistrates. I'll call you out, damned if I won't, and face the consequences if I put a bullet in you."

The threat did not intimidate Manaton but it roused him to the extent of understanding some kind of explanation would be necessary if he was to avoid trouble and serious trouble at that. Now that the ache in his testicles was receding somewhat he was able to think clearly, and saw that his advantage must lie in putting that little devil in the wrong. He said, carefully, "I'll tell you precisely what happened, Colonel Swann. You'll hear her account of it, no doubt, and believe her rather than me, but bear in mind she got off with a torn dress, whereas I had my head laid open," and he bent forward so that the Colonel could see the wound and the blood-clotted hair about it. "I've been giving her riding lessons. At her instance I might say. Today, when the storm came on, we went in here out of the rain. There was a kiss or two, I won't deny that. But she began it, and that's a fact, and you're man of the world enough to make allowances for it. The truth is, Colonel Swann, your daughter-in-law gave me every encouragement to treat her the way I did, and ended by asking me to run away with her. It was for turning that down that I got this, not for taking advantage of her. Question her closely enough and you'll find that out."

He paused, undecided how much disposed the old man was to believe this, then went on, "She didn't lose half of her dress defending her virtue, although that's the defence she'll put forward. She used that damned stone on me for deeper reasons than that—pride, I daresay. And don't tell me she didn't know in advance what usually happens when a man and a woman of our age find themselves alone in a place like this. Ask her why she came seeking me out day after day, and why she led the way here instead of taking shelter under the trees within full view of the footpath. All I know is that I got this crack on the head and she got her dress ripped from her back trying to dodge the consequences, for if I had caught hold of her I would have given her the thrashing her husband should give her once a week. Even that isn't the whole of it. When I was on my back, over there near the door, she hit me again in a way that could have maimed me. You saw how it was when you came here."

It did not seem an improbable story and he was content to reserve judgement. He said, "See here, Mr. Manaton. I'll give you two

379

pieces of advice for nothing. Go home and get that skull of yours stitched, and don't show your face around 'Tryst' when my son is at home, for if you do there'll likely be murder done when his wife tells him what occurred this afternoon."

"She'll not tell him if you don't," Miles said, sulkily, "and the fact that she won't should underwrite my version. If ever a woman brought trouble on herself she did, and will again if she isn't watched. As for me, my furlough expires tomorrow, and I'll be serving overseas in a month or two. I don't expect I'll ever see her again, and that's a hardship I can shoulder."

"What's your regiment?" asked the Colonel and when Manaton told him he said, rubbing his long nose, "I might ha' guessed. It was my experience in the field you could always rely on the gunners to stand off out of range and make a pretty fair mess of things every time they went into action."

He rose heavily, feeling his age, impatient with the young and their shiftless ways. Without another word he stumped back across the islet, over the river and down the path towards home, his boots gurgling with the water, his hat brim tipping trickles down his wrinkled old neck. As expected he found the kitchen quarters in uproar, maids running this way and that, and that scold of a housekeeper scampering about like an outraged hen and babbling nonsense about 'the poor lamb having been thrown into the river by a horse'. He said, sourly, "Hold your tongue. If it's true she should know better than to go out riding in a bad thunderstorm!" Then, "Where is she?" and Ellen told him the mistress had retired to her room with a glass of milk and a headache powder. He went into the dining-room and poured a tot of brandy, carrying it up to the big bedroom over the porch and finding her sitting up in bed and drying her hair that was fluffed like a clown's. She looked pale and agitated but by no means prostrate, so that he thought, 'What the devil do any of us know about women? As far as she's aware she might be up on a charge of manslaughter or worse, but all she's concerned about is her appearance!' He said, thrusting the tot in her direction, "Get that down you and let's see if your story matches his. And you'd best tell me the truth, for a rare lot depends on it!"

"I don't like brandy," she said, sniffing the measure like a spoiled child, but he growled, "Get it down, I say!" and she swallowed it in two gulps, spluttering as the colour returned to her cheeks.

"How . . . how was he?" she said, at length.

"A long way from dead," he told her. "He had a bump on a head that is already too big for a hat but I fancy that jab you gave him below the belt will keep him clear of other men's wives for a day or two."

Suddenly, and to his indignation, she giggled. He said, severely, "Listen here, I'll be damned if I can see anything to laugh about! You got off very lightly in the circumstances. You realise that, don't you? For if you don't you're a far bigger fool than I took you for!"

"I got off lighter than he did," she said, cheerfully, and then, composing herself in the way of a mischievous child called to order, "I was only flirting with him, and if he told you anything else he's a liar as well as a beast. Do you think I would have gone riding and fishing with him if I'd had the least idea he was that kind of person?"

"No," he said, "I don't, but what right had you to go riding and fishing with him at all? Dammit, woman, you've got a good husband, a couple of children, a great house, and everybody dancing attendance on you. What more do you want?"

"I don't know," she said, ruefully, "fun, I suppose, and something to occupy me all the time Adam is away. He's not blameless you know."

"Did I say he was? I'll take that up with him, maybe."

For the first time, he thought, she showed deep concern, enough to bring her out of bed and down beside him so that again he thought of her as a child in disgrace. "You'll not *tell* Adam? You'll not provoke another scene, like the one we had over the chimney sweep? Oh, I'm not afraid of what Adam might do, what he has a right to do, I suppose, but if what happened gets gossiped about the entire neighbourhood will think of me as ... well, as that kind of woman, and I'm not. I'm not that kind of woman at all. You must know I'm not."

"Adam needs a dressing down as much as you," he conceded, "but what I tell him is my business. If it's any comfort to you I'll spare your reputation, if that's what you're concerned about. All I intend to do is to make sure this doesn't occur again with that young fool or anyone else. We've had more than enough trouble lately and there's no damned sense at all courting more, the way you did with that gunner. Can I depend on that, Henrietta?"

"You know you can, but I can't be answerable for what Miles might spread about."

"He'll say nothing."

"How can you be sure?"

"He's leaving here tomorrow but there's more to it than that. Womanisers of his type are gamblers and when did you hear a gambler boast of his losses? They'll brag their heads off when they win but judging from what I saw of him, crawling round on his hands and knees, you can be sure he'll keep the facts to himself." He looked at her with a glint of humour. "Did you have to use him so hardly after letting him think you were fair game? Was it done on impulse the moment you realised he wanted more than you were prepared to offer? Or did you have it in mind to teach him a lesson?"

She climbed back into bed. It seemed to her then that anything short of complete honesty would be offensive on her part. "It was both. Manaton assumes that every woman in the world would give all she had to become his slave, never mind his mistress. I knew that, and he knew that I knew it. The trouble was he didn't realise I was married to a real man, someone who doesn't find it necessary to impress every woman he meets. The real difference between them struck me the moment he touched me. There was ... well ... condescension in everything he did and said, in his eyes and mouth and even his hands. He made me feel like somebody's cast-off property and that's something Adam never could do, to me or any other woman."

"Well, that's progress of a kind. Go on."

"I think I hit him not just to get away from him but to show him what I thought of his silly conceited ways. I didn't think about it, I just did it because it showed him what I was thinking. I hit him where his vanity lives. Both places. I'm not pretending, though, I wasn't terrified at the time. Not *of* him, exactly, but for us; myself, Adam, the babies, even for you. Does that sound very likely to you?"

"Far more likely than anything else I've seen or heard since I saw you sneak off to meet him." He looked at her, indulgently, "Get up and dress yourself. No damned sense pretending to be an invalid. Tell Ellen we'll have dinner together and that I shall expect something toothsome for all the trouble I've been put to. Where's that dress you had trailing about you?"

"On the window seat and quite ruined. Throw it away while I'm getting ready."

"Aye," he said, "I'll do that but go my own way about it. They may have pretended to believe that tomfool story of yours about falling in the river but they'll put their own interpretations on it, in the way servants do if they've got a mistress who lets 'em make a fool of her."

He picked up the sodden rags and tucked them under his coat, going out and along the corridor to his own quarters. He was wet, tired and bothered by twinges of rheumatism that had their origin in nights on the slopes of the Pyrenees half-a-century ago. But, taken all round, he was pleased with himself. For the first time in years he felt useful.

5

Truce Terms

ON his way into town the Colonel had plenty of time to trim his brief, deciding to confine himself to broad hints concerning the encounter, and lay the emphasis on the folly of letting her roam the neighbourhood unchaperoned. He also intended to have something to say concerning his son's frequent absences, but he found, after no more than a few words with Adam, that he had underestimated his son's sagacity, and that his mere presence here had been sufficient to plant in the boy's mind a suspicion that he was listening to an edited story. In fact, when the old man got as far as saying that Henrietta should be forbidden to ride out alone, Adam laughed in his face, saying, "Come, now, what really happened? You're the worst liar I ever met. Has Henrietta been kicking over the traces?"

He told him all then, or nearly all, and was astonished when his son showed no signs of outrage either against his wife or that popinjay of a gunner, but said, equably, "Well, I'm obliged to you for keeping track of her and it was lucky for all concerned you were there when it happened. But it's a relief to learn she can handle someone like Manaton at a pinch. In a way, I suppose, I've only myself to blame for the scrape and should think myself fortunate she was able to fight her way out of it." He stood musing a moment. "One on the sconce and another where it hurts most, you say? Well, that saves me the trouble of doing it myself and making bad blood between neighbours. I wouldn't care to tangle with Henrietta if she was desperate for there's more of Sam Rawlinson about her than she realises."

His son's imperturbability irritated the Colonel, who saw it as yet another indication of the renunciation of values that had been standard currency for centuries. "God damn it, boy," he burst out, "shouldn't a man show more concern over someone's attempt to use his wife as a doxy? Time was when a husband would have called that fellow out, then gone home and given his wife reason to eat her meals standing for a fortnight!" but Adam smiled, blew a

384

smoke ring and said, easily, "Ah, I don't doubt it. But times change, and knowing Henrietta as well as I do I can read more and less into this than you can. More, because she's in desperate need of something to absorb her energy—and that's something I intend to remedy, less because she was telling the truth when she said it was no more than a joke on her part to gammon that young fool Manaton. She might have been married five years and presented me with a couple of children, but she's really no more than a schoolgirl, and that's my fault more than hers. I've known it long enough but put off thinking about it until that chimney-sweep business. In a way it's lucky this occurred, for it'll likely soften the impact."

The old man looked pained, recalling his half-promise to Henrietta to make light of the business. "You mean you intend to give her the whipping and let that damn Manaton get off scot free?"

"I don't mean anything of the sort," Adam said, impatiently. "A man who struts round inviting duels and a husband who knocks his wife about is not only a bully but a damned fool living in the past. I've got faults enough but I hope I've more brains than to react like someone in one of those trashy tales she feeds on. I won't tell you what I intend doing, you'll find out soon enough, but I'll give you a hint. I'm going to find her the kind of problems that keep my nose to the grindstone so that I'm not obliged to trot around to Kate Hamilton's plush establishment to prove myself every so often. Meantime I can only thank you again, and ask you to do one thing more for me. Go on home and send her up here. Michelmore can drive her into Croydon and I'll have her met at London Bridge. There's a train that gets in about five in the afternoon and we shall be putting up at the 'George', in the Borough High Street, overnight."

"The children are expecting you home," the old man said, at a loss to know what to make of his son, but Adam said, grimly, "The children can wait. They've got the whole of their lives ahead of them. Hustle on back now, and tell her to put on her smartest clothes and pack an evening gown. But don't plague me with a mountain of hand luggage."

"I hope you know what you're about, boy. It sounds to me as if you were going to indulge her rather than teach her how to behave when your back is turned."

"I've got several surprises for her," he said, "but I've a notion she'll be dipping into a very mixed Christmas stocking," and he led the way down the spiral stairway and handed his father into the gig.

"Take the Peckham route," he said, "the traffic will be lighter," and then disappeared into one of the warehouse sheds.

'Damn my eyes, but he's more of a puzzle than he was as a lad,' the old man reflected, as he gathered the reins and moved off. 'There's more of a French strain in him than there was in his mother and he's even beginning to sound like a merchant, with his bustling ways and that trick of his of keeping all his important thoughts safe in his head. I wonder how his children will turn out, whether they'll be Swanns or D'Auberons?' and he let the horse find its way through the traffic, turning right halfway along the Old Kent Road and threading a way through side streets until he could cross Peckham High Street and head south towards Sydenham. He wondered then why he had not caught a train to carry him across this maze in under the hour, telling himself he had been born too long ago to adapt to the nonstop hustle of the age. More and more these days, and not only in the matter of personal relationships, he felt himself a castaway in a world that had died even before the Duke's funeral carriage went rattling up Ludgate Hill to St. Paul's.

*　　*　　*

It was like a recurrence of the sultry summer night when, as a chit of a girl, she had escaped from her father's house in a green crinoline, a fugitive without a destination, at the mercy of any destiny that blew up out of the storm.

So many experiences had come her way since then but she wondered, settling herself in the first-class compartment and watching Michelmore stow her hand-luggage on the rack, whether she had learned very much from them for, if truth were known, she was more scared now than then, and even more dependent upon the whims of the horseman who had come riding over the moor to catch her washing herself in a puddle. She had never made a train journey alone, and reflected that nobody passing up and down the platform would identify her as the mother of two children. She even wondered whether anxiety about the approaching confrontation showed in her face and in her fidgetings with the jet buttons on her jacket bodice, and it was thinking this, and the vast amount of space a small person like herself occupied, that reminded her of the earlier occasion when she had been similarly encumbered. The only essential difference between then and now was that she would at least recognise the man to whom she had been consigned and that the uncertainties attending his reception of her were now confined to something definite, that is, what he was likely to make of her involvement with Manaton.

The Colonel had been small help in this respect, notwithstanding her importunities. She still had no clear idea of what Adam had been told, or how much his father had left him to guess. The only reassurance the old man had offered was a hint hidden in the advice he had given her when he kissed her good-bye; "There now, put a bold face on it. A man doesn't tell his wife to pack an evening gown if he has it in mind to wallop her. It wouldn't surprise me if you didn't get off with a finger-wagging."

For herself, bowling towards him at fifty miles an hour, she wasn't so sure, and perhaps her doubts had had time to crystallise for even the old man was unaware of what had actually occurred in that dreadful little summerhouse, or how near Manaton had come to condemning her to live out the rest of her life like a felon on ticket-of-leave.

For a day or so she had refused to contemplate what might have happened had her hand not brushed against the projecting edge of that stone. Then news came that Adam was back, and that the Colonel had intercepted him, and she had been obliged to take a closer look at the encounter. It struck her at once that she must have been as innocent as a three-year-old to trust Manaton to the extent that she had, and that she would consider herself fortunate if she was able, in due time, to put it out of mind, in the way she invariably dealt with unpleasant experiences. She had a feeling that this would rest upon Adam's attitude and that attitude would depend upon how much he surmised rather than how effectively his father had pleaded her case.

Forebodings of this kind occupied her until the train chuffed out of Sydenham, heading into the golden-brown pall that stood over the city like a giant toadstool but then, little by little, her anxiety lessened, and she began to feel a small, comforting glow at the prospect of seeing him again for it seemed that he had been absent much longer than usual. Remembering the original quarrel she gave herself a little shake, calling her scattered thoughts to order, and taking advantage of the fact that she was alone in the compartment, she murmured aloud; "I'll be myself so long as we're in public and when he brings it up, as he's certain to do the moment we're alone, I'll burst into tears and bury my head in his shoulder!" It was a promise she knew herself capable of carrying out. She had done it several times in the past over trivial matters and made the discovery that tears muddled his thoughts.

He was not at the London Bridge barrier, a fact that surprised her but his clerk Mr. Tybalt was there, and lifted his tall hat as she handed in her ticket and broke into a trot in order to keep the porter carrying her hand luggage in view. He called, excitedly, "Mrs. Swann ... I've a carriage waiting ...! I'm to drive you to the yard where Mr. Swann is detained, completing some business!" and she allowed the little man to pilot her to a four-wheeler and watched him make a great show of stowing her luggage and tipping the porter. His air of self-importance amused her but she helped him indulge it, reflecting that all the men Adam had assembled around him paid him more genuine deference than the millhands had paid her father and that this was odd, because Adam never struck them or swore at them. It had to do, she supposed, with his army training and it crossed her mind, as the cab passed through the gates of the yard and ran between phalanxes of waggons bearing her trademark, that he was still serving in a kind of army, only now he was the general with the power of life and death over everyone else.

She looked about her with a keener interest than she would have expected, wondering why she had never visited this hub of his life, and deciding that it had more to offer in the way of a spectacle than Sam's mill that was really no more than a large brick box, enclosing a nonstop racket. Tybalt must have noticed her interest for he began pointing out various features of the place, as though he had been a Beefeater at the Tower of London showing a distinguished visitor the Crown Jewels. "There, Ma'am, straight ahead, that's the counting house where I spend my time. Those sheds are our transit warehouses, where we stow goods consigned to the docks for shipment overseas. That's the weighbridge—the checker holding the lading bills is weighing the contents of the pinnace—a one-horse van, and people new to the game always want to know how he arrives at a total when the waggon is weighed with the goods. He knows the *unladen* weight of the vehicle you see, and all he has to do is subtract. .... Ah, there goes the whistle. That means the end of the day shift and two-thirds of the men will leave now, but the late shift will stay until the last waggon comes in from the Triangle or The Bonus. There might even be a long-distance delivery, for if we're transporting priority goods it's often quicker to send them the full distance by road on account of the delays in the goods yards, especially the London termini."

Most of his commentary went over her head but enough made a lodgement to introduce an element of wonder concerning the size and complexity of the undertaking. Not once, in all the time she had been married to him, had this occurred to her, for she had always thought of his obsession as something childish, almost like a boy building a dam in a stream at the bottom of his father's garden, or a man of fashion slum-visiting in the company of other men of an equally eccentric turn of mind. Now she realised that it was not like that at all, that this was a real place of business, just like Sam's mill and just like Matt Goldthorpe's rent-collecting agency, and that all this time he and she and the children and everyone else at 'Tryst' had been fed and housed on the proceeds of what was done about here. She said, sombrely, "Where does he ... where does Mr. Swann *work* when he's here in London, Mr. Tybalt?" and Tybalt blinking, said, "Why right here, ma'am. Here with us. Up there in that little tower, for that's the hub of the place and always has been!" and as the cab ran down alongside the warehouse and came to a stop he pointed through the window at a square tower that looked like a church lost in a welter of bricks and sheds, as though it represented all that survived of an age of piety.

Tybalt handed her out, telling the cabby to wait for luggage and a fare to the 'George', and she followed the clerk up a narrow winding staircase into an octagonal room with latticed windows overlooking the river. Coloured, hand-drawn maps, of a kind she had seen him working on, covered every wall, and between the desk and the door was a strange-looking object like a huge, dress-display stand that moved on a pivot but she only glimpsed it for he was sitting at the desk working and she noticed at once how fit and tanned he was looking, and also how pleased he was to see her. As he looked up his quick smile made her heart beat in a way that not only surprised her but convinced her there was really nothing much to worry about, for he was clearly in one of his exuberant moods. He said, leaping up, "Ha, Tybalt, thank you. Train on time?" and Tybalt replied, "Bang on time, sir. That superintendent at London Bridge has a reputation to maintain," and then bowed himself out, ostentatiously closing the door so that they were alone in this queer, ecclesiastical-looking room, crammed with the apparatus of his life.

It was absurd, she thought, but she found herself blushing furiously, as though she was alone in a room with him for the first time, and he was not slow to notice it saying, gaily, "Why, Henrietta, you're bringing us 'Tryst' roses in your cheeks!" and he moved round the desk and put both hands on her shoulders, holding her off but looking at her very intently, as though searching out traces of

Miles Manaton's kisses. She thought that if he did this a moment longer she would have no need to conjure up tears in order to postpone his cross-examination, so she dropped gloves and reticule on the desk and threw her arms round his neck, kissing him hungrily on the mouth and saying, "Oh, Adam . . . *dearest*! I'm so glad to *be* here, so glad you asked me! I've been very wretched, for such a long time it seems . . ." and then he embraced her in the way he usually did when they had been parted and she wished heartily they were anywhere but here, where any one of his acolytes might come tapping at the door and there was nowhere they could sit apart from his swivel chair and a stool under the maps.

Some such thought must have occurred to him for he said, passing his hands over her and finally (reluctantly, she thought) letting them rest on her hips, "I've reserved a room at the 'George'. We'll stay in London a day or two for I want to show you the city. You've seen most of the famous places but never this London, the liver and lights of the country, and I should like that because I've something to explain that concerns you more than it does me." He bent to retrieve her gloves and reticule and she noticed how young and supple were his movements, as though he had been two and twenty instead of a man approaching middle-age. She said, knowing it would please him, "Tybalt explained all manner of things as we went along. I had no idea it was so . . . well, so *organised*," and at this one of his booming laughs escaped and he said, "What did you suppose we did up here? Play skittles? Look, I'll give you some idea before we have dinner and later on, if you're interested, I'll show you the stables, forge, yard and warehouses, but that can wait on a meal. I don't know about you but I'm very peckish. I've been arguing with lawyers all day." He led her across to the window that looked directly across a jumble of tile and slate, sliced here and there by narrow threads of traffic moving towards the river that swept in a brown curve both sides of the bridge. To the left she recognised the great dome of St. Paul's and to the right, a reach down-river, was a dock that seemed to contain all the ships in the world. Straight ahead, on the far bank, was the Tower, crowned by the familiar centrepiece that reminded her of a toy fort owned by David, the younger brother of her onetime friend Sarah Hebditch. The atmosphere, for a city far larger than Manchester or Liverpool, was relatively clear at this season of the year, but the brown mushroom of smoke she had seen from as far away as Sydenham had now changed into a semi-transparent pyramid, rose pink and chrysanthemum gold under the westering sky. The smoky smell, that found its way through the upper part of the casement, was much homelier than the reek of Seddon Moss. It wrinkled the nose, and made the eyes smart, but it contained elements other than grime and furnace belch, a whiff or two of cooking and the acrid, not unpleasant smell of horse droppings churned under wheels.

He said, cheerfully, "Well, there it is, and it's never the same from one hour to another. Granted it hasn't the fragrance of the view from our windows at 'Tryst' but it's a permanent reminder to keep at it, at least, that's how it always strikes me. I drew these maps in the first weeks I was here, and never a day passes when I don't study them, and old Frankenstein over there." He pointed to the nondescript thing she had thought of as a display stand and she saw that it was an encyclopaedia with a hundred faces, made up of well-thumbed wedges of cardboard, scrawled all over with squiggles of the kind one might expect to find on an Egyptian monument but when she looked closely at a particular section she was aware that the squiggles were really lists of minutely-written names, flanked by columns of figures and, here and there, pieces cut from the maps like those used as wallpaper in this mysterious sanctum.

"You surely know I can make nothing whatever of that," she said, and he told her, smiling, that nobody save him could, now that Frankenstein absorbed the entire network. "Tybalt could make it produce information in its infancy," he said, "but now he prefers the long way round." He stood thinking a moment, "See here, I could give you the idea by a random example. Think of it as a railway Bradshaw, an atlas, and a trades directory rolled into one. What did you have for breakfast this morning?"

"Two cups of tea and a piece of toast," she said, unhelpfully, "I was too excited to eat."

"Well, then, yesterday?"

She pondered, entering into the spirit of the game, for she understood that it might be important to their relationship at this point. "Eggs and bacon," she said, "two rashers, nice and thick."

He turned to the apparatus and spun it. "Eggs—Bacon, Poultry— Pigs. Eggs we can discount, they come in from all areas by short haul, but bacon means Wiltshire, and a Southern Square bread-and-butter line. *Wiltshire* ..." He spun the frame again, his long fingers probing here and there among the cards. "Bacon—*Wiltshire*— Eli Dawson & Son. Eli has a curing depot and a cut-price contract, on

391

account of him being the first pigman we nailed down in the Southern Square. Calne is five-and-a-half miles south-east of Chippenham, and Chippenham is on the Great Western." His fingers were flying now, reminding her of a spinner mending broken yarn. "Five-miles-plus is a short haul but bacon is heavy freight so we use frigates—two-horse vans." He flipped out a card. "Three miles on an unsurfaced road, two miles plus over a macadamised route. In good weather an hour's run, including loading at the factory and off-loading at Chippenham." Another card emerged. "A goods train goes out of Chippenham at six-five every week night. Dawson's bacon is in a London siding by midnight and collected by the wholesaler before breakfast. If you like Wiltshire rashers for supper you could be eating them the same evening at 'Tryst', and you would be putting ... wait a minute ... three-halfpence per pound in my pocket for getting them there!"

She was so delighted that she clapped her hands, bobbing from one small foot to the other. "Why, that's marvellous! It's like a magician taking doves out of a hat! Who ever invented that wonderful machine?"

"I did," he said, puffing himself up like a robin in the snow, so that she squealed with laughter and then he laughed too, as much at himself as at her.

They went down the stairway to the four-wheeler where the giant Keate, whom she recognised as an occasional visitor to 'Tryst', was talking to the cabby. Keate said, touching his hat, "Good day to you, Mrs. Swann. Forgive me a moment ..." and he turned to Adam, saying, "I'll wait and see Goshen's haul in from The Bonus, sir. He was due an hour ago. He's probably caught up in a cart jam the other side of the bridge. Will you be in tomorrow?"

"Not until about this time. I'm hoping to show Mrs. Swann our workshop after taking her to look at the docks."

"Very good, sir," he said, just like a sergeant-major, and stepped forward to open the cab door and hand her inside.

It was all rather like playing a stately rôle in a play, she thought, a military pageant, perhaps, with undertones of comedy in which Adam was a field-marshal surrounded by a swarm of adjutants, each hanging on his commands. The force and the rhythm of his enterprise began to stir in her imagination and its surge swept her along, as though she was a passenger on one of those expresses that had whirled her south as a bride nearly five years ago. For the first time since she had sat beside him she was conscious of privilege in a way far beyond the conventional sense, for if he was king here then it followed that she was queen, and it was surely something to be queen of an empire that engaged the attention of so many solemn-looking men and so much bustle and precision, even if it was concerned with humdrum things like breakfast rashers of Wiltshire bacon. The thought comforted her, as did the touch of his hand on hers and suddenly she felt very safe and relaxed in his presence, a sensation not entirely unfamiliar to her but one that had never previously made itself felt unless they were alone. She exclaimed, rapturously, "Oh, Adam, I do love you! You're so good to me, you've always been good to me!" and lifted his hand, pressing it against her cheek.

2

She knew very well that he had something important to say but was holding back until they had all but finished their meal and were unlikely to be interrupted by the ministrations of the bald, elderly waiter, who looked such a fixture of this great, galleried inn that Adam said had been doing business for three hundred years, and was a local landmark before Queen Elizabeth mounted the throne. Next door, he told her, was the even more famous 'Tabard', where pilgrims had assembled for their journeys to Canterbury, and not far away was the 'White Hart', where Mr. Charles Dickens met the original Sam Weller and made him famous all over the world in *Pickwick Papers*. Before the railways, he said, coaches ran from these courtyards to every part of the country, but because they were situated here, in the heart of the capital of the world, they had not suffered the decline that overtook their provincial counterparts. The cuisine was good, and the reputation for service and comfort jealously guarded, and even two disastrous fires had not succeeded in breaking their tradition, for the 'George' (once known as the 'St. George') had been rebuilt on its original plan and its galleries, gay with a hundred window-boxes of geranium, lobelia and nasturtium, were still the favourite haunt of city men who sat here discussing odysseys bound for Batavia, Peru and the South Sea Islands. His familiarity with the city background impressed her in the way his fieldcraft had at their Pennine bivouacs during that long, pillion-ride across the fells. Somehow, she thought, one was the complement of the other, inasmuch as he seemed to find it so easy to adapt to wherever he happened to be and this, she was sure, was rare in a man, even one trained as a soldier, for what would a fop like Miles Manaton make of the world if he was stripped of his fine coat and red-striped trousers, and turned out to compete with hard-faced merchants? She was pondering this, savouring his superiority as it were, when the waiter suggested serving coffee on the lower tier of the gallery, where the gentleman might like to enjoy a cigar, but Adam said, a trifle sharply, she thought, "Serve it here. I'll wait for my cigar," and the old fellow shuffled away, leaving her with a qualm or two, for the dining-room was now almost empty and his preference for privacy surely implied he was about to come to the point and what point could that be if it wasn't her ridiculous involvement with Miles?

He said, as the thought made her fidget, "Are you comfortable here?" which was his way of giving her a chance to excuse herself, in the way she had after that gigantic supper at Windermere the first night of their marriage, but she said, with forced brightness, "Oh, quite comfortable, dear. It was delicious. I do wish Mrs. Hitchens could make pastry as light as that," and he replied, with terrifying directness, "I'm going to send Mrs. Hitchens packing the minute I get home. Along with most of the others."

It was said in such magisterial contrast to his indulgent mood since he had greeted her in the tower that she gave a little gasp of dismay, saying, "Oh, Adam, you don't mean to uproot us? We're not leaving 'Tryst', are we?" and to her great relief he shook his head and said, "No, my dear, quite the contrary. I've just bought 'Tryst'. That's what I've been doing all day."

"*Bought* it? You mean it's *ours*? For always?"

"I think that depends."

"On the money you make?"

"No, mostly on you. On whether you're capable of running it as it should be run, without half-a-dozen ignorant women taking the reins out of your hands, and throwing you back on yourself whenever I'm away and unable to keep them to their jobs."

She was not sure what to make of this. Did it imply that he numbered her among the idle, or was it an indirect reminder that she had recently made fools of them both? She said, carefully, "You mean I've been a failure because I'm too stupid to keep accounts and get into such muddles with the bills?" and he said no, he didn't mean that; keeping accounts was not likely to come naturally to someone who had not been trained in the art of housekeeping, and was something that could easily be remedied, for she wasn't in the least stupid, simply inclined to let herself be dominated by people like Ellen Michelmore and Mrs. Hitchens the cook, and even Evans, the parlourmaid, and the new governess, who couldn't be trusted to govern a cat. She understood then what he was driving at and privately admitted that it was true. All the women about the house, and especially Ellen, had been at pains to impress upon her that the mistress of a place as large as 'Tryst' lost caste if she participated in domestic chores, or even directed them save at a remove. She saw too that this decree was linked in his mind to the Manaton débâcle, and the certainty of this terrified her. She was almost sure then that he was about to make direct reference to Miles' attempt to convert a flirtation into a rape, and suddenly the shameful memory of Manaton's outrageous attempt to strip her made her shudder so that he jumped to the wrong conclusion, He growled, his face clouding, "You find the prospect of losing Ellen intolerable? You couldn't face accepting full responsibility for the place? Not even if I found one reliable woman to replace four scrimshankers, with instructions to teach you everything she knew about running a house?"

She emerged from her panic, recognising in his tone and expression the indications of an obvious crossroads, not merely in their relationship as man and wife, but in her personal future within that relationship. Suddenly the alternatives were startlingly clear. She could throw herself at the opportunity he was offering, even at the risk of falling flat on her face, or she could withdraw from the brink and seek temporary shelter behind the skirts of women like Ellen, relying on his physical need of her to hold on to him until she got her second wind. And then she saw, possibly for the first time, how very frail these bonds were, and how easily they might be broken in favour of some other woman, maybe as young and pretty as herself but possessing, in addition, qualities that appealed to that other side of him, the side she had glimpsed back at the yard. Fear made her catch her breath but it also spurred her to make the leap. She said, throwing up her head, "Of *course* I could face it, and of course I realise I should have done it long since, from the moment I begged you to let us live at 'Tryst'!" Then, gaining courage, "But I'm not the only one at fault, Adam! Goodness knows, I was green when we married, and you must have known it, but I'm not a fool and never was, and if I'm to make a fresh start then I'll do it and like doing it, providing you show the patience you did at the beginning but have stopped showing me!"

He looked, she thought, first astonished, then relieved and finally, although she could not have sworn to it, shamefaced, as though she had probed a tender spot in him somewhere and this was fairly evident when he said, with a slow smile, "Well, good for you, Henrietta! That's the answer I hoped for and that's why I took the gamble, for the sum they're asking for 'Tryst' will account for every penny I've got, other than stock and premises. But I've an idea it'll be worth it, for we could hardly continue this way without arriving at some kind of compromise. You're right about my share of the blame. In fact, I'll go so far as to say it's been six of one and half a dozen of the other, for until this moment I could never see you as anything but a romp between spells of hard work and worry, and I suppose you've adapted to that as we went along. Dammit, I don't think I've ever thought otherwise of either you or the children—you as a bedmate, the children as diversions. That's what comes of marrying a girl thirteen years younger than oneself." He leaned forward, pushing his wine glass to one side and she thought she had never seen him look so earnest. "Don't make the mistake of assuming I want you to turn into a frump," he went on, "or a houseproud old besom like my Aunt Charlotte. God forbid! In most ways I like you very well as you are, and I fancy I've told you that often enough. But owning 'Tryst' is very different from renting it. It's the difference between a waggon and team that has cost you good money, and a cart and an old screw to pull it hired from a stable. That place needs more than love, care and attention. It needs *organising*, and I've neither the time nor the inclination to do it, but you could if you had a mind to. It could be one of the finest houses in the country and the best administered, providing you gave it the concentration a man has to give to his business in this day and age."

He stopped suddenly, and again she thought he looked shamefaced. "There I go again," he said, "in spite of my good resolutions," and when she asked him what these resolutions were he said, chuckling, "I made up my mind to talk straight to you but not to bully you. What I'm trying to say amounts to no more than this. From here on we're in partnership. You look to your side of the business, and I'll look to mine. I won't offer advice unless it's asked for and we don't overlap, understand? Now I can move on to the other reason I brought you up here instead of coming on home."

"Oh, you don't have to instruct me in that," she said, but he made an impatient gesture, saying, "I'm serious. I want to see if I can get it into your head that the word 'trade' doesn't necessarily smell of anything worse than sweat, that it doesn't have to be practised the way your father and Goldthorpe and that chimney sweep practise it, that it can take on as much dignity as any other profession, and is sometimes a damned sight more honest than some I could name. You're prejudiced against it because you saw how it was managed up north, and I suppose you'll always look at it in terms of a mill, but I meet merchants of every kind, dealing in every product you could name, and by no means all of them are brutes or scoundrels. A few are even beginning to encourage their employees to stand upright, and walk on two legs. This country lives by trade and nothing but trade. It made its decision to do this long before you were born, and there's no turning back now. Without trade, and expanding trade at that, neither the Queen nor Lord Palmerston, nor any one of us could survive as anything better than peasants grubbing in the fields, and the sooner that principle is taught at our so-called gentlemen's schools the better it will be for every man-jack of us! That's my gospel and you don't have to believe it or practise it. All I ask is for you to try and see it through my eyes and then set about dragging that establishment of yours into the nineteenth century."

He paused, for want of breath she supposed, and his eye caught hers so that suddenly they both laughed and he said, refilling her glass, "Let's drink a toast to it and to being together again in a way we never have been, notwithstanding our 'proofs of affection' as old Aunt Charlotte would say."

She drank with him although it occurred to her that she had already had enough wine to make her reckless, but now that he seemed to have said all he had to say she did not feel reckless any more but somehow older and wiser than she had ever felt in her life and she supposed this was due to a number of things, to the challenge he had thrown down, to the fact that he had spoken his mind on a variety of subjects without even mentioning the one subject she would have thought uppermost in his mind but, above all, to a sense of having drawn almost level with him at a bound. She was not sure how this had been achieved but only that it had, and saw it as an exercise in magic, like the kiss that had awakened Sleeping Beauty from her trance. She could sit here looking across at him and realise that she was not seeing him as husband and provider, or the father of her children, but a friend able to invest her with something very rare among women of her generation, an equality that went far beyond kindness and trust, and this was something to be prized for itself, like the ring he had given her on the road to Ambleside. She loved him then in a way she had not been equipped to love him in the past, for the radiance she had mistaken for love was seen to be sugar-icing and underneath was the cake of comradeship to be eaten in the company of a human being as hard-pressed as herself.

It was not the time for temporising. She had courage but she was still short on confidence. She said, meeting his eye, "I understand what you want, Adam, and all I can promise is that I'll try. Goodness knows, I should be telling a lie if I said I hadn't enjoyed being your wife but ... well ... there was always something missing and now there isn't. I wish I was clever enough to put it into words you could understand but I'm not. All I can say is it's going to be different from now," and she reached across the table and put her hand in his, not caring in the least about the presence of the waiter, still propping his back against the panelling near the door, or one diligent gourmand, champing his way through his fifth course under the window.

It was almost dusk now and the city roar had dwindled to a hum. He said, with reluctance, "That fellow Manaton ... he's still bothering you, isn't he?" and when she said nothing to this, "Don't let him, for he doesn't bother me in the least. I think you'll be able to laugh that off, given time. I have already. I've never had any doubts that you're a one-man woman, my love, so don't expect me to work myself into a blather about a bit of flirting that got out of hand."

"That's all it ever was," she said, earnestly, "you do believe that, Adam? Really believe it?"

"If I didn't I can also assure you I wouldn't have undertaken to come up with the sum of eleven thousand pounds for 'Tryst'."

The sum seemed to her astronomical. "Is that what they're asking? Have you got such a sum?"

"No," he said, "but I think I can raise it, or most of it. However, that's my concern. Would you like to sit out on the galleries now and watch the world go by?"

"Not in the least," she said, "I want to send that poor waiter over there to his bed. I'm sure he'll fall asleep standing if we don't."

"He'll brighten up when he gets his tip," he told her and rose, handing her out of her chair. The waiter stiffened and the gourmand paused in a ferocious attack on the savoury in order to pay them the compliment of an interested glance as they passed out and up the

398

broad staircase into a maze of corridors and dark, wainscotted landings. The old, uneven floorboards squeaked and Henrietta thought, as she followed him through the warren, that the place must have listened in to innumerable conversations over the centuries but none more momentous than the confidences they had just exchanged across the table.

It did not surprise her that the new understanding between them should invade their physical relationship. She came to him gladly and gaily, and it seemed to her fitting that their embrace should be the very first they had shared as equals. Without sacrificing the gusto that attended his approach on these occasions, when they had been parted for a period, he introduced—or so it seemed to her—an element of tenderness that was new and exciting, so that her mind went back to the first time she had shared his bed, a lifetime ago it seemed, but the sense of discovery was there, as though they had consciously retraced their steps over the years to make a new and more equitable beginning. She remembered many things lying there in his arms, basking in his silent appraisal of her body and reminding him by caresses of her own, that she had profited from all the outspoken lessons he had given her in this constantly renewed experience. It crossed her mind that it was a pity this was such a private communion, for tonight, of all nights, she could have shared it with every woman in the world, and perhaps it was this that reminded her that she had a daughter who, one day in the years ahead, would introduce a shy young man into the house and exchange meaningful glances with him under the impression that they had made a discovery that they would be sure to think of as unique and that she, for her part, would be obliged to pretend it was, if only for modesty's sake. But there had been little enough modesty, thank God, about her involvement with the man beside her. In this sense their relationship had been far less complicated than in others, and she had no doubts at all that he found her excessively pleasing as a bedmate, more so now, perhaps, than in the earliest days of their association.

The reflection made her giggle and she lay very still for a moment listening to the familiar sound of his breathing, a close and somehow reassuring accompaniment to the muted roar of the city. She knew him well enough now to predict the exact pattern of his behaviour on these occasions, when he tended to act as though he had been deprived of her for months rather than days. He would lie sleeping like that, his left arm flung across her breasts, until the peep of dawn and the moment he stirred he would stretch, become aware

399

of her and draw her closer. Then, almost absently, he would fall to exploring her with his lips and hands, the one seeking her mouth and neck and hair, the other her breasts, back and thighs. His movements were in leisurely contrast to the relative impatience he had shown the night before. He would go about it as though he was assessing what was his in the unhurried way she imagined he might take stock of inanimate possessions, his waggons, horses and now, she supposed, 'Tryst' and everything in it. His warm firm hands would play contentedly over her loins and buttocks, as though seeking an exact compromise between the assertion of mastery and an act of courtship, so that she found it very difficult to contemplate a more accomplished lover, or a man who possessed a surer, subtler knowledge of a woman's senses. Then, but still only half-awake, he would begin to praise her and it was always his words more than his touch that roused her to a pitch where she felt she could never absorb enough of him, her body opening and contracting to receive and seal that part of him that seemed to her, on the instant, to assume a separate identity that was a contradiction of the man she knew inasmuch as it was overweening, arrogant and aggressive, but not in a way she resented for, by then, the whole ecstatic process of domination and submission was being repeated with her active assistance so that she rarely thought of a time when this compelling act had seemed to her something quite outside the range of human possibility. After that, invariably, she would sleep for another hour, perhaps two, but he, it seemed, had slept long enough, for when she opened her eyes again he was usually prowling about the room in shirt and breeches, with his lean, brown face masked in lather through which he would grin at her approvingly and make some jocular, half-boastful reference to the encounter, as though daylight had no power to abash him as it abashed her. Tonight, however, the room was not dark for light filtered through the curtains from the big courtyard lanterns and she could turn in his loose embrace and study him, comparing him, to his immeasurable advantage, with all the other men she knew, married and unmarried. He always looked, she thought, very young when he was deeply asleep, as though the weight of his concerns added years to him as soon as he climbed out of bed and addressed himself to the business of the day, and his boyishness encouraged her to trace a frivolous pattern down his cheek with the tip of her finger. He talked and thought a great deal about England, and invariably projected himself as an Englishman, but looking down at him she remembered his father was given to saying that he was really only half an Englishman and that his mother had been a Basque, and Basques were, according to the Colonel, wild and unpredictable. Perhaps his mixed blood accounted for his eccentricities. She did not know any foreigners but she assumed they would differ very much from punctilious, predictable men like his father, or aggressive, explosive men like Sam and timid, conscientious men like Tybalt, the clerk. Different or not he was all she had and all she wanted, the man who had enslaved her from the moment she took shelter in that moorland hut, as if to await his arrival. She loved everything about him; his originality, his strange tolerance and basic kindness, and his dynamic self-reliance that was, perhaps, the most singular thing about him, for although she would never wholly understand what he sought to create for himself any fool could recognise it as a deeply personalised goal. But that part of him was still private and would, she was sure, remain so, for she sensed that in a curious way he was very jealous of it and would never lift more than the corner of the curtain on it for her or his male intimates, awaiting, possibly, the arrival of a son before he was ready to share it with another. She meant to give him that son if she could but not Alexander; some other, less important son, whom he could mould in his own image and she did not think he would quarrel with this. He was a man of his word and Alex had been spoken for. Equality she now had and she meant to hold him strictly to the terms of their original bargain, made the day after Stella was born.

She wriggled back into his embrace, running a hand half the length of his firm, muscled body and then, again recalling her wedding night, she lifted his hand and tucked it firmly under her breasts. Its limp presence there had always given her comfort. Tonight it represented permanence and continuity.

6

Flight of a Sleeping Partner

WHEN, in his old age, Adam Swann looked back on what he learned to think of, in retrospect, as the cleansing of his domestic stables, he was able to do so with humour for he saw himself in good company, notably that of the lately lamented Prince Consort, who had faced a similar situation earlier in his career as Master of Windsor.

Albert, Adam recalled, had finally prevailed upon his wife to let him examine the royal accounts and had found, to his astonishment, that he was footing a large annual bill for candles, and that after gas had been installed in the royal apartments for time out of mind. Candles, he learned, had been ordered in bulk during the reign of his wife's grandfather and were now regarded as the perquisites of court flunkeys and this was only one sideline exploited by the swarm of servants whose duties, to say the least, were very loosely defined.

Albert, frugally reared in faraway Saxe-Gotha, had solaced his isolation among the islanders by applying a touch of Teutonic thoroughness to a resentful household but Adam Swann, a man cast in the same mould, went further for, unlike Albert, nobody had ever implied that he was not master of his house in fact as well as title. His cyclonic descent upon 'Tryst' a day or so after he and Henrietta had arrived at their new understanding soon passed into local legend. It was sometimes spoken of, in Twyforde Green cottages and shop-parlours, in terms of a visitation, rather as the ancestors of those same villagers might have referred to the reign of Stephen as 'a time when God and all His Angels slept'.

Having carried all Henrietta's housekeeping books into his study he remained there for two hours, emerging to make a storming descent upon the kitchen. Half an hour later a red-eyed Mrs. Hitchen, the cook, was collecting her things, assuring God and His Angels that a halfpenny-per-pound butcher's meat commission was the acknowledged perks of every cook in Kent, and that 'real gentry' had been known to wink at double the rate. "I haven't a doubt that she is speaking the truth there," said Adam, when Mrs. Hitchen's recriminations were relayed to him. "Her error lies in the fact that we are not gentry, real or counterfeit, but tradesmen and she must be aware that no tradesman worth his salt would pay over the odds for a joint to adjust to her preference for one butcher or another."

After that it was Miss Gage's turn. Celia Gage, a relative of the local rector, had enjoyed a sinecure at 'Tryst' for more than a year as combined governess-nanny. She was not the kind of governess readily recognisable by readers of Miss Charlotte Bronte. There was nothing retiring or self-effacing about Celia Gage, or not after she had taken the measure of her situation and decided that she was answerable to no one but Ellen Michelmore, with whom she shared a predisposition to indulge in what the hen-pecked Ned Michelmore would have labelled 'women's clackety-clack'. It seemed that Celia's fondness for clackety-clack had resulted in overlooked obligations in the nursery and Adam, having satisfied himself that Stella was convinced that 'elephant' began with an 'H', told the governess that he was prepared to overlook this but not the fact that his infant son was still eating porridge with his fingers. The only concession he would make as regards Miss Gage was that she could stay while she sought alternative employment. Her sins, as he saw it, were those of omission, not to be bracketed with those of the cook in the matter of farming out kitchen contracts.

All this, however, was in the nature of an overture and no one was surprised when the outside staff was slashed from five to two after a brisk inspection of the orchard and vegetable garden behind the house. For an hour or so, pending the investigation by Adam into the distributing end of a steady traffic in plums, peaches and greenhouse grapes, the fate of the gardener Dawson hung by a thread but it was then discovered that Dawson's lieutenant, a man called Moffat, had a weekly rendezvous with some notable bottlers of fruit, who were marketing his produce as far afield as Purley. So Dawson stayed on, converted overnight into a hawkeyed martinet whom even the Old Duke would have promoted to the rank of provost sergeant.

There were other minor changes and many adjustments in procedure and the chain of command, but most of them pointed in a single direction. Less than a week after the upheaval Ned Michelmore was summoned to the presence and came away with a gleam in his eye that directed him straight into his wife Ellen's quarters, where a loud outcry was heard within seconds of him slamming the door on all that remained of the indoor staff. Not even Henrietta learned what passed between 'dear Ellen' and her husband, but Stillman, the handyman, whose principal duties at 'Tryst' were to attend to the few wants of the Colonel, formed an opinion of what had been said, recognising the relayed ultimatum for what it was, a choice between instant dismissal and a shift to the county town, where Ned Michelmore had been offered an alternative post as stableman for Blubb's teams on condition he took Ellen with him. Here again Adam found himself in sympathy with the late Prince Albert, having no difficulty in recognising Ellen Michelmore as his wife's Lehzen. So long as she was entrenched, exercising control over the entire household, and flattering Henrietta into believing that no lady of the manor would be seen in her own kitchen or nursery (save for the permitted bedtime visit), it was unlikely that much progress would be made along the lines laid down over the supper table at the 'George'.

The handyman, Stillman, a confirmed woman-hater, had noted the expression on Ned Michelmore's face and had listened outside the housekeeper's door from the moment the first of Ellen's cries of dismay had penetrated to the bootroom. He had gifts as a raconteur and demonstrated them that same night in the bar of the 'King Cade', where he supped his ale.

"In marches Ned, pale about the gills," he recounted, "and when you mind his wife had come to reckon it was her who pays the quarter-rent for the place, tis no wonder Ned was slow in getting round to tellin' her young gaffer's decided to call the tune, and time enough too, as anyone up there could tell you if they'd had an ear to the ground. Ned's bin given the choice o' restartin' the mill, or taking over as stableman at Maidstone, and I don't have to tell none o' you that that ain't a choice at all for that mill been losin' money since Conyer's time and couldn't be restarted on account o' the floods back along. Ned was for taking the job but his missis, 'earing she was to go along whether she liked it or no, threw a fit, an' after that a shelf full o' crocks to keep it company. Then out comes Ellen, with her hairpins fallin' out in a shower, and stampedes all over the damned house in search o' the missus but when she found her she come away without change. What was said between 'em I can't tell, for I got no business upstairs, where they did their talking. All I see is Ellen comin' down again, blotchy about the face but quiet, thank Christ, quieter'n I ever recall, an' now they'm packing. Later on down comes the missis to me with a sparkle in *her* eye and a rare edge to her voice, telling me I'd best put a rare shine on the master's boots, and I take this as a friendly nod from her ladyship that there's been a sorting-out all round. Not that I didn't see it comin', mind, wi' that fat thief of a cook sacked, and that Moffat, who was so generous with other folks' fruit gone, and parson's nominee for governess under notice to quit. Come to think on it, it began brewing a week since, the day young missis comes home on the Colonel's skewbald drenched through, and with her clothes in tatters. There's more'n one story as to how *that* come about, but you'll get none of 'em from me, for I'm walking a tightrope up there myself."

At this stage in the long recital one of Stillman's audience suggested that Swann was a hard man to please but Stillman, after a moment's thought, denied this.

"Nay," he said, finally, "but he's a hard man to best, or to turn aside once he's put his mind to something. Looks to me he's decided it's the missis and not them women who run the place, and good luck to him, and to all you other mugwumps who have been soft enough to let your ole John Thomas steer you to church and lived on to regret it."

The majority of ex-Rifleman Stillman's audience accepted this gibe as the price of a first-class story, that would be something to carry home to their wives when their tankards were empty but Stillman's summing-up was a fair estimate of what had occurred, for the Henrietta who returned from London was a markedly different woman from the one who had set out forty-eight hours previously and even Adam, who looked for a change, was not fully aware of this at first. It was as though, with the title to 'Tryst' in the family deed-box, she summoned the spirits of long-dead Conyers to witness the fact that she had it in her to equal the best of them and it would not be too much to say she sought counsel in the building itself, pausing to listen to the whisper of old timber at the turn of the staircase, or reading something intelligible in the creak of the scullery pump-handle that had witnessed innumerable kitchen feuds down the generations. She seemed to enlarge herself not only in assertiveness and positivity, but in stature, and this despite the fact that she was soon showing unmistakable signs of pregnancy and took no pains to hide the fact. She had plodded through her previous pregnancies with a certain modest pride but concerning this one she seemed to go out of her way to advertise the fact that a third cygnet would make his appearance around February. For she had no doubt whatever that the child had been conceived, as though by decree, in the course of what she had come to regard as their truce talks at the old 'George'

405

where they had, one might say, agreed terms, signed articles, and dutifully exchanged hostages.

It was because she herself viewed it in this light that she never once thought of the child as hers in the way she had indulged herself regarding the foreseeable future of Stella and Alexander. This boy (the child would hardly have the effrontery to be female) was city spawned, a living amalgam of his father's involvement with the capital, as though Adam had set himself to the task of siring an heir to his Thameside sprawl and had gone about it with the thrust and singlemindedness that he brought to all his commercial concerns. It pleased her, indeed, that it should be so. After all, on that memorable evening he had not only presented her with 'Tryst', but had invested her with the authority of a person who was expected to exercise supremacy in her own right and not as a cosseted deputy, and this made the loss of dear Ellen, the cook, the governess, and their cohorts, easy to bear, their very removal from the scene enabling her to settle to the business of grafting a new personality on to the house and finding in this a task that was not only absorbing but extremely satisfying.

This was before he found her Phoebe, who arrived a month or so later, her few belongings enclosed in a basket-trunk of the kind Henrietta had carried out of Scab's Castle. It might have been the trunk that established a rapport between the two women from the moment Adam ushered her into the sewing-room, introducing her as Miss Phoebe Fraser, the daughter of his Border Triangle manager, who had had the advantage of a Scots education, and, for good measure, four years in the service of a Galloway laird, with a reputation for counting the groats and living almost exclusively on gruel.

Phoebe was a small-boned, fresh-complexioned girl of about two and twenty, unobtrusive up to a point but extremely forthright once she had pondered a problem and made her decision. She had, everyone soon discovered, very definite opinions on a wide range of subjects, the benefit of fresh air, good table manners, the improving habit of selective reading, diet, exercise, the hour of lying down and getting up, and particularly the importance of inculcating into children at a very early age the social obligations of the fortunate towards the less fortunate. And yet she was far from being sanctimonious and was certainly not a prig, for she could be very lively and original on occasion. The children took a liking to her at once and Henrietta had never seen them better behaved than they were at the nursery table under the eye of Phoebe Fraser. As time went by she began to consult

Phoebe on all kinds of matters; the best way of getting Stella's front teeth to go straight, and the likeliest means of removing claret stain from table linen, but they were never intimate, as she had once sought intimacy with Ellen. Instead a partnership and mutual respect developed between them, based upon the fact that each secretly admired the other. Henrietta, a naturally impulsive and slapdash person, conceived an awesome regard for the little governess's deftness and self-discipline, whereas Phoebe looked upon Henrietta as a kind of gay adventuress, whose life had been as rich and colourful as her own had been grey and uneventful. She had, Henrietta discovered, a more reverential respect for Adam, looking upon him as a far-ranging and almost celestial being, charged with the fearful responsibility of shifting every product in the country from one point to another with despatch and safety. Perhaps she had gathered this from her father, whom Henrietta had never met or, perhaps, with her traditional northcountry acceptance of the natural superiority of the male, she was only expressing gratitude to the man responsible for winkling her out of a dull and dismal servitude in the bleak borderlands to a comfortable home in a countryside where the sun shone for at least six months of the year. At all events, Phoebe Fraser settled down very quickly and Adam, watching from afar, congratulated himself once again on his knack of spotting a promising deputy when he met one. The children, he decided, were in good hands. Stella was soon learning her alphabet and little Alex, his tantrums exorcised by two sharp slaps on the behind, learned to use a spoon and fork instead of relying on his fingers. Peace and accord descended on the house as the paddock beeches turned to gold and warm September sunshine lit the long façade of the old house where it crouched in its half circle of woods and rhododendrons. Sometimes, as she bustled about her work, Henrietta could be heard singing one of the lively songs Mrs. Worrell had learned from the handsome girl Sam Rawlinson had found on a Liverpool quay a quarter century before, and sometimes, when Adam drove out of blue dusk, he caught a rewarding glimpse of mother, governess, and children standing in a group on the balcony under the nursery window and would run up the shallow staircase to greet them before Phoebe Fraser announced, in a voice that brooked no appeals for a respite, "Awa' to your beds, the pair o' ye!" and Henrietta would say, in response to his query as to how she felt, "Never better in my life. At least he spares me that dreadful vomiting the others brought on. This one seems occupied with his own concerns, for he's never still a moment. I daresay it's on account of having started life among all that bustle alongside that yard of yours." In the next few months she said something approximating to this so often that he began, subconsciously perhaps, to read into her hints that the conception had been a deliberate act, representing a gift from her to him in return for 'Tryst' and the new personality he had willed upon her. And although he did not comment he was none the less grateful for, unknown to her or anyone else save Tybalt, he was himself going through a period of anxiety set in train by the abrupt withdrawal and ultimate disappearance of Josh Avery, his banker and source of credit. By October of that year, the fifth since he had set out to cut his swathe across England, Adam Swann was a desperately worried man.

2

Finance had always been the most ill-defined area of his enterprise and there were two good reasons for this.

In the first place he had never been able to regard money as an end in itself. Most city men, he discovered, thought of money as the base of their pyramid, often to the extent of pursuing profit for profit's sake, and even those concerned with a reputation and the consistency of their service or goods, gave to the financing of their undertakings a great deal of thought, and more of their time than to the competitive aspect of the concerns. It had not taken him long to face the fact that he was not endowed with their perspicacity, that he thought of finance, considered apart, as less important than all the other factors involved in a project. That is to say, it had to take its place in the queue and wait upon other imponderables—the age of a team, the strength of a vehicle, the loyalty of an employee, so that he was inclined to let money find its own level somewhere around the middle of the pyramid, far below the high standards he set himself, and only a step or two above, say, the breaking strain of an axle, or the time factor in a haul over a bad stretch of road.

That was one reason and the other was the instinctive trust he placed in Avery, having formed the habit of consulting him before making important decisions. Only when he needed a fresh injection of capital to get things moving in a new area, or to replace stock that had outlived its usefulness, would he seek out Avery in order to state a case.

The terms of their original agreement presumably reposed in the two letters of intent deposited with Avery's lawyers but he had forgotten all but the general outline. Now that he came to think about it he was not at all clear how their mutual obligations had been defined, for the association had never advanced beyond the gentleman's agreement, spelt out five years before, when he left the remaining rubies in Avery's keeping, partly as collateral for his advance, partly as a reserve. Since then there had been shifts in the arrangement. He was still paying Josh one per cent below the current bank rate for his initial three thousand, and he seemed to recall that Avery's original estimate of the value of the stones had been nine thousand guineas. Twice he had drawn upon the capital represented by them but on each occasion Avery had refused to treat the advances as further loans, stating that he was content with his fifty-fifty split on the overall profits, and Adam had agreed to this readily enough, although he was never sure how much capital Avery was deemed to have invested.

Many might have found it hard to understand how a man who could calculate to the halfpenny the profit on a run anywhere between the Border and the Channel should have been so vague as regards the financial structure of his business but even when allowances were made for the trust he reposed in Josh there were many excuses that could be offered for this omission. Avery had never taken an active part in the business and was rarely seen about the yard. He knew and approved of Tybalt and was on nodding terms with Keate. Apart from these two he would not have known any one of the area managers by name. He lived, so far as Adam could determine, a strange, rackety life, drifting between Stock Exchange, club and racetrack, with an occasional jaunt to Paris, or a call on Kate Hamilton who regarded him as an influential customer. He still kept on his old rooms in Guildford Street, where he employed a moonfaced servant called Vosper, who had once served him as orderly and who seemed to Adam a discreet servitor, short on conversation. Sometimes weeks would pass without a meeting, or an exchange of letters. Smaller sums of money, both in and out of Avery's account, were handled by his lawyer, and often enough, when Avery was in town, Adam was away or vice versa. Neither of them seemed to find anything odd about the relationship. For five years now it had worked well and Adam would have said that he had the better of it for, so long as Avery's lawyer retained power of attorney, he was always able to borrow tide-over money for new stock or premises, and had once drawn a largish sum to replace ageing horses in areas where bad roads shortened their working lives.

It was only after he was committed to buy 'Tryst', and had milked his personal account dry to raise the one third demanded as an advance on signature of contract, that he felt any urgency to consult Josh, or even tell him that he had recently converted the lease into a freehold. It seemed to him then that it was high time they had a talk and perhaps converted some of the remaining rubies into hard cash. He had his own ideas about what the stones were worth on the present market, having recently had Henrietta's ruby valued, and concluded that the total, based on the assessor's estimate, was higher than the initial sum quoted by Josh. The discrepancy, however, did nothing to cause him to doubt his partner's honesty for Avery was known to move in dubious company and the original estimate had almost certainly been that of a fence, who would be likely to strike an exceptionally hard bargain. When he saw how low his personal funds were, and how much next year's team and waggon renewals were likely to cost, he was half-inclined to discuss the financial situation with Tybalt but realised, when he thought about it, that this was impossible, for it would almost certainly lead to a disclosure of the source of the capital, as well as the insecurity of his arrangements with Avery. Tybalt, to whom financial integrity was a religion, would probably react unfavourably to the knowledge that Swann-on-Wheels had been financed by a looted necklace but there was more to it than that. He would also regard his employer as a complete fool to take the risks he took every day of the week on the strength of a partnership resting on a handshake and Adam did not care to look a fool in the eyes of Tybalt or anyone else in his employ. He had put aside most of his military precepts when he went into trade but one he continued to observe was that the commanding officer must appear to know what he was doing, even if rank and file were convinced he was marching them in the wrong direction. He therefore made up his mind to have a full discussion with Avery before he asked Tybalt to prepare a statement of accounts and next year's estimates.

But Avery was not to be found. He wrote twice to his club, and once to his rooms, but receiving no answer took a hansom to White's and made inquiries there of the steward. The man seemed more evasive than he need have been, although discretion was a qualification for a post at this kind of establishment.

He said he could give the gentleman no information concerning Mr. Avery's whereabouts, for he had not been seen in the club for a month. He could, however, disclose his address on production of the caller's card. Adam said, sourly, "I know his address. Damn it, man, he's been my partner for five years. I'm not here to collect a debt!", and turned on his heel, telling the cabby to drive to Guildford Street. Here he had slightly better luck. After pulling the doorbell several times he saw the curtain move on the far side of the area railings and caught a glimpse of Vosper's anxious face. He was now sufficiently frustrated to bellow through the letter-box, stating his identity and demanding to know Avery's whereabouts on matters of urgency. Presently the door opened slowly and Vosper said, unhappily, "Mr. Avery isn't here, Mr. Swann. I haven't seen him since Friday of last week," and then hesitated, as though undecided whether or not to admit the visitor. Adam helped him to make up his mind, putting his foot over the threshold and saying, "Look here, Vosper, it's important I contact him. I've got matters that demand his attention, and they won't wait. Where am I most likely to find him?"

Vosper said, wetting his lips, "I . . . er . . . I don't mind telling you, Mr. Swann, but I've made it my business not to tell them and I hope you'll tell Mr. Avery that if you catch up with him."

It was clear from Vosper's words and manner that Josh was in some kind of trouble, possibly financial trouble and in view of his purpose here the thought was disturbing. He said, urgently, "You know Mr. Avery and I are business associates, even if he hasn't told you we served together in the field. Would I be likely to do anything to make things more difficult for him? I might even be able to help him. Have the bailiffs been here?"

"Among others," the man said, gloomily, and at last stepped aside to let Adam into the hall, after which he locked the door and re-attached the chain.

They went into Avery's smokery, a bachelor's apartment in every particular, although it was cleanly kept and the reek of stale tobacco was due to the windows being closed and the blinds drawn, as though in anticipation of the owner's funeral.

"I'm afraid the Captain has overstepped the mark this time," Vosper said, making it clear that his master had come very close to doing this frequently during his period of service. "It's not just a matter of debts, sir. Mr. Avery is inclined to run them up, but every now and again, once pressure is applied, he settles them out of hand. I sometimes wonder why he puts us all to so much inconvenience."

"Who else has been here apart from the bailiff and the tradesmen?"

"I couldn't swear to it, sir, but it might have been the police. A

411

gentleman making inquiries about this lady, sir. I daresay you recognise her, she is very well known I understand," and he took from his pocket-book a sepia photograph mounted on stiff card showing a woman in a Spanish dress, posing in the middle of a dance. One hand rested on her hip and the other was raised high above her head, both being fitted with castanets.

It was a conventional pose but the dancer was anything but convential. She had a hard, predatory beauty rare among Latins of her type that suggested the Andalusian gipsy, or possibly someone with a strong dash of Moorish blood. Her features had classical conformity and her figure, emphasised by the highwaisted dress, was broadhipped and sensuous without losing its feline mobility. Adam recognised her instantly, as would almost anyone with a casual knowledge of the London entertainment scene.

"That's the Seville dancer, Esmerelda, isn't it?"

Vosper confirmed that it was, adding that Mr. Avery had been squiring the lady about town during her recent engagements at the Star and two other music-halls.

"He squires a great number of ladies. Is there anything particularly significant about this one?"

Vosper looked away and Adam had the impression that anxiety concerning his personal future was doing battle with Vosper's professional discretion as the valet of an acknowledged rake.

"It's my belief, sir, she's bled Mr. Avery white. Her and her partner. He sometimes accompanied her here."

"They've been here? Recently?"

"As recently as a few days ago."

"And Mr. Avery? When was he last here?"

"Two days ago. I didn't see him, sir, I was marketing and it seems he called for a change of clothes and left again in a matter of minutes. He left my wages and this note. It doesn't help us much, I'm afraid."

He produced a sheet torn from a pocketbook on which was written, in Avery's neat, legible handwriting, *'Stay here until I write. J.A.'*

"When did the man you thought of as a police-officer call?"

"Two hours later, towards evening. He had no warrant but he was civil enough. I told him I believed Mr. Avery was on the Continent and he asked if he could look round the house. I told him not without a search warrant and he seemed disinclined to press the point and left. Did I do right, Mr. Swann?"

"Quite right. I daresay he'll be back however."

"Yes sir, he indicated as much." Then, doubtfully, "I should feel happier if I could let Mr. Avery know about the call."

"Have you tried his lawyers, in Portugal Street?"

"Yes, sir, but they haven't seen him in weeks. Neither has he written."

"Where would I be advised to look for him? It seems to me he might need a friend and I don't know that he has many, do you?"

"No, sir. A great number of acquaintances but few friends, Mr. Swann."

It was strange, Adam reflected, that he should say that. Five years had passed since his reassociation with Avery began on that same note. He said, "I think he would consider me a friend, Vosper. If not, then he hasn't got one, apart from yourself."

Vosper said, hesitantly, "There are certain places you could try, sir. Do you know Kate Hamilton's establishment, in Princes Street, Leicester Square?"

"Who doesn't?"

Vosper did not smile but ran a hand around his jowls. "You might get news there, sir. I don't know that he'll thank me for saying that."

"I'll try and if I run him down I'll insist he writes giving you proper instructions."

"Thank you, sir, I should be glad of that." He paused and seemed to reflect deeply. "I've valeted him for a good many years now, sir. Sometimes I've thought I should find a more predictable situation but I was never one for change and Mr. Avery has been kind to me in his way, sir. I've no family, you see, but I'm not getting younger and one would like to feel more settled as regards the future." He seemed to be addressing himself more than his visitor but when Adam picked up his hat he emerged from his reverie, saying, "It isn't just a matter of debts, sir. There's something about it that I don't understand. Mr. Avery has been behaving very strangely of late. As though . . . knowing him it must seem a little absurd sir . . . as though he was personally disturbed."

"Wouldn't he be that in any case if he owed more than he could find at short notice?"

"No, sir. He's very comfortably off. The sale of property would see him through the worst of it and, as I say, he was never a man to worry about money matters."

"It's the woman then?"

"Yes, sir. I'm not one to pry but one overhears certain things. The last time that dancer and her partner were here there were high words

413

when Mr. Avery showed them to the door. The partner, he's another foreigner, sounded ... well, sir, high-handed and threatening. I wouldn't have been much surprised if it hadn't come to blows."

"Mr. Avery was always able to take care of himself in that respect, Vosper."

"I'm sure, sir, but ..." suddenly he put aside his doubts, reluctantly but resolutely. "I'd take it as a favour, sir, if you could call at a certain address in Chelsea that I happen to know Mr. Avery once rented on that woman's behalf. I'm virtually sure no one but myself knows about it. It isn't her formal lodging. She was staying with her partner at the Surrey Hotel but I know she and Mr. Avery went there on occasion." He crossed the room and opened a small bureau, taking from it a black notebook and thumbing swiftly through the pages. "It's the Chanticleer Gaming Club, not a formal club you understand but a somewhat rough house, patronised by young bloods and women of a certain kind. There is an apartment immediately above—three or four rooms, with a separate entrance in a mews leading down to the river off Cheyne Walk. You'd find it easily enough. I took a case of wine there shortly before Mr. Avery disappeared."

"Why haven't you looked there?"

Vosper hesitated again and then said, "Mr. Avery's instructions were very explicit on that, sir. I think he was afraid of my being followed and I do know it was his wish the rendezvous should remain a close secret, particularly from the lady's partner, possibly from some of the people he associated with from time to time." A fleeting gleam of humour lit the manservant's pale face and then disappeared. For some reason it reminded Adam of the Irish Member's reference to Sir Robert Peel's smile, 'the wink of a silver plate on a coffin lid'. "There's considerable competition for the lady's favours, I believe."

"I'll give it a try but not tonight," Adam told him. "He hasn't paid me the compliment of getting in touch with me and whilst it's urgent I see him on commercial matters I don't intend to lose sleep over his junketings. If I do find him I'll let you know, Vosper. I take it you'll do the same for me?"

"You can rely on it, sir."

Vosper preceded him to the door and let him out into the darkening street. A cutting wind kept the evening drizzle at bay, chasing leaves from adjacent plane trees along the pavement. No cabs were in sight so Adam turned east, heading for the Gray's Inn Road, where he knew there was a rank. At the corner of Theobalds Road, however, something caused him to stop and scrutinise a hoarding that he had seen out of the corner of his eye. It was a playbill broadsheet, advertising the weekly change of programme and in large type, near the head of the bill, he saw the words '*Notable Attraction*', and below them, in bolder type, '*Esmerelda & Figaro, Exotic Dancers from Spain*'. What really checked him, however, was not the bill itself but a yellow sticker pasted crosswise over the Spaniards' names, overprinted with the words, '*Replaced by Monsieur Vidocq, Noted Escapologist*', indicating that there had been an abrupt change of programme.

He stood studying the hoarding some time, aware of a sense of unease and wondering what the link might be between Avery's eccentric capers and the cancellation of a dancer's contract at a music-hall. That there was some link he felt certain and his doubts extended beyond Avery and his troubles to his own financial situation that was, to a large extent, dependent on the man. A mood of depression entered into him, matching the cheerless autumn evening and the soft skitter of dead leaves in the wind, so that he had an uneasy certainty that he was approaching another, unlooked-for crisis, like the moment he had sat his horse outside the walls of Jhansi, or when he watched the riot build up in Seddon Moss and again, when he went into the double-room at 'Tryst' and saw the corpse of Luke Dobbs in his hearth. He muttered, "Damn it, I'll go there now and if I don't find him I'll take a cab to Kate Hamilton's. If anyone can put me on his track she can," and moved on into Gray's Inn Road.

The cab set him down at the western end of Cheyne Walk and he located the 'Chanticleer' within minutes. It was a seedy-looking place, half a public-house, half a club, not at all the kind of establishment he would have thought a buck like Avery would have patronised. There was, as Vosper had indicated, an outside entrance to rooms above, an open door and a flight of uncarpeted stairs leading up from the mews at the side. The windows above were curtained and the place looked unoccupied, although there was a certain amount of early activity going on at the 'Chanticleer' to the thin accompaniment of a piano tinkling out a music-hall dirge. Standing there in the dark Adam experienced a rare sensation of futility and indecision but then it passed and he went up the stairs to a wide landing, moving with a caution not solely imposed by the blackness for, although a strong draught implied the landing window was open, there were no lamp-standards in the mews below. He struck a match and in its glare saw two heavily-framed doors facing him. He tried both but they were locked and without much hope he knocked on the panels and when there was no response called, softly, "Josh? Are you there, Josh? It's me, Swann."

He could not be sure but he thought he detected the sound of a scrape on the far side of the door farthest from the stairs and called again, "Josh? It's me, Swann, and I'm alone." He heard a definite movement then, very laboured and deliberate, almost as though some heavy object was being removed from the threshold and then the key was turned and the chain moved in its groove and Avery's voice, very hoarse and somehow disembodied, came to him out of the darkness, a darkness that smelled stuffy and cloying, like the smell that would issue from a long-locked chest full of clothes that had been put away damp and left to moulder.

"Adam? Just you?" and on a rising note of urgency, "Step inside, for God's sake. Quickly, man."

Adam went in and the door closed, the key being turned and the chain readjusted.

"What the devil is going on here?"

He heard Avery laugh but there was no mirth in the sound. "A penny-dreadful with a cast of three. You sure you want to make it four?"

Adam's irritation mounted. "How do I know until I can see you?"

Avery said, soberly, "You might not like what you see. However, you came of your own accord. My advice is to leave by it. I'm in deep, my friend, and a great deal deeper than I bargained for. Stand where you are, I'll light up."

He moved away and Adam, even in the darkness, noted his dragging step, as though he was drunk or handicapped in some way. Then, from a corner farthest from the window Avery struck a match and applied it to a table lamp that burned low, casting fantastic shadows round the large room.

It was, as he saw at a glance, in the wildest disorder. Furniture was overturned and one curtain had been ripped from its rings and hooked back over the bracket to shut out any light from the street below. The remains of a china group of figures, nymphs and a satyr, lay in the fireless hearth and fragments had been crushed to powder underfoot. The room was evidently a parlour adjoining a bedroom reached through closed, folding doors, and a plush table-cloth had been half-dragged to the floor and hung like a discarded banner. Its folds shrouded the upper half of a man sprawled on his back, the toes of his yellow, calf-leather boots pointing to the ceiling. Adam took it in at a glance and then looked at Avery, standing in front of the folding

416

doors, blinking as though his eyes were having difficulty adjusting to the light. He looked ghastly, with his clothes stained and rumpled, two days' growth of bristles on his chin, and a pallor the shade of old parchment. His left arm was resting in a roughly-made sling. His right hung down and in the hand, loosely held, was a four-chambered revolver of a kind Adam had never seen. As he stared Avery made a characteristic attempt to outface the circumstances. "Not pretty, eh?" and he drew back his lips in a grimace that was more of a snarl than his usual cynical smile.

"For Christ's sake, what kind of mess are you in, Josh?"

Avery relaxed, laid his pistol on the lamp-table and poured brandy from a near-empty bottle into a tumbler.

"No worse than you'd find yourself in if anyone saw you come in, Adam."

"No one saw me come in. Vosper had this address and gave it me at the last moment. Very reluctantly. Who the hell is that on the floor?"

"A fool," Avery said, offhandedly. "Take a close look. You've seen dead men before."

Adam bent and lifted the trailing edge of the table-cloth. The single eye of a young man with dark, handsome features stared up at him. Where the other eye had been was a hole sealed by long-congealed blood. There was more dried blood on the carpet where the slug had emerged from the back of his skull. A foot beyond lay a short, broad-bladed dagger, with blackish stains spreading almost to the hilt. He stood up and his eye rested on the bulge in the upper part of Avery's left arm. "You're hurt?"

Avery shrugged and the movement made him wince. Adam said, "Lie on that couch and let me take a look at it."

"Presently," Avery said, "after you've seen what you've walked into. There's still no reason why you should stay. If I was in your situation I should walk out of that door, and forget you paid a call."

"You wouldn't," Adam said, "and you must know that I can't, so don't pretend to heroics. They don't suit you, Josh. What else do you want me to see?"

Avery pushed gently at the folding door with his foot and motioned Adam over the threshold. There was light in the bedroom issuing from two half burned candles, set one on either side of the bed In contrast to the parlour everything here was in order, with curtains drawn and the white coverlet stretched tight, its folds meticulously

417

arranged. On the bed, looking exactly like a marble statue carved by a master sculptor, was the dancer, Esmerelda. She was naked save for a wisp of muslin laid crosswise under her breasts and the piece of fabric looked so incongruous that Adam's attention was at once drawn to it. The flesh under the transparent material was dark, as though heavily bruised, and the small blemish emphasised the startling whiteness of the rest of the body, composed and stilled, as was the face with eyes closed and blue-black hair carefully arranged on a spotless pillow. The photograph Vosper had shown him did not come close to doing the woman justice. Stark naked, and in death, she had the perfection of a sleeping goddess painted by someone like Botticelli or Giorgione. He said, over his shoulder, "You killed her too, Josh?"

"No, by God! That bastard Figaro killed her. It's hard to say why unless he was afraid she had access to the loot."

"What loot?"

"Everything I had. Including your rubies."

Adam came out of the bedroom and closed the door. Without moving from where he stood just inside the parlour Avery stared at him, still blinking.

"Well?"

"Let me attend to that wound first. Then we'll talk about it."

Something seemed to ebb from the man. He pushed himself off the wall and slumped a little, swaying as he moved the few steps to the sofa where he sat, almost involuntarily. Removing the sling and his jacket Adam could hear his breath whistling and smell the sour odour of his brandy-laden breath. The wound in his upper arm was not as serious as he had feared. The knife had sliced through the flesh below the biceps but it had missed the bone for Avery could still flex his elbow. It was very swollen, however, and still uncleansed. Avery lay still while Adam washed it thoroughly with a napkin soaked in brandy and water before re-bandaging it and readjusting the sling.

"That's all the damage?"

"A bruise or two. Figaro worked with his feet, but you'd expect that from a dancer."

"You had to kill him?"

"It was him or me. But I'd have killed him anyway. She was dead when I got here."

"Tell me about it."

"It's a tedious story. Most love stories are, told by a middle-aged man."

"You were in love with that girl?"

"How does a man like me define love? I was besotted with her."

"To the extent of letting her bleed you of everything you possessed? A man like you? It's damned hard to believe, Josh."

"I find it hard to believe myself. All I feel for her now is pity. She should have taken her wages and got out ahead of him. She worked hard enough for them, I saw to that. But maybe she had no such intention and I've no means of knowing now. Not that it matters a damn, to me or anyone else. The money and rubies are past recovery, and that disposes of all obligations, mine or yours."

"Why do you say that?"

"What else does a man say to someone whose pocket he has picked? Does he demand the cab-fare out of range of the police?"

"You can leave me out of it for the moment. You killed that Spaniard in self-defence. There's the wound and the weapon to prove it."

"That might serve a hard-used, respectable bourgeois. It wouldn't help me much, except maybe to save my neck and even that's unlikely. A man like me makes enemies, some of them placed to pull strings. Then there's Esmerelda. When the full circumstances are known would anyone believe I didn't kill her?"

"What are the circumstances? Apart from her milking you?"

"What do they matter? To you or anyone else?"

"Damn it, man, of course they matter," Adam blazed out. "What kind of partner would I be to turn my back on you in a situation of this kind?"

"You might if you knew how things stood between us and have done, from the moment you came to me with that necklace."

"I said leave my involvement for the moment. We'll come to that. Tell me what happened, so that I can make some kind of guess at your claim on help."

"Is that bottle empty?"

Adam picked it up and poured the last of the brandy into the tumbler. There was no more than a couple of fingers and Avery contemplated the liquid, swirling it round.

"You could begin by telling me what was so special about that dancer. She's a very beautiful woman, granted, but you've never had much difficulty in hiring bedspace alongside beautiful women. How did it come about that you lost your head to this extent over a particular whore? And don't tell me she wasn't as much a whore as any of those girls at Kate Hamilton's."

A flash of the familiar Avery showed in the green eyes that continued to consider him, coolly. "There are whores and whores. Some are more accomplished than others, or perhaps appear so to a man nudging fifty." He paused a moment, still assessing the man who stood over him, "You took your fun where you found it before you decided to put on that tall hat and watch chain. Before that, when you were younger bones, were you never sexually enslaved? For a brief space, perhaps? A month or less?"

"No, but maybe that was because we were always on the move in those days."

"It happens," Avery said, "it can happen to the cockiest of us. I was capable of astonishing myself. It might have something to do with age." A flash of his habitual charlatanry returned to him. "Take care it doesn't happen to you, Adam. That plump little partridge you married might keep you snug and cosy for the time being but a man oughtn't to take it for granted until he knows all there is to know about himself. He can always turn a blind corner, as I did when I first took Esmerelda to bed." He paused again but Adam said nothing. "That was close on a year ago and I've had no other woman since. Nor wanted one."

"You were thought of as a very warm man. What went wrong? I've heard artistes of her kind are well paid but surely not so well as you could pay her?"

"That's what I thought. It's what any man in his senses would have thought. But it wasn't so. There isn't enough money in the world to satisfy the Esmereldas and when the well runs dry they move on, like any other nomad."

"So you ran yourself down to the last penny?"

"It doesn't happen like that," Avery said, "it's a zig-zag track, a small-time gambler trying to claw back losses. When I began to feel the drag I plunged and when she realised what was happening and applied the screw I went under a second and third time. I wasn't going to lose her while there was breath in my body, and that wasn't solely the need to have her exclusively. It was more of a point of honour. My kind of honour. I knew she was fleecing me and didn't care. What I didn't know was that she was getting her brief from that pimp on the floor."

"What happened here, and when?"

"I heard she'd missed an appearance and that her dressing room had been cleared. The prospect of cutting my losses was more than I could face. I came here with some kind of idea of forcing a decision,

420

of latching on to her wherever she went—making sure of seeing she didn't leave the country at all events; or maybe of getting at least your share of the money back if it was concealed here."

"It wasn't?"

"It's been transferred to the Continent in droplets, and in his name. I found that out going through his pockets."

"He was here when you arrived?"

"Another two minutes and I would have missed him. Did you notice her fingers? He had trouble getting the rings off. You could say he was killed collecting his small change, or most of it."

He took out a ring and Adam recognised one of the smaller rubies, set in a diamond cluster not unlike the ring Avery had had made up for Henrietta. The sight of it recalled his own situation.

"I went to these lengths to run you down because I bought 'Tryst'. Apart from that, expensive renewals can't be put off much longer."

"I knew about the house. I'd like to believe it was one reason why I acted." He studied his empty glass. "They say a man changes every seven years. Maybe a conscience moved in to keep company with adolescent goatishness."

"How long have you been holed up here?"

"They've been dead thirty-six hours."

"Why didn't you make a run for it?"

"It was too risky. There are always people coming and going at that bawdy house below. No. That isn't the real reason. I've kissed my hand to a hundred women. Esmerelda was different."

He leaned back on the sofa-head, closing his eyes. For the first time Adam saw him for what he was, an ageing, used-up rake who had been experimenting with himself and most of those who crossed his path since puberty. A man without any kind of faith, who had shed belief in himself with the erosion of his belief in others, so that cynicism seeped into his mind as Figaro's blood had been absorbed by the carpet at his feet. The one thing that redeemed him, Adam thought, was his courage, and after that a self-mocking honesty that only those who knew him would recognise as such.

"Suppose you got clear. What would you do, Josh?"

"I hadn't thought about it."

"Think about it then."

"They'll soon be looking for her, no doubt. A person like Esmerelda doesn't just disappear without trace. Her things are still at the hotel. I checked there first."

"They're looking for her now. A man wanted to search your

421

COB AT LARGE: 1862–1863

Guildford Street rooms. Vosper thought he was a detective. There's already a cancellation slip on her billing. If she walked out on a contract the theatre people will try and trace her to recoup their advance fees. We don't have long to make up our minds, Josh."

"*We* don't? I told you, I don't expect you to concern yourself in this. Why should you? You're already committing a felony by being here. Lend me what money you have about you and I'll make a run for it."

"A run for where, Josh?"

"Harwich. I've got a standing arrangement with a Dutch skipper there. A man like me has to keep at least one back door unlatched."

"They'll be watching the railway termini. You've never hidden your light under a bushel. Any detective worth his salt would recognise you at a glance."

"I daresay I'll give them their money's worth."

Adam said, slowly, "It isn't just a matter of you, Josh. I'm involved, whether you like it or not. Or whether *I* like it or not. Every London customer on my books knows of our association. I'll have a hard enough task riding this out financially. Seeing you in the dock at Old Bailey wouldn't help and I've put too much of myself into Swann-on-Wheels to see it advertised in the Newgate Calendar. Did that occur to you?"

"Yes, it did. But that isn't the reason you'd run counter to the law to get me clear of the country."

"It's reason enough." He got up, stepped over the man on the floor, and went to the window.

A line of cabs were dropping fares at the 'Chanticleer' and using the mews to turn. The harsh thump of a brass band had replaced the piano and the sound seemed wildly incongruous in that setting, like fiddlers on a hearse.

"When does that place down there slacken off?"

"Round about three in the morning."

"It's not light until seven. I could get in touch with Vosper . . ."

"Leave Vosper alone. If the police have called they'll have a man watching. Either that or the bailiff's men." He smiled. "If you're contemplating cloak and dagger work you'd best leave it to me. I've had more practice over the years."

"What do you suggest?"

"Nothing until you know the full facts. I talked of picking your pocket from the beginning. Well then, before you try and stick your head in my noose you'd best hear I sold those stones for nearly twice the sum I quoted. Notwithstanding that I've still been collecting interest on the initial outlay, plus fifty per cent of your net profit over a long time. I've done pretty well out of you already. I was always one to drain the cup to the dregs, Adam."

"I'll come myself in a frigate and turn in the mews at around three-ten, give or take a few minutes. You be at the foot of the stairs, ready to climb in the moment I stop level with the door. That's your only chance as I see it."

"There are conditions. With a Puritan there always is."

"There's one. Leave that revolver on your shrine in there. It's just possible they'll conclude they killed each other and give us a longer start. If they come before I'm back give yourself up. These people are nothing to me but I'm damned if I'll have a police officer's death on my conscience."

He went over, unfastened the door and let himself out without looking back. At the foot of the stairs the blare of sounding brass hit him in the face like a wind and behind it was a confused uproar of laughter and squealing women. He thought, gloomily, 'Uproar and violent death—they go hand in hand', and three separate images appeared to him, the carnage at Jhansi, the roar of the Seddon Moss rioters, and general lamentation in his own drawing room, the morning Luke Dobbs died in the flue.

3

He came down from the tower about one carrying his overnight bag and a spare topcoat he kept there. The counting house was locked and it occurred to him that if he opened it and the safe with his private keys the night-watchman and stableman would be disinclined to believe the story that he was driving a frigate down to Blubb for a rush removal job within a few miles of 'Tryst'. They had both looked startled when he had issued orders for the team to be harnessed up, and a large, straw-filled crate placed inside the waggon, but it was not for either to question a gaffer renowned for his eccentricities. He managed to borrow a carter's uniform cloak and cap without their knowledge, guessing there would be a hue and cry among the first shift when it was found to be missing from the rack in the waggoners' shed. It was a detail, he thought, that he would have to explain away on his return, like his own two-day absence, and the non-existent

423

house removal in Kent. Money was a problem. He had less than ten sovereigns about him, and the petty-cash box in the tower had yielded five more. It looked as though Josh Avery would have to start again from scratch if his passage money cost him more than fourteen pounds.

The traffic at that time of the morning was light and he could take his time, pulling into a waggon park at Waterloo to change his hat and greatcoat for the uniform concertina cap and cloak of a regular driver. It seemed strange to the point of absurdity to be wearing his own livery and driving one of his own teams, as though he was taking part in some kind of charade that would result in ribald laughter at the yard, and perhaps as far away as the regions if he was seen and identified, but he thought this unlikely. With luck he and Avery should be clear of London by daylight and he had taken care to choose the best team in the stable, as well as the least worked over during the last thirty-six hours.

He crossed Westminster Bridge in thin drizzle and noted the tower clock pointed to ten past two, holding the horses at a plodding walk to save them for the long haul to the coast and trying to put his own pressing concerns out of mind. He told himself that this was not due to despair, and the prospect of running the business from here on turnover alone, but to the experience of his campaign days, when the immediate problem took precedence over the grand design. He thought, bitterly, 'One damned thing at a time! As long as Avery is on the run we're all in pawn and "Tryst" into the bargain. With the German Ocean between us I can at least start thinking and planning again. It'll mean an end to expansion for years probably, and re-trenchment all round', and then he wondered if, in the end, he could hold on to both business and 'Tryst' in the years ahead, and how back-tracking on his bargain with Henrietta might affect the recently-established equilibrium of their relationship. But the thought of Josh Avery's plight obtruded and it struck him how shallow were the judgements of one man on another. He had seen Josh as a man of action, a voluptuary, a gambler, and a person who, stripped of his veneer of cynicism, was capable of projecting highly original ideas. He had never thought to see him as a fugitive from himself and even now did not see him as a scoundrel who had emptied a large sum of money held on trust into the body of a harlot. An idea that had occurred to him when Josh had first admitted the discrepancy between the real and acknowledged value of the stones had taken root in his mind. Avery, a man who had always spurned prudence, had none the less demonstrated it pretty obviously by holding on to the rubies for so long, and feeding money into the business piecemeal. Adam was virtually sure that the same prudence, the same underlying determination to buttress expansion with reserve capital, had encouraged him to lie about the extent of that capital. What had happened to it ultimately was irrelevant. It had no real bearing on their relationship, having been sucked into the vortex of the man's emotional maelstrom. There was another factor that helped to persuade him he owed loyalty to the broken man. Avery's stated reasons for remaining in that apartment for two days and a night with the dead for company had been no more than half-truths. A stronger reason was his need to confess and Adam had a conviction that, if he had not gone to Avery then Avery, in defiance of all risk, would have come to him.

*   *   *

It was coming up to three o'clock when he crossed into Chelsea and walked his team along deserted streets towards the blur of orange lights that represented a subsiding 'Chanticleer'. The place had crowed itself hoarse. One or two drabs passed in and out and two men, supporting one another in the penultimate stage of intoxication, emerged and staggered off in the direction of the river. The bandsmen had gone, replaced by the tinkling piano, playing the same sentimental dirge.

It was accomplished in a moment. Wisps of river mist merged with the persistent drizzle and the mews itself was dark and silent. He turned the team, drew level with the stairway door and checked the Clydesdales, watching their breath rise like the smoke of half-seen cannon. A figure ran crouching from the archway and scrambled through the flaps of the tarpaulin—Josh Avery on the run again at fifty, with another episode of his planless life receding into the murk.

He took his time about it. North of the river market traffic was steady but after Ilford, on the road to Brentwood, he turned east, choosing country routes, crossing the Crouch on the Hullbridge ferry, and moving at about seven miles an hour up the road to Maldon where he stopped to buy beer and bread and cheese. Avery made no attempt to communicate with him through the driving-box curtains and when, on an empty stretch of road, Adam glanced through the chink, he saw him stretched full-length on the sacks and sound asleep, bluish stubble showing on his pale cheeks and small, aggressive chin. Beyond Tolleshunt Major, as dawn crept over the misted fields, he gave the team a breather and took a short nap himself but still Avery did not stir and Adam saw no reason to wake him, calculating that this was his third night on the run. He thought, 'It's under ten miles to Colchester but if we skirt it, and bear east for Wivenhoe, we'll fetch up outside Harwich by dusk', and remembered then that Clydesdales were tireless and could haul two to three tons over a metalled road for hours on end if they weren't pushed.

They jogged on through a sparsely populated countryside, with here and there a cottage light winking through the early morning mist. Now and again they passed south-moving drays but on some stretches they might have been the only living creatures moving across a flat, half-seen landscape. The day wore on but the sun remained hidden, seen as a coy glow over the estuary. By late afternoon beyond Wivenhoe and, by Adam's reckoning, halfway between Goose Green and Wix, Avery's grizzled head popped through the curtains like the devil in a puppet-show. "Where are we?" he demanded, and Adam noted that his long sleep had wrought a decided change in him. Here was something approximating the familiar Avery again, picking his way among a world of fools, all of whom could be bought or cozened, and when Adam told him he said, brusquely, "You don't have to go any farther. I can contact my man at a tavern just beyond the Ramsey fork. Pull in and bivouac. I need a shave and we could both use a hot toddy."

The man's resilience ruffled him slightly so that as soon as they had a fire going under the lee of a clump of pines he pretended to busy himself in the waggon. He was still there when he heard Avery whistling 'Lillibulero' and thought, 'Damn him, he's like a cork. A good sleep, and the prospect of showing a clean pair of heels, is all he needs to salve his conscience', and for a moment his disapproval did battle with his envy at the ability to grow such a damnably thick skin and whistle 'Lillibulero' while someone else pulled your chestnuts out of the fire.

His sourness survived the first pannikin of toddy brewed over the fire, and when Avery said, cheerfully, "Well then, it seems we got off without much trouble," he growled, "Aye, without much on your part. Now I'm left to salvage what's left, while you beg your way across a Continent, I suppose. But you'll manage, no doubt. In a few months' time you'll be wining and whoring again, while I'll still be here with my nose to the grindstone!"

Avery was a hard man to deflate. "You could always come along," he suggested, and Adam said, with a snort, "I like a pattern to my

426

life," and then, as the spirit warmed him, his boorishness moderated and he produced the fourteen sovereigns he had scraped together, saying it was all he could raise without leaving himself open to awkward lines of inquiry from Tybalt and others. Avery pocketed the money and produced the ring taken from Esmerelda's finger. For a moment he studied it thoughtfully, then said, "This is yours. It's a little joker and there's a flaw in it but I daresay you could raise a few hundred on it. No one is likely to question it after all this time. The Sepoy Mutiny is ancient history now."

"I won't touch that either. Fourteen pounds won't get you far and you'll need a stake. Don't look for one from me, Josh. I'll be hard put to it to keep the service running."

Avery glanced at him across the fire, jigging his pannikin on his thumb. Finally he said, "I won't thank you for, in that respect at least, we're alike. Neither of us care to be under an obligation to anyone but I'll give you a piece of advice to reflect on in case you're inclined to take up panic stations as soon as I'm over the hill. You might say I'm not qualified to give a law-abiding citizen like you good advice but I am for all that. I've knocked about, and met most kinds and so have you, but there's a difference. I've little enough character of my own but I'm interested in character. I've made it my business to study other people's and sometimes I bet with myself on their prospects. I'm not often wrong. Those stones aren't important to you and never were really. I'd wager twice their value against a crooked sixpence that you'll achieve any damned thing you want to achieve and no time lost on the way. Why? Because you've got the right combination of qualifications; patience, staying power, a monstrous self-conceit, and a streak of enterprise into the bargain. A good many men who make up their mind to be someone have all that but still come a mucker. You won't, if only because you're uniquely endowed to run a business, any kind of business that involves a big labour force."

"It's late in the day to sit there giving me a character reference, Josh."

"No charge. The fact is you've got what's known as the common touch and don't deceive yourself into thinking it's at all common in this day and age. It's rare, especially among individualists. You've seen very little of me these five years but I've had my eye on you, and I wouldn't have encouraged you to spread your wings if I hadn't known precisely what I was doing. You can command loyalty and that's worth all the backing in the Bank of England. If you find yourself within hailing distance of Queer Street go forward, not back. Double the stakes and push on, so long as you remember to take the men who trust you into your confidence."

It was curious, Adam thought, how the wheel made a full turn every so often and found him sitting over a bivouac fire with a single companion, being preached at concerning his fitness to go out and smite the Amalekites. In his mind's eye he saw his wife, then a slip of a girl and herself a fugitive, suggesting he used his name as a trade mark as they sat under the Pennines. And as recently as last summer another woman, Edith Wadsworth, had given him advice very similar to Avery's—to stick it out, without deviating from his original course, to push on, believing in the certainty of arriving with trumpets in the years left to him. And now here was Josh, a man fleeing for his life, telling him that he could run a freight line on a compound of credit and loyalty, urging him to put aside all thoughts of retrenchment and rely on his own judgement and the men who marched under his banner, notwithstanding the period of extreme financial stringency that awaited him.

He said, "That's well enough so far as the firm goes, Josh, but there's 'Tryst'. I've paid out four thousand on it and am obliged to find the other seven by the end of the year. How's that to be done? Every penny I earn between now and then is earmarked for wages, stable rents, running expenses and renewals. Suppose I found a way to shed that millstone, wouldn't the wisest course be to shut down the least profitable districts?"

"You want to do that?"

"No, I don't want it, I hate retreat. I've got a good marriage but ownership of that house hangs on it. I don't expect you to understand that, and I'm disinclined to spell it out, but you can take it from me that it is so. 'Tryst' is to her what Swann-on-Wheels is to me."

"Then dig your heels in. You can mortgage most things but not dreams. Bluff it out. Bluff your customers, bluff your creditors, and match those tightfisted Conyer lawyers with a better lawyer of your own. But don't bluff your work force. Lay out your hand and let them see you play it. You've lost a partner but I was never important to you. Tybalt, Keate and the depot managers are your real partners."

He stood up, dusting his breeches, and Adam, also rising, held out his hand. Avery did not appear to see it. He said, carefully, "There's just one more thing. You can always give a busy man another job but this one at least won't involve you with the law. You remember Charity Stanhope?"

Adam remembered Charity, the wife of Colonel Stanhope, whose involvement with Avery had rocketed him out of the Company service more than eight years ago. He remembered her as a silly, pretty woman, with a soft mouth and the limpid expression of a not-too-intelligent child, and also that she had believed at least half the lies Josh Avery had whispered in her ear at regimental soirées in Bengal. "She was packed off home, wasn't she? Soon after the scandal broke?"

"Shortly before," Avery told him, "but that old fool Stanhope took her back as soon as he went on half-pay. He's dead now, and she was sharp enough to wriggle back into his will. He didn't leave much but it was enough to get her another husband. She's living near Bath."

"You went on seeing her?"

"God no, not for years. But we had a child. A girl."

"She's with her mother?"

"No. It was a condition of Stanhope's that she should ditch the child before she was invited back to bed. I had the child placed in a convent near Folkestone, the Convent of the Holy Family. She's about eight now, a whimsical little thing, called Deborah."

"Deborah what?"

"Avery. I acknowledged her. Why not? I'm not much for sentiment, and I've no business bringing up children, but I made it my business to call and see her now and again. I daresay she'll miss me. It's been known from time to time. Will you look in when you're that way and see if she needs anything?"

"If she's eight years old she'll want to know what's happened to you. What the devil am I to tell her?"

"Oh, you'll think on something. A man who replaces a swan's wings with a pair of wheels shouldn't be short on fairytales." He held out his hand and Adam shook it. Now that they were parting, with little prospect of meeting again, the last of his impatience with the man evaporated. He saw him as little more than a picturesque vagabond, a leftover from the days when men of good family took it into their silly heads to walk to Jerusalem in topboots, to drive hell-for-leather along the Brighton turnpike with beery old rascals like Blubb, or wager a thousand guineas on the result of a snail race. He had managed to fit Blubb into the pattern but there was no place for an Avery in the new society, where even royalty had become respectable, and where grocers, tailors and ship's chandlers were attending church regularly and building stucco villas to accommodate purse-proud wives and a swarm of dutiful children. He said, "Good luck, Josh. I should take it as a favour to hear how you're faring from time to time."

They shook hands again, lightly and without emphasis, and Avery picked up his valise and moved off down the empty road. For a long time Adam watched him, his jaunty figure silhouetted against the fading light that lay on the dripping landscape. Then, thoughtfully, he stamped out the dying embers of the fire and unhitched the horses, climbing into the box and turning the waggon south. Within minutes the dusk and mist closed in and he settled back in the box, letting the Clydesdales set their own pace for home.

Part Four

Sortie Torrentielle: 1864 - 1865

1

Council of War

NOTWITHSTANDING his ultimate disenchantment with the profession, Adam Swann had been a good soldier. He had imbibed a certain number of sound military precepts and carried them into commercial life where they sometimes served him well, without him being more than half aware of the fact.

They were to serve him now, when he acknowledged to himself that he was being edged into a corner from which it would need more than courage and luck to escape.

Tybalt's spring budget was even more depressing than he had anticipated. Hiding among its neat, inter-related columns of figures were elements of stress that would have worried him if he had still been secured by Avery's credit. As it was, with the balance of the 'Tryst' purchase money due in under three months, the prospect of regaining the initiative appeared hopeless. He was not even sure how he could survive at all without drastic contraction right across the board.

There was no shortage of contracts, and money continued to flow in at a steady and even an increasing rate. Of the twelve districts, eight were showing a profit and two others were breaking even. Only Catesby, in the Polygon, was frozen into immobility by the continuing cotton famine, whereas the Southern Pickings still needed time to establish itself. The need was not increased turnover but a strong injection of fresh capital to replace worn-out teams and waggons and also to meet the flood of quarterly rents on depot premises, stables, and warehouse space. And all the time, like a boulder poised on a hillside above him, was the balance of the money due to be paid over to Conyer's attorneys.

The problem, as he saw it, was both strategical and tactical. The strategic object was clearly defined—to hold on to the ownership of 'Tryst' and avoid wholesale contraction of the network. The tactical remedies that presented themselves were more devious and after studying Tybalt's breakdown figures he did precisely what he would have done faced with a similar situation in the field. He made a series

433

of resolute sallies, aimed at catching the enemy off balance and deceiving him as regards strength and aggressiveness. The first of these carried him into the camp of Conyer's attorneys, Messrs. Stock Frithleston & Stock, in St. Paul's Churchyard.

He was received, in the absence of the older partners, by young Aubrey Stock, recently down from Cambridge, a competent pink-cheeked, unpretentious young man, who looked more like a cheerful subaltern than a lawyer and Adam, sensing that he was more open to compromise than his dry-as-dust father or asthmatic uncle, made up his mind on the spot to come straight to the point. He said, flatly, "I can't find the balance for 'Tryst', or not without selling half my business, and I'm disinclined to do that. It wouldn't be in your true interests or mine, Mr. Stock."

The young man did not recoil, as his father would certainly have done but merely looked solemn, and drummed his long fingers on the blotter, staring down at a brass pentray. He seemed to think hard for a moment and then said, with a glance at the document before him, "The balance is due on 1st January. We've made plans to invest it on Mr. Conyer's behalf. It's to go into a Trust Fund for his heirs."

"I don't give a damn about that," Adam told him, "and I'm not bilking from choice. A partner of mine squandered our reserve capital and skipped the country. As I see it you've three alternatives. To hold fast to the contract and make me bankrupt. To return the initial four thousand I've already paid, less the forfeited deposit, or to advance the completion date and get your money in quarterly instalments. Even if you do that I feel bound to warn you I shall have great difficulty in meeting them. There's one other possibility. You could find me a buyer to take it off my hands. In that case I should have to sell at a loss and would expect to, so long as it wasn't a staggering loss. If it was I'd fight."

Stock said, cautiously, "You would prefer that? Providing it could be done?"

"No, I should prefer to do my utmost to keep up the instalments and eventually clear what remained in a lump sum."

The lawyer sucked his pink cheeks and gave the pentray his dedicated attention.

"Taking that alternative, Mr. Swann. How long would it stand over? Approximately, that is."

Adam took out Tybalt's estimates and passed them across the desk.

"I didn't come here to bluff my way out of a difficult situation. This was my financial position at nine a.m. this morning."

434

Stock took the papers and ran his eye over them. It was, Adam noted, a very cool and judicious eye, despite the man's youth and inexperience. He had the impression that Stock Junior was very conscious of being the new broom about the office and had far less hidebound notions concerning the handling of money and property that those practised by preceding generations of Stocks and Frithlestons. In spite of his conventional frock coat and outward sobriety there was a hint of the speculator about him.

"A little worrying, Mr. Swann," was his comment, and Adam said, sharply, "I'll admit to that, but the business is sound enough. If you won't take my word for it ask around the City."

"I'll take your word for it, Mr. Swann. You were recommended to me as an exceptionally enterprising man and we might even have something in common. Say a predisposition to examine new ideas, without rejecting them out of hand and reverting to rule of thumb."

Adam accepted this as a hopeful sign. "It's encouraging to hear that from the lips of an attorney. Most of them are still quoting precedents in use when we lost the American colonies."

"Ah, yes," said the young man, "but we've acquired another Empire since then, I'm told," and he actually smiled, although it seemed to hurt a little. "Suppose I persuaded my father and uncle to extend the completion date six months, making it 30th June? Would that help?"

"Not enough. I might find half the money by then but if I'm to stay in business on the scale I practise I need the amount I owe you for renewals and quarter-rents, to say nothing of wages. I don't handle large sums. My network pays off in trickles, and my policy has been to plough profit into fresh territory. It may not be your way of doing business but it's the only way that makes sense to me. A static business is half-dead to my way of thinking."

"I told my father that only last week," Stock said, surprisingly, "and in almost identical terms. The trouble is, of course, getting them to regard it as anything more than 'Varsity brag. Suppose I went a step further? Suppose I could draft an instalment plan, spread over two to three years? You would have to pay interest and that would add to your liabilities."

"It would also give me a breathing space and that's what I need. Talk your principal into agreeing to that and I'll be uncommonly obliged to you, Mr. Stock."

The young man was silent for a moment, nibbling his pen. It was curious, Adam reflected, but against all probabilities there

435

was something about him that recalled Avery. You could see the gambler at work inside his narrow head. He said, at length, "These lawyers your partner used. Are you tied to them in any way?"

"Shadwell and Dowse? No, I'm not. As a matter of fact I've never been impressed by them. They move too slowly for my taste, almost as slow as your firm without the merit of being reputable."

"You mustn't expect me to slander fellow professionals," Stock said, with another smile, "but things get about you know, especially at chop-houses where lawyers foregather. This partner of yours skipped, you say. Did Mr. Shadwell or Mr. Dowse show much surprise?"

"I haven't paid them the compliment of discussing his exit with them," Adam replied, but Stock was not disposed to let it rest at that. He said, "I take it he was the man who introduced you to them?"

"That's so, but I never had much to do with them. I give lawyers a very wide berth when I can."

"But a concern as large and as growing as yours, you must get involved in litigation of one sort or another from time to time?"

Adam began to see the drift of the conversation so he said, obliquely, "There are contracts to be vetted, and premises to be conveyed. Sometimes we need to insure high-quality goods and take out standing cover against accidents."

Stock said, "Give me twenty-four hours, Mr. Swann. I think something might be worked out. Suppose you let me give you luncheon tomorrow. I reserve a table at The Mitre on weekdays and the game pie there is excellent."

"I'd be happy to do that," said Adam, and went out feeling a good deal more hopeful than when he had entered.

The upshot of the next meeting was the respite Adam sought. Over their game pie young Stock said, leisurely, "How about a two-year extension at six per cent, Mr. Swann? Too steep for you?"

"It's near-robbery but I won't quarrel with it for I've no real alternative," Adam told him but then Stock succeeded in surprising him yet again. "Would you think it impertinent of me if I asked to look around H.Q.? I've always been interested in haulage and I'm curious about your trademark. It's a play on your name, I take it?"

Adam told him he was welcome to examine the yard and explained the significance of the trademark and how it came into being. By the time he had shown the lawyer round the Bermondsey headquarters he had formed a considerable liking for him, seeing him as a younger edition of himself, about the time he was contemplating resignation from the Company's service. It was not until they were on the point of parting, however, that Stock revealed the underlying reason for his interest. He said, unequivocally, "That six per cent, Mr. Swann. I realise you're not a company, and it's demonstrably clear that you're a keen individualist, but suppose a man like me wanted a flutter? Would my undertaking to take care of that interest over the period make me a minor shareholder, with prospects but no say in policy? Six per cent on seven thousand over two years ... one hundred and sixty pound short of the round sum of one thousand?"

"There's nothing wrong with your mental arithmetic," said Adam and Mr. Stock said that there did not seem to be much wrong with his own.

"Would that mean I'm under an obligation to bring my legal business to Stock, Frithleston and Stock?"

"Certainly not, but it might be in your interests to think about it, Mr. Swann."

Adam said, "I'm not inclined to reject any helping hand just now, Mr. Stock, and something tells me we think alike on essentials. Draw up something along the lines of what you've put forward and I'll sign it without even reading it. I flatter myself I can recognise a man who keeps abreast of the times, even if he is a lawyer."

And so it was arranged, and although the boulder remained poised it was underpinned, to a great extent, by the good offices of the astute Mr. Stock, although Adam would have wagered all the money involved in the transaction that this was an extremely private investment on his part and that Stock Senior, to say nothing of the Frithlestons, would have to console themselves with the thought that the respite meant the purchaser was paying almost a thousand pounds over the odds for their indulgence.

*   *   *

The pressure had eased slightly but his personal account remained empty whereas Tybalt's estimate of income during the next twelve months fell far short of what was required. It was now that he took the head clerk into his full confidence, admitting his reliance upon Avery's finance, and the reason why it was useless to look in that direction for money to tide them over the next year, or the year after that. Tybalt made no attempt to hide the fact that the absence of reserves appalled him. He said, massaging his bald head, as though to help it absorb the truth, "We must find a partner, someone of substance from among our clients. We're well established now, Mr. Swann, and there must be people willing to invest in a firm as reput-

437

able as ours," but suddenly he broke off, warned by the frown on Adam's face, and concluded, lamely, "You don't intend to shed some of the load, sir?"

"Not an ounce of it," Adam told him, "for I built this with my own hands and little else. Mr. Avery had almost nothing to do with the planning of it and never did stand to lose money of his own. Now that he's run off I'm free to develop any way I like. The one compensation this mess has brought with it is complete independence, for I don't count that eight hundred and forty young Stock has just invested. God damn it, man, don't you realise that if we called on some well-heeled merchant to tide us over we should end up working for him? A glance at that budget would give any big investor the right to call the tune."

Tybalt groaned and scanned the columns in front of him. Watching him Adam reminded himself that he was not equipped to deal with a crisis and the clerk was man enough to admit it. He said, "Very well, Mr. Swann. If you won't contract by closing down some of the depots, and you won't call on fresh capital, I'm not qualified to advise you. But Mr. Keate *is*. He told me yesterday that of the four hundred horses in service a third are due to be retired early next year, and another third twelve months later. He's even shown me the age checks, and according to him most of the Clydesdales were more than halfway through their working span when he bought them and we got them cheap on that account. We've been working them hard now for five years plus. I daresay one can give or take a year in the case of a few of them but only at the cost of sacrificing our principal selling point, speed. At all events, that's his view and I promised him I would put it to you."

"That's what I pay you for," growled Adam. "What else have you to say?"

Tybalt went on, red in the face, "Over a hundred new waggons are needed and twelve quarter-rents are due on stables and warehouses. You'll need to find something in the region of five thousand by this day twelvemonth. How do you propose to do it? By mortgaging 'Tryst'?"

"You can't mortgage what you haven't paid for. I've got a better idea. When you're surrounded, and expect an attack, the manual recommends a breakout in force and feints on other sectors, what the French call a *sortie torrentielle*. These weekly conferences we have, the departmental pow-wows within our parish, would you say they have been productive?"

438

"Very much so," Tybalt said, "you know I've always approved of them."

"What actually emerges from them?"

Tybalt looked at him doubtfully, as though he had a strong suspicion his leg was being pulled. "They clear the air. Each of us knows what the others are doing. There is another aspect too ... I don't know how to amplify that without seeming to take a liberty, sir."

"You wouldn't have the smallest idea how to take a liberty, Tybalt."

"Then put it this way, sir. They give subordinates like Mr. Keate, myself and the resident farrier and carpenter, a sense of ... well ... of being consulted, sir, of being something more than hired hands."

"That's precisely what I'm driving at. We call a network conference right here at headquarters and lay the facts before everyone concerned."

The finality of the suggestion startled the clerk. "You don't *mind* these figures becoming generally known, sir?"

"If I continued to work used-up teams and run waggons that spend half their time in the repair sheds every man on the pay-roll will draw his own conclusions, and those conclusions won't be flattering to me or the firm. Convene a general meeting here on Friday, and say I'll pay for return fares and an overnight stay in London. Meantime I'm going to see Blunderstone about new waggons, then McSawney about fresh teams, bought on credit."

He stalked out of the tower, leaving Tybalt stuttering, and buttoning his topcoat set off towards the river at a fast walk.

It was raining, and winter was marching on the city from the east but he had never found the interior of a cab conducive to thought and it crossed his mind that he ought to keep a saddle horse in the yard for rapid movement through streets where the traffic situation was going from bad to worse, and there were sometimes blocks a mile long in the busiest periods of the day. It occurred to him then that, notwithstanding the gridiron, the pace of the new age inside the big centres of population was still regulated by the speed of a horse, for even as recently as twenty years ago there had never been cities as populous as this, where villages, orchards and stubble fields were being devoured at the rate of acres a week. What would happen, he wondered, if London, and all the rival Londons in the Midlands and North, continued to grow at this pace, and people were edged out of the heart of them to make room for more and more offices, factories, warehouses and docks? The London suburbs already lapped halfway across Middlesex and were nibbling the farmlands of Hertfordshire, Essex, Kent, Surrey and Berkshire. Soon, in his lifetime perhaps, it would take a man days to walk the diameter of the capital and perhaps a week to work his way round the circumference. With only an odd glimpse of cherry-garden and cornfield. Change. Movement. Speed. Money. Expansion. Innovation. These were the factors upon which one had to base one's calculations today if one was determined to remain in the swim, and he thought it surprising that this was not generally accepted by a majority of Englishmen. Most of whom were as conservative as their pastoral ancestors. There had been that one big leap forward a generation ago, but by now the sons of the Stephensons and the Brunels had absorbed it and settled on an even course, as though England had always been a workshop with an insatiable hunger for new markets overseas. Men, and women too, thought in terms of hardware and cotton instead of in terms of turnips and the next hay crop, but that was the only concession they made to the century. They still put their trust in eighteenth-century legislation and the navy and at base the social structure of the nation was still rooted in the petty squire and the arrogant politician, typified by Palmerston, who thought of Trafalgar and Waterloo as last week's triumphs.

Here and there certain prophets had raised their voices—John Stuart Mill, Peel, Shaftesbury, that solemn, clever fellow, Gladstone, and the persuasive chap, Disraeli, and because they were vocal they were heard at Westminster but not beyond it, not in the shires, not even in big provincial communities that were becoming semi-autonomous states, ruled by families whom sudden wealth had invested with power that was as parochial as feudalism. Unashamedly these people, who ought surely to have enlisted in the vanguard of progress, were preoccupied with conserving, and conservation was a word that made no appeal to him. Perhaps it should have done. Perhaps he should have taken things more slowly, limiting his field of action, and remaining the tenant of 'Tryst' while he built up his reserves. Then, because he knew himself better than most men, he realised that he would stay on the offensive to the day he died for that was the way he was made and a man never got far if he ran contrary to his nature. Now, with his future in the balance, he could see no other course but to attack, and it was Blunderstone and McSawney who gave ground before the first onrush of his *sortie torrentielle*.

He marched into Blunderstone's waggon yard and declined the

clerk's invitation to be fobbed off with Blunderstone's son, a product of the new type of gentleman currently being turned loose on the city by imitators of the pious Doctor Arnold of Rugby, and better fitted, to his mind, to lead a cavalry squadron than kick their heels here, where a man's word did not rest on a handshake and a work force was not to be rallied by a bugle call.

Blunderstone senior waddled out on demand and Adam, who had always found the coach-builder an honest, imaginative craftsman, was as blunt with him as he had been with Stock. Having told him his needs, he asked for a fleet of two hundred men-o'-war and frigates, in proportions of two to one, delivery to be made in time for the spring hauls.

Blunderstone said, rubbing his hands, "I thought it was time you came to me for replacements, Swann. Some of those vehicles I sold you were refits if I remember rightly, for you were short on capital then. The way you've been working them they must be held together by wire by now. A hundred and thirty flats and seventy two-horse vans? My word, that'll make a hole in your pocket, won't it?"

"That depends on you, for I can't confirm the order if you want cash. Either you accept it on the basis of a spread-over, carrying us into 1865, or I make do with replacements at Gideon's."

Blunderstone looked almost as horrified as Tybalt when told that his employer's personal account was overdrawn.

"*Gideon?*" he said. "You'd haul your customers' goods in a Gideon-built vehicle? They told me you prided yourself on speed and minimum wastage. How can you do that with waggons built for door-to-door deliveries?"

"I should have to overload and make allowances for breakdowns in my quotations. The fact is, Blunderstone, I'm faced with a very heavy outlay this year, and although prospects never looked better I could only pay you twenty-five per cent on delivery and the rest over the next nine months. I've been a good customer to you, and I've never had reason to complain of your vehicles. I've built my reputation on your waggons but now it's Hobson's Choice so far as I'm concerned. You can take it or leave it, I'm not here to beg favours."

"Now hold hard," Blunderstone protested. "Say forty per cent on delivery."

"I couldn't meet it. It's no use pretending that I could."

"Two hundred new waggons will occupy more than half my work force over the next four months. It would mean putting off other customers, with cash in their hands."

"Orders for odd vehicles," Adam reminded him. "I'm buying in bulk and that entitles me to credit."

"What about security?"

"I could offer you existing teams and stock, plus goodwill. Nothing more, I'm afraid."

"I hear you've bought yourself a big place on the Kent-Surrey border. Now I've always fancied myself as a country squire in my declining years. Suppose you deposit the deeds?"

Adam could chuckle at this. "You heard right but you didn't hear enough. 'Tryst' is barely one-third paid for and the rest is left on at six per cent."

"You think too big for an amateur," Blunderstone said, but there was friendliness in his tone. "Suppose you give me a week to mull it over?"

"I can give you two days. I've got a depot managers' conference on Friday, and I'll need your answer by Saturday."

"Waggons are no good without teams," Blunderstone said, "and unless you take half your vehicles off the road you'll have to buy in fresh from McSawney. You won't find him as accommodating as me, he's from Aberdeen."

"I hope to talk him round," Adam said, "for McSawney wouldn't care to see me buy crossbreds in Suffolk."

"Nay, lad," said Blunderstone, paternally, "stick to the beasts you built your reputation on and if necessary double up on heavy loads." He looked at Adam thoughtfully, rolling a cheroot from one side of his mouth to the other. "How old are you, Swann? Thirty-four? Thirty-five?", and when Adam told him he was thirty-six he said, "I wish to God you were my lad. I made a bad mistake about Charlie. Sent him to one of those new gentlemen's schools thinking he'd amount to something and so he has, providing a man's looking for someone who can read Latin on a tombstone. But I see my error now. I should have put him clean through the trade—joinery, wheelwright and coach-builder, same as my old father did for me. Away with you then, to gammon McSawney, and damned good luck to you!"

McSawney, however, was not so easily gammoned. As Blunderstone had predicted he drove a hard bargain and refused to supply teams on the basis of twenty-five per cent down and the rest spread over a year. The best terms Adam could get, and they kept him in McSawney's stables for the rest of the day, was fifty per cent on delivery and the balance in nine months, with a flat rate of three per cent interest on the outstanding debt. Adam would have agreed to harsher terms. Like Blunderstone he had an unshakable faith in his Clydesdales and Cleveland Bays, and his teamsters were now well accustomed to them and knew to a few pounds how much they could draw over a specified route.

It was dusk when he made his way back to London Bridge Station and caught a train for Croydon, and supper time when he drove his gig between the leafless copper beeches and saw the glow in the tall downstairs windows and the one patch of light above, where Phoebe Fraser was patrolling the nursery. He stopped short of the stableyard and looked along the rambling frontage of the old house, reflecting that, when all was said and done, it had been these bricks and mortar, and all they meant to Henrietta, that he was fighting to retain. He thought, 'I daresay I'm a fool to hamstring myself this way. With that four thousand in my account I could have ridden this out in less than a year,' but then he remembered the striking change in Henrietta since the night at the 'George' where they had drove their bargain, and after that the queer satisfaction he derived from meeting a challenge that was tantamount to starting all over again. 'I don't give a damn what figures tell me,' he reflected, 'I'm happier following my nose. Josh was right about one thing. It's folly to dig in when your instinct tells you digging in means getting bogged down, and as for Edith's advice, there aren't many city men who can ask for loyalty over an empty cash-box and be pretty sure of getting it!' He shook out his reins and drove into the yard as Henrietta, hearing the scrunch of gravel, came to the yard door to greet him. He called cheerily to her and she must have gauged his mood by his tone of voice for she hitched her skirts and ran tripping down the stone stair and round the angle of the stable door to a point where they could not be overlooked from the kitchen windows. He said, throwing out his arms, "By God, I've had a day of it and I'm damnably glad to be home!" and then kissed her and slid his hands over her hips in a way that confirmed her belief that she was growing on him at a pace that she would have thought very unlikely a few months ago. She said, trying to keep gaiety from her voice, "The Colonel's gone to bed to nurse a cold so there's only the two of us. Will you say good night to the children while I see about supper?"

"Ten minutes," he said, throwing off the last buckle and turning the horse into the loose box, "and send down for a bottle of Beaune. It's a celebration of a sort." They went out of the yard and up the steps and he walked with his arm round her. It was a gesture, she reflected, that he had not made in public since their clash over the chimney sweep.

2

It was as though, between them all, they were reassembling an engine that had been known to work but did not work now, for it stood in need of so many adjustments and modifications and had, moreover, run clear out of steam.

The blueprint was before them in their collective experience and in the simplified figures of Tybalt and the written statements of Saul Keate, the one proclaiming the facts, the other assessing them in terms of past, present and future.

They sat along each side of the long trestle table, with Adam at the head, Tybalt on his right, Keate on his left, and at the far end the clerk Rookwood, whom Adam thought of as the Artful Dodger. Rookwood's duties were to take careful notes on what might emerge from the discussion.

They were all there, talking little among themselves and each, it seemed, impressed by the solemnity of the occasion. Catesby, with his Caius Cassius look, Bryn Lovell, thoughtful and attentive, and Hamlet Ratcliffe puffing at his cherrywood pipe that he had asked permission to light as an aid to concentration. Wadsworth and his daugher Edith were there representing the Crescent South, the one looking his phlegmatic self, the other dressed in her Sunday best. Immediately below her, representing the Border Triangle, sat the Scot Fraser, making his first visit to the capital and still dazed by the speed of his journey south that had begun twelve hours before. Comparative newcomers were there, some of them meeting one another for the first time; Vicary, from The Bonus; the islander Dockett, from Tom Tiddler's Ground; young Godsall, from the Northern Pickings, secretly assessing Blubb whom he would succeed in a year or two, and thinking it might be sooner than that as he contemplated the old coachman's purple complexion and vast, waistcoated belly. Abbott, the Southern Square slave-driver, was there, a man who begrudged the time spent so far from his patch, and Morris, the Jew recently given the task of seeing what he could make of the Southern Pickings in the Hereford-Worcester area, a man who had impressed Adam with his knowledge of the high-grade china traffic that demanded a specialist's packing. The tally was complete with Goodbody and Horncastle, sub-depot managers who worked under Wadsworth's direction in Crescent Centre and Crescent North, together with Lawrence, the Headquarters' farrier, whom Keate had called in at the last moment.

They heard Tybalt and Keate in attentive silence, the clerk giving a rundown on the year's estimates, the waggonmaster translating the figures into terms of waggons and teams, and as the voices of the two men droned on Adam watched the faces of the fourteen men and one woman for reactions, reading very little in their expressions for, with the exception of old Blubb and the laconic Abbott, each of them seemed awed by the occasion. Only the pink-cheeked Ratcliffe, once again fearing for his future, showed signs of stress when Keate announced that unless the turnover could be doubled in twelve months depots would be closed down, and the waggons and teams absorbed into a truncated network. He said nothing of personnel, leaving them to draw their own gloomy conclusions.

When Keate sat down there was a volley of throat-clearing and foot-scuffling and then everyone was silent again as Adam rose.

He did not make a long speech, telling them simply that the crisis had been brought about by two factors, his backer's unexpected disappearance, and his own over-extension. He owed it to them, he felt, to make this clear, lest any of them should assume he held the view that they had contributed to the situation. He was unequivocal, however, regarding the necessity to bring about a dramatic increase in business within a very limited period, and underlined this by announcing the terms under which he had purchased a new fleet of waggons, to be distributed according to the demand among the districts. It was this statement that made the maximum impression, perhaps because it introduced an element of competition among them. The hint was clear enough. Those who brought new business would qualify for new teams whereas, if there was to be contraction, the sluggish areas would be those selected for the pruning-hook. As he sat down and lit a cheroot he caught Edith Wadsworth's eye and her glance seemed to say, "So far, so good. Now let's see if their loyalty can match mine," and suddenly he felt immensely grateful for her presence, for it seemed to anchor him to them in a way that had not been so obvious when he rose to speak.

Surprisingly, Dockett was the first to comment, a gangling man with a prominent Adam's Apple, who had never had much to say and had seemed, up to that time, a conscientious manager content to work on a very limited scale. He used what Adam thought of as the

445

'Southcountry-Barsetshire' brogue, flattening his vowels and lengthening his consonants, in the manner of the traditional yokel in
a music hall sketch. Standing there, sweating freely and red in the
face, he groped for words, reminding Adam of a recruit facing his
baptism of fire.

"I got somethin' to zay," he began, swallowing hard, "but mebbe
it conzerns my patch on'y. It's shifting chattels, house to house.
That's my strong line on the island. Alwus 'as bin. Dunno why," and
he stopped, as though appalled by his own temerity.

"They got var more'n their share o' fleas over there and it keeps
'em moving," prompted Blubb, and there was a general laughter that
died quickly when Adam snapped, "Hold your tongue, Blubb! You
can joke as much as you like over your pot afterwards but we're not
here to amuse each other. Carry on, Dockett."

Blubb subsided and Dockett plunged again. "It's just we could
zave money on mileage wi' box-cars, same as the railway use on the
mainlan'. We could make one trip take the place of three but charge
the zame."

Catesby said, "Aye, happen you could. But those box-waggons
need a four-horse team to haul 'em."

Blubb spoke up, this time seriously, "What's wrong with a four-
some, if it saves time an' mileage? It never paid to pull a coach
unicorn in my day and the same applies to freight today."

"What do you say to that, Keate?" Adam asked and the waggonmaster said that Dockett and Blubb were talking sense, providing
secondhand box-cars could be bought cheaply from Blunderstone.

"I 'abben vinished yet," Dockett said, still more surprisingly, and
although Edith Wadsworth smiled, this time nobody laughed. "What
I was leadin' up to was this. A chattel haul has been a straight
door-to-door job up to now, wi' the customer packing and unpacking
the goods. That's well enough, and zaves us the trouble I reckon, but
it wastes time and it wastes space, for most o' they vools got no
notion of how to stow an' pile it on any old how. Suppose we make
an overall charge for crating and uncrating? All but the poorest volk
would be right pleased to get shot of the job, for it's a main tiring one
if you don't know how. We could use our own crates and do it in a
quarter o' the time, besides which we'd stow in a way that'd cut down
on damage in transit, and scotch all manner o' claims, just an' false."

"That's more good sense," Blubb said, and there was a murmur
of agreement that encouraged Adam to ask a general question.

"I've always thought it strange that Dockett is the only one here

446

who does a steady line in house removals," he said. "Suppose we charged a standard rate according to mileage and the number of waggons used, how many of you would be likely to increase turnover?"

Half a dozen hands were lifted and Adam said, quietly, "Thank you, Dockett. Mr. Tybalt will go into the figures and I'll see what we can do to replace a dozen flats with box-cars. That's exactly the kind of suggestion I'm looking for," and Dockett sat down as suddenly as a spent mechanical toy, blushing at the round of applause Adam's compliment had earned him.

He had done something, it seemed, to put the others on their mettle. Blubb declared that beyond the London fringe the pinnaces were uneconomical, and should be withdrawn and five other managers agreed with him, it being argued that a carter driving a three- or two-horse waggon cost the firm the same when he was hauling a third or half the tonnage and that all the light vans should therefore be relegated to local runs.

Then Morris, of the South Pickings, said that not nearly enough effort had been made to undercut the railways in the transport of fragile goods, such as his own Worcestershire ware, and that he could vouch for the fact that manufacturers of high-grade china and glass would prefer to see their goods carried the full distance in the waggon that received them at the factories.

"It doesn't need thinking about," he said. "As it is, where we or any other haulier carry a load marked 'Fragile', the risk of breakage isn't in the journey but in loading and offloading. Send a crate by rail and what happens? It gets bumped up into the waggon at the factory, bumped off again in the goods yard, manhandled across platforms at God knows how many junctions, and finally heaved aboard another waggon for delivery to the customer. Goods of that kind are always packed by experts but the breakage rate is enough to turn a man's hair white. I've gone into it and costs rise steeply on account of insurance rates. With a single loading and offloading we could demand a competitive insurance quotation and there would be a saving all the way round. Why don't we all put in for the full journeys and make a bid to cut the railways out altogether?"

Both Keate and Tybalt thought this a very promising suggestion and said so, as did Wadsworth and Godsall, both of whom had been handling fragile goods in the last few months. Young Rookwood's pen was now flying over the paper and Tybalt, anxious that he should not miss a word of the decisions reached, moved his chair round to

447

assist in the notetaking. Everybody, Adam noted with satisfaction, had something to say and once Dockett had broken the ice nobody seemed to mind saying it. Discussions, some laconic, one or two acrimonious, ranged around the subjects of installing a resident far-rier in each area, the life of a tarpaulin sheet, the cost of cordage, the strength of lynch-pins, the balance to be struck between speed and safety, the false economy of using a short, bad route when a longer haul over a good highway was available, and the folly of using an identical waggon for hauling Grimsby fish-boxes and, say, manufactured soft goods that arrived smelling of herrings. They dis-cussed the need for specially-adapted vehicles for very heavy loads, such as Abbott was now hauling out of Portland quarries and Lovell from the Llanberis slate terraces, a demand from the Border Triangle for double teams in order that Fraser could compete for the trans-port of heavy machinery between unconnected rail junctions, and all manner of adjustments concerning the haulage of agricultural products from fleeces, in Crescent North, to hops and root crops in the Kentish Triangle and the Polygon.

By the time Adam called a break, and they had all moved on to the 'George' to drink one another's health and eat bread and cheese, there was hardly a product between the Border and the Channel that had not found its way into Rookwood's notes.

Adam, thinking it wise to give them an opportunity to talk among themselves for a spell, carried his ale to the window of the saloon bar and through the lattice he saw Edith Wadsworth sitting apart in one of the galleries open to the blustery weather. She looked small, lonely and a little out of it sitting there in her neat clothes, a woman far removed from the sunburned lass in clogs, blue woollen skirt and short reefer jacket who chivvied the carters about the Boston yard, and his first thought was to join her and tell her what had come of their extraordinary encounter under the walls of Richmond earlier in the year. Then caution checked him, as he remembered that their names had been linked by the gossipmongers of the network, and that her father was known to be a crusty old Yorkshireman with strong notions concerning propriety. It would be foolish, he thought to jeo-pardise the solid gains of the conference by giving substance to the tittle tattle, so he remained inside and when she glanced in his direc-tion he raised his glass to her and left it at that. Half an hour later, when they reassembled, she merged into the group when Catesby, in the process of airing a theory of his concerning the relative benefits of rail and road haulage, accidentally set in train a project that domi-

448

nated the remainder of the agenda and led to the conference being reconvened the following day. By the time they had dispersed plans were sketched out for a development that promised, if achieved, to recast the entire structure of the enterprise.

* * *

They had been checking routes in relation to the latest maps showing the advances of the various railway companies insofar as they concerned their territories.

In the five years that had passed since the first Swann-on-Wheels waggons had been seen in the lanes of Kent and Surrey, railway expansion and railway-company amalgamation had proceeded unchecked. The new railway map he maintained looked very different from the one Aaron Walker had given him in the Plymouth depot, the day after he had come ashore to hawk dreams. Several of the big lines had entered into mutual agreements to run traffic over one another's tracks so that, to a great extent, the bitter rivalry upon which they had traded in the early days had been moderated and in some areas eliminated.

In addition, scores of short spurs had been run out to link some of the older market towns that lay off the main routes to the nearest junction and whereas, in the late 'fifties, the big companies had concentrated almost exclusively on a profitable passenger traffic, they were now, one and all, out to capture their share of freight, particularly in the larger population centres.

They had always, of course, maintained fleets of freight delivery waggons, but these were reckoned slow and cumbersome by all heavy and light industrialists whose products were transported in bulk, as in the mining valleys of Lovell's territory. Catesby, however, whose routes crossed one of the best-served concentration of towns in the country, had heard persistent rumours of a strong bid on the part of the London and North Western to capture the lighter, short-haul traffic, and now he voiced this threat as a warning. "It was time we met and agreed on a policy, notwithstanding all that's been said about shortage o' brass and overdue renewals. The fact is, we could be run clean off the road in my patch the moment Lee surrenders and the Yanks re-open the cotton ports. From what I hear, and I've had an ear t'ground, we could be back to milk and turnip hauls in the belt when the war ends and the same would be true of any other area where there's a basic industry and plenty of track laid down."

Fraser, whose territory included the Newcastle-upon-Tyne ship-

449

building areas, took up the point. "It depends on rival companies sinking their differences," he said. "Some would as lief go bankrupt as accommodate one another and that kind o' foolishness operates in our favour and always has, to my mind."

"It won't last," Catesby warned. "You'd travel a bloody long road to find a tighter-fisted clan than a railway board, and Fraser's part right, most of them would watch other investors bleed to death before reaching out a hand. But in my area they're beginning to see the mutual advantages of a cartel and when the notion catches on we can look out for a squall." He pointed to the wall. "That map there is about filled in now. The next ten years or so will see a few more new lines opened up but they won't carry fast traffic and we can disregard 'em. I'm thinking on places where t'main lines run close together. Suppose, here and there, they pool their road resources as some have already pooled their tracks? Where do small concerns like ours stand then?"

To Adam the threat was not entirely new. In his movements about the country, and in the work of keeping his railway map up to date, he had foreseen something like this but his thinking had been conditioned by the fierce rivalry known to exist between all the giant companies, whereas the smaller ones had never presented much of a freight challenge. A railway, of necessity, ran from point to point, and short runs were uneconomic. In a sense this had been the strength of their network, for the linking of two big towns by express trains had automatically isolated smaller centres either side of the track.

He said, putting this into words, "We started the business believing that the gridiron brought certain communities closer together and put others back in the days before the coaching companies ran regular services. Blubb can tell you about that, for he saw it happen. But Catesby has a point, and an important one. If the companies sink their differences, as they might well be obliged to do sooner or later, and organise freight lines as cartels instead of individual companies, then it follows they would do their damnedest to cut us out altogether. This won't apply in areas like the Western Wedge and Mountain Square, where the track is thin and the terrain difficult, but it's a real enough threat in the Polygon, in Kent, along the Border, and up in the Crescents. There are only two ways to meet it and we ought to consider both. One is to step up our speed and build on our reputation for punctuality down to the last minute. The other is to take time by the forelock and make a bid for sub-contracts with the railways themselves. Some freight lines have already done that, I'm told."

"Aye, they have," growled Blubb, who had never rid himself of his

450

profound distrust for the gridiron, "and I'm told they run at about a penny a hundredweight above cost. There's no damned sense in kissin' the backside of a goods manager—beg pardon, Miss—for a haul that'll cover the carter's wages, and a bag of oats for his nag, while you turn a blind eye to the wear and tear of your vehicles and teams."

"I'm not suggesting we do that," Adam said. "Tybalt and myself could work out a practical quotation on every regular haul, providing each one of you gave me prospects and data from companies operating in your own areas. Has anyone here already made personal contact with a local goods manager?"

Wadsworth had, admitting to being on friendly terms with the goods manager of the East Lincolnshire line that served the coastal area between Boston and Grimsby, and receiving a black look from Blubb on this account.

"That fact is," he said, "some of the goods-yard men in Brock-worth's situation would welcome us. Those railway flats are well enough hauling heavy loads over short distances but they can't average more than three miles an hour over country roads and less in winter. It would pay Brockworth to hire my teams, if I could quote low enough to give the company its pound o' flesh."

Ratcliffe, Lovell and Dockett withdrew from the discussion for neither one of them were seriously concerned with railway competition, but all the others, notably Fraser, Vicary of The Bonus, Abbott, serving an area crisscrossed with railroads, the Crescent team, and the two depot managers from the Pickings, undertook to explore the possibilities of subcontracting for the haulage of freight consigned to their local railway companies. Only Blubb stood aloof, swearing and muttering under his breath, and saying that no good would come from roadmen consorting "wi' bloody tea-kettle scum". His prejudice did not surprise Adam and it even amused some of the younger men, who had grown up with the railways, and whose childhood memories of the coaching era were growing hazy. Hour after hour, in waning daylight and later in the light of oil lamps brought into the warehouse by Tybalt's clerks, they were hard at it, reducing possibilities to notes, and rough notes to carefully-arranged lists of all likely contracts. When, at last, the conference broke up, and the delegates dispersed to their lodgings with the prospect of a Sunday journey back to their depots, a detailed campaign had been mapped out and Tybalt, flexing his right hand to moderate the effects of penman's cramp, was more elated than Adam had ever seen him. He crowed, in the

451

presence of a more restrained Keate, "Something spectacular might well come of this, Mr. Swann. I feel it, feel it here!", and he beat his pigeon chest with anticipated triumph. "The fact is," he went on, "if it falls out as I think it might it could treble our turnover. Frankly, sir, I've always been disposed to try and co-operate with the railways but Mr. Blubb isn't the only prejudiced man in the yard. Some of the older waggoners stand behind him and at the risk of sounding impudent, sir, I always entertained a suspicion that you yourself enjoyed beating the railway companies at their own game."

"I did," Adam admitted, "but I never made the mistake of imagining that we could stay in business indefinitely without them. Or the nation either for that matter. I've always subscribed to the theory that the history of a tribe is the history of its transportation system, and nobody but a fool would argue that British railways weren't the best in the world, as well as being the first. Catesby's right. We've got to go to work for them, even if we have to do it on a margin of five per cent profit. Cut your estimates to the bone when you get down to them, Tybalt. What we need even more than capital now is a vastly increased turnover. With that I can get credit wherever I need it."

He went up to his tower and retrieved hat, topcoat and gloves, pausing for a moment to look down over the familiar view of the Thames, now picked out in blobs of gaslight so that the surface of the river showed as a linked line of triangular silver pools splashed across a scaffold of black velvet. It was Saturday night, and the weekly Saturnalia was already erupting in the streets between yard and docks, narrow blades of naphtha flares thrusting east-north-east across the bow of the river towards Rotherhithe. High above, stars were beginning to show so that the city looked like a fat, ageing courtesan, displaying the jewels of youthful conquests. He thought pleasantly of all that had been achieved in the last forty-eight hours, and what it promised in terms of expansion of a kind that even he had never contemplated, not even in his most optimistic moments. They were a splendid team, and he owed their selection to no one but himself for he had handpicked every one of them, but in all other spheres he had needed constant advice and encouragement, above all encouragement, and it seemed to him that he had been very lucky in this respect. Not once had he been turned away by the people he trusted.

There was Josh Avery, blast him, whom most men would regard as a damned scoundrel, but whom Adam could still think of as a friend. There had been Tybalt and Keate, loyal and conscientious to a fault, and surely any enterprise would be lucky to have one much less two such men on hand and so deeply committed. There was Catesby, whom he had once thought of as a rebel, but whom he would now trust with his pocket-book. And there was that truculent old diehard Blubb, who had repaid the trust placed in him tenfold over the last few years. Above all there was Edith Wadsworth, and it continued to puzzle him to know precisely how he felt about Edith or, for that matter, how she felt about him, for although she was probably the most committed of all there was restraint in her approach every time they met and he wondered if it had to do with him personally or with events that had occurred before they knew one another, a sense of having been cheated of the sweets of life when her sailor lover drowned off Holy Isle, condemning her to a life of make-do and loneliness. Then, as he was shrugging himself into his coat, he heard a rap on the door, and thinking it was Tybalt with an afterthought, called, "Come on in," and there she was, cloaked and hooded for her overnight journey back to Boston and no time to spare either if Wadsworth had been right about the train he meant to catch.

She said, a little breathlessly, "Father's got a cab waiting. I made an excuse to come back, saying I forgot these," and she held up a pair of cheap cotton gloves. "I wouldn't resort to anything as feminine as that for anyone but you."

He said, "I looked out for you to say good-bye but you'd gone. Your father seemed in a great hurry."

"Well," she said petulantly, "he can wait and if we miss the train we'll catch the next." Then, more directly, "You haven't been near the Crescents since the summer and you haven't written."

"You expected me to?"

"I was curious to know if you followed my advice that time. I gather you took part of it, and bought 'Tryst'."

He told her then, holding nothing back, how he had struck a bargain with Henrietta, and how it had appeared to provide a complete answer to his domestic problems. "Things have been jogging along happily enough," he said, "and that's due to your straight talking. I should have written but it wasn't an easy thing to set down on paper."

"It's a good marriage now? It's working in a way it didn't work that time you followed me up to the Swale in the summer?"

"It was the perfect prescription and gave Henrietta something to think about." He smiled, not quite comprehending her hesitant and pensive expression. "She's expecting another child in February."

Her head came up then and he noticed she seemed not to know what to do with her hands and began to fidget with her gloves. She

453

turned away rather abruptly, crossing to the window and standing with her back to him. "That's what I came back to hear," she said. "I guessed it but I had to be sure," but then, her voice rising, so that it seemed to him almost querulous. "I've wished times enough I'd given you very different advice but that's my handicap. I'm a bad liar and I should always find it difficult to lie to you about anything, much less a matter of that kind."

"I'm not sure I understand."

She turned and looked at him frankly. "No? Well, there's no harm in spelling it out, or not now. I happen to love you, Adam Swann— no, let me say what I've got to say. It's this. I'd come to terms with loving and losing one man and then, when I lost him, making do with what came out of the bran tub, if anything. I thought that was the kind of person I am and must abide by it. But as it happened I was wrong. Oh, I loved Matt Hornby, and it took me a long time to get over losing him that way, but then you had to come bustling up and soon it was Matt all over again. A different kind of love, maybe, but now I'm just as trapped as I was after Matt's brig went down and slammed the door on me." She paused but he said nothing, knowing she had not finished. Presently she went on, "Here's the real reason I made a silly excuse to come back and it wasn't to throw myself at your feet. It was to tell you that we aren't likely to meet again."

"But that's nonsense," he burst out, crossing to her and taking her hand but she snatched it away, saying, "Don't touch me! For God's sake don't encourage me to undo all the good that's been done here in the last two days. Before you know it you'll be in a different kind of trouble. There are plenty of men who can separate private and business life that way, tuck someone like me away in a love-nest and hang up a sign, 'Business as usual'. But you're not one of them, Adam Swann! I know you, and I think I know myself. We'll have it all or we'll have nothing and make the best of it. You're not in love with your wife in the way I think of love but to run an undertaking of this size you need your wits about you twenty-four hours of the day. That's why a settled domestic background is essential to you, as much as it is to men like Keate and Tybalt, and all those others who depend on you. I'd put up a fight against that child-wife of yours, and not think the less of myself for doing it, but I don't propose to pit myself against something as complex as Swann-on-Wheels. It's far more than a means of livelihood to you, and far more than a profession. It's *you*, the real you, and I wouldn't care to put that at risk. That's why I've made up my mind to go."

"To go where? Damn it, this isn't rational. It isn't fair on you or me . . ."

"Not fair? Don't talk like a child! What's the alternative? I could make you a good wife in every way and it isn't solely your bed I want to share, or the sons I could bring you. There's nothing I should like better than to share life with a man of your stamp. But things being what they are it's out of the question, particularly since Henrietta has put her mind to the business. What could we salvage from a situation of that kind? A hole-in-the-corner association, with you dividing your time and energy three ways instead of two. Besides, as I said, I know myself better than that. If you held me in your arms once I wouldn't give a damn what happened to Swann-on-Wheels or your wife."

She walked round him and across to the head of the little stone stairway. "I'll write," she said, "and tell you my plans. I meant to do that when I came down here, and then slip off without fuss. But watching you, being near you again, well . . . it seemed furtive. And now I *am* lying. It wasn't that altogether. I came back to give myself the benefit of any chance there was. It was just possible things were much as they were back in the summer."

He said, desperately, "I'll come up to the Crescent the moment I get things sorted out here. At least we could talk . . ."

"We've done our talking. We've done too much talking. I'll write, but I'll write here. Not that I see Henrietta as a person who would steam your letters open!" and she tugged at the heavy door and went clattering down the steps to the yard.

He rejected the idea of following her, of making some excuse to accompany her and her father to the terminus. Instead he looked down into the dimly-lit yard and watched the two yellow lamps of the four-wheeler swing round in a wide arc as the horse made for the open gates at a fast trot. He could not adjust to the fact that she had gone, out of the network and out of his life. But in the back of his mind he accepted the inevitability of her decision, and the essential rightness of her priorities. Alone among all his associates she had the ability to recognise the dedication he brought to the task he had set himself when he first came here, as well as his close, personal involvement with all the men who wore his badge. She was a strange, fascinating woman, and although he thought of himself as the most obstinate man in the world, he understood well enough that she had courage, refinement and strength of a quality that very few people possessed and that he was not numbered among that minority.

455

2

Byblow

THE Convent of the Holy Family was a gaunt, stucco-faced building that stood in unkempt grounds off one of the residential avenues running at right angles to the foreshore. Its forecourt, carpeted by untrodden snow, was reached through a wilderness of overgrown laurels and leafless elms. From a distance it looked as cheerless as a private gaol.

Adam was old enough to remember a time when the presence of a Roman Catholic teaching order in a sedate English seaside town would have been regarded, by local Protestants, as an outrage, and he wondered if the child's mother had been a Roman Catholic, or if some other reason had dictated the choice of Deborah Avery's dumping place. In spite of the Reverend Mother's letter, politely acknowledging his own, and accepting him as legal guardian of the child during her father's absence, he wished now that he had consulted young Stock before setting out on a cold journey to the coast, with some muddled notion of fulfilling an ill-defined obligation thrust upon him by Avery in the last moment of their parting nearly three months before.

The visit, he had to admit, was overdue and would not have been made now, with the Christmas holiday almost upon them, had he not been so unguarded as to mention the child's existence in the presence of his wife and Phoebe Fraser, the governess, that very morning whilst seeking feminine advice concerning the child's Christmas present.

Their joint indignation took him by surprise, and, almost without realising it, he had told them rather more concerning her circumstances than he had intended. Phoebe said, looking at him as though he was responsible for a string of farmed-out bastards, "A lassie of *eight*? Motherless, and abandoned among Papists?" and then, turning confidently to Henrietta, "We *canna* let Christmas pass without making up a parcel for the bairn, ma'am. Stella and little Alexander have more toys than they need so I'll set about sorting some out!" and with a bob in Adam's direction stormed up to the nursery.

"That's the Presbyterian in her," said Adam, chuckling. "I never could understand why they should berate the Romans, for when it comes to intolerance no Papist could hold a candle to John Knox," and he would have dismissed the matter on the spot for he had an important appointment with Blubb in Maidstone that day.

"Go down there today," Henrietta directed. "Phoebe's perfectly right. You simply can't let Christmas go by in those dreadful circumstances. A girl of eight, indeed! How could a mother let such a thing happen?"

"It was that or starve," Adam said shortly, and explained briefly how Avery had thrown up his commission after seducing his colonel's wife, although he was careful not to say what had converted Josh into a fugitive from the law. Phoebe then reappeared carrying a bulky parcel containing a doll and several other gifts destined for his own children. Within minutes he was obliged to accept the fact that wife and governess had arbitrarily rearranged his day. There was a train to Tonbridge at ten-twenty and a connection to Folkestone ten minutes later. Half-irritated and half-amused by their decree he allowed himself to be driven to Bromley in the gig, stabling it there pending a train journey to the coast where he was lucky to engage an aged cabbie who knew where the convent was and could tell him something about it. The man said it had been established a year or two ago by a refugee teaching order, who made a meagre living teaching French and music to the daughters of local bigwigs, now settling on the coast in increasing numbers since the journey to London could be made in an hour. Beyond that the cabbie knew little about the establishment except that it was still regarded with suspicion by the Anglicans and Dissenters in the district. He seemed to share their views. "All sorts are making free wi' the country nowadays," he growled, with haughty isolationism of his class. "Get 'emselves into mischief over there, come here to catch their second wind, and hatch more devilry while they'm waitin'. The Guvverment should put a stop to it. Nobody minds 'em making bombs to blow up other forriners but will it stop there? I'll wait out 'ere under the trees if you don't mind, sir. More snow before noon be the look o' the sky."

Adam walked up the drive and presented his card, announcing his purpose to the silent nun who admitted him. She showed him into a fireless waiting room opening out of a hall hung with religious pictures depicting a wide range of excruciating martyrdoms, so that he

457

thought, gloomily, 'Josh could have found a cosier nook for the child but when did he care two straws about anyone else's comfort or convenience?' and he sat huddled in his topcoat, awaiting the appearance of the Mother Superior.

When she swept into the room and offered her chilled hand he moderated his opinion somewhat. She was a very striking woman, with fine features over which her pale skin was stretched as tightly as the skin of a drum. She had luminous grey eyes, compassionate eyes he would say, and a distinguished high-bridged nose with sensitive nostrils indicating high breeding that also showed in her carriage and voice. The moment she spoke he set her down as a Gascon and hoping to ease their relationship told her that he recognised the accent, one of the few things he could recall of his mother, a native of St. Jean de Luz. She said, smiling, "You could pass as a Basque yourself, m'sieu, except for your height," and then, wistfully, "It is a very long time since I was there and it seems unlikely now that I shall ever return. Our community was uprooted in the troubles of 'forty-eight, and we have been on the move ever since. First Anjou, then Normandy, now here." She became very businesslike, saying, "Ordinarily, of course, I could not give you access to the child but I heard from Mr. Avery the day before you wrote. He authorised you to exercise full rights of guardianship over Deborah so long as he remained abroad. He will be absent for an indefinite period, I understand?"

"Very indefinite," said Adam. "Probably until his daughter reaches her majority," and looked for the Mother Superior to register surprise but she did not, saying thoughtfully, "It's all somewhat unorthodox, but naturally, on hearing from Mr. Avery, I made inquiries concerning you. That was obligatory, you understand? Not only are we responsible for his child but Mr. Avery is a generous patron. One could say our sale patron."

He began to feel out of his depth. He did not quite know what he had expected but whatever it was it was not this, a link between a man of Avery's stamp and an exiled order of nuns. Neither had it occurred to him that he would be vetted.

"I've been a close associate of Mr. Avery's for a long time, Reverend Mother. First in the army, then in business. I believe I am the only friend he has in England, certainly the only one he would trust to keep an eye on his daughter. But I must admit I'm puzzled to learn that he's a patron of yours. He never gave me the impression that he subscribed to any religion."

She smiled at that and it was such a tolerant smile that he found himself comparing her attitude with the immature outbursts of Henrietta and Phoebe at the breakfast table. She said, "Mr. Avery is of our Faith, Mr. Swann. Perhaps, in the army and elsewhere, he would find it necessary to conceal the fact but it is so. We have explicit instructions from him to raise Deborah in the Faith. He made no secret, however, of the trust he reposes in you. We had detailed instructions to grant you every facility. In his letter he told us a good deal about you and it was his information that made our inquiries straightforward. You would like to meet your ward now?"

"Not before I've cleared up one or two other points. When did you get this letter, and where was it sent from? He hasn't paid me the compliment of writing since he left the country in October."

She seemed to consider a moment. "There can be no harm in letting you know when we received the letter. It was in early December, the fourth of the month I recollect. But as to Mr. Avery's whereabouts, he asked us to say nothing concerning that. He will write in due course, no doubt."

"I hope so," muttered Adam, and it occurred to him that he was probably not the only one in the secret concerning the circumstances under which Avery had fled the country. He said, "Do you have any dealings with the child's mother?" and the Mother Superior said they did not, and that to the best of her knowledge the mother was not aware that Deborah was being educated here.

"What kind of child is she?" he persisted. "You realise we've never met?"

"Mr. Avery was here shortly before he went overseas. He mentioned you then as a possible choice for guardian."

"When *was* that? I'm sorry, Reverend Mother, but I have a right to know. Mr. Avery might have been explicit in his dealings with you but he was very cavalier in transferring his responsibilities to me. As I said, he only mentioned the child's existence moments before we parted."

"Yes," she said, with another sad smile, "I'm afraid that was Mr. Avery's way. It was in October. A rather hasty visit."

"I can imagine," said Adam, grimly, and a possible reason for Avery's delay in putting the Channel between himself and the bailiffs suggested itself.

"As to Deborah," the Mother Superior went on, "she is a rather withdrawn child—how would you say over here? *Biddable*, I think. Would that be right? She is our sole boarder, of course, and thrown on her own resources on that account. It is understandable that she should be lonely at holiday time. We give no lessons to local children for three months in summer and at this time of the year. And not, of course, during Holy Week. Deborah's health is good, and she is very intelligent and observant, but come, as her legal guardian you should judge for yourself," and she led the way out of the room and down the draughty funnel of a hall to a room overlooking a forest of neglected laurels at the back of the house.

It was less forbidding in here. There was no carpet or rug on the floor but the boards were waxed, and a fire burned in a clean grate. More religious pictures adorned the distempered walls and the room was obviously used as a schoolroom, for there were two rows of desks, a blackboard, a rostrum, and a map or two rustling in a strong draught from a garden door that opened on a terrace bounded by a fence in the final stage of dissolution.

In the angle beyond the fire was an unhinged door laid upon four stacks of housebricks, the surface having been used as a platform for a crib, with modelled, plasticine figures of the shepherds, the Three Wise Men and Joseph. A small, flaxen-haired doll had been pressed into service as the Mother of God. Cows, sheep and a donkey with one ear half as long again as the other, were grouped around the manger and over all, suspended on threads of cotton, angels gyrated in the draught.

Deborah Avery, or Deborah Stanhope to be more exact, was making some last minute adjustments to a shepherd's crook and was so absorbed that she did not hear their entry. The Mother Superior said, gently, "Deborah, my dear, this is Mr. Swann, the gentleman I told you about. He is a very old friend of your father's and has come here specially to make your acquaintance."

The child spun round and made a short, Continental curtsey and perhaps it was this unlikely acknowledgement that made pity rise in his throat so that he suddenly felt embarrassed and had to make an effort to smile. He said, taking her hand, and finding it as cold as the Reverend Mother's, "I came because it was Christmas, Deborah, and to give you some Christmas presents your father asked me to deliver because he can't be here himself," and suddenly he felt grateful for Phoebe Fraser's forethought and opened the parcel, displaying the doll, some illustrated books that he guessed would be too juvenile for her, a mechanical toy or two, a box of bricks, and some blue and pink hair-ribbons in a box.

She examined the gifts gravely. She was, he decided, a very solemn

460

and exceptionally well-mannered child, with her mother's eyes and Avery's small, aggressive chin, but it was difficult to see her as the fruit of a brief flirtation between a silly, empty-headed woman like Charity Stanhope, and a cynic like Avery, although a little of Avery's separateness showed in her so that she seemed surprisingly self-contained for a child of eight. He said, making a conscious effort, "Did you build that crib, Deborah?" and she said, with a careful regard for the truth, that Sister Loretta had made the manger and one of the angels but she had been responsible for the rest. He said, addressing the Mother Superior, "When Mr. Avery visited did he ever take Deborah out?" and the nun said that he did in summertime, when they sometimes spent the afternoon on the beach. There was no prospect of taking her out now, with a leaden sky and more snow threatening, but compassion for the child nagged at him and he made a sign, indicating that he wanted to speak to the Mother Superior alone. Like a good Frenchwoman she at once took the hint and said, "Let me show you our little chapel, Mr. Swann. Excuse us a moment, Deborah," and led the way through what had once been a conservatory but was now half-full of rubbish.

"What do you make of her, Mr. Swann?" she said, with the same pale smile, and Adam said, briefly, "I'd say right off she needs the company of other children. Especially now, at Christmas. Perhaps they told you I had a family of my own and plenty of room to spare. Would it be in order for me to take her home for Christmas? My own daughter is rising four, and her governess is a very responsible person."

The request took the Mother Superior by surprise, so that he added, quickly, "I would give you an undertaking not to run contrary to the religious training she receives here. I'm no bigot, like most of my countrymen," and the woman smiled and said, "We are overcoming it but it will take a little time. At least in this country one is guaranteed against persecution. Isn't that why we flock here?"

"Some Continentals don't come here to teach, according to my cabbie," Adam said, warming towards her. "Would it be in order for me to see the instructions Mr. Avery gave you concerning guardianship?"

"I see no reason why you should not," she said, "they were very flattering." Then, but anxiously, "You would return her when we begin school again in late January?" and he said he would, personally.

461

"Then go and make friends," she said, "and I'll instruct Sister Agatha to pack Deborah's bag. If she wants to go she shall, but you must ask her yourself, Mr. Swann."

She went back into the hall, leaving him to return to the school-room. He stood for a moment on the threshold, looking across at the child now sitting on the window seat cradling the doll. The scene had a certain familiarity and suddenly he thought he recognised its parallel, the boy Scrooge revealed by the Ghost in the schoolroom scene, in the popular *Christmas Carol*, rescued and taken home on Christmas Eve. He said, frankly, "You hardly know me yet, Deborah, but the Reverend Mother was right, I'm a very old friend of your father. When he had to go abroad he asked me to be sure to look after you as long as he was away. I have a little girl younger than you, and a boy younger than her. We live in the country not far from here, and I'm sure they would both like you to visit for Christmas. The Reverend Mother says you may go if you wish. Would you like that?" He thought the child looked startled so he went on, "We have a Christmas tree and there are ponies to ride. After all, I am a sort of uncle and I think you might enjoy staying with us until school starts again, and all the other children come back. What do you think, Deborah?"

The child looked at him then without surprise but with a steadiness that he found disconcerting. Her expression indicated that she had already learned to make decisions and that most of them would be based on a sense of detachment inherited from her father. She said, primly, "What must I call you then? 'Uncle' something?" and he said, laughing. "Why, surely. Uncle Adam. And at home you'll find Aunt Henrietta, Miss Phoebe, the governess, Stella and Alexander. Will you come?"

"Yes," she said, "if I could bring Angelica."

"But the Reverend Mother told me you were the only little girl left here. Who is Angelica?"

"The doll," she told him, "I have christened her Angelica. It suits her, does it not?"

Her gravity had a trick of levelling their ages. In a curious way she seemed older than himself or the Mother Superior, and more resigned, he reflected, than anyone she was likely to find at 'Tryst'. He was suddenly conscious of the terrible complexity and unpredictability of human affairs, seeing the child before him as the end product of a casual encounter halfway across the world between a hard nut like Josh Avery and a shallow, pretty woman who could have had no clear idea of the kind of scrape she was getting into. And here was

Deborah, the product of their joint folly, already more truly adult than either one of them, or that old fool of a colonel who had stood by and watched himself cuckolded.

* * *

His sympathy built a bridge between them and they were able to talk, first in English, then in French. He marked her perfect accent, reflecting that it might benefit his daughter who was already beginning to speak French like a Lowland Scot. He wondered how Henrietta, seven months pregnant, would get along with this solemn little thing, and whether she would be likely to regret her insistence that he paid the visit when he returned with the child in tow, but decided that, in her new rôle as châtelaine, she was likely to take Deborah in her stride.

Then Sister Agatha appeared carrying a tartan holdall containing Deborah's clothes, and Angelica was carefully re-wrapped whilst Sister Agatha, somehow managing to convey the impression that she was consigning a helpless child to heathen custody, disappeared again, to return with a blue, scarlet-lined cloak that he took to be the uniform of the convent.

They were in the hall when the Mother Superior emerged from her office to hand him a long envelope bearing a foreign postmark and broken seals.

"You may take Mr. Avery's letter," she said, "but I would like it returned. It is my sole authorisation, you understand?" Then, to the child, "Be good, Deborah. We shall look forward to seeing you again in a month," and as Deborah dropped her little Continental curtsey the nun stooped and embraced her and the gesture comforted Adam who saw it as proof that the Convent of the Holy Family was not as bleak an institution as its fabric and chilliness implied.

They went out into the forecourt where heavy flakes of snow were beginning to fall, and when the cab came out from under the trees he noted the unfriendly stare the cabby gave the nuns standing on the steps. It was, he thought, an indication of the man's built-in hostility towards Rome and all its works, and had its origin, no doubt, in an Englishman's ancestral memories of the fires in Smithfield. Then the cab was jolting towards the town and he glanced at Deborah who was looking out at the whirling snowflakes, for all the world like a prisoner being taken to or from her gaol, he was unable to decide which. The cab reeked of damp horsehair and inside, with both windows raised, he began to feel a curious affinity with the child, as

463

though both of them had been arbitrarily isolated from everything familiar and left to seek solace in one another's society. Then, as the child turned her head, he saw tears glisten on the lashes of her serious eyes and before the first of them fell he reached out and enclosed her hand, finding, to his relief, that it was more responsive than when he had greeted her beside the crib. He said, "You mustn't be scared, Deborah. We shall be good friends once you've stopped being shy," and was gratified to see her force a smile, for somehow the effort she put into producing it at once enlarged him and integrated her into the pattern of his life, so that he saw her not as a stray he had acquired through force of circumstance, but as a link in a chain he and Avery had been forging over the years and would now, he supposed, secure the partnership whether he liked it or not. The fancy absorbed him all the way to the station so that they completed the journey in silence, her small hand in his, and it was not until they were in the train for Tonbridge that she spoke again, saying, "Where is my father spending his Christmas, Uncle Adam?" Her question reminded him of the letter the Mother Superior had given him and he took it out, glancing at stamps and postmark. "Probably in a place called Liège, Deborah," he said, "but I can't be sure. He's a great traveller, is your father." She responded with one of her solemn nods. "Yes, he is," she said, "for he sends me presents sometimes from Switzerland and France. A brooch once, and one of those weathercocks where the lady comes out when it is fine and the gentleman if it is wet. I have it in my cubicle but Sister Agatha will have packed the brooch in the bag, I hope. I think my father might spend Christmas in Holland this year. Because of the Dutch doll he sent."

'By God,' he thought, 'she's sharp! I shall have to warn Henrietta and Phoebe, for she's not likely to take kindly to goo-goo talk and that's a fact!' and he said she was almost certainly right, and that her father must have moved on to Holland after posting the letter, for Liège was not very far from Holland and his letter was several days old.

Gradually, as the train whirled through the snowstorm, she began to relax, shedding her gravity little by little, but even so it was still very difficult to treat her as a child, and quite impossible to connect her with the giddy woman he remembered as her mother who had never, so far as he recalled, had a serious thought in her life. Instead, he found himself confiding in her and even telling her about his business, and was secretly astonished by her familiarity with counties and districts and the kind of activities carried on within their boun-

464

daries. He said, complimenting her, "You seem to know a great deal of geography. Is it your favourite subject at school?" and she even had to think hard about this, replying, after a judicious pause, "No, not really, Uncle Adam. I much prefer history but Sister Albertine, who teaches geography, is very good at explaining, whereas Sister Sophia, who teaches history, is not. That isn't her fault, of course, for she only joined us a short time ago from Pisa, and her English is not good. Pisa," she added, as a kind of postscript, "is in Italy."

"Ah, yes," he said, infected by her pedantry, "It has a famous leaning tower, I believe."

His response seemed to please her for she nodded eagerly, saying, "Yes indeed. It is one hundred and seventy nine feet in height, and sixteen-and-a-half feet out of the perpendicular. I should very much like to see it when I am grown up."

He only just stopped himself exclaiming aloud, reflecting that Phoebe Fraser and that cabby could say what they liked about Papists but they had the edge on Protestants when it came to the art of educating children. It occurred to him then that although he had heard a good deal about why the tower leaned nobody had ever explained how it came to be there in the first place and this seemed a time to find out.

"Why was it built?" he asked, and she said it was once a bell-tower for the cathedral, and that he was not to worry about it falling down for it had stood just so for hundreds of years and was unlikely to collapse, steps having been taken to ensure that it did not.

By the time they had reached Bromley, collected the gig and driven across the silent countryside to 'Tryst', he had almost adjusted to her, but as they crested the drive uncertainty concerning their reception returned to him and he was glad to hand her over to Lucy, the general maid, for a hot drink and a bowl of soup, while he sought out Henrietta, already rehearsing his statement of self-justification.

He found her toasting her toes in front of the drawing-room fire, tired but complacent after helping Phoebe to dress the tree and pack the children off to bed and it was here, a little haltingly, that he told her precisely what had occurred, watching her closely as he did so for it occurred to him that she might see in his introduction of the child into the house some kind of threat to her own children. He need not have worried. Something of the old, feckless Henrietta showed in the twinkle in her eye as she said, "There's really no curing you, is there? You scooped me from Seddon Moor in much the same manner!", and she heaved herself up, saying, "Where is the little mite? I'll go to her."

He said, restraining her, "No, wait, Hetty. It's important to discuss this with Phoebe right away," and her mouth tightened as she said, "Why? What has a thing like this to do with a governess?"

He understood then that she was jealous of her new authority and that there were still latent tensions about the house for which he had not made allowance. There was even a gleam in her eye that introduced a note of wariness into his voice as he said, "Because Phoebe is a strict Presbyterian, and Avery's daughter has been raised in the Roman Catholic faith. I know Lowland Scots. I wouldn't put it past Phoebe to set about the child as she would upon a heathen, ripe for conversion."

"You think that's likely?"

"It's entirely possible."

"Then it's a matter for me, not you." She waddled round him, a small, tubby, determined figure, endowed with a bantam-like air of displeasure, so that he said, with a laugh, "Sit down, Henrietta. Phoebe can see to her, and I'll introduce you to one another when she's fed," but as soon as he had said this he realised that he had miscalculated, for she stopped, pushed the half-opened door shut and stood with her back to it. "I was right!" she said. "You *don't* understand and it's really time you did."

"You don't approve of me bringing the child here without consulting you!" and she burst out, "Of course I do! It's not that at all! No one with a heart could have left her there and gone back when Christmas was over with another bribe wrapped in brown paper. I should have done exactly as you did but that isn't the point, that isn't the point at all, Adam!"

For the first time since the now historic confrontation at the 'George' he was face to face with the fruits of the dramatic change that he, circumstances, and possibly that encounter with Miles Manaton, had wrought in her. He had accepted the fact that she had made great advances in the rôle of housekeeper, that her judgements were maturing with every day that passed, that she was no longer at the mercy of mood and impulse but he had not made nearly enough allowance for the injection of pride that had attended all those changes and the assumption of responsibilities she had consistently evaded over the last five years. He remembered the periods when she had been carrying Stella and Alexander, when she had sometimes been tetchy and sometimes pitiful, scuttling away from even trivial decisions and content to leave everything to him. Now all was changed, as though the night spent in his arms after that unlikely re-union had enabled her to break out of the shell of youth and take on an entirely new personality. And here it was confronting him, a woman intensely jealous of her rights and responsibilities, who found it humiliating to share them with anyone, even him. He understood this and marvelled at it, for it seemed to him something as elemental as birth or death, and brought him face to face with the realisa-tion that he would never again see her as the laughing girl he had met on a moor, courted (if that was the word) and saddled with three children and this great barn of a house. That girl was a ghost and if there was a part of him that mourned her gaiety he had no one but himself and Edith Wadsworth to blame.

He said, coming to terms with the situation, "What is it you want, Henrietta? Not simply in respect of Avery's child, but from me. From all of us here?"

She had no difficulty in finding the answer. A year ago she would have floundered, an inarticulate child seeking to justify a stand dic-tated by instinct, but now words found their way to her with the same facility as she had acquired the apparatus of authority. She said, "That's easy to explain. What I want is to be *seen* as someone who matters. To be able and expected to *decide* things, *all* things, just as we agreed and just as you said you wanted."

He gave this the contemplation it deserved. They had negotiated one impasse but here was another, entirely unforeseen one. Perhaps it was not so much a matter of what she wanted but what he preferred, the girl-wife of the first years of their association, or this indomitable little woman, who not only rejected patronage but saw the least tres-pass upon her preserves as a threat to her stewardship. He made up his mind on the spot. People, he supposed, had to expand and de-velop, and this was as true of a wife as it was of a business. Having encouraged growth why should he complain if the pace dazzled him? The real answer lay not in expediency but in humour that had always resided in their relationship. He had gone looking for an efficient deputy to manage his domestic life while he spent his nervous energy elsewhere, and by God he seemed to have found one capable of surprising him. He crossed the room and took her face between his hands, tilting it and studying it with amusement and affection. He said, gently, "You're a very remarkable person, Henrietta. I must have reminded myself of it at least once a week ever since I winkled you out of that hut on the moor. But a man doesn't really expect to rediscover his own wife when she's seven months gone with his third child, and that's what I seem to be doing at this moment. You were right to flare up in that way. How Deborah Avery is to be received here is your concern, not mine, or Phoebe's, or even Avery's, and I'll not make that mistake again. Others maybe, for I can't promise I can adapt to you without a wobble or two, but one thing you should know. From here on, as far as parish pump politics are concerned, I abdicate. Go out to that child and do what's best for her. I'd back you against a dozen governesses," and he kissed her, reached over her shoulder and opened the door on the hall.

She went out without another word and, watching her sail across the hall towards the kitchen quarters, another thought struck him concerning her singularity. She had never, in the course of three pregnancies, shown a flicker of embarrassment, and this despite the fact that her stature made concealment impossible the moment her figure began to thicken. He thought, as she disappeared, 'She parades a pregnancy like that father of hers parades his power and moneybags', and he reminded himself again how much the two had in common and that, to Henrietta, her womb was the equivalent of Sam's mill.

Safe in his study, that no one in the house entered without an invitation, he ran his eye over Avery's letter, savouring the cool impudence of the man who went his own way in the certainty that others, endowed with a conscience, would pick up the pieces he left in his wake. '*You can repose complete trust in Mr. Swann . . . he has my entire confidence . . . a man of strict integrity . . . noted for high principle . . . my daughter must be encouraged to defer to him as she would to me . . .*' and so on, three whole pages of it, most of it blarney.

He put the letter aside and cocked his head, listening, with half an ear, to the tinkle of a carol trickling from one of his daughter's musical boxes that she collected as other children collect dolls and marbles. There was not much doubt in his mind that, from here on, Deborah Avery was virtually his child; his, and seemingly, Henrietta's too if he had drawn the right conclusions from that scene in the drawing-room just now. He wondered what she would make of the child, with her curious blend of stillness and amiability, sensitivity and self-containment, her solemn prattle about coal seams in Wales and towers in Pisa. Probably they would circle one another for a spell, taking one another's measure like a couple of gladiators, and then, no doubt, arrive at a compromise that would almost certainly involve him. For, sooner or later, everything seemed to revert to

468

him and the older and busier he became the more numerous and complicated were the day-to-day problems he was set to solve. He thought back for a moment to the time when his problems had been few, and confined to a choice of two courses, to kill or be killed, to run out ahead in pursuit of glory and promotion, or to stay under cover and hope nobody would notice. That was all that was required of a man content to cut his swathe with a sword and all the Swanns of the past had sought in the way of a destiny. It was not that simple, however, when a man threw away his sword and taught himself to use more sophisticated tools. Before one realised as much every facet of life reflected alternatives and every personal relationship became infinitely complex, demanding all manner of shifts and adjustments. People moved in and stayed like the Keates, the Tybalts and the Blubbs, and others, the Averys, the Ellen Michelmores, and the Miles Manatons, collided and bumped away out of sight and sound. Predictability he had once had and spurned and only a fool would look for it in business or marriage, certainly not in marriage to a woman like Henrietta Rawlinson. The phrase 'natural selection' returned to him and what else could have dictated that casual decision of his the day Sam Rawlinson came blustering into his father's house on Derwentwater, demanding the return of his daughter? Money hadn't entered into it, for Sam had disowned her on the spot, or wisdom either, for Henrietta, at that particular time, and for a long time afterwards, had shown no evidence of possessing the sense she was born with. And yet, looking back on it all, he regretted nothing and told himself, as he refolded and resealed Avery's letter, that if he was beginning all over again there wasn't a single short-cut he would take from the moment he opened his eyes outside Jhansi and saw cobra's eyes reposing in a shattered casket.

Above him, leaking uncertainly through the chinks and cavities of the old timbers, the nursery serenade continued and for a moment he gave it his undivided attention. 'God rest you, merry gentlemen, let nothing you dismay . . .' an appropriate jingle, he thought, for his mood and the day that had provoked it.

3

Valentine's Day Breakout

IT was said of George Swann in his middle years, that he had been born laughing and the story, no doubt, originated from his father, who had been impressed on the occasion of their introduction.

Henrietta was sleeping then and Adam accepted the midwife's invitation to 'take a peep at the nipper' wondering, as he did so, whether any of the women who came running at the whisper of a birth, could have been persuaded that a male animal actually participated in the process of procreation. This one, Nurse Hoxton, rushed in from Bromley the day before, was particularly patronising, apportioning to herself the lion's share of credit for the presence of a sturdy eight pound boy, as bald as a coot and evidently something of a night hawk, for he was wide awake and taking the keenest interest in everything that went on around him. George, it seemed, had other ideas about the allocation of credit, for he stared Adam full in the face, cleared his throat, flexed his chubby knuckles, put out his tongue and (Adam would later swear to this) winked. Then, withdrawing his tongue, he burped twice and the sound must have pleased him, for the corners of his mouth turned up so that Adam laughed with him and then returned to the dining-room to drink the boy's health and with it his own for, all in all, the day that had just ended would surely rank as one of the most rewarding of his life.

In the years ahead there were to be many such days, occasions when circumstances and the Royal Mail combined to shower him with opportunities, but never a day quite like this so that although he was bad on birthdays he never forgot George's. St. Valentine's day, 1864, a day when anything might happen and whatever did could be turned to account.

It was for the same reason that he later came to associate George with luck as well as laughter, and this may have prepared the ground for the subsequent understanding between father and son that isolated George from all his other children, not as a favourite but more as a pledge that Swann-on-Wheels, now under full press of sail, was

470

under orders to proceed anywhere at all with safety and dispatch. Somehow George represented these certainties, together with one other that his father, warming his behind at the fire, found exhilarating. Already, in his mind at least, George Swann stood four-square for commerce. Nobody would make a drill-ground dummy of someone who could wink within twelve hours of birth.

* * *

The day began ordinarily enough. Doctor Birtles had looked in the previous afternoon expressing an opinion that Henrietta might expect her third child early next week and Adam, privately deciding on a dash north-west before the event, drove off to Croydon before the morning mists had dissolved, catching a train that set him down at London Bridge a few minutes before nine. He bought his *Times* and *Morning Post* at the station exit and was sifting through the mail in his tower when the clock struck the hour and a wintry sun played on the trailers along the margins of the river and then went to work on the brass fittings of a wherry moving downstream at the head of a string of pregnant barges.

The post limited his contemplation of the panorama to a glance. Sometimes, when the mail was commonplace, he would pay the Thames the compliment of an absorbed scrutiny, wondering what the tarpaulins of the barges concealed, and how the devil that daredevil Norman priest Ralph Flambard, had managed his midnight descent by rope ladder from the White Tower opposite in A.D. 1100, but Dockett's letter put these idle thoughts out of mind, for Dockett had not only made good his boast concerning the establishment of a near-monopoly in house-removals on Tom Tiddler's Ground, but had set the seal upon his achievement by inventing a slogan and transferring it to his waggons, without troubling himself to seek headquarters' approval for such a breach of protocol. For so, it seemed, Tybalt had regarded it, having pencilled an exclamation mark, followed by a row of asterisks. Seeing them Adam grinned, as he often did at Tybalt's notations. They called to mind Phillip of Spain's marginal comments on official reports from Spanish governors who had been hustled by Drake and he would not have been much surprised had Tybalt written '*Ojo, ojo, Dockett!*' on the back of the photograph the Isle of Wight manager had taken of his new box-van, harnessed to four Clydesdales, and on the point of making its maiden run.

Adam studied the photograph closely, instantly approving the in-

471

novation. Below the swan insignia, stencilled on the side of the enormous waggon, were the words, *'Swann's House Removals. From Drawer to Drawer'*.

"By God, that's eye-catching!" Adam exclaimed to his friend Frankenstein. "I would have bet a sovereign Dockett didn't have that much originality in him," and then he remembered that it was Dockett who had broken the ice at the December conference, convincing everybody that there was money in house-removals, and that this had led to him being given the first box-waggon delivered by Blunderstone a fortnight ago.

Dockett's accompanying letter, moreover, was very encouraging. He claimed that the van was spoken for as far ahead as May, and that he could use another if others had doubts about their usefulness. He was out of luck, however, for the mail included a request from Blubb for the second van off the stocks, and Adam approved it, wondering if the request had anything to do with Blubb's yearning to drive a four-horse team across Kent again and relive part of his splendid youth.

In rising good humour he went swiftly through reports from the Border Triangle, the Northern Pickings, the Southern Square, and Crescent South. There was nothing from Catesby, in the Polygon, where the cotton famine was grinding through its third year, or from Edith Wadsworth, again deputising for her father who had been in hospital with a hernia since January. Then, with Dockett's photograph clamped to the wall by a drawing pin, and the sheaf of reports earmarked for circulation among the clerks below, he opened a letter addressed to him personally from Morris, manager of the Southern Pickings, the man who had been so insistent about canvassing porcelain factories for the transport of high-risk goods.

It was regarding this that he now wrote, enclosing another letter in the spinstery hand of Bryn Lovell, of the Mountain Square. It seemed that the two managers, who were neighbours, had got as far as hatching a scheme in their mutual advantage, and all they needed to secure an impressive contract was headquarters' approval. Assessing the importance of the letters at a glance, he rang for Tybalt, who must have been anticipating a summons for he popped in at once, wearing the expression Adam had learned to associate with good news.

Responsibility had aged Tybalt but it had also given him a dignity he had not possessed when Keate introduced him into the firm more than five years before. He was now almost bald, with a grey, monkish fringe coaxed into a blunt point between his pink, flattish ears. He wore steel-rimmed eyeglasses secured by a strip of black tape to his lapel and security, plus three rises in pay in as many years, had given him a paunch. He trotted across to the desk flourishing a brace of letters that had apparently been held back and Adam did not need to be told that they related to staff appointments, for Tybalt was a slave of method and invariably withheld letters of this kind to check against the day book in order that he could tell Adam whether or not he would be in London on the dates suggested. He said, breathlessly, "Things seem to be crowding in on us, Mr. Swann. Everything seems to be happening at once. You've looked at the mail, sir?"

Adam told him he had and before showing him Morris's letter sounded him out on Dockett's slogan. He had almost abandoned hope of finding Tybalt ready to welcome an innovation that did not stem directly from him, or from his bosom friend, Saul Keate.

"What do you think of it, Tybalt?" he asked, and the head clerk's mouth contracted, as though he had bitten into an unripe plum.

"Frankly, sir, rather vulgar," he said, unequivocally, and then, as Adam raised his eyebrows, "Oh, I don't have to be reminded that vulgarity is very much in vogue, sir. One has only to study newspaper advertisements to be aware of that, but it doesn't match up to my conception of a sober concern. Too ... er ... facile, Mr. Swann, a catch-phrase that would come better from an American salesman."

"But that's the point," Adam said, seriously now. "It *is* a catch-phrase, just as you say, but catch-phrases stay in the mind. Think about it. *'From drawer to drawer'*; it's got a music-hall ring." and Tybalt said, primly, "Quite, Mr. Swann!" indicating that this in itself was enough to condemn it. Like his friend Keate he equated music-halls with Sin and Saturday.

"Well, whether you approve or not I'm telling Dockett he can keep it, so long as he only stencils it to box-vans. It wouldn't make much sense on the side of a waggon shifting pig-iron or milk. However, that wasn't what I rang about. Run your eye over this, for it seems that Dockett isn't the only one who has been taking vice-regal liberties with headquarters," and he passed over Morris's letter and the letter from Lovell that Morris had enclosed.

News of a big contract always acted as balm to Tybalt's dignity. He said, absorbing the text at a glance, "That's promising, sir! That's very promising indeed! Mind you, it doesn't come as a surprise to *me*.

473

Mr. Morris hinted at the possibility when he was down here."

"He didn't hint to me," said Adam, and Tybalt said, apologetically, "Oh, don't misunderstand me, Mr. Swann. I wouldn't like you to think Mr. Morris took me into his confidence as regards details, but after he mentioned those china hauls, I . . . er . . . took the liberty of asking him if he had any particular factory in mind. He admitted he had, mentioning Royal Worcester. It's my opinion, Mr. Swann, he had as good as secured this contract before he mentioned it at conference, but I had no idea Mr. Lovell would be involved."

He held a letter in either hand and his glance darted from one to the other so that Adam thought, 'By God, he might be stuffy but nobody could be quicker off the mark for he's already reading more between the lines than Morris or Lovell put on paper', and he said, hoping to draw Tybalt out, "An overland haul from the factory to Cardiff docks. The entire distance by road, and half of it through an area well served by rail. *Why?* At first glance it wouldn't seem economical from Royal Worcester's standpoint. Turn up those conference notes, and let's see exactly what Morris had to say about it at the time," but here Tybalt became tutorial saying, with a hint of unction, "I don't need to do that, Mr. Swann. What is it you want to know?"

"Why Royal Worcester have stopped shipping high-grade china from Bristol and switched to Cardiff. Also, given current rates of insurance, why they seem prepared to pay more for a much slower haul than they could get from the railways."

"I can help you there," said Tybalt. "Cardiff is a longer haul certainly but they've been dispatching via Cheltenham or Gloucester over the permanent way of two rival companies. That means the goods are either manhandled or switched in the original waggon over a link line. It doesn't need much imagination, sir, to decide what that kind of usage might do to fine porcelain, no matter how carefully it was packed. If we could examine the claims departments of the Grand Central and Great Western, I think we should be in a position to discover why consignor and consignee have decided to part company."

"There's more to it than that," said Adam, and Tybalt agreed that there almost certainly was, and that it would probably have to do with Mr. Morris's hard bargaining with local insurance companies and also interminable delays due to overcrowding at Avonmouth Docks.

They had formed the habit of communicating one with the other in this rather artful way, Adam using the less imaginative man as a sounding board while they nibbled at an idea, a problem, or a prospective source of income, like two schoolboys planning a raid on an orchard. Adam had often made up his mind on most of the questions and Tybalt was aware of this, but sometimes the gambler in Adam would over-reach himself and Tybalt, drawing on a reserve made up of his prodigious store of trivia, would apply the curb, citing the odds Frankenstein made available to them. Frankenstein helped them now, assessing the profit margin on a four-day haul, two over metalled roads, two down the winding valleys of Bryn Lovell's territory, where gradients were steep and the surfaces execrable. All things being equal, Adam decided, there was certain profit in a quarterly contract with an undertaking as rich and as rooted as the Royal Worcester, but risks in transit made him cautious, notwithstanding Morris's carefully-worked-out insurance schedules. He said, thoughtfully, "We should look for a way to narrow that risk without lengthening the haul. Morris suggests specially-built waggons but the fact is, notwithstanding the obvious benefits of a long-term contract like his, we simply can't afford to invest in new rolling stock. We'll be damned hard pressed to pay for what we have on order."

He knew Tybalt, with his hand forever poised over the purse-strings of the enterprise, would agree with this but the clerk, it seemed, had given the matter a great deal of thought after his exploratory talk with Morris and now he introduced what was, for him, a revolutionary compromise. He said, "I'm with you there, Mr. Swann. It would be folly to spend this income before we get it. But couldn't existing waggons be adapted to Lovell's specifications? A thing like that could be done locally. I could take it up with Mr. Keate."

"Over a period of a year, with bi-weekly hauls using two frigates, how much gross would a contract like that bring in?"

Tybalt had the answer in five seconds. "A hundred pounds a quarter, give or take a sovereign or two, Mr. Swann."

"Right. Then we'll invest the first half-year's income in double-springing and fitting compartments in half-a-dozen waggons, but, as you say, let it be done locally and at a cut price. Take the letters to Keate, put the problem to him, then write Morris at Keate's dictation. I'll make one condition. Our limit on adjustments mustn't exceed a hundred pounds."

They went on to discuss other matters; the demand of Lawrence, the master smith, for a new forge; Fraser's discharge of two dishonest carters, against whom he wished to press charges; the withholding of a quarter's rent for stables in Crescent South that were threatening to fall down, the loose ends of a web in which hundreds of waggons. twice as many horses, and an army of clerks, carters, smiths and saddlers were trapped. Much of it, by now, had become routine to him. He made his decisions quickly, lightly balanced on a see-saw of expenditure and income, short-term and long, seeing himself as a man liable to fall flat on his face at any moment yet relishing the never-ending challenge to his wits, judgement, nerve and initiative. Tybalt said, hovering at the threshold, "Well, that would seem to be all for today, sir. Will you be going north this week?" and Adam, making another off-the-cuff decision, said, "No, but don't ask me why. I planned to go today, at least as far as the Polygon and down through the Pickings to call in on Abbott at Salisbury, but I've just changed my mind. I've got a conviction we've turned the corner. I've no real grounds for thinking that, apart from Dockett's slogan, and this Royal Worcester contract, but it's in there, just the same," and he tapped his chest. "Do you ever pull certitude out of thin air. Tybalt?" and Tybalt said, respectfully, that he did not, preferring to base hopes and fears on the answers to sums in the master ledger.

He went out then and Adam, crossing to the window, watched him cross the yard to the waggonshed where he and his friend Keate would soon be immersed in the agreeable task of cheeseparing. He thought, 'Those two run on rails and I can understand men like Morris and Dockett getting impatient with them, but an undertaking as complex as ours needs a couple of sheet-anchors to hold it steady. The best turn I ever did myself was to sign on Keate and Tybalt at the start of it all.' In spite of a surge of optimism amounting almost to glee he did not feel like sitting still at a desk, and reassessing his chances of paying off Blunderstone and McSawney inside the time limit. His fancy continued to conjure with irrelevancies, the impact that lovable child of Avery's had had upon his household, the impersonal approach his wife had brought to the child she was about to bear, almost as though she was having it by proxy, the health of the old Colonel, now approaching his seventy-fifth birthday, but, above all, his absorbing theories concerning the segments of the English working-class, represented by his own work force. There was an answer here somewhere to the astounding lead the country had gained over all its Continental competitors in the last forty years, and he did not think it had to do with steadfastness on Continental battlefields but was buried somewhere in the seams where the nation's commercial instincts were mined. There were the Keates and the Tybalts, sober, plodding men, buttressed by moral purpose, and at the other end of the scale men like Tim Blubb, who saw any change as a flaw in the national character but who could still be coaxed into adapting, as Blubb had adapted once pride was restored to him. There were the Catesbys, slaves of another kind of morality that had nothing to do with the beatitudes but was the legacy of the Saxon peasant who had made up his mind to screw advantages from his Norman overlord, and dotted here and there, as though to give an added shape and colour to the social kaleidoscope, were young sparks like the ex-ensign Godsall, oddities like Hamlet Ratcliffe, men who walked alone like Bryn Lovell, arrant thrusters like his father-in-law, astute, ambitious men like Morris, and imponderables like Dockett, who looked like yokels but possessed something more than a yokel's brain. What the devil did all these men have in common apart from obstinacy? And what common denominator had enlisted them under his banner? For that matter, what was *he* doing at the head of them, when he might, on the proceeds of that necklace, have lived a life of ease and idleness?

The clock struck ten and he turned away from the window to scan his newspapers. The column headings told him what was happening in the world outside. Federal troops were mounting yet another offensive to bring the South to heel and nearer home Bismarck was rattling the Prussian sabre at the inoffensive Denmark over the provinces of Schleswig and Holstein. Palmerston, he suspected, despite a matching bluster, would do nothing about it, for the Court was against him, the Queen continuing to think of Germany as a pixied fairyland of scented woods and sugarloaf castles where she had once dallied with her adored Albert. Gladstone, who, at fifty-four, was beginning to look like the popular conception of Jehovah, was thundering out more theories of retrenchment. Yet another railway company had gone bankrupt, the twentieth this year. There was agitation among the Radicals for another franchise bill and the abolition of the rotten boroughs on the grounds that it was absurd for Cornwall to send as many representatives to Westminster as all London and Middlesex combined. He supposed he was involved in all this but was able, thank God, to take a detached view of it. His business was not with Danish provinces, rebel states, and rotten boroughs. It was with English counties, English products, English-bred horses and English-built waggons. He made a note or two from the market page of *The Times* and then turned to his memoranda pad, on which was written under yesterday's date, '*Edith. Australia? Wadsworth's hernia.*' It reminded him of two related matters. Could

477

he dissuade Edith Wadsworth from emigrating, as she had indicated last time they met, and, how long could her ageing father continue as general of the Crescents? He picked up his pen with satisfaction. It was always a pleasure to write to Edith but he had only scratched 'My Dear E . . .' when there was a knock at the door announcing the arrival of someone less timorous than Tybalt. He called, "Who is it?" and Sam Rawlinson, his father-in-law, marched into the room.

The leathery old rascal—Adam could never think of him in any other terms—looked very spry for a man in his late fifties. His broad, aggressive face was tanned the colour of a conker, and he seemed to have lost flesh in the last few months. He said, moderately pleased to see him, "You? I thought your capital was Manchester?" and Sam said heartily that it was, and would be recognised as such as soon as those damned Yankees stopped killing one another and got back to shipping cotton, after which he wrung his son-in-law's hand with an affability he never tried to conceal on the rare occasions they met. Adam seated him and grinned down at him. Notwithstanding the alienation of father and daughter he could never share Henrietta's acrimony having long since come to terms with Rawlinson and all his kind.

"I don't recall you showing up in London before," he said, pouring him a brandy, and Sam said that he never had, and what little he had seen of the place had not impressed him. "However," he went on, "Ah've come from somewhere that stinks worse nor river garbage! You're looking on a travelled man, lad. Ah've just stepped ashore from Egypt!"

If Sam had said Tibet Adam could not have been more surprised, and Sam enjoyed his astonishment. "Aye," he said, "Ah thowt that'd bowl thee over, but you're not the on'y one wi' gappy, and the guts to use it! My stocks ran dry last September, so what good would it have done to sit on bloody backside beside looms piping me eye over t'slump, same as all the other noodles? I said to myself, 'Sam Rawlinson, this is t'chance you been waitin' on! Find out why Georgia and the Carolinas have hogged monopoly o' trade and get the missis offen th' back for a spell.' I booked a passage out o' Liverpool and went to see the Pirry-mids." He paused, sucking in his florid cheeks. "Eeee, but there's a bloody waste o' manpower! A million men it took to put 'em there and now what are they good for? I'll tell thee. For catchpenny sideshows, same as they'd set up on Blackpool sands for the gawpers! Did *you* ever set eyes on 'em?"

"Never," said Adam, "but I'm far more interested in what you

478

found out about the cotton they grow there. I always heard it was far superior to American fibres."

"So it is," said Sam, "finest cotton to be had anywheres, but the damn fools raise it on nine-acre plots. By the time it gets to us it's too damned costly to spin. However, that's neither here nor there, for I saw something that'll likely make me another fortune before I'm planted out, and that'd be the third, lad. Is that bad for a bit of a lad who started out as a bale-breaker on ninepence a day?"

"It depends on how you make it," said Adam. "As I've told you times enough, I wouldn't care to go about it the way you did, and still do if the truth's known."

"Ah, you'll have heard from yon Catesby, no doubt," said Sam, but without rancour. "He'll land you in a reet mess before you're as old as me, for I'll tell you what *he's* been about during slump. Organising a teamsters' union, right on my patch, damn his impudence! Do you ever give a thought to what a thing like that could lead to?"

"I can't say as it keeps me awake," said Adam, smiling.

"Then it should, lad. Time'll come when all these tinpot unions'll make ruinous demands on their betters on the strength of withholding labour. I'll be in my grave then but you won't."

They had had this kind of argument before and there was no profit in it. They were so far apart in outlook that it was difficult, at least on Adam's part, to take the man seriously. He represented a generation that regarded a working man's guild as a secret society and if he had his way men like Catesby would have been shipped off to Botany Bay years ago, leaving their employers free to recruit on a work-or-starve ticket. He said, tolerantly, "Oh, come now, you didn't call in to warn me about a Lancashire revolution. Pay me the compliment of asking after your daughter and grandchildren. Don't you ever think of a damned thing but brass and cotton?"

"Not often," Sam said, unrepentantly, "but since Ah'm here how's she shaping?"

"Very well," Adam told him, "and as much of a slavedriver as her father since I cut down on her staff and called her to account. Incidentally, she'll be presenting me with our third any day now."

The news interested Sam. "She *will*? Three, in a little over five years? Well, you could ha' done better but you might ha' done a damn sight worse, lad. You don't lack good sense in that direction for it's the only way with 'em. If Ah'd ha' ketched my Hilda young enough

479

Ah wouldn't have had to take six months' holiday from her tongue!"

"So you haven't started a second family, Sam?"

"Nay," he said, "Ah get nowt from Hilda but impudence," and although he said it carelessly Adam detected a tinge of disappointment in his voice, at least enough to prompt him to say, "Why the devil don't you and Henrietta bury the hatchet? You'd enjoy meeting your grandchildren, and seeing her again, wouldn't you? Be damned to your pride, Sam. You haven't all that time left to indulge it."

Sam said, avoiding his eye, "Ah'm willing, if she is," and then, with a sincerity that Adam found appealing, "Look, lad, I'll show my hand and be damned to it. Ah were wrong about you, wrong as could be! You're all kinds of a fool in many respects but at least you've put yourself on the map, same as I did when I were your age, and I'll tell thee summat else. Folk speak well o' your concern in the Belt. You weren't so daft as I took you for when you started hauling vittles free for those soup-kitchens. Now tell me something in return. Did you have business in mind, or was it what I took it for at the time, pie-faced, Come-to-Jesus meddlin'?"

Adam, laughing, admitted it was a little of both. With waggons idle on account of the cotton famine he saw no harm in using them in a good cause.

"Eeee, but that about settles it!" Sam said. "We'll do business on the strength o' it, and it'll amount to zummat by the time they get that ditch finished, and I get a headstart over every other spinner. You'll have heard o' that canal they're about, no doubt?"

"The Suez? Well, naturally, who hasn't? But what the devil has it got to do with any haulage you head my way?"

Sam said, with the note of gravity he reserved for money talk, "More than you think, lad! Or any other man thinks, so far as I can tell by asking around. I've *seen* it. It's a bloody marvel! It'll make those Pirry-mids sing small I can tell you. One hundred and three miles long an' deep enough to take ships of any draught. T'passage to India'll be halved and have you ever thowt what that could mean to spinners? Even if they haven't bought shares in it, as I have?"

"You've put money into the Suez Canal Company? Good God, man, they say it'll be another ten years in the making. You'll be nearly seventy before a rowing boat sails through it, if one ever does!"

Sam regarded him sadly. "Eeee, and I took you for a lad wi' gumption! Listen here, they'll have that canal open four years from now and cotton'll come as quick as it does from Savannah and Charlestown, and a damned sight cheaper if you ask me, for India's ours, isn't it? We can keep the wholesale price steady and hold the Yankee market in check at t'same time. Then there's the export market that now has to trail around Africa. There's a fortune in it for anyone like me, a man who depends on raw cotton in and cotton goods out, and with a piece of that ditch in my britches pocket how can I go wrong? If I were your age I'd buy all the stock I could get while it was there to be bought. Shares'll rocket the moment the facts sink in but how many have had my gumption to go and see for themselves?"

It made sense to Adam, more sense perhaps than it would to someone who had not endured the tedium of a Cape voyage to India, but over-extended as he was at the moment, it was hopeless to think of investing in such a venture. He said, "I'm having to work hard to keep my head above water, Sam. A few months ago I thought I should have to contract and only now are things beginning to pick up. Besides, I'm a carrier not a financier. One man one trade is my motto. However, it doesn't take much brains to see you're on the right track if you mean to switch to Egyptian and Indian cotton and I take it you do."

"What choice has a man if he wants to keep his mills open?"

"That war won't last for ever. The South is about finished, I'd say."

"Mebbe it is," Sam said, "but you can add another two years before the plantations are back in production. And there's another aspect that nobody but me seems to have thought on."

"What's that?"

"For generations the South has been running on slave labour. When they get going again they'll have to pay hands, same as anyone else. What'll that do to the wholesale price of every bale set ashore at Liverpool? Nay, lad, from here on I buy in our own market. That's why I'm the only spinner in the Belt opening up new premises."

"You're opening a new mill? With things at a standstill up there?"

"Aye, that I am," Sam said, "for did you never hear what that fellow Rothschild said about buying on a falling market? Well, that's what I've done. I telegraphed from Gibraltar a fortnight since and bought a five-acre plot at Rainford, midway between the Liverpool-Manchester and the Liverpool-Bury railways. Land's fair given way up there right now, and bricks'n mortar too, so I got it for the price of a hen-run. It'll be ready in time for my first Egyptian shipload round about midsummer. That's when I thowt o' thee and all those waggons o' yours plying on charity."

He crossed to the wall map representing the Polygon. It was interesting, Adam thought, how, notwithstanding the gulf between them, they could always find common ground in the no-man's-land of commercial exploitation. Sam seemed just as much at home here as in his lean-to office under the loading ramps of a mill, pointing to the thin triangle slanting north-east out of Liverpool and bounded by the two railways he had mentioned. Among the string of villages along roads connecting St. Helens with the Mersey Estuary was one called Rainford. "Right here it'll be. Specialising in high quality cloth, and likely to pay for itself in a twelvemonth. You can haul every bale if we can come to terms, loading at dockside and cutting out bloody railroad. That'll save me time and put money in your pocket. A fleet of three-horse flats it'll mean but mind, I'll have first call on 'em, come boom or slump, wet season or dry."

They got down to detail and Sam made the acquaintance of Frankenstein, for whom he conceived an instant respect. When Adam admitted that he had invented the ready-reckoner their wary relationship entered into a new dimension. "Eeee, lad, but tha've brains," Sam said, admiringly, fumbling with the leaves of the machine and coaxing from it the mileage from Liverpool docks to his new mill-site, at Rainford. "God alone knows how far Ah coulder travelled with a lad like thee to follow me," and then, hoisting his grey bushy brows, "Did tha mean what tha' said a while back? Will that lass o' mine be civil to me if you put in a word, for I'll own I've a rare fancy to see the brats. It's a fine thing for a man to have sons to inherit something he carved from nowt."

"Stay on in London a day or two and I'll stage-manage a reconciliation," Adam promised, "but as to sons to follow me, I don't bank on that. Henrietta is determined to make gentlemen of them and see them in uniform before the middleaged spread slows her down," but Sam said, with a shocked expression, "Nay, lad, but you'll have to beat that dam' nonsense out of her! I'll give you a hand if need be."

"You'll keep a very civil tongue in your head if you want me to patch things up," Adam told him, and they went down into the yard where he took his father-in-law on a conducted tour and afterwards lunched him expensively at the 'George'.

482

Mellowness stole upon him throughout the afternoon as he sat working on the drafts of the contracts for the clerks to copy in time for the evening post. The heatless sun dropped away behind the dome of St. Paul's and mists began to drift upriver like a storming party assembling for a night attack on the city. But the day still held surprises.

The first arrived in the form of an express letter from the west, where Hamlet Ratcliffe, lion-catcher extraordinary, had landed an unexpectedly large fish in the person of another westcountry eccentric, none other than Lord Augustus Courtenay-Hopgood, whose scurrilous condemnation of the railways had made him a national figure twenty years before.

It seemed that once again Hamlet had turned local circumstances to good account. Lord Augustus, a fanatical fox-hunter who maintained numerous packs and country-seats between Exe and Tamar, had already passed into legend, and was now a figure of fun in a nation that had come to take the gridiron for granted. Adam could recall a time when Courtenay-Hopgood's peers, equally devoted to the cult of the horse, had sneered at its challenger, but that was long ago, before men like Aaron Walker had poured molten gold through the chinks in their armour and bought off all but the diehards like Lord Augustus, who still opposed every railway bill that came before the Lords. Now, it seemed, Lord Augustus had taken a fancy to concentrate his packs in the hilly, wooded country behind Barnstaple Bay, not very far (as a hunted fox might run) from the spot where the lion Dante was induced to surrender, making Hamlet Ratcliffe's chubby features almost as famous as those of Courtenay-Hopgood. There were no railways within miles of the new seat—Lord Augustus had made certain of that. Furnishings, Hamlet wrote, were to be drawn from hunting lodges dotted about the two counties, plus sufficient necessities from his main seat in East Devon to keep every waggon in the Western Wedge busy for a month. Hamlet added, as a postscript, that money was no object, Lord Augustus being one of the wealthiest landowners in the country. His agent had given Swann-on-Wheels carte blanche, so long as the firm undertook to have everything in place before the cubbing season opened.

It was as well he had written in detail, giving Adam an inkling of the magnitude of the task, for it was clear that Hamlet loved a lord and had not deigned to consider the needs of his regular customers. Adam said, after ringing for Tybalt, "I don't question it's an order worth having, and it'll keep Ratcliffe out of mischief until the leaves fall, but what about his farm runs? They're his bread and butter and I won't sacrifice them for that old fool's jam. How many frigates has Ratcliffe got down there?"

Tybalt, consulting Frankenstein, said four, adding that the depot manager would probably resort to men-o'-war, but here was an occasion where Adam, considering the problem in the general and dismissing the particular, was prepared to ride roughshod over his clerk. "Good God, man, you can't shift a nobleman's French furniture and bric-a-brac across country on open waggons," he said, "notwithstanding acres of tarpaulin. Down there it rains six days out of seven and, moreover, Ratcliffe's men-o'-war are old and springless. How would it look if the goods were sodden, or shaken to pieces by the time they arrived at his new place? No, my friend, we'll have to shunt half-a-dozen frigates down from the Southern Square, and replace them from here. According to my recollection Abbott has nine based on Salisbury and they won't all be in daily use at this time of year."

"Mr. Abbott won't like that at all," said Tybalt, but Adam said Abbott would have to lump it. The Southern Square manager was an improviser but Ratcliffe had hooked a big fish and it was the business of Headquarters to make sure he landed it.

Twilight stole into the turret while they juggled with teams, vehicles and mileages over the roads Ratcliffe's carters were likely to use in hauls across Devon uplands and along marshy river-bottoms, and it was dark before they found satisfactory answers to the complicated sums. Then Tybalt crept away, clutching a sheaf of instructions that would, Adam supposed, keep the conscientious chap busy far into the night. He said, as the clerk withdrew, "Take a cab home, Tybalt, and do your work at your fireside, after supper. It's damned cold in that counting-house when everyone has gone. Charge the cab to the petty cash. Even you'll agree we can afford it today."

Tybalt said, hovering, "Thank you, sir. Will you be making a night of it?", but Adam said he would not, having decided to spend the night at home and postpone the northern trip until the current problems were settled in detail.

There were one or two items that needed his attention before the last post went out, and he lit the lamp and one of his favourite Burmese cheroots, shooting his long legs under the desk and blowing smoke rings towards the vaulted ceiling. Slowly the clatter of the yard subsided as draymen came and went and Keate's staff walked the horses to their stables. Lights twinkled across the city beyond the river, and in the violet dusk he saw the Conqueror's towers dissolve. He thought, pleasantly, 'What a day! I had a feeling we were turning the corner when I opened Dockett's letter but that was hours ago. Now we've not only turned it but been kicked round it and are running downhill at a pace that's making Tybalt's head spin! Dockett's slogan and removal bookings, Morris's Royal Worcester contract, Sam Rawlinson's dock-to-mill, all-the-year-round order in the Polygon, and now Ratcliffe having to borrow frigates from his next-door neighbour before putting his name to the best contract we've ever screwed out of his patch! If we go on like this we shall be clear of debt by September. One more heave and I could be owner of "Tryst" into the bargain!'

He got his bonus heave. Footsteps echoed on the staircase and he called, in response to a light knock, "Come in, whoever you are. This is Liberty Hall today!" and as the door opened he smelled lavender and looked into the eyes of the woman to whom he had been trying to write a letter all day.

He jumped up, crushing the butt of his cheroot into a saucer and exclaiming, "My God! Now it's *you*, Edith!", and he was so pleased to see her that he did not stop to reflect that she might be here to say good-bye before taking ship from Tilbury for Australia but lunged round the end of the desk, threw his arms round her and kissed her on both cheeks and finally on the lips.

She said, gaily, "Thank you, sir, but you smell of tobacco!" and he said, holding her at arms length, "And you of lavender, and the bonnier for it!" There was, he noted, a latent sparkle about her as though, for some deep-seated reason, she was moderately pleased with him and herself. She said, "As to the lavender, it's my Sunday clothes. I don't go to church often enough and they lay about in closets. However, I didn't come here to discuss clothes."

He said, anxiously, "You're not on your way to join a ship? How could you be? Your father's still in the Infirmary, isn't he?"

"Yes," she said, "and doing well. He'll be home in a day or so, and back at work after a fortnight's convalescence. No, Adam, there's no ship and my father doesn't even know I'm in London, for what I've been about is a hole-and-corner business and I'm not sure he'd approve. He might even regard it as treacherous, for I set to work on his cronies in his absence. Quite shamelessly, I might add."

Her gaiety kept bubbling through and she peeled off her gloves with what he could only regard as a debonair flourish. "Being greeted in that way," she went on, "has unsettled my thoughts and that's a pity for they were very well organised when I entered the yard. Tybalt and Keate know I'm here, by the way, so please behave for we aren't in Wharfedale now."

"You're here on business? *My* business?"

"Very much so." She looked around. "A convent bell-tower may be a romantic place to work but it's too Spartan for women lieutenants. You don't even have a fire."

"Oh, I never feel the cold," he said, "I've never quite shed the relief of escaping from under that steamy Bengal heat. Suppose we go somewhere more comfortable? Down to the 'George', where I could buy you tea and hot muffins?"

"I had tea when I left the train and I've not much time, for I mean to catch the seven-ten back to Peterborough. Why Peterborough? Because I'm established there. Permanently I hope but I can't be sure. It depends on you, I suppose."

"You're talking riddles and that means you're concealing something." An unpleasant thought struck him. "You're not married, are you?", and she laughed and said, with the same note of gaiety, "What if I were? What's it to you?"

"I can tell you that," he said, catching her mood, "I'd be jealous and any blessing you extracted from me would be a grudging one!"

Her eyes danced and he began to sense that the threat of Australia was receding.

"You really are a bit of a Turk, Adam, and it isn't very flattering, even though I've never made much secret of my availability as second fiddle. However, I'll not let myself be sidetracked for, as I said, I haven't the time. I mean to catch that train and make sure you catch yours. Has that child of yours arrived yet?"

"Any day now, and I've just had Henrietta's father here. He's buying up an Egyptian cotton crop for a new mill he's opened in the Polygon and we've landed the haulage contract from dock to loom."

"That's very encouraging," she said. "How is business generally?"

"If you had asked me yesterday I should have said middling but right now it's booming. We've had the best day I can ever remember," and he told her briefly of Dockett's success, Morris's new contract,

Ratcliffe's deal with Lord Augustus and Sam's plans in Rainford.

"Well," she said, "that cuts me down to size. I was hoping you were down in the dumps because I've got something in my reticule that might be the means of getting Swann-on-Wheels out of debt by Christmas. Now it seems, I'm only the fairy on top of the cake."

She opened her bag and took out a folded tracing, smoothing it out on his desk. He recognised it as a map of the Crescents and the northern half of The Bonus, including most of Suffolk, scored by the sinuous 'Y' of the Great Northern, where it ran north to Peterborough and forked, the eastern branch slicing her territory, the western arm taking a westerly course to Doncaster. To the right, a complicated criss-cross of lines, were the arteries and spurs of the Eastern Counties, with its main route stretching from Peterborough to the sea at Lowestoft. A red-pencilled oval ringed the entire network. He said, motioning her to his swivel chair, "What the devil have you been up to while your father was in the Infirmary?"

"You remember that railway contact he mentioned at the conference in December, a nice little man called Brockworth? Well, he's the goods manager for the Eastern Counties, based at Cambridge and often in our part of the world. He's a widower, luckily, with two young children and I ... well, let's say I was able to do him a very good turn. His sister, who keeps house for him, fell sick, so I had the children to stay over the Christmas. It was just before father went into the hospital to have his hernia seen to."

"What's that to do with a shift of base to Peterborough? Unless you intend to take on his children permanently?"

"Oh, he's already suggested that," she said, laughing, "but I politely declined. The children are nice enough, a bright boy we might employ in a year or two, and a little girl called Angela, but Brockworth himself is no catch, not even for a girl like me. He earns a good wage and has money in the bank I'm told, but he's fifty-plus and has a wall eye. You'll have to believe I didn't strike that kind of a bargain with him."

"What kind?"

She took a deep breath, so that for a moment he saw her not as a handsome woman but a vivacious schoolgirl, giddy with enthusiasm for a fad or fashion that pushed everything else out of mind.

"It's astounding what a volume of goods traffic they handle," she said. "Far more, proportionately, than the bigger companies that look on goods traffic as small beer compared with fare-paying passengers. Maybe it's the comparative isolation of their territory, with so many scattered communities. Scattered, mind you, but settled and prosperous, quite unlike the places Ratcliffe and Lovell operate in the West and the Mountain Square. East Anglia is thickly populated, and its industries, although small, are very diverse. But you'd know that."

"I know it. Go on about the Eastern Counties."

"They're not a particularly wealthy company and sometimes I get the impression they'll be squeezed out in the end. They can't afford to invest in more spurlines, like the Great Western and the L. & N.W., and they've gone about as far as they can with the capital at their disposal. You remember a majority of depot managers approved that idea we had of exploiting the rivalry between the companies? Well, I went one better than that. I told Brockworth we could offer him a scheme to cover every town, village and hamlet east of Peterborough to Norwich and beyond, and even down into Vicary's territory in The Bonus. With a difference, however, and an important one. In this case they transport the goods over their lines to a dozen or more dispersal points *but they do it in our sacks, which are sealed on loading.* At each depot we offload them and deliver the rest of the distance in pinnaces."

"Why in pinnaces?" He had forgotten his personal involvement with her, forgotten indeed that she was a woman at all for this was a new kind of challenge and his imagination took fire. He might have been tackling a logistical problem with Tybalt or her father.

"Because the Eastern Counties handle very few heavy goods," she said. "It's all parcels weighing anything between ten to twenty pounds consigned to places like village stores and private addresses, farms and manufactories employing under a dozen hands. Small stuff granted, but an enormous volume of it, and the fact that they make the main haul means we can cut costs to the bone and make it up on turnover. I've even worked out test figures. If we deliver a thousand parcels a month, at an average weight of ten pounds apiece, we could show a net profit of threepence a pound on everything under a twenty-mile haul and more if the haul is not above five miles. Pinnaces are half as cheap to run as frigates and only a third as costly as a man-o'-war. They're faster, too, and we could build on our reputation for speed. We should need a fleet, of course, but outside London you don't use your small vans much. Most of them in the territories are doing odd-job work that can't show you a profit of a penny a pound. I could multiply that by three and keep at least thirty vans in day-to-day use all over Suffolk, Norfolk and Lincolnshire. That's not all, either. If it paid off we could employ the same tactics with bigger lines all over the country, using the Eastern Counties as a pilot scheme. A study of the annual turnover would give us all the information we need to make every railway in the country a sound proposition on the sub-contract basis. You might ask, since they already have the traffic, why they should share it with us but the answer is so simple I wonder we've never hit on it before. The bulk of lightweight traffic carried over the rail in this country is carried at a loss. Some of their sacks and crates go half-empty, except at Christmastime. On the figures I squeezed out of Brockworth on the strength of a pigeon pie I baked him, it never has paid a railway to haul small parcels from door to door. You'll find most companies ready to subcontract, providing you cut them in on the profits. You can't absorb all this at once Adam, it's too complex and will need time and thought. That's why I wrote a detailed report, summarising the information I coaxed out of Brockworth."

She opened her reticule again and produced a little black book. He flicked through the pages, finding them covered with her handwriting and close columns of figures. Here was the answer to most of the doubts and queries he was likely to raise, methodically indexed and cross-referenced, in a style that would have earned the unhesitating approval of Tybalt.

He said, "You're right, Edith. It would need thought and very careful calculation before we were in a position to offer quotations but the idea itself doesn't need a moment's thought. You've done most of the thinking and I don't have to tell you what this could mean if it comes up to expectations, yours or mine. It's the biggest single advance we've ever made, or are likely to make, and I'd be a fool not to see that at once and give you credit for it. Now let's consider the personal element. Do you think I could go forward with this without making some kind of recompense? This map, this report you've compiled must have represented weeks of hard grind on your part, and it doesn't fit in with what you hinted about emigrating the last time you wrote. What's happened in the interval? I have to know that because, if I go forward with the scheme, you would have to be part of it. The most important part."

For the first time since she had slipped into the room some of her composure left her. Then, looking at him frankly, she said, "Nothing very complicated. I suppose I saw myself more clearly than I have in a long time and I didn't like what I saw, a woman racing down the years to middle-age and living off a diet of self-pity and regrets.

First Matt, drowned at sea, then you, married to a woman who loves you well enough to change into the person you need."

"Just what am I to make of that?"

She stood up, brushing shreds of tobacco from the sleeves of her dress where her arms had rested on his desk. "I made up my mind once and for all about you the last time I was here. I've been unlucky myself but that doesn't give me the right to steal some other woman's happiness. I've always despised weaklings, men and women, and I was fast becoming one myself, incapable of standing on my own feet and looking the world in the eye." She paused. "You want the whole truth? Very well, here it is. I've gone through a bad time since you came to me at Richmond last summer. I knew then there would never be anyone else but you and for a time, and I don't mind admitting this, I half made up my mind to get you if I could. I lay awake thinking of little else right up to the time of that conference, and even afterwards. It wasn't fear of scandal that held me back but the difference in you since you put your foot down at home and kept it down. You were still growing, and who was I to check that for purely selfish reasons? I suppose some people would call that conscience but, believe me, it wasn't. Women don't have consciences about men they covet and besides, I'm not a religious person, and I don't even believe in an after-life. It was something more earthy, a sense of fair play if you like, or my own long-term interests and yours. I was quite serious about emigrating and went right ahead with my plans. Then, one night, I found myself looking in the mirror saying, 'Stand up, for God's sake! *Be* someone in your own right. Running away to Australia won't help for over there, a man's country if ever there was one, you won't even get a chance to express yourself, as you can right here on your own doorstep.' I went downstairs in my nightdress, stoked up the stove and burned those emigration papers. You want to hear more?"

"Every word."

"Well, then, the next morning I went out after Brockworth and from there on it was easy, or easier every day. I was doing something, using my brains, being somebody with a job on hand."

"You always had a job on hand, Edith."

"A makeshift one, that didn't require anything more than managing a team and keeping an eye on a few beer-swilling waggoners. This was different. This was creative. I suppose that's why I understand you better than anyone in the network. I don't know what's in your mind but I'll tell you what's in mine. Father is about finished.

490

He's still good for work but only work at a desk, and that isn't good enough in our kind of business. If you adopt that scheme make me boss of all the Crescents and you'll never have cause to regret it. It isn't a woman's rôle, maybe, but I'm not a fashionable woman and never was. My brain is as good as any man's on your list and a lot better than some—Ratcliffe's for instance, and Vicary's, down in The Bonus. I'd get a different kind of fulfilment out of that and you'd profit by it. But perhaps that's another thing you'd like to think on."

"No," he said, sharply, "not for a second. I would have done that much for you before you came to me with this scheme. I never had any doubts about your ability or judgement or initiative. I've never heard a word out of you that I didn't recognise as good sense, and as for your loyalty to me and to all of us in the network, that was never in question, not even when you talked about turning your back on us."

"Then it's done? I take over from my father and I leave here with full authority over Goodbody and Horncastle in the Crescents?"

"Yes," he said, "overall manager of all three territories, back-dated from the first of the year on your father's salary, plus a five per cent bonus on turnover."

"It's generous," she said, "but I can justify it."

There was no more to be said. They went down into the yard and out into Tooley Street, where he found her a growler to take them over to King's Cross. In the semi-darkness of the cab he held her hand and she let him, saying little as they trotted through trailers of river mist. Each had a sense of having arrived at a new point of departure in their relationship and when they parted, after he changed her second-class ticket for a first-class with a small joke about her new managerial status, it gave him the greatest satisfaction to see that the strain and uncertainty that had attended all their other partings was no longer there. He said, taking her hand, peeling down the glove and raising it to his lips, "Pay no attention to what I said about grudging you a good husband, Edith. I never met a woman who deserved one more. Whatever happens from here on you can count on me," and she said, with a smile, "I always could, Adam. In that way I imagine I've been luckier than most women. I've crossed paths with two men who didn't have to resort to pomposity and whiskers to prove their masculinity. Poor Matt drowned but you'll swim on. Away into the next century I wouldn't wonder."

The guard's whistle shrilled and the long train gave its first, convulsive jerk. He stood watching her face until it was swallowed up by

491

the February murk, a small, pale triangle that somehow reminded him of Avery's in its assertiveness and singularity. Then, like a man who has dined well and is conscious of a spring in his limbs, he walked with long strides to the cab rank and made his way to his own terminus.

*   *   *

He could see that something tumultuous was afoot the moment the gig passed the last of the leafless copper beeches. The entire frontage of the house was lit up, as though for a celebration, and the old Colonel, muffled to the eyebrows, met him in the yard, as excited as a schoolboy greeting a companion at the start of a new term. "It's a boy!" he cried, exultantly, "Lively as a cricket and caught the whole damn lot of of 'em on the hop! It was over by late afternoon and the gel is splendid!"

He said, catching his breath, "That about crowns a remarkable day but you oughtn't to be out here with your chest. Let's hurry in and mix you a hot toddy!"

"I've already had three," the old Colonel said, chuckling, and Adam thought the old fellow could have shown no more jubilance had he been the father.

Inside all was controlled bustle. He went softly upstairs and peeped at Henrietta. She looked, he thought, radiant, with a clear, blooming skin and her copper hair spread across the pillow in delightful disorder. Nurse Hoxton told him she had a moderately easy time of it, and had taken her broth and toast before going to sleep. He went along the corridor and looked down at the gurgling, winking George and it was then that the sense of purpose that had dominated the last twelve hours crystallised in an impression of cresting a steep hill and looking down on the prospect below. It had shape and a promise that enfolded him and his, insuring them all against the future. He thought too of Edith, speeding through the darkness towards her private destiny and somehow, he could not have said why, it all converged on that saucy little bundle winking up at him from the cot. He went down again and warmed his hands at the fire. Outside the wind got up, soughing through the bare branches of the beeches and stirring Henrietta's curtains, part of the material ordered for a party that was never held because an unknown waif had died in a chimney flue. He thought, 'Well, that's all behind us now and we're set fair, I suppose, the whole lot of us. It'll be up to me to keep on course.' A little over six years

492

had passed since he opened his eyes on the littered field behind Jhansi and seen what he thought of as a half-circle of cobra's eyes that were not cobra's eyes but the genesis of everything he had achieved, and looked to achieve in the years ahead. He thought briefly of Avery, and of Avery's child down at Folkestone, of Henrietta asleep upstairs relieved, he supposed, of the unspoken pledge of continuity she had made him that night at the 'George' inn. The identification of the child's name with the place where he had been conceived made him smile, a rather vain, self-satisfied smile of proprietorship over a higgledy-piggledy assortment of men and teams and waggons and the generous body of the woman sleeping upstairs who had somehow, in these last few months, found a new identity, much as he had done when he came crashing down at Jhansi and fallen on the means to adopt it. Then, yawning, he was conscious of the demands of the day and climbed slowly upstairs, too tired to eat the supper laid for him but more composed in his mind than he had ever been, at any time in his life.

4

Advance on Most Fronts

THERE is a certain affinity between the growth of a commercial enterprise and the tactics a trained athlete brings to a long-distance event upon which reputation and prize-money are staked.

It was in these terms, or something like them, that Adam Swann gauged the strength of the tide that turned so definitely in his favour on St. Valentine's Day, 1864, seeing himself as a marathon runner nearing the halfway mark, with a prospect of not merely holding on but finishing well ahead of his rivals.

By the late spring of 1864 Swann-on-Wheels had, as it were, caught its second wind, and was settling down to a steady, mile-consuming pace, aware of the hazards of the future but fortified by the achievements of the past. The first, spirited attack of the *sortie torrentielle* had all but spent itself, its ripples spreading out across England and Wales, there to be absorbed in any number of minor forays, but while this was taking place new energy was being generated at headquarters, where the hard-won gains of farflung storming parties were being assessed in ledgers and consolidated on staff maps, so that by midsummer the enterprise was ripe for a second offensive to be mounted on a larger scale than its predecessor. *Sortie torrentielle* had, in effect, transformed itself into an advance on all fronts.

The advance, like any successful breakthrough, was uneven. Here and there, across a front that embraced all England, progress could be measured in yards, while in other sectors the breakthrough yielded sizable territorial gains and a rich haul of booty. Then, for one reason or another, a promising local advance would falter, to be taken up elsewhere, so that Adam, studying his wall maps in his belfry, and feeding them with Tybalt's returns and information filtered to him through the post, could never be quite sure where progress would continue, or where reserves were most urgently needed. For the first time in his life he was able to generate sympathy for a general like poor Lord Raglan, whom he had once written off as

494

a hopeless dolt. It was not so easy, he decided, to make wise, overall decisions on the basis of a dozen conflicting reports, or to make accurate allowance for a time-lag that sometimes tricked him into despatching reserve teams to sectors that no longer needed them, thus depriving those that did. Freakish accidents, and equally freakish weather, often had an important bearing on a situation, and neither Frankenstein nor his experience could warn him in advance of the breaking strain of a worn axle in Cumberland, or an unseasonal downpour that turned a Dorset road into a morass overnight. By and large, however, he made few serious mistakes and even managed to learn something from those errors he did commit. By that summer, when the business was on an even keel again, he had learned how to use philosophy as a recoil and also to rely less upon judgement (his own and his adjutants') than upon luck. One lesson he learned well. Of all the apparatus needed to haul goods from one end of the country to the other the least predictable was human. By June, 1864, he was incapable of being surprised by those who manned his picquet-lines and sapheads from Berwick to Brixham, from Cockermouth to Canterbury. Dockett, who looked and spoke like an overgrown shepherd lad, had cornered the house-removal market in his territory with a slogan and in a sense they were all Docketts. One never knew what would emerge from any one of them.

* * *

Hamlet Ratcliffe, enlarging his hold upon the Western Wedge, had all but accomplished Lord Courtenay-Hopgood's migration to the edge of the Exmoor plateau but the effort of co-ordinating the exodus, without disrupting his bread-and-butter runs, had exhausted him. When the last of his borrowed frigates had trundled up the Exe Valley to discharge its load in the clamorous courtyard of Milord's new headquarters above Simonsbath, Hamlet was a spent man. In three months, the period it took him to shift Milord's chattels over miles of execrable farm tracks, he lost more than a stone in weight. His comfortable paunch had shrunk to three folds of slack flesh that had to be held in by a leather belt, an item Hamlet had never used when the waistband of his breeches was taut, whereas his few grey hairs, that had been regularly plucked by his doting wife Augusta, were now so numerous that it was as well to leave them be for fear his scalp would begin to show.

All through May and June, when the great exodus was building to its climax, Augusta worried herself sick about Hamlet. She had never seen him so nervously extended, not even when terror of dismissal had driven him to catch a runaway lion, and her pitiful appeals to " 'ase off a particle, midear" only made him irritable, so that at last he rounded on her bellowing, "Dornee talk so bliddy daft, Gussie! 'Ase off, you zay, time an' again! But how can I, when I'm zittin yer on me arse all day, trying to pour zix foaming quarts into zix pint pots without spilling the bliddy lot?" She subsided at that, of course, but she went on worrying, neglecting her housework to keep a close watch on him, and surreptitiously dissolving malted-milk tablets into his nightcap cider as well as burying Iron Jelloids, three at a time, in the slice of walnut cake he always ate with his morning cocoa. They must have benefited him in some way for at least he survived and on the final day of June, when the last empty frigate returned to the Southern Square, she crept into his office to find him smiling in his sleep and looking, she thought, like the child she had never given him. She stood looking down at him suffused with tenderness, reminding herself for the thousandth time how fortunate she had been to be chosen by such a genius from all the maids in Devon, and as she gazed it came into her mind that someone should do something for *him* in return for all he did for others. What he desperately needed, she thought, was to be taken out of himself, to be whisked away from all this clatter and excitement and bustle, and allowed to vegetate and grow his paunch again, and it was then she decided that, whether he liked it or not, he would take a holiday before another rapacious ogre appeared to sow more grey hairs over his ears.

It was not often Augusta Ratcliffe made an independent decision but when she did it took a great deal of persuasion on the part of others to alter it. And so it was on this occasion, when Hamlet, refreshed by his nap, appeared for his midday meal long before it was ready. He said, when she proposed the holiday, "Tidden possible, midear. Us've zeen the last of His Lordship, thank Christ, but now us is faaced wi' the job of unscrambling the eggs and getting all the routine runs back on schedule. And a main tiresome job it'll prove, dornee maake no mistake about that!"

She said, with an asperity that startled, "I daresay t'will, Hamlet. But *you* worn be about it. For one thing us dorn keep dogs to bark ourselves, do us? And for another, you worn be on tap, nor me neither!" Her assertiveness puzzled him so much that he decided to humour her, saying, genially, "What was 'ee thinking on, mother? A foo days in Dawlish? Or a week wi' the quality at Budleigh Salterton, while the weather holds?", and Augusta said she wasn't thinking of anything of the kind, for at both places he would be within close range of the stables and would, as like as not, be recalled to unravel some other tangle. "Us'll tak' one of they pinnaces an' move off, gipsy-like," she announced. "You need the change, midear, an' youm 'aving it, for that way us'll zee places us baint never zet eyes on."

It was not unpleasing to hear her lay down the law in this way, so long as she did it on his behalf. As always, he looked to her for enlargement and notion of the pair of them driving into the sunset attracted him for he was, at base, an idler by preference, and had often yearned to visit places to which he dispatched goods within his territory. He said, approvingly, "Now that baint a bad idea at all, Gussie! I'll put me mind to it, zoon as I've got some o' that apple pie down me!"

She had the good sense not to press the point, having learned in twenty-five years of marriage that he preferred to think of himself as the originator of an idea and never experienced difficulty in returning it to its source in the form of an inspiration. And so it proved for that same night, when she was struggling with her corsets, and he was lying flat on his back contemplating the ceiling, he said, suddenly: "I've a fancy to take 'ee to Plymouth, midear, to zee that bliddy gurt battleship that's put in there. Tis an ironclad, the virst they laid down, but why 'er dorn zink like a stone is more than I can zay. Would 'ee like that?"

"Why, for zure I would, 'Amlet," she said, but then, artfully, "zo long as us travels by the coast road, for I dorn fancy crossin Dartymoor, an' passing by that gurt prison. Chock full o' rogues, tis, or zo they tell me, and they'm alwus up to some caper. Us'll go by way o' Dawlish, Teignmouth, Torquay and Dartmouth-ferry. Us can afford it, can't us?"

He chose to accept this as a slight on his qualification as a provider and sat up, giving her a stern look. "Gordamme, o' course we can afford it! We got the bonus commin', baint us? *Afford it?* Why, us'll put up at the best inns all the way down, and maake it a round trip while we'm at it. We'll zee Plymouth, cut across to Bood with a fresh team, move on up to Ilfracombe an' Barum, and then home down the valleys, where I c'n show 'ee where I caught that lion." His imagination took fire as he went on, "Dam' it, it worn cost us a penny piece. I can write it off as a Western Wedge survey, an' get London to foot the bed an' board bills. What do 'ee zay to that, midear?"

She disposed of her corsets just in time to set the seal on his genius with an embrace. "What do I alwus zay, 'Amlet? Youm one in a millyon, and there tis then!"

They set out in the newest light van, harnessed to two of the best pair of draught horses in the stable, for he reasoned that one horse could not be expected to tackle some of the gradients they would meet on their journey. They averaged about fifteen miles a day, winding their way slowly along dusty country roads gay with wildflowers and towards evening, having picnicked en route, they put up at one or other of the old coaching inns that had survived in great numbers down here, despite the blight laid upon hostelries by the Great Western.

She had expected a leisurely progression from stage to stage and looked for nothing more, but she had forgotten his erudition, and how closely he had been involved with all the communities they encountered. He knew the names and singularities of every village, their basic industries, and the distance separating them down to the last furlong, and on the fourth day, when they joined a party of sightseers to inspect *Warrior*, the first British ironclad, he not only astonished her with his store of information concerning the vessel but attracted to himself a party of hangers-on, who seemed to accept him as the official guide engaged by the Navy.

It was this incident that gave her another idea that was duly fed to him, masticated, and regurgitated as an inspiration. As they were ambling north across the peninsula, on the first leg of their return journey, she said, pensively, "Lookit yer, 'Amlet. Seein' as 'ow zo many folk come to the zeaside zince the railroad was laid, why dornee use some o' they ole waggons o' yours to taake 'em around at zo much a mile? Woulden it pay 'ee through the holiday-season? Woulden they *zee* more than they would on Shank's?"

His answer was noncommittal at the time but when they had entered Bude, and were inspecting the wreck of a steamer that had gone ashore in Widemouth Bay and was the season's attraction, circumstances conspired to put a practical polish on the notion. The wreck was some way out of town and the leader of the bedraggled Sunday School outing, caught in a heavy shower, offered Hamlet sixpence per head to convey them back to Bude before they all caught cold. In the drive along the coast towards Ilfracombe Hamlet was very thoughtful, and remained so, even when they were heading over the western spur of Exmoor towards the scene of his lion-catching exploit. He reined a few miles short of the South Molton farm where he had been born, surveying the rolling landscape on his left, "Lookit there, Gussie," he said, with the irradicable pride of the westcountryman in the hills of home, "dorn it maake 'ee wonder why volks who once zeed it dorn bide yer till the'm carried away veet virst?" and when Gussie reminded him that they themselves had exiled themselves after learning that gold pieces were to be gathered on the streets of London, he said, "Arr, and us come posting backalong the minnut us zeed what a bliddy ole lie it was, didden us?" It was at this point, possibly, that the twin trains of thought, set in motion by Augusta's comment and the Bude Sunday School Superintendent's dilemma, struck fire. "*Brakes!*" he exclaimed, "*that's* what us'll use! *Brakes!* Four 'orse if need be, wi' knife-edge zeatin'! Damme, there's no knowing how much we could take in between June and September, when all they bliddy townees descends on us! Becky Valls, Haytor Rocks, Widdicombe-in-the-Moor, Kent's Cavern. *Think* on it, midear. A hundred an' one places to gawp at and no means o' getting there be rail. '*Zee Devon on Wheels*'. That yokel Dockett baint the on'y one who can think up slogans. I'll put young Tapscott to work adapting one o' they old flats we don't get no call for this time o' year."

He saw it all in terms of a succession of hayrides, of the kind that he and his brothers had enjoyed in the days before the railway had come snorting down the river bottoms, and it was in these terms that he put it forward, a little diffidently, promising as a sideline but nothing more. It was Adam, two hundred miles to the east, who grasped the full significance of the idea on the instant, who saw the means of linking it to the modish cult of the seaside holiday, ushered in by the railways. For whereas Hamlet Ratcliffe thought of an excursionist as a purely local phenomenon Adam recognised his national implications at a glance. Having written Hamlet a congratulatory letter, and doubled the bonus due in respect of the Courtenay-Hopgood house removal, he circulated a memo to every base manager whose territory embraced a spa, a ruin, or a seaside resort. Like most of his directives it was brief and factual, reading, '*For General Circulation and Comment Within Seven Days*. It is expected that heavy vehicles will soon be in use in the Western Wedge during summer months as sightseeing conveyances, carrying day excursionists to places of interest. Information required for possible extension of this use of idle waggons in suitable areas is summarised below, viz:

1. Do you consider it a practical proposition in your territory?

499

2. Could available vehicles be adapted on the spot to purpose defined, i.e. fitted with roll-back canopy and back-to-back seat-accommodation?
3. Please supply short list of popular landmarks (i.e. castles, abbeys, beauty spots, etc.) *within an easy day's haul of base,* say 20-mile maximum there and back.
4. Have you on present staff a waggoner able to act as local guide in addition to driving?
5. General comments, if any . . .'

A copy of this directive ultimately found its way to Hamlet Ratcliffe, who read it aloud to Augusta over the breakfast table. By then however, he had three excursion brakes in full service between Exeter and Plymouth and thus had a headstart over Catesby, in the Polygon, and Goodbody, in Crescent North. Only Blubb, with an old coachie's instinctive eye for perks, was mounting a regular run to Chislehurst Caves and Canterbury Cathedral. It was towards September, Augusta noted, when Swann-on-Wheels excursion brakes had been seen and commented upon as far apart as Snowdonia, Rydalwater, Fountains Abbey and Stonehenge, that his pride in initiating such a profitable sideline became tinged with jealousy, prompting him to say, as he surveyed a photograph sent him of a brake setting off for Hampton Court: "Gordamme, Gussie, look at that! You'd ha' thowt it was the Gaffer's idea, woulden 'ee now?" and Augusta murmured her sympathy. She had conveniently forgotten whose idea it was.

2

Swann's holiday excursions was one of those simple, trouble-free ideas that found instant favour among base-managers. Almost all of them had a spare vehicle or two that could be adapted, in a matter of days, as a passenger-carrying conveyance, and soon, with a minimum of capital outlay. Swann's brakes were running almost daily through the summer months to various points of interest, notably ruins of one kind or another, that seemed to have a nostalgic attraction for a nation that turned its back on the past and was crowding into cities where the Gothic past was already dominating the imagination of the architects of so many municipal museums, most of which seemed to be dedicated to the memory of the late Prince Consort.

Blubb and Dockett got away to a flying start with the holiday traffic, and Catesby, with Wordsworth's daffodils on his doorstep, was not far behind. In close pursuit came the indefatigable Abbott, of the Southern Square, whose territory enclosed Stonehenge, Cheddar Gorge and the Rufus Stone, as well as Nelson's flagship, the *Victory*, riding at anchor within hailing distance of the shore. Bryn Lovell, in the Mountain Square, went so far as to open a sub-depot at Caernarvon, catering for summer excursionists, who were trundled along the coast to gaze at Edward the First's castles, or inland to try their luck at scaling Snowdon. Even Edith Wadsworth, who had far more important things to do, gave Goodbody and Horncastle, her deputies in the Crescents, permission to convert a couple of men-o'-war apiece into brakes to convey weekend shrimpers and paddlers to Yarmouth, Whitby and Scarborough, whereas Vicary, in the flat Bonus country below her southern boundary, based his single three-horse brake on Ipswich and specialised in Roman ruins. The traffic had the advantage of demanding no more than a small injection of capital and was, moreover, something that lent itself to long-term planning, so that Adam's commercial instincts prompted him to take two steps towards an extension of the scheme pending next year's holiday season. He compiled a list of local beauty-spots and places of interest, thus adding a new leaf to Frankenstein's encyclopaedia, and he made plans to circulate all the adjoining tea-gardens with the intention of coming to some arrangement on the commission basis as regards excursionists set down on their door-steps. By early September there were twenty-two brakes plying in eleven of the territories, and Blunderstone's designers were at work on a four-horse prototype to be put into commission by Whit Week, 1865.

There was only one manager whose response to the circular was negative. Ian Fraser, one-time carrier who ruled in the Border Triangle, wrote '*Not Practical*' in answer to question one of the directive, and although he submitted a list of targets for jaunts across his territory, including Alnwick Castle, the battlefield of Flodden, Holy Isle, and Grace Darling's tomb, his reaction to the memo was discouraging, for he wrote, in the 'please comment' space, '*The weather up here, even in August, is not likely to encourage excursionists unwilling to do their sightseeing afoot.*' Adam did not press him. He had formed an opinion that Fraser, although dour in all his judgements, knew his business as well as any man in the provinces.

*   *   *

There was, in fact, a good reason behind Fraser's contemptuous dismissal of Hamlet Ratcliffe's brainwave. On the day Adam's directive reached him he was poised on the threshold of an enterprise that promised, at long last, to edge the Border Triangle into the limelight and hoist it into the same bracket as the Southern Square, or the combined Crescents under the vigorous leadership of Edith Wadsworth. Fraser, for some time now, had been sensitive to the fact that he was lagging far behind in territorial turnover, and since his daughter Phoebe had joined the Swann household he liked to think he had formed a special relationship with the young man who had appeared out of nowhere, bought up his rundown stock, and offered him security in his middle age. These factors, however, were only marginally responsible for Fraser's great leap forward, in July of that year. The main impetus was in his blood and bone, and could be traced back to ancestral memories that exerted a strong, subconscious pull upon the character of the Borderer.

Ian Fraser, although the bearer of two good Scots names, was none the less a renegade. Several centuries had passed since his particular branch of the clan had moved across the Tweed, intermarrying with former enemies who raided north instead of south, and there resided within him a profound distrust of Lowlanders whose greatgrandfathers (notwithstanding the Act of Union) had never ceased to look covetously at Berwick and beyond. In the old days they had been content to mount a cattle foray twice a year and an occasional full-scale invasion that took them as far south as the Plain of York. For centuries the ding-dong battle had continued up here, the clang of peel tower bell summoning both sides to resist a raid north or south of the border, but since the final ruin of the Stuart cause, rivalry of a different kind had replaced the incursions of the moss-troopers. Men who had once contended with bow, bill and Lochaber axe, now cheated one another of small change, and commercial competition up here was cut-throat, especially in the carrying trade.

It was this competition that had contributed to Fraser's failure to improve his position in the areas between Berwick, Carlisle and Newcastle. He could hold his own among English hauliers but was persistently undercut by shaggy little carriers who plied their trade in the wild areas of Lammermuir and the Pentland Hills. These gipsies (in his new status as resident manager Fraser could regard them as nothing else) were always liable to make a piratical inroad into his territory and because, as he himself put it, 'They could ply on twopence a day and a bowl of porridge', because they used broken-

502

down transport and the breed of ponies their forebears had used for cattle-raids, they could always undercut his quotations, so that he came to regard them with the same hostility as the most implacable of his ancestors. His greatest wish, and of late it had become an obsession, was to best them, preferably on their own ground, to have his waggons rolling across their routes, loaded down with their products, and the means of achieving this occupied his thoughts whenever he was in the northern sector of his beat. It took a fortuitous summer storm, in the third week of July, to attain his heart's desire.

There was, based on the town of Eyemouth a few miles north of his frontier, a prosperous general wholesaler called McAlpin, who reigned as a kind of king among the Lowland distributors, and had established, by exercising thrift and foresight, a very considerable business along the eastern coast as far as Montrose and beyond. McAlpin owned a small fleet of colliers plying between Newcastle and Leith but he dealt in many other things beside coal, having cornered the wholesale traffic in cheap, manufactured goods in that part of the country, mainly because he could command bulk transportation by sea, enabling him to buy cheaper and sell at the normal price. He was not, in any sense, a direct competitor of Fraser's but McAlpin's haulage contracts, particularly inland to places like Edinburgh, Peebles, Lauder, and Greenlaw, dangled before Fraser's eyes like a long, long row of ripe, juicy plums, and despite the fact that he had been given headquarters' sanction to sally into Scotland if the opportunity presented itself, he never had succeeded in doing so and his failure nagged at him like an old wound.

On the 13th of July 1864, one of McAlpin's colliers lost its rudder in a choppy sea off Burnmouth, drifted ashore and began to break up in Hilton Bay, no more than four miles north of the border. Word of the incident reached Fraser at once and partly from motives of curiosity, partly in anticipation of the pleasure it always gave him to see Scotsmen lose money, he had ridden north along the coast, where he could watch all the layabouts for miles around merrily helping themselves to the old skinflint's coal that was being thrown upon the beach by every successive wave. To add seasoning to his extreme satisfaction he saw old McAlpin himself, wringing his hands over the agonising spectacle, alternatively bellowing for magistrates to intervene and berating his luckless skipper, who had come off in the dinghy as soon as the vessel struck.

It was, Fraser decided, a heartening spectacle. Every tide, he estimated, would cost the miserly old devil a handful of sovereigns, and he kicked his cob a little closer, in order to overhear an animated exchange between the merchant and the local coastguard. McAlpin was bleating, "Can ye do *nothing*, man! Must ye stand by and witness such barefaced thievery? Look at them down there, wi' buckets and barrows and sacks, pilfering ma coal by the hundredweight!" but the coastguard, an equable man, only sucked an empty pipe and said, with quiet certainty, that there was nothing to be done. It was his opinion that coal washed ashore in these particular circumstances ranked as flotsam, and was therefore the legitimate harvest of anyone who cared to salvage it. He saw no reason to add that his own wife was about the business, or that his daughter Jenny had been sent home for the wheelbarrow.

It was the word 'salvage' that recollected Fraser to his duty and after a moment's thought he gave a lad a penny to hold his horse and approached McAlpin, saying, without deference, "No doubt you'll remember me, McAlpin. My name's Fraser, and I'm north-eastern manager for Swann-on-Wheels, hauliers from over the border. I've quoted you from time to time, but you've never paid me the compliment of replying," and the old man replied, ungraciously, "Aye, I mind you, Fraser, and your rates come far too high for my liking. Ye're here to gloat, nae doot?"

"I never care to see good money lost when it could be saved," Fraser said, and although he rarely smiled he made an exception when he saw McAlpin's face light up. "Ye're telling me ye could *save* my coal? Before those damned brigands take the last of it from the beach?"

"I could save four-fifths of it," Fraser said. "I grew up on the coast and the heavy knobs won't wash ashore until the next high tide. That's twelve hours away." He drew a deep, satisfying breath. "Give me the nod and I'll have my waggons here before that happens. Moreover, I know a way to check the tidal drift south, and cheat all the Berwick beachcombers out of a jubilee. But it would stand you in at thirty shillings a cartload."

McAlpin winced and bucked, as though someone had jabbed a nail into the small of his back. "*Nay, man!* That's close on half the wholesale price o' the coal. It's the best house coal, ye mind, for a special customer no more than twenty miles from where we stand!"

"You'll lose the entire shipment if you stand there wringing your hands," said Fraser. "What's more, once the coal is in my waggons, I'll deliver it direct."

"Aye, but ye've a point there," conceded McAlpin, and then, as a boy staggered past carrying two buckets of 'flotsam', "but can ye no *stop* barefaced robbery while you fetch your waggons? Why, man, it'll tak' ye best part o' three hours to get here, and by my reckoning half the stuff'll be stowed by then and past recovery."

Fraser contemplated the beach for a long moment. Then he said, judiciously, "Aye, I could stop it, providing you consigned the cargo to my charge. Are we agreed on thirty shillings a haul?"

"Ha' mercy on a man who's just lost a fine brig! Twenty-five."

"Thirty," said Fraser, "or I ride on home."

"Beach to coalyard?"

"Aye, and the sacks thrown in."

"Ye have my word on it," said McAlpin, but the words issued from him jerkily and breathlessly, like a confession extracted under torture.

Fraser moved lower down the beach and took his stand on a hillock. Cupping his hands he shouted; "I've just paid McAlpin for every knob of coal off that beach and my foreman is standing by to take the names of every man, woman and bairn who lifts a bucketful after turn of tide!"

One or two of the beachcombers faltered in their work but the majority went on picking at an accelerated pace. The tide, he saw, had half-an-hour to ebb and soon, by his reckoning, the sea would make amends to McAlpin. By the time he returned most of the area would be inaccessible. When he climbed the beach again he saw a very rare sight indeed, much rarer, in fact, than a wreck on this section of coast. It was McAlpin smiling.

He was back again at high tide with every waggon he could summon, having left orders for the diversion of any others that came into the Berwick yard. Within an hour of the job beginning he had two men-o'-war, three frigates, and four pinnaces lined up and less than an hour later a tenth waggon, borrowed from a Berwick smithy, appeared loaded with fencing stakes, each of them eight foot in length, for he had made his plan during the canter to and from his yard. The scour ran almost due south to the Needles Eye just above Berwick, and what was needed to check further drift from the wreck was a makeshift breakwater south of the beached *Bonnie Mary*. If there was sufficient time between tides he would try and erect another barrier north of the heeled-over vessel, and he used the time spent waiting for the ebb to assemble materials from the neighbouring area. Logs, a broken ploughshare, a length of wicker fencing bought from an astonished grazier, and sand-filled barrels were piled along the tideline and the moment the water was waist deep round the exposed keel Fraser's team went into action, ramming the piles into the sand and building a curtain wall in the shallows slanting beachwards at about forty-five degrees. Coal cascading from the gaping hold began to pile against it almost at once and before the tide began to flow again they had filled five waggons, that were at once dispatched to McAlpin's customer in the Coldingham area, with instructions to return the moment they offloaded. The improvised breakwaters were strengthened while the men in charge of unladen waggons stayed on the beach overnight, as did McAlpin himself, and work went on by relays all though the next day and the day after that. On the fourth day, when Fraser returned to the scene fortified by a good night's sleep and his first hot meal in seventy hours, quantities of silt and rubble had accumulated under the barrier to make access to the wreck possible at half-tide. Moreover, as the weather improved, and the sea went down, returning waggons could be reloaded from the riven hold on arrival. By the end of the fourth day, Fraser's team working almost nonstop, the collier was empty and McAlpin, who seemed never to have quitted the beach, and was said by some to be counting the knobs as they came ashore, was jubilant. "Aye, man," he said, tugging Fraser's elbow, "but ye're a bonnie worker! There's no' but a few sackfuls o' dust in that brig now, and I'll come straight wi' ye. She's insured but her cargo wasna'! Twenty-five shillings a haul was your price, I believe!"

"Thirty," said Fraser, "and if I'd known what I was up against it would have been thirty-five and cheap at the price." Then, staring the old man down, "Why does a man of your experience cheat himself on every inland haul he makes? Damn it, man, you save pennies and squander sixpences. You say my rates are high and so they are, compared with the trash you use to carry your goods north and west out of Eyemouth. But you can see for yourself the kind of equipment I use, and the men and horses my gaffer in London has me employ. Do you think a reputation like Swann's was built on saddle-galled, knock-kneed beasts, and a few patched-up manure carts bought secondhand from a crofter? Time is money, or so I've always heard, and you often handle more fragile goods than that coal we've been dredging up for close on a week."

"Aye, aye," said the old man, "but you'll own you've been well paid for it."

Fraser said, wiping his grimy hands on his breeches, "I'll tell you summat, Mr. McAlpin. I didn't do this job for money. I did it to prove something. If I had your contracts I could cut your delivery dates in half and offload everything you put aboard intact. Will you not at least think on it, man?"

But McAlpin, it seemed, had already thought upon it. By the end of that week Fraser had established a sizable bridgehead north of the border and Swann-on-Wheels waggons were soon seen as far north as the Royal Mile, hauling coal, timber, and Newcastle-manufactured ironmongery not merely across the border but over the Forth and, now and again, beyond the Tay. Ian Fraser, watching the first convoy set out, experienced a glow of satisfaction that had nothing to do with the boost McAlpin's contract gave his turnover. It was linked, in some way, to long-dead Frasers who had raided hereabouts in the days of Bruce and Wallace, and whose bleached bones, scattered between the ramparts of Berwick and Solway Firth, rested easier on his account.

3

It was not all beer, skittles, hayrides and new contracts. That same month trouble flared in the Southern Triangle.

On the last day of the month, buried in a sheaf of reports from lieutenants trumpeting their triumphs, was a letter addressed to Adam personally concerning the youngest foreman in the network, the pink-cheeked urchin Rookwood, recently promoted from clerk to trainee foreman at the specific request of Keate, his original sponsor. Adam remembered questioning the appointment at the time. Some of Abbott's waggoners were elderly and as set in their ways as Blubb. It did not seem likely that a lad of Rookwood's age, notwithstanding his keenness, would be able to exert much authority over them but after a trial period Abbott, under whom he was placed, had given him an exceptionally high rating, so Adam had concurred. And here, a month or so later, was a lawyer's letter stating that manager and foreman had come to blows and that Rookwood was threatening to sue on charges of assault and wrongful dismissal.

The whole affair struck Adam as ridiculous. Rookwood, he recalled, was one of Keate's Thameside boys, who had shown clerical promise at Headquarters. He was literate and Adam had been surprised when the boy asked for an opportunity to begin managerial training, but this particular letter, he noted, had been written by a stranger signing himself Gilroy, a lawyer's clerk with whom

Rookwood had taken lodgings. Mr. Gilroy, not a man to beat about the bush it seemed, wrote: 'Sir, I write on behalf of my client, Albert Rookwood, a resident boarder in my house, who is claiming two weeks' wages in lieu of notice, namely the sum of £5.10.0 (five pounds ten shillings) being wages plus overtime. On the 27th instant there was a dispute between my client and one, George Abbott, your manager, concerning deliveries to Ringwood. In the course of this dispute Mr. Abbott committed a physical assault upon my client, blacking his eyes and cutting his lip. There was no provocation, other than a formal complaint concerning the use of horses, and my client assures me he did not strike the first blow. Be that as it may, he was not only severely assaulted but summarily discharged without the requisite notice (due under his contract), or the back-pay owed to him from June. My client did not, in fact, wish to take the matter further, but he is under age and not clear concerning his rights. In view of this I persuaded him to communicate through me with his firm's headquarters, with a view of laying the matter before you. In the event of not receiving the money due (slips enclosed) I would be glad to have your comments, if any. Yours faithfully, Cedric C. Gilroy.'

It was the first letter of its kind that had ever arrived on his desk and it puzzled him a good deal. Abbott was known as a hard taskmaster but had never, so far as Adam knew, used his fists on his staff, and the matter was further complicated by the fact that it was the manager who had urged the lad be appointed to a position of responsibility. Not knowing what to make of it he sent for Keate, the waggonmaster, and showed him Gilroy's letter. Keate said, frowning, "Young Rookwood is the last lad I should have expected to be involved in violence. He's one of the best boys I ever had, and one of the first I took home. Amiable, and quick to learn, and with more ambition than most. I taught him to read, I recollect, and I was glad when Abbott recommended his promotion. You'll call him to mind, sir, a quietly-spoken boy, hardworking and easy to get along with?"

Suddenly Adam did recall him, not only as the urchin who had grinned at him from the communal bed on the floor of Keate's upper room, but the eager boy who had shown him Tybalt's personnel map the day he went north to find Edith Wadsworth, and had later assisted the head clerk to take notes at the conference.

"I remember him very well and you're right about him being biddable. That fellow Abbott has me worried sometimes. He's a hard worker but he drives his men like blacks." He made one of his spot decisions. "I'll go down to Salisbury, Keate, for this is something I should look into personally. Tell Tybalt I'll be back before he leaves, probably around six," and when Keate demurred, saying it was surely something that could be dealt with by letter, he said, sharply, "You don't solve these matters by letter and this concerns you as well as me and Abbott. You sponsored the boy, and things like this could set our entire promotion scheme at risk."

He went off then, catching a Southern express out of Waterloo at ten o'clock and two hours later he was making his way to Rookwood's lodging in a narrow street off the Cathedral Close.

Gilroy was at his office but Mrs. Gilroy, a forthright, motherly soul, admitted him and showed him into the parlour, darting about straightening chair covers and antimacassars. "Poor Mr. Rookwood is still abed," she said. "We've had a doctor to him, and there's no damage that won't mend in a week. But, begging your pardon, sir, that man Abbott is a bully and I advised the lad to leave before this happened."

"You've taken to the boy, Mrs. Gilroy? He's a quiet sort of lodger?"

The woman avoided his eye. "Well, yes, sir, but there's a little more to it than that. We've got no son—just the daughter, Hetty—and well, we took to him straight off, the both of us." She looked up, defiantly. "That man Abbott had no call to knock him about that way. My husband says he could be charged for it!"

"Can I see him?"

"Yes, sir, if you give me a minute to tidy." Then, hesitantly, "Mr. Gilroy says he can find him a job at the office. He won't get as much money as he's been bringing home lately but he'll work clean, won't he?"

Adam was familiar with the phrase. It was part of the new creed among people like the Gilroys—better to 'work clean' on next-to-nothing than dirty your hands earning a living wage. It was a point where the fashionable doctrine of self-help verged on the ridiculous, for it took no account of craftsmanship and implied that penmanship in any capacity automatically hoisted a man on to a higher social plane.

He gave her a few minutes and went up, to find Rookwood half-dressed in his attic room, overlooking the Close. The boy's appearance shocked him. Both eyes were badly discoloured and his face was puffy, the lip decorated with sticking plaster. He said, as soon as Mrs.

509

Gilroy had left, "Tell me about it, the full story from the beginning. I thought Abbott had taken a rare fancy to you?"

The boy looked uncomfortable and said, reluctantly, "I reckon he did, sir. Too much of a fancy, mebbe."

"What do you mean by that?"

The boy began to fidget. Then he said, pleadingly, "Look, sir, can't we leave it be? Mr. Gilroy wants me to press charges but I won't, you c'n be sure o' that. It wouldn't do none of us no good, for the truth is Mr. Gilroy don't know all the facts."

"I've got to know them for I employ you both. What happened between you?"

"The rough and tumble started over the 'orses, sir. He works 'em cruel. I warned him offen but he woulden lissen, sir. Ask the waggoners, if you don't believe me. But that warn't the real trouble."

"What was?"

He saw then that Rookwood was blushing and an inkling of what lay behind the assault occurred to him. "He made approaches to you?"

"Several times. But he didn't get nowhere, sir."

It was curious. You could usually recognise the type at a glance but it had never once occurred to him that Abbott was the kind to molest boys. Women, perhaps, although he had no reputation for wenching, but there was nothing in the least effeminate about his mannerisms or outward appearance. He said, thoughtfully, "Listen, lad, I won't press charges either, but I'm damned if I'll sack you under these circumstances. You must realise I can't leave things as they are, for Abbott has access to all the juniors. If it isn't you it'll be somebody else."

"Oh, it didden amount to all that much," Rookwood said, miserably, "just a bit o' pawing in the stable, when the men had gone off. I told him to lay orf. 'Nothin' doin', I said, for I've met his kind before. Who hasn't? It was the 'orses that had me worried, and when I refused to let him harness up a pair that had done one trip, and send 'em out again to the Ringwood, he went for me. To get his own back, I reckon." Suddenly he grinned. "He might be queer, but he's a dab hand when it comes to mixin' 'em, Mr. Swann. Looker my clock."

He said, quietly, "Thank you, Rookwood. That's all I need to know," and went down and out into the Close, without another word to Mrs. Gilroy. It was no good, he told himself, stoking oneself up about this kind of thing. It happened all the time and he had

510

had experience of it in the army more than once. There was very little one could do to protect a man like Abbott from himself, and the only possible course was to get rid of him at once. He did not feel the kind of disgust most men of his generation felt for homosexuality, seeing it as a sickness rather than a vice. That much army life had taught him and he was glad of it.

Abbott did not seemed surprised to see him and they went into the yard office across from the stables. The man's heavy, fleshy features told him something he might not have noticed had he not been looking for it and suddenly he felt less cocksure about his flair for picking deputies. Abbott said, glumly, "It'll be about Rookwood, won't it?"

"I've just come from him."

"What did he tell you?"

"The facts. Did you have to knock him about, just because he wasn't your kind, Abbott?"

The man looked down at the littered table, hands anchored to the projecting edge. His knuckles were gleaming with the pressure he put into the grip.

"Nothing happened between us."

"It wasn't your fault it didn't."

"Is he taking it further?"

"No. But that doesn't help, does it?"

"This is the end of the road for me then?"

"You know the answer to that. It's a pity. You've done a good job down here, but you couldn't stay on after this."

"I wouldn't lay a finger on him again and you say he won't blab. I wanted to talk to him, to explain, but I couldn't get to see him. That lawyer got between us. You won't give me another chance, then?"

"I can't, Abbott. There are other boys and it's not only them I'm thinking of."

"Yes, I see that. I could make promises but I don't say I could keep them." He looked up and Adam thought he had never seen a man look more wretched. "What does a man *do* in these circumstances? I'm forty now. Will it be different when I start ageing?"

"Not if you stay in England. Sooner or later it'll catch up with you, and you know as well as I do what that means among a race of Puritans. Years on the treadmill, maybe."

"What could I do, then? What hope is there?"

"Go to a country where you can expect more tolerance."

Suddenly he felt more sorry for Abbott than for Rookwood. Black eyes and a cut lip healed in a few days but Abbott had to live with his problem for the rest of his life. He said, "Have you saved since you've been down here?"

"I've got a hundred or so put by."

Adam crossed to the window and looked out across the sloping roofs to the point where the cathedral spire soared blandly heavenwards. The men who built it seemed to have had no doubts. What approach did they bring, he wondered, to a situation of this kind. 'We've been practising Christianity for a thousand years,' he thought, 'but how does it help a man like Abbott? If a priest got to hear about it I doubt if he'd visit him in gaol. Whose business is it to help? His bishop's? His doctor's? Where could he expect to find anything but cant?' He said, "You've got a hundred saved and I've no complaint to make about what you've done in the Square. I'll give you a discharge bonus of another hundred, providing you'll undertake to leave the country."

"That's generous."

"It's not, it's just an easy way out of a mess."

They were silent for a moment. Then Abbott said, "Who will you get to replace me?"

"I hadn't thought about it."

"Why don't you give the lad a chance?"

"*Rookwood?* As base manager?"

"I'll tell you something. That boy has a way with men and horses. People take to him and he's got spunk. He might even do well."

"But, good God, man, he's only twenty!"

"All the better. He's got his way to make, and Keate regards him as the most promising of that bunch you started out with."

"Would you be saying that to make amends?"

"I might, but it's true anyway. He knows the territory and a stranger wouldn't. Get Keate down here to supervise for a week and then turn him loose. He'll manage, take it from me." He faltered a moment, still keeping his eyes on the table. Then, "Will you shake hands, Gaffer?"

"Why not?"

He took Abbott's hand, noticing for the first time that it was as soft as a woman's.

"You'll give me a character?"

"As regards your work, yes."

He went out then and felt the man's gaze following him across the yard. Suddenly the air began to quiver with pulsing waves of sound, as the cathedral bells began to peal. He thought, sourly, 'What the devil have you got to sound so smug about', and made his way back to Rookwood's lodging.

The lad was downstairs now, drinking cocoa at the kitchen table and when Adam came in Mrs. Gilroy excused herself so he was able to come straight to the point. "I've seen Abbott and he's leaving. You can go back there as soon as you feel up to it. How would you feel about taking over from him?"

Rookwood gaped and then began to splutter, setting down his mug and groping wildly for his handkerchief. "*Me*, Mr. Swann? Gaffer of the Square?"

"Abbott thinks you could do it. I'd get Mr. Keate down here for a week or so to explain the paper work. Well?"

"I . . . I dunno, sir. Mr. Gilroy was goin' to get me a job at his office."

"You want to be a penpusher all your life?"

"No, sir, I'd sooner work with 'orses."

"Would you like to give it a trial?"

The clamour of the bells seemed to fill the room. Adam got up and shut the window. The boy said, slowly, "I'd do that, pervidin' you don't expect miracles, sir."

"I don't, just patience. Abbott will be gone in a day or so. Keep clear of the place until he has and by then Keate will be here. How are you off for money?"

The boy's ebullience showed in his grin. "I'm not hard up for a shillin'."

"Then there's no more to be said, except to back yourself to win." He went out into the Close and crossed the town to the station.

5

Edith as Thief-taker

RATCLIFFE'S excursions; Fraser's raid across the Border; Abbott's dismissal and Rookwood's promotion. These were matters that came within his personal orbit and found their way into the firm's records. But one incident that occurred that summer was not recorded and he was to remain unaware of it for years. It was, in a sense, as experimental as things that were happening elsewhere, but Edith Wadsworth did not think of it as such. To her it was in the nature of a private gamble, and one that would do well to remain buried.

She first noticed him harnessing a frigate for the regular run to Ipswich, a casual replacement recruited by waggonmaster Duckworth to fill a post vacated by a waggoner unable to pass an inn.

He did not come within her experience of waggoners, a man in his mid-twenties, perhaps a year or so younger than herself, and she was struck by his bearing and good features, gipsy features she would say, for he was very dark, with crisp, curly hair and an effortless way of using well-developed muscles. He was impudent, too, showing his white teeth in an evaluating smile as they exchanged glances when she crossed from office to stables to discuss the parcel run to Harwich. When she was back at her desk she looked him up in her book, finding that his name was Wickstead, Tom Wickstead, and that he had once been a stablelad at Newmarket. The records did not help her much. The name Wickstead did not suit him, for there was a suggestion of the Latin about him and he seemed old for a stablelad, unless he had been employed in some other capacity in the interval. From her perch in the office she was able to study him at leisure, noting his masculinity and deciding, with a grim smile, that he was almost certainly a wencher but an engaging one, of the kind likely to make a strong impression on women. Then she forgot him in order to give her full attention to Beckstein's letter.

Beckstein, a goldsmith and gem merchant, was in a fair way of business in the territory. She had handled his goods in the past but they had been low-value consignments, sporting trophies, flat plate

514

and clocks, passed on to Vicary in The Bonus for transit to London. This latest proposal was something that needed thought, a packet of uncut diamonds consigned to The Hague via the Harwich packet, a routine shipment, no doubt, as far as Beckstein was concerned, but the first of its kind entrusted to her and possibly a tryout on his part. Beckstein's agent asked her to quote, allowing for generous insurance rates, and it crossed her mind that if the terms were attractive this would not be the last high-value goods they carried, for Beckstein did a good deal of Continental business. On the other hand, no haulier liked to handle precious stones and if it had been a matter of taking them overland by waggon she would have declined to quote. The established rail service, however, made a difference. Sealed in a small-parcel bag, the jewels would be safe enough, and might lead to more of Beckstein's Harwich-bound traffic. She worked out a rate, keeping it as low as possible but pointing out that it was safer to send high-value goods without special insurance. In her experience there was security in anonymity, even for small packages. She marked the letter 'urgent' and sent for Duckworth, one of the few who had accepted her promotion philosophically. He said, when she explained the possibility of landing other Beckstein commissions, "I'm not sure I'd want 'em, Miss Wadsworth. Hauling gunpowder and high-grade china is bad enough, but packages of that kind are freight that could keep a man awake o' nights. Why doesn't Beckstein send 'em to Harwich by special messenger?"

"I can make a guess at that. The messenger would need an escort and both would have to be thoroughly trustworthy. He's probably lost jewels en route in his time and is changing his policy. Our responsibility would end with delivery to the purser. They would go straight into the ferry safe and you can depend upon him having made inquiries concerning our reliability."

"They should have satisfied him," Duckworth said. "We've never lost a parcel yet. But wouldn't insurance run high?"

"Not the way I would arrange it. It would go as an ordinary package marked 'Fragile' and we can send someone along to make the actual delivery. This is a sprat to catch a mackerel and I mean to get his contract if it's possible. I'm quoting and I'll let you know whether we land him or frighten him off."

"Aye, do that. But for my money I'd as lief see someone else get the job."

He went out shaking his head like an old collie and Edith pondered the reluctance of men to vary the pattern of their day-to-day routines. Once a man passed thirty, it seemed, he was deaf and blind to adventure, and thinking this she glanced once again at that handsome young spark in the yard, now rolling casks up the steep incline of a plank as casually as though he was pitching marbles.

The post, and a rush of business, drove Wickstead and Beckstein out of mind. It was not until the following Thursday, the day before the weekly parcel run, that she remembered either of them again. Then Beckstein wrote, accepting her quotation and saying that packages would be delivered by hand from three of his branches in time for the evening train. He must have taken her point about insurance, for he made no mention of it and Edith thought, gleefully, "I've netted him, and that's another feather in my cap, for Duckworth would have let him slip away."

She was clipping the letter on the file when she happened to take one of her wardress peeps into the yard to see how things were shaping there, and it was as well she did. A load of cast-iron drainage pipes, piled high upon a man-o'-war, were stacked in such a way as to ensure that the load would slip at the first gradient. She called, "Hold that dray, Bastin!" and went into the bright sunshine where three waggons, the flat and two frigates, were standing in line awaiting their turn at the weighbridge.

She recognised the carter as one who had made no secret of his resentment at taking orders from a woman and now, called to account for slipshod loading, he scowled like an overgrown schoolboy.

"They'm on'y going as far as Oundle," he growled. "Where's the sense in using chains?"

She noticed then that the drivers behind him were watching her, probably to see if Bastin's obvious truculence would cause her to back down. It had the opposite effect and she snapped, "I don't give a damn whether they're going a hundred yards. You'll fasten them more securely than that. There are humpbacked bridges between here and Oundle, and your whole load will likely finish up in Willow Brook. Pull out of line," and she swung herself on to the floor of the flat as Bastin, swearing under his breath, jerked his leader left to make way for the frigate behind.

It might have been bad luck or the sullen force he exerted on the bridle, but the load began to slip just as she stood upright. She heard a shout of warning from behind and then, amidst a vast clutter, she jumped clear as the pipes spilled over the tailflap, crashing down on the cobbles with a din that set every horse in the yard rearing. A length of pipe hummed past her head like an enormous arrow as

516

others poured down either side, like logs spilling over a dam. She crouched there on her hands and knees, fury at such manifest incompetence submerging every other instinct, even that of self-preservation. Then, half-rising, and conscious of a sharp stab of pain on her knee, she realised how she had avoided being buried under the load. Wickstead was braced against the rear of the waggon, supporting the tailboard with his shoulder. He looked, she thought, like a statue of Atlas, arms half-raised, feet planted astride, sustaining what must have been a crushing weight, and it seemed to her that he remained like that a long time while other men ran in to take the strain and Bastin backed his team on to the bridge, so that they were able to force the flap into an upright position and check the cascade. He was beside her then with his arm about her waist, and even the shock and dismay of the accident did not deprive her of the pleasant sensation communicated by his firm, strong touch. He said, breathlessly, "You hurt, ma'am? You fell very heavily," and she said, breathlessly, "I've cut my knee. That's all, thanks to you," as Bastin came prancing up, his face white and his expression confused as he mumbled, "Gordamme, Miss Wadsworth, I made sure you was gone! There's two ton or more up there and when I saw you fall ..." but she interrupted, saying, "See to your vehicle and load up again. I've seen men crippled for life by sloppiness of that kind!" and then her knee began to smart horribly, and she saw blood on her shoe buckle and said, addressing Wickstead, "Give me a hand into the office," but he replied, gallantly, "I'll carry you, you'll need that cleaned and bandaged," and before she could protest he had whisked her off her feet and was shouldering a way through the waggoners who had converged on the spilled load.

There was nothing she could do about it. His grip, although gentle, was very firm, and suddenly the narrowness of her escape caught up with her so that she felt lightheaded but very comfortable there, with her head against his chest, and one hand about his neck. He marched into the office, kicking the door shut with his heel and looking round for somewhere to put her down but the moment they were alone she felt shamed and her anger against Bastin mounted for putting her in such a ridiculous position. She said, "Set me down, for Heaven's sake ... I'm not hurt ..." and he obeyed her but reluctantly she thought, for his hands lingered a moment under her thigh and below the swell of her breast. She sat on her swivel chair, half-expecting him to go and then wishing that he would, for she wanted to lift her skirt, roll down her stocking and staunch the flow of blood

517

from her knee. He must have noticed her embarrassment for he said, with a pleasant smile, "Don't be shy, ma'am. I've got five young sisters and over at Newmarket I worked for a vet. Let me look at it for you've had a rare shock. There's running water out behind, isn't there?"

It seemed ungracious to refuse and suddenly she stopped feeling ridiculous, thinking it rather pleasant to be fussed over for a change. "There's a first-aid box above the sink," she said, "I bought it the week I took over but it didn't occur to me I'd be the first to need it," and he nodded, going into what had been the scullery of the cottage before it was converted into a yard office.

She took advantage of his absence to lift her skirt and petticoat and roll down her bloodsoaked stocking. Contact with the cobbles had jarred the knee badly, and there was a wide area of grazing on the cap. She rested her leg on the visitor's chair and dabbed the wound with a handkerchief, hearing him run water into a bowl, and calling, "It might have been worse! Just bruising and a bad graze. I've a good mind to sack that idiot. Suppose his load had slipped in the town and killed half-a-dozen people?"

"Swann would have had a very long lawsuit on his hands," he said, reappearing with the bowl and the first-aid box, setting the bowl on the floor and the box on her desk. "Keep the leg stretched out, ma'am, and don't worry, I won't touch it. I'll squeeze the rag."

He had, she decided, altogether too much authority for a man in his position. His masculinity reminded her of Matt Hornby and Adam. He had their deliberation too, as she noticed when he stripped off his neckerchief, dipped it, and wrung it out over the wound until he was satisfied it was clean. She was going to tell him there was a tube of salve in the box but he was not the kind of man you directed so she let him find it and squeeze some on to a square of lint, applying it gently and finishing off the dressing with a bandage that was neither too tight nor too loose. She found herself watching the deftness of his supple fingers and wondering how many women they had caressed in their time. A hundred or more she wouldn't wonder, for he certainly had a way with women. She said, for something to say, "That vet taught you a thing or two about bandaging. How do you come to be a waggoner? It's a bit of a come-down from riding at Newmarket, isn't it?"

"Not if you backed a string of losers two seasons running," he said, gaily, and left it at that.

She contemplated the ruin of his neckcloth, noticing that it was silk. "You're very kind," she said, "and I haven't thanked you yet. I should have needed more than a vet's services if you hadn't stopped the rest of those pipes falling on me."

"It was nothing," he said, carelessly, "I saw what was likely to happen and was there before you hit the ground. Give Bastin another chance. He won't forget that in a hurry. It might even win him over."

"Win him over?"

He smiled. "To taking orders from a woman."

"I see. And how do you feel about it, Wickstead?"

"I'll take instructions from anyone who knows their trade, ma'am," and she thought, with a subdued chuckle, 'I warrant he plays every woman he meets like a fish on a line. I wouldn't care to be in love with him,' and she rose, stiffly, saying, "I'll run the tap on that neckcloth. Later I'll launder it."

She carried the bowl into the scullery and gave the square a rinse but when she returned a few minutes later he was still standing with his back to her, seemingly preoccupied with thoughts of his own.

"How long will you stick at this kind of work?" she asked, and he said, with a shrug, "Until something better turns up, ma'am."

"Are you married?"

"No, I'm not that much of a gambler."

It was, she thought a friendly rebuke for prying, so she dismissed him, saying, "Well, I've work to do notwithstanding a cracked knee. Thank you again, Wickstead, and if you care to stay on in haulage I've no doubt my Gaffer could find you a better job than a waggoner."

"What kind of man *is* Mr. Swann?" he asked, unexpectedly and she replied, without thinking, "Your kind. Capable but bossy!"

That rattled him, she thought, and smiled as he absorbed it. Then, with a cheerful salute, he marched out and she was left with the impression that she had had the better of the exchange, for it was clear that, given the slightest encouragement, he would have lost no time at all in exploiting his advantage.

Once again she became absorbed in work and although her knee was stiff and uncomfortable she was soon able to forget it coping with a shower of orders, and the making up of the manifests for the parcel runs to Grimsby, Yarmouth, Leicester, Cambridge and, above all, Harwich.

She had evolved a system by now, converting a shed adjoining the stables into a sorting centre like a miniature Post Office, where frames supported rows of gaping canvas bags, each larger than a soldier's kit-bag and fitted with a chain and padlock. Over every bag was a shingle painted with the terminus of a run, together with a list of dropping-off points en route. Harwich served Whittlesey, Chatteris, Bury St. Edmunds, Stowmarket and Hadleigh and sometimes consignments for this area required half-a-dozen bags. At most stopping-places a Swann-on-Wheels waggon met the train and began the local deliveries and as goods travelled in vans under the eye of the guard there was no necessity to send a man on the majority of the runs. Only when traffic was particularly heavy, or when carters were in short supply in a particular area, was a waggoner sent along with the goods, but it occurred to her that here was a case when an escort as far as Harwich was obligatory.

Duckworth came to help check the manifests and lock the bags with a string of keys, for which waggoners along the line held duplicates, and it was while they were fastening the Harwich bags that he mentioned the escort, saying, "I've detailed Wickstead. We owe him a day, and it so happens he's making a private trip to Newmarket. I asked him to take an extra half-day and see our parcel aboard the ferry at Harwich. He suggested it, as a matter of fact. Seems he lived at Newmarket, and it's well over halfway there."

The coincidence alerted her so sharply that she bit back the comment that rose to her lips and walked the length of the shed, leaving him to fasten the rest of the padlocks. Wickstead—Newmarket—Harwich—Beckstein. Somehow they made a pattern in her mind, but for a moment it was blurred. Then, as she stood in the doorway looking across the yard, another factor clarified it, for she suddenly recalled the incident of the previous day when he had carried her into the office, set her down in her chair and gone into the scullery to run water for her knee. She said, rounding on Duckworth, "I hope you said nothing about the contents of that bag," and he said, in an aggrieved tone, "Why, naturally I didn't. The less anyone knows about that the better. It doesn't even carry special insurance, does it?"

"No," she said, "it's going under a 'Fragile' label," but she answered vaguely because her mind was still occupied marshalling the suspicions aroused by the fact that Wickstead had volunteered for a job, a job he had no reason whatever to anticipate. Then, quite suddenly, she understood that he did know, and that his foreknowledge was related to the fact that, for the space of perhaps three minutes, he had been alone in her office, and within touching distance of Beckstein's letter on the clip over her desk. Thinking back she could see him there when she came out of the scullery, standing with his back to her, as though looking out into the yard, and her stomach muscles contracted as the pattern became much clearer, almost clear enough to assume a definite and sinister shape. She said, "Where is Wickstead now?" and Duckworth replied, "He signed off mid-morning. He was on a night haul to Thetford and promised to report back at four, in time for the parcel-run to the station."

She considered then taking Duckworth into her confidence, and might have done so had he been a younger, quicker-witted man. As it was he would almost surely panic and she had no real evidence at all to lay before him, nothing but the impression that haphazard events of the last forty-eight hours came together in a way that was logical and frightening. She said, abruptly, "I'll leave you to finish," and returned to her office, shutting the door and moving across to the hook where the clip enclosed letters of the last few days. Beckstein's was buried now so she extracted it, clipping it back on top, rehanging the file, and standing where he had been standing when she emerged from the scullery. She found that she could read the letter quite easily, and this converted suspicion into certainty.

She stood there for several minutes, testing the evidence for coherence and conformity. Every circumstance fitted. Wickstead's superior manner, his eagerness to enter the office, his access to the letter and, above all, his action in volunteering for a trip to Harwich, with Beckstein's consignment for company. She was on the point of returning to the shed to ask Duckworth precisely how this had come about but then she had a better idea and turned instead to the card-index containing the names and addresses of all the employees in the Crescents. His card told her that he had lodgings at 'The Wheatsheaf', just off the market. She went into the scullery, collected his neckcloth and put it inside a buff envelope. Then she crossed the yard and walked the short distance to the market.

2

The Boots told her that Mr. Wickstead lodged in the annexe made from part of the old coaching stable, but added that he had just gone out, so she waited until the man's back was turned and then slipped through the arch and up a wooden stair to the gallery. She had no way of knowing which of the four rooms up here was his, but trying the first door found it open. A woman's cape and hood lay on the bed so she moved on and tried the two adjoining rooms, finding them both unoccupied with their beds stripped. The fourth door, farthest from the main building, was fastened but in one of the unoccupied rooms a key had been left in the lock and so she got it and tried it on the end room, finding that it fitted the common lock pattern. She went in, not knowing what she was seeking beyond some kind of confirmation that Wickstead was a trained thief and she did not stop to ask herself whether this justified her ransacking the man's room on suspicion. All she needed, at this stage, was proof that Wickstead was not what he seemed to be, an ex-stableboy down on his luck and currently marking time as a waggoner on twenty-five shillings a week. With that, perhaps, he could be challenged.

She found evidence of a kind at once, a suit of good broadcloth in the closet, and a riding cloak of excellent quality, as were the calfskin boots treed on the rack below. Then, as she was closing the closet door, her eye caught a gleam of metal on the shelf reserved for hats and she reached up to find a heavy, six-chambered revolver, fully loaded. Attached to it was a looped strap, too short to be used as a belt and she had to study the weapon for a moment before understanding its purpose. It was made to buckle round the forearm, so that user and gun could not be separated in a struggle. She was quite sure now, certainty making her perspire under the armpits as she turned to the small cabin trunk at the foot of the bed. In here, among some neatly-packed small clothes, was more positive proof. A young man of his temperament might conceivably own a pistol but what would he be doing with a crêpe mask, of the kind highwaymen used robbing coaches two generations ago? She examined the trunk very closely then, noting a fresh label consigning it to Liverpool. She thought about this, deciding that his plan was probably to send his luggage carriage forward to the port, and claim it there after he had extracted everything of value from the Harwich package on the short journey between terminus and quay. In the bottom of the trunk was a pair of shoes, stuffed with newspaper and they seemed to her, as she turned them over, unusually heavy. She extracted the paper from one and three gold watches and a dozen pairs of ornamental studs and cuff-links winked up at her.

She replaced the shoes, closed the trunk and glanced out into the passage finding it empty. In twenty seconds she had relocked the door, replaced the key, and descended into the yard, passing through the service door and finding the Boots eating his dinner at a staff table. "Mr. Wickstead doesn't seem to be in any of the public rooms," she said, giving him sixpence. "Tell him I called with this on my way out of town," and she handed him the envelope containing the laundered neckcloth and went through the buttery into the street.

Her first thought was to consult the police. That way, she supposed, the safety of Beckstein's goods would be assured, for even if Wickstead could talk his way out of possessing a loaded firearm, a mask, and a shoeful of watches, he would be unlikely to report to the yard after questioning. But two following thoughts occurred to her and both were prompted by her pride. One was that Wickstead, whatever his profession and ulterior motives, had been instrumental in saving her from death or injury under that shower of drain pipes. The other was less easily defined. It had to do with her position in the Crescents, a woman in authority over so many men, and it seemed to her that here was an unlooked for chance of setting the seal upon that authority. Suppose she devised a counterplot? Suppose she was able to catch a thief in the commission of a crime and attach to herself the kind of publicity Ratcliffe had won when he recaptured a tame lion, or Bryn Lovell had gained when he saved the lives of half a hundred miners?

It wasn't an easy decision to make. She had the nerve but did she have the skill to challenge a man as calculating as Wickstead? And suppose she bungled it, and he got clear away with Beckstein's casket, and then it later emerged, as surely it must, that she had known him for what he was long before the Harwich bag had left the depot? She was still undecided when she found her steps had led her past the station and here she suddenly remembered Brockworth, the goods manager, to whom, in a sense, she owed her promotion to the position of manager. Brockworth was an intelligent man, and because he fancied himself in love with her, would be likely to take a good deal on trust. She smoothed her hair, retied her shawl under her chin, and marched into his office, finding him sorting his forms at a counter set against the wall.

He rose with a smile that augured well for the granting of favours. She said, without preamble, "I'm here on business, Edward. We've got a high value package going to Harwich on the evening train. It'll be in one of our usual sacks in the luggage van and I'd take it kindly if you allowed me to travel with it. In the mail van, that is."

He said, with a puzzled look, "But that's flat against regulations, Edith. No one but the guard is allowed to sit in there."

"That's why I'm here asking you to arrange it. The fact is, I don't want that sack out of my sight, for far too much depends on its safe arrival. I could go into details but I don't care to at this stage. All I can promise is this; if you and your guard shut your eyes to my presence in the van I'll explain later, when I get back."

"I couldn't take that risk," he said, unhappily, "not even for you, Edith," but then, seeing her frown, "I daresay Hibbert would let you ride in the brakevan and from there you could watch the sacks through his spyhole. Would that do?"

"Very nicely," she said, "so long as I get aboard before the sacks are loaded."

"That must mean you're expecting trouble and if you are this isn't the way to prevent it."

"I'm not expecting trouble," she said, gaily, "and it isn't that I don't trust your railway. It's just that I have a fancy to prove somebody's worth."

"I'll have to know who that somebody is, Edith."

'I'll tell you that. My escort."

"If you're sending an escort why do you have to spy on him?"

"To see how well he attends to his business. I've singled him out for a more responsible position, but I want to be sure."

He looked at her curiously. He had known her since she was a child but he had never understood her. She was an impulsive, wayward creature, utterly unlike her phlegmatic father and her sweet-faced mother, whose courtship and marriage he remembered. At one time he had thought of her as a lovable, high-spirited little lass, very much the tomboy, and at another time, after she had shown him and his children kindness, he had hoped to make her the second Mrs. Brockworth, but now he was resigned to an avuncular rôle, for what would a lively girl like her want with a middle-aged plodder like him? He said, glumly, "You're up to mischief again and I daresay it's to do with that young gaffer of yours. I don't have to tell you there are folk hereabouts who raise their eyebrows at a slip of a girl like you running a haulage business and lording it over a lot of foul-mouthed old drunkards down at that yard."

"No, you don't, Edward. I see the eyebrows raised and noses tilted every time I give an order but most of them are obeyed and I mean to keep it that way. This 'mischief' as you call it is planned with that in mind. What time do you smuggle me aboard?"

"Be here at five sharp," he said, "and you can watch your bags stowed. What the guard will think is more than I can say."

"Tell him there's half-a-sovereign waiting for him and he'll say nothing, not even to his wife," and she flashed him a smile and blew him a kiss so that he sighed as he watched her walk quickly back across the siding to the street.

3

There was a great deal to be done in the three hours left to her. On the way back to the yard she telegraphed Kitson, the Cambridge agent, advising him that there would be an extra sack in his consignment marked 'Waterbeach' and that it was to be offloaded by him personally and held back, pending further instructions. Kitson had a warehouse and she could break her journey on the way back and reclaim the sack. This seemed to her safer than keeping the Harwich bag on the premises where there was no secure place to stow it, and also eliminated the possibility of alerting Wickstead by withdrawing the parcel from the shed. Then she went to the sorting-house, locked the door and removed the Harwich docket and the 'Fragile' label from the bag, replacing the docket with one made out for 'Waterbeach'. It occurred to her then that a man of Wickstead's daring might have saved himself trouble by stealing the package before it left the premises, but then she realised that this would have reduced his start to about an hour, or even a few moments if anyone had made a final check. His plan was to extend that start into days, possibly until the casket was found to be missing at Rotterdam and the news was telegraphed to Beckstein.

When the decoy bag was ready she went to the far end of the shed where spare sacks and packing materials were stored, choosing an identical bag, stuffing it with paper and three or four half-bricks to make up the weight. She marked this bag with the Harwich docket and a 'Fragile' label, replacing it in the rack. It was then near to four o'clock and she went to the office and wrote a detailed report of everything she had done and proposed doing between the time Duckworth's remark had alerted her and her estimated time of arrival at Harwich. Set down like that it seemed to her a wild and improbable tale, and it was not until she had read it through and signed it that she realised the letter for what it was, a kind of insurance against her losing the package and perhaps even her life. She had a serious qualm then, reminding herself that she was facing a high and unnecessary risk, but the moment passed. Adam Swann required indisputable proof that he had a woman up here who was the equal, possibly the superior of Ratcliffe in the Wedge, and Bryn Lovell in the Mountain Square.

At four-thirty, when she had sealed the report and marked the envelope *'For H.Q. in the event of my absence at lock-up on Saturday, 15th August'*, she saw Wickstead drive his waggon across to the shed, where he was met by Duckworth and the waggoner who was to bring the empty vehicle back to the yard. She studied his bearing intently, searching for signs of tension, but there were none. He vaulted from the box, exchanged a joke with the waggoner, and they all went into the shed, emerging a moment later carrying one sack apiece. As soon as they had disappeared she slipped across to the gate where Hallet, the weighbridge clerk, was sitting on his bench picking his teeth. "Tell Mr. Duckworth I've had an urgent call from Grimsby, and won't be back until tomorrow, around midday. If I'm later he'll find instructions on my desk. Is that clear?" Hallett said it was and made a note of it and she went out through market crowds to the station, arriving in time to inspect the train waiting in the bay and finding it was made up of four passenger coaches, one luggage van and partitioned brakevan combined. Brockworth came up with the guard Hibbert in tow.

"Pleased to have you along, Miss Wadsworth," Hibbert said, but Edward said, "Are you sure you want to go ahead with this nonsense, Edith?"

"Quite sure," she said, "and I'm obliged to both of you."

"You'll call in on your way back?"

She promised she would and they climbed aboard the van. Hibbert had even provided a cushion for his bench beside the brake lever. "You can look into the mail van from here," he told her, indicating the cage reserved for the mail. "She's a rare slow coach, Miss. Stops at March, Cambridge, Newmarket, Bury St. Edmunds, Manningtree, and places you'll not have heard of."

"She's heard of all of them," Brockworth said, sourly, disapproving of his colleague's familiarity. "She's district manager for Swann-on-Wheels, the hauliers," and the guard's chirpiness fell off like a hat. "Is that so? I had a notion we were indulging a young lady's fancy. This is a business trip?"

"Very much so, Mr. Hibbert," she said, with a wink at Edward, "so I'll take my seat if I may."

From the van window she could watch the platform and within

minutes a porter-pushed trolly passed piled with docketed sacks bearing the Swann insignia. Behind the porter, caped and booted, and looking for all the world as though he was a railway director, strode Wickstead, and she watched him superintend the unloading. She was even able to count the sacks dumped beyond the mail cage, noting that he held on to the Harwich bag himself, setting it down near the door. She had no means of watching which part of the train he entered but reasoned it would be as near as possible to the luggage van.

Exhilaration engulfed her as the whistle blew and Hibbert swung himself aboard. She was satisfied that the casket was safe while the train was in motion, and could pretend to listen to Hibbert's conversation, but as they rattled along, with the evening sun flooding miles of sugar beet fields either side of the line, her mind was occupied with the young man sitting farther up the train and she found that she could wonder about him objectively, as she might contemplate Claude Duval, Dick Turpin, or Robin Hood. There was something old-fashioned and improbable about him that divorced him from the common sneak-thief, of whom she had encountered a great number, and she was half-persuaded that he was committed to this profession for adventure rather than profit. There was another professional aspect of him that interested her. Thief he surely was, and something of an artist at the trade, but she would wager he worked alone and had no use for confederates. She wondered about his gallantry, trying to decide whether his dash to the waggon had been instinctive or the exploitation of a lucky opportunity to get inside her office. This led her to speculate whether he had signed on because of foreknowledge of her dealings with Beckstein, or because a waggoner's job in this area promised good pickings.

The guard left her to supervise the offloading of mail at March and she watched through the panel window. Wickstead did not appear and neither did he when the train stopped to drop mail at intermediate halts. At Cambridge, however, she saw him stroll up to watch the offloading of Swann's parcel sacks, including the genuine Harwich bag docketed for Waterbeach. It was lifted off with the others but his eye caught the 'Fragile' label and she had a bad moment as he exchanged a word with Kitson's carter. Whatever was said must have satisfied him, for he moved the decoy bag nearer the cage, then helped Hibbert close the van door. Then they were off again, chuffing east along the Newmarket and Bury extension, with only two more stops before the terminus.

527

Dusk had fallen and the moon was rising before they pulled out of Manningtree and the Stour estuary was seen as a white finger laid across a violet veil of mist, with here and there tiny splashes of primrose light on the northern shore, and away to the right the cluster of lights that was Harwich. Hibbert said, "You'll be staying overnight, Miss Wadsworth?" and she said she would, for she had friends in the port and thanked him again, giving him his half-sovereign which he made a show of refusing but pocketed gratefully enough. "I'm going back on the fast," he told her, as the train began to slow down. "She'll have me home and in bed by midnight. Nice to have met you, ma'am. We handle a lot of your parcels and that's a rare smart system your people have devised, with the railway doing most of the work and you getting the best cut off the joint. Somebody in your outfit is quick off the mark, I'd say." She thought desperately, 'Yes, and I wish you were half as quick, for I'm going to need all my wits about me from here on unless I'm to see him get away with a sack of shavings and half-bricks!', but then she knew she could not leave it like this, that there would have to be a confrontation, although she was by no means sure that she could steel herself to the point of giving him in charge.

Mercifully Hibbert jumped off before the train had actually stopped and a pair of postal clerks appeared to help a Harwich guard empty the luggage van of mail. She stayed watching through the peephole and presently she saw him again, waiting for the mailmen to finish, a cigar glowing under his long, sharp nose. She made her decision then. If he was to be challenged it would have to be here, in lamplight, and in the proximity of other people.

He seemed disposed to take his time, and presently everyone drifted away from this end of the platform. He tossed his cigar butt on to the track and climbed leisurely into the van, ignoring the other Harwich sacks and lifting the decoy carefully, almost tenderly. He had turned, and had one foot on the platform, before she could dodge through the brakevan door and get between him and the station exit. There was not much light up here, just a single gaslamp nearer the barrier. She said, catching her breath, "What about the other sacks, Mr. Wickstead? There might be something worth having in them."

She had never seen a man look more astounded. He stood there, half in and half out of the van, holding his load of rubbish as if it was a lumpish, passive child. His lips were slightly parted and his eyes were dull with bafflement, the eyes of a sleepwalker arrested on his own doorstep. He said, at last, *"You?"* and the word emerged like

528

the single note of a flute. She felt almost sorry for him. Dismay seemed to paralyse him and she could almost hear the jangle in his brain as he fumbled with the alternatives—flight, violence or surrender.

"You can put that sack down for a start," she said, "for there's nothing in it but bricks and shavings. The real one was put off at Cambridge, consigned to 'Waterbeach'."

He said nothing to this but sat down very suddenly on the step, his legs folding like those of a man half-stunned. She said, "Open it," and like a robot he took out a clasp knife and slit the sack its full length. Rubbish, and a single half-brick, rolled out on the plank floor and he studied it, not so much ruefully as contemplatively, as though it would somehow explain her presence. And then he did a strange thing. He threw back his head and laughed, moderately at first as though tickled by a small joke, then heartily and finally uproariously, until he was helpless with mirth.

She let him have his laugh before saying, "I might be a woman, Mr. Wickstead, but I've had a good deal of experience in the trade. The thing I resent most, I suppose, is being taken for a damned fool. Particularly yesterday, when you passed yourself off as Sir Launcelot. That was quite a performance for Jack Sheppard."

"I enjoyed it," he admitted, readily. "You're a very cuddlesome lass and, as to your legs, they're among the best turned I ever saw."

"We're a long way from home now, Wickstead, so spare me your kiss-in-the-ring compliments. The point is, what the devil do I do about you? Can you tell me that?"

"I could offer suggestions," he said, equably, "but I'd sooner know how you rumbled me."

"It wasn't difficult. Mostly a matter of putting two and two together. For a professional thief it was very stupid to volunteer for the trip."

"Yes, it was. I see that now, of course, and I saw it at the time, but there didn't seem any alternative. However, you wouldn't have gone to all this trouble on that much evidence."

"I didn't. I paid you a call and went through your things. You have interesting luggage, Mr. Wickstead. A revolver, a mask, and a fascinating collection of other people's watches."

He blew out his lips, as though on the point of whistling. "You're a corker," he said, "a real corker! I hope that chap Swann realises what a treasure he has on his payroll."

Suddenly she was tired of bandying words with him. The enormity of his deception, and the price she would have paid for it had it been successful put a cutting edge on her voice. "Great God!" she exclaimed, "why does a man like you have to go through life like a jackdaw with his beak in everyone else's property? Why the devil can't you stand on your own two feet, as I have to, and make your own way in the world? It isn't as if you were a cripple, is it?"

"I'm a kind of cripple," he said.

"Because you're bone idle and would sooner steal than work?"

"No," he said, dreamily, "I'm not an idle person. I work harder than most at my trade."

"Trade!" She spat the word down at him. "You call it a trade? Trade has dignity and where's yours at this moment, run into a corner by one woman? Aye, and a woman without a pistol strapped to her wrist."

He seemed to consider this and accept it as valid. He stood up, slowly, brushing shavings from his breeches. "That's fair as far as it goes," he said, "but it doesn't go far enough. To begin with, those diamonds are as much mine as Beckstein's."

"How can you say that?"

"Because it is so. To you Sol Beckstein is a merchant. To me he's something else. I know how he came by those particular stones and why he's using your service to get them off his hands. Being Sol he could find a safer way of fencing them if he wanted, but he's like most of his kind, as greedy as a gull, and couldn't wait for the two thousand per cent profit they'll fetch him."

"You're telling me those diamonds were stolen?"

"Of course. Most of the stones he handles are in one way or another. We take the risks. He takes the profit."

It made a difference. In a way it answered some of the questions she had asked herself about him over the last twenty-four hours. She said, slowly, "Have you always done this? Wasn't there a time when you were like other people?"

"I am like other people. A great number of people. I don't mean like you, or old Duckworth, or any of those pound-a-week carters at your yard, but there's a kinship between me and the kind of men who pay you pence to make guineas. Honesty? Industry? Thrift? What do these words really mean to people in a big way of business? What do they mean to that gaffer of yours, living on strawberries and cream in London?"

She felt the colour rush to her face and turned away from him. "Far more than a cutpurse like you could imagine. Adam Swann puts in a longer day than any of us. He pays good wages and accepts personal responsibility for every living soul he employs."

"Then he must be an exception proving the rule. You called me a jackdaw. All the merchants I've come across are hawks. One was instrumental in transporting my father for twelve years, on account of a single bale of calico. He stole it to provide clothes for my mother and sisters during a workless spell and we never saw him again. You don't have to believe it but it was the first thing he ever stole, other than spoiled vegetables in Covent Garden."

"How old were you then?"

"Nine. And the eldest of five."

She reckoned back, quickly. That would have been getting on for twenty years ago and the savagery of the sentence painted a sequence of pictures illustrating the probable background of the tall, embittered man, lounging on the threshold of an empty luggage van, committed to a nonstop war on society. She said, "How did your mother manage, Wickstead?"

"Indifferently, for two to three years. Then she died in the local Grubber. I saw her in her coffin and calculated her age. She was around thirty-five. She looked sixty."

"And your sisters?"

"The three youngest were taken in by neighbours. Gilda, the eldest, was pretty. She didn't have to steal. She had something to sell."

She had sometimes thought of herself as sorely tested over the years but she saw now that hardship was a relative experience. She had always had a roof over her head and enough to eat. She had always worn woollens in winter, and there were many days in her childhood and girlhood that had kept their colours over the years. It struck her then that by no means every theft he had committed was as calculated as this, and that there had been occasions, perhaps many of them, when stealing had been an alternative to starving.

She said, quietly, "Were you ever taken, Wickstead?" and he replied, casually, "I served three years building their stinking fortifications at Gibraltar. Three of seven I was directed to serve," and then smiled, adding "Long enough to build the muscles that held that load off you yesterday morning."

"Is that why you carry a loaded pistol?"

"I don't mean them to take me alive again."

It was not a threat exactly but a statement, at one with his coolness and impudence and with his resolution too, for he was not in any sense a blowhard. She saw him then as she had half-seen him from the first, not as a stable-lad turned waggoner, not as a professional thief, but as a freebooter as old as time, hammered into the man he was by the hit-and-miss blows of an imperfect society. Whatever thoughts she had of putting the police on his track were washed away by the strong current of sympathy she felt for him.

"They'll take you in the end. This isn't the only way to hit back."

"It's my way," he said.

She thought hard for a moment, contemplating the risks of a compromise. "You could do better. You've got brains and brawn and nerve, and it's all such a terrible waste. I stand in well with Swann and he needs men like you. I should have to tell him the truth but I believe he'd back my judgement . . ."

She stopped because he was smiling, the way he had smiled when he was cleaning the wound on her knee.

"I wouldn't put you or him to the test," he said. "Things have a way of going astray in your kind of business. It's one thing to risk a stretch chasing a handful of sparklers. It's another to have to prove to one's benefactors one wasn't there when a packet of pins went missing. It's handsome of you, none the less, so I'll give you some advice in return. Steer clear of Solly Beckstein. His orders aren't worth having at double the rates you're charging."

"I'd already made up my mind as to that."

"Yes, you would have." he considered her, his eye roving from top to toe and back again. "I said it once and I'll say it again, Miss Wadsworth. You're a corker. Any man on the make would be damned lucky to lay his hands on you. Commercially speaking, that is, although not exclusively so. Do we shake hands now? Honour seems to be satisfied."

She took his hand and shook it, wondering why she felt so diminished, the loser rather than the winner of this curious duel. Perhaps it was a final attempt to draw level that made her say, "If you change your mind I'll speak for you any time. So long as you've thrown that pistol in the river," but he was equal to that. "I'll do as much for you," he said, gaily. "If you change yours, that is. I operate over a wide field but a whisper to the Boots at the 'Wheatsheaf' will always reach me." He tipped his hat gravely but there was laughter in his eyes as he stepped round her, on to the platform and down towards the exit. She saw him for a moment against a tide of passengers moving across the hall to the London train and then he was lost.

* * *

She was still at her desk when Duckworth ambled across the yard and closed the gates after the last, homegoing waggoner. Her leg, coiled in an unnatural position because the scab on her knee was hardening, felt stiff and numb, and she stood up, yawning and at odds with herself, wondering if there were any more loose ends to be tied before she went home to supper. Kitson, of Cambridge, had been wired to extract the casket from the Waterbeach sack and to return it by hand to Beckstein's warehouse, sending the remaining packets on to Harwich. She herself had written and posted the letter explaining to Beckstein that instructions had come from Headquarters prohibiting the handling of jewellery as freight. She wondered what he would make of this but decided she did not care. Duckworth and Edward Brockworth had been given adequate explanations, the one as regards her second thoughts on Beckstein's traffic, the other a fabricated story about suspicions concerning a waggoner's honesty. Both had accepted the stories at face value, just as she had accepted Wickstead's. Arrangements had been made with the Harwich agent to collect bags at the left luggage office and make the local distributions a day behind schedule. She didn't care about that either, although it was the first time a parcel run had lost a clear twenty-four hours.

There was one thing left to be done. She picked up the report for Headquarters, the letter that would have been on its way to London by now had she failed to return from her thief-taking jaunt within the period, and tore it into small pieces, burning them all in the grate. It took a moment or so and then it was gone in a final spiral of smoke, just like Wickstead, just like all the men who touched her life and moved on out of sight and sound. She called to Duckworth, "Go on home, I'll lock up and let myself out the back!", and he raised his arm in acknowledgement and left. Petulance stirred in her when her sore knee came into contact with a stool and she kicked at it like a sulky child. Then, catching herself, she pulled herself together and stared into the tin-lid she used for a mirror, seeing there a new kind of doubt that hadn't been there two days ago, when she had run shouting into the yard, to berate a carter for slipshod loading. For a moment Yorkshire commonsense battled with dragging loneliness and body-hunger, with the impulse to break with a way of life that seemed likely to deny her the security and comfort of a man of her own and children of her own, with all that a healthy woman of twenty-eight took for granted. Wharfedale forthrightness won. She said, aloud, "Oh, give over, you silly slut! Where's the sense in lusting after a footpad, with his neck in a noose?"

She picked up her scarf and drew it over her head, knotting it with such emphasis that the jerk elevated her small, pointed chin. She went out, slamming the door on its spring lock and marched across the yard, her flatheeled shoes raising a scuffle of dust like a series of soundless explosions.

Part Five

Towards the Weir: 1865 - 1866

1

Apogee

HE always looked back on that period—the few weeks leading up to the early summer of 1865—as his apogee, a time when he and all his concerns were riding high, when the sun shone every day and the nights, wherever he happened to be, were redolent with novelty and promise. His domestic affairs had never enjoyed a period such as this, with Henrietta recapturing much of her original sparkle as the household settled to its comfortable collar, and the children seeming to grow a little every day, Avery's rewarding byblow as well as his own Stella, pudgy little Alexander, and baby George, who lay in his cot, chuckling over his inexhaustible stock of private jokes. His financial affairs were stable, with the house paid for, Blunderstone and Mc-Sawney off his back, the quarter-rents paid, and a reserve accumulating against the delivery of more box-cars, more horses and a fleet of holiday brakes in time for the indents of Ratcliffe, Dockett, Catesby and Blubb.

He spent the entire month of May on an extended spring tour, visiting every district in the network, and although he was never satisfied that all were fully stretched, what he found there gave him a personal glow of achievement and private assurance that very little had been overlooked in the regions.

He went first across the Kentish Triangle, finding Blubb established down here like a mellow old potentate, whose shrewdness had gained him the confidence of all his customers and subordinates, so that they tended to speak of him with a mixture of jocularity and awe, a ruler who was admittedly old, gross and beery, but who knew precisely how many beans made five and, moreover, possessed an additional pair of poached-egg eyes positioned somewhere near the top of his spinal cord.

By Mayday he had passed into the Southern Square, to find the boy Rookwood grown to manhood in a matter of months and bringing to the territory a zest and crackle that had not been evident in Abbott's day, notwithstanding the latter's drive and administrative

537

ability. He spent two days here before passing across to Tom Tiddler's Ground, and accompanying Dockett on a rapid horseback tour of the island, counting no fewer than fourteen Swann waggons in their progress across the chines and into the interior. Two days later he was at Exeter, fussed over by Augusta Ratcliffe, and introduced by Hamlet to innumerable country cousins, whose buzzing speech recalled his ride across the full width of Devon after his landfall at Plymouth when the enterprise was a dream.

From Exeter he took a train to Worcester and was conducted by Morris on a tour of the porcelain factory, taking note that Morris was accepted as a man of substance by the merchants on account of cornering the market after his deal to haul china all the way to Cardiff. Morris did not take kindly to supervision so he spent less than a day here and passed on into Bryn Lovell's territory, astonished to find the taciturn Welshman married and legal guardian to a flock of copper-coloured children, the sons and daughters of a pretty half-caste, whose first husband had died of blackwater fever off the West African coast the previous year.

Lovell had always registered at Headquarters as the incorrigible bachelor, who sought the small bonuses of life in his books and social theorising, so that his new status came as such a shock to Adam that he felt justified in demanding an explanation. The old Bryn would have retreated into his terrible personal privacy but marriage, or multiple step-fatherhood, had greatly enlarged him, and he said, with a smile, "We all come to it, Mr. Swann, and I've no regrets for she's a rare woman, with a still tongue and the sense to keep from under a man's feet when he's about his concerns. The truth is, I was nudged into it at Barry dock, where Lottie—Lizzie's youngest that is—fell between jetty and a moored collier, and would have drowned if I hadn't been there to fish her out with a boathook. I gave her mother a tongue-lashing for letting her stray there unattended and then one thing led to another, and here we are, six of us in the cottage where I thought to spend my old age reading books I'll never have leisure to open now. Would you care to make the acquaintance of Lizzie while you're here?"

Adam said he would indeed and was introduced to a slender, sloe-eyed woman, who looked young enough to be the manager's daughter and was, for Bryn said she was not yet thirty. She was very subdued in her husband's presence but he noticed that, for all his long years of bachelorhood, Lovell seemed to adjust naturally to the rôle of paterfamilias and was already teaching the two older boys to read.

He went on to the Northern Pickings in thoughtful mood, reflecting that it did not do to make assumptions about anybody for, in spite of Lovell's casual approach to his new responsibilities, it was obvious that he derived great satisfaction from the reverent ministrations of Lizzie and was very pleased with his readymade family. He met Godsall by appointment at Derby and found him chafing for promotion, although he seemed to be doing well on the fringe of the industrial area and holding his own with competitors in the Dale country, where he had hopes of organising a holiday-brake service, based on Ashbourne. He said, when they were inspecting the stables, "How long is old rascal Blubb going to cling to the Kentish beat, Mr. Swann? He should have died of apoplexy years ago," and Adam said that coachees of Blubb's type had been known to make a century, and there were tombstones around to prove it, but that he intended to retire him on pension in the new year and Godsall should replace him, as promised. "Not that Blubb needs a pension," he added, "the old reprobate has amassed a fortune in tips and commission, for it's that kind of territory. Not like this, where they count the pennies."

He went by train to Manchester, relieved to discover that the city was emerging from its long trance, as trickles of cotton came in from the Mississippi Delta following the surrender of Lee only six weeks before. Sam Rawlinson, whom he met at his new mill further west, told him it would be months before King Cotton settled himself comfortably on his throne again but the stresses of the reconstruction period were likely to bypass a man now buying Egyptian fibres.

"Are you investing in owt else but cattle and waggons?" Sam asked him, and when Adam said he intended to stick to what he knew, his father-in-law shook his head so vigorously that his blue jowls flopped like a bloodhound's dewlaps. There had been a time, he said, when he too had crammed all his eggs into one basket but the cotton famine had taught him that a man who did this deserved 'a mess on his britches'. They could talk this way now. Since presenting himself at the yard on his return from the East, Sam had been a regular visitor to 'Tryst'. Henrietta, Adam noticed, continued to treat the old devil with caution, as though, at any moment, he would box her ears and drag her back to Scab's Castle, but he had adjusted to Sam and they now did a great deal of business together. Sam was too old, however, to respond to the new mood of industry. He still tended to regard a man like Catesby as a potential Robespierre who would, given half a chance, hustle him into a tumbril and cut him down to size in St. Peter's Square, Manchester. He even warned

539

Adam that there was daft talk among cotton operatives of joining with other trades to hold a conference of delegates, and when this happened (if the Government was mad enough to let it) every employer in England had best look out for squalls.

They parted affably and Adam went to Salford to see Catesby, now reaping the benefit of the soup-kitchen hauls instituted at the height of the cotton famine in 'sixty-three. "Not all the cotton-kings are like your father-in-law," Catesby said. "Some get religion once they've made a bloody pile, and those are the ones I go for. That chap Gladstone is God Almighty in the Belt, and they seem to think the Radicals will sweep the board as soon as Palmerston kicks the bucket. Then we might get progressive legislation out of that talking-shop at Westminster, for folk here have sworn they won't stand for t'pay an' conditions dished out before the Slump. Radicals are promising compulsory education, a ten-hour-day bill and extended suffrage. It's been a long haul, since I stood at a loom from six nor ten when I were a little lad."

"Sam Rawlinson seems to think something on the lines of the Oath of the Tennis Court is being cooked up," Adam said, and Catesby replied, "Aye, and he's none so far adrift either. The Association of Organised Trades has it in mind to hold a conference soon and I'll doubtless be called upon to represent the waggoners hereabouts. Would that earn me my notice at Rawlinson's instance?"

"You know me a damned sight better than that," said Adam, grinning, "but don't count on a delegate from my father-in-law's patch."

He left Catesby dreaming of his social millennium, crossing the Pennines to see Fraser at his Hexham headquarters. Fraser was making giant strides up here. The incident of the wreck had injected confidence into him that he had lacked in the early days of his command, and now he had many Lowland customers on his books, and clamoured for more waggons and teams. Adam, seeing the progress he had made, promised him a rise in basic salary before turning south and crossing into the Crescents, calling on sub-depots at Whitby, Market Weighton, Newark, Boston and Spalding.

Like a child emptying a Christmas stocking he saved Edith Wadsworth until last. He approached the Peterborough yard one humid afternoon and saw her before she saw him, framed in the uncurtained window of her office. He was rather shocked at her appearance. Even at this distance she looked tired, drawn, and rather bowed about the shoulders, as if the demands of her command had sapped her vitality. Instinct prompted him to withdraw behind the double gates, thinking, 'If I know her she'll be ruffled if I show up without a warning' and took refuge in a tavern near by, dispatching a note saying he was passing through on his way to The Bonus and would call in around teatime. He spent the interval walking round the busy town, counting the number of his waggons he saw, but the thought of her, slumped over her desk, with the strain of responsibility apparent in face and posture, stayed with him so that he thought, 'Did I do the right thing giving in to her, and making her gaffer of such a slice of territory? It's a big bite to chew on, and I daresay she's had jealousy and surliness from men like Vicary, Goodbody and Horncastle.' He consulted his watch, finding it coming up to four, and made his way back to the yard where the weigh-bridge clerk, seeing him coming, emerged from his shed, saying "Message from Miss Wadsworth, sir. She'll be expecting you for tea at her lodgings. Will you want to look around first, sir? Mr. Duckworth's on hand." He said no, smiling at the way he had been checkmated, and took her address. "Tell Duckworth I'll call later if I stay on," he said, and the man looked relieved and saluted. It was curious, he thought, how almost all his employees continued to behave to him as though he was still wearing a shako, and had a corporal's guard within call, although not one among them had ever seen him in uniform.

2

She had made the most of the respite he had given her. Her house-keeper-landlady showed him into the ground-floor flat she occupied in a row of Georgian terrace houses overlooking a reach of the River Nene, where it wound its way across flat meadowlands on the southern edge of the town. She had changed into what he recognised (having hauled for so many suburban costumiers) as one of the new 'double dresses', with the upper skirt looped at the sides and bunched out behind, a style they were calling the 'Grecian bend' whatever that meant. The colour, olive green, suited her but she had dressed her hair in a bang that did not suit her as well, for it added severity to her expression, as though she was a governess or a vicar's wife entertaining a testy bishop. He soon discovered, however, that the familiar and outspoken Edith was still there for she

541

said, giving him her hand, "You didn't imagine we were caught on the hop, did you? There is such a thing as a grapevine. We've had an eye cocked for you ever since you left town. Our problem, of course, is to decide in which direction you're travelling, up the east coast and down the west, or vice versa. Try a cucumber sandwich. Mrs. Sprockett makes them for all my Grade A visitors."

Her manner, bantering but half-resentful, bothered him a little. It was the first time they had been alone since she descended on him with her armoury of facts and figures more than a year ago, although she had been present at the annual conference, when her parcel-run pilot scheme was adopted by four other districts. He said, hoping to call her bluff, "Don't take that tone with me. I remember you when you wore clogs and fried bacon beside the road. How is it working out, Edith?"

She looked at him sharply, as though he was posing a trick question. "You don't need to ask that, Adam. Tybalt puts my returns on your desk every Tuesday morning," and he said, impatiently, "I'm not referring to turnover and you know I'm not. Is the loneliness of power bothering you? You look to me as if you've been overworking. You've lost weight for a start!"

"Oh, I could afford a pound or two," she said, pouring his tea, and then, "'The loneliness of power'. That isn't original, is it? Someone famous said it about kings and ship's captains. Well, it's a price I expected to pay, for the fact is I carry an additional handicap as an unmarried woman. When I was a glorified waggoner I was at one with the men and their families but as gaffer I have to watch my step, or I find myself accused of favouritism. The wives are the real sinners, of course. They can't or won't accept a gaffer in petticoats. Most of them regard me as a compromise between a lucky harlot and the Tattooed Lady."

"I'd back you to make light of that," he said. "From my standpoint you're a tremendous success. Even sour old crab-apples like Blubb admit to that."

"Ah, yes," she said, nibbling at a sandwich in a way that suggested she would have preferred her bread and cheese, "the New Woman, climbing out of the seraglio and the schoolroom. But it's a long, hard climb, Adam, longer and harder than I expected. You and I are ahead of our time. It'll be another two generations before men as a whole will admit that some women can function outside the kitchen, the nursery, and the double bed!"

"There was Grace Darling and Flo Nightingale," he prompted.

"Freaks," she replied, "patronised by Beards."

There was bitterness in her voice and it continued to worry him although he was not all that surprised by it. He said, "Aside from the business, don't you enjoy any social life? You were always one to make friends easily enough."

"Not here, for I'm betwixt and between; that's to say neither husband-hunting nor qualified to sit among the dowagers and talk scandal. It isn't easy for any spinster but a spinster in authority . . .! I'd be lying if I said I wasn't lonely sometimes. For all that don't go away thinking I regret taking the plunge. It might have isolated me but it paid another kind of dividend."

"Tell me?"

"Do you need telling?"

"I need telling. I'm happier about you than I was but I still worry. You've made a success of the job but that isn't much to crow about if the price comes too high. Does it, Edith?"

She looked across at him with a smile. "You never will take things as read, will you? If I had my time over again I should do the same thing, only sooner. Handling a job like this, standing or falling by my own efforts, has given me back my self-respect and that's worth all the work and worry that goes with it. Now stop turning me over and prodding me to see if I'm done, and tell me what goes on elsewhere. You can begin with the truth about why you sacked Abbott and gave his patch to a boy like Rookwood."

He told her the bare facts, reflecting that he had never recounted them to anyone, not even Henrietta, and he was not surprised by the objective view she took of the unsavoury business.

"You took the only course open to you," she said. "How is Rookwood bearing up?"

"Surprisingly well."

"I gather you were sorry for Abbott. Have you heard from him since?"

"He took my advice and put his money in a half-share of a schooner."

She said, thoughtfully, "I was right about you, Adam. When it comes to handling hot potatoes I've never met your equal." She looked him over with embarrassing frankness. "You've got what amounts to a feminine intuition but the odd thing is it only serves you with men."

"Why do you say that?"

"Because it's obvious. You gave Ratcliffe the credit for that excursion idea when we all know it originated with his wife. You had to come to me to be told why your marriage wasn't successful and how to set it right. And although I've shamelessly spelled it out to you, you've never really accepted the real reason that prompted me to shoulder a burden like this. Shall I refill your cup? It might stop you fidgeting."

"I've done, thank you," he said. "What are you trying to tell me, Edith?"

She stood up, smoothing the crumbs from her bodice.

"Perhaps I can demonstrate it. Put your arms round me. Go on, no one is likely to come in. Mrs. Sprockett is accustomed to me entertaining gentlemen. Put your arms round me and kiss me, the way you did when we parted on the road to Ripon."

He looked so startled that she laughed and the sound of her laughter eased the tension between them. "If I remember rightly," he said, "the last time I offered to kiss you you bucked away like a scared filly."

"Yes, I did. For the simple reason I couldn't trust myself. But a lot has happened since then, to you and to me. I daresay you've already assessed your progress. Now I'd like to take stock of mine."

He stood up and kissed her on the mouth. It was something he had often thought about doing since that encounter beside the Swale but now that he did it surprised him a little to find her lips friendly but unresponsive.

"You see? It's worked for both of us. If that had happened the last time we were alone together in that belfry of yours I wouldn't have made much of a success of what I had in mind at the time. You follow me, I hope?"

"I follow you. But there's something else. My feelings about you haven't changed. I still think of you as very desirable, and also as the best friend I've got. But I know that if it came to a choice between me and the Crescents I'd run a damned poor second, and so would any other man in the offing."

"You're sure about that?"

"Certain of it. So certain that I'll not waste time inspecting your yard and stables."

He stood looking down at her thoughtfully, his regard for her enlarging itself into gratitude that there was at least one person who understood, in depth, precisely what animated him, and what had absorbed nine-tenths of his nervous energy over the formative years of the enterprise. "What's more" he added, "the next time we meet

544

we won't circle one another like gladiators. If I feel disposed to kiss you I'll do it, by God, without having to be coached." He picked up his hat and gloves. "There's a train at five-forty-five. It'll get me back in time to start sorting out the conclusions I've reached on this tour."

"I hope you won't commit your Peterborough conclusions to paper," she said, "but if you do, send me the duplicate. Tybalt wouldn't know where to file it. Shall I walk you as far as the station?"

"By all means," he said, welcoming the laughter in her voice, "but we'll confine ourselves to business all the way there."

She went into an adjoining room, re-emerging in seconds wearing her bonnet and pelisse and it seemed to him, quite unaccountably, that she had laid hands on her lost youth in that brief interval. The metamorphosis comforted him, so that he thought, as they emerged into the sultry heat of the street, 'It's hard to believe she was ever in love with me or that poor devil of a sailor. She only fancied she was, until she saw a way to become her own boss, and in that respect we're as alike as two peas.'

3

The old Colonel could not have said when or why the premonition touched him, causing a small, inward shudder. He was not given to premonitions and today, with a June sun flaming in a cloudless sky, was not a day for gloomy thoughts. And yet the prescience was there, formless but real, and once it had appeared uninvited and unwelcome, it remained, a silent, brooding wraith standing a yard or two behind his right shoulder, refusing to go and yet refusing to leave cover and identify itself as anything more than a shade.

There was no room for trolls of this kind in 'Tryst' nowadays. By a series of imperceptible shifts and adjustments the tempo of the house had settled to the key and rhythm of the enterprise that sustained it but he, as a permanent observer, understood that it was not a theme directed by a single conductor, as was the case with the orchestra beside the Thames. In the stone and timber house the first Conyer had built in a suntrap, it was possible to distinguish individual themes, his daughter-in-law's first violin, the governess's briskly played second fiddle, the incidental harmony contributed by Avery's child Deborah, the toot of little Stella's trumpet and the

545

steady rattle of Alexander's drum. And that was how the old man saw and heard it, a muted, pleasing, tuneful domestic symphony, accompanying the slow march of the seasons.

He was well-placed to watch and listen, for his observation post, an upended, sliced-through longboat, converted into a weird-looking summerhouse and planted on the spur above the house, overlooked frontage, paddocks, forecourt and drive. He could sit here taking it all in whilst pretending to paint, and listen and wonder without embarrassing anyone, often without anyone knowing he was there.

On a day like this, when the sun warmed his old bones he would turn the leaves of his memories like an old, well-loved book, sometimes probing back half-a-century to a time when a stronger sun had flashed on his helmet as he rode along the banks of the Tormes, the Tagus, and the Ebro with his light dragoons, or to half-forgotten garrison posts in the Caribbean, or set on the edge of some steaming jungle. But he was not a man to do more than savour the distant past much as a chef might savour a sauce before serving it. Mostly he lived in the present or recent past and that was odd for a man of his age and ripeness. It was probably due to the satisfaction he derived from his situation, doyen of a household populated by young people and children, a position he had never thought to enjoy until 'that boy' took it into his head to go into trade and found a family.

He missed very little. From his elevated position, with his back resting against the old timbers of the upended whaler, his sharp old eyes could probe the landscape as they had once probed Marshal Soult's position on a distant ridge. It was here that he had first spotted the impact the Avery child was making upon the household, how deftly that prim Scots lass, Phoebe Fraser, had enlisted her as a deputy, how conscientious Henrietta had become concerning her responsibilities as stepmother and how dependent little Stella had become on the older child now that Deborah had been integrated into the family. He noticed, too, the transition of his daughter-in-law from girl to woman, sometimes wondering if that silly brush with that gunner had not had too sobering an effect upon her, converting her, almost overnight it seemed, from a lovable, mischievous hoyden into a matriarch. He would have regretted the transformation had he not been there to see her change back when Adam's horse's hoofbeats were heard on the gravel, for then the way she ran to greet him recalled his own short-lived happiness with the boy's mother, so that he thought, with a smile, 'I daresay he knew what he was about when he threw her across his saddle bow and brought her home like a prize. She only lives for him and his appearances. The rest of us are so much surplus kit she lugs about.'

The children intrigued him. They were already talking about what regiment Alexander would enter at seventeen, and even from here he could spot the boy's qualifications to pick up the Swann tradition where his father had laid it down. There was a foretaste of the parade ground strut in the little fellow's movements from porch to paddock, a touch of the cavalryman's pride in the way he sat his barrel-chested pony at three. There was even a hint of the barrack room in his hectoring approach to Dawson, the gardener, or Still-man, the handyman, and the stuttering questions he put to them, like a young greenhorn making his first tour of stables.

He had his favourites, of course, among them Stella, who often climbed up here to watch him paint. Stella shared his delight in landscapes under rapid-changing conditions of light and shade, and would sometimes challenge his choice of colours when he was trying to capture the green of April, or the russet of October in the copse opposite. Up here they would converse as equals, an old soldier of seventy-five, and a child of five, sharing the pleasures of the long, slow ride from the moment the first daffodils showed on the paddock, to a time when the chestnut leaves were brittle and autumn sat over the woods like a patient mother waiting to put her noisy family to bed.

He was very happy, happier he supposed, than he had ever been, so that sometimes, when this kind of mood was upon him, he would wonder a little tremulously how long it would last. Not long for him, of course, for he had already celebrated forty-nine Waterloo anniversaries, but away into a brand-new century for most of them, he hoped, although sometimes this seemed to be taking a great deal for granted in a world that was changing at such a stunning pace.

Perhaps it was the pace that bothered him, even though he was a confirmed potterer who never hurried anywhere, and yet he was conscious of it, as though, out there beyond the heat haze, he could hear the grinding roar of the big city, and sniff its stale, second-hand air competing with the lilac, mock-orange and cabbage rose, whose scents reached him from the beds between the house and paddock.

He could not settle to his painting, deciding it was a mish-mash and rested with his hands on his knees, trying to match the perman-ence of what he saw and the sense of impermanence that blurred his thoughts. He had a fancy then that it was a premonition of death, introduced, perhaps, by the invitation he had received that same day to attend the Jubilee dinner at Apsley House, marking the fiftieth anniversary of Waterloo. It might well be this and if it was it ought not to bother him, for very few of the originals were above ground now and it was time he thought about shuffling off to join them. He would be sorry, of course, for no one but a fool would wish to be winkled from this particular billet, even though he sometimes suspected they had all come to look upon him as a museum exhibit, like the Old Duke's cocked hat, or the voltigeur's musketball that sent Tommy Picton packing all those years ago. Or perhaps his unease stemmed from something more definite, a heart murmur, or the stumble that had recently replaced the careful, spur-conscious tread of earlier old age.

He sat very still, his eye on the truncated fingers of his right hand, and it was then, for the first time in many, many years, that he saw again the fierce, moustached face of the big cuirassier who had lopped them, a florid, clumsy fellow, who had looked amazed when his opponent had shifted sabre from right hand to left and lunged before he could correct the body swing that followed his own gigantic slash. Then, as the sabre-point glanced from the rim of his breastplate and entered his neck, he had fallen away without so much as a cry, while the Colonel had reined in, staring down at his bloodied gauntlet.

The clarity of the memory startled him so much that he fancied he sensed pain in fingers that were not there and he thought, wonderingly, 'Now why the devil should I recall that on a summer's day fifty years later? Damn it, it's almost as though that poor devil of a Frenchman had been looking for me all this time . . .' and he glanced round the edge of the summerhouse just to satisfy himself that it was not so, and very reassured he was when, instead of a cavalryman's frown, he looked straight into the laughing face of little Stella, who had stolen up on him through the ferns as she sometimes did when she tired of Alexander's demands on her.

The sight of her, with her chestnut curls cascading over her pinafore, and her little mouth puckered in a smile, steadied him for he could see that she was excited and had something to confide. She said, dancing up and down, "Debbie is coming tomorrow to stay until September! Won't you just love having her here?" and when he consented that he would, and that he supposed Phoebe the governess would be taking her to meet Deborah's train, she hopped from one chubby leg to the other, squealing, "Oh, *no*, Granddaddy! You've got it wrong. *We're* going to fetch *her*! On the train! All the way to Folkestone—me and Alex and Mamma and Papa, for Papa will be home in time for tea and it's all arranged. Isn't that wonderful? I mean, not just having Debbie, for lessons, and sharing my room and ... and everything, but all of us going to the seaside as well?" Then, stepping back and regarding him speculatively, "Why don't we ask Papa to take you? He would, I'm sure, and you've never been in a train, have you?"

"No," he said, "I never have, and I'm too old to travel in one now. I like trains, at least I like watching the smoke puffs in the distance, but I wouldn't feel safe nor comfortable rushed along at that pace. No, my love, I'll stay here with Phoebe and entertain young George while you're gone."

Alexander came waddling up the path, just as the bell announcing luncheon clanged from below. "We're g-g-g-going on a t-t-train," he announced, "to fetch Debbie away from the nuns," and the old man chuckled for it was obvious that Alexander regarded a convent as an ogre's castle, where Deborah was held under duress from time to time.

"So your sister tells me but you'd sooner ride there, wouldn't you?"

"Don't be silly, Granddaddy," Stella said, severely, "who could possibly ride all that way? It's forty miles, Miss Phoebe says," and it struck him that people's notions of distance had altered with all the other changes for even after his return from the wars forty miles had still been reckoned a two-day ride and tomorrow, he supposed, they would all be there and back in a matter of hours. He rose stiffly and lifted his easel inside the summerhouse, taking the children by the hand and moving between them down the path to the house. The ghost of the French cuirassier did not follow but remained to brood in the summerhouse beside the half-finished watercolour. Perhaps, the colonel thought, as their pace dragged him on, ghosts were impotent in the presence of laughing children.

4

He had been away longer than usual but at least she had been forewarned of his return, so that she was able, by inventing a white lie or two, to slip away towards the middle of the afternoon and wander down the drive in the hope of intercepting him before the children took charge of him. He usually arrived home at dusk, so that it was not long before they were alone and she could adjust to his presence, but today she did not feel that she had that much patience. Nearly a month had passed since he had set off to pay a call upon those other mistresses of his, dotted all over the country.

It was, she thought, the loveliest summer day she could ever remember, even here in Kent where everyone expected more than their fair share of summer. The air quivered over the paddocks and in the copses every leaf was so still that the foliage reminded her of Mrs. Worrell's waxed fruit under a glass dome. There was not even enough breeze to set the poppies nodding under the paddock rail, but the colour down here was like a long, cooling draught, so that the heat, under the arched chestnuts, was not oppressive. She hugged the shade none the less, following the line of trees as far as the derelict building that had been Michelmore's mill, then climbing the low fence and entering a thin belt of fir and larch bordering the lane. There was a pheasant hide here, a solid little structure built by old William Conyer, the sportsman, and she peeped in, to discover that the children had been using it as a little house and had carpeted the floor with bracken. Outside was a stack of sawn logs striped by sunshafts, and she sat down, cocking an ear for the rattle of the gig and, as always when he was absent, and she was clear of the house, revelling in solitude and the speculation that solitude encouraged. Excitement at the prospect of seeing him again hummed in her like a spinning top, but slowly the silence of the little wood had its way and she leaned back on her hands, luxuriating in a way that was impossible up there at the house, where new demands were made upon her every minute.

Gradually her thoughts formed a pattern that was at one with the scene, having serenity, colour and shape. There was 'Tryst', with its routines; there were the children, who seemed to her to have acquired, of late, not only charm but moderate manageability; there was his business which, judged by his letters, was booming along like a river in spate; and there was her, sitting here on a pile of logs awaiting him, like the Cecil girl who had stolen out of her father's house to meet the first Conyer near this very spot.

The comparison pleased her. Outwardly, she supposed, things were always changing, but the basic things did not change at all or not until people grew wrinkled and frail and breathless, or stiff in the joints like the old Colonel who had seemed so pensive over luncheon. She was twenty-seven now, mother of three handsome children, and the virtual mother of a girl of ten, but at this moment she felt more akin to the novice who had waited beside Derwentwater for a stranger to come back and marry her. How long, she wondered, would she continue to feel like this about a man? How many years would pass before they took one another for granted, before the idea of coming down here to waylay him would seem absurd and undignified? Five? Ten? Not more, surely, for at thirty-six one was nearly old and he would be close on fifty, about as old as Sam when she packed her basket-trunk and fled into the night.

She thought about Sam for a moment, deciding that he had no terrors for her now, and reflecting that Adam had been very wise to promote a reconciliation. Sam had once seemed to her a man capable of anything, but now, with his florid face and heavy paunch, he was nobody special. People could be tamed then by the passage of time and the planless events of passing years. She must have been tamed, she supposed, or she wouldn't be sitting here in a wood listening for the rattle of a man's approach, and hoping to snatch a few moment's privacy with him before he became common property up at the house. She wondered if anyone, least of all herself, would ever subdue Adam Swann and decided not for she saw him now as a member of that select company who had mastered England and were well embarked upon the task of subduing the entire world. Surely it was a privilege to be such a man's mate and bear him children, and she realised now that it was only in the last year or so that she had come to terms with this, for until then, until George had been conceived that night at the inn, she had always been jealous and resentful of his business whereas now she not only accepted it but took a personal pride in it every time she saw a waggon bearing the Swann insignia. After all, it was *her* insignia.

It was only a step from this to contemplation of any future children she might have and there was time, she supposed, for half-a-dozen more. Stella and George were his and Alexander was hers. What arrangement would they come to concerning future children, or rather future sons, for daughters did not count in this context. For a moment her imagination soared as she saw man and wife picking sides, as for a game of tag, as successive sons presented themselves. She was smiling at this absurdity when her ear caught the jingle of harness and the scrape of wheels. She jumped up, assailed by the scent of resin and realising, with a flurry of irritation, that some of the sticky substance had transferred itself to her palms. Then, forgetting everything but his approach, she ran through waist-high bracken to the low bank where she could watch his gig round the last curve in the lane, the lane down which Dancer had rushed them the night Stella was born and she thought she was going to die. It astonished her that she could remember that at this particular moment, when all her senses were strained towards the approaching reunion, and yet she did, and for a fraction of a second relived those awful moments in the lurching carriage, but then he came bowling up, seeing her out of the corner of his eye and pulling hard on the reins as the horse, less impatient than Dancer, came to a halt.

She stood with one hand enclosing a sapling and the surprise and the pleasure in his expression was ample excuse for the ambush. He called, eagerly, *"Wait!"* and jumped down, looping the rein over the whip socket and running out a length of cord as a tether. The cob welcoming the respite on such a hot day, lowered its head and began to crop the long, sweet grass of the verge and for a moment they stood there, she looking down and he staring up, his face glistening with sweat and his hair powdered with the dust of a cross-country ride.

Some explanation, she thought, was necessary so she said, lamely, "The others were all dressing up for you. So ... well ... I thought I'd come on down and wait," but then she stopped, blushing under one of those half-ironic, half-predatory scrutinies he seemed to reserve for homecomings.

"I'm very flattered you did," he said. "How often does a man see a siren in a Kentish hedgerow? And a very pretty one at that? No, don't," as she made to descend, "you'll get hooked up on the briars," and he vaulted upwards as eagerly as a boy on a birdsnesting expedition, throwing his arms round her and kissing her eyes and cheeks and hair and finally, with tremendous gusto, her lips, so that she said, breathlessly, "Adam ... that cob ... No one could get by ..." but he only replied, laughing, "Don't be so coy, woman. It's our right-of-way. Let them shift the gig into the drive if they're in that much of a hurry, for I'm not, are you?"

The boyish spontaneity of his greeting delighted but bewildered her. "Well, no," she said, "I suppose not, for we didn't expect you for an hour, but it's so public here, in full view of the lane ..." and then she remembered the pheasant hide and giggled, reflecting that they really were behaving more like a couple of peasants in a hayfield than a married couple with three children. She took him by the hand, nevertheless, pulling him into the copse and pointing to the

552

little hut in the clearing. "The children have been playing there," she said, "making a little house, I suppose." He glanced inside, then back at her, saying, "Very obliging of them," running his hands over her and holding her off by the hips in that speculative and rather shameless way of his as he said, "They're dressing up, you say? Well, you don't seem to be wearing very much, my dear," but she could match his mood now and replied, saying, "I should think not, in this weather. Besides, I know you of old when you've been away and I should, shouldn't I?" but when he held her to him again delight in his presence and more particularly in the astonishing success of her stratagem, led her to say, without reserve of any kind, "Oh, Adam, I've missed you so! More than ever before. I've ached for you, yearned for you and I wanted you all to myself for a few minutes ...", and with that he practically bundled her into the hide where the sun made intricate patterns through weathered patches in the roof and walls, and she forgot the cob and the gig blocking the lane, and the possibility of people coming to and from the village, and the presence of the Colonel, the children and the staff almost within hail at the top of the drive.

*   *   *

The serene splendour of the afternoon, the weeks they had been separated, and even the brazen nonconformity of the setting might have been contributory factors to the joyousness of the occasion, but they were no more than that. It was as though, at that precise hour, circumstances and experience had contrived to strike an exact balance between them, so that for the first time in the years they had shared as man and wife they were aware of existing momentarily for each other. Their fusion, when it came, was a new peak in their mental and physical experience so that what had begun as a frolic took on a new and spectacular dimension, transcending the passing of seed from his loins to hers and profoundly disturbing their entire ethos, as though the act itself was the apotheosis of a ritual as old as time. Perhaps he was more acutely aware of this than she, sensing it in every shift of her eager body, and in the cry wrung from her at the moment of fulfilment. Something approaching this rapture had attended them in the past but only occasionally and never with the same intensity, for it was as though he had helped her to cross a sensitory frontier into an area of intense personal conceit where, from this moment on, she could more than hold her own with all his other concerns, taking pride of place in his heart and mind.

553

For her it was much simpler than that. She was not concerned with abstracts but her instincts were as sharp as any woman's and much sharper than most, so that awareness of the extension brought her a security and maturity that had eluded her all her life. She had been endowed with one personality and, at his insistence, had tried hard to develop another, but now, crushed under him, and exulting in him, she was conscious of a blending of those two separate selves and had no need to be assured that this was an alliance he not only approved but had been trying, in his own obstinate way, to promote ever since that night of compromise at the inn adjoining his yard. What he had sought, and what so far had eluded him, was a different kind of compromise, the establishment of a working partnership between the impulsive, affectionate juvenile he had married, and the self-consciously dutiful mistress of his household and here it was, achieved almost effortlessly through the alchemy of flesh and fervour on a carpet of dried ferns and bracken on their own doorstep. In a way it was a kind of miracle and she accepted it as such.

He seemed reluctant to withdraw from her and she did not hurry him, even though she was aware that all her artfully arranged hairpins had fallen away and lost themselves in the fronds under her shoulders, and that her carefully-ironed sprigged muslin was a soiled, rucked-up ruin, in which she dare not show herself outside. She lay very still, savouring her triumph, and waiting for him to acknowledge it and presently he did, taking her hot face between his palms as he said, "It's all behind us now, Henrietta, that make-do marriage, the pair of us leading almost separate lives, the way we've been doing all these years. I can't say how or why precisely, but something happened, something we were hoping for and searching for. You can't order these things. Between two people they happen or they don't."

"I've felt it happening all the time you were gone," she admitted. "I suppose that's what led me to get to you before you were swamped in affection."

"It isn't my imagination then? Suddenly we're so much more necessary to one another, in every sense?"

She said, after a moment, "You wanted me to grow up and I did, in many ways. But then . . ." She had no facility with words and stopped. "*You* explain it. You must know what I mean."

"I know exactly what you mean. That we lost something we had in good measure from the beginning but now we've found it again. That's what you're trying to say, isn't it?"

"I never stopped loving you and wanting you this way. Not for a moment. Not even that time we quarrelled."

"I know that. I've always known it. It was my turn to make a move." He kissed her mouth very gently and she heaved herself half-upright, finding a backrest against a sapling built into the structure of the hide. She noticed something else as she did this. Modesty, of the kind she had always acknowledged the moment he was spent, had abdicated, at least for as long as they remained alone in here contemplating their achievement. She made no move to rearrange her dress and petticoat, but pillowed his head on her bare thighs, stroking his hair, absently, and noticing the spreading patches of grey above the ears and the deep, brown patina of the skin enclosing his high cheekbones and jaw like a sheath. Desire still flickered in her, so that she thought, irritably, "Bother the children! Bother everyone waiting for him up there! I'd like to stay here loving him all night and all tomorrow," and looking down at the underside of her dress, decorated with dozens of tiny leaf-skeletons, she felt an irrational impatience, not only with conventions but with clothes, especially the kind of clothes that made occasions like this so rare. She would have liked to have shrugged herself out of the straining bodice and leaned forward so that his lips could caress her breasts but then, remembering Stella's excitement when she read aloud that part of his letter announcing his return, and the proposed expedition to Folkestone to fetch Deborah, she felt greedy and selfish and said, regretfully, "We'll have to go, dearest. If we stay one or other of them is sure to come down and see the gig and they'll start beating the woods for you."

"Before that happens, and before I forget," he said, "the next time I go you pack a bag too. This place is big enough to take care of itself for a spell and I'm not getting any younger. Why the devil should I save you for the odd moments I can spare from that octopus out there?"

She did not remember him ever saying anything that enriched her half as much. He had often praised her physically, both calmly and in the turmoil of a tumble such as they had engaged in a moment since, but this was something altogether different. For the first time he was admitting her to full partnership, to permanent association, and she said, fervently, "I should love that, Adam. It's something I've always wanted, more than anything; except to give you sons."

"It's settled then. From now on we'll travel in convoy, and there's a great deal out there that I should enjoy showing you." He sat up

555

and helped her straighten her wrinkled stockings and find one of her errant shoes, and suddenly she was fully aware of how she must look and lifted despairing hands to her hair.

"How on earth can I show myself? One glance and everyone up there will realise ...", but he only laughed, hauled her to her feet and said, "I've thought of that. Go back through the copse and across the kitchen garden, behind the greenhouse. If I time it well they'll all flock to the front of the house as you slip in the back. Even Dawson and Stillman will come round to the stableyard to see to the cob and carry the luggage in."

She was only partially reassured. "My hair, Adam ... it's awful, and I haven't even a mirror. I could tie it up but if I use a garter my stockings ..." but at this he laughed again, saying, "Turn around," and took off his cravat, looping it round her tresses and tying it in a bow.

"You're quite dreadful," she said, "but you do seem to think of everything. You'd imagine we behaved like this every day."

"Perhaps we will," he said, and they went out into the blinding sunlight where he showed her how to cross to the little wood above the mill, speeding her on her way with a smack on her bracken-strewn bottom. She shot across the road into the trees like a fugitive and he thought, 'She's been running from something or somebody ever since I found her on that moor but now she's home, and so, by God, am I.' He went back over the bank and retrieved the cob and gig, swinging into the box and beginning the steep ascent of the drive.

2

Tumult

As always, in summer, birdsong in the wisteria awakened them before there was any necessity to stir and for a few minutes he lay still, with her head pillowed in the hollow of his shoulder. He said, as though resuming a conversation interrupted by no more than a moment's contemplation, "What I was saying ... a chance for you to see the network first-hand. Why put it off? Why don't we take advantage of Deborah's stay? The children will be wholly taken up with her for a spell, and you've never seen the westcountry, have you?"

No, she said happily, she never had, and it was a part of the country she had a rare fancy to see, especially Dartmoor.

"Why Dartmoor?"

"I read a book a long time ago about a girl who lived in a great house down there and fell in love with one of her father's grooms and ran away with him. Not as we did, for this was planned in advance, and they went all the way to Gretna Green but before they got there he was arrested for abduction and thrown into Newgate. It came right in the end, of course. He was only pretending to be a groom. He was really a French nobleman's son, spying for Napoleon."

"Good God!" he said, chuckling, "the awful trash you read! Don't you ever tackle anything heavier than that?"

"No," she said, unrepentantly, "for I'm not at all good at concentrating. There's always so much to do."

"Well, listen," he said, "when the nights draw in I'll read some of my favourites aloud to you after the children have gone to bed. George Eliot and Charlotte Brontë—they're to your taste I'd imagine, and my old friend Dickens, the best of the lot. Suppose I did? Would you have the patience to listen?"

"Indeed I would. I should like that. It's twenty years since any one read to me, but how can you think of going off like that when you've only just got back? Won't the children resent it?"

557

"Not in the least. I run a poor second to Deborah Avery when she's available. I'll tell you what I have in mind. We'll catch the boat-train back today. Four hours on that beach is as much as your complexion will stand in this weather and you can start packing right away. We could get off tomorrow, or the day after. We'll spend a week at Exeter, going somewhere fresh every day in one of old Ratcliffe's brakes."

"*Ex*-et-er," she said rolling the name on her tongue. "It's a lovely word, I've always thought."

"The Western Wedge is a lovely area. The scenery is superb, and Ratcliffe has made a great start with the excursion trade down there. Later on, around September, I'll show you Wales, and when I go up to the Border Triangle in the autumn you shall come too."

She contemplated his offer in the way she had sometimes contemplated that ring he had given her on the road to Ambleside, something immensely flattering and extremely personal, something that emphasised the certainty of the gains she had made after so many years. Here he was proposing a second honeymoon, as though to compensate for the lack of one when he brought her south and turned his back on her to devote all his energy into launching the service. It was, she supposed, to be expected that their relationship should ripen as time went on, and the house and children drew them closer together, but it occurred to her that his mood was linked in some way to a sense of personal achievement that he had brought home with him after an extended tour of his empire. Something told her, however, that the main impetus was hers, and that it had to do, at root, with his essential physical need of her so that once again she saw him as a reincarnated Conyer, keeping a tryst with that Cecil girl, almost as though something of the satisfaction those two Elizabethans had found in one another was still stirring in the stones and timbers and coverts of this sundrenched corner of Kent. It was an extravagant fancy but it pleased her, emerging as a wordless, self-congratulatory paean, as she went about the business of dressing and braiding her hair, smiling into the mirror when she came across an odd wisp of bracken that had survived last night's brushing.

She assumed, of course, that her triumph was essentially private but it was not as private as that. He was aware of it and accepted it, though it continued to puzzle him, for he began to see it as a transition from a merely physical affection, tempered with tolerance on his part, into a comradeship that was unique in their relationship. It was there in the rather smug, possessive glances he intercepted, and

later in her brisk air of authority as she presided over the hasty
breakfast and issued her orders to children and staff, but, above all,
it was apparent in the clothes she selected for the jaunt, as though,
instead of dressing for a beach picnic, she was on her way to a viceroy's garden-party. He was not alone in noticing this, for little Stella,
her attention almost wholly occupied with the excursion, remarked
on her mother's ensemble as soon as they settled themselves in the
gig for the journey to the branch line, saying as she fingered the
creases of her mother's silk parasol, "You look ... *different,*
Mummy!" and he saw Henrietta colour and caught the sparkle in
her eye as she replied, "It just happens to be new, dear, and Folkestone is very fashionable, I'm told."

It was half an hour later, when they were aboard the train, and
Henrietta was explaining the nature of an oast-house to Alexander,
that he had leisure to observe how very 'different' she did look in her
inappropriately-named 'country toilet' consisting of a tight-fitting
paletot worn over a white muslin blouse, and long trained skirt in
dove grey silk, buttoned gloves and a saucily-angled crinoline hat,
adorned with what they were calling 'follow-me-lad' ribbons, so
that he thought, 'It's astonishing, the confidence she's acquired.
Maybe I underestimated her all these years, maybe I should have
pitchforked her into the network from the beginning', and he recalled the remark of Edith Wadsworth when they parted at Peterborough a few days before, something about him having a feminine
intuition that failed him in feminine society. The recollection made
him smile for this, he thought, was one victory he couldn't go crow-
ing about to Edith.

*   *   *

He put them off at a section of beach above the bathing machines,
promising to be back with Deborah within the hour, and the cab
took him through the town to the western residential section, where
the unkempt drive led up to the featureless house he had first seen
under snow on the day he introduced himself to Avery's byblow. It
was only eighteen months ago but it seemed much longer, perhaps
because the child had made such a comfortable place for herself in
his heart and had been integrated so effortlessly into his domestic
background. He contemplated her as he stood listening to the echoes
of the convent bell, a still, knowing, composed little presence, with
a great reservoir of affection that was at the disposal of every living
creature that crossed her path and dead creatures too, for he

559

recalled watching her conduct a burial service over a kitten that Dawson, the gardener, had inadvertently trodden upon in the vinery. Genes made no kind of sense, he told himself, for who could have imagined a child like this resulting from a casual collision between a sophisticated rake like Avery and that tittupy woman he had set himself to seduce all those years ago? Then the door opened and the Mother Superior was standing there, a little thinner and more fragile he would say, with bright colour spots on her cheekbones that he had not marked when they first met. She said, ushering him into the vestibule, "I'm glad you could come personally, Mr. Swann. Deborah is packed and Sister Sophie will bring her down in a moment. But first we could confer for a moment, yes?"

He noticed a certain hesitancy about her and it disturbed him. "Is anything wrong? Deborah is well?"

"Never better," the Frenchwoman replied, with a smile, "but please to be seated, Mr. Swann. I had it in mind to write but then, when you said you would be calling, I changed my mind. It is presumptuous to talk of such matters but more so, I feel, to commit them to paper."

He waited for she was not the kind of woman one prompted. The morning, so bright at its outset, clouded a little, and it occurred to him that she had received news that Avery was dead, or instructions to remove Deborah from her charge and his. The second possibility alarmed him more than the first, for he had made up his mind that Josh Avery did not deserve Deborah, or anyone as rewarding as Deborah. She said, pensively, "You are corresponding with Mr. Avery?"

"Not a word," he admitted, "and I can't say that it surprises me. Have you heard from him lately?"

"Not directly. Money drafts have arrived through an agent in Vienna. He's a strange man, Mr. Swann."

"Stranger than you imagine," said Adam, feeling relieved, "but if it concerns the child I should be glad to help in any way I can."

She looked down at the worn linoleum. Her skin was like waxed paper stretched on a skull and the two crimson spots glowed like small beacons divided by the high ridge of her nose. "It concerns all of us here," she said, "but essentially me, Mr. Swann. I have not long to live, they tell me. No, please! No condolences." She smiled and he thought he had never seen a sweeter or a wiser smile. "I am much older than you suppose, and I have known the truth for some time now. The fact is, the establishment here cannot continue without me and the sisters must necessarily disperse. That part is arranged and need not concern you. As regards Deborah, I could arrange something satisfactory, for our Order has re-opened several establishments on the Continent. Things are more settled there than they were after the troubles of 'forty-eight. There is, however, the matter of guardianship, and the child's best interests should be considered."

He said, with diffidence, "What are her best interests? In your view, Reverend Mother?"

The answering smile was frank and even tinged with mischief. "Ah, Mr. Swann, what kind of interests are we discussing? Spiritual or material?"

"Do they run contrary?"

"Technically they do. You are not of our Church, Mr. Swann."

"Isn't that for the child to decide? She's old enough, and very mature for her age."

"You do me an injustice in assuming I haven't consulted her, Mr. Swann. That would be very bigoted on my part. You have given her love, you, your wife, and children."

"She's easy to love," he said, "but I think I understand your position. You would only part with her on an undertaking that I brought her up in her own faith?"

"You make it easy for me, Mr. Swann. Would that be possible? If she made a permanent home with you?"

"I see no reason why not. There would be difficulties, I suppose, but they would be practical ones—access to a priest, regular attendance at Mass, that kind of thing. Is there a legal aspect?"

"None that I know of since Mr. Avery seems to have surrendered his responsibilities. That letter he wrote would satisfy any lawyer and as to the quarterly drafts, I could arrange for these to be redirected to you."

"The money isn't important. Apart from her faith I should bring her up as one of my own family, and I can speak for my wife as well as myself. We already think of her as one of us. Will you make the necessary arrangements or shall I?"

"It can be done from this end. We have a legal adviser who will be disposing of the property and other matters."

"Then consider it done." He looked into the deep-set grey eyes of the woman, recognising her disease as a certain killer, probably within the year, but strength of a kind still resided there. "You will be going into a hospital in England?"

"No," she said, "I am going home. A place is being prepared for

561

me in a nursing Order in Languedoc. So you see, I shall have my wish after all. I shall see the south again. For a little while."

He heard the clatter of feet in the hall and saw Deborah and a nun pass under a picture of the martyrdom of St. Sebastian. There were, he reflected, less dramatic roads to martyrdom. She saw his glance and said, with the same quiet smile, "We have said our goodbyes, Mr. Swann. As you say, she is an adult child. One of my rare successes."

There was nothing more to say. Any prolongation of the interview would put an unnecessary strain on her dignity. He took her hand, noting the blueness of the veins as he bent his head. Her smile followed him into the passage and as far as the door where Sister Sophie hovered, holding it open. Deborah was already in the carriage, her usual still self, as though she was taking away some of the Mother Superior's repose as a keepsake. The sun still flamed in a cloudless sky, but for him the heat had gone from it. He thought, 'This will have to keep until I've had time to talk it over with Henrietta. Tonight, maybe, when they've all tired themselves out,' and again he felt gratitude that the decisions he had in mind were likely to be easier than they would have been a few days ago.

2

Blubb's hatred of the railroad had never moderated, not even now, when the stage-coach had taken its place in the museums alongside coracles and Boadicea's war chariot. He still referred to it as 'that bliddy ole gridiron', or, after a fifth, mellowing pint, 'that stinking ole tea-kettle us is stuck wiv'. Alone among the district managers he had made no more than a token attempt to establish the equivalent of Edith's parcel-runs in his territory, declaring more than once that bag traffic, concerned as it must be with small packages, 'weren't worth a farden's pains nor the fag-end of a bliddy candle'. Adam, who had affection for the old rascal, had not harried him, knowing that he would be retiring very soon, but Tybalt, with an eye on the parcel-run income had given him any number of prods, the latest and most vigorous in Adam's absence when a few cases of French wines consigned to a City wholesale vintner were included in a shipment booked to cross Blubb's patch by South Eastern goods train,

The wine order was not important and ordinarily Blubb would

not have made an issue of it, but he saw, or pretended to see, a splendid opportunity to score over clerk and railway, pointing out that it was wrong to subject good Burgundy to the shaking it was likely to get on the gridiron, and although he was overruled, and the cases were consigned to Reigate by rail, circumstances enabled him to make his point in a way that brought him tremendous satisfaction. Due to a series of unforeseeable accidents the wine was mislaid and left behind in a shunted goods waggon in a siding a couple of miles east of Headcorn.

Feeling that here was an opportunity too good to miss Blubb set about tracing it and in the course of his inquiries learned that the South-Eastern track-layers were rebuilding an insignificant bridge over the river Beult that spanned the magnificent racing section of line midway between Ashford and Tonbridge. It was, in fact, due to these repairs that the wine had gone astray, a shunted waggon having developed a fault and been pulled out of line to allow the passage of the boat-trains. It did not surprise Blubb that men mainly pre-occupied with fast passenger traffic should forget its existence for three whole days after the rest of the shipment had gone on to Reigate for distribution.

Discovery of the oversight brought a gleam to his eye. He did not care a curse about Tybalt's London customers, for Reigate was suburban territory and the wine, in any case, was consigned for a London customer. But he saw at once that it provided him with a useful stick to belabour Tybalt and the railway, and that was why he undertook to recover the goods personally, driving down to Head-corn in a pinnace and relishing the prospect of giving a set of tea-kettle lackeys the rough edge of his tongue. He delivered himself to Michelmore, his stableman, before setting out. "They worn know where to look when I show up, wi' my manifest, and lay claim to that there wine! Three days it's bin there, and if I 'adden tracked it down it'd be maturin' beside the track till it was fit fer a Dook's cellar! Pervidin' they didden swig it, mindjew, and I woulden put that parst the thievin' bleeders. The minnit I get aholt of it in goes a report to the Gaffer that'll make ears burn in Headquarters," and he cracked his whip and set off in fine fettle, stopping to refresh himself at four taverns between base and Sutton Valence, where he took the road bearing west of Headcorn for the section of the track under repair.

Two quarts of Kentish ale had moderated his choler somewhat by the time he arrived and located the waggon on the siding east of the bridge. The sun was hot and it was pleasant to sit in the shade of the canopy where the road ran across a swampy field straddled by the bridge. The track, at this point, swarmed with platelayers working against the clock in their efforts to re-lay rails across a forty-foot gap Blubb's side of the bridge. He was a man who set great store on the adage 'Know your enemy' and said nothing for the time being concerning his purpose there, and soon he became mildly interested in the work of hauling the lengths of rail into position, and riveting them to baulks of timber that formed the floor of the cross-over. Presently, noting the flash of a gilded inn sign in the village of Staplehurst close by, he climbed down, tethered the horse to a briar, and waddled up the embankment where he chanced on the foreman platelayer consulting a timetable.

He was tempted then to declare himself, but the ale, the mildness of the day and, above all, a sense of rectitude that warmed his belly like a belt of flannel, had mellowed him to the point of jocularity, so that the fancy took him to discover how well the foreman was up to his work. He said, with a bumpkin's innocence, "What be about then? Opening up a new stretch o' line, mister?" and the man looked at him as though he was an idiot and said, casually, "Are ye daft or summat? This is the fastest stretch o' main line in the system. The boat-train stretch from Folkestone," and Blubb decided to expand the hoax, saying, with a respectful whistle, "You doan zay, mister? But how's a train to cross that gap without wings?"

The man closed his timetable with a sigh. He was accustomed to boys plying him with questions concerning his trade but it was not often he had a chance to patronise someone many years his senior. He said, "There's no boat-train due, you pudden-'eaded Swede. Boat-trains run on the tide, and this timetable tells me the first up train passes Headcorn at five-twenty. Headcorn is two miles away, so that gives me two hours to close the gap, don't it?"

"Ah," said Blubb, hugely enjoying his country-cousin rôle, "It do, pervidin' there bain't no freight trains in between. I see you had one waggon come adrift a day or two back. Now what be stowed away in there, I wonder? Wines, mebbe? That thirsty gentlemen in London is waitin' to drink?"

At this point the foreman tired of Blubb and his bucolic conversation. He was hot, sweaty and working to a tight schedule, and he turned aside to shout instructions to a gang wrestling with a bulk suspended over the last arch by a pulley on a gantry, but as he did this his trained ear detected a disturbing sound, a sustained humming, like the sigh of a far-off wind, and it tensed every muscle in his body. Shouldering Blubb aside he dropped on one knee and laid his ear to the rail and then, like a released Jack-in-a-box, straightened up, whipped out his timetable and flicked through the thumb-printed pages.

Watching him at close range Blubb thought he was taken by a seizure. He went rigid and his eyes seemed to leap from their sockets as he whispered, "Oh, Christ! Sweet Christ, *no!*" and suddenly began to dance and gesticulate, screaming incoherently at the gang handling the baulk and then, when they stopped working and stared at him, breaking into a run down the track towards Headcorn and the coast.

A lifetime of coping with emergencies had equipped Blubb to make very quick assessments of evidence available to ears, eyes and that sixth sense coachees had in abundance. He picked up the discarded timetable and ran his eye down the closely-printed columns, noting that an up train, and a boat-train at that, was due to pass Headcorn not at five-twenty but at three-eleven. He groped for his watch, a cumbersome hunter that had once regulated journeys all over the country, noting that the hands pointed to nine minutes past three. With an oath that emerged like a belch he too began to run as the distant humming enlarged itself into a definite pattern of sound, the noise of an onrushing train travelling at maximum speed.

3

He first saw him as they passed in single file through the barrier to claim reserved seats in the first compartment of the last coach, a man of medium build in his mid-fifties, with a brown imperial and whiskers, and a high forehead that would have been recognisable anywhere in the civilised world.

He was moving leisurely up the platform, accompanied by two women in half-crinolines and there was absolutely no mistaking the profile, the slightly dandified clothes, the general impression conveyed by gait and gesture of an assurance close to arrogance. He said, gripping Henrietta's arm, "Good God, it's *him!* It's *Dickens!*" and when she said, vaguely, "Who, dear?" he turned on them all, his face red with excitement, and repeated "*Dickens! Charles Dickens!* The most famous man in the world!" and that made them all stare so that they blocked the wicket-gate and boat-passengers from the Channel packet began to jostle them from behind, and Deborah, the first to recognise the majesty of the occasion, squealed, "He's on our train, Uncle Adam! He's travelling on our train!" and she skipped ahead with such alacrity that he hissed, "Don't *stare* so, Deborah. People don't like to be stared at!" but he stared himself nevertheless, for it was something to look into the face of the creator of Sam Weller, Scrooge, Micawber, and so many others at a range of a few yards and discover, when you checked your seats, that you were occupying the compartment next-door.

They settled themselves in a flurry of excitement, his awe infecting them all, not excluding three-year-old Alexander, who demanded more information at the top of his voice and had to be shushed. Deborah said, settling him on her knee, "He's a famous story-teller, Alex, the most famous in the whole world. He's called Mr. Dickens, and Papa has a very high regard for him, haven't you, Uncle Adam?" and Adam said he had more regard for him than for any writer alive and that he had read every word written by him. This was an exaggeration but an excusable one in the circumstances. Henrietta, who had never turned a page written by Charles Dickens, was more amused than awed, but it pleased her that the day should provide Adam with a bonus for she had always acknowledged what she thought of as his erudition. "How old is he, dear?" she asked, and Adam said he would be fifty-three, and when Henrietta said he looked older he told them that he had recently suffered a breakdown in health due to overwork, for he was regarded as the most prolific writer of the age.

The presence of so famous a man in the next compartment gave them something to talk about as far as Ashford but they were all sun-tired, and little Alexander took a nap, his fat limbs sprawled on Deborah's lap. "It's odd," Adam said, "you remember it was only this morning I promised to introduce you to Dickens. I said I'd read him aloud to you next winter and, by George, I will, now that you've seen him. I'll begin with *Oliver Twist*, for that's a striking picture of what goes on in the London underworld. Would you believe it? That chap in there sometimes walks about London all night unescorted looking for characters and material. They say he penetrates districts where no policeman would be seen alone. He's not simply a novelist, you see, he's concerned with all kinds of social abuses, and his books have done a great deal to make other people aware of them." He was going to draw a parallel between *Oliver Twist* and Kingsley's recently-published *The Water Babies*, that had roused

566

public opinion over the plight of chimney sweeps, but checked himself just in time. It was not an occasion, he thought, to remind her of that incident, and he saw that he had not only her attention but Deborah's too and, through Deborah, the attention of little Stella, who was gazing up at her friend with eyes limpid with adoration. He thought, 'I'm glad things have turned out as they have, and that child is making her home with us for good. Henrietta will approve, I'm sure, and Stella will be so excited that she'll be sick the minute she learns of it.'

Pluckley flashed by and with Alex soundly asleep, and Henrietta dozing with her head resting on the cushion, the two girls began making holiday plans so that he forgot Dickens in favour of his wife. She looked, he thought, prettier than he ever recalled, with her copper hair trapping the sunlight where it swept in a soft curve from hat to dimpled chin. Odd, irrelevant images concerning her returned to him, like a review of family photographs in the brassbound album in the drawing room—Henrietta as he had first seen her, shin-deep in that peaty pool; Henrietta in ivory satin, standing beside him in the church at Keswick; Henrietta, scared but gallant, in that candlelit room at Ambleside, where he had first held her in his arms, and suddenly a rush of affection for her surged through him and he wished very much that the children were next-door closeted with the celebrity, so that he could slip his arm round her, and tell her how young and pretty she looked, and how eagerly he was anticipating the holiday they had planned.

Then, out of the tail of his eye, he saw the station of Headcorn flash past and a moment later became aware that the train was slowing down, not gradually, as if approaching a scheduled stop, but abruptly, as brakes were sharply applied, and at the same time he saw, on the track below, a man prancing about with a red flag, reminding him of a frenzied sepoy on the walls of Lucknow, and within seconds of his stupefied face being lost to view the carriage itself began to bounce and bucket like a horse out of control and they all seemed to be lifted out of their seats and caught up in a mad, senseless jumble of arms and legs and cascading luggage. Without in the least being aware of what had happened he saw Henrietta open her mouth in a soundless scream, and the bemused expression on his son's face as he was catapulted upwards from Deborah's lap, and after that a long, grinding jangle that obliterated everything, and a rush of suction that seemed to scoop them up and swill them around like so many leaves in a gale.

567

He did not relate all these astounding happenings to the train in which they were travelling, or indeed, to anything that had a place in the ordered scheme of things. They were bizarre, apocalyptic occurrences, associated with a gigantic natural disaster of some kind, a tidal wave, an earthquake or possibly a thunderstorm more violent than any thunderstorm he had ever experienced. And they seemed to go on and on, with the noise getting more deafening, and the gyrations within the compartment ever more violent and complicated, and then, just as suddenly they ceased, or almost ceased, for rumblings and crackings and splinterings continued at a remove like the long, long echo of a thunderclap rolling away into the distance. Then, in the strange silence that followed, he was conscious of a pricking sensation in his cheek and lifted his hand to it, amazed to find that the fingers came away holding a dart of varnished wood about four inches long but feeling no pain and not even realising he was bleeding until he saw blood splash down on to some grey material level with his chin and realised, with sudden and shattering certainty, that the material was Henrietta's paletot, and that the gleaming point sticking through its folds like a lodged arrow was the ferule of her parasol.

Gradually his brain began to clear and he became aware of subdued uproar around him, an outcry quite distinct from the grinding, splintering cacophony that had preceded it, a sound issuing from human throats and lungs, a confused, wailing chorus of shouts and groans and screams, some half-heard, others heard at close range. His military reaction to disaster partially reasserted itself and he dashed the blood from his cheek and tried to stand upright, finding that it was possible, in spite of a variety of obstructions, sharp and solid, or soft and rounded. At last he got his head clear and the first thing he recognised was Deborah's head and shoulders, hunched and withdrawn, as though she was hugging something close to her body, and then he saw that she was cradling his son Alexander, hedged about by innumerable bundles and that Alex, too, had his mouth wide open in a scream.

The steady drip of blood from his cheek maddened him, for it made concentration very difficult, and he clutched at the material it was spotting and wiped it across his face, finding that his vision cleared and his brain with it, so that he could make some kind of attempt to adjust to the lunatic confusion of a carriage tipped almost at right-angles. He knew then, at least approximately, what had happened. The train in which they had been rattling along a few seconds before had all but disintegrated and when, reaching out for Deborah, his eyes came in line with the shattered window, he could look down on a field about fifteen feet below and see men scuttling in all directions, like a swarm of beetles exposed by an overturned stone. Between the window and the field was a wide baulkhead of timber, at least two feet thick and resting, so far as he could determine, on two brick piers that had supported it but there was no track to be seen. To the right, across a wide gap in a bridge, he could see the engine and tender still miraculously upright but listing slightly to one side and half-enveloped in steam. Behind it, and linked to it presumably, were three coaches, but between the last of these and the spot where his own coach hung suspended was the middle part of the train, a horrid jumble of timber and metal bridging the full width of a small river and already erupting with people, as though a whirlwind had stripped the roof and beams from a village street exposing everything that went on beneath thatch and tiles.

He began now to take deliberate action to free himself from what he thought of as a deadly trap, plucking at the ferule of the parasol, drawing the malacca cane free and using the point to break out the jagged edges of the nearest window. The fragments fell with a succession of insignificant crashes and he had his head and shoulders through the aperture and was wrestling with the door handle when Deborah's voice reached him as a high, imploring wail, "Uncle Adam ... help ... help ... Alexander ..." so that he wrenched himself back, twisting a half-circle, seizing the screaming child by his shoulders, hoisting him over the still form of his daughter and somehow contriving to push him clear of the window where he at once disappeared into the outstretched arms of the ex-coachman Blubb, who was standing on the baulkhead immediately below.

It did not astonish him that Blubb, manager of the Kentish Triangle, should be there to receive Alexander, only that the child should be removed so effortlessly from his grasp but as he withdrew himself a second time he became more or less aware of what was happening outside, where the coach hung from a snarl-up of rails and brickwork like a sock from a tangled clothesline. With a sense of wonder and relief that was like the removal of a tremendous weight from his chest he saw too that no one inside the compartment was dead, or even bleeding as he was bleeding, and it seemed miraculous that this could be so, for the woodwork and stuffing of the interior bulged and sagged in all directions, like a sofa that had been ripped and slashed by a dozen drunken swordsmen. Henrietta's voice came to him faintly and he saw her struggle half-upright, her pale face framed in a tangle of bright, copper hair, her hat reversed but still firmly fixed on her head with its absurd ribbons spilling down the front of her corsage that had split across the middle, revealing the pink petticoat underneath. Then Deborah called to him again and he was struck by the steadiness of her voice as she said, "I'm not hurt, Uncle Adam ... but Stella ... *Stella* ... there by your knees ..." and he glanced down and saw his daughter propped like a folded bolster between the seats, with her little white boots braced against the horsehair of the section of the compartment where Deborah had been sitting. He writhed around, fending off a hamper that had contained their picnic and lifted her clear, moving towards the window backwards, turning and finding there another pair of hands, or perhaps several pairs, reaching out for her over his shoulders, so that she too passed from his grasp. A gravelly voice from outside was saying, "The child ... the lady ... pass 'em through, mister, for Christ's sake, before she slips ...", and his body began to respond to orders dictated by instinct, for he was unable to think clearly and logically and all the time that infernal drip of blood pumped from his cheek, splashing everything about him.

His next impression was that of receiving the limp body of Deborah from the hands of his wife, who had somehow levered her from the far corner of the compartment, and it seemed to him quite astounding that she had the strength to perform such a feat in flat contradiction to the laws of gravity, for Deborah had been lying half under Henrietta when she had projected Alex upward into his grasp. He saw blood too, and realised that it was not his own, for it was running diagonally across the child's thigh, but before he could look more closely a bearded face peered down at them from the splintered window frame and he recognised it at once as the face of Dickens and realised that the man was actually addressing him, saying, jerkily, "Door's locked ... they're *all* locked ... wait ... !" and one of his hands disappeared, reappearing almost immediately holding a stone, and then more glass fell with a crash, some fragments inside the compartment, where Stella had been lying a moment ago, but more of it outside on the baulkhead.

He had some kind of grip on himself now and could begin to deliberate as regards actions that, until then, had been little more than reflexes. He could even count and addressed himself to a sum relating to the occupants of this shambles, remembering that he had passed three bodies down on to the baulkhead but the power of concentration came and went so that he could not be sure who they were, or in what order they had left the compartment. There had been five of them and three from five left two, himself and one other. He inched himself away from the window, beyond which all hell seemed to be breaking loose, and moved closer to the jumble at the far end and there was Henrietta, face downwards in a welter of split cushions and bloodied luggage, and he would have assumed her dead had he not remembered that it was she who had been lying across Deborah's legs a moment ago and had somehow changed places with her, pushing the child in his direction. He began to work his way down to her, moving very cautiously, for the gravelly voice was still warning him that the coach was finely balanced and that movement inside it might shake it loose and pitch it through the gap into the river with the others.

It seemed to him a long time elapsed before he could grasp her by the shoulders. Her fine clothes were in ribbons but she did not seem injured, although when he called her name she did not respond but stared at him with a curiously hostile expression. It was when he sat back on his hams, bracing himself to lever her between his legs that the carriage itself began to sway and the movement, no more than a gentle rocking motion, had the power to frighten him as nothing had ever frightened him in his life. In blind panic he exerted his full strength, rolling over on his back and dragging her with him, so that her full weight rested on him, her head level with the window. He could see nothing now but he could hear a confused mutter of voices immediately above and assumed hands must be reaching down through the aperture and plucking at her, for the pressure on him moderated and suddenly she was gone and he was sitting there alone holding one of her elastic-sided boots, half-blinded by blood, dazed, breathless and utterly spent.

The rocking motion he had noticed now became more pronounced and behind it, like the thump of a brass drum, he could detect a harsh, jarring sound, as if the free end of the coach was beating rhythmically on the ground. He understood then that he was lost for very slowly, or so it seemed, the carriage began to spin. He heard someone call out with terrible urgency and seemingly almost in his ear, but there was nothing more he could do to help himself beyond rolling on his side and crouching between the shattered seats. The sliding movement brought his eyes level with the window and suddenly he glimpsed the sky, blue, cloudless and, like everything else in that bedlam, gyrating with a slow, ponderous swing. And

571

after that nothing, only a wall of sound that fell on him like tons of masonry.

4

Blubb, clambering on to the step of the last coach and peering down through a window at his employer, was not much astonished by what he saw. The coincidence was swallowed up in the immensity of the occurrence, a small, insignificant piece of a horrific jigsaw in which Adam Swann, his wife, and his family were somehow trapped and almost certain to die. In a disaster of this magnitude identities went by the board. It would not have surprised him to have seen the Queen or the Shah of Persia and all his retinue stagger out of the debris that choked the valley. As it was he did what he could, and what he achieved stemmed not so much from the man he was, old, gross and short of wind, as the man he had been before those meddlesome fools had laced all England with iron rails, boasting that they could now transport passengers from one point to another at twenty times the speed of the old 'Tantivy' or 'Shrewsbury Wonder'. At a price, of course. Sometimes this kind of price.

Blubb's reactions, notwithstanding his age, his bulk and his mountainous prejudice, were as quick or quicker than those of anyone at work on that bridge at the time. He had read approaching disaster in the face of the foreman before the man had moved two strides down the line towards the distant figure of the man stationed there, waving his futile little flag at an onrushing boat-train, the smoke of which could already be seen in the cutting. He knew then that nothing could avert a tragedy of fantastic proportions, and that here, on this strip of line, many people would die, or be mutilated. There was no time to shift the pinnace out of the line of danger. What time there was he used to save himself, and used it to advantage, plunging down the embankment like a hippopotamus in flight from a dinosaur, then diving under the brick pier supporting his end of the bridge. He gained sanctuary with seconds to spare. A moment later the avalanche came thundering down on them, scattering men from the bridge like a shower of peas and filling the air with a diabolical symphony of screaming brakes, hissing steam, rending metal and human outcry.

From where he crouched, in the limited security of the brick buttress, Blubb had a clear view of the plummeting train, watching, jaw agape, as engine and tender cleared the gap on their own momentum, dragging the first three coaches in their wake and somehow, freakishly it seemed to Blubb, remaining upright on the other side. He saw it all clearly for no more than a moment and then it was enveloped, together with half the valley, in a cloud of steam as the following carriages broke free and slipped away down into the stream like a string of barrels shooting a waterfall.

The spectacle was so awful and so final that it had majesty, rooting him there in a kind of trance and watching the wreckage thresh and flounder before resolving itself into a vast, untidy pyramid. It was not until little spurts of colour began to spill down the sides of the pyramid and roll or bounce across the marshy ground, that he could see the wreck in terms of human tragedy rather than a spectacle involving tons of wood, glass and metal. Then, at last, he crept out, his old heart pounding against his ribs like a sledge hammer, and averting his eyes from the carnage he glanced upward, amazed to see the final coach balanced at a sharp angle, like a diver arrested in the first movement of a plunge. Immediately behind it, and comparatively intact, were two vans, presumably those of the guard and the mail and the phenomenon had the effect of steadying him a little, the sheer improbability of what he saw absorbing the recoil of the shock that was paralysing his brain, so that it struck him at once the final passenger coach had been caught in wreckage ploughed up by the engine and tender, and it was possible, and even likely, that it contained people able to help themselves, if they were encouraged and assisted from without.

He made his decision on the instant. Down on the river banks there was a score of men, and many more, alerted by the uproar were already streaming out of Staplehurst, so he reasoned that they would be likely, one and all, to concern themselves with the first luckless wretches they found, whereas he alone was within easy reach of a coach that might, at any moment, plunge into the chaos below. He clawed his way upward to find the horizontal baulkheads had withstood the shock and were still in position, although there was nothing at all between them and the field below and it was therefore necessary to move cautiously, as upon a catwalk. A middle-aged man with an imperial, whose distraught face seemed to Blubb vaguely familiar, was already half out of the shattered window of the second compartment, wrestling with the door-handle, and as Blubb shouted a warning he lunged himself forward and downward,

573

so that Blubb was there to support his weight for a moment while the passenger's flailing feet found the steeply-angled step. He seemed uninjured and in control of himself, for he said, breathlessly, but authoritatively, "Stay there . . . two ladies . . . pass them down!" and Blubb braced himself to receive the weight of two women, one young and pretty, the other elderly and hysterical. Neither, so far as he could see, was injured and the younger woman scrambled nimbly through the window without much help. The elder was halfway through when she collapsed, and hung there, wedged in the aperture like a rag doll plugging a small hole in a fence.

It was a terrible business easing her through, despite the absence of all but a splinter or two of glass. She was wearing one of those monstrous, box-pleated crinolines, flat at the front but very full at the back, together with armoured stays and innumerable petticoats, some of which caught on the jagged woodwork of the frame and ripped to tatters. The iron-nerved passenger with the imperial beard heaved and strained and Blubb, his chest level with the step, stood like Atlas supporting her weight as she descended on him an inch at a time. By the time she was free two other men were there to help and the younger woman had disappeared, so that Blubb moved nearer the bridge with the bearded traveller at his elbow and heard him say, wheezing for breath, "Party in there . . . children . . ." but he was clearly incapable of hoisting himself up and seemed to Blubb near the point of collapse. He said, "Wait on, sir . . . I'll go up. Could you handle the nippers if I winkled 'em out?" and the man nodded wordlessly, passing his hand across a brow coated with dust and sweat. Blubb grabbed the handle of the compartment and hauled himself up, not without a fearful glance over his right shoulder, for the coach rocked twice and then gave a lurch before settling again. Then, of all people, the Gaffer's face appeared in the window and Blubb, occupied with establishing a precarious balance, muttered, "Christ A'mighty, *you*!" as he hauled himself level with the window and saw what appeared to be a coachload of dead bodies, sprawled at all angles, and between him and the charnel house the face of his employer, Adam Swann, with a great jagged cut below the right eye pumping blood and spattering everything about him.

Blubb thought then that he would die himself, falling backwards over the balustrade of the bridge, and fear prompted him to make the effort of his life, gripping the doorhandle with his left hand and clawing the edge of the window frame with his right. For perhaps twenty seconds he hung there like a fly on a wall, watching Swann grope his way down towards the bodies at the far end of the compartment and then claw himself back again, moving crabwise and dragging behind him a screaming boy, aged about three. The child's screams helped him, stirring in him a terrible compassion for everyone in there, but, rising level with his pity, a terrible hatred and contempt for railways rose in his throat like bile so that he saw himself, in that moment in time, as a man singled out by Providence to avenge all the other victims of the gridiron, living and dead, who had mouldered away in failed inns, in bankrupt livery stables, in tumbledown toll-houses and in want and destitution over the years. The mission acted on him like a cordial, injecting a new and furious energy into muscles that he did not know he possessed, or had ever possessed, giving him the strength and dexterity to improve his position in a manner that left one hand free to drag the child through the hole, to steady him for a few seconds while he levered himself round, and then, with infinite gentleness, to lower him into the upraised hands of the man he had helped rescue the two women further down the coach.

He was no longer aware of the uproar that surrounded him on all sides, or even of the presence of the other helpers scrambling up the embankment in ones and twos, or indeed of anything but the necessity to empty the compartment of survivors before the coach broke away and continued its arrested nosedive into the field. He accepted the fact that this would happen very soon, that every second he remained there, every movement he or Swann made, underlined this certainty, but it did not occur to him to release his hold on the doorhandle and jump clear while there was a chance of extricating the four other people trapped in that debris. The little girl who was passed on to him was much easier to handle for she was unconscious and as light as a feather, but when Swann dragged an older child level with his chest he was obliged to use his teeth as well as his free hand, biting into the collar of the summer dress she was wearing and shifting his left-handed grip on the handle so that he could roll her on his belly and let her fall between himself and the coachwork into the arms of men on the baulkhead. The movement, carefully judged as it was, came near to causing the ultimate disaster, for the coach began to rock violently, flailing its broken coupling against the baulkhead and prompting another chorus of warnings from below. He ignored them, readjusting his grip and finding a blessed purchase for his knee against what he imagined must be the hinge of the door, and it was this anchorage that enabled him to claw Mrs. Swann through the window, although he could never have managed it had she not stirred and opened her eyes as Swann levered her towards him and he got a grip on her bunched skirt. She seemed then to understand what was happening and co-operated to a degree, taking some of her weight on her elbows and getting a purchase with one foot on the split horsehair of the backrest, but she could never have worked herself free without Blubb's leverage from outside and the effort used up the very last of his strength so that when she fell he could do no more than grab at the tatters of her dress that came away in his hand. Those below must have broken her fall for he saw her stand upright for a moment, her mouth open, her arms gesturing feebly towards the place where he stood and he read her message, despite the successive waves of giddiness that assailed him now, causing him to spare a final glance at the interior of the compartment and the mask of blood that had little in common with the man who, so improbably, had appeared from nowhere seven years before and had helped him rebuild his pride. Then, glancing over his shoulder, and perhaps assessing the wisdom of jumping down to make way for a younger, stronger man, he saw that the group under the step had scattered, and at first their abrupt disappearance did not connect with the slow, deliberate slide of the structure to which he seemed to have been clinging for an hour or more. When the connection was made, and he understood precisely what was happening, he gathered himself for a spring, aiming roughly at the baulkhead but knowing somehow that he would miss it and fall through the gap on to the debris below, and this was how it happened and there was no one to break his fall, only spears of splintered coachwork and one steel buffer that struck him above the heart. The buffer absorbed the impact to some extent but the collision was lethal none the less, for it catapulted him clear of the wreckage and he fell like a sack into a patch of spongy marsh, and lay there spreadeagled, half-buried in soggy, trampled grass.

Only one or two bystanders saw him die. Most of them, including those scrabbling frantically among the wreckage of the carriages lying in the stream, ran for their lives when coach and vans crashed down between the piers, remaining upright for a moment before slipping sideways and rolling over on their backs like three grotesque insects with wheels instead of legs.

576

3

Thaw

HER responses during what she later came to regard as the deep
trance period, a matter of ten days or so, must have been as involuntary as they were polite and practical; orders issued; information
supplied; decisions taken, all with that frozen area of her brain that
had governed speech and actions at the scene of the crash, and continued to serve her up to the moment they came to her with the
straight alternative. To amputate, or to let him take his chance. If it
was a chance.

The decision had a curious effect. It cracked the ice that had insulated her to a great extent but, once it was made, a second, shallower
trance succeeded it, so that full awareness of what the disaster meant
to them all in terms of personal adjustments continued to elude her.
This second state of mind prevailed through the remainder of the
summer and, to a degree, until autumn had spotted the wooded spur
behind the house with old blood and guinea gold, reminding her that
the rhythm of the universe was entirely unchanged, that it had not
faltered, as everything else had faltered, because a foreman platelayer had looked at the wrong page of a railway timetable on the
afternoon of the ninth of June.

That same night she paused to do something it had not occurred
to her to do throughout the entire interval. She stopped in the act of
undressing to hold a candle up to the dressing table mirror, studying
the reflection calmly and objectively in a manner uncharacteristic of
a time when she had acknowledged vanity as a vice that a woman
deeply in love was entitled to practise.

What she saw in the oval frame astonished her. A tense, hollow-
eyed woman she would have judged about thirty-four or five. A
woman who had slept very little in weeks and who was convalescing
perhaps but had, in the process, struck some kind of bargain with the
future, exchanging dimples and a ripe mouth for a tautly-stretched
skin and a prim little gash. Someone who had ceased to be concerned
with the clothes she wore, how she dressed her hair, what effect sun,
wind and insomnia had upon her looks.

577

She sat studying this stranger for a long time, moving slowly towards the point of recognition. Outside the night sounds in paddock and copse resolved themselves into a familiar pattern and with that small part of her mind not engaged with the process of adjusting to the transition from polite, disembodied ghost to someone of flesh and blood and complete awareness, she juggled with dates, measuring the most distant of them against the time available for a counter-attack upon the terrible demands of the last few weeks and finding a measure of reassurance in the answer to the sum she set herself.

Spring was the earliest estimate Sir John Levy had given as the time of his return. It would take a man that long, Sir John had said, to learn to walk again, and it was two seasons and a child away. Pregnancy exacted toll from the figure but was, on the whole, an honest trader in that it often bestowed something in return. Bloom to the cheeks, and a definite sense of renewal in terms of youth and vitality, a very comforting thought, to be used as a reserve against months of loneliness and the stresses resulting from the biggest challenge of her life.

Then, as the candle guttered in the draught, another thought occurred to her. Like a whiff of fresh air invading a stale sickroom, like the swift passage of the court jester through a council chamber of sour-faced ministers of State, the enormity of her double deception proclaimed itself, so that the tight little mouth she was studying quivered, experimenting with the forgotten habit of laughter. And it deserved a laugh, she told herself, as he, of all people, would be the first to admit, for how many husbands returned home after a nine-month's absence to learn that they had not only been superseded as helmsman of a business but were obliged, into the bargain, to acknowledge an addition to the family?

The secret smile was like a spring opening a door sealed against the past and, she found, as the door opened, that she had the courage to look and to contemplate, to look back and see herself slumped over that farmhouse table sipping tea from a mug thirty minutes after they had dragged her semi-conscious and half-naked down on to the line. It was good to see herself in that abject posture, drained and vulnerable, for the woman in the mirror was far from beaten. She looked very tired, and desperately overwrought, but she was both armed and armoured against the future and compared very favourably with the complacent little baggage who had used that same mirror the morning they all set out for the picnic on Folkestone beach.

*　　*　　*

The interval between emerging from the wrecked coach and finding herself in the crowded farmhouse kitchen, with her children around her, and so many strangers coming and going, was a very blurred memory. She did not recall how she got there, dazed from the impact and that prolonged escape through the window into the arms of the men who caught her and set her down as tenderly as though she was a bubble that would burst. She had a vague recollection of stumbling across a field, a battlefield it seemed, but unlike any she had seen in the illustrated papers at the time of the Crimea and Mutiny. There was no shape to it, and no dignity. Dead and wounded lay about in abundance but they were not arranged in graceful attitudes as in the pictures, and seemed, one and all, to be in strident revolt against the fate that had spewed them into a water-meadow. Some kind of directing force was present, however, for a stream of walking wounded were all moving in a single direction, through gaps in a hedge, and across a grain-field already trampled flat, to a red-roofed building that formed three sides of a steaming midden. The children, her children that is, seemed to come and go, so that she seemed to be watching them through a thick lens held by an unsteady hand and it needed a tremendous effort on her part to assure herself that they were whole, and present as a unit, but for the time being Adam remained outside the range of contemplation. It was much later that she understood why.

It had to do with the kind of man he was and also, to some extent, with the strength and dexterity he had exerted to drag her free of the wreckage and propel her within reach of the hands that plucked her through the hole and down on to the line. A man who could lift her clear of the floor, whilst lying flat on his back and half-blinded with blood, must surely have been capable of following her down on to the line, but what had become of him since was more than she could say. A man like that, she assumed, must be in urgent demand nearer the river where the main part of the train had piled up along the banks of the Beult. Then somebody was confronting her, a haggard, middle-aged man, with a pointed imperial, and was saying something about a coach that hung over the gap. And then someone else joined him and suddenly, or so it seemed, she was the centre of attention, and knew somehow that this had to do with Adam. The man with the imperial took hold of her arm and she caught a word or two he uttered ... 'went down' ... 'no time' ... 'still there', and suddenly, without much sense of shock, she understood the drift of what they were trying to say, relating it to the reverberating clatter that accom-

579

panied her slither down the embankment to the field. He was not out there helping after all. He was still in that carriage and almost certainly dead and her first, overriding thought was that she must go to him.

They tried hard to dissuade her, not just the persistent man with the beard, but others, including two or three whitefaced men and one young woman, with her dress hanging in tatters, but she pushed through them, saying, "He's my husband! I'm not afraid to look at him."

They went out then, resignedly, a sorry little procession consisting of herself, the man with the imperial, another man in bloodsoaked overalls, and the young woman clutching her rags about her. She heard Deborah call but ignored her, crossing the yard, negotiating the gap in the hedge and moving over the field now dotted with couples hurrying past carrying bundles on improvised stretchers, to that part of the meadow where a single coach and two vans lay upturned, the wheels glinting in the strong sunshine.

There was a group of men at the free end of the carriage using a crowbar laid across a great, squarecut baulkhead and as they sweated and strained the end of the coach rose slightly and tilted, making a sucking noise as it parted from the deep, muddy scar on the grass. Stooping low she caught a glimpse of him, or rather of his sand-coloured coat, together with the picnic-basket they had carried down to Folkestone. The basket was squashed almost flat. She cried out then, dropping on her hands and knees and crawling forward under the leading edge of the roof. Someone tried to hold her but she took a firm grip on a projecting plank and all that happened was that her ripped bodice, already split across the front, parted down the back as far as her belt. She went on, nevertheless, burrowing steadily through an accumulation of loose debris and calling his name and at last she managed to insert her head through the narrow gap between a bulge of leather and the top of the flattened picnic basket.

He was lying on his back in a little hollow formed by the concave slant of the shattered timbers. One leg was clear but the other, splayed out at an angle, was pinned by Deborah's trunk and the trunk in its turn was held by a loose axle, as thick as a man's wrist. His face, turned away from her, was streaked with half-dried blood, his hair was white with dust, and one hand, flung across his chest, still held her boot.

It was the boot, that she had not even missed, that enabled her to piece together those blurred intermittent memories of the last few moments they had spent in the coach as it hung suspended over the gap. She understood then that he had been instrumental in getting the children clear of that shambles as well as herself, but just how this had been achieved she could not imagine. It must have been so however, for all four of them were alive and safe, and only he was lying here in the wreck, crushed, battered and almost surely dead.

They were calling piteously to her now and someone grabbed her by the booted foot but she kicked herself free and thrust her body still deeper into the wreck. She had to know. She had to learn for herself that it was over and done with. She could not compose herself to wait until somebody like that man with the beard, or that man in bloodied overalls, broke the news to her in halting, evasive phrases. She pushed her hand through the gap and tore at the lapel of his jacket, still buttoned to the waist. The cloth came away easily, indicating that it was split down the back and her palm moved under his shirt to the heart. Aware of nothing else around her she tensed herself to distinguish a beat and when it came, faint but definite, she let out a great shout of triumph. Then a firmer pressure closed over both feet and she was hauled backwards, still holding the tatters of his sand-coloured coat.

2

They learned of it on their respective patches within a few hours of the issue of provisional casualty lists, reacting to the dolorous news according to their several temperaments.

Catesby, seeing his name in the critically injured column, told his stableman that Swann would die, was probably dead already, and when the man asked how he could know this he said, savagely, "His sort always do. It's the scabs who survive!" Then he telegraphed Tybalt, demanding to know if there was any point in his catching the night express south.

Fraser read of it an hour or so later, returning from a long haul to Leith and wondered, wretchedly, what would happen to him, and how this tragedy would affect his daughter Phoebe, who had been so happy down there at that great place they maintained in Kent. He wrote at once to her, saying more or less the same as Catesby, but he did not telegraph. Even at a time like this Fraser was not a man to waste money.

Bryn Lovell, in the Mountain Square, was shown a newspaper containing an account of the disaster by his mulatto wife and went out to his office, locking the door and pulling down the blind. He did this not as a gesture of mourning or even grief but because he wanted to study the newspaper undisturbed and evaluate Swann's chances as he would assess the vital aspects of a difficult haul.

Young Rookwood, acknowledging that he owed everything to the man who had come marching into his bedroom when he was nursing a black eye, wept and would not touch his supper, despite Mrs. Gilroy's restrained coaxing. Vicary, of The Bonus, caught the midday train to London Bridge, arriving to find the yard in a terrible state of confusion, with Saul Keate incommunicado in the tack room, and Tybalt almost hysterical with anxiety, running up and down the belfry steps carrying a meaningless assortment of papers, or on his knees in his counting-house cubicle imploring the Almighty to intervene.

Down in the Western Wedge, where even bad news travelled at a countryman's gait, Hamlet Ratcliffe and Augusta learned of it by means of the Headquarters telegram and Hamlet, like his neighbour Rookwood, left his shepherd's pie untasted, declaring that this would spell certain ruin for them all. When Augusta asked why, hinting that a business of this size could surely run itself while Adam Swann was nursed back to health, he reproached her for being so stupid as to assume anyone could survive such a buffeting and adding, with gloomy relish, that the business would go under the hammer in a matter of weeks and old stagers like himself would be shown the door by the new management. For once, however, Augusta took issue with him, saying, sharply for her, "Dornee go to fretting about us, Hamlet. Think on they tackers, fatherless at their age, poor mites! Do 'ee reckon his missis would like to zend 'em down yer out of the way for a spell?" and later, when he was out of the way, she took the unheard-of step of writing a letter to Mrs. Swann expressing her sympathy and containing this proposal.

Morris, of the Southern Pickings, was the first to take positive action, locking his premises well before time in order to catch a train for Abergavenny and consult Lovell, whose judgements he trusted. For Morris, alone among the provincials, knew that two sizable haulage firms would be happy to acquire the Swann network and it occurred to him at once that neither would miss this opportunity of snapping up a competitor. He had no ulterior motive. If Swann died, or came out of hospital too maimed for work, then he felt he owed it to Swann's dependants to cast around in advance for the best possible price.

Of the provincial managers only young Godsall, of North Pickings, noticed the name 'Blubb' in the list of dead. There was no reason why they should as yet, for Blubb's part in the rescue operations was not yet known. Nor was it until Charles Dickens, pursuing private lines of inquiry, identified the gallant, purple-faced, blubbery old man who had clung to the swaying wreck until Henrietta had been lifted clear and had then been abandoned to jump to his death. The body was identified that same night by means of a consignment note found in the coachee's breeches' pocket but Blubb's clumsy act of heroism went unnoticed. Dickens, helping the dazed Henrietta down the embankment had not seen him fall and Henrietta had not recognised him as he dragged her through the window and down to the men balanced on the baulkhead. His waggon was found and commandeered by the rescue service, and it was assumed that he had been standing close-by, awaiting a goods delivery, when wreckage from one of the coaches fell on him and killed him. All that night he lay in the improvised mortuary with the other victims, under a blanket loaned by a Staplehurst villager. Later on formal identification was made by Michelmore, who explained to a bemused Headquarters why Blubb had happened to be on the scene. It was a grim coincidence, Tybalt thought, that two leading men in the network should be struck down within yards of one another, when neither could have known the other was present. Godsall, reading Blubb's name, jumped to the conclusion that they had been travelling in consort and his grief for Swann and Swann's family was mitigated, to some extent, by the certainty of immediate promotion to the Triangle. He thought it in bad taste, however, to mention this in a letter to Headquarters, and wrote instead to Henrietta, offering his services in any capacity. The letter, with Augusta's and many others, lay unopened on Adam's study desk. Henrietta had more important matters on hand than to read condolences.

Edith Wadsworth read of it in an evening paper she chanced to buy when she was returning from an evening visit to the market. She did not usually buy anything but the morning papers, and rarely bothered to scan sensational national news but a railway disaster lay within her new field of operations and the contents bill, propped against the stand, read, 'South Eastern Boat Train Tragedy; Many Dead'.

She took the paper into her office, perched herself on her stool, and glanced through the pages, catching her breath a little at the magnitude of the crash. Then, but still idly, she glanced down the list of casualties, and when she saw the name 'A. Swann' her heart seemed to stop and she said aloud, "It can't be! It *can't*." But it was. Less than an hour later Tybalt's telegram arrived and she sent for the waggonmaster and asked him to circulate it among the staff. He thought she looked shocked but he was a taciturn man and after a few expressions of dismay, he left. She sat on, watching the sun sink behind the high brick wall of the adjacent brewery. The tragedy, to her at least, was a very personal one and unlike all the other managers, even young Rookwood, she did not relate it to her bread and butter or even the future of the firm. Its likely repercussions in this respect did not cross her mind. Instead, she found herself thinking of him as the inheritor of the strange fatality that seemed to account for all the men who had touched her emotions. Matt Hornby, drowned at sea. Wickstead, a professional thief on the run. And now Adam Swann, to whom, at any time in the last few years, she would gladly have given herself. What did that make her, she wondered? A Jonah trailing bad luck wherever she went? His wife and children were safe, it seemed, and she tried to picture their desolation, finding it very difficult for her own wretchedness absorbed her, and she wished now that she had held him in her arms at least once. She recalled then his dedication to eccentric ideals, his tremendous vitality, and his masculinity, understanding that she could not sit waiting for driblets of news from Fleet Street or from Headquarters, and that her presence in the yard, at a time like this, was superfluous, for she could not concentrate on any routine matter for a second. She locked up, crossed the yard to the stable and gave Dymond, the horsemaster, her keys. "I'm going up to town," she said. "They'll probably need help and you can manage here, can't you?" Dymond said he could, making no further comment. It was common knowledge in the network that Edith Wadsworth and the Gaffer enjoyed a special relationship. The older men, like Dymond, thought of it as a business association. Most of the younger ones took it for granted that Edith Wadsworth had earned her stewardship on her back.

3

The succession of hot summer days passed like units of an endless caravan crossing a desert. For Henrietta, for the old Colonel, and

even for five-year-old Stella, there seemed never to have been a time
when the sun did not hang motionless over the spur of the woods,
when people did not walk on tiptoe and converse in hushed voices,
as though in the presence of a corpse, and yet, below the pall, there
was a persistent undercurrent of stealthy activity, a coming and
going of strangers, of telegraph boys, of half-known associates from
the yard like Keate and Tybalt, and a well-mannered young lawyer
who introduced himself as Mr. Stock and claimed to be Adam's legal
adviser as well as a business associate of two years' standing.

Henrietta saw them all, was polite to them all, but she did not
take much heed of what they said, or recognise them when they
called a second time. She was isolated even from the Colonel, who
kept assuring her that there was every reason to hope, especially now
that Adam had been moved from the emergency ward in the hospital
to the home of Sir Nevil Cook, of Cook's Digestive Breakfast Bis-
cuits, whose factory was hard by the Bermondsey yard and whose
patronage, in the early days of the enterprise, had played an important part in getting the business launched in the London area. Tybalt
tried to explain the relationship to her. Sir Nevil and Mr. Swann were
not friends exactly, he said, but the magnate had always thought
highly of the service, and had visited the yard on occasion to confer
with Mr. Swann on provincial distribution. He was a generous man
and it was characteristic that he should propose moving the injured
haulier to his country house near Cranbrook, where the services of
his own specialist, Sir John Levy, were available, together with
trained nurses he proposed to hire. Tybalt knew Sir Nevil as a noted
evangelist, of course, and a Member of Parliament. What he did
not know was that the discussions he referred to were not confined to
business matters, or that Adam had given the M.P. detailed information to help the passage of Shaftesbury's Chimney-Sweep Bill,
assistance Sir John recalled with gratitude as soon as he heard of
the disaster.

She had no opinion to offer concerning the move. The whole thing
was out of her hands so long as Adam remained in a coma and her
two visits to his bedside had brought her close to the point of physical
collapse. He was getting first-class medical attention and was still, in
their quaint phrase, 'holding his own', but that was all and her helplessness to influence the situation built up inside her like steam in a
valveless boiler, so that sometimes she felt that her brain would burst
and render her as helpless and immobile as he. She could get nothing
and nobody into correct focus and this had nothing to do with

585

delayed shock but everything to do with the split-second transition from serene happiness to black and bitter misery. It was no help to remind herself, as she did from time to time, that she had responsibilities to the Colonel, to her children, to Avery's child, and to the future generally. For as long as he lay there, swathed in bandages, with that strange dead look about him, and his crushed leg resting on a kind of gallows, there could be no future, for her or for any of them, and this belief was underlined by the agitation of his associates who kept appearing and disappearing, with soothing words and distraught looks that belied them, as though they already thought of Adam Swann as dead and buried.

The strange thing was she was incapable of finding temporary release in tears. In the fortnight or so that elapsed between her crawl under the wrecked waggon and the appearance at 'Tryst' of two elderly strangers who drove up in a smart, two-horse equipage and demanded an audience with Mrs. Swann, she had not shed a tear and neither, if one discounted an occasional doze tormented with dreams, had she slept. The only relief she could find from the weight of dread that pressed down on her was in the silent presence of Avery's child, whose thigh injury kept her within call when she was not helping Phoebe Fraser to distract the children. For some reason, possibly because Deborah was old enough to appreciate the situation, she felt much closer to her than to her own children and could communicate with her, albeit wordlessly, in a way that was not possible with the Colonel, who she supposed had been insulated against the horror of death and wounds. Deborah would come upon her as she sat pretending to read letters in the sewing-room and take a seat beside her, saying nothing but taking her hand and holding it, sometimes for half-an-hour at a stretch. Then a current of communication would pass between them, as though the physical contact synchronised their grief and then, still without a word, Deborah would lift her hand, kiss it, and steal away and she would feel tenderness for the funny little creature stir under her breast but it was never sufficiently clamant to release a flow of tears.

She received the two elderly visitors in the drawing-room where the curtains were half-drawn and it was cool. They introduced themselves as Sir Nevil Cook, Adam's host, and the specialist Sir John Levy, a surgeon who had, so Sir Nevil informed her, attended the royal family before his retirement to the country.

"Sir John is my neighbour and was good enough to drive over and take a look at your husband," Sir Nevil said, in his curiously squeaky voice. "We thought you should know that hope definitely exists, Mrs. Swann. If only on certain conditions."

She had been obliged to make an effort to concentrate on what they said but the words 'on certain conditions' made an impact. She said, in a whisper, "Conditions? What could anyone do that would be likely to help him?" and Sir John replied bluntly, "Amputation of the left leg, Mrs. Swann. That, in my view, is essential. It should be done at once. Tonight."

"Take his leg off?"

"Unless we do he isn't likely to survive, or not in my view. Even discounting mortification he could never use it again. It is broken in four places and the foot is crushed. We must have your assent, Mrs. Swann, but I urge you to give it. It represents his only chance of recovery, you understand?"

"Yes, I understand," and then, rising, "May I have a little time to think about it?"

"Not much time, Mrs. Swann." He took out a ponderous watch, holding it in the hollow of his hand. "It is coming up to midday and it will likely take us two hours to get back to Sir Nevil's place and possibly another hour to prepare him for the operation. I could operate by four this afternoon and in my opinion every minute counts."

"You're saying I have to decide now? At once?"

"I'm afraid I am, Mrs. Swann."

She moved nearer the window, standing there steadying herself by the heavy, half-drawn curtains. Through the space she could see sunlight bathing the forecourt, flowerbeds and paddock, down as far as the copse at the foot of the drive. There was no heat haze and the row of Scots firs reminded her of toy trees like half-opened umbrellas in the garden of a doll's-house Sam had bought her for her birthday twenty years ago. It was very strange, she thought, that she should remember that now, that and what had occurred behind that belt of firs only a fortnight ago judged by a calendar but as distant, in her present reckoning, as the day Sam burst through the front door of Scab's Castle trumpeting the fact that he had knocked four shillings off the price of the doll's-house and its garden ornaments. To cut off his leg. To take a sharp knife and separate it from his body, leaving him deprived for the rest of his life, whether that life was measured in years or weeks or days. She was able to picture the leg, that particular leg, the one that was nearest the window when they were lying side by side in that great double bed upstairs. A long,

587

hard, well-muscled leg, almost as brown as his face, for he never seemed to lose the tan he brought home from the East, and the contrast between the whiteness of her own body and the brownness of his had always intrigued her. To remove that leg and lay it aside. To burn it or bury it, leaving him to grovel along with what was left of anything that survived the butchery. She heard an apologetic cough on the part of Sir Nevil Cook, and then the steady tick-tock of the grandmother clock the Colonel had brought down from the house beside Derwentwater. She said, without turning, "Do it. Do it this afternoon. What choice is there . . .?" and then nausea seized her and she blundered past them and out into the hall, darting across it to a recess housing the sink where she cut her flowers. She hung over the sink racked with dry retching, eyes misting and the taste of bile souring her tongue until, sensing a movement behind her, she slowly straightened herself, expecting to see the portly figures of her distinguished visitors but it was not them. Deborah was there, her narrow little face as pinched as a starveling's. Responding to a terrible need for strength and succour she reached out, clasping the child to her breast and for a moment they stood there, braced against the sink, Deborah half-supporting her, as though she was the crutch Adam would need from round about four o'clock this afternoon. This time contact with the child broke through the crust of ice enclosing her brain. Silently and steadily she wept.

4

Conspiracy

It might have been any time between midnight and dawn when the bedroom door opened very softly and she sensed Deborah climbing into Adam's side of the bed. She was at war with time now and had banished the clock to the lumber room after a third sleepless night. She said, "You, Deborah?" and the child answered, "Yes, Auntie. Shall I stay awhile?" and Henrietta reached out, her arm encircling the child's thin shoulders as she thought, 'God knows, I need someone. Whatever time it is it's done now and if he lives how will he regard the person who authorised it?' She knew she had not spoken aloud but she well might have done, for the child said, in a level voice, "I *know* about it, Aunt Henrietta. I listened at the door, I had to, you see, for it surely isn't right you should take it all on yourself." Then, more diffidently, "I asked the Virgin what I should do and she told me. Not at once, you understand, but afterwards, when I was asleep."

"What did she tell you, Deborah?"

"To share it if I could."

She had no kind of answer to this. It was as though, by a stroke as sudden and salutory as that which had broken the pleasant rhythm of their lives, their ages had been reversed, and Deborah had attained the status of adult while she had become a child again, younger than Deborah when Adam first brought her here that Christmas Eve. She asked presently, "I did right then?"

"Of course. How could you have refused? How could anyone, who wanted him to get well?"

She lay very still. Outside, far across the downs, an insignificant flicker of lightning shafted the sky producing a candleblink in the room. The following peal was so faint that it was like a child's sleep mutter. She said, "He liked to ride and walk and swim. He was such an active man. I think he would rather have died."

"That isn't true. You know that isn't in the least true if you think about it. He's a fighter and I don't mean ordinary fighting, the kind

589

he gave up, but . . . well . . . fighting for other people. I talked to some of his men who were here and they all said the same thing."

"What men, Deborah?"

"The men who work for him. That big man, Mr. Keate, and that little bald one, Mr. Tybalt. But most of all the young one, the lawyer."

"Mr. Stock?"

"He didn't tell me his name but we talked in the stable. He said Uncle Adam had more chance of getting well than anyone he knew and that when he did he would start all over again because—well—that's the way he's made. I thought about that after Mr. Stock left and it's true."

Was it? She moved closer to the child, marshalling aspects of Adam Swann in support of the theory and was obliged to admit that Deborah's was valid. He was a fighter. Everything about him proclaimed as much and she, of all people, could vouch for it, for she had watched him convert an extravagant dream into reality in seven years, and do it, moreover, without the bluster men like her father regarded as essential to success. She had overlooked this and it was too important to be overlooked. Being Adam Swann it was entirely possible that he might regard a grave physical handicap as yet another challenge to his wits, his patience and to that aggressive ingenuity he had used as a kind of blasting powder to overthrow every obstacle he had encountered since the day they sat over a camp fire in the fells and he told her how he proposed putting that necklace to work. A very great deal had happened since then but it could all be traced back to the obstinacy and self-reliance he possessed in such abundance, a characteristic she had noticed the first day they travelled together.

She saw then how hasty she had been in her estimate of the effects such a deprivation was likely to have on him. She had assumed, and might have gone on assuming, that Adam Swann, short of a leg, would be reduced to a parody of the man she had known, and this was a monstrous assumption to make about someone who had taken such pains to carve a place for himself in competition with ruthless rascals like her father, and old Matthew Goldthorpe, men who only pretended to independence while fattening on the sweat of others.

Drowsiness stole over her and the prospect of sleep, real sleep hovered just out of reach. She said, "Don't go, Deborah. Stay with me until they send word. Phoebe told me Sir John promised to let us know by mid-morning."

She wished then with all her heart that she had the child's faith. She had never extracted the smallest comfort from religion, thinking of it as she thought of institutions like royalty, or a piece of apparatus like the alphabet or the multiplication tables. Something that deserved occasional lip-service, and possibly a passing thought or two, before being set aside in favour of something more amusing and tangible. She supposed she had been taught to look upon Roman Catholics in the way she regarded foreigners, misguided, unfortunate people, much given to rituals of a kind not far removed from those practised by savages and heathens. She realised now how utterly stupid and bigoted this was on her part, for Deborah's God was clearly of far more practical use to her now than the austere Jehovah she had half-accepted as the arbiter of the universe, or the more patrician deity who presided over the parish church at Twyforde Green. She would have liked to have asked Deborah to give her more explicit information about her communion with the Virgin but it seemed an invasion of the child's privacy so she said, "You'll say more prayers for him? Special prayers, until he's well again?"

"Why, yes, of course, and I've written to Sister Sophie to help. I did that the first day. I gave Stillman the letter to post and I wrote again today, as soon as I heard about his leg. It's important as many as possible should help."

Her simplicity was one of the most devastating forces Henrietta had ever encountered for, in a way, it seemed to embrace all the religions in the world, reducing their differences to insignificant proportions, and making nonsense of sect and schism. It was rooted and basic, part of the very structure of society once society was stripped of all its fads and fashions and prejudices. There were human beings, pulled this way and that by temperament and by circumstance, and there was a majestic source of power that left them to flounder or to make the best of things. As long as things went smoothly, as they had for so long now, she had had no quarrel with the divine plan, but when something like this occurred one needed more than conventional belief in her kind of creator, who was altogether too remote and impersonal to be used as a buffer. One needed access to somebody near, warm and sympathetic, of the kind Deborah enjoyed, and she supposed right of access to such a source could only be acquired by training, of the kind the child had received in that community of nuns, or possibly, by self-discipline, of a kind she was never likely to possess. She remembered, however, that there

591

was a word religious people sometimes used in these circumstances —'Intervention' it was, by which, she supposed, the untrained and the undisciplined were enabled to make their supplications. There was also something in the Bible about the special regard in which children were held by God so that it might follow that Deborah's presence among them was not an accident at all but part of a plan, arranged long in advance, and readily available to him in this desperate pass.

She said, at length, "I've forgotten all the prayers I knew. I could make one up I suppose but that isn't the same somehow, and there's no need so long as you're here. Will you pray for me as well? Will you keep praying, until we hear something one way or the other?"

"All the time," the child said, and then, "You're so tired. Try and sleep, Aunt Henrietta, just try, and if you can't then I'll go and make tea. I could use the small kettle for the iron one is too heavy. Suppose I made tea first and then you tried?"

"I can sleep," she said, "providing you stay," and again the curious reversion in their rôles occurred to her as Deborah drew herself half-upright and made a pillow of her shoulder, so that a sense of weightlessness stole over her and she surrendered to it with a gratitude that she could not have expressed in words.

2

It did not take Edith Wadsworth long to decide that the presence of someone in authority at Headquarters was essential to the survival of the firm. She had long known that Swann-on-Wheels was a one-man concern, owing everything to his considerable administrative talents as well as his initiative, but the degree of dependence upon him surprised her, as did the helplessness of experienced men like Keate and Tybalt in this contingency.

She would have thought that, for a week or so, a month even, the network would have run itself but within forty-eight hours of her arrival she realised that this was not so, and that power was so distributed here and in the provinces that no one person, other than himself, was capable of steering the concern. This was partly due, she imagined, to an essential fault in its structure but it also owed something to the very nature of the business. Although, throughout the territories, responsibility was strictly departmentalised, the movement of goods at short notice from one end of the country to the other necessitated a constant crossing of lines of communication and unless endless duplication of effort and double-tracking was to result, someone equipped with cool judgement and an encyclopaedic memory was needed to devote unwavering attention to the inflow of orders, the limitations of teams and rolling stock, the day-to-day staffing situation at every depot, and a dozen other constantly changing factors, not excluding several outside their control, such as weather, and the vagaries of public authorities charged with the repair of roads and bridges.

She understood now the tremendous amount of thought and patience that had gone into the building of the system, and the nature of some of his eccentric apparatus, notably the ready reckoner, part map, part itinerary, part index, that he called 'Frankenstein'. She had always thought of Frankenstein as a kind of joke he played upon himself but now she saw that it was far more than that, that it symbolised his unique approach to the entire field of road haulage, that is to say, ready access to hard facts and their translation into terms of time and distance, from which emerged two end products, the gross cost of a run and the net profit it represented.

But this was only one discovery she made during that first exploratory period when, with one half of her mind, she was trying to hold the business on an even keel, and with the other steel herself against the near-certainty that the next person through the little door at the top of the staircase would bring her news that he was dead.

Gradually the first preoccupation took precedence over the second, and as she became ever more deeply enmeshed in the task of deputising for him, she was able to forget why she was here and whether, in point of fact, all her efforts would prove futile. She had already passed this stage when they brought word of the amputation and the high fever that followed it, but such was the degree of concentration demanded of her that even this could be set aside until the day-shift went off and the clamour in the yard below was stilled. By then, when the heat had gone from the day, and the city lay gasping like a spent old whore supping twopennyworth of gin in the gutter, she was too dazed by the effort she had poured into the task to do more than drag herself to the lodging Keate had found for her, eat her cold supper, and sleep until it was time to clear the pending trays in time for the next avalanche of mail. Then she had reason to be grateful to the impulse that had sent her flying down here to take over in this high-handed manner. Alone among them she could prevent the swift dissolution of all they had worked for and this, she thought, was ironic. With the possible exception of Catesby in the Polygon, she was the only henchman who thought of him as a man rather than an employer.

She soon adjusted to the inadequacies of Keate and Tybalt. The one was no more than a conscientious waggoner and the other an excellent administrator within certain limits but far more equipped to obey orders than to issue them. Neither, she discovered, welcomed responsibility outside their narrow spheres and among their juniors there was only one, an ex-Thameside waif in charge of the warehouse, who could be relied upon to back his judgement without reference to herself. Nobody raised an eyebrow at her usurpation and she soon came to believe that, in the territories at least, her presence as his vicereine was accepted as official. In her correspondence with men like Ratcliffe and Fraser she encouraged this fiction for it made for swifter decisions, whereas down here, where all roads met, Keate and Tybalt were only too glad of someone to whom they could look for a lead.

In less dismal circumstances she would have found the challenge exhilarating. The network was now making over three hundred hauls a day and perhaps half as many deliveries, a total of around two thousand separate movements in a six-day week. Four-fifths of these began and ended within a specified territory, and unless they were complicated by some exceptional factor, such as an insurance claim or a breakdown, the mechanics of each operation did not concern Headquarters, save as a figure on a monthly return sheet. It was the odd fifth that represented the hard work in the way of estimates, advice notes, memoranda, the checking of distances, choice of routes and rapid transfers of reserve teams and waggons, for these involved journeys that crossed from one territory into another and sometimes in as many as four adjoining sectors. Tybalt could give her a good deal of information, and Frankenstein (once she had learned to manipulate him) gave her more, but there were areas where commonsense and guesswork were the only available tools and a mistake could be costly, representing the difference between modest profit and heavy loss. Then there were the maps and indexes to be kept up-to-date, new contracts to be vetted, and staffing problems sorted out, so that sometimes it astonished her that he had been able to spend any time at all with that family of his, much less tour the network twice a year.

Her first big decision was the transfer of Godsall from Northern

594

Pickings to the Kentish Triangle and this was done before the part
Blubb played in the Staplehurst disaster was made public by no less a
person than Charles Dickens, who wrote a letter to the press entitled
'Former Coachman's Heroic Act'. She knew that Godsall was earmarked for the Triangle and went a step further, persuading Tybalt
that young Skillyrated a more important job than warehousekeeping,
and could replace Godsall in Derbyshire. Keate approved, encouraged by the fact that Skilly was one of his protégés, and that
Rookwood, notwithstanding his extreme youth, was making good in
the Square, but Tybalt argued that they could not afford to lose a key
man in the yard at a time like this. She said, shortly, "Fill that yard
vacancy with a clerk. That's what he would do," and it was
done.

She had been there about three weeks when the next crisis came
and went and she learned that Adam had a good chance of complete
recovery, if he accepted Sir John Levy's advice and went into a
Swiss sanatorium for a protracted course of treatment. The amputation had been carried out above the knee and his tough constitution,
they said, had enabled him to survive a battering that would have
killed most men verging on forty. His other injuries, severe but
trivial by comparison, included a dislocated shoulder, severe concussion, a broken wrist and the long, jagged laceration caused by the
splinter under his eye. He was very weak, they said, and bedside visits
were prohibited. Even his wife had been kept away until the effects
of the concussion wore off. As to a discussion of business concerns,
it was out of the question.

She learned all these details from Stock, his lawyer, for whom she
developed a high regard, partly because his advice was always helpful but also because she decided he had a profound admiration for
Adam as a gambler in a world where men habitually played safe. It
was Stock who complimented her on her practical display of loyalty
in taking the Headquarters' tiller and warned her that it was a job
liable to keep her in London for another twelve months. She had
not thought of it in that light until then and now that she did she
hesitated.

"I couldn't stay here that long without official sanction," she protested. "I'm not sure I'd want to in any case and even you must see
that I can't appoint myself to the job. I only stepped in as a stopgap
and he'll have to be consulted before he goes abroad."

He said, smiling, "Oh, I've no doubt we can make a tidy legal
package of it, Miss Wadsworth, and call a general conference if you

insist, but you can rely on my backing, as well as Keate's and Tybalt's. Can you think of anyone better qualified for the job?"

That was the point. There was no one else with her grasp of his affairs and it frightened her to realise that Stock, and probably the more discerning of the managers, were well aware of this, but the prospect of moving into his chair more or less permanently scared her. In a way, it was a tacit admission that all those rumours concerning their relationship had substance but how could she explain this to Stock? She said, uneasily, "I'll tell you what I'll do. I'll go down to 'Tryst' and discuss the situation with his wife. After all, she's his executor, and if this dreadful business had ended as we thought it would she would have been consulted at once."

"That's a splendid idea," he said, genially, "so don't lose a day over it," and he smiled again in a way that left her in no doubt but that he was convinced she had been Swann's mistress for years. The injustice of the situation vexed her and she thought, 'Devil take them and their dirty minds! At this rate it won't be long before the silly rumour reaches his wife and once it does I'll have no choice but to throw in my hand here and in the Crescents!'

She went home in a resentful mood and in the course of the evening, when it was too stuffy to do anything but sit fanning herself at her bedroom window, she made up her mind. Eight-thirty saw her at the yard gate awaiting Tybalt and before he had shed his hat she said, in a tone that cut short his protests, "I won't be here today. I'm going down to see Mrs. Swann. Take your work up to the tower to be on hand for callers. There's nothing that can't be held over for twenty-four hours!", and she marched off without giving him an opportunity to argue.

3

She had always harboured a curiosity about his home, of which she had heard so much, and Henrietta, whom she had never once met but concerning whom she had a confused series of impressions. There was the general picture, common to all the provincial managers, of a pretty, imperious little madam, who had been clever enough to hook the Gaffer before he was in the swim and had since made his money fly.There was her own private picture, built upon the admissions she had drawn from him when he had chased her half across England after that incident involving the death of a chimney sweep, and this estimate of Henrietta Swann was even less flattering, for it projected her as a shallow, heartless creature, the kind of daughter a brute like Sam Rawlinson would be likely to sire. But then, since he had taken her advice, her conception of the woman whom she had always envied and resented had changed again, for it seemed that Henrietta had matured to some extent and had seemed to grow on him, so that his casual references to her lately had been generous and affectionate. It was this, she realised, that had deterred her more than once from pressing her advantage, for her intuition told her he was now a little ashamed of his frankness in that heart-to-heart talk they had had beside the Swale.

The house made an unexpectedly profound impression on her. She first glimpsed it as the self-driven dogcart turned in at the drive, a home rather than the showpiece she had expected, a place of charm and serenity that was indubitably old and weatherworn but not unwieldy, as were most of the country seats of the period. Under the spur of summer woods it seemed to her to draw colour and greenery from all points of the compass and she understood at once the urge that had led Henrietta to nag him to move in at a time when he needed every penny he possessed for the expansion. It had another and entirely unforeseen effect on her, one that almost impelled her to turn the dogcart and drive back to the yard. In an odd way it enlarged his wife and diminished her, so that she saw herself in the guise of a hanger-on, someone who had come here seeking a favour and was liable to be shown into a waiting-room. Then she summoned up her pride, buttoned her gloves, smoothed down her skirt, and rattled on into the yard, telling a man who came forward to take charge of the horse, that she had come to see Mrs. Swann on a business matter and asking where she was likely to be found.

The man looked across at a child aged about ten who happened to be standing on the steps at the rear of the house and Edith thought, 'Now who can that be? She's too old for his daughter but she looks as if she belongs', and the child approached saying, gravely, "Aunt Henrietta is in the drawing-room writing. Shall I take you to her?", and Edith said, "You'd best ask her first. Tell her it's Miss Wadsworth from the yard," and the child disappeared into the back regions of the house, reappearing in less than a minute and saying, with the same adult gravity, "I'm to take you in by the front door, Miss Wadsworth Uncle Adam isn't worse, is he?"

"No, no, I've just called on business. Mr. Stock, the lawyer, sent me."

597

They went through the stable arch and round past a great clump of lilac growing close against the house and the child stopped and sniffed at a sprig, saying incongruously, "It's a pity he missed the lilac. He loves summer smells," and Edith thought it such an unusual remark that she said, "He's going to get well. It'll be a long time but he'll be back," and the child replied, cheerfully, "Oh, yes, I'm sure about that. I always have been."

They had reached the deep porch when Edith asked, "Are you his niece?" and the child said, "Not really, but I spend my holidays here. I'm Deborah Avery. Papa worked with Uncle Adam until he went abroad," and then Edith recalled Avery, and Avery's sudden withdrawal, and the child's bearing interested her so that she said, "What *makes* you so sure, Deborah? Is it because Mr. Swann is so strong and active?" and she said, with innocent directness, "Oh, no, not really, although he is, of course. Do you know him well, Miss Wadsworth?"

"Very well, I think."

"Well, then you'll understand. I mean, he'd put up a great fight, wouldn't he, and wouldn't give up like most people? Not if he was in pain, I mean. Or frightened. I told Aunt Henrietta so and she believes me now, tho' she didn't at first."

She had an impression then that a deep understanding existed between this funny little creature and her Aunt Henrietta and her curiosity about Deborah increased but there was no opportunity to satisfy it for the child led her into a large room where the curtains were half-drawn against the sun and Henrietta Swann was sitting at a secretaire writing. The first sight of her, small, still and hunched, stirred Edith's pity. In that subdued light she appeared scarcely older than the child and far less assured.

"Miss Wadsworth, from the yard, Aunt," Deborah announced as she withdrew and the doll-like figure at the desk rose and Edith saw that the face was drawn and that she was having some difficulty in extending ordinary courtesy because her mind, wherever it was, was certainly not at the disposal of callers. She said, however, "Please be seated, Miss Wadsworth," and then stopped, biting her lower lip and staring down at her hands, very elegant hands Edith thought, with long tapering fingers matching a pair of slender feet encased in slippers that looked like little black chisels.

She was nothing like the woman she had pictured all these years. There was a stillness about her that was not entirely due to the strain to which she had been subjected in the last few weeks. She was prettier, too, with a great cluster of copper-coloured curls disciplined by a piece of black ribbon, a very clear complexion, a large, ripe mouth, now half-open as though to emphasise her uncertainty, and restless green eyes in which fear continued to lurk. For a woman who had borne three children her figure was very good, although she looked as if she had lost weight recently. Any initiative she had possessed, Edith decided, had crumpled under the impact of shock or suspense.

She said, quietly, "I don't imagine you know about me, Mrs. Swann. I've worked for your husband since the beginning, first under my father, lately as a manager in Peterborough. As soon as I heard I came down to Headquarters to do what I could," and she saw a flicker of interest in the melancholy eyes as Henrietta replied, carefully, "I know about you, Miss Wadsworth. Adam often spoke about you and both Mr. Tybalt and Mr. Stock told me how helpful you had been since . . . since it happened. I'm sure Mr. Swann will be grateful." Then looking at her directly for the first time, "You'll have heard what's been decided?"

"I heard Mr. Swann might go to Switzerland to be fitted with an artificial leg. Has anything else happened?"

"No, not really, except that he's likely to be away a long time."

"You'll go with him?"

"No, everyone is against that."

"But wouldn't it help him?"

"It seems not. Sir John, the surgeon, says it requires tremendous concentration to learn to use a . . . a leg of that sort. And . . . well there are other reasons too."

"You don't have to tell me, Mrs. Swann."

"I'd like to tell you. I . . . there's really no one I can talk to about it, not in the way another woman might understand. The Colonel, his father, tries to make light of it, as if it's . . . well . . . no more than getting used to a new house, or a new horse. And Phoebe Fraser, the governess, puts it all on God and just hopes for the best. Deborah, that little girl who showed you in, she's been wonderful. I couldn't have held on without her, but she's only ten and like Phoebe, she leaves everything to God. I can't, you see. I'm not even sure I believe in God any more. Does that sound wicked? Seeing that he lived through it?"

Her heart went out to her in a way she would have thought impossible an hour ago. She supposed it was more than the normal compassion one might be expected to feel for a woman in her circumstances, someone who had leaned on a man as self-assured as Adam

599

Swann for so long. It had to do, she imagined, with their shared appraisal of someone who had been free and far-ranging, self-governing and uncurbed, and was now reduced to a dependent rôle that he would hate and fear.

She answered. "Not in the least wicked. Inevitable, I'd say, for any sensitive person who was close to a man like Adam Swann."

She was much sharper than she looked and did not miss the inference.

"You were close to him?"

"I like to think I was one of the few who understood what he was trying to do."

"Tell me then." The voice was eager and far more alive than it had been a moment ago. She considered, choosing her words carefully. "Well, it wasn't just a matter of running a business and making money. People and trends interest him more than goods and money and that always showed. In everything he did, every word he spoke. I think a lot of us sensed this but he didn't proclaim it."

"He must have to you?"

"To me, and to one other district manager, a man called Catesby, in Lancashire."

She moved closer, sitting directly opposite, her hands in her lap. "What *can* happen now? I mean, how will somebody like him manage with such an awful handicap?"

"People do and with less start than he has. By way of temperament, that is."

"But don't you see, it's temperament I'm worried about. I've been to see him several times and he's different already. I can't . . . well . . . get to him. He seems patient and resigned but that isn't really him. He was never resigned to anything. I'd feel happier if he was restless and resentful, the way he used to be when things went wrong."

"He's weak. He'll need time to adjust, Mrs. Swann. I think we can leave that side of it to him."

"But what else matters?"

"What he's created, what he's worked for all these years. That's extremely important to him. It will make all the difference if it's still there and he can return to it as soon as he can walk."

"There's no risk of it not being, is there?"

"I think there is. It's a very personal concern. It isn't the kind of business that runs itself."

"Is that why you're here?"

"Yes, I suppose it is."

She was silent a moment. Then she said, earnestly, "What could I do to help?"

She had to think quickly and deeply, lest she should convey an impression that she was here for her own advancement or, indeed, that anything was at stake beyond the vital necessity of maintaining the impetus of the concern that offered, to her mind, his sole chance of rehabilitation. And then, like the wink of a heliograph, she saw a solution that could conceivably solve both problems, his deep, personal involvement with the network, and this woman's tenuous relationship with him as wife and partner, someone who could, providing she had the courage and was sufficiently desperate, exploit this situation to tremendous advantage. She said, drawing a deep breath, "I've been running things, Mrs. Swann. I had to because there was no one else qualified to do it. Mr. Stock is now trying to make me take over for as long as Mr. Swann is away and convalescent."

"You don't feel you could do that?"

"Yes, I could do it. Not nearly as well as him but I could do it if I had to."

"But you have other plans?"

"I hadn't when I came in here a few moments ago."

Their eyes met for a moment. Neither flinched.

Henrietta said: "It's to do with me then?"

"Yes. It would be far better if you did it, Mrs. Swann."

"*Me?* Me run the business? How would that be possible?"

"I think it would. Don't ask me to explain why but I do. You could do it as well as me, perhaps better in the end. And I'd help. I'd help in any way I could."

"But suppose that were true. Suppose I could leave Phoebe in charge, and Deborah stayed on to help with the babies, what on earth would be gained?"

"As far as you're concerned? A very great deal, Mrs. Swann."

"I'm sorry, I still don't understand. Do you mean the men would be more likely to take orders from me than from you? Is that it?"

It was a way out but she rejected it. It wouldn't wholly convince her and she needed very much to be convinced. She got up and went over to the window, calculating risks of a kind that had nothing in common with those she had been taking in the tower, risks that seemed at this moment, not to qualify as risks. She said, finally: "I could easily offend you very deeply, Mrs. Swann, but for his sake, and yours too, I'll say what I have to. If you did what I suggest, if you made that kind of effort, it would make a very great impression

on him when he learned of it. It might even give him the kind of courage he needs and has to find somewhere."

"Why should you think that might offend me, Miss Wadsworth?"

"I haven't finished yet. Whoever takes his place and holds the
thing together is going to earn his lifelong gratitude. That person
should be you not me, Mrs. Swann."

She heard the clock in the corner ticking the seconds away and
its plangency seemed to fill the room, reducing the summer sounds
outside to an infinite distance. She heard Henrietta say, in what
seemed an incurious tone, "You're in love with Adam?" and then,
as though debating a point with herself, "You must be, otherwise you
would have made a very different proposal." She stood up and the
scrape of the chair brought Edith round, so that they faced one another. "Is he . . . is he in love with you?"

She could answer this truthfully, thank God, and did with a directness tinged with bitterness. "No, and never was, Mrs. Swann, tho'
there were times when he might have imagined he was!"

"Recently?"

"A long time ago."

"Ah, yes, when we had that trouble here. When the boy was
killed?"

"Yes, but nothing happened. Nothing that belittled you in any way.
You, his children, this home you've made for him, always kept pace
with the network. I was a long way behind, even in those days. Since
things have changed for him I've dropped right out of sight. You
must believe that, Mrs. Swann. For all our sakes."

She was not afraid to look at her now. Her assumption, she supposed, was logical enough and neither of them, so far as she could
see, had much to lose. Only he could lose, lying trussed up in bed
with a stump where his leg had been and his life in ruins. All they
were doing was to try and salvage some of the pieces. She moved to
the door and turned, one hand on the knob. "You'll want time to
think it over, no doubt."

Henrietta's swift movement surprised her. She seemed to flit across
the room like a random shadow and materialise on the threshold.
She said, pushing the door shut, "No, Miss Wadsworth! I don't
need time. I've been all kinds of a fool concerning Adam in my time
but I stopped being one some time ago. I understand that what you
say is true, how much that business means to him, and how important it is that it should be there to come home to. I understand what
it means to you too, not only for your own sake but for his."

"You'll do it? You'll try?"

"If I didn't then you'd have to and I'd deserve all that followed. I love Adam very much. I always have, although I didn't find loving him easy until lately, until just before this awful thing happened to us." A tiny gleam of humour showed in her eyes. "He isn't the easiest husband for someone like me, without much to go on except instinct."

"There's nothing wrong with instinct, Mrs. Swann. Certainly not your instinct."

"No, but more was needed, a lot more. You realised that a long time ago." She stopped, her hand to her mouth, and again Edith saw her as a child but a child from whom a sense of dread had been lifted. "My manners . . .! I haven't even offered you tea . . ." She flung open the door and called into the hall. "Deborah! Tell Agnes to bring tea. Not here, in the sewing-room," and turned back into the room. "How would I go about it? Where would I begin?"

"From here until he left for Switzerland. I could send papers and maps and specimen contracts. It would help you to pass the time and stop thinking. And I could spend Sundays here until I went back to my patch. When does the surgeon think he'll be fit to travel?"

"By the end of the month, if he continues to progress," her fingers twiddled with the tassel of her belt. "You think I should tell him? Suppose, as he gets better, he begins worrying? Won't that be bad for him?"

"It's something we can guard against."

"How?"

"I'll send him the monthly returns. It doesn't matter whether they're accurate or not."

"Miss Wadsworth?"

"Yes?"

"What's your Christian name?"

"Edith."

"I'll tell you something nobody else knows, Edith. *Two* things. You might know one of them but I think not."

"Well?"

"Years ago, before we married, when he was helping me to run away from home, I did make a contribution to that business. I invented the name and trademark. I think he's forgotten that and I've never liked to remind him. It seemed like giving a present, then telling him how much it cost."

She found she could smile at that and did, sharing a little in the

603

excitement that had revitalised her and brought colour to her cheeks. "I see. And the other thing?"

"We'd none of us be alive if it hadn't been for him. He was half-blind with blood, and more hurt than any of us, but he kept his head somehow. He held the children up to that poor man Blubb, the one Mr. Dickens wrote about, and after that—I still can't imagine how—he dragged me across the carriage and lifted me high enough for them to reach."

"Why did you keep all that to yourself?"

"It was something to hold on to. Can you understand that?"

She understood perfectly. If he had died, she supposed, it would have been in all the newspapers but knowing him as Henrietta did it was something she would not dare to broadcast while there was the slightest chance of being called to account for it. A man who had renounced heroics would fight shy of that kind of publicity. She said, "Keep it secret. Most men would enjoy basking in that kind of sunshine but Adam isn't among them."

She would have preferred then to have driven away and been alone with her thoughts but this was not possible. She had to stay and be introduced to the children and Phoebe Fraser, to sip tea in the sewing-room with Henrietta and Avery's child, and all the time the un-expected success of her stratagem dragged at her. It was not that she regretted it, or was daunted by the problems and risks it presented, only that, in a sense, it slammed a door that had remained open ever since that day he ambushed her beside the Swale.

5

Vicereine

TIME was the element that eluded him. He was aware of many things, odd, unrelated things, the fact that it was summer, that he was helpless, that he was in unfamiliar surroundings guarded by friendly gaolers. He had a sense too of having been involved in some kind of catastrophe associated with falling, with water and the smell of bruised grass, indicating a subsidence of some kind, a landslide, a flood, or something of that nature. Beyond that no conclusive indication of why he was here, watched over and trussed like a fowl.

There were pointers but they did not lead him anywhere. The pungent whiff of disinfectant, the occasional appearance of the man he took to be his chief gaoler, a long-jawed, gold-spectacled busybody with a Hebraic nose, who smelled of camphor, a succession of bowls held to his lips, lips that were clothed in bristles and whispered when his fingers passed across them. But time, in relation to phases in his remembered past, eluded him, so that presently he surrendered to it and let it swirl him along like a slow current.

Once he had adjusted to the sense of drift he could focus on landmarks of one kind or another. The Cumberland fells were a constantly recurring background, and so was the Addiscombe riding school, where 'Circus' Howard would entertain them with his acrobatics and Roberts, grave and serious-minded, would be looking on, his face stiff with disapproval. Roberts was a fairly constant travelling companion, sometimes riding beside him through sweltering heat to Cawnpore, or putting his case concerning the ethics of their profession, but then, less probably, so was that bewhiskered ass Cardigan, justifying the destruction of a brigade in a valley between two ranges of hills, and the logic of his dream rejected this for he had never exchanged one word with Cardigan.

Sometimes the images telescoped and then proliferated. Henrietta would appear in that cageless green crinoline she had worn in their ride over the Pennines and at other times—the image was very vivid on these occasions—she wore a dove-grey dress and a severe poke bonnet that made her look sad and remote. Once or twice she appeared from nowhere wearing no clothes at all, so that he could study her as she moved unconcernedly across his line of vision giving him time to appraise the symmetry of her shoulders, thighs and buttocks, and the slow, sensual ripple of her heavy copper ringlets. Other, more shadowy figures hailed him and were lost—Hamlet Ratcliffe, driving a frigate at a furious pace, Catesby reading a letter from his son, Bryn Lovell, swarmed over by piccaninnies, and Edith, tall, swaying and immensely dignified as she picked her way through a maze of waggons, all of which seemed to be driven by Blubb.

* * *

It was Blubb who became his first, fixed point, a moonfaced familiar he could use as a kind of base, and presently he saw him constantly in the same incongruous frame, a railway carriage window through which he stared and stared, with an expression of outrage in his eyes and his slack mouth agape. He became very irritated with Blubb's immobility and understood, for the first time, why Tybalt and Keate disapproved of him and never mentioned his name without frowning. Then, one stifling afternoon, Blubb withdrew from the window and was replaced by the long-jawed gaoler who smelled of camphor, and for once he could comprehend what the man was saying and recognise kindly concern in his serious eyes. He said, apropos of nothing, "Well, now, that's rather better. You won't have much to show for it. Just a seam, like a crease in a sheet." And then, more jocularly, "You've still kept your tan. You'll never win sympathy as an invalid, Swann, but don't let that concern you. You won't be one much longer."

There was more talk of this kind before he slipped away again, and he could not have said how long passed before he opened his eyes again and saw, of all people, old Sir Nevil Cook, the evangelist M.P., who was said to own twenty-three biscuit factories and had been so intrigued by that story of Luke Dobbs, the chimney sweep. He saw and heard Sir Nevil quite clearly and could even demand to know how he came to be there, and what, in the name of God, had happened to himself and everybody else over such a long period of lunatic confusion. The magnate said, anxiously, "Er ... how much do you recall, Swann? Sir John thinks that is important."

"Sir John who?"

"Sir John Levy. The surgeon. He's been looking after you, for weeks now."

"*Weeks?* What the devil happened to me?"

"You don't know?"

"I remember some kind of fall! Did I take a bad toss from a horse?"

The old fellow looked uncertain at this but presently, blowing out his pink cheeks, he said, carefully, "You were in a bad railway accident at Staplehurst. You and your family. It happened close by, on the 9th June. Your wife and children were with you . . ."

"Henrietta . . . the children . . . ?"

"They were unscathed, I'm happy to say. You were hurt."

He digested this. Then he said, thoughtfully, "A railway accident. I remember vaguely. The boat-train—what's the date now? How long . . . ?"

"It doesn't matter, old chap. It's of no consequence at all."

"Tell me, and tell me where I am and how badly I was injured." And when the old fellow hesitated, "I've served through two wars. I've seen everything in my time."

"Very well, it's mid-July. The seventeenth, and you're at my country house, Rising Hill. We brought you over here from Tonbridge shortly after it happened. As to your injuries, you had a very bad gash on your face but that's healed up splendidly, a dislocated shoulder and a broken wrist, both responding well to treatment, severe concussion . . . and . . . er . . . severe injuries to your leg. Your left leg."

"How severe?"

The old man looked as if he was being threatened with a pistol. He said, "Sir John can explain, Swann."

"You explain, Sir Nevil. Come, I'm not a child."

"Very well. As you say, you've seen active service and may take it better than some. Sir John had to amputate. Since then you've been on the mend."

"You took off my leg?"

Sir Nevil nodded and instinctively Adam tried to rise and stare down the length of the bed, but he was unable to do more than raise his head an inch or two and all he saw was a wicker cradle, half-screened by a stiffly-starched sheet. It looked, he thought, like a new, canopied pinnace just delivered from Blunderstone.

For perhaps two minutes he fought the shock. He had known a great number of men who had suffered amputations, both in India and Scutari. They had survived, or most of them, and some had been fitted with very serviceable artificial legs. At least one had retained his commission and converted his disability into a messroom joke, like that cavalry general of Napoleon's . . . what was his name . . . ? Latour something, Latour-Maubourg, who told his orderly to stop

607

blubbering and remind himself that he would now have only one riding-boot to polish every morning.

He lay there staking himself against successive shock waves, trying with all his might to remember the name of the man who had continued to serve the John Company with one leg. A lancer or a hussar ... with a red face and two enormous moustaches, of which he was very vain. *Jack* Something. Whittall, Wyndale, Wisbey ... *Wickett!* Jack Wickett. '*Jolly Jack*' Wickett his squadron came to call him after his return, and the sudden visual memory of him, limping across the parade ground at Meerut, was immensely comforting so that he saw him not as a fellow messmate of years ago but a buoy thrown to him on a line just as he was on the point of drowning. A very odd-looking buoy with a red face painted on it and a pair of enormous moustaches fixed to its widest point. He caught and held on for his life and presently, knowing that he would not drown, he saw the anxious face of Sir Nevil blur and merge into the folds of the green silk screen against which he was standing. And after that he slept, this time dreamlessly.

2

She made a gesture of irritation when Phoebe came in and said Sir John and Sir Nevil were awaiting her in the drawing-room. Of late, ever since she had recovered from the panic produced by the arrival of the first of Edith Wadsworth's packages, she had become so absorbed that she resented any interruption, even by those who could give her news of his progress.

The sewing room was no longer a sewing room. Everything associated with sewing had been banished and replaced with trestle tables triumphantly unearthed by Stillman from the stable loft, scrubbed, and covered with clean brown paper held in place by thumb-tacks. Now the whole of England and Wales was an open book to her and she fancied she knew it as well as the final chapter of *East Lynne*, so that it was difficult to recall a time when she had thought of Birmingham as a place where Adam could have ended his voyage from India. She knew other things besides the frontier towns of all the sections, and the districts those sections served. She could have told anybody who cared to listen that Ratcliffe hauled fish and flowers across Bodmin Moor, that young Rookwood trundled a hundred milk churns a night from Wiltshire villages to Great Western depots, that Phoebe's father, up in the far north, was paid so much a mile for dragging a blast furnace from Point A to Point B, but less for assembling and setting in motion a convoy of oats and barley from scattered areas in the Cheviots. Words that had been commonplace to her since childhood had acquired a new and mystical meaning, translating themselves from mere words into products that could, in turn, be reduced to pounds, shillings and pence and tell her things like the daily wage of a carter, or the carrying capacity of a three-horse flat that was known as a man-o'-war. The vast and complex pattern of his enterprise expanded hour by hour, until it all but filled her mind, leaving little room for anything else, except his progress, and the basic needs of the children about the house. She knew how to draft a contract, how to measure distances, how to look up train departures in a Bradshaw, and how long it took to haul a pinnace between Worcester and Swansea, mostly over macadamised roads but, here and there, over tracks that added hours to a tight schedule in winter. She said, when Phoebe repeated the summons, "I know, I know! Tell him I won't be a minute ..." and kept her finger on a column of Bradshaw while, with her free hand, she jotted down the time of the milk train out of Chippenham and scrawled, in brackets, *'Must check. Should be earlier one'*, before smoothing her hair, following Phoebe across the hall and swishing past her as she held open the drawing room door.

She noticed that they were ill at ease. Not wretchedly so, as they had been on the previous visit, but wearing expressions her father would have called 'downy' as they advanced to greet her. She had learned the art of direct speech in the last few weeks and said, at once, "It's bad news?" and saw that her forthrightness disconcerted them, causing Sir Nevil to shuffle and fiddle with his hat. The surgeon did not fidget but he looked concerned, stroking the long, black hairs on his nose as he replied, "Not in the least bad. Good, I'd say. Taking a long-term view, that is."

"Well?" He continued to hesitate, however, so she said impatiently, "See here, Sir John, wouldn't you agree that I had borne up pretty well in this business? Compared with most wives, I mean, who might have made a great nuisance of themselves, drooping about his bedside asking silly questions, getting in the way?"

He smiled at that and said, gravely, "Yes, ma'am, I would indeed. As a matter of fact, that's why I'm here to put a proposal to you. The fact is your husband has made astonishing progress, physical progress that is, and on top of this, having regard to the kind of man he is,

609

he seems to me to have absorbed the shock of a permanent handicap far better than I would have predicted. That doesn't mean, however, that he hasn't a hard time ahead of him, so let me ask you a question in return. Would you call him a patient man?"

"No, I wouldn't. He's obstinate, but that's not the same thing, is it?"

"Obstinacy can help. In his case it might help a lot." He remained thinking for a moment and having taken his measure she allowed him this grace. Sir Nevil, she noticed, had withdrawn from the conversation. He was inspecting the moulded ceiling as if he might make an offer for it.

"What proposal have you in mind then?"

He came straight to the point. "That we leave him to fight it out entirely alone. He'll do it better that way, I've made up my mind to that."

"You're saying you would prefer me not to accompany him down to Dover on Thursday?"

"I would indeed, but there's more to it than that. What I should regard as ideal is for you to give me an undertaking not to visit him at all, to stay here with your family until he's able to come to you."

The ultimatum, for she regarded it as that, startled her. They had already warned her that he was scheduled to stay at the Swiss clinic throughout the autumn and winter, and possibly well into the spring, depending upon how quickly he mastered the art of using an artificial limb, but the prospect of not seeing him and not exchanging a word with him in all that time seemed to her heartless and cruel. She said, reddening, "Why would my presence hold him back? We're very close, as man and wife. Closer than most married couples I like to think," and he replied, rather too quickly, "I'm sure. And that has a direct bearing on it, Mrs. Swann."

"How?"

Sir Nevil suddenly erupted in a cough, saying, "Excuse me, Sir John ... this is very much between you and Mrs. Swann," and moved swiftly through the French windows and out on to the terrace. The surgeon seemed not to notice the scuttle but said, gruffly, "See here, Mrs. Swann, I'm an old man and I'm a doctor. We ought to be able to talk without embarrassing one another. How long have you been married?"

"Almost seven years."

"You've had three children in that time?"

"That's so."

He looked at her coolly. "You could well have had more?"

"I miscarried twice but what has that to do with it?"

"Nothing to the layman, Mrs. Swann, but it is useful evidence to some one with my experience. I've also had several long conversations with him and only fools keep secrets from their lawyers and doctors."

She found herself blushing then and he must have noticed it, for the twinkle left his eye and he looked at her compassionately. "To be truthful I didn't learn much talking to him but when a patient runs a high fever over a long period one usually comes away with a reliable sketch of the kind of person he is, what kind of life he has led, and more particularly what is important to him. I admit to taking all that into consideration when I came here asking favours. I am right in assuming it to have been a very rewarding marriage on both sides?"

"I like to think so. I was young, and entirely without experience when we married, but I've learned since."

He smiled again and this time it did not embarrass her. "I'm quite sure you have, Mrs. Swann. More than he gives you credit for, I daresay. I said he had adjusted to the shock and so he has outwardly, by which I mean he isn't likely to drown in self-pity. But a strong man, especially a man young for his years, faces innumerable hurdles in a case like this. Vanity is one, and another is his reduced capacity as a provider. He'll need time to surmount those and your best way of helping is to give him that time. All the time he needs. A year if need be."

"A year!"

"Take a minute, Mrs. Swann. Take a minute and think about it," and he carried his sherry glass over to the window through which she could see the spare figure of Sir Nevil, studiously contemplating the ponies grazing in the paddock.

She accepted his invitation and thought about it. Vanity and his capacity as a provider. She had often thought of herself as inordinately vain but until this moment had never included vanity among his weaknesses. Now she saw that she had been too charitable. Or, at any rate, unobservant, for he *was* vain, in many respects as vain as a peacock, and Sir John had pinpointed at least two areas where he was certain to prove extremely sensitive. They were only two among several. He had often, now that she came to reflect, demonstrated vanity as regards his vigour and his power, at any time he chose, to dominate her physically, and she found that this was something she could think of now not merely with humour but with infinite compassion. Mutilated, with his splendid body chopped and lacerated, he would be likely, she imagined, to suffer untold agonies of humiliation and the certainty that deprivation on that scale would only increase her love and respect for him as man and mate was no help whatever while they were separated. She understood that clearly enough and there was no hope of demonstrating this—as she had resolved to demonstrate it—until he could meet her on something approaching equal terms. He could not be expected to take that demonstration for granted and would be likely, stripped of his dignity, to regard himself as something repulsive and obscene, a mere part of a man; truncated, pitiful.

That was one hurdle he had to learn to negotiate but the other was even more formidable. Ever since she had known him he had taken pride in advancing, sword in hand as it were, to meet every challenge that his generation offered. The purchase of 'Tryst' and the constant financial risk he had courted to see his waggons roll on every highway in the land, were only isolated examples of his aggressiveness, his single-minded determination to stand firmly on his own two feet without incurring obligations from anyone, even his closest friends. Moreover, and this seemed to her the nub of what Sir John, in his bumbling way, was trying to say, he had enjoyed fighting his battles alone, and here was one that promised to engage every ounce of self-sufficiency and stamina he possessed. She saw him, fleetingly fighting it out in a strange land and finding a certain amount of satisfaction in a battle that would end, she had no doubt, in the re-establishment of his pride.

She said, with a smile, "Very well, you don't have to think up new ways of persuading me, Sir John. You've been kind and wise, and I'll never forget that, any more than I will Sir Nevil's kindness all these weeks. As to what you advise, it would be a poor return on my part to make fresh difficulties. I'll do as you suggest, providing I can write to him regularly."

"By all means," he said, enthusiastically, "so long as you take care that your letters aren't dull. But I don't have to advise you there, do I?"

No, she thought, you certainly don't, and remembering that absurd, adolescent tumble in the copse the day he returned, she felt a malicious impulse to patronise him and wondered how he would be likely to receive the facts of the relationship that they had all but built a few hours before this terrible strain had been added to it.

He said, picking up his hat and gloves, "I'm grateful to Sir Nevil

612

for introducing me to this case, Mrs. Swann, and I'm not speaking professionally. Perhaps, when things improve for you, I might have an opportunity of getting to know you and your husband as friends rather than patients. May I presume that far?"

"If you don't mind telling me why," she said, involuntarily, but then, thinking that this was rather rude, added, "You must have treated hundreds of people in more or less similar circumstances."

"Ah, that's where you're wrong," he said, with another of his unpredictable twinkles, "for most cases aren't in the least like yours, or most partnerships either. People like me are resigned to having to cut through half-a-yard of sentimental blubber to expose the bare bones of a human relationship and I doubt very much if I could have conducted this conversation with one young married woman in a thousand, or not without hemming and hawing on my part and blushes on hers. I hope you'll take that as a compliment, Mrs. Swann. It's certainly meant as one."

"One that should go to him," she said, as he gave her an old-fashioned, half-humorous bow and strode out across the terrace calling to Sir Nevil, now engaged in making the acquaintance of what, she supposed, he would be likely to call her 'proofs of affection'.

3

Edith Wadsworth's transfer of power to Henrietta was a shift that could not, with the best will in the world, be accomplished at a stroke. Anticipating the demands it was likely to make on her she did not see herself returning to the Crescents in time for the autumn rush, that usually began in the first days of October. Her estimate was pessimistic. In the event she was back in Peterborough by the first week in September and by then she had had to recast her entire estimate of the woman she had once thought of as a flibberty-gibbet, with little to recommend her as a wife, much less an adjutant. Notwithstanding this hasty reassessment the speed with which Henrietta adapted to the task, her perspicacity, her intelligent curiosity and, above all, her easy grasp of essentials, caused Edith to think that perhaps Adam Swann was not such a fool as regards women as she had once supposed.

They had established a routine before he left for Oberhofen, on the shores of Lake Thun, where Sir John Levy's colleague had his clinic. Within a week of his departure Henrietta had absorbed the mass of theory sent her through the post and was clamouring for more, as well as advancing the date when her practical tuition could begin.

Her insatiable appetite for data left Edith breathless. She had made the mistake of assuming that Henrietta's acceptance of managerial status was prompted solely by her desire to serve. It had never occurred to her that she would be likely to find personal fulfilment in the rôle and neither had she reckoned on her keen commercial instinct or her prodigious memory for detail, superior to that of the man whose chair she was occupying. Long before she set foot in the belfry she had memorised not only the names and characteristics of every key man in the thirteen districts, but also the type and number of teams and vehicles he operated, and the variety of goods he hauled. This was surprising enough. What was more so was the lengths to which she was prepared to go to break new ground, using a counterfeit helplessness to recruit chivalry where Edith would never have imagined a single chivalrous instinct existed.

Left alone in the belfry one afternoon she coaxed a contract from a Eurasian tea-importer who had resisted Adam's blandishments for years, and when Edith, quite bewildered, demanded to know how a grasping old cutpurse like Alcibiades had been netted, she replied, "Well, I suppose I simpered a little and then had one of the clerks bring us tea in tall glasses. With lemon, the way foreigners like to drink it in the Cotton Belt."

Soon she was using similar tactics on the Headquarters' staff. In a little over a fortnight she had every one of them dancing attendance on her, in a way that might have soured Edith had it altered the balance of the tutor-pupil relationship, but this was not so. She made it perfectly clear that she was not prepared to be infected by Tybalt's fussiness, or slowed down by Keate's caution, but as regards Edith she showed a circumspection that was touching, deferring to every hint, and putting her questions so humbly that it was not long before the alliance between them developed into mutual respect and genuine friendship, as between a pair of sisters widely divided by age and experience. At least, that was how Henrietta saw it, but to Edith it was more profound, something that made fools of them all, including Adam Swann, who had had her believing (and perhaps continued to believe himself?) that he married a little goose who was a swan by courtesy alone. Soon, as they laboured five days a week through the heat of August, she was able to stand off and look in on the pair of them, seeing herself in the rôle of a sorceress engaged in coaching an apprentice who, given time, was likely to dislodge every stovepipe hat in London. Whatever jealousy she might have experienced at witnessing this phenomenon was moderated by glee, for in a way Henrietta's performance indicated that this was only a man's world because men were determined it should remain so and that one fine day maybe a century hence, they would wake up and find petticoats in all their citadels. She said, when they were drafting Alcibiades' contract, "Weren't you ever tempted to poke your nose into his concerns before?" and Henrietta said no, never, and for a very good reason, for she was sure Adam would have resented it, however much he pretended to despise 'twitterers'. "I suppose I must have kept my wits about me without knowing it," she admitted, "and learned a certain amount listening to my father and his cronies. Up in the Belt a woman gets shushed if she so much as offers an opinion, but it's all mostly a matter of commonsense, isn't it? I mean, if you can run a house you ought to be able to run a business. What astonishes me is that even an old skin-a-grape like this Alcibiades is so full of his own conceit that he doesn't see the obvious. Here he was, offloading tea at docks on the south side and carting it through all that traffic and over London Bridge to wholesalers, north of the river, when he could have saved himself time and money by repairing and using a tumbledown warehouse he owns at Wapping, and stocking up by wherry every time a clipper docked. It was pointing that out to him that got us the contract."

Edith said nothing. She was too busy wondering whether, in years ahead, both she and Adam would find themselves in the situation of the king who enlisted a powerful neighbour as an ally and found, when the war was over, that he had been absorbed along with the enemy. Her assurance was rather depressing when Edith recalled how tiresome and complex the work had appeared when she was up here alone, whereas Henrietta seemed to advance towards it with a kind of girlish gaiety. She would sometimes look across at that tumble of copper ringlets and try and imagine what was going on underneath them in a brain none of them had taken into account before it was confronted with slate hauls from Llanberis, and the profit represented by one of Dockett's furniture removals in Tom Tiddler's Ground. What would Adam be likely to make of it when he returned? Would things ever be the same between them when he came back with his pace inevitably slowed and his confidence in himself badly shaken?

One other aspect of this conspiracy on their part surprised her. Henrietta never made a single reference to what had emerged from that confrontation at 'Tryst', and seemed to take it for granted that any woman associated with Adam Swann would be likely to fall madly in love with him. It was one aspect of their association that irritated her, taking issue with her loyalty and her determination to play fair. She was grateful enough for a clear conscience but sometimes it seemed to her a very lopsided distribution of largesse, for here was a woman several years younger than herself who bore his name, had already borne him three children, was still in possession of good looks and a good figure, and was now seen to possess an agile brain and a self-confidence superior to anything she had to offer. She kept these thoughts to herself, however, and because they were constantly occupied through that sweltering month they did not trouble her overmuch until news came that he had been measured for his leg and was likely, according to the latest bulletin, to be home by spring.

Edith noticed then that the news did not seem to elate Henrietta so much as she would have expected and it even crossed her mind, rather treacherously she supposed, that Henrietta was thoroughly enjoying the challenge and might resent an end to the interlude. This suspicion was so persistent that presently she had to bring it into the open, saying, half-jokingly, "I really believe you prefer it up here and feel more at home in this belfry than at 'Tryst'!", and Henrietta replied, frankly, "In a way I do, and I know why. For the first time in my life I've been useful and it's pleasant to learn you're not such a fool as you took yourself for. Do you suppose women will ever get a chance to prove that they can do anything apart from cooking, scouring, mending, minding children and making themselves available when husbands have time to be affectionate?"

The question was posed with such honesty that Edith laughed outright. It expressed so exactly all the secret resentments she herself had nursed over the years against the assumption by men that women were no more than a piece of apparatus, equipped for reproduction and servitude at the back of the cave.

"I daresay it will come dawdling over the horizon in time," she replied, "but not in your time or mine. Men have been fighting and hunting for thousands of years. All they've done since is to exchange both pursuits for commerce. There's a rumour, I hear, of giving women University places, and training spinsters for professions, but I doubt whether we shall ever be regarded as fit for anything except a little clerking and clearing up after our masters."

"But that's ridiculous," Henrietta protested. "You and I are plain proof that it is, and you especially. It's quite obvious to me that Keate and Tybalt couldn't have managed without you when Adam was injured. They even admit to it, don't they?"

616

"They might, but I don't think Adam will, or anyone like Adam, who isn't already conditioned to receiving orders. Does that bother you? I mean, having identified with this side of his life, will you ever be able to carry on where you left off?"

"I've really no choice," she said, glumly, "for by the time he gets back I'll have another baby to attend to and I don't suppose for a minute it'll be the last."

The casual announcement so stunned Edith that for nearly a minute she was incapable of comment. She stood beside Frankenstein gaping at her partner with amazement that was approaching awe.

"You're *pregnant*? But how . . .?" and she broke off as Henrietta, discerning the other's incredulity, said, "Why do you find it surprising? It doesn't surprise me, although I must say it's a perfect nuisance in the circumstances."

"You're saying you're upset about it?"

"Well, no, not upset exactly, but I do wish it could be told to wait its turn." She rose, standing in such a way that Edith could see then there was not much doubt about her condition and she was surprised she had needed telling. "After all, I oughtn't to grumble. I've always wanted children, a whole tribe of children. Stella was difficult but the other two came easily enough, and I'm not scared of having more. It's just that I'll have to go home around Christmas and I'd set my heart on carrying on until the last moment so as to surprise him."

"You'll certainly do that. Have you told him?"

"No. I was only sure myself a fortnight ago. I put it down to the shock and worry."

"You'll tell him now that you are certain?"

"No, I won't."

She stood there looking, Edith thought, like a plump, stubborn child refusing to apologise, and in response to an impulse in which comradeship and humour were combined, she crossed the room and put her arm about her shoulders. "But why ever not? It isn't likely to worry him, is it?"

"Oh, it's not that," said Henrietta, "it's just that I want to hold it in reserve. It'll give him something to think about the moment he crosses the doorstep."

She considered this, finding in it further evidence of this indomitable woman's knowledge of the man Edith had once supposed she knew better than anyone alive. It was a very chastening thought and one that had the effect of removing yet another prop of self-esteem. She said, "I suppose you're right," and then, grudgingly, "You know

617

him far better than I do," and Henrietta said, lightly, "Well, I know that side of him. Better than he knows himself."

"You're proposing to work here five days a week until Christmas?"

"Why not? So long as I'm well and I've felt well ever since I took your advice. I'll stay at the 'George', and go home every Friday afternoon. One good thing has happened that I didn't hear about until after it was fixed. That convent Deborah attended is closing, and Adam arranged for her to live with us all the time. I suppose he was going to tell me that night, the minute we were alone. Did Mr. Avery's child impress you?"

"Very much indeed."

"She's a strange little body. Sometimes she doesn't seem like a child at all, more like someone studying to be a saint. That sounds rather silly, I suppose, but I couldn't have got through those first days without her. Or without you for that matter, Edith."

"You'd get through anything," Edith said, "anything at all, Henrietta!" and she meant it.

"Will you come up again in the New Year?"

"That won't be necessary. By then you'll know enough to run Headquarters at a distance."

She saw Henrietta's eyes sparkle. "You think that would work?"

"Of course it would work."

She realised then that she had removed a weight from the other's mind and it did not need much reflection to understand why. To have him come home, and find his wife in the nursery and herself back in command, would have cancelled out their entire strategy, but so long as she could continue to exercise control from 'Tryst' Henrietta was likely to reap the benefit of all the work and enterprise she had contributed to the plan. It was well enough from her viewpoint, Edith supposed, but it was difficult to suppress a sense of being pushed even further into the shadows, where nothing awaited her but a lifetime of watching waggons through that office window at Peterborough.

She said, with an effort, "Well, I'm glad for you, Henrietta, and for him too. I'll go back to my lodgings now and start packing."

"You're thinking of going back to the Crescents already?"

She managed to smile. "Why not? You're perfectly capable of managing here, and my patch is in dreadful disorder after three months with no real supervision."

She went out quickly then, for fear of betraying her feelings. It was ungenerous, she supposed, but she could not prevent envy mounting in her for the woman on the other side of the desk, someone who seemed to have virtually everthing when she had so little. The fact that Henrietta had earned her bonuses did not help.

4

When she saw him standing by the window, legs widely planted, hands deep in his breeches pockets, and an expression of uncertainty in his eyes, she could only think of him as yet another problem that had materialised out of a fog of dejection through which she had been walking ever since Henrietta had told her she was expecting a child in early spring.

It was irrational that she should feel deprived on this account. The plan to involve Henrietta in his concerns had been hers, and the certainty of its succeeding beyond all expectations ought surely to have been an occasion for the greatest satisfaction. But she found as the train rushed her north, that she could not defeat envy with logic, or derive comfort from a sense of rectitude that Christians reputedly enjoyed when they had made a sacrifice, and she supposed this had to do with the near-certainty that she would never have a child. By Adam Swann or by anyone else.

The mood endured all the way home as she reviewed successive phases of her life with a kind of gloomy relish, seeing very little that afforded her satisfaction. Society, she thought, was badly organised for people of her temperament, possessing vast reserves of affection fated to remain untapped. A man, even a fool of a man, could make any number of attempts to track down happiness, addressing himself to the task until he was toothless and senile, but a woman had so little time at her disposal and time for her was running out. Fulfilment was not to be found in a job of work. At best it was a distraction, of the kind she had found at Headquarters and now that she was resuming the rhythm of her old life it seemed scarcely worth the effort. For a woman as resilient as Henrietta there was a sense of purpose in everything she did, together with a sense of moving towards some definable goal, but up here, surrounded by men who looked to her not as a woman but as a gaffer, there was nothing to set one's sights on but increased turnover, or the satisfaction of beating men at their own game, sources of inspiration that were beginning to run dry.

She had intended on arrival to go straight to the yard and take a look at the tangle she would have to unravel in the morning but now she was here she jibbed at the prospect. The yard could damned well look to itself. There were days, weeks, even years to attend to anything she was likely to find down there, so she directed her steps towards her lodging, reflecting that the last time she had passed along this road she had thought of Adam Swann as a dying man and the time before that, on the occasion of his last visit, had lectured him merrily on the art of handling women. She must have made her point. He had gone straight home and handled Henrietta with such address that she was now carrying his fourth child in her womb and his business concerns in her head.

She let herself in, expecting her landlady to call from the kitchen but there was no greeting and she thought, with a spurt of irritation, 'The old slut is over at that sister of hers, and now I shall have to get my own supper if I want any', and she opened the door of her sitting room to see Wickstead standing there, gazing thoughtfully into the street.

. She exclaimed, dropping her hand luggage with a clatter, *"You!"* and he turned and looked at her, as though by no means sure of his reception. He recovered almost at once, however, smiling his slow, impudent smile, so that she remembered his perfect teeth and at the same time was conscious of a rather disturbing sensation under her breasts and rush of colour to her cheeks that caused her to fall back a step. He was beside her then, heaving her bag on to the sofa and saying, "Did I frighten you? I'm very sorry, I didn't think that was possible," and she snapped, "For God's sake, don't treat me as if I was a dragon! How do you come to be here? Who told you where I lived? How did you get in?"

"Well, now," he said, genially, "let's take those questions in order. I'm here to ask you advice on an important question—important to me, that is, and I was given your private address at the yard. As to getting in I didn't pick the lock as you're entitled to expect. Your landlady told me you would be home on the afternoon train and that I could wait if I cared to. She's had to go out and asked me to apologise. It seems her niece is having a baby and she was in a tizzy on account of it having arrived a week early." He dropped his bantering manner and suddenly became solicitous. "You look tired and hungry. Your dinner's in the oven, shepherd's pie and apple tart, and I went out and bought this as an appetiser," and he produced a bottle of hock and set it down on the table. She said, impatiently, "Wait here. I am tired and I am hungry." Then, more affably, "Have you eaten?"

"Yes, but I should enjoy sharing a glass of hock with you."

His charm was infectious and she suddenly felt very glad to see him, not only a liberty, but apparently as irrespressible as when she had parted from him on the Harwich platform some months before. It seemed much longer, like meeting someone remembered from childhood, and as she went into the kitchen, retrieving her warmed-up meal, she thought, 'Something very odd is happening to me! Why should I feel so wretched at the prospect of Henrietta's baby and so delighted at meeting up with a professional thief? Am I so far reduced that I welcome a scoundrel, so long as he has a pleasant smile?', and suddenly she felt more excited than hungry and spooned a small helping of pie on to a plate her landlady had left to warm, carrying it through to the sitting room where he was uncorking the wine. She said, trying hard to sound casual: "I've been in London since June. Mr. Swann was badly injured in that rail crash at Staplehurst," and he said, "Yes, so they told me at the yard. How is he?"

"Making very good progress in Switzerland. He had a leg amputated."

He looked at her curiously and she wondered how much he knew of her involvement with Swann. More than was good for her, probably, if he had taken heed of gossip at the yard, and thinking this she said, "You took a mad risk to go back there. Weren't you afraid they would send for the police the moment you showed up on the premises?"

"Not in the least," he said, "I wouldn't have bet much against you not showing me the door but I'd have staked all I have you said nothing about that job of mine that misfired." He found glasses and poured the wine, and it occurred to her that this trick of knowing where things were, and making himself at home in a stranger's house, was part of his stock-in-trade. She sat and began to eat while he remained standing and lifted his glass. "Here's luck," he said and then, swallowing hard, as though in need of stimulation, "You once hinted your firm could use a man like me, so long as he kept his hands in his pockets when he wasn't driving. Was that Bible Class talk, or did you mean it?"

"I meant it then but I've revised it since."

For a moment he looked dismayed but his mercury bobbed up as he said, with a wry grin, "Oh, well, it was worth a try," and reached for his hat.

"Don't be in such a damned hurry," she said, feeling a malicious pleasure in regaining the initiative. "I simply don't see you as a waggoner and that's all I meant by revision. You'd get bored in a month and go to stealing again. If I was employing you, and had

621

the slightest expectation that you would adapt to honest work, I'd give you real responsibility. I'd put you on commission, too, so that the harder you worked the more you'd earn."

"You'd do that? Without worrying what I was up to when your back was turned? How could you, when you know I've never done an honest day's work in my life? Unless it was a plant, like that time I was hanging around waiting for Beckstein's diamonds."

"Because I got the impression you don't steal for gain."

"Why else would a man steal?"

"For all kinds of reasons. From habit. From necessity. From motives of pride and revenge. Even from a love of walking a tight-rope."

He looked across at her steadily and there was mischief in his eyes. "You've thought about it a great deal, haven't you?"

"I've thought about you, yes. Wondered about you, too. What you were doing, whether you were back in prison or still on the run. But mostly, as I said at the time, what a waste you represented."

He pondered this while she finished her pie and started on the apple tart.

"Don't you want your wine?"

"Does that mean you want it?"

"Yes, it does. It wasn't easy to bring myself to this point. It was the most difficult decision I've ever had to make."

She tasted the wine, set down her glass and refilled his. "Drink if it helps," she said, but he left the glass on the table and said, slowly, "I'm not on the run. I didn't tell you the full truth about that. About everything else but not that. I'm out on licence, with two years unexpired sentence hanging over me but if I'm caught on a fresh crib it would mean seven to ten years, plus the outstanding two. That's slow death. There'd be no going back after that."

"Why did you lie about that?"

"It seemed the best way to head off a lecture on the rewards of industry."

"And the real reason?"

"I doubt if you would have believed it. It would have sounded too unlikely in the circumstances—me having been on hand to save you from those drainage pipes."

"What's the connection?"

"It was something similar that earned me a big cut in sentence. I'm a good swimmer and in Gibraltar harbour I saved two marines from drowning when their gig capsized. Their Commandant wrote to

London, and because he was highly-placed, and could pull strings, they gave me a conditional pardon; with instructions to report weekly, of course."

She stopped eating. "You mean you deliberately threw away a chance like that?"

"It wasn't much of a chance. I had a record, and no trade. I knew I could do better than beg and I have." He began to brag. "These aren't the usual swagman's duds. This suit of clothes was made to measure."

Suddenly she wanted to laugh. His mixture of vanity and jaunty self-justification were so much at odds with what she took to be the real Wickstead, a man who had come near to admitting that he was lost in the dark. She said, "You've come so far, Wickstead ... What's your other name?"

"Tom."

"You've come this far, Tom, so why sit there fidgeting, like a young man trying to nerve himself to ask a girl for a dance? I mightn't say no and if I do I'll spare your pride. You've been thinking, too, since we last met. You've been assessing your chances of starting out all over again. Well, that's the most sensible thing you've ever done, so you don't have to apologise for it. I've been thinking along the same lines concerning myself."

"*You* have?"

"We'll come to that. For the time being let's confine ourselves to you. If you'll give me your word that you genuinely want a job, that you would give it a fair trial and promise to come to me if you decide you made a wrong decision, then I'd find a place for you. Old Duckworth has come into a little money and only stayed on to oblige me. You can take over tomorrow as yard foreman, at fifty shillings a week and the standard rates of commission on new business. It isn't much but it could be. More than half of Swann's foremen have moved on to a deputy manager's post, and that carries a bonus rate of two per cent on local turnover. I know a man much younger than you who is making three hundred a year. Will you want time to consider that?"

No, he said joyfully, he wouldn't and she remembered Henrietta had made an identical reply when she had put her proposition to her back in July. It reminded her that she was so concerned with solving other people's problems that she never had time to solve her own. She said, as he began to stammer his thanks, "That's you accounted for, and I don't want any earnest protestations until the trial period has

623

expired. In the meantime there's one small thing you could do for me, Tom."

"What is it?"

She measured him with her eye and stood up, having emptied her glass and set it down with a flourish.

"You can do what I asked Swann to do the last time he was here. You can come round here and kiss me."

He looked so taken aback that she felt sorry for him, but then, as he hesitated, she felt less sorry than indignant. "It's not a condition, damn it! You won't be expected to do it every morning you report to the yard. It's a ... a gesture, and I'm terribly much in need of a friendly gesture. More than you are if the truth's known!"

He moved in smartly then and his gaiety reassured her, so that when she felt his arms encircle her she changed her mind about the kind of kiss she had in mind. She was in no doubt as to the reason behind the invitation. It was just the same as when Adam had stood there. All she wanted, but that most desperately, was to feel a woman again, and he seemed to understand this very well, perhaps too well. He kissed her fondly but expertly, more expertly than she had ever been kissed, and the sensation under her breasts returned so that she was unable to conceal the pleasure his embrace brought her. She could have stood there being kissed for as long as he was disposed to remain but when his pleasure revealed itself in a slight increase of pressure at her waist and shoulder she quietly disengaged, remembering that Mrs. Sprockett might come bustling in at any moment, and that her personal dignity would be involved. She wanted him, as much as she had wanted his predecessors, but not furtively, the way he had always lived until now, but she was exhilarated to note that he was the more breathless of the two when he said, in a rather hushed voice she had never heard him use, "Is it because things have gone wrong with you since we parted?"

She replied, equably, "No, Tom, or not in the general way. Certainly not any way I could explain. Let's just say I suddenly felt very lonely; as lonely as you appear to be."

"You mean, we might give one another a hand?"

"Why not? Without obligations on either side. And I mean what I said about a trial period. You can walk out on the job at any time and all I ask is that you will tell me, and not just disappear, with anything that belongs to us, or our customers."

He said, thoughtfully, "That quip of yours—about walking a tight-rope—it probably seems an exciting life to safe people looking in but it isn't, you know. It's hell all through unless you're drunk, and if you're drunk you botch it sooner or later. That brush with you in Harwich did more to destroy my nerve than anything behind me, and you can't play my game if your nerve isn't up to it. I walked about all that night, seeing how it would end. Early one morning in a prison yard, with the chaplain snuffling his prayers, and a drop straight out ahead of me."

"Don't, Tom. Don't talk that way!"

"I have to. If you're prepared to take me on trust you should know how it is. The truth is you can't really worst them. Nobody has that much luck and this kept recurring to me. Before it was light I dropped the revolver into the dock and I haven't done a job since. Unless you count fencing those watches you found in the trunk."

"Where have you been?"

"Tramping. Thinking things over flat on my back and looking up at the sky." He was silent for a moment. "Are you religious? I don't mean in the going-to-church sense. Do you believe in a plan of some kind?"

"If I do it isn't the one they preach about in pulpits."

"That's what I decided. That's based on property and education and the handicapping is badly arranged. Brains, background, the kind of upbringing a person has . . ."

"People like you put too much emphasis on those things."

She was thinking, curiously enough, of Henrietta, and the neatness with which she had eased herself into the management of the network with no other qualification beyond a need to hold fast to a man's affection. She thought of Adam, too, in his earlier days, with nothing to guide him but instinct and a muddleheaded obstinacy, who had yet succeeded in translating extravagant dreams into realities. "The important thing is to be ready to back yourself and then find people willing to cover the bet. That, and to guard against self-pity. I should know."

She felt immensely comforted in his presence and in his need of her, and the emotion demanded assurance of a kind she had never sought from anyone, not even Adam.

"You're not married, are you, Tom?" He did not seem to put the obvious construction on the question but replied, simply, "No. I never cared to involve anyone fond of me in the life I led and the risks I ran."

"There was somebody?"

"No one in particular. I suppose I took my fun where I found it."

So had she, she reflected, except that there seemed to have been precious little fun all told. She was glad then that Mrs. Sprockett would soon be back, for she understood quite clearly what she would be inclined to propose if they were alone and it seemed very unfair to rush him to that extent. So she compromised, saying, "We might have fun working together, if you were so disposed. And that isn't a roundabout leap-year proposal. At least we could get to know one another," and he replied, soberly, "I don't need time to get to know you. I've not thought about anyone else in all this time and what you might find harder to believe is that it didn't begin with that ambush on the train."

"When you were working in the yard? Nonsense, Tom."

"It isn't nonsense. You fascinated me from the first day. I used to watch you when you didn't know it through that office window. When I heard you giving the orders, and men twice your age taking them, it sometimes seemed as if you were married to everyone in the yard and had brought everyone a dowry."

She laughed and it struck her that he could make her laugh without any trouble at all.

"Is that all? A loud-voiced gaffer in skirts?"

"No. As I say you always intrigued me but the real impact was when I saw those pipes slipping and had what you could call a cast-iron excuse to put my arms about you and satisfy myself that you handled like a woman."

It was an odd sort of compliment, she thought, but it pleased her. She said, "Kiss me again then and go before we scandalise Mrs. Sprockett," and he kissed her but with a mildly abstracted air. He had, she decided, a very rare technique, half drollery and half male gentleness that was new in her experience.

"Where are you staying, Tom?"

"The Wheatsheaf. I'm paid up until Saturday."

"You want an advance on your wages?"

"No, I'd much prefer to earn it."

He made ready to go then and she saw him as far as the door, smiling when he tipped his hat as he turned into the street and wondering if his elation matched hers, and whether a man like him would settle to any collar for more than a month. It was unimportant. A month would be long enough to enable her to readjust to the rhythm of things and stop feeling so damned sorry for herself. She closed the door, went through to her little bedroom, and began to unpack. As she did she caught herself humming.

6

Petticoat Government

THAT was the autumn and winter of seeping, pitiless rains, of swiftly alternating gales, frosts and thaws, that made the life of every man and beast in the network a torment. A time when thoughts turned yearningly to the summer that was gone, and forward to a spring that sometimes seemed reserved for the next generation.

Henrietta, clinging to her five-day stint at the yard until the Christmas break, was there to hear the dolorous pleas of Ratcliffe in the west, the first domino to fall, setting off a chain reaction among the southerly regions. His initial bleat reached them as early as late October, after a fortnight's torrential downpour had smashed the banks of the Exe, the Taw, the Torridge, the Bray, the Dart and many lesser streams, inundating all the valleys along which his bread-and-butter runs travelled, and spilling millions of gallons of ruby floodwater across the grazing grounds of his regular customers between the Channel and Barnstaple Bay.

Then the Tamar and the placid Camel followed suit, and in a single disastrous twenty-four hours he lost eight loaded waggons and three teams, two of his waggoners barely escaping with their lives when a wall of water engulfed them north of Tiverton. That same week, with half his routes under water he had to turn to the railways for succour, not only in Devon but in Somerset too, in order to fulfil his commitments, but as every other carrier in the west was in similar straits, deliveries piled up on sidings right across the region and railway embankments were beginning to shred at a dozen places between the Vale of Taunton and Bodmin Moor. After his St. Thomas's sub-depot had been flooded to a depth of four feet he sent a despairing wire for reserve teams, declaring that unless Rookwood in the Southern Square could help him, he could not undertake to keep his traffic moving for another week.

They sent him a convoy and at once had cause to regret it, for large-scale subsidence along a stretch of the Wilts, Somerset and Weymouth Railway north-west of Salisbury swamped Rookwood with a

627

flood of a different kind. Every farmer for miles around began to clamour for road transport to haul London-bound produce to departure points further east, so that Rookwood, in his turn, had to call on the Kentish Triangle for help.

Then the implacable downpour moved east and Vicary, his low-lying territory laced with estuaries, was soon in difficulty, flooded roads necessitating complicated detours where the usual routes were blocked by a dozen or more collapsed bridges. The strain on the draught-horses was killing as they churned their way through seas of liquid mud and slewed into open country where landslides had obliterated the highways. Horses foundered, loads shifted, axles broke, canopies were stripped by high winds, and journeys that had been made in a few hours stretched into a day and a night throwing every timetable in the south into disarray.

Early December brought a brief respite when temperatures fell and the ground hardened, but a quick thaw followed and stream beds brimming with snow water washed down a wilderness of up-rooted trees and tangled underbrush, so that conditions were soon chaotic in all four regions and reserve teams were just not to be had. It was then that the game of general post they had been playing with one another had to cease.

About a fortnight before Christmas, when things were at their worst but the most dreaded months of a haulier's calendar were still to come, Henrietta made her decision but in obedience to her policy of giving the professionals first call, she summoned Keate, Tybalt, Godsall of the Kentish Triangle, and the lawyer Stock to the belfry, asking them what they had in mind to guard against a complete standstill when the regions advanced into the new year with depleted teams, broken-down vehicles and a sullen, exhausted work-force.

They had ideas of a sort. Tybalt proposed a head office edict, forbidding the acceptance by any district manager of a single new commission, all efforts being bent to meet the requirements of customers whose loyalty had been tested over the years.

Keate, whose cautious nature had been eroded to some extent by Adam's expansionist creed, had an alternative solution. Setting his face against the rejection of new business (especially when it was there for the taking), he suggested an overall abandonment of time-schedules right across the affected regions, a concession, he said, that would ease the tremendous burdens laid upon men, waggons and horses operating over half-ruined roads, particularly in the soggy Western Wedge and The Bonus that was now like a gigantic sponge.

Godsall, declaring that his loans to Vicary and Rookwood had left him dangerously under-strength, was more revolutionary. He recommended a cancellation of all long-distance hauls and a new understanding with the railways on the basis of bulk shipments over a limited period, to carry them over into the spring.

Stock, the lawyer, offered no solution, having decided that Henrietta's recent probing into the financial aspects of her husband's concerns indicated that she had a sweeping decision of her own and was merely indulging in a cat-and-mouse exercise with her lieutenants. He was, as it happened, quite right as regards this although, as soon as she spoke, he thought himself a fool for not having seen through her request for a summary of the reserve accounts when she called on him the previous afternoon.

By now, of course, they had all adjusted to her presence behind that great desk of his, with her little feet on a footstool, and her artless way of playing them against one another. They were a generation of men who had grown to maturity under a small, plump woman ruling large slices of five continents. Perhaps this helped them to accept her invasion of their spheres of influence.

She said, rather pertly, Stock thought, "All very practical, I'm sure. But there must be a better way, a more *daring* way of going about it. What I mean is ... well, why couldn't we turn this run of bad luck to our advantage, seeing that it must have thrown all our competitors into a regular whirl? Wouldn't *you* say it has, Mr. Keate? Knowing as much as you do about what one can expect of the strongest teams?"

It was one of her artifices, Stock thought, smiling his discreet lawyer's smile, to flatter a man before she knocked him over the head and he wondered how Swann had managed this sharp little filly before his accident. Pretty firmly, he would say, so that now she was making the most of a loose rein and enjoying every minute of the canter.

"The point is," she went on, "and do correct me if I'm wrong, all those suggestions would help to keep us marking time but they wouldn't do anything to prove we were the best hauliers in England. They would show we were just as dependent upon weather as anyone else owning a horse and cart. Isn't that so?"

Stock saw Keate wince and guessed the reason. Keate thought of himself as a waggoner, not a carter, and there was a subtle difference, although it was not one a pretty woman like her could appreciate. In fairness to them all, however, he decided to give her the opening she

629

was seeking and said, "Come now, Mrs. Swann. You've got the advantage of us, for you've slept on this and unless I'm mistaken you already have something in mind."

She smiled then. It was one of her advantages as an amateur among professionals that she could have her bluff called without losing face. She said, "Well . . . yes, I have. Ever since poor Mr. Ratcliffe wired that he was in trouble. But I didn't like to put it forward until I was sure it was in my husband's mind as long ago as last December, when we had all that snow in the north. Now I *am* sure, because here's a file on it," and she produced a buff folder entitled *'Central Pool. Team Allocation Account'.*

None of them had ever seen the folder and she did not tell them where she had found it. There was very little in it but some pages of jottings and a map, and it was the map rather than the notes that interested them. It was a sketch of the regions, with three place names ringed in pencil and decorated with question-marks. Keate, studying it closely, said he could make nothing of it, but a small bell tinkled in Stock's mind, recalling Adam's approach over a year ago when he had suggested deducting five per cent of the net annual profits and building up an account specifically earmarked for renewals. For the moment, however, he could not remember whether any decision had been arrived at, and saw no reason to link it to a map starred with the words 'Harrogate', 'Derby', and 'Oxford'. He said, "I take it you've studied this file, ma'am?"

"I didn't have to. The map, and Mr. Tybalt's statement that there is already over four hundred pounds in that account, tells me what Mr. Swann had in mind for the winter. What's happened proves what a good idea it was."

She had their attention now and made the most of it. "This continual shuttling we've been doing for months, it's silly and wasteful, and beyond a certain point I think it makes matters worse in the long run. It would do as a stopgap if we had the worst of the winter behind us but we haven't. In January and February the weather might well be worse, especially up north, and for heaven's sake, where will that leave us? Borrowing teams and waggons from one another so often that not even Mr. Keate will know who has what, or for how long. What we should have is a fixed reserve of waggons and teams waiting at specially selected points, and that was what Mr. Swann had in mind when he pencilled in those towns. Mr. Tybalt says refuse new business. Mr. Keate says cut the time schedule, Mr. Godsall says go cap in hand to the railways. Well, I can't believe Mr. Swann would approve of any of these courses. He was never one to miss a chance of making a new customer. He built his business on speed, and from all I hear he only made the railway serve him when and where it's useful. I'll tell you what I think we should do. Draw on that account, buy fresh teams, and base them on stables where they can be rushed in wherever they're needed as soon as we get a call for them!" She searched her mind for a phrase, something that had reoccurred very frequently in newspaper reports of the Crimea and Mutiny she had read long before she got involved with waggons, sides of bacon, slates and foundry machinery, and suddenly she remembered it. *"A strategic reserve!"* she concluded, triumphantly, "that's what's needed, *a strategic reserve!"*

Stock had the greatest difficulty in restraining a very unprofessional yelp of laughter. It was not that he found Henrietta's proposal funny, indeed, it struck him at once as a brilliant piece of improvisation, but the expressions on the faces of the three other men were those of children who had just watched a magician pull a rabbit from a hat and hold it up by the ears. He covered himself by thumping his knee and exclaiming, immoderately, "That's capital, Mrs. Swann! That's clearly something Mr. Swann meant to guard against when he opened that account!" and then, "I ... er ... don't suppose you've consulted Mr. Swann about it? If you have we could wait ..."

She flushed, perhaps at the implication that the idea was not strictly original. *"No* Mr. Stock. I haven't written and I don't intend to! He's not to be worried and I've had the strictest instructions to that effect."

Keate said, slowly, "Teams like that ... dotted all over the country. They wouldn't be earning anything ...", and then Tybalt, wearing that agonised expression that settled on him whenever the outlay of capital was proposed, said, "Four hundred wouldn't cover the cost of a scheme of that kind, Mrs. Swann. It would only buy around half-a-dozen teams, to say nothing of waggons to go along with them," and Stock thought it a stupid remark, for he must have known Henrietta had already calculated the sum needed. She said, patiently, "Why, of course it wouldn't be enough. Mr. Tybalt. We should have to dip into the general reserve, to the extent of at least another thousand, but who knows what a hard winter in the north and Midlands might cost us in lost business, spoiled goods, ruined waggons and worn out teams? How many Clydesdales could we buy for fifteen hundred, Mr. Keate?"

Keate did a sum in his head and said round about fifty, making available an additional twenty-five frigates or seventeen men-o'-war. He wouldn't recommend the use of pinnaces, they were too light for hard work in heavy weather. Stock gathered from this that he was all but won over to the proposal already.

"Well, then," she went on, gaily, "let's put it in hand tomorrow morning. Mr. Stock will tell you I've got power of attorney, and can draw eleven hundred from the general account and put it into the other one but Mr. Tybalt would have to countersign, so it's important he should agree. You'd best say now if you don't, Mr. Tybalt, for then I should have no alternative but to write to Switzerland."

It was a naked threat and Tybalt cowered under it, inserting a finger between his thin neck and what the vanboys called his 'Come-to-Jesus' collar. He said, miserably, "It's more a matter for Mr. Keate, ma'am. After all, he's waggonmaster," and at once looked relieved at having found a way of shifting the burden of responsibility on to the shoulders of his friend.

"Well, Keate?" asked Stock, thoroughly enjoying the session, and Keate said, deliberately, "If time is a factor we can forget new waggons. Blunderstone couldn't supply them at such short notice but we can make do with what we have if we've available horses to double up in overtaxed regions. That's the real answer. With fifty more Clydesdales we could keep moving, short of a month of blizzards." Suddenly he became enthusiastic. "It's a good idea, Mrs. Swann, and we'll set about it at once. If I could make one suggestion—we'll need five reserve stables, not three. Harrogate and Derby are well enough. Harrogate will serve the Polygon, the Border Triangle and Crescent North, Derby the Crescent Centre, Northern Pickings, and the northern half of Mountain Square. Teams can be rushed where they're needed, by train if necessary. Down south we'll need to divide our strength and one depot at Oxford couldn't serve such an area. I suggest we make Oxford the main depot but put in a couple of teams at Cheltenham and one or two more between Aylesbury and Chesterford, to keep an eye on The Bonus and Crescent South." He got up, looking, Stock thought, like an Old Testament prophet about to address himself to the task of chastening the ungodly. "I'll go and see McSawney if you'll excuse me. No sense in wasting a day. None at all," and stalked out, his boots hammering the stairs as if to emphasise the completeness of his conversion.

"That's splendid," said Henrietta, clapping her hands like a child at a party. "Now I wonder if you would be so good as to go and see to the money side of it, Mr. Tybalt?" and Tybalt rose but without taking his eyes off her and slowly backed away so that Stock, unable to see him as a recognisable Old Testament character, thought of him as the murderer in *Maria Marten* withdrawing from the grave of his victim. He said, chuckling, as soon as the clerk and Godsall had excused themselves, "Well, you've got them all tamed, Mrs. Swann. I can't think they would jump through hoops that readily for your husband. Have you got any one in mind for the job of supervising these depots?" and she said, "Indeed I have, Mr. Stock. Miss Wadsworth has a new yard foreman called Wickstead, and she seems to think of him as a real treasure. He's worked at Newmarket racing stables, and I'm going to propose him. Subject to Miss Wadsworth's agreement, of course."

He said nothing to this, reflecting, as he shook hands, that whether Miss Wadsworth agreed or not there would be a vacancy on her Peterborough staff before the week was out.

2

The new year was hardly more than a fortnight old, when the snow Henrietta had predicted was blocking the old turnpike roads that ran east and west of the Pennines, and over the two-thousand-year-old mosstrooper tracks of the Cheviots.

Down south the weather had moderated, giving men like Ratcliffe and Rookwood time to lick their wounds and marshal their scattered forces against the prospect of fresh assaults from the North Atlantic. Flood levels had receded, and there was even some bleak sunshine in and around the pitheads of the Cornish tin mines, but further east Rookwood had already made his first call on the reserve depot at Cheltenham, and over in The Bonus country Vicary had reason to be grateful for the availability of two spare teams to double up on a haul of timber for repairing damaged bridges that spanned his bread-and-butter routes.

Kent, for once, escaped the snow, and Godsall thanked his stars, for it gave him a chance to settle to the collar in Blubb's old territory. He found it less difficult than he had imagined for down here, where there were innumerable military depots, he was able to add to the old coachee's long list of contracts by using his army background to make new friends in the garrison towns.

It was bitterly cold in the Crescents but the snow held off and the teams stationed there were not called to face the hazards and hardships in the north where Fraser was fighting it out both sides of the Border, sometimes in drifts of upwards of six feet. The northern reserve depot was a great boon to him and three times in fourteen days he called up reinforcements by rail, enabling him to make hauls he would have had to cancel without means of harnessing six horses to flats pulled usually by three.

Over in the Polygon Catesby was also fighting a nonstop battle with the weather, and in some ways it recalled the cotton famine, for in this kind of situation railway spurlines, on which a score of towns depended for food and raw materials, failed in a way that confirmed arguments Blubb had often advanced against the gridiron. Points froze at several junctions, and even main line locomotives were sometimes baulked by iced inclines, proving that there were still times when horseflesh was the more reliable form of transport.

Bryn Lovell, down in Abergavenny, had trouble in the central part of his region, where every road was treacherous and even double teams could not pull full loads over the icy hills of Brecon and Radnorshire, but the reserve depot at Derby helped him out with his more northerly hauls and when it came to his knowledge that the scheme had been proposed and pushed through by Swann's flibberty-gibbet wife, he asked Morris of Southern Pickings, if this titbit of network gossip was well-founded. Morris, who missed very little in his interpretation of day-to-day grapevine intelligence, admitted that it was, but he was not so surprised as his colleague. He had quite a different attitude to women and simply said, with a shrug, "That accident of his was the making of her. Maybe he didn't know the woman he married before it happened and she had a chance to show her mettle."

*   *   *

She had the business, that demanded most of her physical and nervous energy, and she had the family, still looking to her for comfort and affection, but neither business nor family could claim any credit for keeping loneliness at arm's length throughout the long winter. This was the achievement of the child within her, after it had assumed a unique identity round about the fourth month of pregnancy.

Private communion with a child she was carrying was not new to Henrietta Swann. Through her first pregnancy Stella had been her EXPERIENCE, and she always thought of her that way, that is to say in capitals. She had presupposed Stella to be a boy and the overriding aspect of her first pregnancy period had been curiosity that remained as a permanent guest in Henrietta's mind when Stella assumed an identity. For she never did succeed in coming to terms with the child's unwavering idolisation of Adam, to the virtual exclusion of herself. She admired Stella's prettiness, and what Phoebe Fraser called 'the bairn's biddability', but she was never able to identify herself with her in the way she could identify with Alexander and George, whose pre-natal personalities persisted in a way that almost persuaded her she had made their acquaintance months before they were born and that they were only following a plan mutually agreed upon in advance. Alex, stocky, masterful and entirely untroubled by imagination, was clearly destined for the barracks, whereas George, adventurous and highly original from his earliest infancy, was also adapting to the rôle he had been allocated, that of inheriting responsibility for the network and, very possibly, carrying it into the twentieth century.

It was not like this at all with the child conceived twenty-four hours before calamity had engulfed them. For a long time, throughout the initial shock period and the slow, agonising acceptance of the new situation, she had been unaware of its existence, and later on, when there was no longer any doubt that she was pregnant, she had resented the physical handicap the baby represented in her new rôle. But then, by a process that seemed to have no real starting point, something rather dramatic happened. The child stirred in more than the physical sense, virtually announcing itself as a confidante and a co-conspirator, so that it seemed eager to share with her the sense of adventure and achievement that carried her through the eventful autumn and into the new year, their comradeship maturing day by day and more so by night, when she was alone with those grey-faced twins, fear and uncertainty. Then the child that was part of her stood sentry, and she was tremendously comforted by its presence, its serenity and its steadfastness, and found that she could commune with it as readily as she had once exchanged confidences with Sarah Hebditch, her Seddon Moss friend, or Mrs. Worrell, when she was not much more than a child herself.

It was a weird, exhilarating sensation, this reliance upon a foetus for solace, for although she could recall the exact circumstances of its conception it seemed to have neither physical nor spiritual links with the man fighting his private battle far away to the south-east. Its duty, its very purpose there in her womb, was to sustain her and her alone, and its message was always one of hope that more than compensated for the aridity of his short, impersonal letters, that seemed to have been penned by a polite stranger marginally involved in her concerns.

Sir John Levy, who had been to Switzerland in November, paid her a visit around Christmas time, perhaps with the object of setting her mind at rest about those letters and said, with a frankness she had learned to expect from him, "No matter how ridiculous it might sound to you the truth is he hasn't time to write. Writing a letter, particularly a letter to you in these circumstances, would call for concentration. His working day is entirely given over to a very complicated and demanding schedule of exercises. Let me tell you something, dear lady. I've seen many people address themselves to the task of learning to live with an artificial limb, and roughly speaking they fall into three categories, the Can't-be-Dones, the That-will-Doers, and the Perfectionists."

"But even a Perfectionist would be likely to show an interest in those most anxious about his progress, wouldn't he, Sir John?"

He rubbed his nose at that, contemplating her gravely for a moment. Finally he said, "To be frank, dear lady, I don't think he has a thought in his head beyond learning to walk and how to disguise his disability, but does that surprise you?"

She had a mental picture of him then, a lean, tall, thrusting man, fanatically self-contained but capable of odd impulses of humour, tenderness and compassion. But he was the last man in the world to spare himself and from her new standpoint she could relate this absent, lonely figure to the great web of enterprise that ran out from that belfry tower to the remotest corners of the country. She said, "No, not really. Not at all when I think about it. Thank you for coming," and relieved him of the slim bundle of letters she had produced as evidence.

After that she went back to her confessor and together, without haste or exasperation, they examined this phenomenon, a man rising forty with a great lust for life, learning to walk again and gammon everybody into believing that he was afflicted with a slight limp but nothing worse.

3

Edith had no wish to hurry him. As the weeks passed and he showed no sign of backsliding, she understood that it was vital not to harass

636

him in any way, neither as a man finding a foothold in unfamiliar country or as a lover. His past stood between them like a wall of glass, very thin glass but able to distort the glimpses they caught of one another as man and woman each in search of solace.

At first, until she came to know him well, she mistook his reticence for timidity. He was always affectionate but never in the least enterprising and this, she thought, was strange in a man who had lived outside the law most of his life. Then she understood why he lacked boldness as a lover for he did not see her as an eager, yearning woman but as a fairy-godmother to whom he owed this unlooked-for opportunity to develop into the man he undoubtedly was and banish the fugitive society had made of him and this, in turn, inhibited her from behaving as she longed to behave when they were alone and off-duty. For while it was one thing to throw one's cap at a shy lad who stood in need of a little encouragement it was quite another to risk making him feel he was under a virtual obligation to take her as his mistress. She understood this quite well but understanding it did very little to promote resignation. There were times, when he kissed her goodnight after one of their decorous walks along the towpath, or a visit to a chophouse or a theatre, when she could have pulled him over the doorstep, slammed the door on the complaisant Mrs. Sprockett in the kitchen, and left him in no doubt at all what was expected of him but she had sufficient self-discipline to resist the impulse. Their relationship at this stage was still tenuous. She dare not subject it to such a severe jolt for she knew she was unequal to the strain of readjustment if she scared him off and also that his chances of making good without her support were negligible. So she waited and waited, substituting gaiety and comradeship for passion, and gaining some slight relief from tension by lying stark naked on her bed after he had walked whistling into the dark and holding imaginary conversations with him until her longing had induced a physical climax and she could go to bed and hope to sleep on an opiate composed of hope, faith in him, and a sense of security that strengthened with every week he stayed in her employ.

She had never felt this way about any man but she was long past making excuses for herself. There was no need for that now that she knew herself committed and deeply in love. She was aware that the change wrought in her must be obvious to all her associates but, unlike the time when gossip in the network was rife concerning her and Adam Swann, she did not give a damn. She had had a surfeit of independence and virtuous isolation, and saw them for what they were, a couple of sour grapes; and juiceless grapes at that. All the authority and independence in the world was not worth the prospect of entering one's thirties without a man to care for, cosset and keep one warm in bed on a winter's night.

In the meantime, however, there was nothing to be lost by encouraging him at his work, and this was why she welcomed Henrietta's suggestion to employ him as overseer of the reserve depots that were established in the new year. He was very much astonished that he should be considered for the post and gave her a bad moment when he hinted that she might have engineered it as a neat way of disposing of him. This, she decided, was a libel she owed to herself to scotch on the spot, so she handed him the Headquarter's circular, to which Henrietta's note was attached. He said, after reading it carefully, "Surely I'm no more than a name on a list to Mrs. Swann, or to anyone else down there."

"No one in this outfit is a name on a list, Tom," she replied. "Swann didn't work that way and she's using his apparatus. The only issue is, do you feel qualified to take a job of that kind? It calls for more initiative than you can exercise here, where I make all the decisions. You haven't forgotten what I said about responsibility when you decided to give it a trial?"

"I've not forgotten anything you said or did on that occasion," he told her, and she was wondering what to make of this when he added, smiling, "I could do a job like that standing on my head but there's one aspect you've overlooked."

"And what would that be?"

"That you're the only one aware of the fact that you've got a professional thief on the staff. If Headquarters knew that would my name have been put forward?"

"They don't have to know. Nobody has to know, and nobody will if I can help it."

"It'll leak out sooner or later. You know it and I know it."

"And suppose it does? Do you think I would profess ignorance?"

"No," he said, "I flatter myself I know you rather better than that, but it isn't the same thing, is it? Working here under your supervision, or ranging the whole country in an executive position."

"I'll take my chance on that. Why shouldn't they?"

"You aren't taking a chance. I wouldn't steal from you and you know it. But can you guarantee my loyalty to strangers, some of whom aren't above a bit of pilfering themselves, unless Swann has handpicked four hundred men and I'm quite sure he hasn't?"

"Loyalty to me amounts to loyalty to Swann, doesn't it?"

"It might," he said, "but again you can't bet on it. If goods went missing, and I was within fingering distance, can you honestly tell me it wouldn't set you thinking?"

It seemed to her a crisis in their relationship and something warned her that he needed very positive reassurance. Because of this she took her time answering and said, at length, "No, I can't deny that, Tom. It must occur to me, but now you're overlooking something. Win or lose it wouldn't make a ha'porth of difference to me. It should, I suppose, but it wouldn't. I've passed that point as far as you're concerned and if you haven't realised as much it's because you've been deliberately looking the other way. Are you going to go on doing that?"

"Not indefinitely," he said, calmly, "only until I've something to offer in exchange."

It would have been easy, she supposed, to have accepted this as a supreme compliment, of a kind nobody had ever paid her before. Not poor old Matt Hornby, who had been a very uncomplicated soul, and not Adam Swann, who had much to offer but all of it spoken for. But time pressed her so hardly she was tempted to reply, 'What the devil do I care what you bring, apart from yourself, Tom Wickstead? I'm twenty-nine, and next Mayday I'll be thirty, so in God's name, don't waste any more time proving yourself!', but then she saw she was confusing his needs with hers, and that panic of this kind would help neither one of them, and might even stunt the appreciable growth of the confidence she had nurtured in him. She said, with a sigh, "Well and good, lad. That's progress of a kind, and I was in need of some sort of a sop to my pride. Can I take that as a very qualified proposal?"

He looked at her merrily but also, she thought, with a certain caution. "I'll do my own proposing in my own time, not in Swann's," he said, and she thought grimly, 'We'll see about that, lad, now that you've let the cat's head out of the bag,' and dismissed him, addressing herself to the task of studying Henrietta's scheme to establish reserve depots at selected points throughout the network.

It wasn't much, perhaps, but the guarded exchange helped to boost them a little, partly by reason of the fact that he was now liable to be out of touch three weeks in four, ranging the triangle between Harrogate in the north, Cheltenham in the west and the unnamed depot that was to serve the south-east. At the depot discretion was essential. The office was a relatively public place and there were always waggoners coming or going.

Then, in late January he went off, reappearing only occasionally and very briefly, and she missed him intolerably, sometimes cursing Henrietta for creating the post and herself for persuading him to accept it. These were days when she fancied she carried a ticking clock about with her and it was no help to remind herself that she could consider herself spoken for and that it was now his prerogative to name the day or the occasion.

It was irrelevant whether she had him as husband or lover. All that was necessary was that she should find release from the most obsessive emotion of her life and it was far more than a predominantly physical manifestation, of the kind she had found so disturbing before she had good reason to hope. She yearned, with the whole of her being, to be of real service to him, to prove beyond all doubt that she was able to more than compensate for his hunted, wasted years, but there seemed no immediate prospect of this. On the few occasions they were together there was neither the time nor the opportunity to enlarge their relationship without appearing to harass him and it sometimes seemed to her it was losing a little of its impetus and would develop into one of those placid 'understandings', where a couple mooned along year after year saving money to set up house. She had forgotten, or had never really known, that a deep emotional involvement with a man had its waste areas where the tares of self-doubt took root and because he made no unmistakable sign, or spoke no irrevocable word, she sometimes half-believed she was mistaking gratitude, or at best friendship, for reciprocal love that waited upon pride. Then she would torture herself, putting various interpretations on that admission of his about taking his fun where he found it, and wondering if, during his jaunts up and down England, he solaced himself with some little trollop at an inn, or some wench out of his roystering past to whom he owed nothing and who made no claims on his loyalty.

This kind of torment persisted all through March and well into April, when he was absent for three weeks at a stretch collecting spent teams and distributing them about the country for a period out at pasture, but he had promised to be back in Peterborough by the end of the month. On the strength of this pledge she had herself fitted for the most expensive walking-out dress she had ever bought, together with a *rotonde* of the same material and a puff bonnet that perched high on the head above a chignon arranged in massed plaits, a daring experiment she had read about in the journals.

The new clothes and daring hairstyle at least occupied her mind for a day or so, until the letter came from Henrietta (whom she had all but forgotten) announcing that her fourth child, a boy, had 'presented himself with remarkable punctuality', and that Adam was expected home in a fortnight or so and might be discharged as early as the first week of May.

* * *

She could not have said what really decided her, what small incident or series of incidents resolved her to jog Time's elbow and stake everything on a privately mounted sally into his camp. It was probably a combination of factors coming together in her mind to form an impulse she was incapable of resisting.

There was the tang of spring, with the old lilac burgeoning in the cottage garden between her office and the yard gate. There was the thought of Henrietta, away to the south, giving her breast to her fourth child and now nursing a couple of surprises, either of which was calculated to overset a man with an artificial leg. There were those swift glimpses of lovers every time she went along the towpath to get the smell of the yard out of her nostrils, but, above all, there was the calendar in her bedroom, reminding her that in a few days she would be thirty and reckoned middle-aged. All this and the bitter disappointment of his note, saying that he could not be there for her birthday after all, for he had new instructions from town that would take him to the Cotswolds, the New Forest, and farms along the eastern frontier of the Mountain Square.

The letter, delivered to the office, brought her to the verge of tears, and after that put her into a fury that would have vented itself on the entire yard had it not been succeeded, almost at once, by a mental vacuum, in which she could stand outside herself and admit that this silly game of catch-as-catch-can was no longer compatible with human dignity and it was time for a gamble that would resolve things one way or another. Once she accepted this she felt more in command of herself than at any time since she had read Adam's name in the list of casualties at the Staplehurst disaster.

There was, as she saw it, no other course but to confront him and discover precisely where she stood in direct relation to his future, and once she had made up her mind to this she went about her preparations with the precision she would have brought to planning a complicated crosscountry haul for an unpredictable customer. She studied her maps, noting his itinerary over the next fortnight, afterwards doing the kind of sums in her head that came very easily to her after so long at the game. The answers told her that on the night of 30th April he was due at a farm a mile or two south of Ludlow, and that the Headquarters' mail clerk would be forwarding his next moves to an inn called 'The Garland', at a hamlet near the pasture. The winter ordeals were behind them and the spring rush of business had not yet begun. She told the yard foreman she would be away for two days and expected to be back on 2nd May, and that he was to call for her in a pinnace in time to catch a train that left Peterborough at 9.15 the next morning. Then, having consulted her Bradshaw again, she locked up, went home and spent the evening making last-minute adjustments to her new ensemble and after that, having given Mrs. Sprockett instructions to call her at seven o'clock, she packed a night-case and went to bed. One thought only interposed between her and sleep. By this time tomorrow, she told herself, she would be equipped to face life with or without him and that, however it resolved itself, was an improvement on what she had been doing for longer than she cared to recall—hang on a bough hoping that a passing male would possess enough gumption to pluck her and sample what she had to offer. It was a desperate and shameless solution, but it had the merit of positivity.

4

Improvisation attended her like a well-trained lady's maid.

Experience in his field of operations helped. Before she booked in at 'The Garland' as 'Mrs. Wickstead' paying a surprise visit, she had traced him via a stableman, who told her that Swann's agent had arrived last night with a string of fagged-out Clydesdales and left early for Bringewood Chase, where the pasture was situated. She said, carelessly, "What a nuisance! Would you get a message to him for half-a-crown?", and the man said he would go all the way to Leominster for that and the farm where Mr. Wickstead could be found was only a mile from his own hearth and he could run the errand as soon as he went off duty.

"I'll write a note and bring it out," she said, and sought the housekeeper. She had then to think herself into the kind of rôle he must have played over the years, bland, casual and friendly but with overtones of patronage. She had no intention of installing herself in his room but booked one of her own, the best in the house, giving as a reason the fact that Mr. Wickstead had to leave early the following morning and might or might not cancel his own room when he learned she had joined him. That way, she reasoned, he could stay or go without loss of face, and as to supper, well, they might or might not partake of it, depending upon how soon he returned. She played her part well and the housekeeper seemed not to find anything unusual in such an arrangement. Keepers of inns, Edith reflected, were proof against the vagaries and eccentricities of guests.

She had her writing case and took it into one of the public rooms to write the note. 'Dear Tom', it said, 'I arrived at ten after five *in my own time, not Swann's*, and booked separate accommodation. If you are back before I retire I suggest supper up here, but leave the decision to you, Edith.'

To any other man in the world, she supposed, the message, loosed like an arrow from ambush, would be incomprehensible, but not to him, a man who had once lived on a diet of bluff and bluster. In a sense he was being matched at his own game and would probably recognise as much. He might be amused and he might be indignant, but he would not be surprised. How could he be after their original confrontation over the matter of Beckstein's diamonds?

She sealed the note, went out to the yard and gave it to the stableman, together with his tip. Then, fortifying herself with two glasses of gin and bitters, she went up to her room, where the maid had already turned back the bed and laid out her slippers, robe and nightgown, setting a can of hot water on the washstand.

She felt calm to the point of resignation, the way he must have felt when, in his own terminology, he was 'inside a crib and sifting the swag'. It did not seem in any way remarkable that she should be here in a strange town, under a false name, bluffing or blackmailing a man into sharing her bed. On the contrary, in a devious kind of way, it seemed a fitting climax to their association. She dipped her fingers in the can, finding the water lukewarm. It was only just after seven and there was ample time, she reasoned, for a makeshift bath in the copper bowl they had provided. Unhurriedly she removed her dusty clothes and sponged herself from head to foot and there seemed little point in dressing again. She put on nightdress and bedgown and rang for the girl to carry the water away, declining her offer to send up supper on a tray pending the gentleman's arrival. She had eaten practically nothing during the long crosscountry journey, but she did not feel hungry. She opened the window and stared out across the yard and stable buildings to a belt of woodland threaded by the river Teme, looking down on a peaceful, fruitful, settled England more tamed than the north, more lush and civilised than the flat farm-studded areas of her own patch, a country that hadn't changed much since the great-battlemented castle that dominated the town had been garrisoned by those same Nevilles who occupied Middleham in her native Yorkshire. It was strange that—the way these Neville ghosts seemed to follow her around, as though they found adventurers like Matt, and Adam, and now Tom Wickstead, far more to their taste than the tophatted merchants who had succeeded them as the policy makers of England.

She stood at the window for a long time, watching the westering sun tip molten gold over the wooded hills of the Marches. Dusk stole into the valleys and the sky over Wales turned coral pink, streaked with crimson and heliotrope. Hobnailed boots clattered on the cobbles and the murmur of voices reached her from the stables and street below. Her sense of detachment, that had never left her since she had resolved upon this crazy enterprise, settled in the room and suddenly the prospect of stretching herself on that comfortable-looking bed was irresistible. She thought, 'Suppose he makes a night of it with that farmer out at Bringewood Chase? Or suppose he calls my bluff, lights his pipe with my note, and comes rolling back here drunk as a fiddler at three in the morning?' and suddenly she was too tired to care one way or the other. She half-closed the window, shrugged herself out of her bedgown and slipped between lavender-scented sheets. In a matter of seconds she was asleep.

*   *   *

The rattle of china awakened her and she sat up, at a loss to know where she was and then, half recollecting, astonished to find it still daylight.

The door was opening and the maid appeared, a smile on her rosy face, and before Edith had knuckled her eyes he appeared, striding across the room in his high, brown riding boots, saying, with quite unnecessary gusto, "Why, *there* you are, my love! God bless my soul, what a pleasant surprise! Have I disturbed you?" and to the girl, "Over there by the window and draw the curtains. Here, catch!" and he spun her a coin that earned him a curtsey. Then she was gone and he was standing over the bed looking down at her with laughter in his eyes and the corners of his mouth puckered with the joviality he had apparently assumed for the benefit of the girl. The expression left him, reluctantly she thought, as though he had not yet made up his mind what expression should succeed it.

Suddenly, and treacherously, all the confidence that had carried her across the full width of England was banished from the room by his presence and she saw now, when it was too late to do anything but blink, that she had lost the initiative by falling asleep in that inexplicable fashion and that he was not a man to let her regain it. She wondered why, having gone to such pains to obtain the advantage, she had neglected to rehearse a speech, or at any rate an attitude. As it was, with him standing there like a doctor attending a scared child, her mind had never been so blank, or her tongue less ready to frame words, and this sense of bewilderment persisted, even when he sat down on the bed, saying, "Oh, come now, don't look at me as if *I* was demanding the ransom. I was obliged to put on some kind of show, wasn't I? They said you had gone to your room supperless, but it didn't occur to me that you . . ." and suddenly he stopped and she saw, with tremendous relief, that his quick wits were already at work on the reason for her stupefaction. He said, laughing, "You didn't intend to be caught asleep. You just dropped off," and she nodded, so that the expression in his eyes was tolerant and he lifted his hand touching her hair, still dressed in its chignon, with the carefully-poised coils specially arranged to offset the new puff bonnet she had travelled in.

His touch was light and playful, and again she had a vivid sense of being whirled back to her girlhood, this time into the presence of a cheerful young doctor, who was kindness itself but represented, by his presence at the bedside, a crisis of some magnitude. She said in a voice that did not seem to be hers, "You . . . you don't *have* to stay, Tom. Not from kindness, that is," and then, despairingly, "It seemed a simple thing to do. I just thought of it and then . . . well, I did it. Without thinking. In a kind of trance."

"You regret it now?"

"Yes, I do. Very much. It's a trick. A silly, shabby trick, and I can't begin to think . . ." and she stopped because suddenly the enormity of her behaviour, and the cold, calculating way in which she had gone about the business, revealed her to herself as someone who was incapable of unselfish affection.

"Not a trick. Let's say a hoax."

"No, not a hoax! I didn't come here to play a joke on anybody. I had quite a different idea when I set out and after I actually got here until . . . well, until just a moment ago, when you came in with that girl."

645

"I see. And then?"

"Now it seems quite monstrous that I should do this to you. For the purpose I did do it."

"You left the backdoor open. The woman said something about my room being available, on account of an early start I'm supposed to make. That puzzled me but I played up. I said I'd take the key, and perhaps go to my room after supper, and that puzzled *her*; that a man should occupy two beds in one night."

His tolerance began to mellow her, not dramatically but gently, so that she was at least capable of peeping round the door of incredulity and contemplating anew the motives that had brought her to this sorry pass. She said, "That note . . . I must have been coming to my senses even then. I said it was up to you, didn't I, and it is, even now. You've got your key. Take your supper along and go about your business in the morning."

"Don't make my decisions. Make your own, Edith."

She considered, thinking it strange that he could command that much generosity, and also, perhaps, that he should confuse her embarrassment with fear, or modesty.

"I made mine by putting myself in this position."

"That's true, but you mentioned the word 'trance'. People can think themselves into extraordinary situations and still be scared of the consequences. That's something I have to be sure about, my dear."

It was true, she supposed, and it meant that she owed him an explicit explanation.

"I haven't the least doubt that I'm very much in love with you, Tom. I didn't think myself into that."

"It's possible."

"Not at my age it isn't. What's the time?"

"What the devil does it matter what time it is?"

"It matters very much."

"About ten."

"In two hours I'll be thirty. That's one reason why I'm here. If you hadn't written, to say you couldn't get back as arranged, it's possible I shouldn't have made such a fool of myself."

He put his hand in his breeches pocket and drew out a little package that he tossed on the bed. "Open it."

Her fingers plucked awkwardly at the wrapping and it came away, revealing a small, five-sided leather box, fitted with a tiny thumbspring. She pressed the spring and the lid popped up. Inside, on a bed of blue velvet, was a thin circlet of gold, set with three small diamonds, hardly more than large chippings. There was something else too, a screw of tissue paper, and for some reason this deflected her attention from the ring so that she set the box in the hollow of the coverlet and unwrapped the paper. It was a broader, heavier ring, gold and unembellished.

She held it in the hollow of her hand, sensible of its weight and peering down at it in the fading light. She heard him say, "Not quite up to Hatton Garden standards but I at least acquired both conventionally. They're the first rings I ever handled in that respect."

She could have wept for him and for herself too. She knew very little about jewellery but enough to tell her that what she held in her hand represented about two months' wages on his rates. She wondered why, since he had gone this far, he had not tossed the latest batch of Headquarters' directives over the nearest hedge, and come flying to her from wherever he was the minute he walked out of the shop with that package in his breeches pocket, but then she saw that this would have undermined the flimsy structure of a life he was rebuilding, not only for himself but for her.

She said, "Dear God, Tom, if I'd known ... guessed ... This makes my coming here so wrong ... so unfair. I should ask you if you've got second thoughts?"

"Well, now," he replied, with his characteristic blend of irony and gaiety, "that's one way of looking at it, for you do have a tendency to stampede a man. But I'd be a fool to hold that against you. Nobody could say I was much of a catch and to have a busy woman chase one across England could be regarded as very flattering."

She held out her arms and he threw himself forward, showering her face with kisses. The box slipped away in the folds of the bedclothes and her hand blindly pursued it, capturing it and pressing it or him but without separating her mouth from his.

"Slip it on, Tom. Now!"

"You mean both, I take it?" and, finding her hand, "Since you announced yourself as Mrs. Wickstead, didn't it occur to you to wear ring?"

"I kept my gloves on."

He slipped both rings on her finger with a flourish that seemed to her to proclaim all those aspects of him that she found so boyish and endearing, aspects that most men seemed to leave behind with their childhood. He was tremendously elated by the neatness with which he had trumped her ace and she supposed many women would have thought of this as naïve but she did not. It was an essential part of him explaining, to her mind, both his male gentleness and his joie de vivre. He said, kissing her ringed hand with a final flourish, "Are you hungry, Mrs. Wickstead? There's cold ham, tongue and pickles over there. Raspberry tart, too, with custard pie and a bottle of Beaune."

"Later," she said, "I don't think I could do justice to it yet. Could you?"

"No," he said, "It's too late for supper and too early for breakfast."

He stood up and she saw him whirling his key on his forefinger. "How soon can a man get married if he's in a prodigious hurry?"

"Three weeks, I believe, since you've already established residence in Peterborough."

"It's far too long," he said, tossing the key on the night table, "so I'll have to trouble you to help me pull off these boots, Mrs. Wickstead. They're a snug fit."

She skipped out of bed and pushed him into the basket chair, kneeling and grasping heel and toe as he wiggled his toes, bracing himself against the pull. They struggled then for a moment and when his boots were off he lifted her back on the bed, saying, "Now do something else for me. Loosen your hair," and she reached up, withdrawing the fastenings, so that the carefully-arranged chignon dissolved and cascaded over her shoulders. He reached behind her, stroking it gratefully. "You've never made enough of your hair," he said. "It's pretty and strong and plentiful but whenever I've seen it it's been bundled up any old how as though it was a nuisance."

"Sometimes it is," she said, "when I'm busy and doing a man's work."

They might, she reflected, have been man and wife a very long time and gaily celebrating some private occasion of their own, a homecoming or an anniversary. He ran his hand down her cheek, his fingers moving deliberately and possessively. "Somebody has been tinkering with your entry in the parish register," he said. "Thirty, indeed! We'll give it as twenty-three. That gives me a five-year start and the necessary authority. Get back to bed, wife," and crossed to the closet, loosening his cravat.

Re-encounter:
1866

1

DILIGENTLY and with characteristic tenacity, he went in search of compensation. His ensign, in the earliest days, was desperation, but later on, when he had adapted to the routine of the clinic, and had been fitted with his leg, his inspiration and talisman was Jolly Jack Wickett, the maimed lancer, so that he began, little by little, to graft humour on to his hurt like a new skin.

Humour, until then, had never been a strong point with Adam Swann. He could see a joke with the next man, and was far from being a solemn man, of the type common enough in the mess and the city, but he had always regarded the antics of clowns like 'Circus' Howard and Hamlet Ratcliffe with mild impatience. Later on, when he was waging his own private war, there had been no time for levity but now, committed to the battle of his life, humour stole upon him like a genial, uninvited guest, and was presently made welcome and accepted as the life and soul of the sorry party.

The hall of mirrors was his playground for here, with reflections cavorting along on four sides of a room adjoining the gymnasium, he could keep track of his progress, from the first lurching stagger to the ultimate sailor's roll, and glimpses of his profile, as well as his gait, sometimes struck him as droll, so that the transition from the first ironic smile to a full-blooded chuckle was inevitable. He acquired the trick of escaping from the bumbling, lopsided creature who moved clumsily between the handrails, and learned to study it from afar, noting its slow, desperately earnest grapple for balance and dignity. And presently, in a strange and secret way, he formed an alliance with it, so that the relationship between them ripened into affection, and the essential Adam Swann would goad it to perform prodigies of enterprise, despite the nag of the tender stump under the pad.

His initiative came to play too, so that he evolved, as time went on, all manner of tricks, subterfuges, and even mechanical adjustments, and had the more conservative of the doctors trying to slow his pace but he ignored their cautionary protests. He knew precisely what he was about and by the turn of the year was virtually his own physician, so that they said of him, among themselves, 'Let Swann set his own pace', and he did, stumping along the gravel paths as far as the lodge gates, and presently, when spring sunshine glittered on the snow-capped peaks across the lake, as far as the lake itself, where he would watch paddle-steamers churning the bilious blue water and test his footing on the slippery planks of the jetty.

Ultimately, to their collective astonishment, he demanded a horse and they stood around watching him master the art of mounting from the right and settling himself in the stirrups with his left leather four holes lower than his right, because he still found difficulty in adapting to the springs of the kneecap; after that, of all things, he wanted to row and did, learning to offset the stronger pull to starboard induced by the superior brace of his sound leg. From the first stumbling weeks he had been their star pupil but now, as he worked his way doggedly towards a provisional discharge date, he became a kind of elder statesman in a cabinet of cripples, and they took to consulting him on points involving techniques and new apparatus for patients less equipped for such a struggle. It was, they all decided, a virtuoso performance, and secretly he thought so himself. Jolly Jack, he decided, would have to look to his laurels if they ever met in the future.

*　　*　　*

He was not alone in his sense of renewal that spring. Unknown to him, the experience was shared all over the network, from Fraser away in the far north, to Dockett, reining in above Freshwater Bay to watch a full-rigged ship cresting up Channel before a westerly that would soon carry it beyond Beachy Head if the skipper knew his business, and the crew were not as worked over as Dockett felt after such a winter.

A sense of survival permeated the network. Fraser had shifted his main base from Hexham to Berwick, reckoning that at least half his hauls struck north and north-west across the Border, so that his present headquarters might have done duty for the camp of a mediaeval raider planning a big-scale foray as soon as the Cheviot streams were fordable. And this, in a sense, was how Fraser thought of it, as he planned his routes and costed his hauls under the walls of a town Scotsmen had coveted for a thousand years.

Over in Salford, where Catesby's pinnaces plied in enclaves formed by the most congested rail network in the island outside the metropolis, the man Adam thought of as a visionary, and his father-in-law regarded as a potential Danton or Marat, had his worries, but they were of a private nature. The much-publicised lockout of the

652

Sheffield file trades in February acted as a spur to men like Catesby, who had never lost faith in the dream of a Trades Congress, embracing every factory, yard, mine, ropewalk and distillery in Britain. Now that the winter crises were behind him he could devote time to stump oratory, preaching with the fervour and consistency of Peter the Hermit recruiting for a crusade. Unite! Amalgamate! Select your delegates! Eschew parochialism! Take up the cause of unity in every sphere of exploitation of man by man! Oh, hear ye and heed ye, at pithead and foundry! Pass the word among the spinners, the weavers, the colliers, the potters, yes, even among the Swann carters, secure in their minimum wage and maximum working day. For in unity alone at the Sheffield conference, planned for July, could reciprocal agreements pioneered by men like Swann be forced on diehards like his father-in-law, to whom the workshop was still an arena.

Over in the Mountain Square, Bryn Lovell heard echoes of these rumblings, but he paid small heed to them. His reading taught him that justice was not to be sought in platform resolutions but in the observances of certain moral laws, of which keeping faith with the source of one's bread and cheese was the most important. His industrial philosophy was very simple. One contracted and was therefore obligated, and the dedicated would have dismissed him as a lickspittle which he was not. Of all Swann's mandarins in the period that was just behind them only Lovell had never botched a run, or failed to deliver on time. It was on this, inside his own patch, that Swann's reputation rested, but it was equally characteristic of Bryn Lovell that he worked less overtime than his contemporaries, for he had other matters in train, among them teaching a flock of stepchildren to read and write. As the days lengthened he could have been seen any evening in the garden of his cottage, hard at work with primer and blackboard, and surrounded by his attentive coffee-coloured class, so that passers-by (if they were strangers to the district) might have mistaken him for an usher rather than what he was, the man who earned his bread hauling goods all over the Principality and had won his footing winkling fifty-seven Welshmen from a living tomb.

Far to the west, where the wild daffodils were done but primroses lingered in the high-banked lanes of his enormous beat, Hamlet Ratcliffe embarked on his customary spring tour. He no longer thought of himself as Swann's emissary but a merchant adventurer in his own right, obligated to keep in personal touch with all his customers and the new holiday centres growing up along the indented coast of

653

the Wedge. He had no need to drum up trade nowadays and did not care to be reminded of a time when he had done it by recapturing a fugitive lion in a North Devon valley. He was a man of substance and prestige, whose waggons could be seen anywhere between Truro and Taunton, but who tended, of late, to identify himself with a revival of the coaching era. For at any time between Whitsun and mid-September you might encounter one of his three-horse brakes, bearing the Swann insignia and any number of parasols, bowling along the leafy approaches to Torquay, Devonport harbour, Bideford Bay, and sometimes tackling the fearful descent into Lynmouth, and he thought of these excursions as his private contribution to the enterprise, as indeed they were if you denied his wife credit she never claimed. It was enough for Augusta that 'poor 'Amlet was 'ome and dry', with his string of false starts behind him. He had at last found a calling where his rare and diversified talents could be channelled into a single impressive outlet.

The winter exertions had left their mark on the smooth face of young Rookwood, master of the Southern Square, whose terrain stretched from the Cotswolds to the Channel, from the Bay of a Thousand Wrecks to the roadstead where Nelson's flagship rode at anchor, reminder of a day when a plump little Corsican had spent himself trying to ruin British trade.

Fraser, Catesby, Lovell, Ratcliffe and Rookwood. Godsall of the Kentish Triangle and Dockett of Tom Tiddler's Ground. Vicary in The Bonus, Goodbody and Horncastle of the Crescents; Morris, on his small, profitable patch in the Pickings and Henrietta at 'Tryst'— all to some extent, warmed themselves in the sunshine of personal achievement, reminding themselves that a leap of six per cent in winter turnover was something to crow about in the circumstances. But satisfaction is one thing and exaltation another and there was at least one zealot among them who did not spare a thought for Swann's balance sheet that spring. For Edith Wadsworth, styled Edith Wickstead from eight a.m. on a day in the third week of May, Swann's waggons rolled unheeded, and carters, resigned to having their manifests challenged and their vehicles turned back at the weighbridge for shoddy loading, suddenly learned the true reason behind a complacency (sometimes amounting to slackness) that had been noticeable in the gaffer's attitude since her unexplained sally into what the company maps defined as Lovell's territory.

She, for her part, was not in doubt concerning their speculations. Gossip regarding her had been flying up and down the network grapevine for long enough, and it was probable that, within hours of the event, Fraser in the north, and Ratcliffe in the west, would hear about the early morning wedding, performed by a nervous young curate in front of two random witnesses.

2

She had never thought that such happiness was attainable, that such an exquisite harmony of the senses could be achieved. Her state of mind was one of blissful suspension, in which past, present and future fused so that all her thoughts, assembling like a confused cavalcade, led back to him. And there seemed not to have been a time when it was otherwise.

They were lying on a deserted strip of shingle a mile north of the lighthouse, she with her back against a groyne, he with his head on her lap and seemingly asleep. They had exchanged no word for some time now and he lay perfectly still, with the sun warming his face and his long limbs in an attitude of graceful relaxation.

The sky up here, as always in East Anglia, seemed much higher and wider than anywhere else, an enormous cavern of blue that shaded off into the sea, relieved, here and there, by little streamers of cloud jockeying for precedence like her thoughts in the stream of time. Inconsequent thoughts they were, some of them probing back into her childhood, when she had sat beside her dour father, fishing in a Yorkshire stream. Proud but out-dated thoughts, of her determination to make a place for herself in this man's world. Jocund thoughts, of their brief association, beginning with her pursuit of him down to Harwich and ending here on this beach, with his head on her lap. But predominantly sensual thoughts that could make her smile but glow with tenderness as she recalled his light, fleeting touch on her hair as he initiated protracted but infinitely restrained caresses down the full length of her spine, over her buttocks, and between her thighs, so that contemplation of his gentle, possessive handling of her prompted her now to extend her hand as far as it would reach, touching his exposed wrist where it lay beyond the shadow of the groyne, to reach out and stroke it with the tips of her fingers, like a child satisfying itself that a gift had substance and was not part of a Christmas dream.

He was real enough and she compared him, as man and lover,

with his predecessors, matching his restrained curiosity against Matt Hornby's bumbling enthusiasm and Adam Swann's steadfastness, and finding it strange that she should have persuaded herself she was ever in love with either of them, for they had both been men dedicated to their own concerns, whereas Tom Wickstead was a giver in the sense that he did not take devotion for granted but set himself to earn it without diminishing himself as a man in the process.

She had understood this the first night she lay in his arms, when he had, she supposed, every excuse to assume an aggressive, proprietorial rôle, and it seemed to her restraint and consideration in those circumstances was rare in a man, something to be highly prized. Neither had he changed since, reserving for her a lover's courtesy that was surprising in a man whom life had used harshly and pitilessly. It was there in his humour and essential boyishness, in his tolerance and his willingness to embark upon marriage as an equal, but it was in the rôle of a lover that it found its richest expression, for he came to her shyly, almost reverently, when he must have sensed that nothing he did or demanded had the power to frighten or affront her, that she was eager to indulge him to the limit of his capacity and had said so in the moment of stillness that succeeded their first rapturous embrace.

He was not asleep after all or, if he had been, her touch had roused him. Without opening his eyes, he brought her hand up to his lips in a gesture that underlined the central theme of her thoughts and said, mildly, "Do you want children, Edith?" and she replied, "Yours, Tom? More than anything in the world."

He considered this and she supposed he was reviewing it in terms of his past but she was wrong, for presently he said, "Then it can't be helped and the sooner you cut the knot the better. Providing you're sure, that is." Suddenly he opened his eyes and looked straight up at her. "Wait a minute tho'. Isn't it dangerous for a woman to have a first child at thirty?" and she laughed, not because the question was characteristic of him, but because it underlined his curious innocence.

"Nonsense. It depends on health and mine is extremely robust. I've known women to have their first child at nearly forty but it won't take that long if I can help it. But what did you mean? *What* can't be helped? What knot had better be cut?"

"You leaving that yard. I was waiting for you to bring it up but since you haven't I will. Write about it today, before that chap Swann comes back and pushes your nose on his grindstone again."

"Is that an order, Tom?"

"Yes, it is, if you want children, my dear."

His way of putting it touched her but it did not obscure the practical issues. She said, doubtfully, "Children will come, I daresay, but we've got more immediate problems. You haven't a penny, and I haven't either for I was never the saving sort. Here we are, man and wife, and not a stick of furniture or stitch of linen. That's bad where I was reared."

"Then you mean to keep that job and have me keep mine?"

"It makes sense, for a spell anyway." His frown made her laugh again. "Oh, come, do you take me for one of those women who have to be carried upstairs, and fed and watered like a sick cat from the minute she blushingly announces she's in a delicate condition? Henrietta Swann stayed on at Headquarters into her seventh month. Can't I do as well as her?"

"I should hope better," he answered, seriously, "but that isn't the point. Not now I come to think about it," and unpredictably he relaxed again, closing his eyes and pillowing his head comfortably on her thighs.

"Very well, what is the point? Before you doze off again."

"How the devil can I give you orders with my eyes open?"

"Why can't you?"

"Because the gaffer is there when you've got your hair up. Tonight, maybe, when you've let it down again."

"I can't see us conducting a serious discussion in those circumstances. Not for a month or two any road. And if you have it in mind don't look for encouragement from me, Tom Wickstead. I've got you, and I mean to make the most of the novelty. I was ladless a long time, remember, and it was a cheerless business."

He opened his eyes again. "Here's the point then. I don't fancy sharing a wife with forty waggons and two score stable loafers. Not even for a year or so, so to the devil with the money it brings to the housekeeping purse. That's no kind of marriage, unless . . ." and he stopped, and she saw a troubled look in his eye.

"Unless what, Tom?"

"Unless you see it differently. Apart from being ladless how well did you like that life? How much of it was choice, how much necessity?"

She had to think about this. The easy answer was that she liked it well enough but that wasn't what he was asking. His question had to do with Adam Swann and it frightened her a little to realise this, for it implied somehow that he was not nearly so sure of her as she was of him, and this seemed to her a lamentable state of affairs, for it was so long since she had stirred jealousy in a man. She said, at length, "It was a good second-best. Never more than that, Tom."

"You were always hankering after Swann?" He said it like a man cautiously emerging into the open but for all that she respected his honesty.

"Hankering is a hard word, Tom, but it's the right one."

"You met him a long time ago?"

"Not all that long. Soon after he launched out."

"But wasn't he married when you met him?"

"Well married. With one child."

"And now?"

"There's nothing now, or nothing but loyalty. It was loyalty that sent me scampering down there to do what I could after that crash although, if I'm completely honest, I suppose I was still half-hoping. Until I made her acquaintance, that is."

"What then, Edith?"

"The spark went out and I was glad of it. In fact I was deeply grateful."

"Grateful? To her?"

"To her and circumstances. It meant that I could stop day-dreaming, stop lying to myself, stop pretending every damned thing I did for the firm was prompted by pride and self-respect. I was far luckier than I deserved. When I got home you were waiting. The sword came out of the stone. It hurt but it healed. Does that answer your question, Tom?"

"Most of it."

He did not have to explain the reservation either. He had made no reference, not even an oblique reference, to the fact that she was not a virgin when she came to him and he was not as innocent as all that. "It wasn't Swann," she said, suddenly understanding that this was important, "for Swann was never my lover. One man was, a very long time ago," and she told him of Matt Hornby. He said, thoughtfully, "You were in love with that sailor?"

"I thought I was and he would have married me. There was never any doubt about that. But you learn a lot in twelve years, Tom. I don' t have to explain that, do I?"

"Not to me," he said, and was silent awhile. She knew then that they were safely past yet another crossroad, and that his confidence had reached a point where she could put it to a different kind of test, one that would not have been possible had she admitted to having been Swann's mistress.

"I'll give up that job right away," she said, "but there's a condition. You take on where I leave off."

It did not startle him as much as she had anticipated. He might even have guessed what she had in mind.

"You think I could hold that down? Gaffer of three areas?"

"If I was behind you you could and in a few months you wouldn't need me, you'd have plenty of ideas of your own."

"Would they give me a chance like that?"

"I'd see that they did and they aren't likely to question my judgement in the Crescents."

"Very well. I'd like it that way."

He was silent for a moment and she wondered whether he was juggling with the mechanics of the yard, with waggons, freight, teams, insurance rates, and the idiosyncrasies of half-a-hundred hired hands, but she was wrong again. With him you never could tell, for suddenly he said, with the utmost seriousness, "Can you *sit* on your hair? Like the Empress Elizabeth of Austria?"

"Just about," she said, laughing, "with a little cheating."

"How could you cheat?"

"By tilting my head and throwing out my chest."

"I should like to see that," he said, chuckling, and she said. "You shall then, tonight, but I couldn't possibly do it in a corset."

"That's better still," he said, and throwing up his arms pulled her face down and kissed her on the lips.

"What a wife!" he said, smiling up at her. "She finds a way of trebling my income on her honeymoon. Why didn't I think of that when I was skulking around with my eye on Solly Beckstein's sparklers?"

3

There was talk of travelling down to Marseilles and taking a sea voyage as a final stage of convalescence but in the end he came overland by chaise and train to Basle, to Dijon, over green Burgundian hills to Picardy, and thence to the crowded harbour of Calais, where every other ship flew the British flag and quays were piled with packing cases, some of them stencilled with names he recognised.

For the first time in months he adjusted his mind to commerce, pondering the implications of what he saw among the bales and boxes of the harbour, and remembering that France was a highly-industrialised rival, and that an even bigger rival lay just across the Rhine. If British goods were accumulating on the Calais quays how many were being lifted at this moment from the holds of vessels in far-off places, where the British exercised a monopoly? He thought, with satisfaction, 'Nothing's changed much and I'll be back in the thick of it in a week or two', and then, watching a string of handbarrows trundle past carrying baggage and plastered with English labels, 'God is an Englishman, sure enough!' and cheerfully acknowledged his insularity, as well as the ache of homesickness soon to be appeased.

* * *

The first thing she noted about him was his fitness.

Even from a distance he looked bronze and taut, with a tan that was deeper and healthier than the legacy of the Indian sun she recalled from earlier days. He seemed to have filled out too, especially about the shoulders, and there was a certain jaunty confidence about the way he carried himself, like a boxer advancing into the ring against an opponent he was sure of beating.

Another novelty about his bearing was present in his gait, a movement that seemed to match a breezier, saltier personality than she recalled, in that it suggested humour and a kind of mockery in its long, easy roll and the casually-attained precision of its stride, but before she had time to think about all this his arms were round her and because, for so long now, she had thought of him as an invalid, she was quite startled by the ease with which he swung her clear of the ground and held her half-suspended, her new green bonnet pushed slightly askew, her body crushed against the solid bulk of his chest.

She had rehearsed all manner of things to say but forgot them all, or perhaps she could not have said them in any case, for he drove the breath from her body, and all she could do for the moment was to dangle, the toes of her tasselled Polish boots clear of the ground. Then he set her down and the children clamoured for attention while she self-consciously straightened her bonnet and tried to come to terms with this ridiculous parody of a cripple, and the first, immensely satisfying thought that occurred to her was that he had not only retained the power to make her head spin and her knees buckle but seemed, in some fashion, to have been improving on the art all the months they had been separated, and this recalled to her the thought of the shock he was likely to get when he climbed the staircase to the paint-scarred nursery to find he was the father of four children not three. She was glad then that he was engrossed with an armful of children and that there was bustle and scurry all around them. It gave her time to compose herself as they trooped away to the boat-train and fussed over luggage that had already replaced him as focal point in Alexander's eyes, once he had announced that it contained presents for each of them. Hearing him say this, she reflected; 'I should be wary of that word, Adam Swann. You've surprised me I'll own, and a very pleasant surprise it is, but you'll need all your bouncing good health to absorb the surprise I have in store for you in an hour or so!'

There was nothing important they could say to one another until the children's excitement had subsided, and little George (it would be George!) had been persuaded that a boat-train was not the best place to exhibit an artificial leg. She wondered if he was thinking she managed them badly but he seemed not to notice, sitting there beaming down at them and indulging them in a way that was so uncharacteristic of him that she wondered if his experiences had blunted his ambition and whether, in fact, he would see her assumption of his place at the yard as anything remarkable once he had learned that he was the father of a ten-week-old son.

They were a long time getting round to it and she was relieved when she saw Phoebe awaiting them on the terrace, with the old Colonel standing beside her leaning on a stick and looking small and frail beside the great oak pillar that held up the porch. She said, as a ruse, "If their presents are all in one bag, dearest, then for heaven's sake open it and hand them around. We aren't likely to get any peace until you do!" and he seemed to think this was an excellent idea and Stillman was summoned to cut the ropes, and so many presents emerged that it might have been Christmas again, with the floor strewn with wrapping paper and string, and all of them jig-jogging with glee. Even Deborah, whose greeting had been watered with tears, perked up when he presented her with a musical box that played an Austrian folk tune said to have been written to celebrate the victory over the Turks, in 1663.

Then, at last, she was able to draw him away, whispering that she would like a private word with him, and he nodded and led the way across the hall into her sewing-room, which was not according to plan for in here was irrefutable evidence of her involvement with Swann-on-Wheels, any number of files, folders, maps and timetables resulting from the regular visits of Keate and Tybalt after her January withdrawal.

It was too late to head him off so she hung on his heels when he stopped on the threshold, staring at the row of trestle tables and then, stumping across, picking up a quarterly return from The Bonus and gazing at it like a man returning home to discover his house has been ransacked.

He said, at last, "All this clutter . . . stuff from the yard filling the room. . . . Did *I* leave it here? Was I in the middle of something . . .?" and then she laughed, for she realised that he wasn't annoyed but merely astounded, and said, unthinkingly, "No, dear, you didn't leave it. This was my sewing-room but I had to work somewhere . . ."

He spun round. "*You* had to work? *You?*" and she said, faltering a little, "Well, yes . . . you see, I didn't mean you to walk in on it in this fashion. I intended to tell you piecemeal, and let you get used to it gradually. However, it's done now, so it won't need much explaining. When it was certain you would be away nearly a year, I took charge. That is, I . . . well . . . made it my business to do what I could. They were in a frightful tizzy up there. Tybalt, and those others are loyal and hardworking, but they're very short on initiative. Edith was quite right about that."

"Edith Wadsworth?"

"She came here. The minute she heard about the crash she left Peterborough and went to London to sort things out, and she did it very well—anyone will tell you that. Later on she came to see me and . . . well . . . we talked." She saw him grimace at this and wondered how much she should admit to at this point, but then she remembered it had no longer a bearing on the situation for Edith Wadsworth was now Edith Wickstead, and as cockahoop, judging by her last letter, as a mill girl who had married a duke.

"You talked about the business?"

"About you too. She was nice. I liked her very much, even though she was quite frank about being in love with you!"

"She owned to that? In this house?"

"Well, not actually, but I got it out of her and it doesn't matter any more, because she's married."

"Great God! Married to whom?"

"To a man called Wickstead she signed on after she left me in charge. I'm afraid it's all rather complicated. Won't you sit down while I explain?"

He said, taking a deep breath, "Let's get one thing straight, my love. I'm not an invalid. They stopped treating me as one months ago. I can ride and swim and row with the best of them, and walk too if I take it gently. There now, that's enough about me. Go on about what happened," and he propped himself against the door and folded his arms.

"Well," she said, "it went rather like this. They went to pieces at the yard, so poor Edith did her best to take your place, but then she saw they couldn't be left, and it was a case of staying on indefinitely or getting someone like Catesby to take command. She came here to see what I thought and then, like I say, one thing led to another and she suggested 1 have a try at it."

"What on earth put that into her head?"

"She had a reason. It seemed to me a silly one at the time but now it doesn't. It was extremely sensible of her."

"What was her reason?"

"She said that the business meant everything to you, and you wouldn't want to come home and find it in ruins, or even losing ground. I said she was the obvious person to take over and I'd get Mr. Stock the lawyer to authorise it but that didn't suit her at all."

"I suppose she was in a hurry to get back to this chap Wickstead in Peterborough?"

"Oh, no. He hadn't appeared then. At least, I don't think he had."

"Well?"

"It was because of you. She said whoever held on, you would have good reason to thank, and it ought to be me not her."

"And then you accused her of being in love with me?"

"It was as plain as a pikestaff and I wasn't in the least jealous of her. What I mean is, we didn't quarrel over it. Don't you understand?"

He understood better than she imagined, finding the gesture was typical of all he knew of Edith Wadsworth, and it humbled him. He said, "I'm absolutely delighted she's married and I only hope that chap Wickstead deserves her." Then, quietly, "There was never anything but close friendship between us. You believe that, I hope?"

"Of course I do, and I did then. But even if there had been . . ."

"Well?"

"I'd still be grateful to her. It was a wonderful idea for it got me through a bad time by giving me something else to think about. Sometimes I didn't have time to worry about you until Fridays."

"Why Fridays?"

"Well, Friday evening I came back here until Monday mornings."

"You *stayed* in London? You ran the firm from the premises?"
"Why, of course. How else? It wasn't nearly as difficult as I supposed, or not once I'd got into the swing of it. I even learned how to work Frankenstein."

He had never looked at her quite like that before and it made her feel slightly embarrassed, the way she felt the first time he looked at her without her clothes. But now it was with a different kind of approval, as though, in addition to pleasing him as a woman, she had just said something devastatingly clever and original. She felt herself blushing as he heaved himself away from the door and moved across to the nearest table with that strange, rolling gait he had acquired and once there he began sifting through files, letting his glance rove over a map of the eastern counties. Then his eye fell on a return from Wickstead, scored over with the tally of horses he had moved in to the reserve depots, and she said, trying to sound casual, "That will be new to you. Sir John said you weren't to be bothered, so I did what seemed obvious when trouble came down on us."

"What trouble was that?"

"Weather trouble. We had a dreadful winter, with floods, landslides, broken bridges, all kinds of things. Then snow and more gales right into March."

"You set up four new bases?"

"Not bases exactly, depots for reserve teams. It cost a great deal but I think it was worth it. Before Christmas they were borrowing each other's horses and waggons like a lot of crazy bankrupts and we got into a frightful muddle. So I emptied that reserve account you started, and drew on another fifteen hundred to buy stand-by teams. When the snow came in January we were better placed than any haulier in the country and got a lot of new customers."

"This was *your* idea?"

"Well, yes. Stock backed me and Keate came round to it, but it frightened poor Tybalt half out of his wits."

He laid the sheet of paper with the others and stood thinking a moment, his hands resting on the table. He said, "I'll take that chair now," and when she placed one for him he sat heavily on it, his sound leg outstretched, the gammy one bent, with one hand resting on the knee cap. She did not know quite what to make of his posture or his expression and waited, not altogether happily, for somehow she had not expected him to be so overwhelmed and even now she could see that he had not yet accepted the situation. Possibly she underestimated her own achievement. She had no means of knowing that he was busy comparing it with his own of years ago, when he had wrestled with the terrible complexities of the network, sometimes despairing of making a coherent pattern of factors that were now commonplace but were, in those days, so inter-related that it required tremendous concentration to find a loose end and follow where it led. Yet she had mastered this same trick in a matter of months, without training or experience, relying on an instinct, and wits that he had not even realised she possessed. The papers on the table told him this much but that admission about the reserve depots told him something more profound. She had discernment that men like Keate and Tybalt would never acquire, not in a lifetime of association with him, the ability to read his mind at a distance, to put herself in his place and make the decision he would make in identical circumstances, and he supposed this derived, in some way, from the act of bearing a man children, as though the habit of physical union between a man and a woman over the years gave private access to unspoken thoughts, and this seemed to him a conclusion that he had never read in a book, or heard the wise pronounce upon but was nevertheless valid.

He said, "Come here, Henrietta," and she stood before him, rather doubtfully, as he raised his hands and placed them on her hips, as though posing her for a picture.

"Sit down. Sit on my knee."

"Can I?" and he laughed, saying, "It won't break! See," and thumped his knee with his fist, producing a dull, metallic sound that made her conscious of the leg as a separate entity, something peculiarly his yet possessing a very definite individuality. She lowered herself gingerly, and still laughing he threw his arm about her waist.

"It doesn't hurt? Not where it . . ."

"Where it joins? No, not unless I overdo it. It seems I was cut out for tin legs. I heal up and harden quicker than most. There's not much to show for that cut under the eye, is there?"

She looked closely at the scar and saw that it was just as Sir John had predicted, a thin crooked seam, like a premature wrinkle.

"Now listen carefully," he said, "for I want you to remember this. You could have sat here thinking up a welcome-home gift for the rest of your life without hitting on something that gave me more satisfaction. Don't ever forget that. From here on I'll take far more pride in you than I ever did in that network. Later on I'll want to hear everything, every last detail, from the minute you walked into that belfry to when I saw your bonnet bobbing up and down at the far end of the gangplank today. Not for reasons of idle curiosity either. I'm as rusty as an old lock and I wouldn't care to make a fool of myself in front of Tybalt and Frankenstein. Meantime, however, the network can go hang. Give me a real kiss and let's go back to the children. Unless you've any other surprises, that is."

It was odd, she thought, that he should have to remind her in that way of the child upstairs. The children and Phoebe had entered into the spirit of the game, and not one of them had so much as hinted what awaited him in the nursery but somehow his reaction to what she regarded as her secondary surprise packet had put the real one out of mind. She had not given it a thought since following him into the sewing-room and said, with a gasp, "Great heavens! I'd forgotten! There *is* another surprise and if this one astonished you I daren't think . . ." and she slipped from his knee, seized his hands and dragged him to his feet. "It's . . . it's upstairs," she managed to say, "but for goodness sake don't alert the children, not until you've had time to . . . to get used to it."

"Can't it wait on their bedtime?" he said, and she replied, positively, "No, it can't! It's been waiting far too long already," and led him up the staircase, out of range of the chatter and laughter that still issued from the drawing-room.

She stopped on the threshold, saying, "Over there, by the window," and threw wide the door, watching him stump across the waxed floor, the old boards complaining under the impact of his boots. Then he stopped, just short of the cot, his body rigid, a stunned, frozen man, bereft of the power to exclaim, to gesture, even to turn his head and look back at her for confirmation that he was really seeing what he saw.

*   *   *

Until that moment it had been a rich collective joke practised upon him not only by her but by all of them here. But suddenly and unaccountably, it ceased to be a joke at all, and took on an entirely different aspect, endowed with any amount of dignity and solemnity, a tangible consummation of every rewarding aspect of the years they had spent together but by no means confined to that. Simultaneously it was a benediction, exorcising all the pain and anguish that this confrontation represented, so that she was aware of a terrible and compelling pity for him, and a vast wave of gratitude for his presence and for the child's. It seemed to her then that it would be almost blasphemous not to acknowledge the miraculous aspect of the occasion, the three of them, man, woman and child, meeting here for the very first time, and she rustled swiftly past him, lifting the baby from its cot and presenting him to the half-comprehending man in what was a kind of symbolic gesture.

He reached out and received the child wordlessly, his glance moving down to it, then up again, so that she remembered he had always held babies awkwardly, as though they were sides of Wiltshire bacon his waggons hauled from the Southern Square every day of the week. She had never seen him so stunned, so utterly deprived of the power to adjust to a situation, for his reactions had always been swift, too swift for a person like her, who needed time to make judgements of any kind. And yet now, with him standing there like a mute, the child passive in his arms, she did not seem able to help him by some kindly coaxing remark that would establish a bridge between them, for what she had seen as no more than a piece of mischief had enlarged itself into the most majestic moment of her life.

He said, at last, "I don't understand . . . when . . .?" and she replied, "Ten weeks ago. It was meant . . . I thought . . ." and stopped, wondering if words existed that could explain her original purpose in withholding the news from him all this time, for now she saw it as part of an unconsciously pursued policy on her part that might have been inspired by that talk she had with his surgeon, when he had told her Adam was diverting every ounce of his nervous energy into re-equipping himself to play an active rôle in life. She supposed, after that, she had done all she could to shield him from worries of this kind for how would it have been possible for him to apply himself exclusively to such demanding work if, with half his mind, he had been wondering how she was managing with three children dragging at her skirts and a fourth in her womb?

The thought fed confidence to her, so that she could say, unequivocally, "What would have been gained by telling you? I was fit and well all the time I carried him, but would you have believed that if I had put it on paper and posted it to Switzerland? You needed isolation, all the isolation we could give you, and it worked, Adam. It worked quite splendidly, for I watched you mount those stairs a moment since and if I hadn't known . . ." but there was no need to argue her case further. She sensed that some part of the revelation she was experiencing had passed to him and the blank, wooden look lifted from his face as he carried the child to the window and stood there, looking down on the paddock where the sun threw long, slanting shadows across buildings that had once been Michelmore's mill.

667

She had another thought then. In a way they had come full circle, for when all was said and done their marriage had not really begun in Keswick Church, or at that lakeside hotel where they spent their first night together, or even in that rented house, where he had dumped her like excess baggage while he addressed himself to the task of launching his precious enterprise. It had been founded right here one April evening when old Dancer, the homing carriage horse, had rattled them along that lane and come close to upsetting them both on the doorstep. And from here it had been as ordered as one of those complicated crosscountry hauls they had worked out in time of flood, frost and used-up teams. Everything that had contributed to their partnership had happened in this place where all their children had been born, where all their mutual adjustments had been made, where she had found maturity facing any number of demands on her patience and ingenuity. All their real loving had been done here and down in that thin belt of woodland he was looking at the first book of their marriage had been closed and a new one opened.

He said, addressing the child, " 'Ten weeks', she says. And here I am, not knowing whether you're son or daughter," and he turned in a half-circle so that she could see he was smiling because he had suddenly recalled the significance of that wood at the foot of the drive.

"You can't guess?"

"If I had to I'd say a boy."

"You'd be right."

They were silent for a moment. Then he said, "Is he christened, or were you waiting for me?"

"We were waiting."

"Ten weeks and not even a name!"

She hesitated, wondering if it was possible to convey to him the communion she had established with the child without sounding like one of those heroines of Mrs. Henry Wood or Miss Braddon.

"I thought we'd call him Edward, after your father. Unless you had a preference. I think of him as Friday, Man Friday. I even call him that when we're alone." Suddenly she felt closer to him in every way than at any time in the past and this had nothing to do with that clutter downstairs in the sewing-room, but everything to do with the child he was holding. She said, "It isn't easy to explain, Adam, not even to myself. But it isn't fanciful either. Stella, Alex, even George who seemed to represent something special between us, didn't really exist for me until they were born, but he did. He was always a person—no, person isn't what I mean—a *presence*. Could a man understand that, I wonder?"

"I daresay this man could if he put his mind to it."

"Well, then, suppose I put it like this. When we knew you stood a chance, and afterwards, when it was clear you would be away almost a year, everyone helped, particularly Deborah, who was a tremendous comfort, so much so that I can never look on her as anyone else's child. But with him it was more than that. We were never separated you see and we did everything together, and that meant I was never really separated from you, not for a single moment. I don't have to tell you where and when he was conceived. You were remembering it a moment ago, but perhaps you've forgotten that that day, when I met you on the edge of the copse, everything changed between us and I suppose this had a lot to do with how I felt about what came of it."

She stopped, wondering if she was making sense to him.

"Go on," he said, prompting her, "there's far more to it than that."

"Yes, there is. He wasn't just *you* in the physical sense, but in every way. That's what I mean when I say he was a person months before he was born. Up at the yard, and through all the worrying times when your letters didn't mean much and there was so much to see to he *was* you. We sorted things out together and waited and hoped as one person. There, I can't do better than that, no matter how hard I try."

"You've done very well," he said. "I doubt if that chap Dickens could do much better. There's one thing, however. You asked if I had any preference for a name and I have, in view of what you've just told me. Call him Giles."

"Giles." She savoured the name and found it crisp and pleasing. "I like that. Yes, I like that very much. It suits him."

"You can be sure as to that," he said. "Giles is the patron saint of cripples."

"Nobody will ever think of you as a cripple."

"No," he said, cheerfully, "I'll make sure of that. But I think you might have, if it hadn't been for him," and he lifted the child and kissed it. The salutation had a proud and possessive element she had never witnessed in greeting his other children. There was nothing more to be said and even Giles acknowledged this for he began to whimper, so that she reached up for him, saying, "Give him to me. Any other child would have been bawling his head off long since but even Father Confessors have to be fed," and she sat and settled the child on her lap and unbuttoned her blouse.

He stood there musing, his back to the light, and although she was absorbed with the child she knew that his mind was occupied assembling the pieces of the new pattern of their lives and that whatever he might make of the task it would bring him infinitely more fulfilment than he had derived from the years behind them. He said, as she freed the top tapes of her corset and shrugged herself half out of her chemise, "Would it embarrass you if I watched?", and she replied, "That's a silly question coming from you. Especially in the circumstances." She lifted the child to her full rounded breast and then, without being aware of her absorption, settled herself more comfortably and forgot him.

She would have been interested, however, had she happened to glance up, for he was looking at her more objectively than he had ever looked at anyone. He would have said, an hour ago, that she could never hope to surprise him much, not if they shared another half-century as man and wife, and yet she had and that very dramatically, and he wondered how he could have been so blind and deaf to her potentialities, for until then he had always thought of himself as more discerning than most. He told himself that all her best qualities had been latent, awaiting a time to emerge and proclaim themselves but he knew this was a makeshift excuse. He had hints over the years but had ignored them and wryly, half-reluctantly, he acknowledged why. Obsessed with her physically he had never deployed her as he might have done, to the advantage of both of them. It had taken circumstances that would have crushed most women to establish beyond doubt that the rôle she had played in his life up to this moment had been no more than adequate, and the fault for this omission lay with him not with her, for what had he ever demanded of her but functions that could have been performed by a middling-to-good housekeeper, and one of those forlorn girls in Kate Hamilton's establishment? He thought, 'Well, I've had my lesson, and I'm not likely to forget it in a long time', and he bent over her, brushing her hair with his lips. Then he stumped across the room and out into the corridor as she called, gaily, "We'll have supper at seven. Take them all outside, I'll be down in thirty minutes!" and he lifted his hand in acknowledgment as he closed the door He could not trust himself to speak.

4

At this season of the year it was light on the flat lands of The Bonus a few minutes to five and if the sky was clear, as it was today, the first rays of the sun went exploring up the estuaries of the rivers, skimming over the surface of slow-moving currents and under bridges that Vicary, Swann's adjutant hereabouts, had hauled timber to rebuild after the spates of the winter. The river levels were very low now after a month without so much as a shower and Vicary's teams, still on charter to the bridge builders, could cross at a dozen points, saving as much as a mile in a five-mile haul but Vicary never harried his carters. Working for municipalities he was acquiring municipal habits and took his time about things. He could not be chivvied, as his colleagues in the Crescents further north had been chivvied by that hustler in petticoats at Peterborough.

At precisely twenty-nine minutes past seven, therefore, when the sun was already high, Vicary lit his pipe, gave the yard porter a nod, and watched him draw back the bolts to let the first frigate through. Then, pondering the morning's mail, he returned to his office, glancing anew at the round robin Tybalt had distributed with a view to collecting for a staff presentation to the Gaffer, now back at his post after an absence of almost twelve months. Vicary, an amiable, unambitious man, wondered if the loss of a leg would slow Swann down and hoped, without malice, that it would. To Vicary's mind there was altogether too much bustle about the world these days and for himself he could not see where it was leading or what it achieved. Settling himself in his chair he waited for his kettle to boil on the spirit stove that a grateful Harwich skipper had given him when he had delivered a spare sail days ahead of schedule. There would be time enough to go through the day's invoices and begin the day's route-plotting when he had finished reading what his newspaper had to say about the defeat of Mr. Gladstone's reform bill, and the current shindig brewing between Austrians, Prussians and Italians. Vicary took a mild interest in world politics but it was the kind of attention a man at home in bed might pay to a gale that was rattling his windows.

Up-to-date as regards what was happening at Headquarters, in Westminster and the Chancellories of Europe, Vicary was out-of-date as regards affairs on his doorstep. His sympathy for Goodbody

671

and Horncastle, deputy managers of the Crescents Central and North, was wasted for, by now, they were both aware that a happy set of circumstances had shifted them beyond the range of Edith Wadsworth's goad and each approved heartily of Edith's successor, a very amiable young fellow called Tom Wickstead, who had appeared from nowhere and succeeded, to everyone's astonishment, in belling the cat. He had not only prised the Wadsworth lass from the seat of power along the East Coast but had unaccountably married her and given her something to think about apart from goods consigned for Grimsby that somehow found their way to Hull. For Wickstead, it was decided in territory reaching from Spalding to Redcar, was a coaxer not a chivvier, and men like Goodbody and Horncastle were relieved to get their orders from a man again. They had conceded Edith Wadsworth's ability, initiative, and diabolically accurate memory but both, at one time or another, had cowered under the lash of her tongue. Now, with male arrogance, they were satisfied that they could identify the source of the Wadsworth woman's tiresome pursuit of perfection. She had not been Swann's mistress after all, it seemed. All she had wanted, when it came to bedrock, was someone—anyone—to tuck her up at nights and someone, thank God, had volunteered for the job. Throughout the whole network that season a period of unwonted somnolence succeeded the ardours of a long, hard winter but nowhere was the respite more noticeable than in the Swann provinces reaching from the north bank of the Thames to the south bank of the Tees, where Wickstead shared the credit with the June weather. There was, in fact, a grain of truth in this, for once Wickstead's appointment was confirmed Edith was seldom seen about the yard but could be sought more profitably in the market, where her familiarity with wholesale prices enabled her to fill a shopping basket at half the cost demanded of the average housewife. Cooking and house-scouring kept her busy during the day but in the evenings she had leisure to address herself to a more familiar task and might be said to have adopted the rôle of governess between supper and bedtime. Anyone passing the Wicksteads' uncurtained downstairs window at this time of day could have seen her putting her pupil through his paces with a day book, a Bradshaw, various ordnance maps and other primers. The exchange of conversation on these occasions was not what one might expect between newlyweds, home from a three-day honeymoon at Cromer, but was concerned, in the main, with haulage rates, weight capacities, distances between points A. and B., and the integrity of a thousand and one local merchants who used Swann-on-Wheels to shift goods from warehouse to customer.

Perhaps it was these evening lessons that enabled Tom Wickstead to surprise old hands like Goodbody and Horncastle that summer and later, when the quarterly returns were sent in, to confound Tybalt, who remarked to his friend Keate, "That new chap, Wickstead, the one who married Miss Wadsworth. We were mighty lucky to find him. For a Johnny Raw he seems to me to have an astonishing grasp of essentials!"

* * *

The early morning sun that probed the sluggish rivers of Bonus country never caught Fraser by surprise. Often, by the time it had touched the eastern folds of the Cheviots, or the long slopes of the Pennines where they fed the Tees, Tyne and Tweed, it would light on a load of plate glass he was hauling inland from the coastal industrial complex, flashing a heliographic message across the heedless dales. Fraser was now indifferent to who ruled at Headquarters, being obsessed with a personal ambition, or rather two ambitions. He meant, before he put his feet up, to win the Swann accolade for the highest annual turnover, and was in fact already lying third to Catesby in the Polygon, and Godsall in the Kentish Triangle. He reckoned on doing this within two years, when he would be sixty but in the meantime his sights were set on another target. Week by week he was slowly enlarging his Scottish bridgehead, and if this luck held he would soon be hauling as far north as the Tay, and perhaps even beyond, into the heartlands of his ancestors. The time would come, perhaps, when Swann would open a Scottish depot, and if he did who was better qualified for the post of gaffer up here? He would sit pondering this under the walls of Berwick during his rare slack periods. It would be very pleasant, he told himself, to return home after a lapse of two centuries with a title of Viceroy bestowed on him by the English.

* * *

West of the Pennines, in the rich agricultural districts where Catesby could sometimes be found roving the triangle between the cotton belt, the north-western coalfield, and the pastoral country watched over by Skipton Castle, the men of the Polygon were forgetting there had been a four-year famine, due to a bloody family quarrel on the far side of the Atlantic. But Catesby did not forget. Whenever he

673

came out here—to give his lungs a spring-clean as he put it—he would reflect upon the tendency of Lancastrians to cram all their eggs in one basket. To the north and east, over the fells and the backbone of England, the sky was washed clean, but to the south the pall of a resurrected King Cotton hung like a saffron banner over a score of cities, all within artillery range of Manchester, and it would occur to him that the Belt might not survive a second beating like the one administered by the war between the states. He did not mourn his son Tam now, having satisfied himself that the boy had died in a bonny cause, but he would have preferred to see mill owners like Rawlinson learn something useful from the long ordeal, if only for the sake of the men and the lasses who looked to them for wages. For of all Swann's managers, Catesby was the only one who understood the real reasons for his employer's spectacular success. First Swann had won the confidence of his employees by letting it be seen that he did not regard them as surly beasts, or expendable machines. Secondly, he made sure that the net he threw across England was so finely meshed that it could trap anything from a pin to a blast furnace, and this, to Catesby's way of thinking, was proof of a prescient mind. Lancashire would do well to follow Swann's example and diversify while there was still time, for who could say when some other calamity halfway across the world would bring every loom in the country to a standstill? It had happened once and it could happen again, but next time, please God, it would not find the workers defenceless. A way must be found to divert some of the wealth accumulating to the few to the many, and the only way this could be achieved short of revolution was by instituting a system of collective bargaining. It seemed to Catesby that there was more chance of squeezing this kind of concession from a variety of trades than from the closely-knit, brass-knuckled association of master-spinners, who ruled Lancashire like a consortium of feudal barons. The war in the States was over but it would be a long time, he supposed, before the bugles blew the cease-fire up here, or in the mines, or in the Black Country beyond the southern skyline.

*   *   *

Bryn Lovell was the last manager to hear that Adam Swann was back at work. When Tybalt's round robin reached the Mountain Square Lovell was not at his headquarters. He was enjoying his first holiday in ten years. The day his mulatto wife opened the Headquarters' letter marked 'urgent' Bryn was in the far north-western corner of his do-

674

main, having made up his mind that it was time his coffee-coloured stepsons learned something of their national heritage. Nobody was likely to mistake Bryn's stepsons for Welshmen but they were Welsh for all that, having been born and raised in the Principality, and it did not seem right to Lovell that they should grow to manhood unaware of the privilege conferred upon them in this respect.

He took advantage of the warm weather and a long, cross-country haul to Llanberis quarries, packing them all into a frigate as supernumerary teamsters, even though the eldest was not yet twelve, and the youngest, a merry little fellow called Shadrach, only six. Sleeping in the waggon, and cooking meals by the roadside, they crossed Wales from south-east to north-west, and while the waggons were loading Bryn accompanied them on an ascent of Snowdon by the Beddgelert track.

They made an improbable picture climbing the steep, tussocky path in single file, and occasionally disappearing into streamers of mist that drifted across the mountain buttresses like bonfire smoke. With Bryn in the van, and his four dark-skinned boys in his wake, anyone could have taken the procession for a safari that had strayed ten thousand miles off course and when at last they reached the summit and the mist lifted, as Bryn had promised it would, there below was half Wales, 'the real Wales' as Bryn was careful to explain, adding that they were looking down on it from 3,560 feet, the highest vantage point in the land.

"Except Pen Nebblis," prompted Enoch, the eldest and most promising of Bryn's geography class.

"Ben Nevis," said Bryn, gently, "and that's in Scotland, Enoch."

They gazed at the unimaginably beautiful vista of lake, peak and forest, elated by the view but even more by their achievement in getting here.

"There's another thing," Bryn said, solemnly, "that as Welshmen you must never forget. The English took the plain from us and built their castles there but they never reached us here, you understand? And now let's eat our snap and go down again, for they'll have finished loading and we'll have to go part way home by train or your mother will wonder what has happened to us." They sat under the lee of a great boulder and ate their sandwiches, one spare, greying man, and four copper-coloured, woolly-headed boys, munching, gazing and wondering, and it crossed Bryn Lovell's mind that a day like this was worth a lifetime of book-reading and that he was fortunate to have discovered this before it was too late and the years had nothing to offer but a lonely dotage.

* * *

Down in the Western Wedge and across the Dorset border to the Southern Square, two other adjutants of Adam Swann had no such thoughts. Hamlet Ratcliffe, fearful of diverting Augusta's attention from himself, had never wished for children, whereas young Rookwood would not be thinking of them until some weeks from now, after he walked out of a Salisbury Methodist Chapel with his landlady's pretty daughter on his arm. Both, however, wished Adam well when news reached them that the Gaffer was back among them and that the days of petticoat government were over.

Reading the Headquarters' circular aloud over his boiled eggs that morning, Hamlet gave expression to this relief, saying, "Us'll be able to put our veet up now, midear, for although I alwus reckoned Swann was a rare one fer stirring us up yereabouts, his missus, an' that fancy woman of his, could best him at it, as you'll own after the winter us had wi' the pair of 'em hounding us up hill an' down bliddy dale."

Augusta (who nursed a secret admiration for Mrs. Swann but dare not admit to it) said that no doubt Henrietta would be glad to get back to her kitchen, and that nothing was to be feared from Edith Wadsworth now she had a kitchen of her own, to which Hamlet replied, "Arr, an' time enough too. For if there's one thing I can't abide it's a woman outside one. You can't never tell what mischief they'll be at if they get where they'm no bliddy bizness to be!"

He said this so emphatically that Augusta interpreted it as a rebuke. "Baint your eggs hard enough, my love?" she asked, timidly, and Hamlet, who was never loath to proclaim himself champion wife-spotter of all England, patted the back of her freckled hand as he said, "They'm just right, midear. And I wasn't implying nothing personal. Why, damme, youm a woman in a millyon, Gussie, and it baint the virst time I've said zo, be it?"

"No, it baint, my love," said Augusta, and blushed, as she always did when he paid her one of his rare compliments.

* * *

The very last man in the network to learn that Headquarters was drumming up subscriptions for a welcome-home gift to Adam Swann was its youngest, and probably its most conscientious manager, Rookwood of Southern Square. The letter arrived at Salisbury in early May but Rookwood inadvertently pigeon-holed it, together with a number of other directives, and this was uncharacteristic of him, as indeed was his state of mind at the time. For the fact was Rookwood was not himself these days and might be said to have been bewitched, all his faculties having treacherously deserted him in a matter of seconds after intercepting a single smile across the breakfast table on the day after his landlady's daughter Hetty, eighteen, pert, dark-haired and devastatingly pretty, had arrived home for good from her Ladies' Academy in Torquay, whither she had been sent three years before to be trained in grace, dancing, music, sewing, drawing and deportment.

He remembered Hetty vaguely, a giggling schoolgirl with long, coal-black plaits and a merry mouth, scampering about the house in the days when he was learning his trade under Abbott, but since then (although she had visited from time to time) he had been so busy that he had no opportunity to learn how a young man might armour himself against the shattering impact of a carefully-calculated glance, directed by a pair of brown eyes veiled in long, curling lashes.

Rookwood, man and boy, had come a long way since Keate had prised him out of the Rotherhithe mud and Adam Swann, prince of gamblers, had casually promoted him to the position of manager over one of the largest segments of the network. All in all he had responded well to the opportunity the chance had offered him, and the territory, under his earnest and attentive direction, had maintained its initial start over its nearest rivals gained by Abbott in the first days of the expansion. He had overcome the handicap of youth by strict attention to duty, by long hours of study, and by a tendency to watch the pennies that was a legacy of his vagrant days on the banks of the Thames. In addition, he had at last, by dint of endless coaxing and the application of several jars of Howarth's Graded Moustache Oil, succeeded in growing an impressive pair of whiskers that would not have disgraced a young Sicilian bandit and these, reinforced by a wary expression and a permanently outthrust jaw, had aged him by a decade, so that carters had ceased to refer to him as 'young Rookwood' and knew him as 'Young Gaffer', which could be regarded as promotion.

For all that he was still young inside, still very much inclined to doubt his potential and still morbidly sensitive about his obscure origins, so much so that he had commissioned his landlord, in the capacity of a lawyer's clerk, to trace his ancestry. No documentary

677

evidence had emerged proving that Rookwood was the missing heir to a ducal inheritance or even that he was the byblow of a raffish earl out of an obliging chambermaid. He remained what he had always been, and what he had always thought himself, a piece of flotsam on the bosom of the Thames that had drifted in on the tide, or possibly downstream from Westminster, to mingle with other flotsam near Brunel's Tunnel.

The failure of Mr. Gilroy's inquiries had not worried Rookwood at the time. By now he had a modest pride in himself, as well as money in the bank, and an assured future in the firm. And yet, to Rookwood's disciplined mind, there was something missing, and he was uncomfortably aware of this the moment he intercepted Hetty Gilroy's frank, tender smile. For how was he to know that Mrs. Gilroy had acquainted her pretty daughter with every relevant detail of her lodger's past, or that she had been enjoined, by both father and mother, 'to go out of her way to be nice to that dear boy and treat him like a brother'. Hetty, an excessively amiable young lady, was perfectly prepared to do this, particularly as the dear boy was in possession of good looks and was also, according to her father, putting money by at a prodigious rate and already earning twice as much as, say, the music master at the Torquay Finishing School.

Pondering these facts on her first day out of school, she looked and she smiled over her morning porridge, unaware that this mild show of courtesy would have a calamitous effect upon the time schedules of Swann-on-Wheels all the way from the Solent to the Cotswolds, or that Rookwood, a victim of love at first sight, would be thrown into a turmoil of self-doubt that ruined his appetite, reduced his sleep to a few fitful hours a night, and set him contemplating the terrible disadvantages of not knowing who he was, where he came from, or even if his name was more than a label attached to him by some forgotten circumstance in the days when he had slept out under tarpaulins opposite the dock where they had once hanged pirates.

He had never been troubled by thoughts such as these in what he could now look back on as his happy-go-lucky past, but now he began to see all manner of gloomy possibilities in his situation and his first step was to instruct Mr. Gilroy to cease his search of the registers of Thameside parishes for a Rookwood male, born about 1844, give or take a year or two. When Gilroy demurred, saying that information might be gleaned from the books of recently-registered baby-farmers, he said, desperately, "Leave it be, Mr. Gilroy. I don't want to know, for what I don't know I can't fret about, can I?"

678

It might have stopped there had not the Gilroy home been a matriarchal establishment. Fortunately for all concerned, Mrs. Gilroy (who had long since elected herself Rookwood's foster-mother) heard about it that same day and set herself to watch. It was not long before she discerned the hidden reason behind her young lodger's disinclination to meddle with his ancestry and in passing she noticed something else but at that time preferred not to confuse the issue. She put her afterthought on one side as it were, merely thanking God that Hetty had come home from that genteel establishment prescribed by her father with her sense of values relatively unimpaired.

For her part Mrs. Gilroy had never favoured the idea much, having a suspicion that a girl who had been taught music, painting, dancing, housewifery-by-the-book and not by-the-kitchen-stove, might become petulant and unmanageable when she found herself all dressed up and nowhere to go. Her observation, however, told her that this risk had been exaggerated. Hetty returned to them more polished, certainly, but otherwise unchanged. She was not above giving her mother a hand with the cooking and cleaning, and it was soon demonstrably clear that she was very intrigued by the shy young man with the worried look and the carefully-cultivated whiskers, notwithstanding the fact that in Mrs. Gilroy's estimation the frenzied application of Howarth's Graded Moustache Oil had aged the boy ten years.

The ageing process, due to the whiskers and the stain of the winter's work, led Mrs. Gilroy somewhat astray in the first instance. She set the blame for his drooping spirits and loss of appetite squarely upon Adam Swann's shoulders, jumping to the conclusion that the dear boy had been overtaxing himself of late. She made up her mind, therefore, to have it out with him, and persuade him to take a holiday, but on the very day selected for the confrontation Rookwood himself brought the issue into the open by hinting that he might soon be leaving the district, and seeking a transfer back to London.

The prospect of losing him appalled her. She had become accustomed to having him there in place of the son she had been denied and the thought of having no necessity to prepare his breakfast kippers was a foretaste of death. She was very sorry then that she had not made more of a stand when that boss of his came posting down from London, and talked the boy into accepting the post vacated by that dreadful man Abbott and said, with a quaver in her voice, *"Leaving us?* Leaving me and Mr. Gilroy? After *all this time?* For

London? Why, Mr. Rookwood," (she had avoided using his Christian name all these years to help buttress his dignity) . . . "that's unthinkable! I won't hear of it! *You* mustn't think of it! There must be another way of easing that cruel workload they put upon you!", and at this, Rookwood looked very puzzled so that she added, "That *is* what's bothering you, isn't it? That's why you don't like my kippers any more and why you toss and turn so much of a night? Oh, I hear you, and so does Mr. Gilroy, and we're very worried about it. He said it's those inquiries he's making about your parents but I told him nonsense, the boy has more sense than to fret over *that*. I said it was all the work they put upon you, and you not much more than a lad, however well you stand up to it, but how will working for the same people in London help? If I was you I'd send in my notice and look about for another position right here. Hickson and Dacre are reputable hauliers . . ."

She could not have said anything more calculated to expose the true source of Rookwood's disenchantment with her kippers. Hickson and Dacre were his most dangerous rivals, and the prospect of transferring his allegiance to a firm that had refused to rent him a single waggon when all his spares had been sent to help Ratcliffe in December was so outrageous that he fell headlong into the kind of trap barristers set for unsuspecting witnesses, exclaiming, *"Me? Move over to Hickson and Dacre? Leave Swann for those brigands? Good Lord, Mrs. Gilroy, I'd sooner sign on before the mast and go to the South Seas to forget!"*

He realised his mistake at once and could have clipped an inch from his tongue. He went very red and gestured with his hands, trying to think of something that would repair the gap torn in his defences. It was a vain attempt. A strong, white light lit up the twilight areas of Martha Gilroy's logical brain and suddenly, as though he had proclaimed it in unequivocal terms, she perceived the real reason for his rejected kippers and rumpled sheets. She saw something else too and it made her bubble with excitement. Suddenly a tremendous prospect opened up before her—a daughter off her hands, the dear boy officially enlisted in the family, and the near-certainty of grandchildren to spoil in her old age.

"Hetty!" she gasped. "Dear life, what a fool I am! It's Hetty, isn't it?", and he nodded, morosely, but this did nothing to prevent her from grasping him in a fierce maternal embrace, something she had so often longed to do but never had, for fear of embarrassing him. Then a sobering thought occurred to her and she clapped both

hands over her ears as though to ward off bad news, and said, "You've not ... not spoken to her? She hasn't said no, has she?" and Rookwood, now so far out of his depth that he despaired of touching bottom again, mumbled, "Spoken to her? Good heavens, you can't know me if you think ... what I mean is I wouldn't presume. ... Speak to her about it behind Mr. Gilroy's back? Good Lord, ma'am, as if I would ..." and he tailed off, muttering something about being shown the door, or invoking Mr. Gilroy's unspeakable indignation but precisely what it was Martha Gilroy never did learn, for suddenly his modesty struck her as something that deserved more than a push; it needed a well-judged kick, and if no one else was there to administer one then she was, praise God.

"Stop it!" she shouted, "Stop talking like that! I won't listen to a word of it and neither will Mr. Gilroy when he gets home. Whatever is wrong with you courting our Hetty? That's what I'd like to know, for if she doesn't jump at you she hasn't the sense I credit her with. As for me, I can't think of anyone I'd as lief see wedded to my flesh and blood, for I'll have you know, since you don't seem to know it already, that I don't give a thimble who you are or where you come from! It's plain to me you're a good, steady lad, and very biddable with it, to say nothing of keeping clear of taverns and bad lasses all the years *I've* known you! There, now I've made you blush, but I'm not sorry for it. It's time someone told you and if you want to begin courting Hetty you can start at any time you've a mind to, with my blessing!" She paused just long enough to draw a single, whistling breath. "Do I make myself clear?"

He was standing in front of her with his mouth open, his hands limp and his knees slightly bent, so that he seemed to her to be cowering and it was this pitiable aspect of him that caused her to lead him to a chair and give him a chance to make some kind of attempt to pull himself together. He said, at last, "You've not ... not mentioned it to her?"

"Indeed I haven't," she replied, tartly, "for in my day lads didn't need sponsoring. Mr. Gilroy took his time, now I think on it, but that was on account of him being a lawyer. All the other young sparks I knew wanted holding off not setting on!"

"But, don't you see, Mrs. Gilroy? Hetty's educated, besides being ... well ... beautiful. She could have anyone, anyone at all, and I don't even know who I am. I thought ..." but Mrs. Gilroy was not in the least disposed to listen to a recital of his disqualifications.

681

Modesty in a man was becoming but only up to a certain point. Beyond that point it became nauseating, so she said, quite sharply, "I told you to stop talking that way and I meant it, Albert Rookwood! Now you listen to me, and stop sitting there looking up at me like a stranded codfish! I've told you what Mr. Gilroy and me think of you, and as to Hetty, I've got my suspicions as regards her, but we'll cross that bridge when we come to it and that can't be soon enough to my way of thinking. No mother wants to see her only child make a fool of herself, and what with her music and painting and all the what-not her father would have her learn there's no knowing what kind of loafer she might introduce into the house as her intended. Now me, I like to see what I'm getting in advance, and you've been as good as a son to me and Cedric, so there's no question of us buying a pig in a poke, is there? I'm sorry to speak that plain, but circumstances demand it. If you fancy Hetty that much then all I can say is she's a very lucky girl, so, for pity's sake, stop fretting about who you *were* and try and remember who you *are*, a lad holding down a job that would tax the wits of a college man, and the patience of Job into the bargain. What's more you've been taking more money to the bank every week than most lads your age save in a month, so if you'll take a final word of advice, say your piece to Hetty right now, without giving yourself time to think on it. If I'm any judge of my own flesh and blood you'll have occasion to thank me for it, and so will she when she gets used to the idea. Then you can go back to eating a proper breakfast again, and go to bed with the prospect of a good night's rest. Are you man enough to try, or do you prefer to stay hanging about while she has her bit of fun keeping you waiting?"

In the last few years Albert Rookwood had been called upon to make any number of quick decisions but never one like this. Perhaps, however, the uncertainties and the manifold hazards of his profession, had tested him in a way he had not acknowledged up to that moment for now, faced with a straight choice, he did not hesitate long. He said, lifting his hand to his long, drooping whiskers, "I'll do it now, Mrs. Gilroy. I'll get it over with, for I couldn't stay on not knowing, any more than I could if Hetty didn't see it your way. Give me ten minutes and I'll come down and perhaps ... well ... perhaps you could pretend to be doing something out in the kitchen."

"Aye, I could that," she said, smiling, "for there's always one woman's work waiting out there, notwithstanding the way you've been picking at your food ever since our Hetty ogled you!"

She went out then and down the stairs, calling sharply to her daughter who was playing with the fat marmalade cat in the backyard. He resisted a temptation to listen at the head of the stairs and resolutely closed the door, peeling off his jacket, rolling up his sleeves and studying himself in the mirror clipped over the splashboard of his washstand. He stood there for more than a minute and then he made another decision. Breathing hard, and holding his face so close to the mirror that it began to mist, he groped for a pair of scissors he kept in his oddment drawer, alongside his razor, his Moustache Oil, and a pipe he had laid aside after a few whiffs had made him as sick as a cat. With the solemnity of a mayor snipping the tape of a new bridge he made two cuts, reducing the carefully cultivated moustache to a ragged fringe extending about two inches beyond each nostril. The alteration was not a success. It gave him the look of a young Irish navigator who shaved by candlelight so he dipped his fingers in his water can, finding the water lukewarm. "Better start fresh," he said aloud and began to lather. It was his final misjudgement that season. The first thing Hetty did was to insist that he grow it again.

5

It was Rookwood he remembered as he stumped across the sunlit yard that July morning, a month or so after his return to bondage, for somehow Rookwood symbolised the entire experiment; something permanent, promising and substantial, emerging from a hotpotch of unlikely components, a coming-together in this place of any number of men and boys with no common background, widely separated by the nature of dreams that some called ambition but were more fundamental to his way of thinking. For a man's dreaming proclaimed his essential personality.

He remembered Rookwood because the vanboys were much in evidence at that hour, a few of Keate's originals but a greater number of recruits, for Keate was still dredging along the banks of the Thames. He watched them idly, swinging like monkeys from the tailboard ropes, exchanging the kind of chaff with which the Cockney armours himself against those who trespass on his individuality. Cockneys, he recalled, made excellent private soldiers and good N.C.O.'s but were too gregarious to hold rank above sergeant. Rookwood was the exception. Somewhere along his genetic line there was good blood, possibly the blood of kings. Who knew? Who knew the truth about anyone? Hadn't he been completely ignorant of the potentialities of a woman who had shared his bed and board for years?

Something alerted him, something in the way they looked at him, as though trying to compose their urchin features into expressions of respect, but only succeeding in looking very artful, and it was the same when he called in at the stables and counting house, finding both Keate and Tybalt missing, and this was strange at nine o'clock on a summer's morning.

He went back across the yard knowing that eyes were following him from several scattered points, gauging no doubt, the effort he was making to conceal evidence of the contraption braced to his thigh but not caring much, for he had seen enough of himself in mirrors to convince him his limp was hardly noticeable. As he approached the belfry door, however, he saw Keate and Tybalt scuttle down the stairway like a pair of guilty schoolboys and dart into the passage that led to the warehouse. He was inclined to hail them and demand to know what they were at but he checked himself. Whatever it was it was clear they did not wish to see him at that moment, so he turned in under the little Gothic arch and mounted the spiral stairs, thankful that it was his left leg and not his right that was artificial for the stairway ran clockwise and he could place his left foot squarely on the broadest section of the tread.

He saw it the moment he opened the door, a shrouded, irregular lump, standing on the map table between the window and Franken-stein, and at once he related it to the glances of the vanboys in the yard, and the furtive haste of Keate and Tybalt in the passage below. He lounged over, his curiosity fully aroused, and yanked the covering free. Underneath, worked in silver, was a scale-model of a frigate harnessed to two Clydesdales, clearly the work of a master silversmith, for every detail of the vehicle was faithfully represented and the horses were superbly modelled, with riffled tails and manes, and every pulling muscle visible on their contours. He thought, 'By God, but that's a wonderful piece of work! I wish it were mine ...' and then he realised that it was, and that Keate and Tybalt had placed it there a moment ago, and that everyone in the yard must know about it, and everyone in the regions too judging by the engraved shield on the starboard side of the waggon.

He was so moved that his eyes misted and for a moment he was unable to read the names engraved on the plaque, or the lines of fine writing below, where the shield merged into the Swann emblem.

He read the tailpiece first—*'Presented to Adam Swann by the employers of Swann-on-Wheels, July 1866, on the occasion of his recovery and return'.* That was all, save for the initials of the silversmith, a simple, straightforward expression of goodwill and collective satisfaction; in a way a kind of cheer for something witnessed, marked upon and approved.

And yet it touched and troubled him deeply, for he saw it as the identification of every name on that plaque with everything he had achieved since he set foot in Plymouth more than eight years before, and was given his first, fleeting glimpse of possibilities by that stationmaster, who had mistaken him for a spy. It had been an essentially private dream then but now it was shared among many and he read the names through very carefully, noting, with a tinge of sadness, that someone had seen fit to give poor old Blubb pride of place at the top of the wedge, so that it read:

Blubb,
Vicary, Goodbody, Horncastle,
Wickstead-Wadsworth, Fraser, Catesby,
Morris, Lovell, Ratcliffe, Dockett, Rookwood, Godsall,
Tybalt, Keate, Stock.

There was music in the names and if their respective territories had been defined the plaque would have resolved itself into a litany or a prose poem. His fancy played with this for a moment—

'Vicary of The Bonus,
Wadsworth of the Crescents,
Ratcliffe of the Western Wedge,
Rookwood of the Square . . .'

and as he did this he saw them all as segments not of his private enterprise but of the tribe to which they belonged, so that they and their territories assumed a national significance, symbolising all he felt about the country and the era and his personal involvement with it. Their diversity was immense but in that, he supposed, lay their value to him and to the age. Three things they had in common. Courage, an obstinacy that some would call cussedness, and a queer, grumbling loyalty to the thing he had conjured out of that Ranee's necklace when he first set foot in this seedy little tower overlooking the busiest river in the world. And this led him to reflect upon the two functions of the place where he stood, the old one, that had been to summon cloistered women to acknowledge the majesty of God, and the new one, concerned with the worship of Moloch. Most people, he imagined, would regard this as an incongruous change of usage, but today he did not, perhaps because it occurred to him that traffic in money was only an insignificant aspect of their collective strivings here in this place, where the prayer bell had once clanged. Their real purpose, as individuals and a team was more interesting and more human, an exercise in comradeship and interdependence, a pooling of talents, a collective contribution to the creativity of the race to which all of them belonged. His idle thought on the quay at Calais returned to him and he smiled, telling himself that if God was an Englishman, then Swann's Yard had as much right to be recognised as a temple as Wren's church across the river, and this was not really such an extravagant thought, of the kind that would be likely to find favour among a thousand counting-house Christians within slingshot range of where he stood. It was dedicated to the making of money certainly, but it had a deeper, broader significance. You could, if you wished, regard it as a staging-post between a whole range of extremes —progress and *laissez-faire*, splendour and squalor, ignorance and expertise, affluence and grinding poverty. If it and its like closed their doors then the wheels of this teeming city would cease to turn and beggars would swarm in their thousands in those streets, spilling out into the countryside and carrying their indigence with them like a plague. Before long, in a year or so, Britain would return to the anarchy that had reigned for six centuries after the Legions went home, everyone awaiting the arrival of that cropheaded Norman, with his passion for public order, to move in and build that square tower across the Thames. There were people who liked to sneer at money even as they spent it but he was not one of them. Progress was the daughter of trade and how could the trading instinct, almost as deeply rooted in man as the sexual urge, find articulate expression without the unrestricted flow of gold and silver from one pocket to another?

He read the names yet again, recalling something specific about each of them, and this time they subdivided into companies, each company standing for a different England. The Headquarters' trio marched under the banner of the metropolis. Vicary and Edith Wadsworth stood for the green, flat river lands, where Baltic sea-raiders had called to pillage and stayed to colonise. To the north and north-west men like Catesby appeared to him as relative newcomers, milking a profit from farmlands that had been sacrificed to mill and foundry, whereas Fraser and Lovell were proof that the Celt had never been conquered or even absorbed by thrusters from the south and across the sea. East, from the Lizard, a fifth company plied their trade across an unspoiled landscape, where men had been lifting fortunes from the soil for a thousand years and one would have thought it was asking altogether too much of a man to look for harmony and a net profit from such a polyglot assembly. And yet harmony of a kind was there and the silver model on his desk was proof of a unity forced on these stubborn men by French kings and German princelings, who had themselves been absorbed into a way of life peculiar to this offshore island. It was all that had emerged from this process of absorption that was so astounding, so improbable—a race of men with as many facets as a giant diamond, projecting aspects of national character that seemed at first to be in direct contradiction to one another and yet were not. There they were, displayed for all to see any day of the week including Sunday—piety and high jinks, an intense love of personal freedom and a willing submission to laws, old and new; kindness and compassion, laced with an occasional streak of cruelty and intolerance; honest trading bedding down with sharp practice, and experimentation living side by side with a profound distrust of everything new and useful. It added up, to his mind, to a singularity that could be sought in vain anywhere else on earth, and the sheer unpredictability of what would emerge at any one time made working here a great adventure. A dictum of Napoleon returned to him, something about bad troops not existing, only bad officers. It certainly applied here, where his officers held his fate and fortune in their hands.

He decided to whistle down the tube for Tybalt and order a general assembly for drinks all round, but before he did he clumped across to the window of his eyrie and looked down on his favourite view of the Thames, watching the never-ending procession of barges and wherries, then shifting his stance to take in the forest of masts on the right, and the bridge and bridge approaches jampacked with crawling traffic. It was strange, he thought, that a man who professed to love the open air, and had cherished movement from boyhood, should feel more at home here than anywhere else in the world.

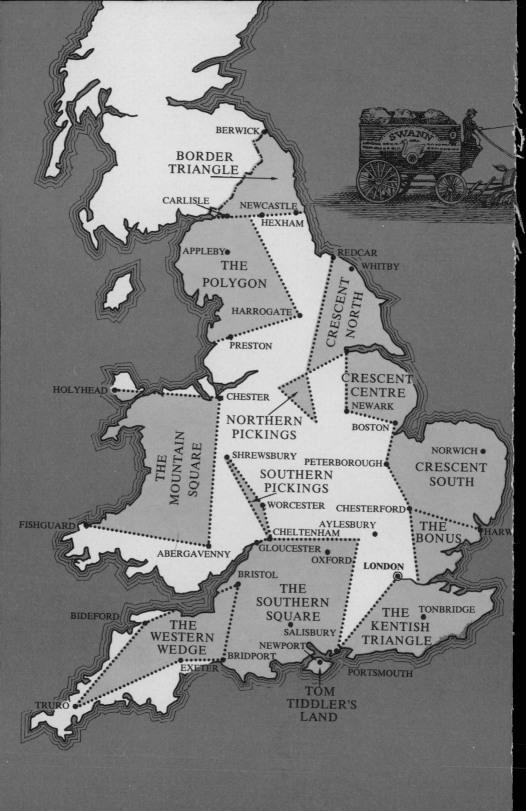

BERWICK

BORDER
TRIANGLE

CARLISLE

NEWCASTLE
HEXHAM

APPLEBY

THE
POLYGON

REDCAR
WHITBY

CRESCENT NORTH

HARROGATE

PRESTON

HOLYHEAD

CHESTER

CRESCENT
CENTRE
NEWARK

NORTHERN
PICKINGS

BOSTON

THE
MOUNTAIN
SQUARE

SHREWSBURY

PETERBOROUGH

NORWICH

CRESCENT
SOUTH

SOUTHERN
PICKINGS

WORCESTER

CHESTERFORD

FISHGUARD

AYLESBURY
CHELTENHAM

THE
BONUS

HARW

ABERGAVENNY

GLOUCESTER
OXFORD

LONDON

BRISTOL

BIDEFORD

THE
WESTERN
WEDGE

THE
SOUTHERN
SQUARE

SALISBURY

THE
KENTISH
TRIANGLE

TONBRIDGE

NEWPORT

BRIDPORT

PORTSMOUTH

EXETER

TRURO

TOM
TIDDLER'S
LAND